KAZAN THUNDERBOLTS

by
Stuart Slade

LION BY LION
PUBLISHING

Dedication

This book is respectfully dedicated to the memory of Andrew Jensen, a long-time friend and valued member of "The Board" whose extensive knowledge of a wide range of subjects was matched only by his good sense, courtesy and gentlemanly conduct. His passing at a comparatively early age was a great loss and he is much missed by everybody who had the privilege of knowing him.

Acknowledgements

Kazan Thunderbolts could not have been written without the very generous help of a large number of people who contributed their time, input and efforts into confirming the technical details of the story. I would especially like to thank the veterans who flew P-47 Thunderbolts in World War II and shared their memories with me. Some of these generous souls I know personally. Others I know only via the internet where they have posted their stories as an invaluable historical resource. I also wish to thank the collective membership of "The Board" whose communal wisdom and vast store of knowledge, freely contributed, has been truly irreplaceable.

I must also express a particular debt of gratitude to my wife Josefa for without her kind forbearance, patient support and unstintingly generous assistance, this novel would have remained nothing more than a vague idea floating in the back of my mind.

Caveat

Kazan Thunderbolts is a work of fiction, set in an alternate universe. All the characters appearing in this book are fictional and any resemblance to any person, living or dead is purely coincidental. Although some names of historical characters appear, they do not necessarily represent the same people we know in our reality.

Copyright Notice

Contents

PRELUDE

Soviet Government Train, Heading East From Moskva. December, 1942

After 180 days of siege, Moskva was dying. The red glow of its funeral pyre could still be seen on the horizon to the west. Looking at it, Lavrentiy Pavlovich Beria marveled that there was still enough in the ruins of the city to cause that fire. Moskva had died slowly and painfully. It was commonplace to say that, at the end the defenses "crumbled" or "collapsed" but that hadn't happened in Moskva. Beria was prepared to bet that there were defenders holding on there yet, in what had been rooms, or basements or sewers. They'd fight on until they'd died. Another commonplace saying "fight to the last man and the last bullet" but Moskva had gone far beyond that point. When the last man had been killed, the women and children had fought on. When the last bullet had been fired, they'd fought the German infantry with iron pipes, bricks, stones, broken glass, anything that could kill or maim.

And now, despite it all, Moskva was dying but in doing so it had achieved something of profoundly important significance. Once again, the great strategic decoy of Moskva had saved the Rodina. Moskva's agony had bought the time Russia needed to survive.

STAVKA, the Soviet High Command which effectively meant Stalin himself, had known that a new German offensive would start once the mud dried in the spring of 1942. The question was, where? Would the Germans strike north, at Moskva and what they thought was the center of Soviet political power and authority? Or south, at Stalingrad and the oil fields of the Caucasus?

The choice was argued backwards and forwards even as the Soviet winter offensive ground forward, painfully rewinning some of the ground lost in the dreadful months of 1941. Would the Germans strike North or South? The arguments raged on until the answers came from two strange sources, ones nobody could quite explain.

1

Kazan Thunderbolts

One was "Lucy". Nobody knew who Lucy was, whether the name covered one person or many, a single spy or a whole network. What they did know was that Lucy supplied top-grade strategic and operational intelligence on German military and political plans. Not just what the Germans planned but why they were making those plans. In 1941, nobody had known whether Lucy was reliable or whether the information was a plant, intended to deceive and mislead. Now, there was no doubt about the messages from Lucy. Whoever he, she, it, they or whatever else applied might be, the information was genuine.

The other source was even odder. On its face, Beria knew more about it than about Lucy. "The Red Orchestra" was based in Geneva and was an organization of economists and bankers who used their contacts to get military and economic information on German plans and intentions. They provided details of German military developments, new aircraft, tanks, guns and ships. They provided current production numbers and totals and what future output would look like. They provided information on how the Germans planned to use those assets. But, with that data, the information on "The Red Orchestra" hit a dead end.

In a way, Beria admired them; their security was so tight that it made the NKVD look amateurish. Agents he'd sent in to infiltrate The Red Orchestra had just vanished. The Germans had the same experience and were equally frustrated. The Red Orchestra was there, in plain sight, yet mysteriously out of reach and untouchable. Every time somebody reached out, the image shimmered slightly and just wasn't there anymore. A mirage, easily seen, but perfectly untouchable. Beria had the faint image of mocking laughter every time he grabbed at what he thought was a solid lead and it vanished from within his grip.

The information from both Lucy and the Red Orchestra had agreed perfectly. The Germans weren't going to choose North or South; they were going to do both. They planned to launch two hammer-blows in quick succession, the first during spring and early summer in the North to take Moskva, the second in late summer and fall to drive south to take Stalingrad. The news had first thrown STAVKA into deep gloom. They could defend against one or the other but not both.

Then glee had slowly replaced gloom. The German plans were complex and interlocked; the two attacks were sequential and used many of the same resources. Executing the second depended absolutely on success in the first. If Moskva held longer than expected, the second offensive would be thrown back accordingly and would take place later in the year, perhaps much later. Enough to leave the Germans trapped deep in Russia for another winter. So Moskva had been reinforced, turned into a fortress, its industry and surplus population evacuated.

The hammer blows came, just as Lucy and the Red Orchestra had predicted. Moskva had been assaulted from the north and west. After bitter fighting, the Germans had enveloped the city, almost. Not quite though. Distances prevented that and a slim lifeline was left along which the STAVKA funneled just enough supplies to keep the city fighting.

The fighting had raged for six months, block by block, street by street, building by building, and room by room. In the open country, the fighting had been by division and corps, in Moskva it was by battalion, then by company, then platoon and squad. That led to a strange change, for in open warfare, the kill ratio had been lopsided in the German's favor. In Moskva, the ratio dropped to near one German for one Russian. STAVKA watched and smiled as the cream of Germany's infantry, its hardened veterans, were ground away in the ruins of Moskva. Meanwhile, from the south, people, equipment, industry, all was evacuated eastwards. When the blow fell in the south, there would be nothing left for the Germans to seize.

There had been one problem. To make the great strategic decoy of Moskva credible, it had to be seen as the vital command center, the seat of Soviet power. That it was nothing of the sort was irrelevant, it had to be seen that way. So Stalin and the more prominent Soviet politicians had to stay in the city, at least in the early days. They had been filtered out, one here, another there, a slow transfer of the government away from Moskva.

Then, as the German noose contracted, as the ruined city fell into their hands, the time had come to evacuate the few that were left. This train was the result, a train that had gone down the narrow lifeline that connected Moskva to the rest of the Soviet Union to the unoccupied countryside beyond. Now, that train was heading for Gorkii where a new administrative center was being set up.

Beria sighed and turned around from the window of the train. Then, he knocked on the wooden door behind him. "Joseph Vissarionovich, you require my presence?"

"Enter." As the door closed behind him, Beria reflected on the ironic fact that few Russians would recognize either occupant of the room. Beria's official picture was deliberately distorted for security reasons as befitted the head of the NKVD but that of Stalin was more than just revised, it was changed out of all recognition. The heavy scarring from a brush with smallpox had been airbrushed out and that alone made Stalin unrecognizable. Also, Stalin was a small man, a fact he disguised by wearing built up shoes and having photographs taken on steps where he could stand higher than his companions.

"Lavrentiy Pavlovich, We have lost Moskva."

Kazan Thunderbolts

Beria nodded; this had been a defeat but an expected one. By sacrificing Moskva, they had bought the time to save Russia. They had sacrificed a rook but trapped the enemy's queen. Then Stalin's next words came as an icy shock.

"This is the result of treason, the work of wreckers and saboteurs. It is time for another purge, Lavrentiy Pavlovich, another cleaning out of those who scheme and plot against us. When we reach Gorkii, that work must start. We must arrest them all, Zhukov, Koniev, Rokossovski, Budenny, Timoshenko, Kurochkin, Yefremov, Belov, all of them. They must be tried before the people and executed. At once before they can conspire further with the Germans. See to it, see to it well Lavrentiy Pavlovich."

Beria looked at Stalin, appalled. *To eliminate the entire high command of the Soviet Army now? It was madness, madness. They might as well surrender to the Germans. 1941 and 1942 had been terrible but they had burned the fat and incompetence out of the Soviet Army. It was now commanded by men who knew what they were doing. To throw all of that away?*

Suddenly, Beria's appalled eyes saw Stalin's face undergo a subtle change, the eyes become larger, fixed and glaring, the nose extending in an exaggerated hook, the skin reddening. For a brief second, Stalin looked like one of the medieval paintings of the devil, then Beria blinked and the vision, the result of exhaustion and shock, vanished.

"I have the list here. Read it well Lavrentiy Pavlovich and bring these saboteurs to justice!"

Stalin turned away briefly and Beria seized the chance. In his pocket was something the Americans called a sap and the British a cosh. A thin leather tube, about 15 centimeters long and filled with lead shot. A simple weapon but one few knew how to use it properly. Beria was one of those who did. In one smooth action he drew the tube and brought it in a long sweeping arc that ended in a very specific point below Stalin's ear.

The effects of the blow were to completely disrupt the circulation in the blood vessels of the neck. A different placing would have brought unconsciousness but this blow did something quite different. It caused a surge of blood to run through the vessels inside his skull. Stalin's blood pressure in his brain peaked at over 240 and more than a dozen of the affected blood vessels, some large, some small, ruptured.

The effect was that of a massive stroke that paralyzed the right side of his body. Stalin saw and understood what was happening but his body would not respond to the brain's directions. Beria paused and took a second swing, striking in almost exactly the same place. The second blow sent a massive surge of blood through the torn vessels, finishing the work the first had started. Blood already seeping from his nose, ears and eyes, Stalin slumped forward onto his bed. Beria left, quietly closing the door behind him.

The next morning, Stalin's guards thought it odd that he did not rise at his usual time, but they had strict orders, he was not to be disturbed. Only at mid-day was he found, lying in a pool of blood in his compartment. The doctors were summoned and immediately diagnosed a massive stroke. One that they had been warning Stalin of for years.

"He has but a few hours at most." The senior doctor looked around. As he did so, Stalin's eyes opened and he cast a terrible glance over everyone in the room. Stalin had never been short of willpower and what happened next was an example of that. He lifted his left hand and pointed directly at Beria, standing by the door. "You." Stalin managed to say before slumping back into a coma from which he would never awake.

Beria shook his head, overcome with grief at the death of his beloved friend. "With his last breath, he appointed me his successor," he marveled. Nobody disagreed. The train was, after all, full of Beria's loyal NKVD guards.

Soviet Government Train, Gorkii.

"Welcome to Gorkii, Comrade Chairman." The Soviet Army Captain was obsequious as he met Chairman Lavrentiy Pavlovich Beria. "The meeting of STAVKA awaits you. We have a car here for you." The officer opened the door of the limousine and ushered Beria inside. Beria's driver took the wheel with three of his bodyguards occupying the other seats. Then, the little convoy pulled off, a truck with infantry in it, a T-34 tank, Beria's limousine, another T-34 and then another truck with infantry bringing up the rear.

The little convoy set off. Beria sat in the back of his car, tussling with a problem that had concerned him for two days. Should he tell the Generals of Stalin's plan to kill them all and thus earn their gratitude at a cost of admitting what he had done? Or simply stick to the story of Stalin having had a massive stroke? One was safe but offered few rewards, the other risky but offered much more. What was it to be? Beria continued to puzzle over the conundrum until a terrible shock shook his mind free.

The T-34 in front had stopped and then backed into the limousine while the one behind kept going and crashed into the back. A limousine, no matter how strong, was no match for a 30 ton tank let alone a pair of them. The bodywork crumpled with the impact, causing the glass to explode from its frames. In front, the driver seemed to be dancing only it was bullets from a PPSH-41 submachine gun that were killing him. The front seat bodyguard was already dead, the victim of a second soldier with another PPSH.

Kazan Thunderbolts

Even as Beria tried to take in the scene, additional short bursts killed his remaining two bodyguards. Beria was dragged from the car, his hand roughly tied behind his back and he was thrown into the back of one of the trucks. In the distance he could hear gunfire and, for a moment, he thought he was back in Moskva. Then reality struck, it was his NKVD people on the train being killed.

Beria was half-dragged, half-carried into a room at the Gorkii main hall. Thrown to the floor he saw a table with five men, Generals, sitting behind it. Zhukov was there, in the center seat with Rokossovski on his left and Koniev on his right. Chuikov was there also with Vatutin making up the fifth. Beria dragged himself up, no mean feat, and his voice was hoarse with rage. "Do you know who I am? I am Chairman Lavrentiy Pavlovich Beria. You will pay for this."

Zhukov's voice was cold and even, almost robotic. "You think we would let a pustule like you rule our beloved Rodina in this, its darkest hours?"

And that told Beria all he needed to know. There was a vivid image of how the Soviet Union worked: A giant bear between two men that each had a leash around the bear's neck. As long as each man held the leash taut, the bear could not harm either. But if one man let his leash slacken, the bear could turn and eat the other. Only having eaten the one, the bear would be free to kill he who had first slackened the leash. The Bear was the Soviet Army, the leash holders were the Party and the NKVD. Only, with the siege of Moskva, the Party had let the leash slacken. The Army had broken free, had destroyed the Government and was now devouring the NKVD. Zhukov's next words confirmed that picture.

"Lavrentiy Pavlovich Beria, you are charged with crimes against the Russian People and the Rodina. Crimes without number or parallel. Do you have anything to say before we pass sentence upon you?"

"You will never get away with this."

"How very unimaginative." Rokossovski's voice was almost droll. "You would think that after hearing so many condemned men, he would come up with *something* original."

Zhukov very nearly smiled at that. "Lavrentiy Pavlovich, your time has passed. Unitary Command has been restored to the Russian Army; the NKVD formations have been disarmed. Those worthy have been incorporated into the field formations, those that were not....."

Zhukov waved his hand. It hadn't been bloodless but the price had been marginal compared with the rewards. A Russian Army that stood proud again, one that did not need to fear NKVD machine guns to its rear. Now those machine guns filled a nobler, almost holy cause, killing fascists and Hitlerites, not Russians. And officers could command again. "And now you will join those who were not. Take him away."

Russian Army. *Russian* People. The *Rodina*, not the Party. *Russia*, not the Soviet Union. Beria knew that his time was indeed past. Suddenly he wondered. *Had Stalin found out? Had he found out that the political leaders filtering out of Moskva were being intercepted and killed? Not by Germans but by Russians? Had that been the treason he had spoken of? In killing Stalin, have I also killed myself?*

He was dragged again to a courtyard filled with rows of men, a few women but mostly men. He was pushed into one of those lines. To him it appeared to be at random but he had not seen the Army officer behind him consulting a piece of paper.

"In Roman times, those groups who disgraced the name of Rome suffered a terrible fate. Decimation. This will be yours."

Watching from the window, Zhukov looked down at the men below. Some, he recognized. Mekhlis, for example, who had gone to units with the specific intention of humiliating and destroying its officers. How many men had died because of his destruction of command structures?

In the coup, the political officers, the Zampolits, had been treated as they deserved. Some, Zhukov had been surprised how many, had been loved by their men and respected by their officers. They had used their skills and their power to help and assist the units they were attached to, not to hinder and subvert them. Such men had been sent to officer schools and would return as unit commanders. Others had been inept, incompetent but had the sense to do nothing. Those men were now in the rifle battalions. What was left in the courtyard and others like it all over Russia, were the dregs. The scum who had destroyed and defiled everything they touched.

Zhukov watched as the executioner stepped out and approached the first man. He leveled his Nagant revolver at the back of the man's head and fired. *Crack!* The man pitched forward and lay on the ground, a pool of red staining the stone. The executioner walked behind the line of men. "Two, three, four, five, six, seven, eight, nine, ten," *Crack!* "Two, three, three, four, five, six, seven, eight, nine, ten," *Crack!* "Two, three, four...."

Some men were quicker on the uptake. Every tenth man was being shot and the smarter started counting for themselves. Were they the unfortunate tenth? Some sagged with relief, some with despair. Some squared their shoulders to accept death with dignity, others wept. And still the count went on as the Executioner walked down the lines shooting one man in ten. Every seventh shot he would take a new revolver from his assistant who would then empty and reload the other. Finally, the executioner was on the last line, reaching the end of the last line.

"Two, three, four, five, six." He reached the end of the line and stopped. Then he returned to the point where he had started, stepped over the body of his first victim and stood behind the next in the first line. "Seven, eight, nine, ten." *Crack!* "Two, three, four......."

And so it went on, down the lines again, shooting one man in ten, then back to the beginning and starting afresh. Zhukov was fascinated to see that not one man tried to run; none tried to attack the executioner. They wept, they stood motionless, some fouled their pants, but none tried to fight or run. Eventually, only one of the prisoners was left standing in the courtyard. Lavrentiy Pavlovich Beria for his position had not been at random at all but carefully chosen so that he would, indeed, be the last left alive. *Crack!* And he too joined the rest.

Zhukov turned away. A dreadful chapter of Russian history was ending. Now the Rodina had to survive so that there would be another chapter could be written. The first step was a paper on his desk. Zhukov read it. A simple decree announcing that the NKVD was disbanded. In its place was a new organization that reverted to the old name, CheKa.

From 1918 until its name was changed to the OGPU in 1926 and the NKVD in 1934, the "All-Russian Extraordinary Commission for Combating Counter-Revolution, Profiteering and Corruption", or "CheKa", had been the Soviet Union's secret police. Even after the name had been changed, Russian secret police agents still called themselves Chekists. *Every state needs a secret police force* mused Zhukov. *They might like to pretend they don't but they do. But, the old NKVD really only defended the Communist Party; the new CheKa must protect the whole of the Rodina.*

Zhukov signed the decree and CheKa was reborn. *Now to deal with other things. There is so much to be done.*

"Valeri Ilyushin?"

"President Zhukov. We must appoint new managers for the big plants. And new Oblast administration, to replace those who are unfit. Who shall we choose?"

"The best Valeri, only the best and most competent. The Rodina cannot survive with anything less. No matter who they are, pick the best. The time has gone when we could worry about what people thought or what they believe. All that matters now is the Rodina. We must do whatever we must; appoint who we must, if the Rodina is to survive. Only the best, Valeri, no matter who. In all your decisions, Valeri, be guided by this. The Rodina deserves only the best. It is served only by those who succeed."

"Comrade President...." Rokossovski's voice was urgent, his usually lazy, relaxed manner gone.

Zhukov smiled sadly. "Gospodin President if you please Konstantin. Comrade is a term that has been dishonored. Let it only be used by those on the front line to those with whom they have shared the loss of blood and friends until its honor has been restored. Is the train sorted out?"

"Yes Gospodin President. Our people have eliminated the NKVD guards and those of the passengers we decided were incorrigible. They have disposed of the bodies; they are being burned in a pit outside the town."

"Including that body?"

"Including him, Georgy Konstantinovich. As we predicted, he was not recognized."

"Very good. Konstantin, hear me now and remember this. Nobody must know what has happened. Nobody. The units we have used, put them against the Germans until they have all gone. And let not one word of what has happened pass your lips to anybody outside. We have cleared up our own foulness; there is no need for others to know of it. And let the word spread that Joseph Vissarionovich Stalin died a hero, fighting in the ruins of Moskva."

Zhukov turned away and picked up a message, a diplomatic telegram from Washington. He opened it, his hands trembling. Just a couple of weeks before, Stalin had sent a message to the Americans, pleading for American troops to come to Russia, to help hold the line against the Germans. Troops to fight in Russia but under American national control and command. This plea for aid wasn't just an admission of how near Russia was to defeat but a massive, fundamental change in policy. The offer of national control was one that had never been made to foreigners before.

The reply to his pleas was simple. It could be summarized in one word. *YES*. An expeditionary force would be sent. Four divisions in six months time with further forces to arrive throughout 1943. The target strength was set at two Army Groups, a total of 72 divisions by 1945. Zhukov sagged in relief. 72 American Divisions, all fully mechanized, each with more tanks than a German or Russian Tank Division. Over a million men and a flood of air power such as the world had never seen before.

The message went on. The Americans requested that they hold the center of the Russian line, with Russian Armies to the North and South. Zhukov understood the message there. With the Americans in the center of the line, they couldn't leave, couldn't sign a separate peace. With that simple request, the Americans were telling him that the Russian and American armies would live or

9

die together. With the Canadians already arriving in Murmansk and lend-lease supplies pouring in. . . .

Zhukov looked at the courtyard where the bodies were already being cleared. *The fascists have six months more. Winter and spring, that is all. And winter is ours. All we have to do is hold on. Then summer will come and with it the Americans. They will bring endless supplies of weapons and equipment from their factories. The Rodina will live.*

Because the Americans are coming.

Kazan Thunderbolts

CHAPTER ONE: NEW ARRIVALS

Airfield 108, Privolzhskiy na Volga, Moskva Front, June 1943.

"How do you intend to evade the fascists?" Guards-Lieutenant Aleksandr Ivanovich Koldunov was genuinely fascinated by the P-47C in front of him. "Run around inside the fuselage perhaps?"

Lieutenant Montgomery Edwards shuffled his feet slightly at the jibe. The truth was, he could see the Russian pilot's point. His Thunderbolt dwarfed the Yak-9 parked next to it. In the end he decided attack was the best form of defense and pointed at the eight .50 caliber machine guns in the wings. "I'm not here to evade the Huns, Alex; I'm here to shoot them down."

His reward was a healthy clap on the back that sent him staggering. "Well said, Misha. And with all those guns, the fascists will have good cause to fear you."

Now it was Edward's turn to score a point. The Yak-9's armament was pathetic by American standards. It had a single 20mm cannon and one 12.7mm machine gun. "It's the old principle at work Alex, if some is good, more is better."

That got him another ferocious clap on the back. "Spoken like a true capitalist, my friend."

The two fighter pilots burst out laughing. When the Americans had started to arrive in Russia, it had been decided to "pair" American and Russian units. So, Koldunov's 866th Fighter Aviation Regiment had been paired off with Edward's 356th Fighter Group. The groups were split between bases in the area with one squadron from each per base. And so it was that Base 108 had its complement of sixteen P-47Cs (with eight more to come) and fifteen Yak-9s.

The partnering of American and Russian fighter outfits had another role as well. The Russians had been careful to select bilingual pilots for their units. Not just fluent in English and Russian but also able to instruct the American pilots in the subtleties of how to phrase their opinions and thoughts to suit a Russian environment that was still technically communist.

Edwards was about to get one of those lessons. Koldunov looked at him thoughtfully. "Misha, let me give you a little advice. We have a secret

11

advantage for the fascists have made a foolish mistake. Their 109 climbs almost twice as fast as anything we have so they have taught their pilots to climb away from us. It is a bad mistake for all we have to do is lift our nose and we can rake his cockpit as he starts to climb."

It was a standard piece of advice, an experienced fighter pilot speaking to a new arrival, but it was phrased in a uniquely Russian manner. It was unacceptable, not to mention very unwise, to suggest that their training or tactics might be in error for that would imply the communist party was fallible and everybody 'knew' it was not. But, attributing the same lesson to a 'fascist mistake' was safe and acceptable. The message remained the same. 'This is a bad move, don't do it.'

Edwards nodded, taking in the lesson. There were those in the group who had derided the Russian pilots, pointing to the number of victories scored by the German experten as evidence of Russian incapability. Edwards took a different viewpoint. He conceded the lop-sided kill-ratio but noted that this was mid-1943, not 1941. The Russian pilots they met now were the survivors of two years of that brutal punishment. To have simply survived was proof that they knew what they were doing. "We've been taught to dive away from the Huns. The Jug here is so heavy that we pick up speed quickly in a dive. Once we're clear and out of range, then we climb for another pass."

"That will work, Misha. But, be sure to extend and separate properly. Now, let us go and celebrate your arrival suitably. With vodka."

The two pilots stepped outside the hangar. Although it was intact, the Russians had placed debris on the roof and painted the result black. There was also black paint staining the walls around the windows. From the air, a perfectly-serviceable hangar looked like a burned-out ruin. The Russians had placed mud circles on the runway and taxiway to give the impression both had been bombed and were unserviceable. As soon as the Thunderbolts had landed, workers had gone out to relay the circles. At night, some would be taken up and replaced by others in new positions. That way, German photo interpreters would assume Airfield 108 was suppressed and, at best, used only as an emergency landing field. Just to drive the impression home, every time a Yak was written off in a crash landing, the wreck was placed in a revetment and made to look as if it had been bombed or strafed there. Edwards had been taught the Russian word for this systematic deception. Maskirovka.

The fine detail that went into supporting maskirovka amazed Edwards. Although there was grass between the buildings, walking on it was severely discouraged. It would only take a few people walking along the same piece of grass for the effects to be visible on aerial photographs. That could give away the fact the base was fully operational. Instead, Edwards and Koldunov walked down one concrete path, across a set of stones carefully placed in the grass and back up another concrete path. The extra distance was better than being severely reprimanded for 'sabotage' or 'aiding the fascists'. Another thing that struck him was the trash left where it had fallen. Paper, empty oil drums, garbage that would have been cleared instantly on any American base. The reason was supremely logical though. If trash was cleared up, that meant somebody must have cleared it up. And that meant the base was still in use.

The building they entered looked just as destroyed as the hangar they had just left. Koldunov pushed open a rickety door and ushered Edwards in. Once inside, the room was clean and well-maintained. It also had a bar with an interesting array of vodka bottles behind it. Most were unlabelled. That made Edwards grin to himself; one thing all the American pilots had learned was that their Russian comrades were experts at setting up and running stills. In some ways, that was fortunate since the level of drinking that went on in the 866th Fighter Aviation Regiment would never have been tolerated in the 356th. Officially, each American pilot was entitled to a shot of whisky at Uncle Sam's expense after every mission. Unofficially, bottles would appear if they were really needed but there was little doubt that American branded spirits were in very short supply. Nevertheless, there was also a pair of bottles of whisky behind the bar. Republic had a custom; every new Thunderbolt they delivered had a bottle of whisky hidden in the cockpit. It was technically a gift from the machinists' union. The Americans had donated the bottles to the bar but they were the only ones who drank the contents. The Russians preferred their home-brewed vodka.

To Edward's surprise, there was a woman sitting at the bar, wearing the high-necked Russian military uniform. His eyes took in the curled peroxide-blonde hair and the dark blue silk scarf with white polka dots wrapped around her neck. When she heard the door close, she looked around. The first thing that Edwards saw was the faint scars on her forehead, under the hairline. All the Yak fighter pilots had them. They came from bellying a fighter in and the pilot's head striking the heavy frame and exposed bolts of the cockpit. They were as much a badge of an experienced fighter pilot as pilot's wings or decorations could be. The woman was attractive but could have been much more so had her eyes not been so heavily shadowed. They were a dark, steely gray and, to Edwards, they seemed to be looking straight through him. Uneasily, he noted there was also a hint, a tiny suggestion, of madness in them.

The woman switched her gaze to Koldunov. "Dos vedan'ya, bratishka. Who's the drug?"

Edwards bristled at that. He knew that to be referred to as a drug wasn't quite an insult, but it was condescending and dismissive. It was a term all the Russian veterans applied to new recruits who had yet to prove themselves worthy of being regarded as a brother. There was only one way to prove that worthiness. Kill a fascist. Koldunov stepped in quickly. "This is Lieutenant Montgomery Edwards. He flies one of the Thunderbolts that arrived today. Misha, allow me to introduce Guards-Captain Lilya Litvyak. Eighteen kills."

"An honor to meet you ma'am." Edwards decided to be very formal and polite. He'd heard the Russians had women flying their fighters but he hadn't expected to meet one of them so quickly. "You fly a Yak?"

Once again, the steel gray eyes seemed to look right through him. "I saw the Thunderbolts landing. Too big."

Edwards wasn't going to let that pass. "Eight fifty-calibers. Great for killing fascists. And lots of range so we can hunt them down."

His words made the eyes and the face soften suddenly. There was a hint that she recognized his existence and that made Guards-Captain Litvyak much more attractive. "You will learn, drug."

Then she put down the empty glass in her hand and left. Edwards turned to Koldunov who already had a glass of vodka in his hand. "Did I say something wrong Alex?"

Koldunov shook his head. "Tovarish Lilya is like that with everybody. She has been flying for 18 months without a break. She is tired, bone tired, deep in her soul. More importantly she has seen everybody she knows killed. All the veterans are like this, they will not allow others close to them for they know they too will be killed. Do not take it personally, Misha. The loss of friends has hurt her so often, she just does not want to be hurt again. Now, a whisky?"

Edwards wasn't a big drinker. In fact, he rarely drank alcohol at all. But, after his meeting with Guards-Captain Lilya Litvyak, he felt like he needed one. "I'd like to try your vodka if I may."

"Good choice." Koldunov appreciated the gesture. "We have three kinds. Special reserve; that has been aged for thirty days in the bottle. Then we have standard; that has been aged in the bottle for thirty hours. And we have the new."

"How long has the new been aged in the bottle for?" Edwards had guessed the answer but gave Koldunov the chance to say it.

"Thirty minutes. I think we had better start you on the Special Reserve."

River Gunboat PR-73, Staraya Mayna, Volga River.

"What are we doing this time, Skipper?"

Lieutenant Kennedy shrugged. "Another supply run. One of the midstream islands is running low on ammunition and rations. We have to resupply them and take off a couple of wounded. Get the charts out, Lenny; we'll have to think about this one."

Kennedy looked at his command with a singular degree of affection. The river gunboats were the direct descendents of the flotillas that had fought on the Mississippi during the Civil War although there was little in common between them and their ancestors. PR-73 was armed with a three inch 50 caliber gun forward and a quadruple mount for 1.1 inch machine guns aft. She also had an Army 60mm mortar mounted amidships and four .50 caliber machine guns in two twin mounts. All the guns except the mortar had once been installed on warships as anti-aircraft guns but replaced by more modern weapons. Surplus to the fleet's requirements, they had found their way to the river gunboat force. PR-73 had originally been ordered as an 80-foot Elco PT boat from the Herreshoff yard up in Rhode Island but the original order had been cancelled and replaced with one for the river gunboats desperately needed on the Volga.

PR-73 had inherited her engines from the PT boats. She had two 12-cylinder 1,500 horsepower gasoline engines that were equipped with underwater exhausts and carefully muffled. Combined with a hull that was designed for shallow draft, she could go right up to the enemy-held west bank of the Volga without alerting any sentries there. That ability was the cause of one of the more exciting jobs the crew of PR-73 could get assigned. Take a team over to the other side and wait while the rangers kidnapped a couple of German sentries and brought them back to the waiting gunboat. Then, get everybody back to the east bank where the captured Germans could be interrogated. *Exciting stuff.* Kennedy thought to himself. *I wonder if Joe realizes how much fun I'm having out here.* He actually felt sorry for his brother, trapped Stateside learning to fly B-29s. Their father was grooming his elder brother for a political career and that had left Kennedy free to follow his own star. As a keen small boats man, that star had led him to the river gunboat fleet.

"Got the charts, Jack. For what they are worth." Ensign Leonard J. Thom wasn't too impressed with the Volga River charts they had received. They compared very poorly with the British Admiralty charts everybody used in the oceans. These river charts were inaccurate, missed important details and were often poorly reproduced.

Then there was the Volga itself. The islands in it were rarely more than mud banks that extended above the water by a bare meter or two. They, and the ones that remained below the river's surface, constantly changes shape and moved as the flowing water either eroded them a way or deposited more mud. Or both. A clear channel one night could be obstructed by a mudbank the next. Navigation on the river was a skilled art that defied even the most careful analysis.

"Here we are. Mordovo   The objective is this island here." Kennedy's finger stabbed at the chart. "It's a rock outcrop, 10 meters above the river level. According to the brass, it's an essential observation point, allows us to see what's going on in the town and along the west bank for miles. The Huns know that of course, and they try and throw us off every so often. So far they've failed. It is an outcrop, the sides are as sheer as it gets and landing there is difficult. There's one small spot our side of the island where we can get our goodies ashore. When I say small, I mean small. A few feet wide at most."

"Going to be a navigation problem finding it then." Quartermaster 3rd Class Ed Mauer sucked his teeth. "We can't show any lights that close in and I'm leery of using the radar. We'll be doing well just to find the island."

The Volga had a lot in common with the Mississippi although the Russian river was wider and didn't twist around quite as much. Not quite. On the other hand, the towns and villages on the Volga were either blacked out, destroyed or both. The Russians had destroyed all the navigational aids on the west bank before they had retreated. Sailing on the Volga at night, in pitch darkness, was hazardous enough. When the constantly-shifting mudbanks and islands were added into the stew, conducting operations became an extremely unsafe occupation. Which was why, of course, young men like Lieutenant (jg) John F. Kennedy found it irresistible.

"Any word of opposition?" Thom had referred to the third element of the dangers they faced. The Germans had started to move their own fast attack craft into the area. The German S-boats were dangerous adversaries, at least 10 knots faster than the Russian and American river gunboats although nowhere near as well armed. They were still weighed down with torpedoes which the conditions on the Volga made worse than useless. The good news was that the S-boats were heavily outnumbered.

"There's reputed to be two S-boats based at Mordovo. There to stop us doing exactly what we plan to do. The Huns want us off that island as much as we want to stay on it. What I suggest we do is this. We hug the east bank all the way south to where the river splits at Scary Belly. Then, we hug the west bank for five miles until we're past the split. That points our bows straight at the island. We can't go far wrong in a mile or so. Then, once we've delivered the cargo, we head north again, back on the east bank."

"Sounds good to me." Mauer looked again, noting the position of the town of Staryy Belyy Yar. "Coastal batteries?"

"88s at Sengiley. Navy Intel thinks four of them. As long as we make sure we stick close to the east bank down by Scary Belly, we should avoid them. Ed, keep a close eye on the radar warning receiver. The Intel weenies want every scrap of information we can find on Hun radars. Doesn't matter how vague or imprecise it is. Any other questions? Comments?

There was a generalized shaking of heads. Everybody knew what had to be done and there was no point in repeating it. Kennedy looked at his crew and nodded to himself. *These are good men, a crew to be proud of. Damn, I'm glad to be out here, not pushing a pen in an office somewhere and my father can keep his opinions to himself.* "Right people, let's lock and load then."

The crew split up into their work details. Kennedy had already learned the most important rule for a young officer. Let the senior petty officers know what was wanted and then get out of their way and leave them get on with it. So, he retreated to the tiny cubbyhole laughingly called the wardroom while some of the crew started checking over the guns and ammunition while others loaded the supplies they had to deliver. The rations and ammunition were stowed in modified 55 gallon oil drums to protect them from the river water. Each drum had to be carefully sealed once its contents had been checked. The process was an example of the way Kennedy ran PR-73. It might be slack and informal but the jobs that had to be done were done fast and with meticulous care.

A few minutes later, Mauer knocked on the door of the wardroom where Kennedy was having a coffee. He had a very strange look on his face. "Skipper, the troops on the Island, they're Russian Marines, right?"

Kennedy nodded. "That's right. They're supposed to be good."

"And they've got Mozzy-Nags, with 7.62 Russian?"

Kennedy shook his head. "Tokarev SVT semi-automatic rifles. Like our Garands. Same round as the Mozzy-Nag though, 7.62 Russian."

"That's what I thought. Well, I took a look at the ammunition we're supposed to be delivering." Mauer handed a round over. "That ain't no 7.62 Russian. Take a look at the headstamp, Skipper. It's Canadian-made .303 British."

B Company. 802nd Tank Destroyer Battalion, 83rd Infantry Division, Klimovo, Chuvashskaya Bridgehead, June 1943.

Digging in was the eternal task of the soldier. If Private Eugene Searle had not known that before coming to Russia, he certainly knew it now. It didn't help that the weapon he was helping to position was a 90mm M2 anti-tank gun. At eight tons, it was a lot of gun to dig in. It was time to start grumbling.

"Why are we putting this damned great thing here?" Searle suddenly realized he was missing an even more important question. "And why are we here, come to that?"

Kazan Thunderbolts

"We're here because we're here." Sergeant Jeremy Perry looked at the private with measurable disdain. He was well aware that it was Searle who had given him the nickname of "Jelly Belly". In fact, that was one reason why Searle was a member of the detail digging the gun into position. "And that's because we're here. We'll stay here until one of the brass decides that they want us there. Then, to there we'll go and we'll be there because we're there. Get it now?"

Sergeant Perry was actually well aware of why the 331st Regimental Combat Team of the 83rd "Thunderbolt" Infantry Division had been stationed in this particular location. The Kolkhoz, the collective farm, they were setting up in was the key to defending the pass behind them. The Kolkhoz Pass wasn't much of a pass by normal standards; to conventional eyes it was merely a strip of land that was a bit better, a bit more traversable, than the ground on either side. Nevertheless, that small difference still made it a key strategic piece of ground.

The Germans had launched a major offensive in the spring of 1943, aimed at clearing Russian forces from the west bank of the Volga. The assault had been, at best, partially successful and had only succeeded in reducing the size of the Russian bridgeheads on the west bank. Of all those bridgeheads, the most important and the one that had seen the bitterest fighting was the Chuvashskaya Bridgehead. It protected the approaches to the city of Kazan and prevented the Germans from closing on that city. Viewed a different way, the Chuvashskaya Bridgehead was also a potential springboard for an Allied offensive to retake the city of Nizhny Novgorod to the west. This double importance made it a critical piece of ground for both sides and there was little doubt that another German offensive was being planned.

The Russians had been pouring troops into the bridgehead. Not just troops but tanks, artillery, anti-tank guns, landmines and every other defensive asset they could find. Then, when the first American division had arrived, it too had been sent to the Chuvashskaya Bridgehead. And so it was that the 83rd had found itself defending the village of Klimovo. It had taken Perry one look at the map to see how critical this sector was. The Chuvashskaya Bridgehead was a mixture of open, rolling farmland interspersed with patches of dense forest. Here, at Klimovo, those patches of forest had spread and joined together so that any possible advance was funneled into a narrow front that also contained three major east-west roads. The bottleneck at Klimovo was the key to any further German movement east.

The German infantry formations had never recovered from the blood-letting they had experienced at Moskva and Stalingrad the year before. They were all desperately under strength and had only a fraction of the fighting power they had deployed before the Russian Campaign had started. Their panzer and panzer grenadier formations were the key to any offensive but they couldn't operate in the forests. So, their eyes also focused on the clear terrain at Klimovo. That meant one thing to Perry; it was at Klimovo that the American Army would meet the German Army for the first time. It was Perry's most sincere wish that the meeting would come as a nasty surprise for the Germans.

"Your gun in position yet, Sergeant?" Perry's reflections were cut short by the voice from behind him. Lieutenant Irwin Grisham was in command of the platoon of four 90mm guns assigned to support the infantry battalion holding the Kolkhoz. In Perry's opinion, he had the makings of a really good officer so he snapped out a perfect parade-ground salute.

"We're just finishing digging the first gun in now, Sir. " He gestured over to a ruined building where the muzzle of the 90mm gun peeked out through the remnants of a window. The collapsed stone walls protected the gun on three sides while the back was open so that the half-track prime mover could back up to it and tow it clear. What had once been the floor of the building had been packed earth. Now it had been dug away to lower the gun and the earth had been piled up on either side to add to the protection afforded to the gun.

Grisham looked at the position of the gun in the ruined buildings. "That's the best of the four positions. You've got a direct line of sight right down the center of the valley. Guns two and three are in the woods on either side of us. We couldn't find anything like this position so the men are digging deeper pits and trying to camouflage the guns with branches and foliage. Gun four is further back so that it can cover our flanks if the Huns try to outflank us. The infantry are fanned out in a clover leaf to cover the approaches and we've got the tank company sitting back as a reserve."

Perry thought about that. It was a standard infantry defensive position, almost straight out of the book, but it was one remarkable well-suited to this particular location. It blocked this part of the Kolkhoz Pass and the flanks of the position were held by the other two battalion combat teams of the 331st RCT. The 330th RCT was defending the front further north, around Novye Achakasy while the 329th RCT was being held in divisional reserve. Perry reflected that, as usually, the Sergeants Grapevine meant that everybody was much better informed about what was going on around them than most of the officers. Thus was it ever so.

"Sounds good to me, Sir. I reckon the Huns are going to get a real nasty surprise when they run into this lot."

Grisham gave a confident smile. "I reckon you might be right there, Sergeant. More than you think; the tank battalions have got the new M4 Mediums. They'll give the kraut Mark Threes and Fours a hammering. Carry on the good work here."

Kazan Thunderbolts

Gunboat Squadron GunRon 5 Headquarters, Staraya Mayna, Volga River.

"Hi, Ray. Could I see the old man for a moment?"

Lieutenant Commander Raymond Blake looked up with an expression of unmitigated shock on his face. "See the old man? Impossible, quite impossible. You need an appointment with at least three week's notice, endorsed by a Senator, two Congressmen and a naval officer who has served on a battleship. On the other hand, John, if you'd like to grab a cup of coffee and sit there for a few minutes, I'll slide you in at the end of this meeting."

"Thanks Ray." Kennedy took a small cup of coffee form the machine and sipped it. It was freshly-brewed which was a wonder. Coffee was a serious problem this far along a precarious supply line that stretched from Vladivostok by way of the Trans-Siberian Railway to Kazan. And yet, the brew was as essential to running the U.S. Navy as fuel oil and ammunition. So, the Navy had made sure at least some of the precious beans made it out to the Volga Front. There, shortage of supply meant that the cups served were small and the grounds reused until no hint of flavor was left. No brew was ever thrown away be it ever so old and acid. The half-full mug in Kennedy's hands was fresh-brewed and the grind was being used for the first time. As such it was nectar and balm for a troubled soul.

Ten minutes later, Blake saw some officers left Commander Henry Farrow's office. He picked up the telephone and announced Kennedy's presence. "The old man says, send you in."

"What can I do for you, John?" Farrow was sitting behind a desk loaded with paper. Keeping a U.S. Navy river gunboat squadron operational on the Volga River in Russia was an interesting administrative challenge.

Kennedy knew just how bad the administrative burden was and hated to add to it. Nevertheless, Farrow had to know what his men had found. "Henry, we were loading the cargo for tonight's run. The boys were about to seal the ammunition drums when one of them thought it would be wise to check the contents before we sealed it up. It's lucky he did; the ammunition we had issued to us for delivery is .303 British. Canadian-made, but still .303."

"Are you sure John?" Farrow didn't sound disbelieving; he knew his officers too well for that. Kennedy had reached into his fatigue pocket and brought out some of the ammunition. After the first round had been found, Ed Mauer had checked every ammunition drum. They had all been loaded with .303 British. "Who found this?"

"QM3 Mauer, Henry. Good man."

"They all are." Farrow's comment was almost inadvertent but it was true. GunRon 5 was noted for having highly competent personnel along with a complete disregard for conventional naval discipline. Some heretics had even suggested the two facts might be connected. He picked up his telephone. "Ray, ask Captain Lapshin if he could step in for a moment please?"

It took about five minutes for the Russian naval officer to arrive. "John, I'd like to introduce Mihail Stepanovich, our Russian Navy Liaison officer and deputy commander of our base here. Mihail, this is Lieutenant (jg) John Fitzgerald Kennedy, commander of PR-73. He's got a horror story to tell you."

Kennedy repeated the story of how the ammunition had been identified. By the time he reached the end, Lapshin had gone pale. "What have you done about this?"

"I've located a supply of 7.62mm Russian we can take. One of your gunboats, the BK-241 got involved in a shoot-out with a shore battery last night. She's not hurt bad but she'll be in dock for a few days. She's got 7.62 Russian for her twin machine guns. We asked the Captain of the 241-boat to hang on to his ammunition. Didn't explain why but he agreed to delay debombing for a few hours. We can take that with us, in addition to the British .303. We've got room for both and there might be something going on we don't know about."

"Nobody is using Canadian weapons down this way. Up around Petrograd and Archangel'sk, yes, but not down here." Lapshin was an extremely worried man. An accident or error of this kind could easily be called 'sabotage' or even 'treason and aiding the enemy'. Either could get a man shot or worse. Anybody who believed there was nothing worse than being shot had never seen the CheKa at work on a fascist. "But taking both types of ammunition is a good precaution. And the ammunition was in drums before you got it?"

"It was, but the drums weren't sealed. Thank G . . . . errr . . . . . Thank good fortune that they weren't."

Lapshin almost smiled at the near-slip and recovery. There were many who saw the growing presence of the American Army in Russia as just another group of foreigners on the sacred soil of the Rodina. But, the Americans were trying very hard to be good guests and Kennedy's mid-sentence change of course was a good example. "Just how could this have happened? The trains from the northern ports don't come down this way. I can't see ammunition being put on the wrong set of trains."

Kennedy glanced at Farrow and got a slight nod. "It is possible; the wrong wagon may have been placed in a consist. That happens sometimes. Alternatively, the ammunition may have been shipped here deliberately for the Partisans or rear-area troops. I believe the Partisans have been given some Canadian lend-lease weapons?"

Lapshin nodded. "They have."

"So, that explains why it might have come here. But reaching us, that's different. There is no way that could happen by accident. This was deliberate. And that makes me ask, why?"

"There is only one reason that makes sense. The Hitlerites plan to attack our outpost and they wanted our Marines to find they have the wrong ammunition so that there will be much reduced resistance."

Kennedy thought about that. "There's a way that can be useful to us there. We deliver the ammunition; if there's an attack, then we know that supplying the wrong ammunition was part of the plan and your CheKa go . . . investigators can get to work finding out who on our side is working with them. If there is no attack, then the fact the wrong ammunition was sent to us is an accident and we need say nothing about it."

Lapshin thought about that very carefully. "If I have read your American hard-boiled detective stories correctly, 'goons' is a good description of the CheKa operatives. I think you are right. If there is an attack, then it is treachery and a CheKa responsibility. If not, it is incompetence and ours."

"As a matter of fact, sir, we have another opportunity here as well. The Huns will be watching the island to see us make our delivery. Why don't we hang around after we've unloaded, just out of sight? Then, if there is an attack, we can close in and support the Marines?" Kennedy half-smiled at a sudden thought. "You know, the Huns may have done us a favor by trying this. They've outsmarted themselves; given us warning of the attack and revealed they have a sabotage cell in place."

"That'll mean you'll be close to the west bank come daylight. Bad news if the Luftwaffe comes calling." Farrow could see the loss of a gunboat and its crew featuring in one of his reports.

"I don't think so, Sir. We've been there before. The Luftwaffe boys aren't so hot when it comes to hitting moving ships. We'll be O.K."

"Mihail, does this seem to you to be a good idea?"

"The marines will value the support certainly. And the more our forces work together the better. I can speak with the Army and see if their fighter regiments can provide some cover if needed. And, yes, John, you are right. The Hitlerites have tried to be too clever. You will find this is very common. They will come up with a cunning plan that has every prospect of success but then ruin it by adding unnecessary details that undo all the care they took."

"Gentlemen, I think we have a plan." Farrow leaned back in his seat and folded his arms behind his head. "Good work today, John. And make sure Mauer gets a reward. If he hadn't kept his eyes open . . . ."

305th Bombardment Group, Bolshaya Tarlovka Airfield, Russia.

"What's the worst thing we have to face over there, Sir?"

Colonel Frederick Anderson thought carefully about that. 'Over there' meant the west side of the Volga, enemy territory. He had commanded the first bomber detachment to arrive in Russia, a group of two dozen old B-17Ds, sent to hold the line while the more modern B-17Es were made combat-ready. That had been six months ago and it seemed like an age. He'd gone 'over there', he'd dropped bombs and he'd been shot at. That had made him a veteran. He'd seen his friends go down, B-17s folding up in mid-air, exploding or spinning in at the end of a trail of fire. That also had made him a veteran. Now he was going home to take command of a new bomb group. These boys would be continuing the fight for him and for that he owed them the best advice he could muster.

"A lot of people, especially those back in the world, will tell you it's the fighters. They'll tell you about the 109 that can climb like a rocket or the 190 that has wings lined with cannons. Or about the twin-engined heavy fighters that have their noses stuffed with guns. Yeah they're bad all right but if you pilots keep your formations tight and you gunners keep your eye on the ball, you can fight them off.

"The worst thing? It's flak. The German flak is really terrific. They've got predictors down there that can lock the guns on to you in a flash. If you fly straight and level for as much as ten seconds, they'll put a shell straight into your belly. If you don't take evasive action all the way in, you're dead. I don't mean a few gentle curves; I mean constant changes in all three dimensions. Throttle up and down to vary the speed, climb and dive, constantly keep turning. Stop twisting for just ten seconds and they'll shoot you down for sure."

The room went silent as the implications of the message sank in. Another pilot broke the silence by standing up and speaking. "What altitude did you bomb from, Sir?"

"We went in at sixteen to eighteen thousand feet. That's all our D-ships could manage. Also, we didn't bring the Norden bombsights with us so we had to fly lower to compensate. You've got E ships and the Norden so I think the plan is to send you in at twenty thousand."

Anderson knew there had been a lot of opposition to sending B-17Es equipped with the Norden bombsight to Russia, mostly based around the fear that the bombsight would be copied by the Russians. Senators had been threatening to stop the deployment, how Anderson wasn't quite clear about, until Hap Arnold had taken them to one side. He'd pointed out that the B-17s would be hitting critical targets and using older, less accurate bombsights would mean fewer hits on those targets. That meant the bombers would have to go back to those targets more often and would suffer greater losses as a result. Did the Senators really want to be publicly blamed for the death of American boys? The opposition had ceased almost on the spot.

"How deep did you go over there, Sir?"

"Deepest raid we did was to Sarov, 200 miles the other side of the Volga. Oddly, that one was a milk-run. The Huns weren't expecting us to go that deep and we took them by surprise. Also, we had MiG-3s escorting us. They're the best high-altitude birds the Russians have. They broke up the fighter attacks before they got to us."

"High-altitude, sir?" The questioner sounded confused.

"This is the Russian Front. Everything over 16,000 feet is high altitude here. The Russians are completely committed to supporting their ground troops so almost everything they do is below five thousand feet, ten thousand at most. So the Germans fight down there as well. Their Focke-Wulf is good at low altitude but loses its edge higher up. The 109 is good all the way up to thirty thousand, but not so hot low down. So, you can expect to see mostly 109s."

"How did the fighters come in, Sir?"

"From the tail. Our D-ships were blind there and the Huns exploited it. We had a field-expedient fix in that we sawed the tail cone off and had the radio operator go back there with a spare .50 caliber. That tail stinger gave the Huns a nasty shock but they still come in from aft. Your E-ships have got twin .50s in a proper tail position so you'll be able to give the Huns a good, American welcome."

That remark caused a thunderstorm of cheers and war-whoops. Anderson looked around at the room full of bomber crews and reflected on something else he hadn't mentioned. He had brought 24 B-17Ds to Russia. In six months, 14 of them had been lost. In the back of the briefing room, the commander of the 305th Bombardment Group, Lt. Col. Curtis LeMay was glowering even more than usual. He'd arranged for his old friend Fred Armstrong to give this briefing so his crews would learn the bitterly-won experience the D-ships had gathered without taking the casualties. Only, he'd spotted the terrible flaw in the information Armstrong had provided. *If my Flying Fortresses are gyrating all over the place to avoid flak, just how in hell are we going to hit anything?*

CHAPTER TWO: FIRST CONTACT

River Gunboat PR-73, Entering the Ulyanov'sk Narrows, Volga River.

"This is the first crunch point." Kennedy swung his binoculars along the west bank of the Volga. Everything over there seemed quiet and dark but he was very well aware that could change in an instant. There was still fighting going on in the city with Russian hold-outs defying the German occupiers three months after Berlin had claimed Ulyanov'sk had fallen. Some of the missions PR-73 had completed were running supplies to those hold-outs. They had been . . . interesting. PR-73 still had a scratch on one bridge window where a .32 caliber pistol bullet had hit the ship while her crew was unloading. That was closer combat than anybody on the gunboat had thought appropriate.

When planning an operation, Kennedy's habit was to identify the places where things had the highest probability of going wrong. He called them crunch points and passing each one meant he and his crew were a step closer to completing their assignment. So, he studied each crunch point especially closely and tried to work out as many alternative plans to handle its specific dangers as possible. When they had to go down river, the Ulyanov'sk Narrows were the first crunch point.

To Kennedy, calling this spot the "Narrows" was an absurdity only understandable when one saw the Volga for the first time. The Ulyanov'sk Narrows were more than two miles wide but that was 'narrow' on a river that often exceeded twenty miles in width. The problem at Ulyanov'sk, though, the problem that made it a 'crunch point' was that the Russians had built a railway bridge over the river before the war. They'd built two stone causeways, each half a mile long, out into the river and then erected a steel bridge to span the rest. It was the only crossing of the Volga in the 400 km stretch from Kazan to Tolyatti, so obviously when the Germans had assaulted Ulyanov'sk, the Russians had blown the bridge up. That had stopped the German advance dead in its tracks. It had also left the Ulyanov'sk Narrows reduced to a single mile between the causeways and that mile was partially blocked by the tangled wreckage of the bridge.

What all that meant was that the gunboats using the river had to edge out into the middle where the water was deepest and the bridge wreckage least obstructive. Kennedy had always wondered why nobody had ever thought of putting guns on the causeways. A quad-20 on the German side or a twin-37 on the Russian could make life really bad for a gunboat trying to get past. Strangely, nobody had tried it. Both sides had tried everything else though. Mines, booby traps, the occasional fougasse. Each gunboat commander had his own theories about how best to run the Ulyanov'sk Narrows. Kennedy was a firm believer in clinging as close as possible to the east bank and sliding through unnoticed. It might not be the most glamorous or heroic of methods but it worked more often than not.

This night, though, something was different. Something had been niggling at the back of Kennedy's mind ever since he had spoken with Lapshin in Farrow's office. He wasn't able to quite put a name to it but he had decided that hints from a Guardian Angel were enough. Tonight he would do things differently. He'd taken PR-73 across the river a few miles upstream and was now sliding down by the west bank. He knew, because he had checked it, that no lights were showing anywhere and the dark green and dark gray camouflage made the gunboat invisible except at close range. Strangers to the river found it hard to understand how far away even a dim light could be seen or how even the softest sound carried across the water. So, all the lights were out, every shutter was screwed down and sealed and the crew didn't speak, even in whispers. Especially not in whispers for a whisper actually carried further than softly-spoken words.

Kennedy's reverie was interrupted by a series of rifle shots from an area of the rubble that had once been Ulyanov'sk that lay just in front of them. His night-accommodated vision placed the outbreak of shooting as inland, close to the ruined railway bridge. The firing increased quickly as other riflemen joined in, followed by the crackle of machine gun fire. Kennedy and Thom exchanged quick glances, each thinking the same thing. *The Germans have claimed that Ulyanov'sk has fallen. Perhaps they should tell that to the people still fighting there.*

Ashore, the fighting was picking up intensity with the explosions of grenades and light mortars joining the gunfire. *Whatever is going on in there is more than just a brushfire skirmish. Either the hold-outs ambushed a German supply convoy or the Germans tried a night attack to mop up the holdouts.* Overhead, a train-like roar announced the sound of the Russian artillery on the east bank opening fire. Kennedy heard the shells pass over and descend on the firefight. *Obviously somebody out there with a radio had called for help.* The shells exploded in the ruined city, a tight-pattern that revealed the guns had been carefully laid. Then, the radio on PR-73 crackled into life, in English and in clear.

"PR-73, PR-73, this is Grigor-53. There are German engineers and infantry in the wreckage of the bridge. They are trying to seize our embankment and lay mines in the safe passage. Turn back, you cannot get through until we clear the fascists out and make the passage safe."

Kennedy and Thom exchanged grins again. They'd just heard a beautiful piece of maskirovka. The Russian commander knew that PR-73 would be coming down the west bank tonight but also that the Germans knew the supply boat must be PR-73. Otherwise, why would they have arranged the wrong ammunition? Kennedy was prepared to bet that the people who had set that up had a file on him. That might well include the fact that he preferred to hug the east bank. The radio message would have confirmed that PR-73 was by the East Bank and focused German attention there. *Sometimes,* Kennedy reflected, *people forget how sneaky the Russians can be. And I bet the fighting in the city was a German diversion to cover the attack on the bridge.*

Kennedy swung PR-73's bows out until she was rounding the end of the western embankment. To his delight he saw a stream of tracer fire; a quadruple 20mm gun was his guess, raking the area of the river's east bank upstream of the wrecked bridge. The next task was to get through the wrecked bridge itself. The situation was complicated by a wrecked S-boat that had sunk just off the end of the embankment. Kennedy smiled to himself at the thought of that kill. PR-57, one of the larger Huckins boats with two three inch guns, had ambushed the S-boat and pummeled it into a wreck before sending it to the bottom. That had been the American's first kill on the Volga and the celebrations afterwards had been legendary.

"Here we go." Kennedy barely did more than mouth the words. He could see the broken mast of the sunken S-boat off to starboard, the wreckage of the bridge to port. There was barely a thirty foot gap where the water was deep enough to allow an Elco boat through. The catch was, the Elco boat had a 28 foot beam. He kept his eyes glued on the broken mast, wondering of the Germans had deliberately let the boat sink there in order to block this gap. His mind was filled with the image of the underwater hull of the wrecked S-boat and the ruins of the bridge. The cargo he was carrying was making PR-73 sit deeper in the water as well.

Over on the starboard side, Mauer was staring at the steel girders of the bridge, his hands held up to give the clearance. They were barely more than a foot apart and the sight of them closing made Kennedy hold his breath. He was deliberately trading off starboard side clearance to put more water between his vessel and the sunken S-boat. Mauer's hands kept closing until the space between them was little more than the thickness of a piece of paper. That's when Kennedy gave a slight degree of port helm and edged his craft through the gap. Mauer started to spread his hands again while the mast Kennedy had his eyes on was falling away astern. They were through.

The underwater exhausts proved their value then. PR-73 accelerated from her previous walking pace up to eight knots and then to ten. She was the downstream side of the bridge now and the western embankment was shielding her from the fighting and gun batteries on the upstream side of the bridge. They were through Crunch Point One.

305th Bombardment Group, Bolshaya Tarlovka Airfield, Russia.

"Damn it, where is the bomb damage?" Lt. Colonel LeMay rubbed his eyes. They would have been sore anyway after many hours staring at photographs of targets hit by the B-17Ds earlier in the year. They were made worse by the effects of Bell's Palsy that had paralyzed much of his face. He had a bottle of eye-drops prescribed by the base doctor and he used them carefully. They did seem to help. His attention was diverted away from the photographs on his desk by a knock on the door.

"Enter."

"Captain Richard Gonzalez, Sir. I understand you're looking for a reconnaissance pilot? I volunteered."

Bell's Palsy had its virtues sometimes. LeMay remained expressionless while he looked at the Captain. "Why?"

"My squadron is doing mapping flights, Sir. The Russian maps are dreadful and we just can't use them. So, the Lightnings are doing photomapping flights to get the information we need to make our own. It's boring, Sir. So, when the request for a volunteer came in this afternoon, I grabbed it."

"You fly an F-4A?"

"F-5B Sir. The F-4s are all stateside, used for training. I got a nose full of cameras. You just tell me what you want photographed and I'll get the shots."

"You'll need to do more than that. I want bomb damage assessment pictures. You'll follow the raid in. I want to know where our bombs land."

"Are you sure, Sir?"

LeMay glowered at the young pilot. "What do you mean by that?"

Gonzalez seemed remarkably unintimidated by the glare. "I mean, Sir, I've been photographing the west bank of the Volga for a couple of weeks now. If there's bomb damage down there, I can't see any. Nor can our photo-analysts."

That was what LeMay had been worried about. "Got these pictures. They're the only ones we have. We'll go through them. If there's no bomb damage, I need to know that."

"These are bad pictures, Sir, quality is terrible. My guess is they're Russian. To be frank, Sir, the Russians don't give a damn about photographing what's going on behind enemy lines. They rely on reports from their partisans for that. Their recon squadrons use old biplanes to provide visual observation and reporting over the front lines. Their optics are crap; that's how I guessed these pictures were Russian. Frankly, Sir, we'll be wasting our time. Even if their cameras were capable of picking up bomb craters, they're not stabilized so vibration from the aircraft blurs them. And that's assuming there is something down there to see."

"Keep speaking frankly and we'll get along fine." LeMay looked at Gonzalez again. "Where do you come from, Captain?"

"The Philippines, Sir. My parents were born in Manila but they immigrated and settled down in California before I was born. My father always said that the best way to do a job is to get it done."

LeMay grunted. "Good advice. Now start looking."

River Gunboat PR-73, Off Sengiley, Volga River.

"There's a radar transmitting out there." Radioman 2/c John Maguire had a truly enviable battle station. He was in the wardroom, sitting in the only comfortable chair on PR-73. "It's on our starboard beam."

The cut was only accurate to within 90 degrees but that close enough. Ahead or astern would put the radar transmission on the Volga. To port would put it on the east bank and that would imply it was friendly. Starboard put it on the west bank and that alone meant it was almost certainly German.

"Frequency?"

"55 centimeters."

"Mark it down. Take her as close to the bank as we can Lenny. We'll try and get lost in the bank clutter. Cut the speed to four knots."

The helmsman edged PR-73 closer to the east bank. The gunboat had crossed the Volga as soon as she was clear of Ulyanov'sk and made her way south under the protection of the Russian-held bank. For a while, the river had been almost ten miles wide but now it was narrowing to barely four miles. To make matters worse, that four mile wide stretch of water was guarded by a battery of four 88mm guns. Now, it appeared as if those guns had been given a radar search capability and possible fire control. That made them much more dangerous. Kennedy thought about that carefully. "If they were tracking us, they'd have opened fire by now. Keep the speed right down, I've heard that the faster we move, the more likely it is the radar will pick us up."

PR-73 continued to drift south. The radar trace on the intercept display obdurately remained marginal, just barely visible on the outside edge of the display. Maguire shook his head. "I don't think he can see us, Skipper. We're only just picking his signal up. I don't know why it's so weak. It's as if something is blocking the transmission and we're only getting a glimmering of what's out there. I've heard about this from other guys on the river. Some nights we can see something from the bridge but the radar swears blind there is nothing there. Other times, we can get a return off something that is miles away, even around a bend in the river. Then again, we can get a strong and clear echo and there's nothing there. There's a hell of a lot about radar transmissions we just don't understand right now."

"I don't want to understand it, Johnny. That's your job. I just want their set to keep not working if you get my drift."

"I wish I could guarantee that." Maguire looked at his screen again. "On paper I can pick up a radar transmission from three times the range it can detect a return echo from us. With all these weird things going on, I just don't know whether that is true or not. Hello, he's gone. Now does that mean he's switched off or we just can't pick him up any more?"

"It means he's given up and switched off." Kennedy was looking out of the bridge windows. Two beams of white light were methodically sweeping the river where it reached its narrowest point. He gestured at them. "Take a look at that. German searchlights. They're searching for us."

Kennedy watched the beams sweeping cross the river, analyzing their pattern and trying to work out how to slip past them. A single searchlight on its own was easy to beat. Two working together was much harder and four would be almost impossible.

"What are we going to do, Skipper? Shoot them out?"

Kennedy shook his head. "They're three and a half miles away. Only our three incher will reach that far and as soon as we open up with it, everybody will know where we are. I don't fancy taking on four 88s with a single three incher, do you? We'll just have to try and slide through. Damn, those crews are good though."

The two searchlights were weaving an intricate net over the three-mile wide narrows in front of them. Even when they reached the shore and the town of Staryy Belyy Yar, known irreverently to the American gunboat crews as "Scary Belly", there was enough light left for the sailors to make out the shape of some of the buildings. The town itself was completely blacked out, not a light to be seen anywhere.

"Sometimes I think the Russians are more on our side than the east-coasters are." Thom had a measurable amount of dislike in his voice and it wasn't directed at the Russians. The U.S. Navy in general had bitter memories of how the east coast cities had refused to institute a black-out and left the ships offshore silhouetted against the lights. They had proved easy prey for the Germans submarines prowling off the coast. A lot of good ships had gone down and a lot of good seamen had died before the Federal government had forced a black-out.

"Cape Cod shut down as soon as war was declared." Kennedy protested. "We even sent sailing boats out every evening to make sure nobody in Hyannis Port had a light showing."

He would have said more but he was interrupted by a sudden explosion of fire on the west bank, just inland from Scary Belly. For a moment, it looked like a massive bomb going off but it started to stretch and lengthen, reaching out across the river in a sheet of orange flame. Kennedy recognized them instantly. They were Katyushka rockets, also known as Stalin's Organs.

One of the stories that did the rounds about the siege of Moskva was that Stalin had been trapped in a building while fighting with the city's defenders and his last act had been to call in the Katyushkas on his own position. Kennedy had no idea whether that was true or not but he did know that the salvo rocket launchers were immensely destructive.

The Germans knew it too, and the searchlights on the opposite bank shut down as their crews crashed out. They had their searchlights mounted on trucks and the drivers kept their engines running for just this eventuality. They would also set up well-removed from the guns they had been supporting so there was little chance the Katyushka salvo would take out any of the German 88s but they would certainly blind them.

"Hit the throttles. Take us through fast." Kennedy gave the order and PR-73 surged forward, accelerating up to her maximum speed of 28 knots. "We're through Crunch Point Two."

"Thanks to the Guards Special Artillery. Lucky for us they were there." Thom was watching dead south for the shape of the island that was their next navigation point. The river was widening rapidly now and the danger from the shore batteries had faded.

"No luck about it. The Russians had them there waiting to support us."

"Then why didn't they tell us?" Thom sounded aggrieved.

"Haven't you noticed? They don't tell anybody anything they don't need to know. They call it compartmentalizing. We didn't need to know those rocket launchers were there so we didn't get told. Those guys worship operational security. Now, swing west and we're about three miles away from our friendly local Marines."

B Company. 802nd Tank Destroyer Battalion, 83rd Infantry Division, Klimovo.

"What the hell is going on out there?" Private Eugene Searle peered out into the darkness that lay in front of his anti-tank gun. The nights on the Volga in mid-June were short, six or seven hours at best but the early pre-dawn hours still made it hard to stay awake. Chatting with fellow-sentries or lighting up a cigarette or pipe was one way to ward off the all-pervading drowsiness. The regular visits made by Sergeant Perry to supervise the sentries gave the men on watch at least one excuse to exchange all the latest rumors.

"Damned if I know, kid." Perry looked out into the darkness surrounding the anti-tank gun position. "The infantry have their wire loaded with tin cans so they'll hear anything that goes on. The Ell-Tee has ordered them to send up a flare if they hear or see anything out of the ordinary. The infantry up front has been here long enough to know the ground around their positions. They'll see if anything has changed."

A few yards away, Private Eli Dugan listened to the exchange, filing away any valuable information for future contribution to the rumor mill. In the week since the 802nd had moved into this area, he'd steadily improved his sentry position, adding some scrounged barbed wire and tin cans half-filled with stones to provide warning of intruders. Covering the same ground from the same position, night after night, he could understand how the infantry sentries further up front would be able to spot anything threatening. That started a train of thought in his mind that led to a critical question.

"Any word how long we're going to be here, Sarge?"

"The Ell-tee hasn't had word of any move yet." Perry called back to Dugan. "So, we'll be staying put for at least another week or so. You keep your eyes peeled."

"I wonder where the Huns are." Searle looked out into the darkness again. It was odd the way there seemed to be nobody in front of them. Before he'd come to Russia, he'd assumed that a battlefield would look like the films he'd seen of the Western Front in the Great War. *But, they don't even seem to have trenches here. Just the two-man foxholes we dug when we arrived.*

"Probably tucked up in bed like good little boys." Perry sniffed slightly. "Our infantry will be sending out their scout sections at dawn. We'll see what they're up to then."

River Gunboat PR-73, Island 10, Off Mordovo, Volga River.

"Get the rafts in the water." Kennedy had seen the coded flash of light from the shore and knew that the Russian Marines were ready to help him land his cargo. PR-73 carried eight large rafts, each of which could handle a cargo drum and two men to paddle it ashore. The problem was, he didn't have enough crewmen to put all eight in the water. By the time he had manned his guns and had an engine room ready to go, he had just six men available to row rafts. That meant he could only use three rafts. On the other hand, it would be a short trip each way. The craft's shallow draft had allowed him to bring PR-73 to within a few yards of the shingle beach.

The rafts seemed to glide across the short stretch of water. As soon as they beached, men came out of the rocks, seized the drum and rolled it ashore. Then, one of the shadowy figures boarded the raft for the return trip. By the time the raft and its passenger reached PR-73, the other two had unloaded their drums and were on the way back for the next.

"Tovarish captain, I am Marine Lieutenant Yevgeny Petrovich Brusilov. Thank you for bringing us our supplies this night."

Kennedy was surprised at the fluency of the English and slightly ashamed of his own inability to speak Russian. "Lieutenant John Fitzgerald Kennedy. Tovarish Yevgeny Petrovich, it my honor to be of service. First I must ask you, do you have weapons here chambered for British .303?"

Brusilov frowned. "No, we have weapons chambered for our own three-line ammunition and some weapons we captured from the Hitlerites. But no British. Why do you ask?"

"Because we were issued with British .303 to bring down to you. My men spotted it and we loaded 7.62 Russian as well. It was just possible you might have received British weapons so we brought both calibers."

Brusilov's eyes opened wide. "Borgemoi! We owe your men a great debt. This was deliberate sabotage?"

It's funny how the Russians immediately assume sabotage when something goes wrong. Never allow for the possibility that shit sometimes happens. Kennedy spread his hands in the internationally-understood gesture of 'who knows?' "We are not sure. There were two ambushes set for us on the way down but with help from your artillerists, we got through untouched. If there is an attack tonight, then giving us the wrong ammunition to bring here was indeed sabotage."

"Then you may assume that it is, indeed, sabotage. The fascists are getting ready for an attack now. We have received news of them loading into barges and a tug over at Mordovo. They will come before dawn. That way, they hope to have taken the island by daylight. Tovarish Captain, you should unload and be on your way first."

"Yevgeny, my orders are to stay down here and help you hold the island. Where would my gunboat be of greatest service?"

Brusilov looked at the gunboat a few meters offshore and thought carefully. "The fascists will try and land here, where our men are now working together. The side of this island that faces the west bank is all steep cliffs. Only here, on the side that faces the east bank is there a beach that can be landed on. So, the fascists will cross the river on their barges and small boats to come around the island to reach here. Their boats are rowed or have weak engines. They will not come against the current. So, they will try to come here around the northern end of the island."

Brusilov put his finger on the map, north of Island 10. "If your gunboat can be waiting here for them, we can catch the Hitlerites in a crossfire before they even leave their boats. With good fortune on our side, they will never reach land."

Kennedy nodded. "This seems a good plan, Tovarish Yevgeny. Let us both hope it meets with success."

River Gunboat PR-73, Between Island 10 and Mordovo, Volga River.

"I can't see or hear anything skipper." Thom scanned the river carefully. PR-73 had just enough engine power operating to fight the current. Since the Volga current was sluggish, that wasn't very much and the two Allison V-1710s were throttled right back. Combined with the underwater exhausts, that meant PR-73 was making almost no noise. The rippling of the water in the great river and the lapping noise it made against the wooden hull were the difference between absolute silence and the noise of a river at night.

Kennedy found himself thinking back to the days before the war, when offering to take a young lady out for a day cruising on Long Island Sound was an excellent first step on the path to enjoying her favors. Oddly, the conquest of even the most beautiful of the girls gave him nothing like the satisfaction he felt here commanding a gunboat on the Volga. *Because out here, I'm doing something useful, something that matters to more people than just myself. Here, I'm doing some good.*

Memories of the days spent on the rivers of Maine and Rhode Island or the coastal waters of Long Island Sound and Cape Cod made Kennedy look at his charts again. In his own eyes, he had been a rich layabout, an idle preppy with more money than sense. In fact he was being extremely unkind to his former civilian self. He was actually a natural sailor with a seaman's eye for the interaction of wind and currents. That seaman's eye was now telling him that things were not quite as they seemed. He could see the water marked in blue on his charts rolling down the Volga to the point where it hit this bend and was joined by the Cheremshan River. His mind pictured the two masses of river water joining and mixing in a complex maze defined by the formations of the banks.

"We've got this wrong, Lenny. We're in the wrong place." Kennedy looked at the charts again. "Look how the two rivers join here. All the water from the Cherry Mash is coming in on the eastern side of the Volga. The current will be very strong here, just the way we found, but it won't be that way on the western side. It wouldn't surprise me if the rivers actually wrap around each other here and the current on the western side flows northwards to remix with the water coming down the Volga and come south again. Like a big whirlpool. Those German barges won't have to fight the current; they'll have slack water at best. Yevgeny said the barges were loading at Mordovo. They're not going north then south, they're going straight across. We're in the wrong place. We need to be further south."

"That'll put them on the wrong side of the island. Under the cliffs." Thom could see what his skipper was getting at despite his objections.

"Look, Lenny, those cliffs are, what, thirty feet high? Tops? A good man with a rope and grapnel can toss the hook up there and climb those cliffs. Used to do that all the time up in Vermont.   Then they can take the Marines in the back. Take my word for it; the Huns are coming across lower down. Try to see them."

"We still can't do that." Thom scanned the river again.

Kennedy thought about that for a second. "What the hell is the point of that radar on our mast if we don't use it? Johnny, get that weird box of tricks you're so proud of on. Search south of us."

"Got them!" Maguire reported the radar contact within seconds. "They're about a mile out – oh Lord, skipper, that's a big boat, a tug or something. There's a half-dozen small ones and well and they're less than a hundred yards from the island. They'll be on our Russian friends in seconds. They damned near slipped past us."

"Damned near isn't there, not yet." Kennedy snapped out his orders, all trace of the genial skipper gone. "Mortar crew, drop some flares on the west coast of the island. Point-fifties and 1.1s, get ready to open up on the Hun landing party. Three incher, lay on to that tug get ready to fire on it."

"Those sixty-mil flares are useless, Skipper. They can barely illuminate themselves."

"Doesn't matter Lenny, they'll still tell Yevgeny and his Marines what is going on. Damn it, I knew something was wrong when we were talking. I just didn't put my finger on it."

Marine Detachment, Island 10, Off Mordovo, Volga River.

"What the devil is the American doing?" Sergeant Petr Ivanovich Lashkov looked over his shoulder towards the other side of the island where the first of a series of flares were descending. They gave a weak and feeble illumination that only just managed to highlight the crest that ran down the middle of the tiny island. It was some measure of how feeble the 60mm flares were that the streams of tracer fire from the gunboat outshone them. Lashkov could see the tracers spraying out from the mid-ships machine guns on the gunboat and the slower, heavier fire from the quadruple gun on the stern. It was the sight of the gunboat pouring fire into the western side of the island that told him what was happening.

"Zhenya, they're behind us! The American is shooting them up on the cliffs."

Brusilov looked quickly at the streams of gunfire being directed at the western cliffs. *Eto pizdets. And it was such a beautiful ambush we had set up for the fascists.* "Pasha, Vova, stay here with the machine gun. Watch the beach and guard our rear well, bratishka. Rest of you, come with me. Along the hillcrest. Quickly or we will be too late."

The ridge down the center of the island was barely two meters high but it had been enough to shield the fascists climbing up from the foot of the cliff. They had thrown grapnels at the end of long ropes to help them climb and the first men up were already in firing positions to cover the ones following. Whether there would be any more was something that Brusilov seriously doubted. The twin .50 caliber machine guns were sweeping backwards and forwards along the foot of the cliff, making any attempt to break cover and go up the ropes suicidal. The big quadruple mount at the rear of the gunboat was firing in short bursts.

Brusilov guessed that the heavier guns were being used when the crew spotted some of the fascists braving the .50s and trying to make the climb up to the level ground. *It wasn't,* Brusilov reflected, *quite as suicidal as it seemed. Those American flares give hardly any light and there are plenty of shadows for the Hitlerites to skulk in. That gunboat needs a bigger mortar. I just hope they don't shine searchlights on us.*

Brusilov saw muzzle flash from the cliff-top. *Perhaps the fascists saw some of my men moving up?* It didn't really matter, his men were spreading out along the shallow ridge, taking advantage of the flimsy cover it offered. Lashkov had seen the muzzle flash too and he was quick to return fire. As a Sergeant, he had an AVT rifle, the selective fire version of the SVT that all the others in the unit carried. There were few AVTs for, when fired on automatic, their recoil was brutal. The AVT needed a strong man to fire it and Lashkov was all of that and more. There was a unit joke that his mother had conceived him after doing unspeakable things with a particularly large and savage bear. So, the Sergeant was able to hold the AVT down when he fired a burst and his effort was rewarded by a scream from the cliff top.

"Well done, bratishka!" Brusilov's call echoed across the night. Along the shallow crest that ran down the center of the island, the Russian marines started to fire on the handful of Germans who had made it to the cliff top.

Detachment SS Jägddivision 502, Island 10, Off Mordovo, Volga River.

Stabsscharfuhrer Johannes Gottschalk heard the scream from the top of the cliff and knew that one of his men had been hit. There wasn't much he could do about it since the fire from the gunboat offshore was pinning his unit down. *It is those damned .50s* he thought. When American units had started to arrive along the Volga, their .50 caliber Browning machine guns had been a nasty surprise for the Germans. Not so much because they were effective although they were all of that but because there were so many of them. Sometimes it seemed as if every American soldier and every vehicle carried one of the big machine guns.

A week or so earlier, his detachment had been sent to ambush an American supply convoy and take some prisoners for interrogation. They'd slipped through American lines on the Chuvashskaya Bridgehead easily enough. The sentries talking and smoking had made sure their lines could be penetrated any time the SS-men wanted to. Then, his unit had ambushed an American supply convoy just as ordered. Six of their big six-wheel trucks escorted by a pair of armored cars.

It should have been easy and it would have been except for those Brownings. Every truck had one and the armored cars had two each. The vehicles had simply sprayed gunfire in all directions. In fact, Gottschalk actually believed that the Americans liked being surrounded so they could fire at anything and everything with a clear conscience. *They were bungling, stupid amateurs with no sense of fire discipline.* Nevertheless, realizing there was no way around that wall of fire, he and his men had given the raid up as a bad job.

"Johannes, Stieber's bought it. Took one in the head. They've got machine guns up there and they know where we are." Dietmar Schreiner had slid down the rope from the cliff top to make the report.

Gottschalk felt his mouth twist. Olaf Stieber had been a member of his unit for years. They were both veterans of the long 'phony war' between the June 1940 armistice with Britain and the occupation two years later. They'd fought alongside each other in the fight to take over the airfield at Tangmere and hold it while the transport aircraft had brought in reinforcements. Now Stieber was dead on the banks of the Volga, deep inside Russia and there was no sign of the war ever ending.

The gunners on the gunboat offshore must have seen something because the quadruple gun started cracking out its shots in a slow, steady cadence. The track of each bullet ended in a small, brilliant flash. They were explosive rounds and the wounds they could inflict were ghastly. Technically, they were anti-aircraft guns but, like the German 20mm and 37mm guns, they had found their niche as support weapons for the Army. Gottschalk and Schreiner huddled behind the rocks at the foot of the cliff until the firing stopped. Only, when it did, it was replaced by rifle fire from the top of the low cliff. Gottschalk realized the Russian Marines must have advanced up to the cliff top and were now firing down at his men.

"It's time to get out of here." Gottschalk made the decision quickly. "Tell the men to get to the rafts. We'll shove off and let the current take us downstream, away from that gunboat. He's got a nasty surprise coming and he won't be worrying about us."

Gottschalk knew that the men in his group didn't need to be told to stay in the shadows and move in the gaps between the flares. The man under his command were some of the most experienced special operations troops in the German Army and their exploits had thrilled the whole nation. Seizing this little island should have been a routine, almost boring, operation. However, he was uneasily aware that this was the second time he had run into the American Army and the second time they had frustrated his plans by doing things that didn't make any kind of sense. *Nobody arms their truck drivers with heavy machine guns and rifles. And nobody just sprays gunfire around in the hope that one of the rounds will bite. And yet, these people do. They must be mad. Why the hell can't they learn to fight like a real army?*

Gottschalk had reached the area where the rubber assault craft had been stored. The men piled on board and pushed themselves out into the darkness. As they did so, Gottschalk made a quick count of those embarked. Olaf Stieber was dead and three other men were badly wounded. Otherwise, the detachment had made it out unscathed. That, at least, would please Otto Skorzeny. The commander of SS Jägddivision 502 didn't like failure but he disliked wasting the lives of his men after all hope of success had gone even less.

Airfield 108, Privolzhskiy na Volga, Moskva Front

"Up, drugs. The Rodina cries out for aid while you lie skulking in your beds! Briefing in 30 minutes."

Edwards opened one eye carefully and looked across the room at the Russian officer at the door. Briefly, he contemplated shooting the man but he realized this would probably result in a lot of paperwork before breakfast. Then, as life slowly returned to his sleep-saturated mind, he remembered he was in Russia and the Russian attitude to summary executions was a lot more . . . . flexible . . . . than in the U.S. forces. But before he could react to this revelation, the Russian was gone and was hammering on the door of the next room.

Around him, the other three pilots in the room were hauling themselves out of their cots and trying to shake themselves out of their sleep. Edwards screwed his eyes up, trying to read the face of his watch in the gloom. "Hey, it's four in the morning. What gives?"

The question went unanswered in the scramble of pilots trying to get their morning routines finished before the mission briefing started. By the time they had grabbed their early morning ration of black bread and fruit preserve washed down with copious quantity of tea, the briefing was already about to start. Edwards was reduced to licking what was left of the preserved apple paste off his fingers while sitting down.

"Your mission for today is to provide cover for one of our gunboats returning from a resupply mission to an island approximately 200 miles south of here." Major Gregory Young tapped the map showing the position of Island 10. "The 360th Fighter Squadron will provide close cover for the gunboat; the 866th will fly free chase missions over the west bank of the Volga. The general plan is that the 866th will break up any German attack before it reaches the river while the 360th knocks down any Huns who break through the Yak screen.

"Jackson, you take Barnes, Walker, and Edwards. Taylor, take Green, Anderson and Foster. You'll be the first wave of cover. You'll be relieved by Russell with Hill, Powell and Griffin and by Johnson with Ward, Carter and King. After that, the 359th will be providing escort.

"This started off as a routine supply run but it's turned into a major battle down there. It seems as if the Huns tried to attack the island just as our gunboat got there. The gunboat stayed around to help the island garrison hold out and really got stuck into the Huns. That means they'll be coming back in daylight and we can assume they've got substantial damage. After take-off, you'll fly on course 135 at less than two hundred feet to Kuyuki. There, you'll climb to cruise altitude for the run down to Staryy Belyy Yar where you will rendezvous with our gunboat. You'll fly down there at 25,000 feet." Young stopped at the gasp from the Russian pilots. For them, flying at 25,000 feet was unheard-of feat. "We're hoping that the Huns will be looking down, not up and we can do it on them from a great height."

There was a ripple of laughter that swelled as the Russian pilots who understood the joke explained it to those who did not. Young was not one of those who laughed. He had felt a strange sensation in his stomach as he'd said the words and a shiver had run down his spine. Something had chilled his soul. "You also have a secondary mission. A Regiment of Sturmoviks will be attacking some coastal defense guns at Sengiley. We can expect Hun fighters to try and drive them off. You will make sure they fail to do so. Thunderbolt take off is at oh-five hundred. We'll fly down at night so we can be on station when the sun comes up. The Yaks will leave at dawn."

Guards-Major Stepan Petrovich Ganin took his place and repeated the briefing in Russian with specific information for the free-chase Yaks that would be flying over the west bank of the Volga. Then, he switched back to English and, when he spoke, it was with solemn intensity. "All Russian pilots know this, but it is worth repeating for our American friends. If your aircraft is hit over territory occupied by the Hitlerites, you must try to make it back to our side of the lines. If this is impossible, you can be sure the Partisans will have seen your aircraft crash and will be looking for you. Try to link up with them as soon as possible. Above all, do not allow yourself to be captured by the fascists. They murder most of the prisoners they take and send the rest to slave labor camps where a slow, miserable death is inevitable."

That sobered the audience on the spot. It was in a subdued mood that the briefing broke up with the pilots heading out to check their aircraft. Edwards stopped by the breakfast table, hoping there might be some of the apple preserves left. On the way in, he'd found them unexpectedly tasty, thick and so laden with fruit it had to be cut with a knife. Quite unlike the jams he was used to. Now, when he reached the table, there was none left but that only made him realize he didn't feel like eating anymore.

River Gunboat PR-73, Between Island 10 and Mordovo, Volga River.

In an odd way, the original mis-positioning of PR-73 had turned out to work in the gunboat's favor. She was now slightly behind the invasion force and moving between the landing boats and the tug that had brought them over. If the infantry who had just landed on the beach were forced off the island, PR-73 would be well-placed to cut them up. In the meantime, her automatic guns could continue to spray the landing area while her three inch gun could deal with the tug. As if to emphasize Kennedy's thoughts, the forward gun fired, its brilliant muzzle flash lighting up the bows. *I wish we had flashless powder for that damned gun.*

The first round was short, only just but enough to send up a column of water instead of the orange flare of a hit. It occurred to Kennedy that the muzzle flash had revealed their position to everybody within miles and there was little point in trying to be discrete any more. "Searchlights, light up that tug. Three incher, put as many shots into the damned thing as you can. Starboard twin-fifty, spray it."

Damn, this is exciting! Kennedy realized that PR-73 was firing all ten of her guns at once, for the first time since he had taken command of the gunboat. The two 24 inch searchlights converged on the tug, revealing that she was turning and trying to get away from the suddenly-savage battle in mid-river. She was too late. Kennedy saw his three-inch gun score a direct hit on the bridge while the tug's own searchlight was extinguished almost as soon as it was tuned on. Then, a second orange ball spiraled upwards as another American shell smacked into the tug's hull, right on the waterline. Kennedy watched in glee as the tug slowed and started to list. *That one hurt her.*

There was a smattering of machine gun fire coming from the stricken tugboat but it was obvious that she hadn't been armed to take on a proper gunboat. From the tracers flashing across the river, the tug had a pair of MG-42s in a single twin mount to provide rudimentary defense against aircraft. Kennedy heard the ringing sound as the rifle-caliber bullets bounced off the 25mm armor protecting the bridge. His own .50 caliber gunner swung his stream of fire on to the source of the tracers and the German gunfire stopped instantly. *Damn, I actually felt guilty about that. Something so one-sided just wasn't fair.*

"Skipper! Another boat out there, she must have been masked by the tug. Oh, crap, she's an S-boat."

"Quad 1.1, get on to that S-boat now. Take her out."

The 1.1 inch mount was powered but the whine of its training motor was drowned out by the intense gunfire. Forward, the three-incher had fired again, scoring direct hit on the tug's stern. The German craft was burning, the orange light from the fire engulfing her bridge casting an eerie light on the river and highlighting the sleek shape of the S-boat as it tried to run interference for the crippled tug.

More tracers joined the criss-crossing streams as the 20mm guns on the German craft opened up. PR-73 had shrugged off the machine gun fire from the tug but the 20mm guns were an entirely different matter. The shells punched straight through the bridge armor, ricocheting off the equipment and sending fragments bouncing around inside the conning station. Kennedy and his bridge crew dived for cover, leaving PR-73 to swerve out of control. In front of him, Motor Machinist's Mate William Johnston reached up and grabbed the wheel, swinging PR-73 back on course. That had the happy result of bringing the three-incher to bear on the S-boat. The gun flared out its muzzle flash again and Kennedy saw the shell strike the S-boat dead amidships.

Fast Attack Craft S-38, Between Island 10 and Mordovo, Volga River.

"Ganz und gar beschissen!" Oberleutnant zur See Oskar Wuppermann knew when things were not going well and tended to express himself clearly on the matter. In his opinion, this whole stupid mission had been doomed right from the start. Skorzeny's men had arrived with a plan that reminded Wuppermann of an Austrian cream cake. Basically, simple ingredients but buried under a mix of over-elaborate and sickly-sweet decorations. Heer units had failed to take the island on three occasions so the powers that be had decided to replace a regular Army unit with a smaller group of specialist SS commandoes.

The basic plan had been quite good; just tow the boats over to a point above the island and let them drift down to the landing beach. Then use climbing equipment to scale the cliffs and take the Russians from the rear. Only, with each level of command, somebody had added extra details until the simple plan was quite forgotten. The Navy had taken one horrified look at the result and made their own addition. S-38 was to go out with the tug and cover her from the looming disaster. *It wasn't as if tugs are in copious supply on the Volga. In fact they are worth their weight in gold.*

"Drive that gunboat away from here. All guns, concentrate on her bridge."

"Yes, Herr Oberleutnant." The twin 20mm gun amidships and the bow single 20mm opened up, the tracers from their fire coning in on the gunboat's superstructure. The low shape was covered with flashes as the shells started to hit home. Wuppermann guessed that they were doing less damage that the display suggested; unlike the S-boat, the river gunboats were armored, sometimes quite heavily.

What really worried him was that he'd expected to hear the deeper thud of the 37mm gun mounted on his S-boat's stern. *In this kind of fighting, that gun was the S-boat's primary weapon. Our torpedoes are useless here. I keep asking for them to be removed and replaced by more automatic weapons. But does anybody ever listen to me?*

He looked aft and saw that the enemy gunboat had got in first. It had brought its quadruple stern mount to bear and the heavy shots from the mounting had smashed the 37mm gun to junk and left its crew dead on the deck around it. The stream of shells from the quad mount was working its way forward and the guns were soon engaged in a private duel with the German twin-20.

42

The night seemed to be driven into retreat by a massive flash from the bows of the enemy gunboat. For a brief moment, Wuppermann believed that he had been blessed by the enemy gunboat exploding. Then he realized that it was just the muzzle flash of the heavy gun mounted forward. *That means the gunboat has to be an Ami. They have a big gun forward. The Ivans just have a 45mm in a tank turret.*

The shot had struck the water just short of the S-boat's hull, showering it with spray and fragments. S-38 hadn't taken lethal damage, not yet, but the accumulation of minor damage from the machine guns and cannon on the gunboat was mounting up. *My primary job is to get our tug clear, not take on an Ami gunboat. And our slackening volume of fire makes me think we have lost the twin-20 as well. Time to get us out of here.*

Wuppermann looked at the tug that was limping away back to the other side of the river and the safety of the port at Mordovo. "Make smoke! All pots, I want the biggest cloud we can make."

River Gunboat PR-73, Between Island 10 and Mordovo, Volga River.

"We got her skipper, she's burning!"

Kennedy looked out over the edge of the armored bridge side and saw the enemy S-boat was belching black smoke and turning to run away. The stern had been reduced to a complete shambles with fragments of wood and metal still being hurled into the air as the quadruple 1.1 inch mount tore up the lightly-built German ship. *Our Russian friends had it right; armor means more than speed in this kind of fighting.*

The volume of smoke from the stricken S-boat redoubled, the whole boat vanishing under the thick, oily cloud. Kennedy was in no doubt she was going down. Nor was anybody else on PR-73. The cheers of the crew rang out across the water and Kennedy's order was only a confirmation of a fact that already existed. "All guns, cease fire. We got her, boys. And the tug. Set course for the Island; we'd better check in with our Russian friends before we go home."

Airfield 108, Privolzhskiy na Volga, Moskva Front

Edwards settled himself into the cockpit of his Thunderbolt and took a deep breath to steady himself. *Time to do the preliminary check. Let's go for it.* His mind dropped into the rhythm that he'd been taught, with each setting heavily emphasized so the litany formed a beat in his head. *Gear handle DOWN, flaps handle UP, Generator switch ON, Intercooler shutters NEUTRAL, oil cooler shutters NEUTRAL, propeller switch ON and selector AUTOMATIC. Fuel boost pump to START and ALTITUDE, fuel pressure satisfactory, gun switch OFF, ignition OFF. We're ready to start up.*

Outside, in the slowly brightening pre-dawn light, his Russian ground crew were standing by the propeller, ready to give it the several revolutions by hand that would begin the process of bringing the big R-2800 engine to life. He watched the Russians turning the prop to disperse the oil that had gathered in the lower cylinders of the engine overnight.

That was his key to start the next series of actions, once again the steps echoing in his head as he went down the list. *Master battery switch ON, supercharger lever OFF, fuel selector valve MAIN, throttle 1/4" to 1/2" open, mixture control IDLE CUT-OFF, propeller switch AUTOMATIC, circuit breaker ON, propeller control maximum, 2700 RPM, fuel boost pump control to START and ALTITUDE, prime with SIX strokes, ignition switch to BOTH and here we go, energize and engage starter.*

Edwards heard the click and the clanking noise as the propeller started to turn. He could also hear the electric hum of the starter motor as it turned the propeller over. He found himself counting the rotations seven – eight – nine and was giving up hope of the engine ever firing when, on the tenth rotation, the R-2800 finally caught with a roar that shattered any remaining traces of the pre-dawn stillness. Blue smoke was pouring from the top of the engine cowling and under the fuselage enveloping the Thunderbolt in a choking light blue cloud, shot with spurts of dark brown. He rammed the mixture forward to AUTO RICH.

His engine was running roughly, not settling down and the blue smoke kept pouring out from under the nose. Then it faded away, the engine smoothed out and the Thunderbolt suddenly became alive. Instead of sitting on the taxiway, it was twitching, its tail moving from side to side. Edwards had once owned a dog who had reacted the same way when he saw a particularly succulent-looking cat. He set the throttle to 900 RPM and allowed his P-47 to edge forward.

Beside his aircraft, the other three Thunderbolts were also edging forward, each seemingly reluctant to allow the others the honor of moving first. He checked the controls, the ailerons and elevators working as intended. He checked his rudder in the mirror, making sure that it too responded to the pressure of his feet on the rudder bar. Then he unlocked the tailwheel and started to taxi out.

This was no easy task. Maneuvering on the ground was something that required great care since the mighty R-2800 blocked out most of the vision forward. The situation was made much worse by the open cowl flaps that obscured a full eighth of what little vision was left after the Thunderbolt's tailwheel undercarriage and massive radial engine had taken their share.

This was an issue that the other American fighters didn't face. The P-38 Lightning and P-39 Airacobra both had tricycle undercarriages and the vision over their noses was excellent. The P-40 Warhawks had tailwheels like the P-47 but their water-cooled Allison engines were much slimmer and masked out less of the ground in front. For a P-47 pilot, there was only one real option and Edwards took it. He taxied his Thunderbolt forward in a series of S turns so he could check that nobody was about to walk into his propeller.

Once he had reached the runway, Edwards saw that his Thunderbolt was now third in the line of aircraft waiting to take off. He was getting his P-47 ready to roll. Once again, the litany, hammered into his mind during the long hours of training sounded. *Set trim tabs: elevator NEUTRAL, aileron NEUTRAL, rudder TAKEOFF, fuel selector valve on MAIN TANK, Flaps UP, Cowl flaps OPEN TRAIL, LOCK tail wheel. And now open throttle; set takeoff manifold pressure to 52 inches, RPM: 2700 And GO!*

The engine roared, the sound echoing off the hangars and half-ruined building. What had been a spluttering rumble had turned into a full-blooded growl that pulled the big P-47 down the runway. Edwards felt the smooth acceleration, the thunder of the tires on the rough-surfaced runway that only ended when his aircraft lifted off and started to climb away from Airfield 108. He retracted the undercarriage, feeling the main wheels thump into their recesses under the wings. As usual, the right hand wheel was the first to close fully, followed by the left.

Ahead of him, his flight was assembling into the finger four formation that would take them to the Volga. There would be a low-altitude leg first, to clear the airfield and not give the German radars any hint from which base the aircraft had taken off. *Those radars are a pain in the ass,* he thought. *We'll have to do something about them.*

The Russian ground crews and airfield staff had assembled to watch the take-off. This was something new, something that marked a profound change in the war. There had been scattered American units in Russia for weeks but this was different. Every day, trains from the east brought more American troops, more equipment, more supplies. Now, there was an American division holding part of the line alongside Russian divisions. American gunboats were operating on the Volga alongside Russian Marines and this very night they had given the fascists a bloody nose indeed. Now the Thunderbolts would be flying alongside Yaks and Lavochkins to hunt down the Hitlerites and claw them from the endless steely gray Russian skies.

It all added up to one thing. The Rodina was no longer fighting alone. After two desperate years of fire and death, of defeat and seemingly never-ending retreat, an ally had come to the aid of the Rodina in its hour of greatest peril. With them, they had brought something that ultimately meant more than tanks, ships and aircraft. The Russians had never been short of courage or the dogged determination to win this war whatever the cost. Now, the sight of the

Kazan Thunderbolts

Thunderbolts taking off added a new ingredient to the mix, one that both strengthened its power and lightened the load it represented. With them, the Thunderbolts had brought hope.

Because, from today onwards, the White Star would be flying alongside the Red Star

CHAPTER THREE: LESSONS LEARNED

Briefing Room, Airfield 33, Surovka, Moskva Front

"The target for today is the Freya radar station at Lomy. This will be the first raid in a series intended to blind the German radar coverage over the Volga and allow us to operate over the eastern side of the river without tipping the enemy off to our plans and operations. The elimination of the Freya radar chain on the west bank of the Volga will be a major step forward in restoring our control of the air.

"The attack will be carried out by twelve aircraft of the 391st Bomb Group. The Marauders will each carry eight five hundred pound bombs internally. The aircraft will fly at 12,000 feet until they cross the Volga at Andreevka, and then drop to treetop height for the final run to your target at Lomy. That treetop portion of the flight will last for some 15 miles from the Volga to the target. After exiting the target area, you will head north for 10 miles to reach the Volga again at Novoulyanonsk whereupon you will climb to 16,000 feet for the flight back to this base. Note the heavy flak concentrations at Sengiley, Tushna and Gulyay. They are south of your planned flight path so do not deviate to the south. Flying at treetop height will mean that the heavy flak there will not be able to range on you. There are also concentrations of flak at Klyuchishky and, most critically, in and around Ulyanov'sk. Be very certain that you do not go too far north and overfly Ulyanov'sk. The flak there is ferocious.

"Why are we doing the dog-leg over Andreevka? If we did a direct flight to Lomy it would take us further away from that flak." One of the navigators was studying the charts with a frown creasing his forehead.

Colonel Gregory Hughes had expected that one. "It's deception. A feint. We can assume that the radar chain we are attempting to disrupt will be tracking you all the way down. They'll see you heading south west and project your course. That will take them to Sengiley. Now there is a coastal battery at Sengiley that is causing the Navy a world of grief.

"This is the important bit. What you don't know is that there has been a big rumble down that way. The Krauts attempted to attack an island held by Russian marines and one of our gunboats got stuck into the invaders. Beat the crap out of them as well, sank an S-boat and a large tug. That gunboat is coming north again but it's making the run in daylight. It's being covered by Jugs out of 108. The Russians will be hitting that battery at Sengiley as well with their Sturmoviks. So, looking at all that going on, the Krauts will assume that this raid is part of covering the gunboat's withdrawal. Probably backing up the Ilyushins hitting that shore battery. So, they'll be expecting you to go south. Only, you'll swing north and in the four minutes it'll take you to get to that radar station, they won't have time to respond. You should get in and out clean. Any more questions?"

"Are we getting fighter escort?"

"No." Hughes noted the disturbance at that. "You'll be in and out so fast that you won't need it. You should be over hostile territory for ten minutes, tops."

"Ten minutes can be a long time, Sir."

Hughes pretended not to hear the somewhat insubordinate tone to the question. Sitting in the back of the briefing room, the Russian Liaison Officer winced and then shook his head in wonder. A Russian pilot speaking to his commander like that would already be under arrest. "Yes, it can. But, we'll be going flat out all the way before we get back into friendly airspace. If the decoy works, the Kraut fighters will be in the wrong place and won't be able to catch up. Fighter escort may even work against you by revealing your course change. If there's nothing else, navigators and bomb-aimers, pick up your packages."

Control Tower, Airfield 33, Surovka, Moskva Front

"And so the B-26 goes to war." Brigadier-General Clayton Adkins looked down upon the twelve twin-engined bombers waddled down the taxiway towards the runway.

"Against whom, Sir?" Hughes was watching from beside the general, inspecting the Marauders as they prepared to take off.

"You name it. The War Department still isn't convinced that air power will win this war. The War College still insists that airpower is of limited value when employed independently and should be restricted to direct support of the ground forces. The only good thing that came out of that is that the department cancelled B-17 production for 1938 and 1939 in favor of the mediums we are flying now. Our own people aren't helping matters by stressing strategic bombing with those four-engined birds. They don't seem understand that we can have two Marauders or three Mitchells for the cost of a single Fortress. Hap Arnold got the B-17 back into the budget in 1940, mostly on the back of British orders. So now, we've been scratching around for B-26s while we waited for the next production lots to start to reach us."

"A little bird tells me that the big boys might not be the favored sons anymore." Hughes looked a sinister combination of furtive and delighted. "I've heard they're finding it impossible to get any decent number of bombs on targets. Like, they have a job getting a bomb within five miles of the aiming point."

"I've heard those stories. The problem isn't bomb-aiming so much as the German flak. It's forcing the bombers to dodge all over the sky and that throws them miles off. That's why this raid is going in over the tree-tops. We've got to get good, tight bombing patterns if we are ever going to do much damage. And we have to start doing serious damage if we're going to keep the War College from talking everybody else into cutting funding for bombers.

Thunderbolt PI-H, Over the Volga, South of Sengiley, Moskva Front.

"My God, have you ever seen anything like that? The Mississippi is a dribble compared with that!" Edwards was looking down on the Volga beneath him. Mostly, from 25,000 feet, rivers looked like rivers. They had banks and curves, all of which were visible and recognizable from the air. The Volga was different. Beneath him the river was more than eleven miles wide and this was one of the narrower sections on the Kazan Sector. Even here, the banks were vague shadows on the horizons and the immensity of the Volga made its twists and turns difficult to perceive. They would have to be much higher, Edwards knew, before they could see the river in context with its surroundings. The sight below him seemed to hammer home the endless immensity of Russia. Americans had always been amused by Europeans visiting the United States who had failed to understand how big the country was. Now, here in Russia, they found themselves in the same position. The Russian steppes were truly endless in a way that had strange effects on the human mind. It was easy to lose oneself in their vast emptiness. Literally and metaphorically.

"Stop yakking on the radio, Edwards." Lieutenant Terry Jackson snapped the rebuke out. A native of Mississippi, he didn't appreciate having his state's namesake river being disparaged. Especially since the sight below drove home how justified the denigration was. Jackson was also being forced to realize that in coming to Russia, the American pilots had entered a different world where the scales of measurement were bore no comparison with those familiar to them.

Behind the American pilots, the rising sun was reflecting off the steely-gray clouds that, like immensity, seemed to be a constant companion to the Russian skies. The sun had turned the clouds into a glowing mass that seemed to cover the whole sky. It suddenly dawned on Edwards that aircraft coming in from the west would find seeing the Thunderbolts against that glowing mass an almost impossible task. Growing up in Pennsylvania, Edwards had been addicted to the movies about fighter pilots in World War One. Films like 'Dawn Patrol' and 'Hells Angels' had stressed the advantages fighting from the East had brought

German pilots and coined phrases like 'Beware the Hun in the Sun.' Now, they were coming in from the east and they had the sun at their backs.

Far down below, there was a small white arrowhead on the dark gray-brown of the Volga. Edwards clicked his radio. "I think that's the gunboat below us. Too small to see though."

Jackson's voice showed uncertainty. "It's the right position. Their last message said they would be a little south of Sengiley at dawn. Keep your eyes peeled. The krauts will be coming at us any minute."

"Gutsy bunch on that gunboat, coming back in daylight like that. Reckon they're asking for trouble."

"Walker, I told Edwards, now I'm telling you. Stop yakking on the radio. Rest of you, the same. Can the crap. Any of you want to miss a warning a kraut has you in his sights because Walker and Edwards are babbling to each other?"

There was an abashed silence on the radio. All eight Thunderbolt pilots in Eagle Section were scanning the western bank of the Volga for any signs of hostile aircraft activity. This was the mark of a fighter pilot, the ability to see the tiny dots in the distance that could quickly turn into hostile aircraft. Everything was geared up towards that single goal. In training, the pilots had been selected for their visual acuity. On the ground, their cockpit canopies had been meticulously cleaned so that not a single speck of dirt would distract them from their search.

It was a flash of light from the rising sun that gave the inbound German aircraft away. A brief flash from the front windscreen of one of the Messerschmitt 110s was enough to alert the Thunderbolts. It was Edwards, who had the keenest vision of all the fighter pilots in the American formation that saw it and realized what it meant. This was the formation sent to attack PR-73 as it retired from the battle around Island 10. "Enemy sighted. Flash off the cockpit, directly ahead."

"Got it." The voice from Lieutenant Jack Taylor was both relieved and excited. He'd had visions of the Thunderbolts missing the inbound raid and suffering the humiliation of having the gunboat sunk under their noses. The flashes of light quickly transformed into the shapes of a dozen twin-engined aircraft. Edwards compared them quickly with the recognition charts he'd learned off by heart. Square wingtips, twin tail. *Me-110* he thought and then corrected himself. Bf *110. The Army Air Force might call it the Me-110 but Aeronautics Magazine had revealed the German name.*

"Jackson, take Barnes, Walker, and Edwards down and break that formation up. We'll stay up top and cover your ass from any fighters that show up."

"Roger." Edwards heard the message acknowledgement and the orders that followed. "We'll hit the middle flight. Barnes, Walker, concentrate on the leader. Edwards, join me in hitting the plane on his right. After that, general chase. As soon as they run for it, get back to covering that gunboat."

Edwards saw Jackson's Thunderbolt make a wingover and start the long dive that would end with a head-on pass against the German fighter-bombers far below. His hands moved on the controls and he did the same, forming up beside his flight leader. Below them, the 110s grew steadily larger, their green and gray dappled camouflage losing its effect as the enemy aircraft filled his gunsight. At 300 yards, he opened fire with all eight guns.

Attack Group, Zerstörergeschwader 1, Over the West Bank of the Volga

Colonel Joachim Blechschmidt saw the fighters peeling off and diving on his formation of Bf 110F fighter-bombers. *Something is wrong, something is different. The Ivans don't do 'different'. They have a set pattern and they stick to it. Their fighters fly in a staggered formation, the lowest elements at around fifteen hundred to two thousand meters, the highest at four or five thousand meters at most. These Ivans started at seven or eight thousand meters at least. The only Ivans that fly up there are the MiGs. And they are coming at us head-on. That's suicide. We'll blow them out of the sky before they get close enough to open fire on us. The Ivans are trained to close to point-blank range before opening fire. With all our guns concentrated in our nose, we can take them out before they get that close.*

"The Ivans are coming in, directly in front of us. Start to climb towards them and hit them before they close in." Blechschmidt started to follow his own orders before he had finished the radio message. The enemy fighters were closing in very fast, much faster than usual. A great stirring of unease was beginning to sweep though Blechschmidt; whatever was going on was indeed very different from the experience the Luftwaffe had amassed over two years of war in Russia. He noted another change in the situation; only four fighters were making their attack; another four were remaining up high to guard their comrades against any escorting fighters. This kind of coordination was something the Ivans just did not do. The lack of radios in their aircraft precluded it. It was that fact that finally opened his eyes. *These aren't Ivans, these are Americans.*

It was Blechschmidt's habit of flying with the third rotte of the Staffel that saved him. He did that so he could coordinate the bombing runs of the formation and make sure that all the targets in the designated area were hit. It also sent the novices in first when the anti-aircraft fire would be weakest and least-coordinated. That way they stood a greater chance of living to become experienced. The Americans had obviously assumed that the formation leader would be in the center of the three rotte and concentrated their attack on it. More specifically, the four aircraft concentrated their attack on the two central aircraft of that four-plane rotte, again obviously assuming one of them would be the formation leader. Blechschmidt saw the American fighters opening fire at a far greater range than he had expected. *Two hundred meters at least, perhaps three hundred?* A moment later he saw the white stars painted on the wings and fuselages of the attackers.

He could also see the streams of tracer bullets from their wing guns concentrating on their selected targets and the devastating effects of the attacks. One of the Bf 110s simply blew up under the impact, its fuel tanks erupting in a fireball that engulfed the entire aircraft. The other aircraft selected for destruction physically staggered under the concentrated fire of the two American fighters. Streams of flame erupted from both engines, spreading quickly along the wings as the Bf 110s structure disintegrated under the intense machine gun fire. The 110 was already heading down, its green-gray shape the head of a black-and-red comet trail. To his relief, Blechschmidt saw at least one parachute emerge from the stricken aircraft but then he realized it was too late. The bailout was too low and the parachute had barely opened when the escapee hit the trees below.

The attacking fighters were close enough to be recognized now. *In fact, they're far too close for comfort* Blechschmidt thought. *They're Republic P-47 Thunderbolts. They've never been seen in Russian before. Our Luftwaffe intelligence people laughed at them, saying they were too big, too clumsy to be real fighters. They ought to be here today. Those Republics might be big but they are blindingly fast and armed to the point where they are death on wings. Just how many machine guns do they have? Eight? Twelve? Sixteen? And they are the American fifty-calibers that will punch straight through the armor on our aircraft. Scheisse, we're in trouble.*

He was trying to set up a trap for the Thunderbolts, turning inwards so the P-47 would fly into a crossfire. The problem was that the bomb-laden 110s were too slow and unwieldy and the P-47s were too fast. The American fighters were through the German formation and gone before the trap could be set. Blechschmidt knew that his formation was now fighting for its life. There was only one thing to do. "Get rid of your bombs. Run for it."

By the speed of response, Blechschmidt guessed that the pilots had been waiting with their thumbs over the bomb release. The explosions of four 550 pound bombs from each aircraft scattered across the ground below. *I wonder if anybody's down there. Still, they're only Ivans.* All around him, the 110s were diving for the woods, hoping to shield their vulnerable bellies by flying at the lowest altitude possible. The Zerstorer crews had learned that lesson over France in 1940. The Bf 110 was terribly vulnerable to an attacker that came up from below and behind. The gunner's single 7.92mm machine gun couldn't be brought to bear and the enemy could gut the Zerstorer like a fish. The problem was that flying low enough to prevent that happening meant that the crew had no chance of bailing out.

Blechschmidt looked over his shoulder. The Thunderbolts were racking around in tight turns to engage the rest of the formation. Two had separated out and were in pursuit of the fleeing survivors of the first rotte. The other two had pulled around and, with grim resignation, he realized they were coming for him. *Too large and clumsy for fighters? In einem Schweinearsch. They may be big but they're light on their feet. I bet they can turn with a 109. And they can roll like the very devil.* He had just watched them do that. He guessed that torque from the big radial engine had to help the Thunderbolts roll and turn. *Whatever it is, they will do for me if I am not very careful.*

For a moment hope surged in him. Both the Thunderbolts were coming in from above and behind, right into the arc of fire from the 110s rear gun. Then hope died. Russian fighters had come in close and taken a beating even from a single rifle-caliber machine gun. The Thunderbolts hung back, opening fire at three hundred meters or more. The fire from the rear 7.92 machine gun seemed weak and feeble by comparison with the torrent of tracers coming in. Blechschmidt saw the 110 beside his own suddenly lurch in mid air, pieces flying in all directions as the fifty caliber bullets chewed up its structure. Then, there was a brilliant white flash and its entire left wing, complete with engine, blew off. The 110 rolled over on its back and dived, still upside down, into the pine trees underneath.

My turn next. Blechschmidt watched the Thunderbolt behind him open fire. He wrenched the controls over, putting the 110 into a wild skid that would undoubtedly have made the design crew go white with shock. It seemed to do little good. He saw the Ami tracers bite into his left wing, just outside the engine and chew along the metal, spraying fragments and shards of skin as they went. There was a scream from behind him; blood sprayed the cockpit canopy making him ashamed to be relieved it was the rear gunner's not his. Then, the whole world seemed to go black in a cloud of oily smoke from his engines.

Thunderbolt PI-H, West of the Volga.

It was the first time that anybody had ever tried to kill Edwards and the momentary physiological reaction to the realization disconcerted him. The tracers from the rear gunner on the 110 floated past his cockpit but, as far as he could tell, his Thunderbolt ignored them. He even got a slight feeling that the mighty P-47 was offended at the idea it could be perturbed by a mere 7.92mm bullet. He squeezed the firing button, hearing the battery of .50 caliber machine guns going off on either side of him over the snarl of his engine. The stream of tracers hit the 110's wing just outboard of the port engine, causing an immediate stream of white smoke that went gray then black. The 110 suddenly skidded hard to the left, taking Edward's stream of fire across the long glasshouse cockpit and into the other engine. The undercarriage wheel dropped down amid a sudden burst of black smoke that almost completely masked the Messerschmitt and the twin-engined fighter started to angle down towards the trees.

Edwards swung to fire on another 110 that was desperately running to get clear of the Thunderbolts. His first burst, hastily aimed and at a poor angle, clipped the tail and walked along the rear fuselage. Before he could correct his aim and take out one of the engines, the radio burst into life again. "Break it off, Jackson. Bring your flight back to the river and take over screening the gunboat. We'll take covering the Sturmoviks for the next part of the run."

Reluctantly, Jackson and Edwards broke off the chase and headed back to the Volga. On the way, they saw the dappled dark gray of the gunboat in the river in front of them. "OK, guys we'll buzz them. Let them know the Army Air Force is looking after them."

As far as Edwards could see, every man on PR-73 was out on the decks, cheering. As the Thunderbolts flashed over, he wondered what the white shower around him was. Then he realized: it was the sailors throwing their hats in the air.

River Gunboat PR-73, Off Sengiley, Volga River.

"Roughly sixty nautical miles, Skipper. Say four hours with this current against us?" Ensign Thom was well aware that his skipper already knew that. The problem was that they were approaching Sengiley again and this time, they didn't have the cover of darkness to help them run the battery. Nor, Thom suspected, would they have the unexpected assistance of a Guards Special Artillery battalion to help them get through.

"Four hours. Assuming nothing goes badly wrong here or at the Ulyanov'sk Narrows." Kennedy looked over the bows of his gunboat and up at the river ahead. "The current has picked up a bit. We should be home just after noon though."

"Any word what's going on up at the narrows?"

"Not a one. You know what the Russians are like and our brass are picking up the same bad habits. They never tell us anything we don't need to know until we have a need to know it. We won't find out what's going on up there until we have to run the narrows."

Any further discussion was made impossible by the ship's siren blasting out an air raid warning. "Skipper, aircraft coming in. Twenty, thirty of them. Coming in from both sides. They'll have us in a hammerhead."

Kennedy gave a curt dip of his head in acknowledgement. "Order all hands to battle stations – again. Stand by for air attack. Redline the engines."

A hammerhead attack was bad. Faced with an enemy coming in from one side only, a gunboat could turn its bows to face the threat, making itself a very difficult target. However, two formations coming in at 45 degrees off the bows from each side were a very different matter, Turning the bows to meet one meant exposing the gunboat's broadside to the other. The good news was that the Germans very rarely mounted hammerhead attacks on the Volga. Doing so meant flying over the Russian east bank and they preferred to avoid doing that unless it was absolutely essential.

"Raid count now twenty aircraft skipper. A dozen coming in low from port, designation Bogey-One eight up high to starboard designation Bogey-Two."

"Bogey-Two are dive bombers?" Thom was confused. The Germans had once made a specialty of dive-bombing but their Ju-87 was too slow and vulnerable to survive and it was now rarely seen except where the air opposition was very limited.

"Can't be. Johnny, what's the radar telling us now?"

"Bogey-Two aircraft are circling us. Bogey-One, still coming in from the west. Wait, wait, wait. Bogey-Two is splitting, half staying over us, the other half diving on Bogey-One. Redesignating. Bogey-Two is now Angel-One and Angel-Two. They're our fighter cover, Skipper."

"Thank God for that." Kennedy ran out to the bridge wing and scanned the sky with his binoculars. "Got them! Radial engines. Must be Lavochkins. No, by God, they're Thunderbolts! They're ours."

He managed to keep the binoculars on them as the olive-drab P-47s swept overhead in their dive to attack the German bombers but he lost them as the battle was engaged. All he heard was the faint snarl of engines and the vicious hammering of machinegun fire. What he did see were the columns of smoke that rose over the pine trees that lined the banks of the Volga. Steadily, he counted them. Two, then two more and another one beyond that. Whatever was happening out there, five aircraft had been destroyed. Then, he saw four black dots reappearing. They quickly resolved into the olive drab P-47s that had flown over a minute or two before.

Below him, word of the Thunderbolts had spread and the whole crew of PR-73 poured out on to the deck to cheer them on. The P-47s got the message and were rocking their wings in acknowledgement of the storm of cheering and blizzard of caps. Then, they were gone, climbing up to rejoin their formation.

Behind them Kennedy looked at the river around him. PR-73 was surrounded by floating seamen's caps. Already the crew was at work with nets and boathooks, trying to salvage what they could. "Lenny, looks like we'll need to indent for a new set of covers. We'll drift for a minute or two, give the boys time to catch their breath, then we'll hit full power and run the guns at Sengiley."

It was so rare for a gunboat to be operating in daylight on this stretch of the river that Kennedy couldn't recognize the surrounding terrain. It was only when he saw the sharp neck of the river where it narrowed to a mere three miles wide that he realized he had reached Staryy Belyy Yar. There was no sign of gunfire from the much-feared coastal battery at Sengiley and the radar trace they had noted on the way down was gone.

Thom shook his head. "It's real quiet over there."

Kennedy couldn't help smiling at the reference. "Yeah, pardner, too darned quiet."

The west bank of the Volga was indeed unnaturally quiet. Indeed, it appeared almost tranquil. Kennedy found himself resenting the report that came from the "radar room" as the gunboat thumped its way upriver. "Formation inbound from the East Sir. Dozen aircraft designated Angel-Three."

"That'll be the Sturmoviks." Kennedy tried to spot them with his binoculars but they were still too far out. The plan had been for the guns at Sengiley to unmask themselves firing on the gunboat so they could then be dive-bombed by the Sturmoviks. It wasn't a brilliant plan, all things considered, but Kennedy had thought it was reasonably workmanlike for a scheme that had been thrown together in a few hours. Sometimes improvisation beat preparation and this was supposed to have been one of those times. The one thing that hadn't been expected was that the guns would remain silent.

The Ilyushin Il-2s were in four neat Vs, each of three aircraft. They started to circle over PR-73, the crews obviously confused by the silence underneath them. Not only was the American gunboat not under fire but there was no trace of anti-aircraft fire coming up. Thom shook his head in bewilderment. "Do you reckon that rocket attack last night took out the entire battery?"

"And its flak? Not a chance." Kennedy was scanning the area where the battery had been located. "Well, we've had our fun. Let's wake them up. Gun crews man your guns. Three inch, bearing two-seven-zero, range three thousand yards. Fire when ready."

"Isn't this a bit like poking a bear with a stick, Skipper?" Thom was deeply interested in what the result of this apparently foolhardy action might be.

"The bear is on our side, Lenny. This is closer to trying to take a haunch of meat from a wolf. The official name for doing that is reconnaissance by fire." Kennedy heard the bang of the 3 inch gun firing and was surprised by how little the flash registered in full daylight. A second or so later, he saw the shell strike home. "Hmm, no secondaries. Three inch crew, fire a dozen more rounds into that area. Minor variations in range and bearing as you see fit. We're trying to get a response out of them."

A dozen rounds later, the west bank of the Volga around Sengiley was still silent. "Now what do we do? Land a landing team and steal their schnapps supply?"

Kennedy laughed at Thom's joke and then suddenly realized that it might not be a bad idea. It would certainly be giving the finger to his father. Before he could reply though, the next step came down via the radio. "Gunboat, this is Eagle Section Commander. I'm sending two of my boys down to have a look. The Sturmoviks are ready to make their run as soon as we see something."

Thunderbolt PI-H, Over Sengiley, West Bank of the Volga.

"Edwards, follow me in. If you see anything, call it out. This is the one time you are welcome to start yakking on the radio."

Jackson's P-47 did a wingover and started to dive on Sengiley. Edwards followed him, staying well behind and off to one side. Below them, the silence was eerie. He could see the town of Sengiley grouped around a small estuary that obviously provided a small harbor. Edwards guessed that it would be a very basic and rudimentary anchorage; all the ones on the west bank of the Volga were. It was the ones on the east bank that had been developed into proper ports. The river leading to the estuary quickly fizzled out though. He thought it was five miles long, six at most.

The town grew beneath him. At first it looked a very pleasant place. The roads were narrow but they had been surfaced and were lined with trees. The buildings on either side were a pleasant light gray stone with yellowish roofs and white highlights. It was only as the two Thunderbolts got lower that Edwards could see the trees were yellowing and dying and the buildings were burned out. As he started to pull out of the dive, he could see the blackened holes in the roofs and the stains around the windows that told of the fighting that must have taken place in Sengiley.

"The guns were supposed to be over there. Can you see anything Edwards?"

The gun positions were supposed to be just north of the city and, like every other German installation, were supposed to be ringed with anti-aircraft guns. Only there were no guns Edwards could see and no streams of tracer fire from the 20mm guns that would have protected them.

"My only theory is that mice ate them." Jackson sounded puzzled by the absence of the expected battery.

Edwards had a sudden, insane desire to rebuke him for yakking on the radio. Prudence almost succumbed to the devilment that lay in the heart of every nineteen year old but he saw something and curved around to take a closer look instead. "Track parallel to the river. There's other paths coming in at an angle from the northwest. See them. I think there's a circle at each intersection. Like a gun revetment?"

"Just like a gun revetment. Only it's empty. There are no guns down there."

"There's nothing of anything down there. No trucks, so searchlights, nothing. What gives?"

"Don't ask me Edwards. This position was giving the Navy fits. Why the hell should the Krauts just abandon it?"

River Gunboat PR-73, Off Sengiley, Volga River.

"Why the hell should the Krauts just abandon it?" Thom was unconsciously echoing the thoughts of Lieutenant Jackson.

"God knows. We'll have to make sure the brass finds out about this. Whatever made them move those guns after all the trouble they've caused must be important."

Kennedy looked up overhead. The Russian IL-2s were departing for their secondary target while the eight Thunderbolts continued their lazy figure of eight over PR-73. It was, in fact, turning out to be a peaceful, almost bucolic day on the river. And so it remained for the 25 miles upriver, to the Ulyanov'sk Narrows.

B-26B Marauder AN-J, Over the West Bank of the Volga.

"How sure are we that the radar station is where they said it is?" Major Benjamin Wood was a staunch believer in the theory that everything that could possibly go wrong, would go wrong.

"They're sure." Bombardier-Navigator Eddie Greer had put the B-26 on the right heading that would take it straight to the target. Now, he was getting ready to shift to the nose position where he could stage the attack on the radar site. Three more B-26s would drop their bombs on his command. Behind them, a second formation of four would bomb a few seconds later, again under the command of a master-bomber in the lead aircraft. Then, the third section would bomb to complete the destruction of the target. "The Navy has been collecting intercept cuts on these places for weeks. One intercept doesn't tell us much of anything; two gives us a really rough position. The cut gets more accurate with each track. We got a dozen or more on Lomy. I'd say we have the position pinned down to feet."

"I hope you're right." Wood sounded unconvinced. One of the problems with flying at treetop height was that he couldn't see anything outside a very narrow arc forwards. The trees seemed to come straight at him and then flow away on either side. All he could see sideways was the blur of their passing. The doctors called it 'tunnel effect' but to Wood it meant he had to fly on courses set by his navigator – who could see as little as him.

Greer took off his parachute. That was one of the bad things about his job; climbing down the narrow tunnel that led from the cockpit to the bomb-aimers position in the nose was impossible while wearing a parachute. If his aircraft was hit while he was down there, he would have to climb up the passage, put on his parachute, make his way to the escape hatch and then bail out. All while the B-26 was going down, probably burning and in a tight spin. The only redeeming factor was that the Marauder was a tough aircraft and took a lot of killing.

Down in the nose, the sensation of the trees flowing past the aircraft was even stronger. Several times, Greer thought an especially tall tree was directly in front of them and would crash through the transparency but each time it seemed to dance to one side at the last moment. Then, over the treeline, he could see the large, square mattress-like antenna of the Freya site. From his briefing package, he knew the Lomy site had two Freya radars and two smaller Wurtzburg sets. All four were closely grouped so they could be guarded more easily against Partisan attacks. The Russians had a lot of aircraft but nearly all of them were tasked with supporting the troops fighting on the front. Their ability to penetrate much behind the front lines and hit rear-area targets was very limited. On the other hand, the U.S. Army Air Force made doing just that one of its top priorities. Partisans had suddenly ceased to be the German Army's worst enemy.

Once he had sighted them, the Freya antennas seemed to approach with terrifying speed. Greer thumbed the intercom and gave a terse, "I have the aircraft. Opening bomb bay doors now."

Then, he lined up carefully on the more distant of the two square grids that rotated slowly over the treeline. There was a logical reason for that as well. In any bombing run, each successive group of aircraft would drop its bombs just a little earlier than the one before it. That way the patterns of bombs would walk back across the target area and the bomber formations had a better chance of avoiding the blast and fragments from the aircraft in front of them.

Greer barely had time to settle down on his bomb sight when the radar site was in front of him and the central cross-hairs beginning its run over the perimeter. A tiny alteration of course lined them up perfectly with the rearmost radar tower then, as the cross touched the base of the tower, he pressed the release. He could feel the eight five hundred pounders stream from the bay.

Almost immediately, he also felt the blast from their explosions surge up fling the bomber skywards. "Pilots, all yours."

In the cockpit, Wood saw the radar tower being lifted bodily into the air. Greer had done a fine job, placing his bombs right across the radar tower and into the operator's hut behind it. The great square radar antenna was slowly peeling downwards as its supporting tower collapsed. He continued to lift his B-26 up, clear of the mass of explosions that marked the first load of bombs to be dumped on the target. Already, the second flight was making its run, adding to the chaos and destruction that had once been a perfectly-organized radar surveillance system. By then, Wood was already putting his Marauder into a dive and turning for the course that would take them back to the Volga and safety. Beneath him, he could see Greer struggling up the passage out of the nose so he could resume his seat as navigator. By the time he made it, all twelve Marauders were crossing the Volga, leaving a huge pyre of smoke in the sky where a Freya site had been.

Bf 110F Blue-One, Approaching Saranov.

Colonel Joachim Blechschmidt lived in a world that was entirely composed of burned engine oil. The engine nacelles were spewing it, the wings were coated with the stuff, the shattered cockpit was a mass of thick, black, semi-carbonized slime. He was coated with the filth to the point where he dare not rub his eyes for fear of the particles scratching his corneas. He wasn't certain what the rear of his cockpit looked like because the sight was blocked by the headless corpse of his rear gunner. *Come to think of it, I'm not sure I'm still alive. I don't think I should be. Perhaps this is hell and I'm doomed to fly like this for all eternity.*

He looked around, trying to work out how to land. Only one thing was running for him, the course home was due west. As long as he kept the rising sun at his back, he would be fine. He would find Saranov. *Now, what do I do when I get there? I can't read the instruments, both my engines are shot to hell, I've got one wheel hanging down and the other jammed up. Oh, yes, and my ailerons and flaps are wrecked.* A look at his wings showed him how true that was. Both ailerons were hanging off their hinges, stuck at awkward angles to the wing. The flaps were hanging off as well, swaying in the airflow under the wings. *I've got to be dead. No aircraft can fly in this condition.*

Ahead of him, he saw a pencil-like line on the ground. It was almost directly in front of him and it resolved quickly into a long rectangle with a shorter, narrower one beside it. It was Saranov. It had to be. When he and ZG-1 had moved into the base, they had thought it was a slum. Now, it was the most beautiful thing he had ever seen. He lined up on the runway, not absolutely certain how he was steering. Red flares were shooting up, warning him that his undercarriage was still up. *Or, at least, not right.*

And yet it was the wrecked undercarriage that saved him. The one that was hanging down collapsed as soon as it touched the runway, dropping Blue-One onto its belly. The 110 slid down the runway in a shower of sparks and a cloud of black smoke but it came to a stop safely. The ground crews were on it immediately, smashing what was left of the cockpit open and heaving the crew out. Blechschmidt felt himself being pulled from the aircraft and laid down on the grass clear of the wrecked aircraft. Beside him, a stretcher covered with a sheet held what was left of his gunner. They had been together since Barbarossa had started two years earlier.

In front of him, Blechschmidt saw what could have happened had his undercarriage not collapsed. Another 110 was attempting to land, also shot into a wreck and streaming smoke. Its undercarriage was lowered and it touched down on its main wheels perfectly but then everything went wrong at one. The nose dipped, the tail rose, the propeller tips dug into the surface of the runway. The aircraft flipped over in a forward somersault, landing upside down in the grass beside the runway. The fuel tanks exploded and Blechschmidt believed he could hear the screams of the crew as they were burned alive, trapped in their wrecked aircraft. Suddenly, he felt immensely grateful to Blue-One.

Then, he saw the man standing over him and tried to struggle to his feet. General Alexander Holle reached down and stopped him. "Rest, Jogge. You are lucky to be alive. What the devil hit you?"

Blechschmidt looked up at his commander. "Not devils, Alex. Thunderbolts."

River Gunboat PR-73, Entering the Ulyanov'sk Narrows, Volga River.

"This is the last crunch point. After this, we're clear." That wasn't strictly true as Kennedy well knew. PR-45 had gone down after she'd hit a mine barely a hundred yards off the gunboat base entrance. They weren't clear until they were tied up alongside and even then, safety was conditional. Air raids were frequent enough to make any idea of real safety an illusion.

"Bootlegger, this is Graziano. We need some help at the bridge."

Thom had the codebook open. "Graziano is PR-61. She's a 125-foot Huckins boat."

"Damned battleship sailors. Why can't they forget my old man exists? I'd sure like to." Kennedy picked up the radio microphone and almost snarled into it. "Graziano, this is Bootlegger. What's the problem?"

"I say, steady on. We've got a problem here. After you went through last night, our friends counter-attacked and seized most of the bridge. They've been working their way across all morning. We're backing them up. Problem is, we're too big to slip through the wreckage of the bridge the way you little ones can. So, we need you to run along the downriver side of the wreck and shoot up the Huns from there."

"Wait one." Kennedy switched off the microphone and turned to Thom. "What is it with that guy?"

"He's Canadian, Skipper. PR-60 to 65 went to the Canadian Navy as Lend-Lease. I thought they were up north on Lake Ladoga but obviously not."

Kennedy frowned for a second. "Graziano, what are you doing down here?"

"Got a refit at Starry May then this whole thing blew up. We stayed down to help out and now we need another refit. Look, we're in a bit of a jam here. We really need some help on the downriver side."

"All right. We're coming around the bend now. What and where?"

"Thanks Bootlegger." The relief in the voice was unmistakable. "After you bust through last night, the Russians counter-attacked. The Huns had placed duck-boards over the wreckage of the bridge and they didn't get time to toss them in the river. It was pretty bad all night but by dawn, the Russians had taken the ironware and were on the western causeway. They've been inching along it all morning. Now, here's the tough bit. There's a group of partisans and hold-outs in the cluster of fishing huts around the landward end western causeway. They're not much and they're separated from the city proper by what's left of a park but they're still a part of Ulyanov'sk. If we can link up with them, we'll have a lodgment in the city and that's a big propaganda thing according to the brass. If we can't link up, they're all dead. We need you to support the Partisans on the downriver side."

"Got it. How will we know you?"

"Oh, you'll know us." The voice on the radio sounded smug.

Once again, seeing a familiar stretch of the river in daylight gave an entirely new perspective to the area. Kennedy had always assumed that the built up area of the city extended right down to the river bank but the real situation was rather different. There was a strip of parkland, almost 300 yards wide, that separated the city proper from the river. He could see that it had once been developed as a recreation area with seats, bandstands and play areas but all of that was now ruined. He was also surprised to see just how much the city towered over the river banks; he guessed the ridge on which Ulyanov'sk had been built was at least 400 feet higher than the river bank. Despite the destruction that characterized all contested Russian cities, he could see that the buildings had once been a cut above the usual monolithic Stalin-era Soviet architecture. In fact, Kennedy couldn't help but think that Ulyanov'sk had probably been a very attractive city pre-war.

That was then, this was now. The area of Ulyanov'sk that could be seen from the river was ruined. The fighting in the city during the German assault on it had reduced it to ruins and then the continuous exchange of artillery fire across the river had completed the work of destruction. Kennedy had little doubt that the area of the city on the reverse slope of the ridge was less damaged than the areas he could see but he guessed that the difference was not that consequential. The Germans had learned that taking a Russian city meant a long, hard, bloody and extremely destructive fight. There was usually little left standing by the time it was over.

The extent of the fighting now in progress was also obvious. Kennedy guessed that the situation was one that military historians might describe as complex. The Russians advancing from the east bank had indeed seized the wreckage of the bridge and the duckboard footways put in by the Germans. However, the west bank causeway was shaped like a capital P on its side with the loop upwards and on the river side. There was a quartet of buildings in that loop and they were obviously still held by Germans. Kennedy could see mortar explosions around the four isolated buildings which showed the Russians were still pressing in on them

The rest of the Russian force had indeed pushed past the loop of the P and was halfway down the stem of the P towards the shore side. Their way further forward was blocked by another German force which was itself cut off by another Russian force that held the cluster of buildings around the area where the causeway met the riverbank. That clustered force was itself under siege from the main German force in Ulyanov'sk that was in the parkland and obviously trying to push the Russians out the way so they could relieve their troops on the causeway. The battle going on was obviously desperate.

"Look over there skipper." Thom pointed at the middle section of the wrecked bridge. A burned-out gunboat was hung up on the steel spiderwork that had once been the bridge trusses. The blackened structure had multiple hits, from the picture in Kennedy's binoculars most likely caused by anti-tank guns. "She's PR-59. One of ours. I'd guess if anybody got off her, they're fighting alongside the frontoviki right now."

Gunboats, even one of the Huckins battleships, up against PAK 75s is a chancy proposition at best and we're about to do the same. Kennedy thought for a second. "What's our target?"

"Group of buildings south of the Russian position. The krauts are in there and getting ready to push up the river bank. The 61 boat is going to hit the Hun hold-outs on the causeway loop. There she goes now."

Ahead of them, PR-61 was moving up to the loop where the Germans were still holding out. Kennedy fixed his binoculars on her, noticing the damage to the bridge and upper works from shore fire. *The battleships are too big a target for fighting on the river. My Elco is a much better design. I'd guess she tried to take on the krauts on the causeway earlier and got shot up by those hold-outs on the loop. So, now she's going to take them out first.* Then he looked at PR-61 a bit harder. There was something unusual about her but he couldn't quite make out what it was.

That question was answered suddenly and quite horrifyingly. Two great arcs of flame spewed out from the fore and aft positions that should have held three inch guns. Kennedy could hear the low-pitched roar of the heavy flamethrowers rolling across the water. The sheer weight of the jets seemed to make the buildings on the loop stagger under the impact before the dissolved in flame. PR-61 had obviously practiced with her weapons because the crew had the art of rolling balls of flame across the water and into the selected targets perfectly. It was an inspiring and terrifying display even from the distance away that PR-73 stood. By the time PR-61 turned away from her run on the loop, the Russian infantry were already beginning to close in on the scene of the holocaust.

"My God, she's a Zippo boat." Thom was awed by the display of fire that had engulfed the first German position. The sight of the balls of fire rolling across the water had given him a nightmarish picture of what would happen if they hadn't stopped and had engulfed PR-73. Fighting S-boats and anti-tank guns was one thing. The oily balls of flame spewed by a Zippo Boat were something quite different. That brought another thought to Thom's mind. *What would happen to a Zippo Boat if a kraut gunner hit those fuel tanks? Nothing good is a sure answer.*

"Order all guns to open up on the large white building bearing two-eight-zero." Kennedy could almost feel it in his heart to be sorry for the next group of isolated Germans. They were on the causeway itself and they were more or less in the open. They had erected crude barriers to protect themselves from rifle and machine gun fire but they would do nothing to defend them against the flamethrowers on the Zippo boat. He dismissed them from his mind; he had much more important things to think about at this point and he tried to ignore the heavy rolling thunder of the flamethrowers and the screams of the men trapped on the causeway echoing over the slate-gray water of the Volga.

Their initial target wasn't really much of a building even when it hadn't been damaged by the fighting. It looked a little like a small sports stadium; a square iron structure with an open front containing rows of seats. Perhaps it had been a sports stadium, Kennedy had noted that the Russians seemed to like those and had built them everywhere. Or perhaps it had been a café where people could drink a cup of tea while watching the Volga roll past. Whatever, it had been, it wouldn't be that any more. PR-73's forward gun dropped its first three inch shell right through the roof. Others followed quickly, the gun crew knowing the quicker they drove back the Germans occupying the cluster of buildings, the quicker they could be through the narrows and on their way back home. Under the lash of gunfire, the little iron building seemed just to melt away.

The crash of the three inch gun was joined by the slow, rhythmic thumping of the quadruple 1.1 inch and the rattle of the fifty calibers. It was also joined by a new sound, a flat, vicious crack that sounded remarkably like that of a 60mm mortar round. That dark suspicion was confirmed when Kennedy saw his 60mm mortar lobbing shells at a German position that the flat trajectory guns couldn't get at.

"All right Lenny, we're not supposed to have 60mm high explosive on board. Where did it come from?"

"I believe some crates, quite a lot of crates in fact, went missing from an Army depot, Skipper. It seemed a shame to waste them so they got shared out amongst the boats." Thom might have explained further (or perhaps not) but he was stopped by a shell that threw water and fragments off the bridge windows. The supposedly bullet-proof glass stopped any damage but there was no guarantee the next shell wouldn't be a direct hit. "Pak gun, skipper, a 50mm I think. Bearing two-six-five."

The 1.1 crew were already on the ball and their shells saturated the area. The Pak gun didn't fire again. PR-73 swung around for another pass at the target but Kennedy knew this would have to be the last. His gunboat had already fought two actions in the last eighteen hours and he knew his ammunition had to be running low.

"Bootlegger, Graziano here." The Captain of PR-61 sounded much more subdued than before. Seeing his flamethrowers at work would do that to a man. "The troops crossing the river have linked up with the rest. We can go home now. Keep close to the west bank causeway."

Sailing between the abutments and listening to the Russian infantry running across the boardwalks overhead was a strange experience. Just as PR-73 cleared the wreckage of the collapsed bridge, the crew hear the "URRAH, URRAH" cheers of the Russians. The cause was obvious. Some of the troops that had crossed the river had hoisted the Hammer and Sickle over the largest of the captured buildings. The building was a wreck, roofless, windowless, doorless, but the flag flew over it anyway.

Then something happened that struck Kennedy almost dumb with shock. Beside the Hammer and Sickle, a new flag was hoisted. It had obviously been made quickly, on the spot from whatever materials were available. A surviving bed sheet, perhaps, and whatever red and blue paint the frontoviki could find.

Kazan Thunderbolts

The flag had a simple blue square and some red stripes but it was enough to bring tears to the eyes of the gunboat crew in a way a formal, authorized 'real' flag would not. The makeshift 'Stars and Stripes' flying alongside the Hammer and Sickle over a tiny area of Ulyanov'sk was a very personal mark of recognition from the frontoviki to the gunboat crews who had fought beside them.

Airfield 108, Privolzhskiy na Volga, Moskva Front.

The P-47 shutdown drill was much simpler than the start-up. Edwards applied his toe brakes and set the parking lever. That caused a brief smile to cross his face; back in Pennsylvania he and a friend had long arguments over when to use the hand brake on automobiles. That random thought made him consider the possibility of a cold-weather start. It was June but this was Russia. Despite of his mental association of Russian with endless snow, he decided not to hold the oil dilution switch down. That would delay things for four minutes and the briefings all stressed the need to get the aircraft under cover quickly. Instead, he opened the engine to 1,000 rpm, placed the mixture control in 'Idle – Cut off' and waited until the engine stopped. Then it was simply a matter of turning the ignition and fuel selector switches to off. Then he flipped off the cockpit lights, pitot heater switch, generator and master battery switches. His first combat mission in Russia was over.

By the time he got to the ground, his Thunderbolt was already being pushed back into its apparently derelict hangar. Around him, the other seven aircraft in his flight were following suite. Teams of workers were hard at work, returning the airfield to its apparently derelict state. The flight surgeon came up to Edwards and ceremonially handed him his shot of whiskey, courtesy of Uncle Sam. He took one look at the small glass and decided that the day needed celebration. He tossed the brown liquid back and wondered briefly why Uncle Sam couldn't have stretched his purse a little and got them bottles of single malt. Then, he went into the hangar where the debriefing team was waiting. His flight leader, Lieutenant Jackson had just finished his session and Edwards took his place.

"Lieutenant Edwards. You flew Thunderbolt PI-H this morning? Could you tell us what happened."

Edwards told the story of the battle against the Bf 110s, using his hands to show the movements of the aircraft in the traditional manner. When he finished, his interviewer tapped his pad reflectively. "You saw the aircraft hit by Lieutenant Jackson blow up?"

"No, Sir. It had an explosion in its left wing. Odd explosion, brilliant white color. Not like the fuel burning. That blew the left wing off completely. Then it rolled on its back and went in nose-first. I saw it going in."

"Right we'll count that as a confirmed kill for Jackson. With the one you hit together, that gives him one and a half kills. The second aircraft you hit, did he explode?"

Edwards was tempted to say yes but he stopped himself. "To be honest, no Sir. I hit both engines and he was a mass of black smoke. He was heading down but I did not see him explode nor did I see him hit the ground."

The interviewer nodded. "That's very candid of you. I'm sorry, Edwards, I can't give you a confirmed for that one. I'll give you a probable. The third one you shot up, we'll call a damaged."

Up on the board at the end of the hangar, Edwards saw his name being followed by three numbers, a half for the "kill" column, a one in the "probables" and another one in the "damaged. To his dismay, he saw that Jackson, Barnes and Walker had all been credited with one and a half kills and a damaged each. The probable didn't seem much of a consolation.

"Sorry." The interviewer was apologetic. "It does work out though. Both the gunboat and the Partisans reported five kraut aircraft going in. The numbers do add up. If it's any consolation, if the partisans find another 110 wreck on the way back to their base, you're first in line for it."

Edwards nodded and looked up. The chalkboard now had four more names on it, Johnson, Ward, Carter and King. Each had three zeros beside their names. Suddenly his half didn't look so bad.

He decided that a visit to the Officer's mess might not be a bad idea. His hands were beginning to shake slightly and the idea that somebody had tried to kill him was gaining prominence in his mind. He was just about to go in when a hand fell upon his shoulder. "Misha, my American friend, how went the day for you."

"Alex, I was hoping I'd meet you here." *Meaning I was hoping you'd made it back and I think you know that.* "We ran into a gaggle of 110s. Dozen of them. We got five and a probable."

Koldunov nodded. "And you? How many fascists did you kill?"

"A half. And the probable. What about you Alex?"

"110 has a crew of two. So your half means you have killed your first Hitlerite. Well done my friend. For it was strange. Normally we run into many fighters the fascist side of the lines but this time there were few. They have all gone. That is very worrying."

Koldunov pushed open the door and ushered Edwards in. He hadn't scored a kill in the free-chase mission and that meant Edwards with his half-kill had pride of place. Once inside, Koldunov looked around before announcing proudly, "Comrades, we have a new Brat today."

"What did you get?" Guards Captain Litvyak actually showed some awareness that Edwards existed now.

"Half of a Bf 110 and a probable on another. Damaged a third."

"How do you shoot down half an aircraft?" Litvyak sounded curious but there was also a derisive note to her voice.

"Two of us concentrated fire on it and it blew up in mid-air."

"Huh."

"In ours, where several pilots share responsibility for a kill, it is not credited to the pilots but to the group as a whole." Koldunov explained.

So, that's why you get in so close. Edwards thought. "The other 110, I raked him from wingtip to wingtip. I left him with both engines burning and the cockpit shattered. I didn't see him explode or crash so it's only a probable but I think I got him."

Litvyak looked at him and smiled. Suddenly she became a very attractive young woman. "Yes, I think you did. The Partisans will be looking for the wreckage. Come, Bratishka, let us share a drink together. Of the Special Reserve I think."

Three shots of Special Reserve Vodka arrived on the bar in front of them. At that point, something occurred to Edwards. "Alex, you said the fact you didn't run into kraut fighters was worrying. Why?"

"If the fascists are going to launch an offensive, they pull all their aircraft back for maintenance so they can put in a maximum effort on the first day of their attack. So, when the fascist aircraft disappear, it shows an offensive is coming."

"When we were coming back, we found the . . Fascists . . had pulled their guns out of Sengiley."

"That too would fit. The Hitlerites are short of guns. They concentrate them where they are needed and remove them from less important areas. You reported this. Edwards nodded. "Then, we know that the fascists are planning an attack somewhere in this area."

Gunboat Squadron GunRon 5 Headquarters, Staraya Mayna, Volga River.

"So, Tovarish Lieutenant, when did you find the wrong ammunition had been supplied to your gunboat for delivery? The Chekist was far removed from

Kennedy's mental picture of an investigator from the CheKa. Drawn from pre-war newspaper stories about the activities of the notorious NKVD, he had expected a swarthy, unkempt figure in blood-stained overalls whose belt was festooned with clubs, thumbscrews, fingernail extractors and other tools of his trade. But, he reminded himself, Beria was dead, Stalin was dead, the NKVD had reverted to being the CheKa and this man was nothing like the image. He was tall, elegant and young. In fact, Kennedy felt he was remarkably like the young men of the Kennedy family in general appearance. What was different was that the Chekist had an air of grimness about him. He gave every impression of being a man entrusted to do a vital but distasteful job and who was determined to do it to the best of his ability.

"My Quartermaster took delivery of the drums and decided to ensure that the contents matched the manifest. This is standard procedure in our Navy. If we receive fuel oil, we check to make sure it is not gasoline. If we receive rations, we check to make sure they did not expire during the Civil War. The American Civil War of course." Kennedy was determined to make sure that his crew was protected from the attentions of CheKa.

"So, you do not trust our supply personnel?" The Chekist leaned forward as he asked that question. Kennedy looked at him harder, realizing there was something odd about his left eye. *It's almost as if . . . I think it is.*

"We have an old saying in our Navy. Trust but verify. I trust your supply personnel as much as I trust our own. But, mistakes happen. When they do, it is best to catch them before they become important."

"After you found the wrong ammunition, what did you do?"

"We went to a Russian gunboat that had just come in for repairs and borrowed their supply of 7.62mm Russian. We then took both types of ammunition down with us."

"Was your 'borrowing' of the ammunition authorized?"

That was when Commander Henry Farrow cut in. "Of course it was. I authorized the loan of ammunition in my capacity as base commander. Better to borrow some ammunition from a gunboat that needed a week's repair than leave the fighting men short."

The Chekist nodded. "You took both types of ammunition down. Why?"

"Because I thought that the Marine unit on Island Ten just might have Canadian-supplied weapons and needed the .303. So, it was prudent to take both."

"Prudent indeed." The Chekist nodded. "It is obvious there is no blame to be assessed here. Indeed, Tovarish Lieutenant, I find your actions commendable. But, to have the wrong ammunition shipped this far south, means there must be a major sabotage ring operating."

"Not necessarily." Kennedy couldn't help himself. He was a Harvard-trained business manager and had seen his father at work. "I have some experience in my family's railway interests back home. In an American yard, it is quite frequent for a wagon to be accidentally attached to the wrong consist and go astray. I would say it happens daily. Usually the wagon turns up in a few hours or a day or so but sometimes the missing wagon turns up hundreds of miles from its destination many days after it went missing. In such cases, if the goods are spoiled, the railway is liable for the loss and must compensate the owner. My work for my father often consisted of investigating such losses and paying the compensation. If this took place in our yards, I would assume that the misrouted wagons were an accident but that somebody at this end saw the useless ammunition waiting to be shipped back north and decided to send it where it would do most damage."

Did I do that right? Kennedy thought. *I described problems that occur on American railways and how an American railway company might go about things. I didn't criticize the Russians or how the Communist Party does things.*

Captain Lapshin caught his eye and nodded slightly. Kennedy guessed he had done well. To confirm that, the Chekist was nodding thoughtfully. "This would be a lesser problem and gives us a start to our investigation. A single Hitlerite would be a much less significant problem than a large ring of them."

"If this was an American yard, I would look for a disgruntled worker, one who feels neglected or unrecognized. The fascists prey upon such weaknesses. Such a person may not even know he was being used by the fascists. He may see himself as striking back at those who ignored him or even see himself as a patriot alerting us to a problem."

The Chekist nodded again. "A good suggestion. When we find the man, we will soon know the truth of the matter."

Kennedy couldn't resist it any longer. "Tovarish Chekist, may I ask a question. Is your left eye glass?"

"It is. How did you know?"

"It has a kindly look to it."

There was an appalled silence in the room. Captain Lapshin was goggling in sheer disbelief. *Nobody* ever talked to a Chekist like that. The silence was broken by the Chekist snorting with laughter. "A kindly look, you say Tovarish Lieutenant? CheKa cannot have that. I will see that it is replaced by a more severe model immediately. Goodbye, Tovarish Lieutenant. The Rodina recognizes your services and thanks you for them."

305th Bombardment Group, Bolshaya Tarlovka Airfield, Russia.

"Captain Richard Gonzalez to see you, Sir."

"Send him in."

"Photographs, Colonel." Gonzalez had picked up LeMay's habit of phrasing everything as tersely as possible. "First set. The four targets you listed. All recent enough for bomb damage to be visible. There isn't any."

LeMay looked at the pictures, his habitual scowl deepening as he examined them. "Good pictures. Sharp."

"They're the forward obliques taken with my nose camera. They're the best for bomb craters because the circular shadows show up. They don't in the belly verticals unless you use a stereoscope. The side obliques show the craters up as well. I brought a viewer for you Sir. It shows everything much more clearly."

Gonzalez opened up the box under his arm and set up the viewer. LeMay peered down it with great interest. "Your cameras are stabilized? There's no blurring from your evasive action."

"Evasive action Colonel? Don't take it. Straight and level over the target area. That gives the best shots."

"For the Huns too. Surprised you're still alive." LeMay was scowling again but this time because he was thinking hard. He had the feeling he was learning something really important.

Gonzalez hesitated a little but felt that his Colonel needed an explanation. "Colonel, Sir, with respect, anti-aircraft guns don't aim at individual aircraft. They aim at a box in the sky through which the targets have to fly. The size of that box depends on altitude but generally the higher the aircraft fly, the larger the box. Now, once an aircraft is in the box, its chance of getting hit is dependent on how long it's in the box for and how much of the box it occupies. My F-5 is tiny and I go through that box at 20,000 feet like a bat out of hell. I got water injection and increased boost. Makes me at least 20 knots faster than the P-38s. Flak's not a problem. Fighters are different. Only thing I can do there is run fast and far."

"How do you know all this?"

"My brother is in the Navy, Sir. When the fleet started expanding he got into gunnery school and specialized in anti-aircraft. He's on the *New Mexico* now. He's striking for Petty Officer and I helped him with his books. Learned a lot myself in the process."

LeMay grunted and looked through the viewer again. All four targets he had given Gonzalez were virtually undamaged. His analysts would calculate the

71

exact figure later but it looked as if the average bombing error was something in the region of five miles. From a crude count, at least half the bombs dropped were so far off target Gonzalez hadn't included them in his runs. Then, he felt a sharp stabbing pain in his eyes. They were getting sore and he took a minute out to apply some eye-drops.

"Second batch, Sir. The B-26 strike this morning. This is what the target looked like before the raid." LeMay slipped the photograph into the viewer and solemnly inspected the image. He could see the two Freya radars and two Wurtzburgs along with the huts for the operators and the perimeter fence. The images were good enough for him to make out the beaten tracks where the site crew had walked around the site and the disturbed ground that told of minefields protecting the perimeter.

"And this is what it looks like now." There was nothing left. What had once been a trim, very Germanic radar site was a mass of overlapping bomb craters. As far as LeMay could see, over a hundred bombs had fallen inside the perimeter fence. It was like looking at a heavily-plowed field or a World War One battlefield.

"Damn. They scored more hits in a morning than we've done in six months."

Gonzalez's mouth twisted slightly. "They did, once. I hope they don't try it again. Next time the krauts will be waiting for them with quad-twenties. Anyway, third package, Colonel. I got these by accident. I turn the cameras on before I start the run and keep them going until I'm well out of it. That way, I know I've covered the target area properly. I found these on the excess films. This one seems to show tanks under camouflage netting. At the tail end of two runs, I found I'd taken these of what appear to be infantry units moving into place. Here, I think we have temporary supply dumps. I'm not an analyst but if I picked these up more or less at random, I'd say there are concentrations of German troops, armor, infantry and artillery, around the Chuvashskaya Bridgehead. I might even say they're massing for an offensive there."

LeMay nodded. "Ask Colonel Holland out there to send these to the Army immediately. Well done, Captain. And thank your aircraft for me. She's done well."

Gonzalez gave an appreciative grin, saluted and left. Behind him, LeMay went over to his book case and searched through it until he found an old artillery manual from his ROTC days. Gonzalez hadn't known he had been speaking to a man who had trained as an artilleryman before transferring to the Air Corps. He wasn't quite sure why he had brought that old manual for the French 75 along with him; he'd just thrown it in with his kit when he was on his way to Russia. *Now, the Germans use 88s, not 75s but I can make allowances for that.*

What I have to do is create a fire plan on a target the size of a B-17 sitting on the ground 25,000 feet from the gun. Then modify it for an aircraft moving at 200mph. His fingers and pencil scribbled, adding, subtracting, allowing for dispersion, allowing for the arcs of fire of the guns, allowing for fire concentration.

In the end, he stared at the figures in front of him. *Three hundred and seventy two rounds. That's what the krauts will need to put into the box Gonzalez was describing to score a hit. Three hundred and seventy two rounds to get a B-17 flying straight in. It'll take a single kraut 88 twenty five minutes to get that hit. Not ten seconds, twenty five minutes. A battery of twelve guns might get one plane or two but that's all. Close the planes up tight so they fill less of that box. Keep straight and level so we get through the box as quickly as possible. So where did that ten seconds figure come from? I bet it was a "let's scare the fresh meat" joke that somehow got accepted as fact and passed on unquestioned. That does it. From now on, everything gets written down. Everything. From tomorrow, forget about gyrating all over the sky. And then we start retraining the pilots to close the formations up tight. The formations need attention as well. Every gun has to count. I'll need Gonzalez to give me a fighter pilot's view on that.* For a brief moment, LeMay wished he had stayed in fighters rather than transferring to bombers. Then he reminded himself of the star he had set his course by. *Fighters are fun; bombers are important.*

LeMay put his pad to one side, laid down his pencil and washed his face. Telling his bomber crews that they were go into the dreaded German flak flying straight and level was going to be interesting. There was only one way he could pull it off. He would fly the lead B-17.

B Company. 802nd TD Battalion, 83rd Infantry Division, Klimovo, Chuvashskaya Bridgehead.

"What is it, Searle?" Perry had walked up to the forward positions screening his anti-tank guns in response to the whistle.

"I don't know Sergeant. I heard something really odd a few minutes ago. A sort of scraping noise. Then, just a minute or two ago, I heard it again."

Perry listened hard but the night was about as silent as it ever got. Then he heard the sound Searle had tried to describe. A metallic scraping noise that seemed to be coming from the left. "You're right kid. I hear it too."

"What is it, Sarge?"

"Dunno, Searle. Let's find out." Perry shouldered his M-1 Garand and fired three shots in the direction of the weird sound. The result was startling but not in the way Perry had expected. His three shots had triggered off a wild outburst of firing from all of the foxholes in the area. Semi-automatic fire from the Garands was joined by long bursts from the Reising submachine guns carried by some of the soldiers. The unit's machine guns cut in as well, adding streams of tracer fire to the mix. The epidemic of fire spread along the defensive positions before fading slowly away.

"Who the hell fired those first shots?" Lieutenant Irwin Grisham was furious. Quite apart from the waste of ammunition and the ill-disciplined fire, he knew as an absolute certainty he was going to be the subject of a serious ass-chewing by the Captain in the morning.

"I did, Sir."

"You, Perry? Just what the hell did you think you were doing? You're supposed to be an experienced man, not firing off ammunition like some raw recruit."

"There was noise out there, Sir. We kept hearing it."

"Noise? Like this perhaps?" Grisham took a thread of barbed wire and moved it so that it grated against a metal support pole. "Barbed wire, blowing in the wind."

It made exactly the same noise that Perry and Searle had heard earlier. Perry didn't have to confirm that was what he had heard although the blowing in the wind part didn't seem plausible. It was a relatively still night for the Russian Steppes. "Yes, Sir."

"You'd better buck your ideas up, Sergeant, or you won't have your stripes much longer. Now, carry on."

Perry paused for a second, took a deep breath and had a momentary fantasy of taking a hand grenade and tossing it at Grisham. Then returning to reality he looked at the men clustered around him. "Show's over. Everybody back to their posts. And keep your eyes open. What we heard may have been wire rubbing on a support but something moved it and we don't know what for sure."

Most of the men were convinced that the fun was indeed over for the night. They started to disperse back, Perry getting some sympathetic grins as they went. Then, there was a loud shout from one part of the line. "Sarge, you'd better see this!"

Perry ran over to the source of the call. Two men were standing over the foxhole Eli Dugan had converted into a mini-fortress. It was now empty. The only sign that Dugan had ever been there was his bayonet jammed into the earthen wall of the dugout, pinning up a sheet of paper. Perry took it and read the note written on it. The handwriting was neat and perfect. "If we want you, we'll take you."

CHAPTER FOUR: EXPERIENCE GAINED

Briefing Room, 305th Bombardment Group, Bolshaya Tarlovka Airfield.

"The target for today is the railway marshalling yard at Penza." Colonel Robert (Dutch) Holland tapped the map with his pointer. "It is 200 miles behind the front lines, giving us a total flight of 350 miles to the target. Weather forecast is good, at most one-tenth cloud cover and an easterly wind, 10 knots at ground level, 25 knots at altitude. Assembly point is over Ishteryakovo. The formation will then fly on a course of two-five-five degrees at an altitude of 22,000 feet, crossing the Volga north of Ulyanov'sk. You will cross into enemy-held airspace approximately seventeen miles after you go feet-dry on the west bank of the Volga.

"From there, you will proceed to the Initial Point, 17 miles out from the target, where you will swing to two-seven-zero for your bomb run. This will align you with the long axis of the marshalling yard. Note the two large semi-circular structures at the west end of the marshalling yard. These contain a railway turning compass. This is a priority part of the target area since such turning compasses are uncommon in Russia and its destruction will seriously impede German use of this railway facility.

"You will be picking up fighter escort when you reach the Volga. They will take you all the way to the target and then bring you back." Holland paused for a second. This was the good news. "The escort will be provided by the Thunderbolts of the 356th Fighter Group. All three fighter squadrons will be covering you; excluding any aborts, that should total 48 P-47s."

"We got fighters all the way?" Several pilots shouted out the question. "*American* fighters?"

"That's right. The P-47s should solve the problem of the Yaks and Lavochkins losing peak performance at the best operating altitudes for the Fortress. We expect you will run into fighter opposition from the Me-109s based at Petrovsk, Trud-30 and Kamenka. Trud-30 is on the edge of the 109s operational radius; if they turn up at all, it will be at the last minute. You will also be facing Focke-Wulf 190s based at Penza North itself. They will probably be the most serious fighter threat. Expect about two dozen 109s and a dozen or so 190s.

"The 305th will be leading two other groups in this attack. The 19th Bombardment Group and the 35th Bombardment Group will be following you. The 19th is assigned to bombing the central section of the yard while the 35th will hit this spur yard to the north east. Each aircraft will be carrying a full bomb load of six 1,600 pound bombs each. Each group will release under the control of its lead bombardier.

"These pictures show you the position and orientation of the marshalling yards. Observe how the yards are surrounded by apartment blocks and other residential areas. Those areas house Russian civilians; it is essential we reduce collateral damage to a minimum."

Holland looked at the assembled pilots for a moment. This was the bad news. "For this reason, aircraft will not, repeat not, repeat again not, take evasive action during their bomb runs. All aircraft will fly straight and level for the entire duration of their bomb runs and maintain their formation."

The explosion of noise in the briefing room was remarkable. No individual words were audible but the howling roar of anger and discontent blanketed everything. Eventually, one pilot managed to get his words through. "You damned fools. You've killed us all."

Holland waited until the outburst died down. Looking at the rows of furious aircrew, he got the unpleasant feeing that most of them envisaged lynching him. He also got the feeling that he was on the verge of seeing an entire bomb group refuse to fly a mission. The impact of that would be catastrophic.

"Over the last week, we have been carrying out a detailed study of all the targets we have bombed. We can't find half the bombs we know we dropped. Certainly they are nowhere near the target areas. Our average bombing error – of the bombs we can find – is more than five miles. We're not bombing targets; we're scattering bombs at random over the Russian countryside.

"Every one of those raids, we're losing aircraft to flak and fighters. We've lost four aircraft in seven missions since we came here. And you know what else; we haven't damaged a damned thing. So, we keep having to go back to the same targets, time after time. Every time we go back, we lose another aircraft or two.

"There's something else. We've watched what other people do. We've watched German medium bombers do their runs. They don't gyrate all over the sky; they run in straight and level – then they get nice tight patterns. Our mediums went in a few days ago – straight and level. No casualties and they put every single bomb into a five hundred yard square. We're the only people who dodge all over the place on their bomb runs and we're the only people who miss by miles. We know the bombs are good, we know the bomb sights are good, we know the planes are good and we know you are good. The only thing left is the tactics and by a process of elimination, they must be wrong.

"So, we change tactics. We go straight in. Think about it guys. How many of you would have shot a qualifying score if you'd been zigging around every ten seconds? Fly straight and level and we're through the target zone faster and we get fewer shells fired at us."

The current of anger was slowly being replaced by a thoughtful consideration. "What about the other two groups? What are they doing?"

"Straight and level, same as us. This is their first mission so they don't know any other way of doing things. This is another change in procedure. Up to now, we've been throwing small packets of aircraft against targets. A dozen or so here, a dozen there. Now, we're changing that as well. We're throwing a hundred aircraft against Penza. We've got the force level needed to do some real damage this time."

"Who's leading us in?" The voice was the same one that had thought the straight and level bombing run was certain death.

"I think we can take it and to prove it, I'll fly the lead plane." It was a myth that Colonel LeMay spent all his time shouting at people. In fact, he very rarely raised his voice and was often difficult to hear well. "The krauts use the lead aircraft of the lead element as their reference point. I'll be flying that bomber. If anybody gets hit, it'll be me."

"Di you think this will work. Sir?"

LeMay looked at the map for a second and then turned to the audience. "Damned sure of it."

B-17E Flying Fortress LG-O, Over Alexeyevskoye-na-Volga

As it happened, Colonel LeMay wasn't actually flying LG-O. Holland was doing that while LeMay sat into top turret, coaxing his crews into the proper positions. In his opinion, the formation flying ability of the 305th was far less than it should be and that of the 19th and 35th was lamentable. For bombers that depended on the massed cross-fire of their machine guns to beat off fighter attack, that was a serious issue.

"LG-E, move to your left. Your other left LG-E. Bring her right in. Now our top turret can help protect your belly while your ball turret can cover our tail. You can do better than this."

The eighteen bombers were in three flights of six. Each flight was organized as two Vs of three bombers each with the second V following behind and above the first. The second flight was to the right, below and behind the lead flight while the third flight was to the left, above and behind the first. The whole formation was called a combat box. The 305th had put up two more combat boxes, each behind the lead box, one above and to the left, the other below and to the right. Then, there was the second formation with one combat box from the 19th and two from the 35th. All in all, 108 heavy bombers carrying almost five hundred tons of bombs.

"LG-E, now hold that position. LG-A, move in and position yourself beside LG-E. Now we're in a Vee with you below and behind LG-O. That way all three of us can fire on anybody coming in from directly in front or behind. If the krauts come in from below and behind, the second Vee will get them. Closer we are together, the shorter range we fire at, the more hits we score."

There was another reason as well for the tight formation. The smaller the formation, the less likely it was to get hit regardless of the number of aircraft in the formation. The lower limit to that was the distance at which a single shell going off could do lethal damage to two aircraft. LeMay had worked that distance out and wanted to position the aircraft slightly further apart.

What was surprising him was that the pilots were quickly adapting to flying in much closer formation than they'd done before. It was a theory of his that most people were much more capable than they realized and only needed to be challenged for the extra to show. For all that, they were still too far apart.

"All right. LG-K move in on . . . . . oh." LeMay has swung his turret around to look at the second flight only to see that all six aircraft were already in position.

"Monkey see, monkey do." The flight commander had a somewhat impudent tone to his voice. LeMay reckoned that seeing what was required and copying it on his own initiative had earned him a little latitude. Just a little.

"LG-K, you are in the correct position. I have no cause for complaint. LG-C, close in on your flight leader."

Slowly, methodically, the 305th sorted its 18 B-17s into the combat box formation LeMay had painstakingly worked out. It wasn't as neat as he would have liked and the spacing between the aircraft was greater than he had calculated but the formation was as good as these pilots at this time could manage. Whether it was good enough to get at the Penza marshalling yards without excessive casualties was another matter.

Thunderbolt PI-H, Over Polyanki on the Volga, Moskva Front.

"Eagle Three to flight leader. I can see the big boys." Eagle-Two to Eagle-Three was a promotion of sorts. The flights had been reorganized so that each pilot who had a kill – even a fraction of one – was now a section leader while the pilots who had yet to score were relegated to their wingmen. Edwards now led the second section of the flight with Ward flying his wing. His flight leader, Jackson, had Carter on his wing.

"See them, Eagle Three. They look grand, don't they?"

Edwards saw the stream of B-17s heading westwards, their thick white contrails painting streamers across the sky. *They sure are a grand sight.* The three combat boxes leading the formation were tightly grouped but staggered to give each aircraft the maximum possible fields of fire for their guns. The two formations following them were much more ragged while the box at the rear was all over the place. Edwards somehow knew that the Germans would see that and the rear group was in for a bad time.

"Listen up. The krauts are going to see what we can see and they'll hit the rear formation first. Eagle and Falcon Sections, stay with them. We'll cover the rest." To Edwards it seemed a bit ignominious to be assigned to covering the rearmost combat box but he told himself it made sense. The B-17s were obviously flown by novices and if he could see it, so could the Germans. Eagle Section had the four pilots who had actually seen combat. The escort force commander was speaking again. "Hey, Big Boys. Your little friends are here."

"Why, hello Little Friends. It's good to see you." The straight, white contrails of the B-17s were being joined by the long sweeping curves of the trails left by the Thunderbolts. The two flights of P-47s stationed themselves either side of the 35th Group combat box and started a series of interlocking curves that allowed them to keep station on the much slower Flying Fortresses. The constant shifting of position and changes of course also allowed Edwards to keep a sharp watch out for enemy fighters. In front of the great formation of American aircraft, the grey expanse of the Volga grew nearer and its width began to dominate the panorama in front of them. *Russia's great moat* Edwards thought, *almost ten miles wide where we're going to cross. Just how the hell do the krauts think they're going to cross that?*

Then another thought occurred to him. *If we lose the bridgeheads on the west bank, just how the hell are we going to cross the Volga when the time comes? That's why the Russians are so desperate to hang on to the Chuvashskaya and all the other bridgeheads on the west bank. A moat works both ways. If we lose those bridgeheads, we've accepted German domination of everything to the west of the Volga.*

The course for Penza took them along the west bank of the Volga for about ten miles. This was the southern edge of the Chuvashskaya bridgehead, an area that had been the scene of heavy fighting earlier in the year as the Germans had driven north from Ulyanov'sk. Not far off to their right was Bolshoye Nagatkino where American units had fought for the first time on the Russian Front. Their counter-attack had driven the Germans back almost three miles and straightened the line. From 25,000 feet there was no sign of any fighting; the ground looked peaceful and undisturbed, a vista of farmland, villages, roads and rivers. Yet, Edwards knew that it was a battlefield down there, one that had already cost tens of thousands of lives and would undoubtedly cost many more.

At Gorodishchi, the river bank swung due south and the American formation moved inland. That meant they were just 17 miles from enemy-held territory. Edwards knew that all the briefings said that German fighters would not cross into hostile airspace but he guessed that the Germans knew the briefings said that as well and one day they would, hoping to catch the escorting fighters off-guard.

"All aircraft, we are forty five minutes from IP. Keep your eyes peeled. They're coming for us any moment now." The words were accompanied by black bursts in the sky around the formation. Somewhere five miles below, German anti-aircraft gunners had calculated the formation's speed, course and altitude and trained their gun accordingly. They had set their shells to explode at the right time and in the right place. Edwards could hear the 'crump' noise as they went off. The bombers seemed to ignore them, wading through the swarm of black bursts with serene calm. He guessed that the flak and fighters were cooperating, the gunners hoping to break up the formations so that the fighters wouldn't have to face the murderous crossfire from the B-17s protecting each other.

"There they are, 109s coming in 1 o'clock high!" The warning on the radio was terse, only its increased pitch telling of the pilot's tension.

"Eagle Section, break, drop tanks and engage. Wingmen, cover your leaders. Buster." Jackson's voice was calm and level. After all, he'd been in combat the day before and that made him, if not a veteran, at least a man who had seen the elephant. Buster was the order to use war emergency power on the R-2800 engines. A spray of distilled water into the intake manifold entered the combustion chambers as a fine mist and cooled the fuel, resisting pre-detonation and giving a sudden burst of power.

The eight Thunderbolts swept up and away from the Fortresses to meet the German fighters diving in. The pattern of German attacks was becoming understood now. Their first waves of fighters would make diving attacks on the bomber formation to soften it up and split the combat boxes into isolated groups. Only later would the fighters come in massed groups to overwhelm those isolated sections and bring them down. That was the theory of it anyway. The combat boxes had always held together so far but the German attacks on them were getting more determined with every mission.

The B-17s in the rearmost combat box were already firing on the attacking fighters. Long bursts at long range that expended precious ammunition for little return. Edwards had selected a group of three Bf-109s that were diving on a group of Flying Fortresses in the middle of the ragged formation. His Thunderbolts were climbing to meet them and he could see the brilliant flashes in the nose as they opened fire. The 109s, he knew, had to do that. Lightly-armed with only a 20mm cannon and two .30 machine guns, they had to deliver as many rounds into their target as they could. It also meant that their pilots would be concentrating on the target picture in their gunsights. He swung his aircraft around so that he was leading his selected target by the correct amount and opened fire.

The white streaks of tracer seemed to take forever to reach their target. When they did, they seemed to go above, below, in front and behind the 109 but never actually hitting it. They certainly had an effect on the pilot though, one that Edwards instantly understood. Under heavy fire from escort fighters, the German pilot broke off his attack. Pulled his nose back and did a bunt, a sudden sharp climb upwards, in order to break clear.

It was exactly the mistake that Koldunov had warned Edwards about a few days earlier. All he had to do was continue lifting his nose and his second burst of fire ripped into the 109. He saw the brilliant flashes as .50 caliber armor-piercing incendiaries hit the nose, cockpit and wing roots of the fighter, sending fragments flying off the airframe and causing a massive gout of black smoke to erupt from the engine. Then, there was a brilliant white explosion from the wing root that blew the left wing completely off. It went spiraling in one direction while the 109 flipped over on its back in a wild cartwheel before exploding in a ball of orange and white flame. *There's no doubt about that one,* he thought.

The combination of the climb, the sharp turn and the recoil of his battery of .50s had caused his Thunderbolt to start slowing down. By this time, he was well above the bomber formation and he could look down on it. He counted all eighteen bombers still there although one of them seemed to be trailing a thin stream of white smoke from its outer right engine. It was holding position and altitude so obviously whatever had happened, it wasn't that serious. Yet.

"Eagle Section, resume escort position."

Kazan Thunderbolts

The eight Thunderbolts moved back into position. Edwards glanced down at his fuel gauge. He was flying on internal fuel only now, his 108 gallon belly tank was somewhere on the ground below. He guessed that he would be part of the escort force that handled the next attack, then he would be ordered to go home with the rest of Eagle Section. It wouldn't help anybody if he ran out of fuel on the way home.

"All aircraft, we're forty minutes from IP. Well done little friends. We got away with that clean."

B-17E Flying Fortress LG-O, Over Sharlovo

The Flight Engineer was back in the upper turret, Colonel LeMay was back in the chief pilot's seat and all was back as it should be. LeMay took a firm grip on the controls and relaxed. "I have the aircraft, Dutch. How are we doing?"

"Pretty good, Curt. We're approaching Sharlovo now, 96 miles from IP. Thirty minutes out. No losses to date, the Thunderbolts beat off the first attack before they got through to us. The 109s steered clear of us. Our gunners did good. Held their fire, snapped out short, aimed bursts and sent a couple of 109s away streaming smoke. 19th behind us, not so good. Their formation is ragged and their two combat boxes are looser than ours. But, they got away with it allowing for a few scares. Some Forts were hit but nothing serious. 35th, different matter. Their combat box is all over the place and their gunners need to learn their job. One Fort is damaged and has casualties, several others were hit. Escort commander is shifting his fighters to give them more cover."

"Flak?"

"Scattered. No damage reported. I'll tell you this Curt; we're flying straight and level. If that ten second thing was right, we should have lost aircraft by now." As if in answer to his comments, LG-O lurched as another pattern of black puffs surrounded the aircraft. The crump of the shells going off was clearly audible over the roar of the four Wright Cyclone engines. The aircraft lurched again but LeMay caught the movement and kept LG-O in position. To his private delight he could see the other pilots in the box doing the same. Suddenly, the flak stopped. That meant the fighters were coming in again. LeMay peered into the sky around the bombers, wondering if the enemy fighters were in the scattered puffs of cloud or hiding up sun where the glare blinded the gunners and the pilots of the Thunderbolts.

"Fighters, at six o'clock high." The enemy aircraft were black dots, sweeping in on the rearmost formation, picking on the Fortresses that could put up the least effective defensive barrage. The blinking lights from their noses showed that they were already firing on the B-17s. The Thunderbolts were already peeling off to break up the attack. That was when LeMay saw another advantage of the close-packed formations of the 305th. The more dispersed the formation, the longer it took the Thunderbolts to get to a threatened area. The 35th at the rear of the formation were in trouble.

"Fighters, one o'clock high." A pause and then "Oh crap, 190s and they're coming for us."

LeMay was about to rebuke the speaker for the non-standard warning but he held his tongue. In the battle that was about to start, the B-17s intercom system was the most valuable weapon they had and the fewer messages on it the better. He could hear the hammering of .50s as the top turret he had been using only a few minutes earlier opened up on the attacking fighters. The messages coming through on the intercom were anonymous yet they allowed him to follow the battle perfectly.

"Coming in, one o'clock high. There's four of them. They're coming around, watch them."

More machine gun fire, with the beam positions opening up as the 190s entered their arc of fire.

"Two fighters, six o'clock, coming in." The tail gunner was joining in the battle, his twin fifties engaging the lead fighter.

"B-17, in trouble, two o'clock. Watch him. He's got an engine on fire."

LeMay looked at the B-17 in question. She was streaming white smoke from her left-hand inner engine but the pilot was doggedly holding position within his formation. It was LG-K, the Fortress whose pilot had given the cheerful 'monkey see, monkey do' message earlier. Already, two FW-190s had seen he was in trouble and started to close in on him but help was at hand. A pair of Thunderbolts swept in, their battery of point fifties blazing. The range was too long for accurate fire but that didn't matter. Their objective was to drive the 190s away from the damaged bomber and that they did.

The 190s, faced with the Thunderbolts on their tails, tried to dive away. That was a critical mistake; the heavy Thunderbolts dived faster than any other fighter. They closed the distance on the 190s rapidly, then both concentrated their fire on the rearmost 190. It staggered in the air under the onslaught and erupted in a thick stream of black smoke. It reared up in a curve to its left then exploded. The other 190 continued to dive away. The pair of P-47s broke off at that point; the 190 was out of the battle and they had to get back to covering the bombers.

"Thanks Little Friends. The beer's on us." The lead Thunderbolt waggled its wings in acknowledgement, then, without warning, both Thunderbolts did wing-overs and swept away. Another Flying Fortress was under siege and needed immediate relief.

Kazan Thunderbolts

More machine gun fire, this time from the cheek guns and the upper turret. "There's two more diving on us. Two 190s, nine o 'clock. Keep your eyes on them boys."

"Coming around to ten o'clock. Watch them waist. Keep your eyes open. Breaking in at eleven, breaking in at eleven. Watch them."

"I got them. Firing" A stream of tracers slewed out from the left cheek gun, the vibration of the .50 shaking the cockpit windows. 'He's coming around underneath us. Get ready ball turret. They're coming through from ten."

"I got them. Got my sights on him. Firing. See that baby burn. He's streaming smoke."

"Watch that B-17 at three o'clock. One with the burning engine. Cover him."

"Fighters at ten, coming around."

"High or low?"

"Both! Get them!"

"B-17 out of control at eight o'clock."

LeMay twisted around in his seat to try and see the stricken bomber. A B-17 from the 35th Group combat box was falling out of the sky, slowly, almost gracefully. It had started to climb, then slowly turned over on its back before its nose went down and it started the long spin down to earth. *Had the flight deck crew been killed?*

"Come on you guys, get out of that plane." The anonymous voices on the intercom suddenly had personality and emotion. "Bail out."

"There's one. He came out of the bomb bay."

"I see him. There's the tail gunner coming out."

"Watch out for fighters."

"Keep your eyes on them, ball turret. See any parachutes."

"Parachutes opened. Both of them"

"190s nine o'clock. Watch them."

"Crew still in that B-17. Come on you guys, get out of there. Bail outs, two so far."

"Three more chutes. Five out so far."

"Fighters, eleven o'clock high. Three 109s. Six more 109s at six o'clock."

"Little friends are taking them apart. Look at them go!"

LeMay was grimly holding LG-O straight and level. It was obvious the steady course was helping the gunners put up an effective barrage. It was also making the Thunderbolt's job easier by not having to evade the maneuvering bombers. *Freddie, you meant well, but that 'advice' you gave us must just about rank as the worst anybody ever gave anybody.*

"More 109s coming in at three high. Take him, waist."

"I'm on him. Come on in, you son of a bitch. . . . . " The shaking from the B-17s guns was easily detectable on the flight deck. The next message from the waist gunners was a scream of triumph. "I got him! He's going down. Look, he's bailing out!"

LeMay glanced at the scene. A 109 was streaming black smoke from its engine and wing roots. A figure was detaching from the aircraft. Obviously the pilot was leaving and that made it a clean kill. "Chief pilot. I see it. Now, dammit, don't yell on that intercom."

"Fighters, ten o'clock low. Watch those two 109s, they're coming in."

"Get that ball turret on them." There was a prolonged burst of fire from under the aircraft. "Save ammunition as much as possible."

"Watch that 190 coming in at three o'clock, he's coming in with a half-roll. We got them running scared guys."

"Shoot her up, shoot her up. Hurry up, get him before the Thunderbolts do."

Behind and below them, another 35th Group Fortress was hurt. She'd lost two engines and was quickly loosing speed and altitude. That was taking her away from the protection of the combat boxes, drifting down alone and helpless. A straggler. Within a few seconds the fighters would be swarming in like buzzards for the kill. LeMay knew they could watch but there was nothing anybody could do to help. The B-17s had to keep their formation.

Thunderbolt PI-H, Over Bazarnaya, Moskva Front.

"Jackson, take Eagle section down and cover that Fort. Move your ass, the krauts are already closing in on her."

The eight P-47s peeled off and started their power-dive to join up with the stricken B-17. To Edwards, the decision to detach Eagle Section had been logical. They had been first to drop their tanks and the long running battle had left them low on ammunition and fuel. They would have had to turn back anyway so escorting the damaged B-17 was a good way for them to end the mission. Below them DE-B had stabilized its flight pattern. One engine was definitely out, its feathered prop stationary. The other inner engine was emitting spurts of black smoke at irregular intervals but was still running. From his long experience building and maintaining motorcycles, Edwards guessed that the engine was generating an impressive selection of bangs and coughs.

"Hi, Big Brother. We've come to take you home."

"Good to see you Little Friends." The voice on the radio was weak and shaky. "We're in a hell of a mess. Cannon shells exploded in the radio cabin area. Our navigator and flight engineer are dead, the radio operator and two of the gunners are wounded. 190 came at us head on. Are we going the right way?"

Edwards could sense Jackson struggling with his maps. "Yeah, we're heading west. Once you're over the Volga, we'll get you to the first available airfield."

"Fighters, five o'clock high." Edwards had, once again, seen sunlight flashing off the cockpit of an enemy aircraft. Three 109s had formed up and were diving on the crippled B-17. Edwards hit war emergency boost again, feeling the cough and surge of the extra six hundred horsepower as the water injection system cut in. Jackson was leading the four aircraft in a long climbing curve that would intersect with the three German fighters well short of their target.

"Concentrate on the leader." Jackson's order made sense. The firepower of four Thunderbolts concentrated on a single aircraft would make short work of the target. That would leave just the two wingmen who would have been split apart by the destruction of their leader and could be picked off individually. To Edwards, the maneuver was almost distressingly familiar. The whole long running battle with the German fighters from Sharlovo to Barzonaya had been a long succession of the Thunderbolts charging into one attack after another, forcing the 109s and 190s away from the bombers. The individual battles had become blurred in his mind, one continuous montage of aircraft turning, firing and swerving, his Thunderbolt snapping out bursts at the German aircraft as they were briefly in his gunsight. He wasn't certain whether he had hit them or not, far less whether he had inflicted any real damage on them. All he did know was that they had driven the German fighters away from the Fortresses.

Ahead of him, the three 109s had seen the Thunderbolts closing in and broken off their attack. Now Edwards thought about it, that was happening more often. The lightly-armed 109s were becoming reluctant to mix it with the massive and heavily-gunned P-47s. This time, the 109s had climbed away and were running for home. That made Edwards think hard.

"We're doing this wrong. Those guys are going home. They'll get their crates repaired and put their heads together and talk about what happened today. Tomorrow they'll be back and know better."

Edwards was expecting a rebuke for yakking on the radio but Jackson's reply was thoughtful. "So what do you suggest?"

"We chase them, right back to their base if necessary. Strafe them on the ground if all else fails."

"And who looks after the bombers while we do that?"

"Yeah little friends, what about us?" The radio message from the crippled B-17 was almost plaintive.

"Getting you home is top priority." Edwards was thinking hard. "But the way we're doing this now gives all the initiative to the krauts. What we need is to get the Russians to do a free-chase sweep ahead of the bomber stream and break up the kraut fighters before they get to us. That way they won't be able to coordinate their attacks. Then, we chase the cripples home and kill them. We won't need so many fighters around the bombers because most of the work will have been done."

"190s coming in, four o'clock high."

"Here we go again. Write that up, Edwards."

B-17E Flying Fortress LG-O, Approaching IP

"Thank God for that. The flak is back." Holland didn't realize the irony of what he had just said.

LeMay did. The flak barrage meant that the fighters had given up their attacks. Another B-17 from the 35th had gone down, leaving a long trail of fire across the sky but, after a thirty minute running battle, the German fighters had been driven off. That thirty minutes had changed the opinions of the bomber crews completely. The flak had done little damage even though they had been flying straight and level. It was the sustained, coordinated attacks by fighters that had done the harm. For all the false alarm about flak, it was now in its proper place. A menace, certainly, but one that was now seen in its proper context.

LeMay knew where Armstrong and the others had made their mistake. They were probably right about the German predictors although he very much doubted whether they were actually any better than the U.S. equivalents. The problem for the Germans was that they were just one part of the system. They had built-in errors; so did the gunlaying system, so did the time fuses on the shells, so did the guns themselves and the crews that served them. All those errors mounted up so that the shells wouldn't explode exactly where the predictors said they should but somewhere within an area around that point. And that area got bigger as the altitude went up. Since the explosion of any shell within that area was at random, a bomber taking evasive action was as likely to turn into a shell burst as away from one.

"We have Initial Point. Turning to two-seven-zero. Five minutes, 32 seconds from target. Damn, look at that flak. It's dense enough to walk on."

LeMay looked at the sheets of black bursts covering the sky. They did indeed look dense enough to walk on. He felt an almost irresistible urge to start maneuvering but he beat it down. *All those cumulative errors in the system mean that the point picked by the predictors is probably the safest point in the sky.* He decided that even he didn't find that argument convincing.

LG-O was lurching constantly with the flak bursts around her but LeMay's sure grip on the controls kept her flying steadily on course. There was a thrumming noise from the airframe as a shell fragment struck home somewhere but nothing caught fire and there were no damage or casualty reports so it seemed as if it wasn't important. Another B-17 was trailing white smoke from a damaged engine but there was nothing like the carnage the pessimists had reported.

"One minute from drop point. Bombardier, you have the aircraft."

LeMay took his hands and feet from the controls. Now, he had a chance to look at the target area. The city of Penza was spread out in front of him with the thick brown line of the railways coming in from the northeast, heading southwest to the city limits them turning west to go through the city before turning and heading southwest again. At each turn, a junction led to a large marshalling yard. The system formed a giant cross in the heart of the city. *Target for today*, he thought, *that would make a good title for a film.*

"Bombs gone." Each of the three combat boxes of the 305th released on cue from the bombardier in their lead aircraft. LeMay waited as the long streams of bombs descended. The first few bursts on the ground seemed scattered but they were all in the approximate target area. Then, the rest of the bombs hit and the bursts merged to a massive cloud that obliterated the target area.

"Pilot. You have the aircraft." The Bombardier sounded quite excessively smug.

The 305th exited the target area, still jolted by flak but without losing an aircraft. Behind them, the 19th and 35th had hit their targets although the patterns were a lot looser and messier than that of the 305th. They were going home now and that was all they cared about. Around them, the Thunderbolts closed in and started to shepherd their charges back to the Volga. Then, about twenty minutes after the raid was over, a single F-5 Lightning streaked over Penza.

Woods, West of Sharlovo

It wasn't bailing out of a crippled B-17 that was the problem nor was it the long drop to earth. That all sort of happened naturally. It was the last ten feet of the fall that gave problems. Sergeant Charles Schultz had been hung up by his parachute for nearly five minutes before he'd managed to cut the cords and drop clear. Then, he'd managed to wind himself on hitting the forest floor. It was not, he opined, turning out to be a good day. He knew well his first job was to put as much distance between himself and the scene of his landing as possible. He couldn't do anything about his parachute tangled up in the trees and it was an unmistakable pointer straight to his position. He had no doubt at all that the Germans would have search parties out for survivors from the downed bombers. From the dire warnings given by the Russians, being found by them was not advisable.

What to do first? Get away from here obviously, but which way? It's afternoon, so the sun will be to the west, and that way lies safety. But, the Germans should know that as well and they'll be hunting to the west of the crash site. Should I go east for a bit and then loop around?

"Go south, Tovarish American."

Schultz spun around at the voice behind him. Three men had emerged from the trees, one armed with a submachine gun, the other two with pistols. They were dressed identically, overcoats reaching down to their knees over white shirts open at the neck, nondescript trousers that might or might not have been Soviet Army issue and knee-high boots that certainly were. Each man wore a flat, peaked cap. The man with the submachine gun was bearded and obviously their leader. He was also the one who spoke English. "South?"

"South, bratishka. Go west and the forest ends very soon and there is nothing but open country. As I think you know, the fascists are hunting for you and your comrades there. East will keep you in the forest but within five kilometers is Glotovka where there is a major fascist base. North, now north is possible and you could go to the American lines in Chuvashskaya. But, the Hitlerites have moved many troops into that area and it is densely patrolled. South, now south has fewer fascists to worry about. The forests give us good cover and there are many comrades in them who will give us aid. Then we head west for the Volga and a gunboat can pick you up."

Schultz looked at them suspiciously. "How do I know you aren't Germans leading me into a trap?"

Two of the Partisans scowled at that but their leader nodded. "A reasonable question, but think on this. The fascists have no need to deceive you. If they had found you first you would now be hanging from a tree. Or worse."

That makes a lot of sense. I suppose. "We had better get started. The krauts will be here soon."

The leader nodded. "Two of your bombers at least were shot down. So there are many of your crewmen in these woods. We of the Partisans are trying to find them before the Hitlerites do."

There was not much more to be said. Schultz followed the three men south. It seemed like the only sensible thing to do.

The forest reminded Schultz of the hillsides he used to hunt in with his father. The pine trees were straight and widely spaced enough to allow a generous layer of undergrowth. There were wide paths through the forest but the undergrowth meant that people moving a few yards to one side of those paths needed only to drop flat and they would be invisible to people walking on those tracks. It was great hunting country. Schultz quickly got the feeling that in these forests, the creatures hunted were now German.

He noticed something else. There were paths through the undergrowth as well, hidden ones. The ground level vegetation as cut away but the overlaying levels were not so the cleared strips were invisible. They were only a few inches wide but they made moving through the ground cover fast and easy. They'd been walking on one such path for a few minutes when the leader of the group held up his hand and pointed at a bush just to the left of the concealed path. A twig was broken, about a finger's length from the main stem and then again two finger's length from the first break. The leader carefully parted the undergrowth to reveal a wire stretched across the path. Even when exposed it was almost impossible to see. Schultz believed that a sharp wire positioned that way would inflict a nasty cut on the leg of anybody hitting it. He also believed that the tripwire was arranged to set something off that would do a lot more than just inflict a cut. *A grenade perhaps? Or some explosive and nails?* The belief was reinforced when he saw the exaggerated care with which the partisans stepped over the wire.

The problem was that the forest never changed. The pine trees were randomly spaced in a pattern that gave no easily distinguishable landmarks. The trees themselves were also nearly identical; the same numbers of branches at roughly the same places. The undergrowth was just that, undergrowth without any real character or unique identity. Even the sunlight was dispersed by the overhead cover so that it gave little to help those trying to find their way through the maze. *The trackless Russian forest goes on forever*, Schultz thought. It was hard to measure time or distance travelled in the characterless surroundings. He could see how people could easily get lost in the trees and never be seen again. Eaten by the forest that almost seemed to be a single, dispassionate entity that watched what happened in and around it with a disinterested, merciless eye.

Eventually, after an indeterminate number of hours, the partisan leader held up his hand. "Bratishka, we must wait here. There is a crossroads up ahead where the fascists will be assembling with any of your comrades they have captured. They will wait there for transport to take them back to their base at Glotovka. We can move a little to see what is going on but we must use great care. If we can see them, then it is possible they can see us."

There were about a dozen German troops on the road, close enough for their voices to be audible. They had two Americans with them, easily recognizable by their leather jackets. Schultz peered at them. Despite the distance he was able to recognize both. "That's Alf Niksa and Ed Rosenblum. Tail and beam gunners on DE-G."

The partisan leader nodded. A few minutes later, another group of four German soldiers arrived with a third American prisoner. Schultz recognized him as well. "Frank McDermott, ball turret gunner on DE-G. He was lucky to get out."

"I do not think so, bratishka."

They continued to watch. The group had settled down now, the three Americans sitting on the roadside bank while the Germans kept a watchful eye on the woods. Eventually, two of the small Opel trucks that seemed characteristic of the German Army pulled up. Two sergeants jumped out of the back and went to speak with some of the troops surrounding the prisoners. The conversation lasted a minute or two, then the Sergeants both turned around. To Schultz's shock they had both brought their submachine guns up to the firing positions and they raked the prisoners with two long streams of bullets. Then, when the bursts of fire stopped, one of the soldiers brought a jerrican of gasoline from one of the trucks. One of the sergeants poured the contents over the three bodies and tossed a light match at them. Schultz could hear the wumph noise as the gasoline caught fire and he imagined he could hear a scream from inside the blaze. Down below, the Germans had boarded the trucks and were pulling out.

"Oh my God. Oh my God. Why? Why did they do that?"

The partisan leader looked at him sympathetically. "You said so yourself. They were gunners. They had nothing of interest to tell the fascists. Pilots, radio operators, navigators, bombardiers, they can tell of things the Hitlerites wish to learn so they would have been taken back to Glotovka for interrogation. Only when the fascists had learned all they wished to know would they have been disposed of."

"We got to get down there. Please . . . . ." Schultz realized he didn't know the partisan leader's name.

"We do not use names in the partisans. That would tell the fascists where to find our families. Instead, we each have a conspiratorial name. We use only that and then only when we have to. Mine is Orlan. Now, we cannot go down there yet. The fascists are cunning and sometimes leave a detachment behind in case we do just that. We cannot even cross the road until we are sure they have gone. Then Gratch and Voron will sweep the area to check. If we are clear, we can go down to your comrades. Quickly, for we have far to go."

The two men with pistols slipped away, leaving Schultz and Orlan by the road. Schultz was in a state of shock; the sight he had seen was something quite outside his experience. He knew that if he had been told of the incident, he would not have believed it; he would have assumed it was just propaganda. Orlan was looking at him with sympathy in his eyes. "Bratishka, I am sorry I do not know words of comfort for you. We have all lost so many that we have all forgotten such things. All I can do is promise that we will do everything we can to get you back to your comrades so you can tell them what happened here today."

305th Bombardment Group, Bolshaya Tarlovka Airfield, Russia.

"We didn't lose a single aircraft. Not to flak, not to fighters. The 19th lost one and the 35th two, all to fighters. The ten second rule is history as from now." Any other man might have sounded triumphant or even gloating. LeMay was matter-of-fact. A problem had been resolved and the emphasis had now moved on to the next.

"The fighter groups are reporting in as well. We lost two P-47s shot down, both nailed by 190s. Neither of the pilots made it, although there is at least one report that says one of them was killed after bailing out. The fighter groups are claiming two dozen enemy aircraft shot down. Our gunners are claiming thirty." Dutch Holland looked extremely dubious.

He was saved from a pungent comment on the probability of fighter pilots over-claiming kills being exceeded only by that of bomber gunners doing the same when the telephone on LeMay's desk rang. Holland picked it up. "Commanding Officer's desk. I'll pass that through right away, Sir."

"Humph?"

"That was headquarters, 40th Bombardment Wing, Curt. They want to see the pictures of the Penza Marshalling Yards as soon as we have them."

"They'll get them as soon as Gonzalez rushes them through processing. What we really need is our own photo-processing laboratory here."

"I'll get onto that." Holland had noticed something rather unusual since the 305th had arrived in Russia. Every time the group put in a request for something, it arrived with uncanny speed. *It's almost as if somebody back home has a watchful eye on our group and was making sure it got everything it needed. Is that a good or a bad thing?*

The sound of a jeep pulling up outside was quickly followed by a bang of the outside door. LeMay's telephone rang again, only to be answered by the man himself. "Send him in.'

Gonzalez burst into the office waving a stack of prints. "Oh boy, Colonel, you gotta see these."

LeMay looked as if he was about to say something but changed his mind. "We hit the target?"

"Hit it, Colonel? Your boys devastated it. These are down-and-aheads, using my nose camera. It's the big one that gives the greatest magnification and the clearest shots. This is the big marshalling yard, the one the 305th hit? Just look at it. Or look at what it is now. I don't know what you'd call it but it ain't a marshalling yard anymore."

The prints were 11 by 17s and they were crystal clear. What had once been a marshalling yard was now a sea of bomb craters, most of them interlocking. The two great semicircular buildings surrounding the turntable were gone, completely. LeMay had trouble finding where they had been and only found them by spotting the ruins of the turntable. He started counting the bomb craters in the marshalling yard, appreciating the way the others in his office kept quiet while he did so. Eventually, he straightened up. "I make it we got about a hundred and sixty three bombs inside the yard out of three hundred and twenty four. That's over half – just. That's good. Nowhere near good enough but good."

"These are more down-and-aheads, Colonel. Same camera but wide-angle. You can see on these that a lot of the bombs fell short. I think the lead bombardier mistook this small marshalling yard short of the main target area for the primary and dropped on it. It's smashed up pretty good as well."

LeMay looked at the second set of pictures closely. "That was the target allocated to the 19th. These must be their bombs."

"I don't think so, Sir. I'll show you why in a moment. Before we move on, some more of your bombs hit this group of large buildings to the south east. They look like warehouses, or just possibly factories. The rest of the bombs are scattered over the surrounding area.

"Next set of prints were taken with my belly cameras. I have two of them and they work as a pair. Each pair of belly-vertical shots look like duplicates but they're not quite. If we put these in a stereo viewer, you'd get a three-dee picture of the target area."

"Dutch, put one of those on a requisition as well. Go on, Gonzalez."

"Well, these shots tell the same story as the down-and-aheads only they show us the damage from directly overhead. Those big buildings I pointed out? They're shells. Walls are left but the roofs have gone. The railway system is chewed to hell and gone. I can't see a single line undamaged.

"The third set of prints is using my side cameras. These shoot side-panorama wide-angle shots only and cover the areas to the sides of the main run. The interesting ones are these, Colonel. There's another marshalling yard in Penza, to the north of the ones you were hitting. It's big, at least twice the size of these three and its orientated north-south not east-west. Anyway, you can see it's been hit as well. Looks to me as if the 19th hit the wrong marshalling yard. I could still see the fires there so I did a second run over it."

"That was taking a chance." Holland was familiar with German flak and fighters and he couldn't imagine himself doing a second run through them by choice.

"*Lailani* didn't mind, Sir and the shots were worth it. Look at the down-and-aheads from the second run. The 19th hit across the yard rather than along it and their pattern is a lot more scattered but that yard was full of wagons and they were loaded. There's been secondary explosions and fires all over the place. I think the belly verticals will be very revealing here. They should give us an idea what got blown up there.

"Third set of shots are back from the first run. They're the third target area. The one hit by the 35th? It's been hit but the patterns are weak and the bomb damage is scattered. I'd say only about a quarter of their bombs landed in the yard. One thing, Colonel. Take a five mile circle around the aiming points and every single bomb is in there. That's better than anything you've had me shoot before."

LeMay nodded slowly as he looked through the pictures. "I have no cause for complaint here Gonzalez. What do you call your ship? *Lailani*? You need to thank her. These results are entirely satisfactory."

"Thank you, Colonel. One last thing. I overtook your Fortresses on the way back and took a side-panorama shot of the formation." Gonzalez took out another picture, this one at least 14 by 21. It showed a combat box of six B-17s, streaming contrails and surrounded by scattered black flak bursts. "Although I say it myself, Sir, that's a museum-quality picture. I thought you'd like an enlargement for your wall."

LeMay pursed his lips slightly. "Dutch, get it framed and hang it up behind my desk."

Gonzalez broke into a broad grin and bounced out of LeMay's office. Holland relaxed slightly. "I thought you were going to rip his ass off when he came in like that."

"Dutch, that kid's greatest virtue is his enthusiasm. Give him a job and he throws himself into it, body and soul. You heard him. He flew back into that flak again to get the shots we needed. Because it was the job we gave him and it never occurred to him to give it anything less than his best. If that means putting up with his excessive eagerness, so be it."

Holland nodded in agreement. He'd actually found Gonzalez's enthusiasm refreshing. "So we smashed up a target. It's about time."

"It's a start, Dutch. We smashed up our target pretty good. We have to do better. We need tighter formations so we get more concentrated bomb patterns. We need to fly steadier, give the bombardiers more time to get set up. We sent six combat boxes to Penza. Of those, three hit their assigned targets and three bombed something else. This time, it worked in our favor. One of our combat boxes covered for the error made by the 19th and the two combat boxes of the 19th did a number on a high-value target not included in the original plan. That doesn't mean target recognition isn't a problem. It is and we need to solve it.

"But what Gonzalez has shown us is that we have a lot more problems than just what we're doing. We need much better intelligence on the target areas. How the hell did Wing miss that other marshalling yard? It was probably more important than the three we did hit put together. I'm going to Wing this evening. There's a lot we need to discuss."

Ruins of Kolkhoz 223, Novyy Dol

The forest did devour things that had once been human and was also quick to reclaim its own. The ruins of Kolkhoz 223 were already overgrown and the first of the new trees were taking root. Mere saplings of course, but one day they would be proper trees and all trace of Kolkhoz 223 would have gone. *Except for the smell* Schultz thought, *and for the brooding sense of tragedy here. That will never go away.* "What happened here?"

"Nothing that has not happened in tens of thousands of other small settlements across the Rodina." Orlan spoke with immeasurable sadness. "One day the Hitlerites came in their trucks. They surrounded the Kolkhoz and herded all the livestock and the inhabitants into the barns. Then they set the barns on fire and listened with joy to the screams of the people and the animals as they were burned alive. They blew up and burned all the other buildings and when there was nothing left, they got back into their trucks and went away. Bratishka, we could walk from here to the border and stay every night in Kolkhoz that has been destroyed like this and still have only seen a tiny fraction of the destruction the fascists have wrought."

Kazan Thunderbolts

Schultz looked around at the ruined buildings and shuddered at the mental picture of what must have happened that morning. The massacre of the inhabitants seemed to have left an indelible imprint somehow, as if their ghosts still haunted the ruins. Schultz was standing by what looked like the destroyed relics of one of the barns. The ground there was stained black by what appeared to be ashes ground into the soil. He really didn't want to think what they were ashes of. Almost completely unaware of what he was doing he dropped to his knees and started to pray for the people who had been murdered here and across Russia.

When he got up, he found that Orlan was standing behind him. "Bratishka, as a good Communist, I must ask why you pray to a non-existent deity? But, as a good Russian, I must also thank you for doing so. Where do you come from in America?"

"Pennsylvania. A town called Lancaster. It's just north of Philadelphia, right in the middle of Amish country."

"What is Amish?" Orlan was puzzled.

"It's a religious group that doesn't like the modern world very much. There's quite a few groups like that in the general area I come from. My folks are Pennsylvania Dutch. Quite a few generations back, we left Europe because of religious persecution. We were farmers for a long time but my father worked in a steel mill."

"Ahhh, Dutch." The relief in Orlan's voice was obvious and he relayed the news to the other two partisans. It was the first indication Schultz had had that his name had been a problem. "And you are Amish?'

Schultz shook his head. The truth was that he hadn't been to Church since he was a child and he couldn't quite remember what type it had been. "Protestant. Truth is, though, I seriously lapsed a long time ago. I haven't been to church for years."

Orlan smiled at that. "We will make a good communist of you yet, bratishka. I will tell you this though. Nobody likes to come to this place. Even the fascists stay away from here. Which is why we use it as a rendezvous."

"It makes my skin crawl. I can feel the ghosts watching us."

"That isn't ghosts, tovarish. That is another group of partisans watching us to make sure we are not bait in a trap. And we are watching them. There is one thing I must tell you. The people we are meeting here are escorting one of our agents to safety. A few weeks ago, a partisan group attacked a fascist convoy and destroyed it. Amongst the dead were a small group of Luftwaffe women auxiliaries going to an air operations control center. One of the partisans was a young woman, a teacher before the war, who spoke fluent German, and English.

Also, she looked very much like one of the dead women. So, the partisan group came up with a plan. She dressed in the uniform taken from the dead fascist, took her papers and orders then hid in the woods. When the Hitlerites came to the ambush scene, she claimed to have survived the attack.

"This was a very brave thing for her to do tovarish. There was only a small chance of it succeeding and she knew nothing of the background of the woman whose identity she took. At any time, she could have met somebody who knew the real woman and been exposed. But, she was fortunate and the plan worked. She worked at the operations center, nothing important, just pushing wooden markers on a map to plot aircraft movements. But, she listened and watched and has learned much of great value. A few days ago, she sensed that something was going wrong and escaped. Her partisan group managed to spirit her away by faking her death. The Hitlerites think she was abducted and killed by them.

"It is of the highest important that we get our comrade to safety. The information she has gathered is critically important. It is also crucial that we do not allow her to be taken by the fascists. If they do, and find out who she is, they will understand how she made fools of them. Then they will kill her a little bit every day for many, many days. We all have a duty towards her, one which now becomes yours as well. You have a pistol; you must share the responsibility of not allowing her to be taken alive."

And if anything will stop a conversation stone dead, that is it. Schultz thought. At that point, a single man left the trees around the ruined kolkhoz and walked slowly towards the buildings. Orlan went out to meet him. The two talked for a while, then the newcomer waved. Three more partisans left the shelter of the trees. One was obviously a woman. Schultz guessed she had to be the one who had infiltrated the German base.

When the group came closer, he realized that there were two men and two women. One of the women was the girl he had already spotted. The other was almost her opposite. Stocky where the first woman was slender, ugly where she was attractive. Her face was roughened and reddened by exposure to sun and wind while the other had the pallor of somebody who worked indoors all the time. What shook Schultz was the attractive woman's attitude. He had expected her to be triumphant at having pulled off a remarkable infiltration and obtained important information as a result. Instead, she was palpably miserable and seemed to want only to be ignored. The three partisans with her seemed quite happy to go along with that.

It was fortunate the night was warm for it would have been suicidal to light a fire in the darkness. The partisans had only some black Russian bread and scraps of cold meat to eat for the smell of cooked food would have carried far enough to attract attention. Schultz did have something he could contribute to the meal though although he wasn't quite sure whether he was doing the group a

Kazan Thunderbolts

favor or not. He had some blocks of D-ration, a fortified chocolate survival ration intended for emergency use. It was as hard as iron and tasted only slightly better than boiled potatoes but he guessed it would be welcome, as a change from the sparse and bland food the partisans could obtain.

"I have some Army chocolate, May I share this with you?" He produced one of the four-ounce bars and started to unwrap it. It was wrapped in gas-proof paper and was hard to open.

"You cannot buy my body with chocolate." Schultz was startled by the bitterness and venom in the attractive woman's voice and he suddenly got a feeling he knew the reason for her misery. Orlan was about to speak angrily to her but Schultz made a small gesture of negation with a hand she couldn't see.

"Comrade partisan, back home when American women are unhappy they eat chocolate to cheer themselves. I can sense you are deeply unhappy but I do not have real chocolate to offer you. All I have is this chocolate-flavored emergency ration issued to air crew in case they are shot down. You and your comrades have shared your food with me and now I offer to share mine with you. 'From each according to his ability, to each according to their need.'" That was just about the only bit of Marxist theory Schultz knew. "This chocolate is very hard; we have to shave pieces off the bar with a knife. Hold the shavings in your hand for a moment and they will soften a little. Now, let us all share chocolate in comradeship."

He took out his survival knife and started to shave pieces off the bar. He passed them around to the whole group. They might have been tasteless by American standards but to the sugar-starved Russians, they were a delicacy indeed. "I have five more bars. We can eat them all now or have one every night until we reach the Volga?"

The partisans had a quick, whispered conversation and a vote. Only the girl didn't take part; she just sat with her knees drawn up, her arms wrapped around her legs and her face buried. Schultz wanted to put his arm around her to comfort her but he reasoned that if his suspicions were right, being touched would not comfort her.

"We have decided, by four votes to two, to have one bar per night." Orlan made the announcement with mock gravity.

"Thank you for the chocolate, tovarish American. I am sorry for my rudeness." The girl looked up and it seemed like she wanted to say something else but couldn't bring herself to do so. Then, she returned to her shell of silent misery.

CHAPTER FIVE: CATCHING BREATH

River Gunboat PR-73, Staraya Mayna, Volga River.

"**A**re we going out tonight, Skipper?"

Lieutenant Kennedy shook his head. "We haven't finished repairs yet and we've been stood down for tonight at least. Henry had some bad news for us as well. Both the S-boat and the tug we shot up got back to port. They were seen in Mordovo earlier today. Both appear badly chewed up but they survived. For a while anyway. Now, show me how the repairs are doing."

In fact, they were going well. The bullet-proof glass on the bridge had already been replaced; the instruments damaged by 20mm gunfire from the S-boat were being taken out and replaced. Russian workers were laboring hard to get the armor on the outer bridge structure replaced. The American gunboats might only have been deployed on the Volga for a few months but they had already learned that large quantities of relatively minor damage were typically the results of gunnery duels on the river. So, they had brought the art of making large numbers of minor repairs quickly to a pitch of perfection. In the spring, they had been the inexperienced novices feeling their way in the art of riverine warfare. Now, when it came to repairing the damage, they were teaching the Russian dockyard workers how to get a boat back into service with minimum delay.

Kennedy was so busy helping to get some of the damage squared away that he didn't hear the truck pull up on the quay. In fact, he was holding a piece of damaged mast in place so it could be welded when he heard Maguire call out. "Skipper! Somebody here to see you. Russian."

Kennedy straightened up and went to the side of PR-73. Unexpectedly, the Chekist he had met the day before was standing by an American-supplied Studebaker truck that was towing a large, short-barreled mortar.

"Tovarish Lieutenant, may I come aboard?"

"Tovarish Chekist, welcome to PR-73."

Kazan Thunderbolts

The Russian scrambled on board in a way that revealed unexpected familiarity with small craft. "Tovarish Lieutenant, I was reading the reports from the action at Island Ten two nights ago and I was struck by one thing. Lieutenant Brusilov remarked on how useless your 60mm flares were. So, I brought you something better. A few years ago, our arsenals developed a short-barreled, lightweight version of the Model 1938 107mm mortar for mountain and paratroop units. It was not successful; the reduced charge and short barrel made it too short-ranged and only a few were made. But, I think it will be a good replacement for your 60mm mortar. If your men would like to install it, we will see if it works."

"Hey, Lenny, Johnny, our friend ... Tovarish Chekist I do not know your name?"

"I am Ivan Mihailovich Napalkov."

"John Fitzgerald Kennedy. Hey, wait a minute; Ivan is the Russian for John isn't it?"

"It is indeed." *And you probably think that is a coincidence.* Napalkov knew that Kennedy's father was a very important and influential man. Becoming friends with his son could have many, many advantages.

"Most of my friends call me Jack. Now, Lenny, Johnny, Ivan had brought us a lightweight 107mm mortar. Get the useless 60mm out of the pit and work out a way of installing the new one there. Ivan, our mortar pit was designed for an 81mm but there's a shortage of them so we got a sixty instead. That 107'll make a big difference. Thank you."

"I have more yet. When I came here, there were some boxes waiting for you in the depot. Apparently they came in by train so I brought them down."

PR-73's crew descended on the Studebaker and started to unload the boxes. Maguire's voice echoed across the quay. "Hey skipper, we've been issued some rifles."

Kennedy's head jerked around. "Garands? Or Springfields?"

"Neither, skipper. Crates are labeled Rifle, .30-06, semi-automatic M2 Johnson. There's enough here for one each and a few left over."

Kennedy's eyebrow lifted slightly. "Never heard of a Johnson. Break one of the boxes open. Let's have a look at them."

The rifle was quite unlike the Garand. It had a rotary magazine and the barrel was exposed from the hand guard to the muzzle. Kennedy took one and looked it over. It was stiff with grease and badly needed a good cleaning. Obviously the crew was in for a hard evening of Cosmoline removal. *Oh joy. That almost beats scrubbing out the heads for fun and laughter.*

"You didn't have rifles before?" Napalkov was surprised.

"Pistols and two Thompsons." Kennedy looked more closely at the Johnson. "This is a step in the right direction. Thanks for bringing them, tovarish. And very much thank you for our new mortar."

"Knowing that it will help kill more Hitlerites is thanks enough. I will be away for a few days. I must go to Archangel'sk to find out what happened with that ammunition shipment. Jack, you know the operational side of railways much better than I, could you help me investigate here when I get back?"

Kennedy felt trapped after the largesse that had been displayed. *I bet you think I believe that us having the same first name is just a coincidence. And that I believe you're not aware of who my father is. I'll help you all right but don't ever believe that I trust you.* "Of course, Ivan. Any help I can give you, you're welcome to."

"Thank you. Also, I have received a new glass eye. What do you think of this one?"

Kennedy made a show of inspecting the glass eye. "Much fiercer. Definitely a better choice for a Chekist."

"Excellent. I will see you when I return, tovarish."

Once the truck had been unloaded and the mortar uncoupled, the crew of PR-73 started to dismount their 60mm and replace it with the much heavier 107mm. Thom looked at it suspiciously. "The pit will be a bit cramped. I wonder if that thing will fire our four-deuce ammunition."

Kennedy shrugged. "Probably not. The four-deuce is rifled. Tuck the 60mm away somewhere just in case we need it in the future. Now we've got rifles, we may be expected to form landing parties and go ashore."

The quayside telephone rang. Thom picked it up and answered. The conversation was very brief indeed. "Skipper, Henry wants to see you right away."

Gunboat Squadron GunRon 5 Headquarters, Staraya Mayna, Volga River.

"Hi, Ray. The old man wanted to see me?"

Lieutenant Commander Raymond Blake waved Kennedy through. Commander Henry Farrow was sitting behind vast piles of paper that completely covered his desk. "Hi Jack. I understand you have some new toys?"

"Rifles at last. We got enough for the entire crew. Something called a Johnson."

"Yeah, heard about them. The Army is grabbing every Garand they can find and there's none for the Marines or us. So, we're getting the Johnsons. Army don't like them very much, say they're too delicate and hard to maintain in the field. So, we're going to get them instead. So are the Marines which all goes to prove the Marines can make things work where the Army can't. You got a new mortar as well?"

"Our friendly local Chekist turned up with one. Some sort of lightweight 107 that never saw much production. For paratroopers I think. We've got it in our mortar pit now; it's a bit tight and the ammunition takes up more room but it looks pretty impressive."

"Good. Report on how it works out. If it's an improvement, we'll see if we can get a modified version of our four-deuce. I'll tell you what; it's a fine day out there. I'll walk back with you to PR-73 and you can show it to me."

Once they were out of the office and in the open, Farrow's demeanor changed. "Jack, a word to the wise. Don't get too deeply involved with CheKa or our Chekist comrade. Your family background and influence makes you a prime target to be compromised or converted. That guy is one of their top men and you can bet your life – in fact you are betting your life – he has ulterior motives for everything he does."

Kennedy nodded in agreement. "He reminds me of the people my old man did business with when he was bootlegging. No matter how nice they seemed – and to a kid my age they were very nice indeed – they always had something going on in the background. And it never worked to anybody else's advantage but theirs."

B-26B Marauder AN-J, Over the West Bank of the Volga.

"Take the formation down to the treetops now." Major Wood was leading a formation of twelve B-26 Marauders on their second radar suppression mission. The first mission, three days earlier had opened a small but significant gap in the German radar chain. The B-26 formation had flown the 180 miles from its base at Surovka through that gap in coverage and was now turning south-west for the next leg of their flight. Then, once they were to the west of their target, they'd make a final turn on to the remaining 25 mile run to the radar site at Lugovskoy. The dog-leg course meant that they'd be hitting the site from the rear. The hope was that the Germans would assume that the B-26 formation had continued to fly southwest to hit one of the transport or communications sites around Novospasskoye.

"Going down." Eddie Greer felt the B-26 formation go into a dive that would take it down low for the run to the target. One of the good things was that the Russian forest was remarkably even in height so the treetops lacked the sudden changes that distinguished more varied woodland. It made flying with one's belly tucked into the trees much easier. "Bring the aircraft around to one-six-five."

Greer knew that hitting the Lugovskoy radar site was important. The attack on Lomy had opened a crack in the radar screen that protected the German-held west bank of the Volga. Taking out Lugovskoy would open that crack into a gaping hole that exposed the German lines besieging the Samarskoye Bridgehead. The Samarskoye was much smaller than the Chuvashskaya Bridgehead further north but it was, if anything, even more strategically vital. The Samarskoye Bridgehead protected the great Samara hydro-electric dam and the associated ship locks. If the Germans got too close to them, both the dam and the locks would have to be destroyed with incalculable economic damage.

He also had a theory that the Russians were planning an offensive of their own. He knew the maps of the area almost by heart and he'd worked out a war-winning plan. All it needed was for the Allies to strike south from the Chuvashskaya and north from the Samarskoye and they could encircle the German army around Ulyanov'sk. The two bridgeheads would be linked and a massive hole drilled in the front. Everybody knew that the fighting round Moskva and Stalingrad had bled the German Army white and that they didn't have the reserves to fill a gap in their front that big.

Underneath his Marauder, Greer could see that the woodland had cleared for a short distance. There were a few scattered buildings in the open ground, clustered around a crossroads where two dirt tracks converged. A little beyond that, the forest closed in again and the ground rose up to a ridgeline that was substantially above the present altitude of the bombers. The target was on top of the ridge. Just over two miles away.

Lugovskoy Radar Site.

"Here they come. Bearing three-four-five, all guns prepare to fire." Captain Christoph Löwe threw the field telephone back into its cradle with one hand while working his stop-watch with the other. The forward observer had been five kilometers out and he had reported exactly when the lead bomber had passed over his position. He knew the Ami B-26 flew at 430 kilometers per hour which mean they would come over the treeline exactly 36 seconds after overflying the spotter. Löwe had his nine self-propelled quadruple 20mm guns arranged in an equilateral triangle, each section of three guns forming one side. He had assumed that the aircraft would come directly from the North but the fifteen degree difference was insignificant. The section facing north would engage the aircraft as they approached, the other two would take the bombers in a crossfire as they crossed the target area.

Thirty five seconds after the warning from the spotter, the three quadruple guns opened up at apparently empty sky. For one second, the streams of tracer fire seemed to be wasted on empty sky, then the leading B-26 erupted over the treeline, straight into the waiting gunfire. The stream of orange tracers seemed to wave slightly as the gun crew corrected their aim, then there were brilliant flashes all over the aircraft. The left hand engine erupted into brilliant red and white flame that quickly spread along the whole wing. Then, the fuel tanks exploded, the wreckage of the wing spiraled off and the aircraft rolled on to its back before crashing into the trees. Löwe watched, almost horrified, as a second B-26 was caught by another one of his guns that walked its shells along the stricken aircraft's fuselage. It went straight into the trees, its grave marked by another pyre of orange flame and black smoke. He had been so intent watching that one that he had missed the death of the third Marauder. Yet another B-26 was going down, not burning but its wing had been shot off just outside the right-hand engine. It was too low for the crew to bail out before it spun into the trees and exploded.

By now, the surviving B-26s were crossing the radar site while being flayed by the anti-aircraft guns. Löwe saw one, hit from both sides by the long bursts of gunfire break in half just behind the trailing edge of its wings. The tail half just dropped out of the sky but the nose half seemed to tumble end-over-end before crashing into one of the Freya radar sets. The gunfire was remorseless and apparently never ending with the bombers seemingly supported on a tripod of orange fireflies. More than one simply exploded in mid-air or dived into the ground when the flight deck crews were killed. Others were streaming fire from burning engines or ruptured fuel tanks. Most were destroyed before they could release their bombs, others died as they did so. By the time the raid was over, the radar station had been damaged but was surrounded by the pyres of smoke that marked the graves of the attacking bombers.

"Well, they won't try that again." Löwe looked around at his gun crews who were cheering wildly at each other's successes. "Well done boys. They definitely won't try that again."

Bf 110F Blue-One, Over Lugovskoy

"We got them." Colonel Joachim Blechschmidt saw the black streams of smoke first, then the olive-drab B-26s that were streaming them. Of the dozen Marauders that had attacked the radar station at Lugovskoy, nine had been shot down by the anti-aircraft guns surrounding the site. The other three were limping home. *Or trying to.* Blechschmidt thought. *I doubt if they will get very far even without us to finish them off.*

He was still trying to get used to his new aircraft. Although it was still technically an F-model, it had several detail improvements over the earlier types, most notably a twin machine gun mount in the aft cockpit. *A lot of good that will do facing a Thunderbolt.* He also had a new gunner to operate them. *A gunner who is barely seventeen if that and probably fresh from school.* In front of him, the three surviving Marauders had bunched tightly together in an effort to protect each other from the coming fighter assault. Blechschmidt picked the central one of the three. It had an engine out, the propeller looking eerily still. For all that, it was probably the least damaged of the three and the only one that wasn't streaming smoke.

The rotte of four Bf 110s was heading directly for the surviving B-26s in a near head-on pass. Defensive fire from a single machine gun in the nose of each bomber arched out to meet them, driving home to Blechschmidt how ineffectual his own defensive fire must have seemed to the Thunderbolts a few days earlier. He squeezed both firing buttons on his joystick, using both his two 20mm cannon and four machine guns simultaneously. The first few tracers went in front of the Marauder but the rest plowed into the cockpit of the bomber, shredding the transparencies and sending fragments of metal arching into the air. The B-26 reared up out of the formation, rolled over on to its back and dived straight into the woodland beneath. Over to his left, a second B-26 was a sheet of flame, almost everything between its two engines burning furiously. The central spar must have given way in the intense heat because the wings suddenly folded upwards, wrapping around the fuselage before what had once been an aircraft just fell out of the sky.

Blechschmidt pulled up and looked around for the lone surviving B-26. It was surprisingly far away and making for the Volga. *Damn, those Martins are fast.* He knew his 110s couldn't catch it up before it crossed the Volga and Luftwaffe aircraft were not supposed to cross the river without special permission. Pilots shot down over the east bank of the Volga had little or no chance of making it back to safety and the Luftwaffe was too short of trained aircrew to accept any losses they could avoid. He would have to accept that the lone B-26 had made it to safety. The only one of twelve to do so.

391st Bomb Group, Airfield 33, Surovka, Moscow Front

"Where the hell are they?" Brigadier-General Clayton Adkins was scanning the horizon with his binoculars. He knew that the raid had run into heavy opposition but that was all.

"They're already late." Colonel Gregory Hughes was scanning the horizon as well and a sickening feeling was beginning to grip his stomach. There had been 64 B-26Bs based at Surovka, divided into four squadrons of 16 aircraft. Today's raid had been drawn from the 574th Bombardment Squadron and Hughes had a bad feeling that squadron had just ceased to exist.

There was a sudden surge of excitement on the base and Hughes was sadly reminded of the advantage young, eager eyes had over his own middle-aged versions. People waiting for the bombers to return were pointing at the horizon to the west. Then, Hughes saw it as well. A black stain in the sky that quickly resolved into a Marauder, staggering through the air, right hand engine dead, streaming black smoke from the left and gray/white vapor from its wing roots. The aircraft was lined up on the runway and obviously coming in but its wheels was up. Hughes saw the red warning flared going up but knew they were pointless. If the undercarriage was capable of being lowered, it would be. This Marauder was coming in on its belly. Fire engines, ambulances, wrecking trucks, all were racing to the estimated position where the crippled aircraft should end up. The 391st had crashed enough B-26s in training to be quite familiar with what was about to happen.

The Marauder hit the runway fast. All the Americans had expected that; the B-26 had a landing speed of 150 miles per hour and woe betide the crew who reduced speed to less than that. A brutal stall and spinning in was the penalty for doing so. What had surprised Hughes was that this smashed-up wreck of a B-26 could do 150 miles per hour to start with. The Marauder was already beginning to turn when its belly kissed the steel planking that surfaced the runway. The stricken aircraft slid down the runway, spraying pieces of its belly all around as it started to spin on its vertical axis. The wing spar on the right had obviously been weakened by the heat from the burning engine and the stress of the spin was too much for it. The wing snapped where it joined the fuselage, the broken sections sliding across the grass.

And that was where the B-26, at last, had some luck. The broken wing burst into flames but by the time it did so, it was well away from the fuselage and the fire was harmless. The B-26 itself rolled over, now sliding on the wing root with the remaining wing almost vertical. Hughes wasn't certain quite how the aircraft remained in that position for as long as it did but when the Marauder came to a halt, the wing slammed back down on to the runway. There, it also broke away from the fuselage.

Rescue workers had already descended on the wreckage and were fighting to get the crew out. Hughes saw some of the Russian laborers pounding at the tail turret with pickaxes, sledgehammers and anything else they could find. The plexiglass couldn't withstand the onslaught and shattered. Hughes heard the "Urrah" from the Russians as they pulled the tail gunner out, alive and apparently unharmed. Another group of Russians had formed a human pyramid to get two of their fellows on top of the rotund fuselage of the Marauder. Those two were also pounding on a gun turret, the mid-upper, and they too gave a cheer of triumph as they pulled the gunner out. Around the nose of the crashed bomber, the Americans were pulling out the crew from the nose and the cockpit. Two sergeants went inside the smoldering wreckage of the fuselage to search for any more survivors. They came out, carrying a badly-wounded flight engineer.

General Adkins went over to them. "You two deserve a Bronze Star for that. What are your names?"

The older of the two men took the lead. "I'm Sergeant Wint, Sir. This is Sergeant Kidd. We're both with the ground echelon."

"Well, you sure earned your pay today. I'll put in the recommendation for a Bronze Star each. Can't promise you'll get them of course." Adkins went over to the Russians, shaking hands and slapping backs. He knew that they would prefer vodka to compliments or medals so he had sent an aide to get some of the good stuff.

The crew, the living and the dead, were on the grass well removed from the wreck of their aircraft. Adkins and Hughes looked at them. The bombardier, copilot and radio operator were dead. The pilot and flight engineer had been wounded. Only the upper turret and tail gunners had survived unscathed.

"What happened?"

"Flak, Sir. They were laying for us. And there were fighters waiting for anybody who escaped them." Major Wood couldn't quite comprehend the fact that he was alive and back on his home base. "The fighters came at us, head-on. We only had the nose .30 to shoot back with."

"I'll need a full, written, report as soon as you're able." Adkins was watching as the wounded were loaded into an ambulance. The handful of unwounded airmen were also being given an ambulance; they were suffering from delayed shock at least. "We need to know exactly what happened today and why."

"I can tell you the why right now." Wood was still traumatized from watching his entire squadron wiped out. "We can't take big aircraft like the '26 in that low. The light flak is murderous low down. The Fortresses proved they can fly through the medium and heavy stuff higher up. We have to do the same."

Forest, north of Polivanovo

They were eight now. *In body at least. In spirit, I don't know where Olen is.* Schultz glanced at the young woman who had pulled off the incredible feat of infiltrating the Luftwaffe operations center and now seemed to wish that she had never been born. Overnight, Schultz had learned her conspiratorial name. Olen meant a doe, a female deer, and it was surprisingly appropriate. She had the delicacy, the natural grace of a doe. Only, she was a doe that wanted to be dead.

The partisans had spread out around them. Two were providing flank guard; one was up ahead scouting while another brought up the rear. The remaining pair provided close-in guards for Schultz and Olen. It was a jarring reminder to Schultz of how seriously the partisans took the task of getting him back to allied lines. He also had a suspicion that it was to prevent Olen putting a gun to her own head. He was searching for a way to talk to her, to try and get her to come out of her shell and become part of the world around her. He thought he would try something that probably had good memories for her. "I am told you were a teacher before the war?"

To his relief, it was indeed a good start. Olen actually smiled slightly as she remembered the pre-war days before the misery and despair closed down again. "I was. In Saransk, far to the west of here. I taught the children German and English as part of the school complex subject "the life and labor of the family in village and town". I also instructed them in dialectics and woodcraft as part of the Young Pioneers so that they would grow up well as small comrades. That is how I learned to survive in the woods when the fascists came."

Her voice had gained a little life as she had spoken about the days before the war but, like her smile, it had faded away again as her memories associated with the war came back. Still, sensing perhaps that somebody cared enough to throw her a lifeline, she tried to make something of the contact Schultz had offered. "What did you do before the war, tovarish?"

Schultz noticed that she hadn't used his German-sounding name. "My name's Charles. Most people call me Charlie or Chuck. I left school right after graduation but there weren't any real jobs to be had. So a friend of mine and myself, we opened a motorcycle repair business in my parent's garage. People couldn't afford a new motorcycle so they'd bring an old, worn out one and we'd fix it up for them. I got to be real good with a spray gun. First year was real hard but we did good work and people started coming in from the neighboring towns. End of the second year, we were doing well enough to rent a workshop. Third year we were earning enough money to considered pretty well-off. Then, news of the *Taney* came in. Next morning Doug, that was my business partner, and I were down at the Army recruiting office. We would have gone to the Navy but the line was already three times around the block."

"*Taney?*" Olen sounded confused but Schultz mentally cheered. He had got her engaged in something and that was a big step forward.

"*Roger B. Taney*, a Coast Guard cutter. She was torpedoed by a Ger . . . by a Hitlerite submarine. After the crew abandoned ship, the submarine machine-gunned the survivors in the water. Killed them all. Almost a hundred men murdered. I know it sounds small compared with what the fascists have done here but the Coast Guard sailors; well, they've got a special place in the hearts of people who live along the coast. You see, they're the ones who come out to rescue us if we get into trouble at sea. They have a motto when people call for help, 'We have to go out. We don't have to come back'. So, when the bodies started being washed ashore, people went a bit mad I guess. It was the last straw, the last little thing that pushed us too far. Then, when we heard how brave a fight you Russians were putting up, how you made the fascists bleed and die for every foot of ground. Well, we had to help and here we are."

"So, here you are." Olen seemed thoughtful about that, then she started talking in a rapid spray of words that seemed to erupt as if they had been held under great pressure. Schultz guessed they probably had been just that. "When we hit the fascist convoy and I saw the dead girl, the one who looked so much like me, I knew what I had to do as well. She'd been hit in the head so her uniform wasn't too badly bloodstained. I changed into it and hid until the fascists found me and took me to the air operations center. The deception had worked. Only what I didn't know was that the Hitlerite officers looked on the enlisted women auxiliaries as their own private harem. They would call the women to their quarters at night. They thought I was one of those women so they called me as well. I had to pretend this was the most wonderful thing that had ever happened to me and that I enjoyed everything they made me do. These were the fascist swine who killed our fathers, our brothers, our sisters, destroyed everything we have built and I had to pretend that getting into their beds was everything I had ever wanted in my life. When they touched me, I had to give great cries of joy even though their fingers felt like acid. After they had finished with me I would wash and wash, but I could never make myself clean again. Everything they touched is foul. If I could cut it out I would."

Schultz looked at her crying and mixed with his pity for her was guilt. *Doug and I made a real success of our business. We did the right thing at the right time and we were raking in the dough. We must have been one of the first little companies to start recovering from the Depression and we weren't short of girls throwing themselves at us. How many of those girls felt the way this girl does? How many of them went with us because they were hungry and we had the money for a good meal and a show? Doug's back home now; his feet and eyes were too bad for the Army and our business is making money hand-over-fist producing motorcycle parts for the Army. He's putting half of everything we make aside for me. But how did the girls feel?* "Olen. Have you ever seen a Flying Fortress?"

She shook her head, confused and bewildered as well as exhausted from the outpouring of emotion. Schultz spoke very carefully because he didn't want to be misunderstood. "There are ten men in a Flying Fortress. The bomb aimer right in the nose with the navigator behind him. Then, there's the pilot and copilot in the cockpit with the flight engineer – that's me – behind them. Then, there is the radio operator in the aft cabin, the two beam gunners, the ball turret gunner and the tail gunner. Ten men. The Army puts the older, steadier men in the bombers. Fighters are a game for younger men. In my bomber, five of my crew were married, another was engaged. Two of the married men already had kids. Our bomber was typical, they're all like that. Olen, I'm not trying to belittle what you have suffered but if what you did saves just one bomber, that's six wives or fiancées who will see their men again when they wouldn't otherwise have done. That's two sets of kids who will grow up knowing their father, knowing him as something more than an old, yellow picture on the wall. Because of you. And that's one bomber, in one flight, in one squadron, in one group, in one wing, in one division. By the time this war is over, what you learned may have saved hundreds of bombers and their crews."

"Hundreds? I think you exaggerate."

"Olen, this war will go on for a long time. We fly twice a week, Every time we do, we lose one or two Flying Fortresses. We have 72 Flying Fortresses in a group. We can all do the math. For us, you have sacrificed more than anybody has a right to ask but you have also given us a gift beyond price. A better chance to go home."

Fast Attack Craft S-38, Repair Yard, Mordovo, Volga River.

"Herr Oberleutnant, the armor kit for your bridge has arrived." The yard superintendent had a big, beaming smile on his face. The arrival of the pre-fabricated armored cupola for S-38 brought the time when he could get the wretched ship and its demanding Captain out of his nice neat yard.

Oberleutnant zur See Oskar Wuppermann was not impressed. Or particularly grateful come to that. In his opinion, while an armored cupola for his bridge was very nice, it didn't mean very much when the rest of S-38 was made out of wood. S-38 showed the effects of American gunfire on such a lightly-built hull. Everything above the turn of the deck was tangled wreckage. The stern 37mm was smashed, the midships twin 20mm gone completely. Only the bow single 20mm was still operational and that only because its mounting was recessed into the raised forecastle. The bridge and midships structures were bullet-riddled wrecks. *It is more guns I need, not a little bit of armor on the bridge. The Ami gunboats outgun by us so much that after their first burst of fire, we have little left to reply to them with.*

"That is good. While your men are installing the armor panels, perhaps they could make a few more minor alterations. I want the torpedoes and their tubes removed and the 20mm guns replaced by 37mms. One on the stern, one amidships, one on the bows. I want twin MG42s, one each side of the bridge." Wuppermann bitterly thought of the way the American heavy machine guns had ripped up his S-boat. As far as he knew, there was no equivalent of them he could get access to. *The MG42 is the best we have. It's nowhere good as the American heavy Brownings, but it will have to do.*

"I already have a 37mm gun waiting for you." The Yard superintendent was not an unreasonable man and he really did try to do his best for the crews that operated out of Mordovo. "It is a 3.7cm Flak M42U. A lighter weight gun than the one it replaces. I have six of them here, intended to arm a small freighter for use as a gunboat. But, the freighter was sunk before it could be converted. S-38 is so smashed up aft of its bridge that almost everything there needs to be repaired. We do not have another twin 20mm to give you so perhaps I can give you another M42U instead? Would two 37mms be acceptable?"

Wuppermann wasn't an entirely unreasonable man either. A little brusque sometimes and he didn't suffer fools gladly. But, he would go out of his way to help those who made efforts on his behalf. "That would be a great help my friend. Is there any chance of mounting a third 37mm gun forward? Very often on the river, it is the bow guns that open the fight and that is why the Amis have a 75mm gun. Often, one shot from that gun ends the battle. Another M42U would ease things greatly.

The Yard superintendent shook his head. "I would give you another 37 gladly but the problem is mounting it. The 20mm gun pit is too small for a 37mm and enlarging it would mean completely rebuilding the bows. Removing your torpedo tubes has the same problem. If I propose a reconstruction like that, it will have to be officially approved and the navy will insist they do a proper design. You might see the result in a year's time or more. Now, if the bow gets damaged badly enough I might be able to work the larger gun in without going through all that."

He was prevented from saying anything more by the wailing of sirens across the base. Wuppermann looked up and saw streams of white vapor high in the sky over the eastern bank of the Volga. One set formed a long, straight sheet in the sky while others made equally long, graceful curves around the first set. *American heavy bombers and their fighter escort. The world is changing while I watch.*

There was something terrifyingly implacable about the bombers. Through his binoculars, Wuppermann could see the B-17s flying in a tight-packed formation. He started trying to count them but the numbers were too great and they were packed into too small a space. *More than a hundred I think. Probably twice that.* Around the bombers were the small black puffs of anti-aircraft fire bursts. The bombers seemed to show a mighty disdain for the weak flak concentration for Wuppermann found deeply disturbing.

"I wonder where they are going?" Wuppermann spoke to the yard superintendent beside him. "Wherever it is, they seem to be heading right over us."

The two men stared at each other as realization dawned on them. When they spoke, it was in perfect chorus. "Scheisse!" Then they started running for the air raid shelters.

They made it, just. The first bombs were already exploding to the north west when the two men hurled themselves down the concrete steps into the shelter. Wuppermann was relieved to see his crew, or the survivors of his crew after the duel with the American gunboat, was already inside. The concentrated roar of the bomb explosions was getting steadily nearer and dust was already beginning to fill the air in the shelter. Wuppermann saw the yard supervisor and his workers were visibly shaking as more and more American bombers delivered their loads on to the harbor and Navy base at Mordovo.

"Relax my friend; we made it to the shelter." Wuppermann made allowances for the yard supervisor. He was only a civilian, after all.

"For all the good it will do us." The man's voice was shaking, both from the explosions of the bombs all around them and from his own fear. "These shelters were built when the Ivans were the enemy. Their bombers were little biplanes that came at night. They dropped ten or twenty kilogram bombs. Then the Americans came and their viermotorens drop five hundred or thousand kilo bombs. A dozen or more of them from each aircraft and any one of them can crack this shelter open like an eggshell."

That made Wuppermann nervous as well. He'd assumed that they would be safe once they were in the shelter. Obviously, that wasn't going to be the case. The dust and smoke in the shelter was so thick that it seemed to have a jelly-like consistency making it hard to inhale and even worse to breath out. The temperature was slowly but steadily rising; leaving no doubt that the bombers had started fires in the dockyard area. Grimly, Wuppermann expected that S-38 was one of those fires. There seemed to be no way she could have escaped the terrible hammering that was being handed out.

He understood now why being on the receiving end of an artillery bombardment or a bombing raid was such a morale-shattering event. The constant rumbling roar of explosions was shaking his body, making his joints scream with pain at every new set of blasts. The closer explosions made him feel as if he really was being hit with a giant hammer, driving all the breath from his body. Given that he felt as if he was suffocating from the smoke and grit in the air, that wasn't completely a bad thing.

Finally, after what seemed like an eon but was really less than twenty minutes, the bombardment ended and the all-clear sounded. When he and the yard superintendent left their shelter, they could see that what had once been a small but trim repair yard was a blasted ruin. The buildings and warehouses were down and burning, the quays and their installations had been shattered. Out in the river, the tug that Wuppermann had saved a few nights earlier was a burning, sunken wreck. A column of smoke was rising from the other side of the river, indicating at least some of bombers had hit targets there.

"They hit Vyrystaykino as well." The yard superintendent pointed to another pyre of smoke upriver. "There was another small repair yard up there. The Amis do that. They always hit the main target and a few smaller ones around it. That was they disperse our repair capabilities. But, we're getting the measure of them. As soon as we get the all clear after their viermotorens hit a target, everybody rushes in to help fight the fires and rescue the wounded. That way we can control the damage before it takes too bad a hold. Let us go and see what has happened to your S-38."

Wuppermann saw that the damage was nowhere near as bad as he had expected. S-38 was still afloat and hadn't caught fire. However, a heavy bomb had hit the quayside in front of her and the blast had wrecked the bow section of the ship. The wooden forecastle that contained the torpedo tubes had been riddled with fragments from the bomb blast and the alloy frames had been distorted.

The yard supervisor shook his head. "There's no way we can fix that. We'll have to rebuild the whole bow section in front of the bridge and above the waterline. It looks, Herr Oberleutnant that we can mount your third 37mm gun after all. We'll remove the torpedo tubes and the reload racks in the process. It'll take time, especially with the damage from the Ami air raid, but we'll get her fixed up the way you want."

305th Bombardment Group, Bolshaya Tarlovka Airfield, Russia.

"A milk run." Gonzalez had brought the photographs in with him. It had been an easy, almost risk-free effort for him as well.

LeMay grunted. He had been opposed to using his B-17s against targets so far forward but the request to eliminate the port at Mordovo had been an urgent one from the Navy. As he had looked at the map, he had realized that the raid would be a perfect training exercise for his inexperienced crews. The Navy had asked if a single bomb group could drop on Mordovo. LeMay had gone two better and sent the 305th, 35th and 19th, a total of 162 B-17s and 96 P-47s as escort. Not one aircraft had been lost although some of the Fortresses had minor damage from flak. The B-17s had spent the whole hour-long flight to the IP being jockeyed into closer formations and then practicing holding those formations. Then, they had made their turn from the IP and held those tight formations through the scattered flak. As a training exercise, it had been near perfect. LeMay thought that he would generously approach the navy and ask them if there were any more west bank targets they wanted hit.

As a bombing raid, the pictures Gonzalez had taken would tell that story. "We'll start with the verticals. The stereoviewer we asked for has arrived."

Gonzalez looked at one corner of LeMay's office where photo-interpretation equipment had been set up. The stereoscopic viewer held pride of place. The very fact that it was there impressed Gonzalez. It had arrived only two days after the requisition had gone through at a time when other units were waiting weeks for essential equipment. Then he looked at the stereoscopic viewed more carefully. "That's odd, Sir."

"Something wrong?"

"No, Sir. Quite the reverse. But this isn't an Army stereo-viewer; it's a pre-war civilian one. Got a lot of bells and whistles that the Army discarded to speed production. Somebody made sure you went first-class."

For the next hour, Gonzalez and LeMay went carefully through the bomb damage assessment pictures. Right from the start, it was obvious that the B-17s had come a long way since the early missions. Gonzalez could see that the bomb patterns were highly concentrated and had – mostly – been put in the right place. Six of the nine combat boxes had unloaded on the proper target, the Mordovo port. One combat box had unloaded on a small cargo handling wharf the other side of the river, two more on another port, Vyrystaykino, further inland. At least two thirds of the bombs had landed within the target areas with the crater count suggesting all of the thousand pounders were within the scan of the pictures. Both areas had been devastated but in some ways that made the fact they were the wrong targets all the more frustrating.

"Nine boxes and three of them hit the wrong targets. We have to do something about that." LeMay was thinking over the problem. "*Why* do they do that? Captain, you never take photographs of the wrong target. Why?"

Left to his own devices, Gonzalez might have made a smart-ass remark about that and under some circumstances he would have done. But, he knew LeMay wanted information to solve a problem and didn't want to be bothered with small-talk. He was beginning to understand the man he worked for and had realized that to LeMay work and relaxation never mixed and the first always took precedence over the second. He wondered, briefly, if the 305th Bomb Group realized how lucky they were.

"Colonel, I'm on my own, remember? When I get to the target area, and it isn't hard to know I have these days, I stooge around for a bit to get familiar with where I am, exactly. Then, when I am quite sure I am where I am supposed to be and know where everything is in relation to everything else, I make my photo-run. Your bombardiers don't have that luxury. They see the target area just once and have to make a decision based on that one look and a few minutes studying some pictures a few hours earlier. It's not surprising they make a few mistakes."

LeMay thought very carefully about that. His mind stripped Gonzalez's statement down to its bare essentials and dug out the key point. The Filipino Captain knew his business and was an expert in what he did. In this case, the concept that was central to his performance was familiarity. He made sure he was familiar with the target area and its surroundings before he made his run.

The key to hitting the right targets was there. "I understand. Oh, Gonzalez, I've spoken with Wing and from now on, you're Major Gonzalez. I've got your gold oak leaves here. You can assume this means I have no complaints over how you perform your duties."

Gonzalez snapped out a salute and took the oak leaves. Since he was beginning to understand the Colonel, he realized that he had just received a serious compliment.

Headquarters, American Expeditionary Force, Seitovo, Chuvashskaya Bridgehead.

The installation was a disgrace, an insult to every American soldier. Colonel Ryan Anderson could think of no other way to describe it. Major General Lloyd Fredendall had used an entire engineer company of the 19th Engineer Regiment to build a large, heavily-fortified Corps headquarters at Seitovo, almost 75 miles behind the front line. The engineers had blasted and drilled two U-shaped complexes running 160 feet into a solid granite ridge just north of the little town. It had taken three weeks to construct. An entire anti-aircraft battalion, equipped with desperately-needed 90mm guns, was emplaced to protect the headquarters.

All this was at a time when the crossing points over the Volga were strained beyond capacity and forces were backed up on the west bank, waiting for a chance to get across. There was one American Division, the 83rd Infantry, holding the line in the Chuvashskaya but there were six more, including the 1st and 2nd Armored as well as the 1st, 2nd, 9th and 34th Infantry in Russia but they were backed up and awaiting a chance to cross into the Chuvashskaya. In fact, one of the reports Anderson had with him was that the 1st Armored was now beginning to cross the Volga, ready to enter the line. Three weeks later than planned. The same three weeks that it had taken to build this headquarters and that wasn't a coincidence. The plan to replace the Russian force holding the Chuvashskaya with an American Corps was drifting steadily further behind schedule.

Virtually everybody in the base complex was acutely aware that General Fredendall had never been up to the front lines. Not once. All he knew of the terrain and situation on the front was scavenged from reports and he was content to direct deployments, sometimes down to company level, based on map readings. He was rapidly getting the nickname 'Vetrenyy Freddie' which he had interpreted as 'Veteran Freddie' and boasted about. He did a lot of boasting. In fact, vetrenyy was Russian for 'Windy' and implied the same lack of moral fortitude in Russian as it did in English.

That pointed to another problem. After four months in Russia, Fredendall hadn't bothered to learn a single word of Russian. Sometimes, his staff believed he didn't speak a word of English either. When he did send out orders, usually by radio, he used a combination of slang and obscure phrases designed to baffle any enemy monitors. Unfortunately, subordinates were equally baffled. Anderson was reasonably sure that the confusion meant that the exact deployments on the front line were nothing like those envisaged by the General.

"The General will see you in a few minutes, Sir." The clerk was apologetic. Fredendall was in the habit of keeping everybody waiting, sometimes for up to an hour or so. Anderson supposed it was a way of asserting his authority. This wasn't the first time he had run into the situation and he had come prepared. He had a paperback book in his briefcase and he settled down to read about the continuing adventures of the Continental Op.

The problem was that even Dashiell Hammett's terse phrasing couldn't drive the tactical picture from his mind. Fredendall had small packets of troops dispersed over a very large area in positions that were only marginally supportive at best. One battalion of the 83rd Infantry Division was at Khornzor, another blocking the Yamashevo road to Kanash. Combat Command A of the 83rd Infantry was at Klimovo but Combat Command B was near Khormali.

Fredendall had the option of reinforcing the Russian forces north and south of the American positions, keeping his forces concentrated in a central location and ready to counterattack, or striking north to open the way for an assault on Nizhny Novgorod. He had done none of these things. *In fact, it is very hard to see exactly what he has done.*

"Colonel, the General will see you now." Anderson couldn't help but glance at his watch. He'd been kept waiting for 35 minutes. That wasn't bad by Fredendall's standards.

Once inside and having exchanged the customary courtesies, Anderson got straight down to business. "General, we have received a considerable amount of intelligence that suggests a major German offensive is about to take place. The first pictures of a German build-up opposite Klimovo came in about a week ago, from an F-5 doing bomb damage assessment. The 10th Photographic Squadron followed up, flying missions all over the area to the west of the Chuvashskaya. They've found large numbers of German troop positions and depots.

"To make matters more worrying, when they reflew some of the same missions a few days later, the number of positions and stockpiles had increased. They've found tank laagers, artillery parks, infantry encampments and supply dumps. All along the front line of the Chuvashskaya but with a major concentration opposite the line held by the 83rd."

"Let me see those." Fredendall was brusque. He looked through the pictures quickly, shaking his head as he did so. "The krauts haven't camouflaged them very well."

"The Russians have virtually no airborne photographic reconnaissance capability, Sir. Just a few old biplanes with crude cameras. They've got nothing like our F-5s. The krauts are used to having everything secure as far as the air is concerned and they've got into bad habits. It'll only last until they shoot an F-5 down and realize how good they are but at the moment, they don't hide much.

Fredendall snorted in derision. "I can think of a much simpler reason. The krauts make the best cameras in the world; they know what we can see. They set these up to be seen. They're decoys."

"Sir, when the B-17s hit Penza a few days ago, they caught a marshalling yard full of rail cars stuffed with explosives and fuel. The secondaries from the bombing ripped the place apart. The krauts really are shifting large quantities of supplies in. Ammunition, fuel, everything."

This time the snort had graduated from derision to contempt. "The railway from Penza also runs to Syzran in the Samarskoye Bridgehead and that's a much more strategically important target. If there is anything going on, that's where it will be. But I wouldn't take anything the fly-boys say seriously. They'll do anything to defend their belief in air power."

"Sir, the railway to Syrzan is only a single track line. The one heading north to Shumerlya is four-track."

Fredendall waved his hand irritatedly. "Do you have anything else?"

"The reports from the air groups show a marked fall in kraut air operations. The Russians say this always precedes an offensive. The planes are down for maintenance so they can have the maximum number operational when they start the attack."

"The Russians say. Well, I suppose they would be looking for a reason why they keep getting beaten. I see nothing to worry about here, Ryan. Dismissed."

River Gunboat PR-73, Staraya Mayna, Volga River.

"Where we going tonight, Skipper?" Thom sounded almost ghoulishly cheerful as he asked the standard question that greeted Kennedy every time he came back from the Command headquarters,. PR-73 had finished her repairs in record time, she had a new heavy mortar amidships, her crew had proper rifles at last and all was well with the world.

"Back down river. We're going to a place called Podvalye. This one is a simple job. We don't have to worry about the Ulyanov'sk Narrows; the troops who fought their way over a few days ago have held on. More than that, they've extended their bridgehead a little." Having seen the geography of the city in daylight now, Kennedy could envisage what was happening. The allied troops who had managed to force their way ashore were spread out along the bank at the foot of the park-covered ridge Kennedy had seen. The Germans were on the other side of that ridge and would, no doubt like to cross it and push the allies back. Only, the moment they reached the crest of the ridge they would be exposed to Russian artillery from the east bank. Kennedy guessed that the Russian guns would be firing over open sights and that would make any attempt at an assault on the Russian positions futile. He'd heard through the grapevine that additional guns had been brought up from the American divisions waiting on the east bank to reinforce the artillery cover for the newly-established bridgehead.

"And Sengiley?"

"The Army sent a reconnaissance aircraft over there today. The guns are gone. One of our missions tonight is to land a Marine reconnaissance squad there and see what is going on. We'll land the team, wait for them, then head south to Pod Valley, make a pick up and come straight back. In fact, I think our guests are arriving now."

A truck had pulled up by the quayside and a small group of Marines were scrambling out of the back to assemble beside the gangways on to PR-73. This wasn't the first time PR-73 had carried a raider group on one of its nefarious missions on the West Bank but this group subtly differed from the previous landing teams. For one thing, they were wearing the standard American olive drab uniform rather than the Frog Skin pattern they had worn previously. Kennedy knew the reason for that; the Marine Corps Frog Skin was all too similar to the blotched uniforms worn by SS units and that similarity had, it was rumored, led to some unfortunate incidents.

"Sir, Lieutenant Kennedy, Sir?" The leader of the raider squad halted at the top of the gangway. "Gunnery Sergeant Custer reporting."

"Welcome on board, Gunny. Uhhhh, any relation to THE Custer?"

"Sir, no sir. And, with respect, Sir, all the jokes anybody can possibly think of got old a long time ago."

Kennedy chuckled at that. "I can imagine. Come below Gunny and we'll discuss tonight's work. Larry, get our guests bedded down as best we can."

In the wardroom, after pouring small glasses of whiskey, Kennedy sat down. "Gunny, I suggest we start off by comparing orders. Make sure we're on the same page. We're a bit jumpy here on crossed wires at the moment."

"Sir, heard rumors about that, Sir. My orders are to land at Sengiley and check the guns are actually gone. Then to search the area for any intelligence material we can find. It's surprising, Sir, what the krauts will miss. They don't often make mistakes, but when they do, it's a big one. They'll carefully incinerate all their trash but leave behind the envelope marked 'Top Secret, burn before reading'. After we've done, we'll re-embark and land again at Pod Valley. There are three people we have to collect and escort back to this gunboat. One escaped aircrew, two special persons."

"That's more or less what I have. We didn't know the number of people you'd be bringing back from Pod Valley but three is no problem. We'll put you ashore in two rubber rafts. My boys can stay on the beach in case you have to leave in a hurry."

"Sir, sounds good to me, Sir." Custer looked at the small wardroom of PR-73. "Last gunboat we were on as a Higgins boat. PR-109. You've got a lot more space here."

Kennedy looked pleased. "This is an Elco Boat. She was designed as a gunboat with some helpful Russian advice. The Higgins boats are redesigned PT boats. A bit smaller than us, they've got a small bridge and their twin-fifties are echeloned rather than side-by-side. They've got an old 23 caliber three incher instead of the 50 caliber three inch we got. 109's a good boat though."

"Got us in and out without a shot being fired." Custer sounded almost reminiscent. "His crew cleaned my boys out at poker though."

Kennedy laughed at that. "McHale and the crew of the 109 boat have, shall we say, a reputation for doing the impossible. Now, time to look at some charts."

Railway Yard Traffic Office, Archangel'sk.

"Tovarish Chekist, our marshalling yard here is the most important on the northern coast. Even before the war we handled large volumes of cargo going both in and out of the oblast. We also handled the supplies for the Northern Fleet at Severodonetsk. Since the war started, the tonnage we handle here has doubled, and when the convoys started arriving, it has doubled again. We run at least two hundred trains a day from this yard. Most of the supplies for the Karelia and Kostromo Fronts go through this yard. Other trains go south, to Cheropovets and Kazan. Then we also handle cargo that comes in and out by way of the Northern Dvina Canal and the White Sea/Baltic Canal. The latter brings us in cargo from the White Sea to Lake Ladoga, and thus to the Volga through the Volga-Baltic Waterway. The problem we face here is not just the volume of shipping but the complexity of the routing and the transport modes we have to use."

Napalkov knew and understood all that but he let the yard supervisor explain it anyway. "You are not the only person who faces a difficult task tovarish. These are desperate days for the Rodina and such times demand the most strenuous of efforts. Every error made by each Russian directly aids the fascists in their efforts to destroy the Rodina. That is sabotage."

Kazan Thunderbolts

The Chekist's voice had dropped to a menacing hiss that made the marshaling yard superintendent go white. Sabotage was an offense that got people summarily executed – or worse. "But, we handle more than 4,000 wagons a day here. Just one went astray."

"And twelve good men, brave Marines fighting for the Rodina, might have died because of that error. It was only the Americans with their meticulous attention to detail, who saved their lives." Even with fear clenching his stomach, the railway supervisor recognized the significance of that last comment. *The Americans saved our soldier's lives and CheKa are making sure everybody knows it. That means it is official that the Americans are indeed our valued friends and trusted allies. At the same time, our performance is being compared to that of foreigners and found wanting. That is far from good – for me at least.*

Napalkov thought carefully, reading the expression on the superintendent's face. "There is blame to be assessed here. Send in the dispatcher who sent the train out and the clerk who typed out the manifest."

The superintendent sent a messenger out for the staff in question. In the meantime, Napalkov looked at the manifest for the train at the root of the problem. One glance told him what the problem had been. The manifest was hand-written. He picked up the telephone and gave the local CheKa office some terse instructions. By the time he had finished, the clerk and dispatcher had arrived. The clerk was a young man approaching his thirties. The dispatcher was older, in his middle forties. Both were terrified.

"Comrades, the wagon that caused this problem was registration number 139-555. I do not see this number on the manifest. Explain yourself." The last remark was addressed to the dispatcher.

The man took the list and scanned it. "Here it is, Comrade. Ohh."

"Ohh indeed. The wagon on the manifest is registration number 139-556. Here we have the reason why twelve of our Marines so nearly died. Are there extenuating circumstances you wish to claim before I pass judgment upon you?"

"Comrade Chekist, the list is hand written when it should be typed. The six is so badly written I read it as five."

Napalkov turned to the clerk who had gone white and was shaking. "So blame falls upon you. Why was this list hand-written?"

"Comrade Chekist, our departmental typewriter is forty years old. It was made before the war with Japan. It types so badly that the words are hard to read even with a new ribbon and the only ribbon I have is pre-war. We have to re-ink it if we are to use it at all. To make the list out by hand was clearer and easier to read."

"Did you report this?"

"Yes, Comrade Chekist."

"I see. Turn around." Napalkov caught the hopeless despair on the man's face as he obeyed his order. His eyes were clenched shut and his lips moved silently as he expected the traditional pistol shot to the back of his head. Instead, Napalkov made a tiny gesture to one of his assistants. The man's fist, reinforced by a brass knuckle-duster swung in a punch that had all the force he could muster behind it and drove wrist-deep into the clerk's stomach. He doubled over and fell to the floor, writhing from the blow but without the breath left in his body to make a sound. He was desperately trying to suck some breath into his lungs but the force of the blow had paralyzed him. Eventually, he managed to suck air into his body with a great whooping sigh.

Napalkov turned to the dispatcher. "You were in doubt of the information yet you did not ask for clarification. You do not deserve the privilege of having a reserved occupation far from the front. Comrade Belyakov, take this recruit to the nearest infantry battalion and see they find him a suitable posting. In a rifle squad perhaps."

On the floor, the clerk had stopped whooping for breath but he had vomited on the carpet. He looked up, obviously expecting the beating to continue. Instead, Napalkov shook his head. He had little doubt that a female clerk in his section had actually hand-written the manifest but he was taking the penalties for the error himself to shield her. In his eyes, that was enough to buy him clemency. "It is enough. You may return to your duties. As for you, Comrade Superintendent, you are demoted to dispatcher. Your deputy will take over your position. Perform your new duties with greater diligence than you have done to date or we will meet again. Now clean that mess on your carpet up before you leave."

A few minutes later, Napalkov walked up to the desk occupied by a female clerk. She flinched when she saw him and had obviously heard what had just happened to her superior. It was obvious she feared that her culpability in the error had become know. Her eyes were fastened on two of Napalkov's assistants who were carrying a large box. A third removed the antique typewriter from her desk. Then, they unpacked the box and put a brand new IBM Electromatic 01 typewriter in its place. "Tovarish Irina Gregorskaya, the Americans have sent us electric typewriters like this as part of their aid to us. They have even included an adaptor for our power and a handbook in Russian. And a large box of spare ribbons. Use it well, tovarish and let there be no more errors such as we have encountered today. Remember, it is the duty of CheKa to punish error but also to aid those who truly labor on behalf of the Rodina."

The woman nodded, excitement at her new typewriter overcoming her fear of the Chekists. Napalkov watched her exploring the new machine with interest. *Beria's NKVD treated people with unremitting brutality and the result people became numb and brutality lost its power to bring about the desired results. Now, we in CheKa follow severity with kindness and generosity. The contrast between the two emphasizes both. One drives home the lessons but the other gives people cause for hope and belief in the fundamental justice of our cause. Irina Gregorskaya will remember the blow that put section leader to the floor as just punishment for his carelessness but also remember that it was our help that will make sure it need not happen to her.*

Watching her tentatively typing a new manifest and being delighted by the clarity of the results, Napalkov had another thought. *People think that Lend-Lease just supplies us with tanks and aircraft but I suspect the office equipment that allows us to administer our work with greater efficiency will be just as important as weapons and supplies.*

Headquarters, 40th Bombardment Wing, Kolosovka.

"The 92nd, 303rd and 306th Bombardment Groups will be declared operational soon." General Ira Eaker sounded pleased with the results of six months hard work. The three new groups would mean that the 40th Bombardment Wing would have a total of six groups available. A total of 432 Flying Fortresses. There were two more groups scheduled to come out later in the year to bring the total up to 576. At that point, the 40th would be split into two Bombardment Wings, each with four groups.

LeMay grunted in acknowledgement of the news. "We should put them on to some west bank targets first. Giving the crews a few milk-run missions makes a big difference when we try something more ambitious. We still frozen at eight groups?"

"We are. In fact, B-17 production is already beginning to wind down. Boeing will be rolling the last ones out in August. The 2nd, 7th and 58th Bombardment Groups are already starting to convert to the B-29." Eaker hesitated for a moment. He was prohibited from flying combat missions – or indeed any missions that might expose him to risk. The reason for the prohibition was simple. He was one of the very few men who knew the secret of what lay beyond the B-29. "Of course, they haven't got any aircraft yet. The first service test YB-29 only flew last week. Boeing still hasn't cured the engine fire problem."

"We can't take the B-17s in deep." LeMay sounded cautious. "Not yet at any rate. We're surrounding them with a cloud of Thunderbolts but the kraut fighters are getting the measure of us."

Eaker sighed slightly. The quality of the German fighter force had come as an ugly shock. Their pilots were skilled and showed the benefit from years of experience and that was measured by the steady toll of B-17s and P-47s that were being lost. "I know, Curt. Germany will have to wait for the B-29. The fact is, you're out here to find what the problems with strategic bombing are and to find solutions to them. You've solved the accuracy issue and your new formations are allowing the Fortresses to fight off fighters the way we always thought they would. Everything you find out here is going straight back to the groups forming up on the B-29s. So, where do we go from here?"

"Moskva." LeMay had the answer ready and waiting. "There are two marshalling yards in Moskva, both vital for the supply of forces in the Kazan area. One of those marshalling yards is also the site of the Kolomna locomotive factory. They produce most of the rolling stock available to the krauts. Take out those two yards and the Kolomna factory and we can permanently damage their whole logistic infrastructure. There's a political side to it as well. The Russians want us to hit Moskva, so they can claim the city is still in contention, that the German occupation of the city isn't accepted by them.

"I thought you didn't want to send the B-17s deep. Moskva is almost three hundred miles behind the lines."

"If we swing north and cross the Volga at Nizhny Novogorod, it's only 230 miles. That's in range and the P-47s can cover us all the way to the target. We can send the three new groups by a northern route. If they cross the Volga at Kostromo, they'll only be 140 miles from Moskva. The first force will come in from due east. Half an hour later, the second group will cross the Volga and come in to Moskva from the north east. If they even see the second group, they'll assume its new arrivals making a milk-run against a target on the west bank. The krauts will see the first group, assume that's the main attack and send their fighters south. The newbies in the second group will just have flak to worry about. "

Eaker thought the plan over. "Escort?"

"First group, Zemke's 56th. Second group, Blakeslee's 4th."

"They're both new groups. What about the 356th? They've got missions under their belt." Eaker was entranced by the scheme unfolding before him.

"We cut them loose. You said it; they're our most experienced group. One of their pilots wrote a memo, suggesting some fighters go on Free Chase ahead of the bombers. Try and break up the kraut fighter attacks before they get close to our B-17s. What he says makes sense. The Thunderbolts running Free Chase will force the kraut fighters up early; by the time the Fortresses arrive, the Huns will be low on gas and ammunition. The Thunderbolts can chase them back to their base to make sure they stay out of the battle."

Eaker carefully thought over the proposal. "Plan it, Curt. Make sure everything is timed properly. One addition. There's a radar station south west of Marfino. We'll send the 391st to hit it. From medium altitude of course; after the disaster a few days back, there's no way we're sending the Marauders in low again. With two groups of Fortresses and one of Marauders in play plus the 356th on Free Chase, the krauts will have a hell of a time working out what is going on."

Site of German River Defense Battery, Sengiley, Volga River.

"Check each pit carefully. The krauts booby-trap everything." Custer repeated the caution to his reconnaissance team as they spread out across the deserted earthworks. The pits were surrounded by high sandbagged walls that protected the guns within from blast and fragments that were the inevitable result of counter-battery fire.

"Gunny, who's Mrs. Laf?"

The whisper came from one of the recon Marines who was searching round a gun-pit for trash. He had a piece of paper in his hand, to Custer's experienced eye it looked like something that had been torn off as an ammunition box had been opened. It read 'SK C/28 in Mrs Laf.'

"Calm down, McBride. There's no lonely German woman around here waiting for your attentions. That's Heerese for 15 cm Schiffskanone C/28 in Mörserlafette. Or, as normal people would say, a 5.9 inch naval gun on a land mounting for use by the army.

"Those poor bastards on the gunboats thought they were taking on 88s when really they were up against six-inchers? These are cruiser guns. What the hell are they doing here?"

"88s are bad enough. Those five-nines are long-range guns. They were probably here to shoot at targets over on the other side of the river and got moved to somewhere more important. Must have been high-priority, moving those guns isn't easy. I'd say that was behind the light display Jack and his pirates reported last time they were down this way. Krauts put on a display for them to convince them the guns were still here." Custer nodded to himself.

Slowly, the recon team moved across the site of the artillery battery, picking up scraps of paper and other items left behind by the departed gunners. Eventually, McBride straightened his back. "When I volunteered for this lot, nobody told me I would be collecting garbage at night."

Custer could sympathize. He was an experienced frogman and had more hours underwater wearing an aqualung than most pilots had flying. Other members of his unit were veterans also in a wide variety of specialties. They had all volunteered for this assignment under the impression that they would be going on to beaches prior to an amphibious landing, to clear mines and booby-traps and to scope out the enemy defenses. Only, the expected war in the Pacific hadn't started. So, his unit and others like it had been retasked for reconnaissance and infiltration work along the Volga. As McBride had said, collecting garbage seemed like a menial tasks for the specialists who made up his team.

"Gunny, does that look suspicious, or does it look suspicious?"

'It' was what appeared to be a full bottle of schnapps on the ground near one of the gun pits. It was the sort of sight that might easily temp a soldier, particularly one from the perennially thirsty Russian Army. Custer was also of the strong opinion that picking up said bottle would be a sovereign cure for drunkenness. In fact, his only question was whether the bottle would detonate the booby trap under it by means of a pressure switch or a pull-wire.

McBride had knelt, very carefully, beside the bottle. "We can't leave this here. Some poor civvie is likely to pick it up."

Custer agreed. In his opinion, leaving booby traps like this around was unforgivable. Booby-trapping weapons and equipment that would attract soldiers was one thing; doing the same to things civilians would find irresistible was quite another. On a previous incursion, they'd entered a small village that the Germans had passed through. There had been a child's toy, a rag doll, left in the ruins. It had been booby-trapped. They'd disarmed that one as well.

"OK, Gunny, I know this one. They've wedged the bottle between two sticks so it won't roll and there's an egg grenade under it. Lift up the bottle, the lever goes free and it goes off. I've heard the krauts do an instant, no-delay fuse for these." McBride looked up to find he was on his own. It was a lonely feeling but the German egg-grenade had a lethal radius of around thirty feet. It didn't make sense for anybody else to be in that radius. He slid his fingers down, carefully feeling for the level on the grenade. When he had it secured, he removed the bottle and rolled it away. Then, he slid a new pin into the grenade to safe it. As soon as he gave the all-clear sign, the rest of the team reappeared.

"Welcome back," he said ironically.

With prizes that were undoubtedly valuable intelligence material but still looked amazingly like bags of trash, Custer took his men back to the waiting gunboat. On the way, McBride took the opportunity to throw the safed grenade into the Volga. He was reasonably confident that it would sink into the soft mud and be harmless but also that Kennedy would not thank him for bringing a booby-trapped hand grenade back on board his command. The Force Recon Unit spotted the sailors securing the landing site long before they were aware the Marines were approaching but that didn't really worry them. They were used to slipping in and out unseen.

Kazan Thunderbolts

A few minutes later he was on the bridge of PR-73, reporting back to Kennedy while the banks of the Volga rolled past in the darkness. Kennedy nodded slowly as the tale unfolded. "What was in the bottle?"

"We broke it. It was water; may have been poisoned. Whatever it was, it won't hurt anybody now."

The words seemed strangely at odds with the weirdly peaceful situation. The blacked-out banks of the Volga seemed to complement the gentle purr of the engines under their feet. "How do you manage to slip in and out so easily? Don't the krauts have garrisons along the banks?"

Custer shook his head. "They don't have enough men. If they put out a couple of men as a picket, the partisans will kill them or we'll stage a raid and take them. If the observation team is large enough to deter a partisan attack, they'll nickel and dime their manpower to death and they won't have enough strength anywhere to resist a push. So, they group their forces in battalion or even regimental cantonments and then run patrols between them. Usually motorized patrols; half-tracks and armored cars. As long as we aren't where they are, everything is just peachy. Most of the time we slip in, do our thing and slip out again before the krauts arrive. This time I thought the krauts might leave an ambush team at the artillery site but they hadn't. Not enough men again I guess. A lot of the time, we probe around those cantonments, see where they are, what units are stationed there, what their defenses are like. People say the krauts hold the west bank but they don't, not really. It's more like no-man's land."

"Pod Valley coming up Skipper." Ed Mauer looked up from the chart table. "The inlet should be dead ahead."

Kennedy scanned the black mass of the bank with his binoculars. One of the small streams that fed into the Volga ended in a small inlet, wide and deep enough to allow a gunboat to close the shore and be shielded by the banks yet have enough room to maneuver. There was a flicker of light on the downstream side of the inlet that resolved itself into a series of red flashes. There was a pause, and then the sequence was repeated in yellow. On the conning station over the bridge, Thom flashed the return sequence, blue light, then green. Contact was made. That didn't necessarily mean all was safe. Recognition signals could be compromised and when they were, the result was a vicious short-range action. "All hands, General Quarters. All hands, General Quarters. Man your battle stations. Prepare to engage shore targets"

For Custer and his men, it was their third trip that night in the rubber rafts that lined PR-73's bridge. The water in the inlet was smooth and the bows of the rafts touched the shore almost before the occupants were aware than the riverbank was close. The Marines disembarked and spread out to form a defense perimeter. In doing so, they realized that their landing point was in the midst of a dozen or so partisans. Without having to discuss the matter either with each other or with the other team, both groups quickly decided that it was fortunate they were on the same side.

"Tovarish Sergeant." One of the partisans moved forward to greet the new arrivals. "Welcome to the west bank."

"Privet bratishka. We have some supplies for you. Radios, explosives, rations. The sailors are unloading them from the rafts now."

"Gunny, if you have D-ration chocolate, these guys will really appreciate it. Sergeant Schultz, flight engineer, Flying Fortress." Schultz stepped forward. He was disheveled and obviously exhausted from the march out of occupied territory. But, Custer saw there was something else as well. A blend of anger, shock and outrage that had sunk deep into his soul.

"Welcome back Schultz. You're the first bail-out we've picked up."

"That doesn't surprise me. Gunny, you've got to get word back if we don't make it. The fascists are killing our guys who bail out. I saw it myself. Three guys from the 35th, Niksa, Rosenblum and McDermott bailed out of DE-G on the Penza raid and got picked up by the Hitlerites. The bastards killed all three of them and burned their bodies. I got their dog-tags after the fascists left. You got to tell the brass about this."

"Damn." Custer was shocked. He'd heard, of course, about the way the Germans behaved towards Russians but he'd assumed they'd treat Americans differently. Thinking about it, he realized how mistaken that belief had been. This was the Russian Front. "Schultz, you can tell the brass yourself. We'll get you home. Now, we're supposed to be picking three people up?"

"There's a girl with us, Gunny. Bravest woman I've ever met but she's had a real bad time. Worst kind of time a woman can have I guess. She needs to be treated like eggs but the things she knows are . . . . well. I guess they're priceless. I don't know who the third is."

Schultz turned around and waved. The girl came out of the trees and joined him. Custer looked at her quickly, noting that she was standing close enough to Schultz to get support from him but far enough away to avoid contact. She was looking at the Marines with an odd expression on her face, a mixture of deep-rooted fear and something else. Something much deeper and more primeval than just fear. Custer thought it was hatred at first but understood that was wrong. Then, he realized it was dread. She was looking at his men with the same horrified dread as somebody who had woken up and found a poisonous snake in their beds. That was when he grasped what Schultz had been trying to tell him.

"Schultz, take the lady to the gunboat in the first raft. When you get there, ask the Captain, he's Lieutenant Kennedy, to get every bar of D Ration on the ship ashore. Now, the third pick-up?"

"That's me I think." The voice had a British accent which surprised Custer completely. "Name's Fleming. I was in British naval intelligence but I'm doing other things now. Pleased to see you, Gunny."

"Right, Sir." Custer was in no doubt the Brit was an officer. Somehow it showed. "Please get on the second raft and we'll get you aboard."

The banks of the Volga were still black and silent and a blacked-out PR-73 still slipped through the current almost soundlessly but this time her bows were turned north and she was heading home with her precious cargo. She had already passed Island Ten where the crew had made mental salutes to Brusilov and his Marines still holding doggedly on to the outpost. Soon, they would be taking the turn that would lead them past Sengiley and up the river towards Ulyanov'sk and then home. Kennedy's navigation plot had them reaching their base at Staraya Mayna just before dawn. It was a very different mission from their previous journey down to this part of the river; then they had got back to base with their magazines almost empty and paint peeling off overheated gun barrels. This time around, they hadn't fired a shot. Nor had the Marines they were carrying.

That brought Kennedy's mind to the next order of business. "Tovarish Partisan. We have very limited living accommodation on PR-73 There is a small compartment in the aft end of the bridge you may use if you wish to have some privacy. Nobody will disturb you there."

"I made you these." Ed Mauer had heard about the problem with this woman and had tried to help. He held out a pair of triangular wooden wedges he had carved from damage control timbers. "If you slip them under the door, it will make sure nobody can open it. As the skipper said, nobody will disturb you but the boys thought you might be more comfortable with these in place."

She nodded and tried to smile her thanks. Mauer had purposely used non-naval terminology when speaking to her and she had understood both his words and the thought behind them. It was an act of kindness that had penetrated some of the grief and shame that still fogged her mind. "Spasibo, tovarishch moryak. This was a thought of great kindness but I feel I am safe here with you and your crew."

That was something that touched Mauer deeply. "Thank you. I'm Ed Mauer."

"Tatiana Timofeevna Pavlova."

In the background, Kennedy relaxed. At least one potential problem had just evaporated. He turned to the Englishman standing in the tiny wardroom. "Since we're exchanging names now, I'm John Fitzgerald Kennedy; everybody calls me Jack or JFK. What's a British naval officer doing on the west bank of the Volga or is that a rude question?"

'I'm Fleming, Ian Fleming. My conspiratorial name is Atticus. We're trying to start a partisan movement in Britain but it's not as easy as we made it sound three years ago. We've got a resistance movement all right, but getting it to do something is proving much harder than we realized. And it doesn't help that the Huns are already infiltrating our ranks. So, the Russians offered us help and advice and my brother asked me to come out here and start to learn where we were going wrong. I've been with the Partisans for the last three months and so far, the answer is 'everything.' We thought we knew it all. We'd read all the books and got advice from so-called experts but none of it amounted to a damn. We're starting from scratch."

"Like us on the gunboats." Kennedy was much more curious than he let on. "We're having to learn the job from scratch as well. What did you do before the war?"

"I was a writer, a journalist but I always wanted to write adventure novels. You know, I think I'll make that girl the heroine of one. Anyway, I joined the Navy in 1939 and was in Canada when That Man betrayed us. What really worries me is the possible installation of Axis radar and long-range reconnaissance equipment in the U.K. Kondors and Ju-90s based there could do a lot to contest control of the Atlantic. Making those bases insecure is going to be a resistance priority. That's why I've been in Russia since February 1942, getting the Russians to help us plan the guerrilla campaign and sabotage in Britain. The joint operation between us and the Russians is called Goldeneye by the way. A few weeks ago, I met a friend of your father's, William J. Donovan? He's from the something called the Office of Strategic Services."

"I've heard of him." Kennedy's voice was terse, a fact that seemed to amuse Fleming. He was well aware that there was no love lost between Kennedy father and son.

"Well, he doesn't really have a clear moral definition of right and wrong."

"Nor does my father. That's why he's in the U.S. and I'm out here. At least out on the Volga, I'm doing right by the good guys."

"If you don't mind me saying so, Jack, I didn't mean that as a criticism. In a resistance movement, right and wrong get very blurry, very fast. But, I fear your father is typical of many Washington politicians. I don't think they've realized yet that this war is going end with them as the single dominant power and they are totally unprepared to rule the world that is soon going to become theirs."

Kennedy thought about that. Despite his dislike for his father, he had finely-tuned political antennae all of his own and they were telling him a rather different story. His political instincts were telling him that, underneath the usual bluster and politicking that distinguished Washington, there was some very cold-blooded calculation going on over the shape of the post-war world to come.

"I wouldn't be too sure of that, Ian. Our people tend to grow into their jobs. The next generation of American leaders won't be coming from Washington, but from here, on the Volga. They're being prepared for whatever the post-war world needs right now. The leaders in Washington represent the 1930s and the 1920s, decades of peace. The 1940s and 1950s will be led by the men who were tempered by war, here."

"I hope so. When I get back to Perm, my first job will be to expand the Goldeneye operation to include the United States so we can ensure smooth coordinated operations. That will need an assessment of the facilities and equipment for the gathering and evaluating of intelligence from all across Europe. Donovan wants one centralized, coordinated intelligence system to monitor and control the stepped up surveillance and sabotage activities by the Allies to support the military actions taking place here in Russia." Without actually saying anything, Fleming had made his distaste for that opinion quite clear.

And that has my father's opinions written all over it. Kennedy thought over what he had just heard. *If there is one centralized intelligence service, then there is one – and one only – source of information. So, whoever controls that source of information also controls the policies that are decided on the basis of that information. If this scheme goes ahead, that will be Kennedy, Joseph and Donovan, William. Not a happy thought. I can't see the Russians liking that either.*

That was when an anvil dropped on Kennedy's head. *So that's why Napalkov was so keen to make my acquaintance. He and his bosses want this idea stopped and are looking for allies.*

305th Bombardment Group, Bolshaya Tarlovka Airfield, Russia.

Officially, the 305th was supposed to have 96 crews for its 72 B-17Es. Reality being reality and this being the Volga Front, it had 72 crews for its aircraft. That meant it had 72 navigators and 72 aircraft commanders. Put another way, the 305th had four squadrons each of eighteen aircraft. Each squadron was divided into three six-aircraft flights. A combat box also contained three flights of six aircraft even though those flights might not come from the same squadrons. At most, three of the four squadrons would fly on a given mission although LeMay had already modified the lowest of the combat boxes to contain an additional three aircraft in order to strengthen its gun power. The Germans had already spotted that the lowest combat boxes were the least well defended and concentrated on them.

Over the last few missions, Colonel LeMay had carefully selected the twelve best navigators, the twelve best bombardiers and the twelve best aircraft commanders, shuffling the crews slightly so that they were teamed together. Tonight, he had explained why. They were now the lead crews for their flights. Each combat box bombed as a single unit, dropping when the bombardier of the lead aircraft did so. So, he had selected the best key personnel he had to lead the boxes in.

"You're the lead crews. That means each of you gets a one-step promotion as long as you are a lead crew. Screw up, don't perform, you all go back to your permanent rank. Another crew will be appointed as a lead crew to take your place."

LeMay hesitated for a second before continuing. "We have received the planned list of targets for the next quarter. So far, we have received twenty four sets of target folders. Each of you crews will receive folders for four targets. Study them every moment you get. Navigators, work out the best in and out routes, be familiar with every river, every road, every railway, every landmark that could help you reach your targets. Bombardiers, you will study the pictures of the targets until you can see them in your sleep. If you think the pictures of the targets aren't good enough, report it immediately and we'll get better ones. That's what the F-5s are here for. When the target in your folder comes up, you will be the lead crew for your formation. On our raids so far, at least a third of the combat boxes are hitting the wrong targets. That must change. If bombardiers hit the wrong target in future, your entire crew immediately loses lead crew status. So study those target folders. Is everybody clear?"

"What happens if hitting the wrong target isn't our fault?"

LeMay stared at the bombardier coldly, already wondering if looking for excuses had revealed the man's selection had been an error. "I have neither the time nor the inclination to distinguish between the incompetent and the merely unfortunate."

That chilled the air. After a few seconds, one of the Navigators asked another question, one LeMay found more to his taste. "Do we get bragging rights when we flatten the target?"

"Absence of punishment is usually the proper reward for adequate performance. Drawing attention to excellent performance serves a useful instructional function and I will have no issues with that."

LeMay left his new lead crews hard at work studying their target folders. There had been objections to allowing them to see the planned targets and the Russians had nearly had hysterics at the breech of operational security it represented. But, he had patiently pointed out, anybody who had a map and crude operational details on the B-17 and B-26 could work out the likely targets. When they were going to be hit and in which order was entirely another matter. LeMay didn't know that himself; nor did anybody else. He suspected though that events would have a major impact on plans. There was an odd electricity in the air. LeMay could sense it and knew that something big was about to happen.

Walking back to his quarters took him past one of the B-17 hangars. On a whim, he went in to see how the ground crews were performing. There were two B-17Es in the hangar. One was having some minor damage to its tail patched. The other seemed undamaged but there was a distinct smell of fresh paint in the air.

"Colonel, Sir!" The First Sergeant snapped out a salute, his greeting alerting the other airmen in the hangar to LeMay's presence.

LeMay returned the salute gravely. "Carry on, Sergeant. These two aircraft need much work?"

"No, Sir. LG-J caught some flak but nothing serious. We were just doing a paint job on LG-K. Coffee, Sir? It's fresh."

LeMay nodded, also noting that the Sergeant was subtly keeping him away from LG-K. He was well aware that the First Shirt was responsible for the morale, welfare, and conduct of all the enlisted members in a squadron and was the chief adviser to the squadron commander concerning the enlisted force. So, there was something about LG-K the First Shirt did not want him to see. He started to walk around the aircraft and then stopped dead. Painted on the side of the nose was a full-length portrait of a young woman in a state of extreme undress. Under that startling portrait was the name *Sally B.*

"Sergeant, is the job done . . . . oh. Colonel, Sir." The young captain stopped dead and froze into a near-perfect salute.

LeMay returned it and stared at the artwork. His wife was an accomplished painter and he recognized high-quality art when he saw it. This one showed a touch of the Vargas style. He also recognized the aircraft commander's voice. "Captain Barker . What would your wife say about that painting?"

"I think she would be flattered, Sir. You see, that is my wife. Look." Barker got a picture out of his wallet. It was obviously the same woman as in the painting, only the photograph showed her demurely dressed in her Sunday best outfit. Then he sighed. "I'll have it removed, Sir."

"Army Air Force regulations do not forbid the painting of names or artwork on combat aircraft where the markings serve an operational purpose. That includes maintenance of morale. That being the case, I see no cause for complaint. You may keep your nose art Captain." LeMay had an odd feeling that he was looking at the solution to a problem that he wasn't yet aware of. "First Sergeant. I wish to speak to you."

The Sergeant arrived bearing the promised cup of coffee. It was indeed fresh and LeMay enjoyed it, allowing the tension to build while he drank it down. "Sergeant, how many of the aircraft have names?"

"All of them, Sir. LG-K is the first one to wear hers openly though."

LeMay nodded. If nothing else, the artwork would indeed be good for morale. "Spread word that the painting of names and artwork on the aircraft is viewed with favor. Between ourselves, make sure any of the enlisted men who do the paintings are properly rewarded for their efforts."

"Sir, yes, SIR."

"Colonel, we've got a message from Wing." Colonel Holland looked highly disturbed. "All hell is breaking loose over there. We need to get there right away."

Headquarters, 40th Bombardment Wing, Kolosovka.

If German bombers had been operating this far behind the lines, they would have found the concentration of leadership at Kolosovka irresistible. There were staff cars lining up to discharge their occupants before the cars were driven away to dispersal points.

"Curt. Long time no see. How are your bombers doing in Russia?" Colonel Hubert Zemke had also just arrived by staff car.

"Blowing up the Krauts standing on bits of it. Getting better at it too. How are your Jugs?"

"The 56th Fighter Group was declared operational two days ago. Fly it right and the Jug is a hell of a weapon. Can dive and roll like nothing else. Want us to ride shotgun on your 305th?"

"Mostly we run with the 356th, another Jug outfit. But, my boys will be right pleased to see yours alongside sometime. Yours too, Don." LeMay had just seen Colonel Donald Blakeslee turn up from the 4th Fighter Group.

"Do you know what this is about, Curt? I got called out of my cockpit to come here." That caused a laugh amongst the assembled group commanders who knew Blakeslee was notorious for flying every chance he got. His pilots were cut from the same cloth.

Kazan Thunderbolts

Despite the recent arrival of the 4th, it was recognized as the most experienced fighter group in the area. Most of its pilots were already veterans. Some had flown with the Russians before the official arrival of the American Expeditionary force, serving with either Russian fighter regiments equipped with Curtis P-40s 'as instructors' or with the first American "Volunteer" squadrons to arrive in Russia. Those squadrons had established a legendary reputation during the ferocious battle around Moskva. The press had christened them the *Flying Bears* in parallel with the *Flying Tigers*, the volunteer fighter unit in China. All of the 4th's pilots spoke nearly fluent Russian and most had seen the horrors of the German invasion at first hand.

"No. I see all then fighter group commanders are here though. Frank James from the 55th is back there. His P-38s are just about operational now." Eaker chose not to mention the problems the 55th were having keeping their P-38s in service. The twin-engined fighters were temperamental and didn't like the primitive conditions in Russia at all.

"And Harry, George. His 31st has P-39s." That made the group think. In six weeks, the U.S. fighter force in Russia had gone from one group of P-39s to a total of six groups and more than 600 aircraft. Half of them were Thunderbolts. All the Colonels gathered outside the 40th Bomb Wing headquarters knew that this was just the start. The stream of aircraft pouring into Russia would soon become a torrent.

Inside the headquarters building, the Commanders of the bomb groups were already in their places. Four B-17 group commanders, two B-26 group leaders, representing more than 450 heavy and medium bombers. It shook LeMay to realize there were already more than a thousand American combat aircraft in Russia. The land force might have been taking its own sweet time about building up but the air power developing over the Volga was building up with remarkable speed.

One thing that surprised him was that a large area in the center of the briefing theater had been curtained off and the seating had been re-arranged so that the audience surrounded that area. Once everybody was seated, the curtains pulled back to reveal an operations room. To LeMay's eyes it was more or less any operations room, a large table on the ground with counters on it to represent aircraft formations and a bank of telephones on one side. There was something wrong with it though and it took him a few seconds to realize what it was. The operations table was arranged so that it looked at the Volga from west to east. That's when the realization sank in. *This is a reconstruction of a German fighter command station. Made by somebody who has been inside one.*

His impression was reinforced when a group of personnel entered the reconstruction and took positions within it. LeMay recognized some of the women as being Women's Army Corps or Women's Air Service Personnel but they were wearing German Luftwaffe uniforms. So were the men who took position by the telephones.

Only one person in the reconstruction was not in German uniform. A young woman wearing the uniform of a Major in the Russian Army. She seemed to be in charge of the display and LeMay guessed she had to be the one who had been inside a German air control station. How she had managed it was something he failed to understand.

In front of him, the demonstration had started. The table operators started placing markers on the map as sightings of allied aircraft were reported. It quickly became apparent that the situation was the Penza mission a couple of weeks earlier.

Suddenly everything stopped and a single man was picked out by an overhead spotlight. The Russian major stepped forward and her voice echoed around the stage. "This man is the Jagdfliegerführer. He is the regional commander for the German day-fighter control organization. All available incoming information about Allied air movements – radio intercepts, reports from radar stations, visual sightings goes to him. He will prepare a concise assessment of the incoming American raid which will then be relayed to the various units under his control."

The spotlight went out and the simulation continued as the 'Jagdfliegerführer' assessed the information and made his decisions. As he started to issue them, the re-enactment stopped again with a group of men sitting at the back of the stage being picked out by the spotlights. Once again, the Russian major started a commentary. "These men are the Jägerleitoffiziers from the Luftwaffe signals service and are in touch with the various Geschwader involved. Ideally, the Geschwader commander will decide which of his Gruppen would attempt to engage any fighter escort and which would go for the bombers. Note that the control by Jagdfliegerführer is restricted to ordering take-off times and giving the fighter units initial courses and heights to help them reach the probable combat area. Once a unit has taken off, its airborne commander – usually the Gruppe commander – takes all tactical decisions."

LeMay's eyes followed the marker representing his bomber formations, watching as the fighter controllers on the telephones alerted the bases and steered the fighters in on the approaching bomber stream. Every so often the action would stop and the spotlights would pick out one or more of the actors playing the German staff. The Russian major would explain who they were and what they were doing. Then the reenactment would continue. The sight told him that the careful plotting of evasive routings intended to conceal the target of the bombers had been a waste of time. The German system was such that it simply didn't matter. The fighters were steered to the bomber formations regardless of their course.

There was also a tote board that showed how many bombers had been shot down and by what. To LeMay's amusement it seemed that the Germans were over-claiming B-17 kills almost as enthusiastically as his gunners had been claiming excessive numbers of fighters. According to the final tote board, the defenses had claimed twelve B-17s and ten P-47s against real losses of three and two. Of course, the same tote board showed that the Germans had lost seven fighters against the American claims of 54.

Eventually, the re-enactment ended with the bombers withdrawing to the East. General Eaker left the audience and paused for a moment before speaking. "The re-enactment you have just seen was prepared by Major Tatiana Timofeevna Pavlova of the Partisans. At great personal risk and with great personal sacrifice, she infiltrated the fighter control station by impersonating a Luftwaffe female auxiliary and spent three weeks memorizing the operations and techniques in use around her."

Eaker paused because Zemke had jumped to his feet and started applauding. He was joined by every group commander, the re-enactors and the other senior officer in the room. The thunder of applause rolled around the operations room, echoing off the walls and sending Pavlova bright red with embarrassment.

Eventually, Eaker held up his hand. "Quite, gentlemen. I am pleased to inform you that Major Tatiana Timofeevna has, with the agreement of our Chief of Staff, General Marshall and the Russian Commander of the Second Volga Front, Marshal Koniev, been awarded the Distinguished Service Cross for her extraordinary heroism in connection with military operations against the enemy. She has also received the Order of Alexander Nevsky for her acts of great personal courage and sustained heroism.

"Now, before we move to a question-and-answer session, we have another report from the West Bank to hear and this one is much more disturbing."

A Sergeant stepped forward and took Eaker's place by the microphone. "I am Sergeant Charles Schultz, previously Flight Engineer on the B-17 DE-G of the 35th. DE-G was one of three Fortresses shot down on the Penza mission. I, and three other crew members, Airman First Class Alfred Niksa, Airman First Class Edward Rosenblum and Airman First Class Frank McDermott managed to bail out. I was contacted by the Partisans very quickly and taken to safety. Niksa, Rosenblum and McDermott were all taken prisoner by the German Army. All three were murdered, shot, and their bodies burned. I managed to collect their dog tags after the fascists left.

"According to the Partisans, the fascists kill all shot-down aircrew except the ones who are taken for interrogation. Those are killed later after they have been drained of any information they have."

There was a stunned silence around the room. Eventually, it was Zemke who stood up. "There have been rumors in the Jug units for some days now that the Germans have been shooting our pilots who bail out of crippled aircraft. We haven't been able to prove these accounts but from what Schultz has just told us, I think we can regard them as plausible."

Blakeslee was nodding in agreement. "Ever since this war started, the fascists have been murdering shot-down aircrew and machine-gunning pilots while they hang in their parachutes. The Bears used to cover bailed-out pilots while they dropped. Sometimes, they'd land and pick up a bail-out. Something we should think about. We need to get our bail-outs home."

"Contact the Partisans as soon as you can." Tatiana Timofeevna was earnest. "We will be out there looking for you. We can get you into cover and take you to the river where you can be picked up."

"We should really come and get them, not leave your partisans to carry all the burden." Blakeslee was thinking hard, drawing on all the experience the pilots of the 4th had accumulated. "The risk to your people and ours grows exponentially the longer the pilots and crews are down on the east bank. And we need to get support to the Partisans."

"We are supporting the Partisans with supplies and weapons right now. We will be increasing that effort. As to going in and getting them, that will be considered. I heard about the Bears doing pick-ups and wondered why. Now we know. If you can do a pick-up without unduly risking another aircraft, do so. That will be a matter of judgment for the pilots in question."

"We don't leave our people behind, Sir. Not where those murdering fascists are concerned." Blakeslee's words met with thunderous applause.

General Eaker looked grim. "I must admit that I never believed aviators would treat other airmen in such a scandalous manner. If any of you gain additional definitive evidence of pilots and crews being murdered after bailing out or being captured on the ground, you are to report it immediately. Now, Major Tatiana Timofeevna speaks fluent English as does Sergeant Schultz despite him coming from Pennsylvania. Both will answer any questions you may have. Rank will not be considered a relevant factor in this discussion."

The discussion got lively as the assembled commanders tried to dig out information that was relevant to their groups. Eventually, as the questioning started to slow down, LeMay got to his feet. "Tovarish Major. How do the fascists recognize which groups are inexperienced and concentrate on them?"

"By listening to your radio communications. Your aircraft refer to each other by squadron code. The fascists have at least one major spy ring operating on the west bank and they know which codes are associated with which units and when those units arrived. You should stop using those codes. They are a security breach. The fascists also know when your aircraft take off and land the same way. Our security agents are working on this problem and we will solve it."

That was when all the pieces fell into place. "Gentlemen, ladies. In the 305th, all our crews have named their aircraft. I have given permission for the crews to paint those names on their machines. If we use the same names as our call-signs, they will be meaningless to those outside the units."

It was Zemke who added the final thought. "And some of the names our crews will come up with are damned sure to drive the krauts pure batshit crazy."

CHAPTER SIX: HARSH LESSONS

B Company, 802nd TD Battalion, 83rd Infantry Division, Klimovo, Chuvashskaya Bridgehead.

Normally, the prevailing wind over the Volga blew from east to west. Usually, in summer, it was a dry, cool wind that broke the sultry heat of the summer and made the lives of the people who lived along the river more tolerable. Sometimes, though, the winds changed and there would be a wind from the west. It would be a hot, wet wind that brought rain and thunderstorms. There was a westerly wind blowing tonight that had caused heavy clouds to form in the sky over the Chuvashskaya. The sun about to rise over the east bank of the Volga (which wasn't a given; there were places where the sun rose over the west bank such were the vagaries of geography) was already reflecting off the bottom of the clouds, filling them with an angry red glow. It was the traditional soldier's warning of bad weather to come. Sergeant Perry knew that, he knew why the old traditional verse was true and he took heed of the warning.

Only, it wasn't the threat of bad weather to come that was worrying him. Some of the concern came from the troops that made up his unit. They were National Guardsmen, mostly unmarried men from eighteen to thirty-five years of age. Two-thirds were high school graduates; about one-third had some education beyond high school. Quite a few men joined the regiment in 1941 to avoid the draft. The pre-draft volunteers looked down on these late-comers. Come early or come late, each man had each received one dollar for attending a training session. It was not a princely sum but a dollar was a dollar in the depths of the Depression and it had been important in attracting members.

They met every Monday evening and practiced close-order drill and the manual of arms. They occasionally performed small-unit maneuvers on a football field or in a city square. Once a year, their armory would be inspected by a regular Army officer. That annual inspection had been linked to a military ball where officers and men of the Guard had worn their uniforms proudly. It had been the highlight of the social season and, perhaps more importantly, the unofficial start of the courting season.

Kazan Thunderbolts

Perry knew that the men in his unit were not ready for war. He was even astute enough to suspect that his own readiness was questionable. His men had many deficiencies in basic soldiering skills and shortages of weapons and equipment were still evident. The fact that his tank destroyer outfit was equipped with the massive and bulky 90mm guns was an example of that. They were officially dual-purpose guns and their anti-tank ammunition made them deadly tank killers. Only, they were tall and had been hell to emplace. They simply didn't belong here. That was symptomatic of a lot that was wrong.

The 83rd Infantry was still not proficient in the doctrine, weapons and equipment, and skills required for the modern warfare of the 1940s. They had no real instinctive understanding of the accelerated tempo and increased distances of the battlefield. Most crucially, they did not have the necessary speed of reaction so well understood by their adversaries.

Yet, for all that, what was worrying Perry most deeply was something unique to this night. The wind was blowing from the west and it was bringing sound from the German side of the lines with it. All night, that sound had been dominated by the rumble of engines. The Germans were on the move and that couldn't be good.

Over to the east, the dark red light reflecting off the clouds started to lighten as a patch of yellowish-orange formed on the horizon. Almost by instinct, Perry glanced at his wristwatch. It was 0329, the exact moment when sunrise was starting when the first hint of daylight started to dispel the darkness and signal the beginning of a new day on the west bank of the Volga. The howl overhead told Perry exactly what sort of day it was going to be.

"INBOUND!" His scream of warning was drowned out by the shattering explosions that slashed across the positions held by the 331st Regimental Combat Team. The big 90mm dual-purpose gun so carefully emplaced by Private Eugene Searle and his team was the first to go. The German artillery fire was deadly accurate and the ruined building seemed to dissolve under the impacts, pieces of the old brick and stone rubble hurled through the air. Mixed in with them were parts of the gun that had caused them so much hard labor. The crash of the shells exploding was a higher-pitched noise than Perry had expected and it seemed to echo longer than he had anticipated but it was hard to tell for each successive salvo was arriving before the sounds of the others had died away. Then it was over and the position his unit had dug was destroyed.

There was a brief pause, then the guns switched their fire to the treeline where the second and third 90mm guns had been concealed. With a sick feeling on his gut, Perry realized the Germans knew where every single one of the anti-tank guns had been emplaced. He had very little doubt that the methodical destruction of the guns was taking place long the entire length of the front covered by the 802nd.

The momentary quiet resulting from the shifting of the heavy artillery fire highlighted the sounds of fighting to the front where the 331st's infantry teams were dug in to screen the front. The battering of the heavy guns was replaced by the popping of mortar rounds exploding amongst the foxholes. The lack of noise confused Perry for a few seconds until he saw the billowing white clouds of the smokescreen splitting up the American positions. Helplessly, he watched while German assault teams moved into the attack.

At some point in the night, sappers had cut the wire and lifted the handful of mines that had been placed amongst the tangled threads. The German infantry slid through the area that had once been wired and mined with the slick expertise of long practice. They were moving in small teams, each group isolating and pinning down the foxholes in front of them with machine gun and light mortar fire while the other teams closed in. From his position near the wrecked anti-tank gun positions, Perry watched the battles around each of the foxholes as the defenders tried to keep the Germans away from them. They were fought hard, but were slowly worn down by the bursts of rifle and machine gun fire and the thumps of mortars. Eventually, each isolated foxhole was the target of German grenadiers hurling their stick grenades into the pits. There would be a series of sharp explosions, perhaps a scream or a sob and then the rattle of submachine guns as the German infantry swarmed over the positions.

The center of the American line was collapsing faster than Perry could have thought possible. As each foxhole was taken, the advancing Germans used it as a forward position to bring down more machine gun and mortar fire on the ones in front and on either side. To Perry's eyes, the rain that was beginning to fall was almost a mercy in that it masked out the scene that was taking place in the infantry front line.

"Damn, it would have to rain today." Lieutenant Grisham slid into position beside Perry. "That kills off any chance we had of getting air support. Where are the krauts?"

"Working their way through our infantry right now. We'd better get out of here, Sir."

Grisham thought about that. "Our orders are to hold on here. But that was when we had our guns. We've lost all four of them. The krauts knew just where they were and dropped 88s right on top of them. We're not infantry, there's nothing we can do here now."

"I was watching the krauts. They know exactly how our defenses are laid out. They're just picking off our positions one by one." As if to emphasize the point Perry was making, the sounds of gun fire and grenades exploding was getting closer.

Kazan Thunderbolts

Despite that, Perry's words had told Grisham what he had to do. "Well, we won't be there when they get to us. Get the gun crews together. Order them to grab their rifles and we'll fall back towards Klimovo. There's a ridge about 200 yards back along there. We'll set up a new defense line along that ridge and bounce the krauts as they assault our old positions. This rain will give us some of the cover we need."

"Sir. Searle, Hill, Curtis, Martin get the crews together, we're moving back."

Perry wasn't certain whether it was the rain or thickening resistance amongst what was left of the infantry positions that bought the time for the anti-tank gun crews to disengage and move back to the ridge. The rain was getting heavier, coming down hard enough to sting exposed skin. The ground was already beginning to soften under the men's feet by the time they reached the shallow ridgeline and that aided them in making a few shallow scrapes to give them a vestige of cover. The ridgeline wasn't much of a ridge at all, barely fifteen feet with slopes so gentle they were hardly noticeable.

Over on the American right was a small village, Koshmash-Toysi. Perry guessed that it would be the rallying point for more of the 331st retreating from the fiasco of the attempt to defend the front line. The sounds of firing and grenade explosions had ceased but the men on the ridge could hear the Germans shouting at each other as they worked their way forward.

Then the noise changed again as the mortars and artillery resumed their fire, the shells striking the positions abandoned just a few minutes before. Perry glanced along the thin skirmish line that had formed on the ridge behind those positions. It was easy to pick out the men who had grown up in rural areas; they had picked positions where they were shielded by rocks or given some cover by bushes. The urban kids had no such appreciation of the terrain. Most of the men had the new, small M1 carbine. It was light and handy, especially for troops whose primary responsibility did not include fighting enemy infantry. One or two men, again, Perry noted it was mostly the country boys, had "acquired" Garands. Perry and the other Sergeants all had Thompson guns. *At this point*, Perry thought, *I would sell my soul for a Ma Deuce.* Then he looked nervously around in case one had miraculously appeared.

To his relief, one hadn't although the German infantry were beginning to emerge out of the driving rain. They were still in the small assault groups that had sliced through the infantry screen but they were slightly disorganized. Perry guessed that the abandonment of the original defenses had disjointed their plans and they were now having to feel their way forward instead of knowing what lay in front of them. It was a small change but a significant one.

The first assault group to emerge from the rain was met by a blast of semi-automatic fire from the carbines and the handful of rifles. The men were bowled over by the fire, some obviously being hit several times by the rapid succession of bullets. Perry had grave doubts about the killing power of the small cartridges fired by the carbines but they did have the advantage that the men were able to carry a lot of them.

More groups of Germans were leaving the wall of mist and rain but the fate of the first few to do so had alerted them to the new defense line. They went to ground and opened fire on the ridgeline, obviously making a very accurate guess of where the fire was coming from. The machine guns were joined by the thump of infantry mortars delivering their rounds into the American positions.

Perry fired a burst from his Thompson, hoping that it would be mistaken for a machine gun and hold the attackers up a little. Whether it did or not he couldn't tell. Another sound, much more ominous than the rattle of gunfire, seized his attention. It was a roar, a low rumbling roar mixed up with a squeaking and squealing that told of a large tracked vehicle approaching fast.

A sleek, low-slung tracked vehicle slowly emerged from the rain. It had the lower hull of a tank but instead of a turret it had a raised superstructure with a short, stubby gun. Perry recognized it instantly. A StuH-42; a StuG-III assault gun with the usual 75mm gun replaced by a 105mm howitzer.

The gun edged forward a little, then halted before firing a shot at the ridgeline. The machinegun and mortar fire directed at the ridge had done little damage that Perry could see but the StuH was an entirely different matter. The commander had obviously seen where the greatest volume of fire was coming from and the 105mm, fired over open sights at almost point blank range, was deadly accurate. The scream of the inbound shell ended in a shockingly loud explosion that silenced much of the fire coming from the American positions.

The StuH started to edge forward, the German infantry around it moving with it to take advantage of the cover it offered. The American riflemen on the ridge tried to engage them but their fire simply attracted the attention of the assault gun crew and resulted in the delivery of another one of the lethal 105mm rounds. Perry knew that the men up on the ridge were doomed. They might – might – have held the line against infantry but infantry with armor in close support was too much. Already, the thin skirmish line was breaking up as the men in it fell back to avoid the shells from the assault gun.

Once again the situation changed as a result of a single appearance. Private Eugene Searle had moved forward, rather than back, and was now in the cover offered by a rocky outcrop. He had with him something new; a weapon that had only been issued to a few units of the 83rd Infantry over the last few days. Nobody quite knew how to use it properly but Searle had found a manual and quickly read it. He had actually thought it was a comedy book by Bob Burns but found it was an operating manual for the anti-tank rocket launcher M1A1, better known as the Bazooka. Still, it had been the only thing around to read. Now he both found the information useful and slightly regretted knowing it.

It was a measure of how much the visibility had been degraded by the rain and early mist that Searle was less than 30 yards from the StuH yet remained unseen by either it or by its accompanying infantry. He took careful aim, remembering the manual's advice and picking a spot low down on the vehicle's side where its armor would be thinnest. He had positioned himself carefully, exactly according to the picture in the manual, so that no part of his body was exposed to the bazooka's backblast. Then, he took a breath, held it and squeezed the trigger.

A streak of orange fire shot out and raced across the short distance to the assault gun. It hit above the third and fourth road wheels, just below the return rollers. The explosion seemed to engulf the side of the vehicle. Searle was disappointed; the book had led him to expect the destruction of the armored vehicle, not just an explosion on its side. Then he saw that the whole engine compartment was a mass of orange flames and that the fire was spreading rapidly.

Before he could properly absorb that, there was a massive explosion and a jet of white fire shot upwards from the assault gun's main hatch. In its midst was the blackened figure of a man, his arms and legs flailing as he was blown through the air by the mass of white hot gas. More explosions racked the stricken assault gun, tearing it apart and sending fragments of steel whirling through the air. *Dear God, did I just do that?* Awed by his own success, Searle decided discretion was the better part of valor and made a tactical withdrawal to the rest of the American force.

Perry watched the German infantry disengaging and fading back into the driving rain. "Well done, kid. I guess you're our official tank-killer now. You done better than those damned great guns we hauled up here."

"Sergeant, we've got to pull out." Grisham spoke very urgently. "The krauts are in Koshmash-Toysi and there are reports their tanks are closing in on Timyashi and Khormali. We have to retreat to Klimovo right now or we'll be cut off."

Barely half the men who had taken position on the ridge were left alive to retreat. As they did so, hunched against the driving rain, Perry reflected that the top brass probably called this a tactical withdrawal. Gresham had called it a retreat. To Perry, it looked unpleasantly like the start of a rout.

Kazan Thunderbolts

Headquarters, 746th Tank Battalion, North of Lenino, Chuvashskaya Bridgehead.

"Just what the hell does this mean?" Lieutenant Colonel William E Long held the order from General Fredendall as if it was infected with something virulent. "Let me read this damned thing to you. 'Move your command, i.e., the walking boys, pop guns, Baker's outfit and the outfit which is the reverse of Baker's outfit and the big fellows to L, which is due south of where you are now, as soon as possible. Have your boys report to the Russian gentleman whose name begins with J at a place which begins with D which is five grid squares to the left of K.' Can anybody make any sense of this? Any sense at all?"

"Vetrenyy Freddie has really outdone himself this time." Major Barndollar shook his head. "Let's take this piece by piece. Walking boys must be infantry and I suppose pop guns must mean artillery. What the hell is Baker's Outfit? We don't have an outfit commanded by any kind of Baker."

"Perhaps he means the regimental cooks?" Corporal Larson was the battalion clerk. In the American Army, the company and battalion clerks were allowed an unprecedented level of liberty and Larson thought the time had come to indulge in a little judicious goading. He was sadly disappointed at the results.

"Makes as much sense as anything else." Barndollar frowned again. "But 'the outfit which is the reverse of Baker's outfit'. I'm foxed."

"Gravediggers?" Larson tried again.

Barndollar was silent then his face brightened. "I think you've got it. Assume the big fellows are the tanks, this could read. 'Take your command including infantry, artillery, armor and all support troops to L. L is obviously Lenino. Well done Larson. We'll make a general of you yet."

"That leaves us with the rest of the text. Report to the Russian gentleman whose name begins with J at a place called D? Any offers?"

"If the J means Jerries and the D means Deutschland, it could be 'attack the Germans in occupied Russia.' That would make sense of the last bit. 'Five grid squares to the left of K.' Assume he's holding his map north at the top, to the left means west. So, could he be ordering us to move the whole unit to Lenino and attack the Germans advancing on Khormaly from the west?"

Long sighed. "Given what we know of the situation, that makes sense. God knows if it's what Vetrenyy Freddie actually meant. And we don't have our whole unit here anyway. He's detached my light tank company and a platoon from a medium company and sent them God knows where. We don't have any infantry or artillery. That's been detached as well."

Long sighed again. One of Fredendall's worst habits was sending orders directly to battalions and companies without following the chain of command or advising intermediate commanders of what was happening. Even platoon commanders had been bemused to receive orders directly from AEF Headquarters. Especially when those orders contradicted the ones they had received from their company commanders.

"OK, we'll go with our interpretation of what we got. One thing about orders nobody can understand, it gives us a chance to respond to the situation as we see it. The 331st Infantry is retreating along the road to Klimovo and the armor advancing on Khormaly could cut them off completely. If they move fast enough, they could put the whole 83rd Division in the bag. Hitting them in the flank from Lenino will slow them down and let the infantry get clear. Do it, Bill and we'll just hope that's what Vetrenyy Freddie wanted."

746th Tank Battalion, South of Lenino, Chuvashskaya Bridgehead

For all the prominence given to Lenino in the orders they had received, it was hard for the tankers in the 746th to take the hamlet seriously. It had about a dozen small houses arranged along a single road. As far as any of the Americans were could see, the place was devoid of any serious tactical importance. Timyashi, ahead of them, was a different matter. It was a major road junction with half a dozen minor lanes converging on it. It also formed the stopper in a large gap in the dense woods that ran north and south of the town. As far as Long could see, the Germans were advancing along the two major roads in the area, the Klimovo Road that led slightly north of east and the Tugaevo Road that led southeast. The problem was that as the two roads diverged and the forward troops of the 83rd retreated along them, a gap was opening between the two. Long had little doubt that the Germans would push their armor through that gap. Doing so would mean they would have to pass through Timyashi.

In fact, they were already doing just that. The rain had slackened significantly during the battalion's advance to Lenino and the visibility had improved enough to give the tanks a good field of fire. It wasn't going to last; the clouds on the horizon were an ominous dead steely gray, but the 746th had the weather working for it for an hour or so.

It was not working for a German reconnaissance section that had been caught by the brief improvement in weather conditions. The section of three half tracks was caught out in the open less than four hundred yards from where one of the American tank companies had formed up. The first 75mm shell hit just in front of the half-track, probably because the panic-stricken driver had slammed the brakes on. A second shot landed just short, rocking the vehicle from side to side. A third shot hit the side of the driver's cab and plowed in the engine compartment. The whole front end of the vehicle disintegrated into a cloud of flying fragments propelled by a rolling cloud of black and red smoke. The second half-track was hit two or three times and burst into flames while the third was stopped in its tracks by a near-miss that impacted inches in front of its nose. Before the driver could get it moving again, another tank put an explosive 75mm round into its side and the light vehicle collapsed into wreckage.

One full company of M4 Sherman tanks started to move forward while the other full company and the under strength unit remained on overwatch. The objective of the advance was a series of dried-out gullies to the south of a small outcrop of trees in the middle of the fields surrounding Timyashi. At least, the gullies had been dried out before the rain had started. Now, there was free-flowing water in them and the banks had turned to a glutinous mud that caused two of the Shermans to bog down. The sound of their diesel engines being revved in an effort to get free of the slime clogging their tracks drowned out the vicious flat crack from the patch of trees. A third Sherman in that platoon started belching brown and black smoke and the crew bailed out. The anti-tank gun hidden in the trees fired again and a fourth Sherman in the luckless platoon caught the round neatly in the side. Again, the tank started to burn and the crew started to bail. This time though, only two of them made it out before the ammunition exploded, sending a jet of pure white fire skywards from the turret.

The crew of the last mobile tank in the platoon had finally worked out that they were facing an anti-tank gun position concealed in the trees. The lesson was reinforced by another shot from the gun that hit their forward armor at a shallow angle and bounced off. The tank started to back up immediately while the 75mm gun in its turret fired on the estimated position of the enemy gun. Whether the shell had the desired effect or the tank had moved out of the gun's arc of fire remained unknown to the tank crew. Once they had backed up a hundred yards or so, the tank stopped; its crew uncertain over what to do next. That was when a second anti-tank gun in the trees put a shot straight through its frontal armor.

Looking at the destruction of his southernmost platoon from the overwatch position, Long was trying to work out what to do next. His original plan, to seize the gullies and use them to hit Timyashi from two sides, wasn't working out. It was obvious that the Germans had fortified the patch of trees with anti-tank guns and an infantry screen. One possibility was to use his tanks to support an infantry assault on that position so he could recover the two bogged-down vehicles and outflank Timyashi. The problem was, he didn't have any infantry in support. Another possibility was to use artillery support to pound on the trees until the Germans abandoned the position. Only, he didn't have any artillery supporting him either. What he did have were the 75mm guns on his Sherman tanks. Those guns were descendents of the old French Soixante Quinze artillery piece and were quite respectable field guns in their own right. The Sherman had, after all, been designed with supporting infantry and engaging strongpoints in mind.

"All overwatch units, load explosive. Open fire on the woods, bearing 175, range 400 yards."

Twenty nine Shermans opened fire almost simultaneously on the woods that had concealed the German forward position. A split second later, the woods vanished in a rolling barrage of explosions that tore the trees and undergrowth into shreds. Secondary explosions marked the positions of the anti-tank guns that had stalled the advance of Able Company.

"Charlie Company, stay here on overwatch. Baker Company, advance by bounds. Able Company, hold positions and support us as we advance. And recover those two stranded tanks."

"Already on it Colonel." Long looked at his radio with surprise. His realized his engineer section had, on its own initiative moved two armored recovery vehicles up to the bogged-down Shermans and were pulling them out of the mud. The engineer half-tracks were picking up the survivors of the three knocked out tanks.

"Well done."

Baker Company and the battalion headquarters was already moving up fast on Timyashi. The Shermans were plowing through a field of corn as high as a tank and could see little of what was happening around them unless they ran across one of the cuttings or roads that serviced the fields. "Watch it. Kraut tanks up ahead."

The message had come from Able Company. Their overwatch position was on a mild rise and it had allowed them to look over the corn and they had caught a glimpse of a German tank advancing towards the fast-moving American tanks. Long saw the angular shape of a Mark Four tank up ahead of them, indistinct in the rain and partially masked by the standing corn.

"Stop. Gun sight – 30 degrees right, Mark Four tank at range of 400 yards."

Long snapped the order out, realizing that the two tanks were on converging courses and would run into each other unless somebody fired first. Long heard the whine of the turret traversing as the gunner pointed the gun to the right as the Sherman advanced towards the next cutting. He could see that the German Panzer Four had spotted the Sherman as well and was also swinging its turret to bear on the target that had suddenly loomed out of the rain and mist. Long was using the panoramic periscope to watch the German tank moving into the optimum line of fire. Sure enough, it came into view right where it was supposed to emerge, just off to the right. Long remembered the advice he had received from the Russian tankers. *The moment you see a Hitlerite tank, you must fire at him. At that very moment! The only way to stop him killing you is for you to kill him first. If you allow the fascist to fire first your only hope is that he misses. He probably will not but if he does, if you are that lucky, you had better shoot fast because his next shot won't miss. Such tough guys are the Hitlerites. Give them the slightest chance and they will kill you.*

Long gave the order to his gunner: "The tank, over there, take it out!"

And nothing happened even though at least half of the Mark Four's hull was already out. Long realized he couldn't wait any longer. Seconds had already passed and the long barrel on the German tank was shortening as it swung to bear. Then, he saw his gunner sitting, staring at the German tank as if hypnotized by the sight. Long seized him by the scruff of his neck and threw him out of the way. Quite how he managed it in the confines of the Sherman was something he would never be sure about. The gunner landed on the ready rounds rack and rolled to the bottom of the turret. Long was already at the gun sight, the gun was already trained on the target and an armor piercing round was up the spout. He fired it at the tank's side, sending it straight through the armor, just underneath the turret. The enemy tank burst into flames, but nobody bailed out. Long looked around, seeing the admiration on the faces of his crew. They knew that if it hadn't been for him, the enemy tank would have fired at them first and they would have all been dead. The gunner, Nicholas Drew, was still crouched on the floor of the tank, white and shaking.

The Shermans of Baker Company continued moving forward until they had seized a road that ran through a cutting between the fields. It gave them good cover and was a perfect place to hold, south of Timyashi and level with the western outskirts of the small town. Even better it was on a slight rise, allowing them to look out over the cornfields. It was an excellent overwatch point so Baker Company covered the below-strength Able Company while it dashed forward.

That was when Long saw the tanks to his left and to the right catch fire. He had no idea where the shots had come from and, to make matters worse, the rain was beginning to close in again. There were more German tanks out there, he knew that, and he also realized that he had become a primary target for enemy fire. There was a sudden, ear-bending clang from outside that told him his tank had just taken a direct hit. The impact caused sparks to flash around the turret, then a bright light picked out the smoke and dust particles as ghostly bluish specks floating in the air. Long thought the tank had blown up and he was dead but that impression only lasted a split second. Then he assumed that the shock of the impact had blown the main turret hatch open.

"Drew, get that damned hatch shut!"

"We can't, Sir." As loader, Private Colin Green was the lowliest member of the crew. He also was in the worst position to escape. Nevertheless, he rose to the occasion. "The hatch is gone, blown off."

A quick inspection confirmed that. An armor piercing shot had hit one of the eyelets holding the hatch in place, sending the hatch spiraling into the air. Before Long could appreciate the luck break, a German armor piercing shot smacked straight into the Sherman's frontal armor. The tank rocked on its suspension but didn't catch fire, at least not right away. Long blessed the Russian tankers who had been so emphatic about the advantages of diesel engines over gasoline. Shermans had been built with both types, but after the American planners had finished listening to the Russians, the diesel-engined versions had been sent to Russia while the gasoline-powered tanks were kept in the States for training or sent to the Pacific and the Philippines.

That decision, taken at rarified levels of industrial planning, bought Long a few seconds to get a handle on the situation. The solid shot had pierced the armor near the radio operator-machine gunner, killing him with metal fragments, and wounding the driver. It had then passed low down through the hull, underneath the gun loader's seat. Ironically, if Drew had stuck to his post, he would have survived but curling up on the floor of the tank had put him right in the path of the shot.

"Out! Now!" Long was already on the way out with Green close behind him. The two men pulled the driver out of his compartment and then took cover in the cutting. Mortar rounds were exploding around them. "We got to get out of here. Mortars mean the kraut infantry is closing in."

"Don't leave me behind." The driver was pleading.

With a name like Solomon Yablonski, I can see why Long thought. *If the krauts get him, he's dead.* "Of course we're not leaving you behind. Do you have any idea how difficult it will be to get a new driver?"

And that is the God's own truth. The driver plays a critical role in fighting a tank. An experienced driver means salvation for the whole crew. He can create relatively secure positions by hiding behind cover or maximizing gun power by selecting flat ground. Yablonski had boasted that he would never be killed, because he would position the tank in such way that a shell wouldn't hit where he was sitting. I'm not parting with him.

The brief respite from the rain had ended and the downfall was even heavier than it had been early in the morning. Visibility had dropped down to a few dozen yards and it was pointless to try and carry on the fight. Long guessed that Major Barndollar would be consolidating the ground they had gained and setting up some form of defense. Exactly how he would do that without infantry support was a good question. *I am beginning to get the feeling that we are not doing this armored warfare thing quite right*

When Long saw that his battalion had lost twelve of the 46 tanks they had started the battle with, his pessimistic reflection seemed an understatement.

Airfield 108, Privolzhskiy na Volga,

"We will not be flying in this weather." Koldunov did not sound overly disappointed at the fact his squadron was grounded by the heavy rain.

"I wonder of the Americans will be grounded as well?" Lilya Litvyak sounded more curious than anything else. The Russian pilots had already noticed that the large Thunderbolts were much better instrumented than the Russian fighters and their pilots were more comfortable flying in bad weather than the Yak pilots. Also, the Thunderbolts had radios and the Russians were painfully aware of the tactical advantages that conferred.

"Not if they can help it." Koldunov sounded grim and a touch envious. The Russians had an in-bred sense of caution, one based on the experience that to try something and fail could be personally disastrous. In case of doubt, it was best only to do thing one knew would work since failure was such a risky concept. The Americans had a very different attitude. Faced with a dangerously risky venture, they'd dive in and give it their best shot. If it worked, they'd pass the knowledge on how they'd done it to everybody else. If it didn't, they'd work out what had gone wrong and try again. And they would keep going until they had succeeded.

"I have been watching how our American bratishka fly." Litvyak was thoughtful. "Their tactics are crude and elementary. Their teamwork is good but they are novices at air combat. They rely on their speed and gunpower to win their victories for them. But, when they finally gain enough experience, the survivors will be formidable indeed."

"Tovarish Lilya, they are formidable now. Take our friend Misha. Do you know how many hours he had in his Thunderbolt before he came to Russia? Four hundred! And before that he spent a hundred and fifty hours in basic training and two hundred in advanced! And this for a man who had soloed *before* he joined the Army. He must have almost a thousand hours of flight time. Five times as much as a fascist pilot has logged and ten times more than us. I had fifteen hours in Yaks before I joined the front. Did you have so much more?"

Litvyak shook her head. "I've been flying since I was 14 and went solo at 15. Then I graduated from the Kherson military flying school. I had three years experience and about 400 hours when the fascists invaded us. I tried to volunteer but the Army wouldn't take women who had less than a thousand hours. So, I went to a different recruiting office and faked that answer. But I had 15 hours in a Yak-1 before I came to the front.

"Fifteen hours – and Misha had four hundred. I have also watched the Americans fly. They know their aircraft and are supremely confident with them. They push those Thunderbolts to the limits of their performance and often a little bit beyond. There is not one part of the envelope of those aircraft they do not feel comfortable in or use in every way they can imagine. Their Thunderbolts have faults, that is certain. They are slow to accelerate and their rate of climb is leisurely. But those crude and elementary tactics you describe are those needed to play to the Thunderbolt's strengths and minimize its weaknesses. Tovarish Misha, are you grounded?"

"Nah." Edwards sounded flustered and worried by the sudden events of the early morning. "The fascists have hit all along the line in the Chuvashskaya. They've kicked in the whole front position held by the 83rd. The rain will stop us giving direct support for several hours so the bombers are going to hit the supply lines behind the weather front. The Forts are going to Moskva, to smash up the marshalling yards there. We'll be flying Free Chase ahead of them."

"Free Chase Bratishka?" Litvyak was impressed. To her, assignment to the Free Chase mission was to be recognized as a true fighter pilot. The simple fact that Edwards and his fellow pilots had been entrusted with such a mission made her take them seriously at last.

"Free Chase Tovarish Lilya. We'll be trying to catch the fascist fighters before they get close to our bombers. This time the weather is working for us. We've just been briefed that the skies over Moskva are clear but we'll have cloud closing down the fascist fighter bases most of the way in."

"Watch your rear, bratishka." Litvyak turned slightly to face Edwards. "The fascists have a habit of doing the unexpected."

"We've been told there are Wild Boar units in the region we'll be going over. Focke-Wulfs with all-weather flight instrumentation and beefed up armament. They're supposed to be night fighters but they haven't got radar. They'll be able to operate in this rain though but they're a bit more sluggish than the normal 190s. We're hoping we'll get at them when they climb out of the clouds."

"I wish you every success, tovarish." Litvyak actually sounded sincere. "Who will be with the bombers?"

"The 4th. Don Blakeslee's outfit. Their first escort mission in Thunderbolts but all the pilots are veterans. The 4th was built up from the *Flying Bears*, the three volunteer squadrons that fought around Moskva last year. I think they flew P-40s then. The Forts will be in good hands."

Thunderbolt FiveByFive *Over Polyanki on the Volga, Moskva Front.*

The first enemy and the one Edwards truly feared was vertigo. The flight instructors had described it as a state of temporary spatial confusion resulting from misleading information sent to the brain by various sensory organs. To the pilot, it more often meant "Which way is up?" The most difficult adjustment that the trainee pilots had to make was to understand that, under certain conditions, their senses could be lethally misleading. Seated on an unstable moving platform at altitude with their vision cut off from the earth, horizon, or other fixed references and exposed to angular accelerations or centrifugal forces indistinguishable from gravity, they were susceptible to innumerable confusing, disorienting experiences.

Nobody had taken vertigo seriously; after all, it couldn't happen to them, until an overcast day when one of the class was climbing through the clouds in a P-44A. He had emerged from those clouds in a vertical dive that ended only when the P-44 smashed into the ground. Nobody ever actually worked out what had happened but it appeared that the pilot had been in a standard rate 3 degree/second turn when increasing airspeed in the turn had fooled him into thinking he was in a level dive. He had pulled back on the control column, tightening the turn and caused the P-44 to stall out and dive into the ground.

That evening the instructors had used the accident to hammer the lesson home. *Without instrument training, the chances of maintaining normal aircraft attitude in limited visibility are non-existent. In a level turn, you may think you are in straight flight or climbing. In a coordinated, banked turn you may believe yourself to be in straight and level flight. In recovery from a level turn, you may feel as though you are diving. In a left turn - if you suddenly bend your head forward - you may think you are falling to the left. The only things you can trust are your instruments. Read your instruments! They are the best insurance you will ever have.*

Edwards had listened carefully and disciplined himself into flying by his needle and ball when in clouds. He was doing that now as his P-47 clawed its way upwards through the rainclouds. He mostly ignored the sights outside the cockpit and refused to recognize the information that his ears and sense of balance were forcing on him. He kept a minimum level of his attention outside his aircraft as a guard against another Thunderbolt looming out of the clouds. It only took a moment's inattention, a movement of the head perhaps, to cause a pilot to drift to one side, into the path of another aircraft.

It was that modicum of awareness, that part of his attention that was not devoted to his instruments, which alerted Edwards to the slow brightening of the sky around him. Seconds later, his Thunderbolt punched out of the cloud and he could see the sea of dark gray clouds apparently reaching to the horizon. After the dismal gray of the clouds, the bright sunshine hurt his eyes, making him blink and turn his head.

Alongside him, the Thunderbolts were emerging from the clouds, their formation ragged from the long climb in zero visibility but they had all made it. One Thunderbolt was well out of position, so far off to the left that he seemed to be a formation all of his own. Edwards guessed that the pilot had allowed the torque of the R-2800 to deceive him and had started a slow left turn in the clouds. It was lucky he had been on the left of the formation to start with.

FivebyFive looked different from her earlier missions. The identity letters on the aft fuselage had been painted out and replaced by much smaller ones that were only readable close up. . Instead, the engine cowlings on the 356th P-47s had all been painted bright red with small blue diamonds. The rudders had been painted red as well. The orders to paint visually distinctive markings on the engine cowlings and rudders had come right from the top and been marked top priority. With the order had come a "suggestion" that pilots could paint their aircraft's name on the nose and *any* artwork they felt appropriate.

The night before that order had arrived, Edwards had been in the squadron craps game and rolled a hard ten. The two fives had been staring at him but he had made his point with the first roll. A few minutes later, his roll came up again with another hard ten. That time it had taken him two rolls to make his point. The third time he saw the double-five of a hard ten staring at him, he guessed somebody, somewhere was trying to tell him something. That time it had taken him three rolls to make his point and, by next morning, PI-H had become *FivebyFive* with a pair of dice showing two fives painted on the nose.

The errant Thunderbolt had rejoined the formation, the pilot looking decidedly sheepish even through his flying helmet, oxygen mask and goggles. It was *Jeanie*, Bill Anderson's aircraft. Edwards stopped himself for a second. Orders had said that aircraft were now to be called by their names, not by the pilot's name or the squadron identity letters. That was taking a bit of getting used to. "Stay beside me on the left, *Jeanie*."

"Roger, *Fivebyfive*. Sorry about the drift."

Sixteen P-47s of the 360th Squadron, 356th Fighter Group were heading north. The plan was for them to rendezvous with the Fortresses at Khakhaly and then sweep west ahead of them for as far as they could. A little to the east, the 359th Squadron would be doing the same with 16 of its Thunderbolts while to the west, the 361st would also be sweeping ahead. Together, the plan was for the three squadrons to clear a path almost sixty miles wide right through the enemy defenses.

The issue was fuel consumption. The R-2800s guzzled gasoline at a prodigious rate and fuel management was going to be essential. The 356th had just received an ordnance modification that installed wing hardpoints capable of carrying either a 108 gallon drop tank or a 500 pound bomb. Engineers and technicians from the Republic plant at Evansville, Indiana had arrived in C-54s and made the installation before flying on to the other Thunderbolt groups. Today, the aircraft had taken off on internal fuel but switched over to their wing tanks before their wheels had fully retracted. Now they would have to drain those tanks of every last vestige of fuel before dropping them.

Edwards took the first step by leaning out the fuel-air mixture in his engine to the point where the engine was on the verge of stalling out but not quite doing so. Of course, leaning out the mixture made the cylinder head temperature rise since manual mixture controls were designed to put out a rich mixture so that excess fuel would help cool the engine at high power. The trick was to accept the rise and carry on leaning out the engine at constant altitude. This would cause the temperature to peak out and then decrease as the excess air took over the cooling job. Edwards had found, by trial and error, that the most efficient mixture in terms of horsepower as a function of fuel flow was well down on the lean or "air cooling" side of the power vs. mixture curve. To his great surprise, he found out that most of the other pilots in his class had discovered the same thing.

There was one last trick in his arsenal of fuel-stretching strategies. Down in one corner of his cockpit was a small gauge that recorded fuel pressure. When his drop tanks were on the verge of being empty, the needle would flick to zero for a fraction of a second before returning to its normal position. A second or two later, it would flick to zero again and that time stay there. The drop tanks would be empty and his engine would cut out. Switching fuel to internal on the first flick would prevent that and allow him to drop his tanks with minimum fuel wastage.

Up ahead, Edwards could see the milky white sheet formed by the closely-packed formations of B-17s. Above them was the long, curving trails of the escorting P-47s from the 4th Fighter Group. That gave him something of a pang; a bit like leaving a pet dog in somebody else's care. Up to now it had always been the 356th Group who had shepherded the bombers to and from their targets. He was a bit reassured when some of the 4th Group Thunderbolts detached to investigate the arriving aircraft. 4th Group also had new recognition markings; they had painted the noses of their Thunderbolts a checkered red and white with the whole vertical stabilizer painted bright red. Reassured at the sight of the 356th P-47s, they turned back and resumed their places around the bombers.

And that left the 356th to start their Free Chase mission. If the 4th had failed to make their rendezvous and the bombers were unescorted, then the 356th would have gone to Plan B and taken over escort duties. There was a Plan

C in case the 356th hadn't made the rendezvous. The 55th Fighter Group, assigned to run a sweep along the Volga in its P-38s would have been diverted to cover the B-17s. There was even a Plan D in case the P-38s couldn't make the rendezvous. That saw the B-17s fighting their way through to the target alone. There was a growing confidence that the tightly-packed formations of B-17s could do just that if need be.

The formations of the 360th were already turning on to their west-bound course that would, if held long enough, take them to Moskva. There were a lot of American groups up today. A second formation of B-17s was heading to Moskva from the northeast, escorted by the 56th Fighter Group. Both B-26 groups were up also, one tasked to hit a radar station, the other the Luftwaffe airfield at Balakhna. How they were going to hit either target through the cloud cover foxed Edwards but he knew it really didn't matter. The B-26s were essentially decoys, intended to confuse the tactical picture and help to overwhelm the German control system with multiple criss-crossing flight paths. Combined with the bad weather holding most of the German fighters down, the planners were hoping that the Flying Fortresses would have a head start over the defenses.

Gunboat Squadron GunRon 5 Headquarters, Staraya Mayna, Volga River.

"Gentlemen, we have to move fast. Our outpost on Island Ten near Mordovo has reported that a group of kraut riverine craft are moving upriver. The force consists of two S-boats, one identified as S-38, the other as S-67, and two small S-boats, LS-9 and LS-12. The force also includes a converted river steamer, we believe the krauts have armed with a pair of 88s. There are also six MFP landing craft carrying, we believe, the best part of a battalion of SS assault troops. Watch those MFPs, boys, they've got a short-barrelled 75 as well as two machine guns." Commander Henry Farrow looked around at his audience.

"We've been caught flat-footed, the other gunboats are heading north to support the troops on the Chuvashskaya. The krauts hit us early this morning and have broken through on a twelve mile front. Last we heard, they've advanced at least six miles and the 83rd Infantry is falling back with heavy losses. We think this invasion force is intended to land behind their positions and cut the whole Chuvashskaya bridgehead off. The fighting at Ulyanov'sk has probably screwed their plans up and we're going to try and intercept them there.

"Good news is that the rain will prevent any kraut air operations and your radar will give you a terrific edge. Also, the rain is making the river run faster than usual so the current is in our favor. That gives us a little time to get ready. Kennedy, you will be in charge. Take PR-73 to intercept them along with Kauffman in the 84 boat, McHale in 109 and Jennings in 57. Two Russian gunboats, BK-116 and BK-119 will be going with you. Get under way in an hour."

Kennedy strode out on to the stage in the briefing room. "Right, this is how we'll do it. PR-73 will lead with the two Russian boats on either side. Andrei Egorovich and Sergei Petrovich, the battle will start at short range just south of the bridge. Your boats with their fast-firing 45mms will be crucial in establishing fire supremacy. It will be for the three of us to get rid of the S-boats. Jennings, you'll be next in line. Your Huckins boat will take on that river steamer. Use your firepower to kill him fast. Kauffman and McHale, you two get loose in those landing craft and sink them. They're SS troops on board and you all know what they've been doing to our shot-down airmen. Time for a little pay-back. McHale, if all else fails, get those MFP crews in a craps game and *win* the damned things."

A roar of laughter went up around the briefing room. His rounded face beaming brightly, McHale got to his feet and took a bow from the audience. "Can we use our own dice, skipper?"

"Of course." Kennedy chuckled. "Never thought you'd do otherwise."

"Thanks skipper. I think."

"Skipper, those MFPs carry at most a couple of hundred men or two or three armored vehicles. That means they've got a battalion with minimal transport at best. Is that so much to be worried about?" Jennings looked confused.

"I can answer that." Farrow looked at the room. "Our information is that the landing force is a battalion supported by three Stug guns. The battalion is one of the detached elements of an SS division, SS Jagddivision 502. Jagddivision 502 is the elite special warfare unit of the entire Hitlerite military establishment. It was Jagddivision 502 units that seized the airfields in southern England prior to the fascist assault there a year ago. They also undertook special warfare missions in the Middle East and during Barbarossa. These men are the absolute best the Hitlerites have. If they get ashore as an organized unit, there will be hell to pay. Just like there was in England."

That caused the room to go silent. Everybody was remembering the news a year ago of how small SS special warfare teams, disguised as Luftwaffe police detachments, had seized a string of airfields across south east England. They'd held those airfields long enough for the Heer and SS to fly in air landing units that had secured their hold on those airfields and turned them into airheads for an assault on the ports nearby. By dawn, they had taken enough of those ports to bring in regular infantry and tank forces and the invasion proper had started. Military experts in the War Department had described it as a superbly-planned and brilliantly-executed operation that had also been granted far more than its fair share of good luck. Ever since then, SS Jagddivision 502 had been carefully watched and its destruction was a high priority.

Kennedy looked at the commanders of the gunboat fleet. "I think it's about time that SS Jagddivision 502 got taken down a peg or five don't you? The Marines down on Island Ten showed they could be beaten. They're not supermen, just good at their job."

Suddenly he stopped and thought. His casual comment had given him an idea. "We've got two or three Marine Corps recon sections here. We better take them along as well. This could get bloody. Lenny, find Gunnery Sergeant Custer and invite him to join us. Henry, can you clear it with the commander of the Marine detachment here?"

Farrow nodded. "No problem. The Marines have been itching to create a little mayhem."

That was when Kennedy had another thought. "Another thing Henry. SS Jagddivision 502 always specialized in attacking key targets that had a value out of all proportion to their size. A simple flanking attack doesn't seem their style somehow. Using the river they could attack more or less anywhere from Ulyanov'sk to Kazan itself. In fact, hitting the crossing points at Kazan would be more in their style."

"Or Vetrenyy Freddie's fortress at Speedy Valley." Farrow was thoughtful.

"I doubt it Henry. SS Jagddivision 502 isn't on our side." Kennedy's quip was received with applause by most of the Americans present and stunned disbelief by the Russians who still hadn't got used to the American irreverence where their senior commanders were concerned.

Then Kennedy looked at the map again. "You know, there is one key target on the Volga that does stand out. Here, Starry May. We've been raising hell along the Volga for months now. This is exactly the sort of target 502 would look on as a suitable objective. A battalion of assault troops hitting this base would be the sort of high-risk, very high gain operation they specialize in. If they seized this base, they'd eliminate a serious threat to their front line, establish a foothold on the east bank of the Volga and have a useful base to interdict the crossing points at Kazan."

"Damn." Farrow was staring at the map. "We've got a Marine battalion for base security and the Russian Marines of course. I'll make some calls and get reinforcements sent down here. God knows, there's enough American troops backed up this side of the Volga; there shouldn't be any problems in getting some sent down here."

Kazan Thunderbolts

Headquarters, American Expeditionary Force, Seitovo, Chuvashskaya Bridgehead.

"Does anybody have any idea what is going on?" Colonel Ryan Anderson was bewildered. *As far as I can tell, nothing here is what it seems to be. We're getting orders sent to units that make no kind of sense and we're getting reports from units that show they are nowhere near the positions they should be holding. The whole 83rd infantry is so spread out that none of its units are mutually supporting. We've got infantry trying to hold without armored support and tanks trying to counter-attack without infantry support. We can't use our strongest card, our artillery, because we don't know where our own units are, much less the enemy. If this carries on, those guns will be firing over open sights soon enough. And they won't have any kind of support either.*

"Permission to speak freely, Sir?" Major Jordan Swanson was earnest, young and extremely competent.

"For God's sake, yes." Anderson almost snarled the response. "Somebody needs to speak clearly around here."

"Sir, I think the front-line units have given up trying to understand the orders they are getting. The General is using his own slang and his own cryptic comments instead of procedure. He refuses to use standard military map grid-based location designators or to use standardized order formats. I think they are using the opacity of the instructions they receive as a rationale for following their own instincts. I think, Sir that we should forget about trying to interpret the orders going out. Instead we should analyze reports coming in to work out where units really are, then use our own judgment to work out what we would be doing if we were in their position. That way we will at least have some idea of what is going on even if we can't control it."

"What a hell of a way to run a war. No wonder we're getting our ass kicked. All right, we'll go for it. Jordan, I am ordering you – and I will take a lesson from our Russian friends and put this in writing – to take your best signals experts and anybody else you deem appropriate and find out where all our forces are. If you can find out what they are doing as well, then go for it. Keep a map but be discrete in who you let see it." *And I hope you understand that is the strongest possible suggestion that you keep it away from Vetrenyy Freddie. He'll hit the roof if he finds out we've been keeping our own command plot.*

"Colonel Ryan, should I tell General Ward what we're doing?"

Ryan hesitated. General Orlando Ward was in command of the First Armored Division that was currently crossing the Volga. He had had a stand-up fight with Fredendall when the AEF commander had tried to split the First up

159

into small penny-packets all over the Chuvashskaya. Ward had threatened to go direct to General Marshall over the issue. Fredendall had backed down but afterwards had deliberately left General Ward out of operational meetings. In fact, the two Generals were barely on speaking terms.

"Yes. Unofficially of course and keep it quiet."

"Very good, Colonel. One thing we have been able to make out. It seems like our boys up there are forming up and blocking every cross road they can find. The krauts are largely road-bound and they have to have those crossroads. That's holding them up more than anything else right now. We've identified one such blocking action taking place at Klimovo, another at Timyashi and a third at Koltsovka. If that delineates the front line, it seems that the krauts have pushed at least seven and a half miles into our lines in less than four hours."

Thunderbolt FiveByFive *Over Balakhna, 239 miles from Moskva*

The sea of gray clouds below seemed to be endless. The weather officer had said that the cloud top was at fourteen thousand feet and would remain at that level until the front had passed. The Thunderbolts were holding relaxed formations to save on fuel. At 22,000 feet, they were well clear of any residual turbulence from the storm. A few minutes earlier they had passed a B-26 Marauder formation bombing blind through the clouds. Edwards had assumed that there had to be something going on there that he didn't know about. All the time, his eyes were scanning the clouds below for the first shadows of German fighters about to break through yet one part of his attention was never diverted from the tell-tale fuel pressure gauge.

A movement caught his eye but it was not the awaited arrival of the Focke-Wulfs. One of the Thunderbolts nearby had jettisoned its drop tanks. *One of those occasions when being first isn't such a good idea. It tells the boss who needs more instruction in fuel management technique.* The first aircraft to drop its tanks was followed by others in quick succession as their external tanks were emptied. Then, the pressure gauge in Edwards' cockpit flicked to zero before returning to center. He switched to internal and thumped the drop tank release, allowing the tanks to blow clear without the mighty R-2800 missing a beat. He felt *Fivebyfive* surge forward. The drag of the drop tanks cost the P-47 45mph off its maximum speed. Even with the tanks gone, *Fivebyfive* was still 15 mph slower than she was with clean wings but she was fast enough for that to be a minor concern. Up here, at 20,000 feet, there wasn't a German aircraft he knew of that could match a Thunderbolt for speed.

Down below, the sea of gray clouds was suddenly disturbed. For an insane second, Edwards thought that some giant sky-sharks were surfacing through the undulating waves. Fins were appearing, cutting through the cloud in the same way that sharks surrounded a sinking boat. The illusion continued as the dark gray Focke-Wulf 190s appeared out of the clouds, looking for the bomber formation that should have been in front of them. The few Thunderbolts that still had their drop tanks, jettisoned them and the whole 360th Fighter Squadron peeled over to dive on the aircraft below them.

"*Jeanie*, we'll concentrate on the trailing 190, rearmost section." There were sixteen 190s in four groups of four, exactly matching the 360th in numbers and formation. The American Free Chase fighters had the advantage of altitude and speed. That was one reason why Edwards had ordered his wingman to join him in firing on a single aircraft. It would make certain the advantages from the first pass were exploited to the full. There was another reason as well. Edwards was fed up with being teased about his half-kill and sharing one with his wingman would bring him up to a nice round three. American pilots had given up bothering with claims for probable and damaged aircraft; now they, like the Russians, were only interested in kills.

The 190s had wasted a few seconds of precious time looking for the bomber formation. By the time they had realized there wasn't one, the Thunderbolts were a step ahead in the game and that counted for everything. At 300 yards, *Fivebyfive* and *Jeanie* opened up on their selected target with the concentrated firepower of sixteen .50 caliber machine guns. The German fighter rolled frantically in an effort to escape from the deadly web of fire, swerving into a diving turn that transformed itself into a barrel roll. The tracers from the two Thunderbolts were going in front, behind, above and below the twisting target yet none seemed to strike home. Then a wave of brilliant flashes swept along its fuselage, shredding the structure and causing a stream of fire to erupt from the engine. The stricken fighter curved away with the .50s still hammering into it. Then, there was the unusual brilliant white explosion that Edwards had noted before, the one that blew the left wing clean off. The ruptured wing went spiraling one way, the rest of the burning 190 the other. It was a clean kill.

"Watch it, *Fivebyfive* and *Jeanie*. 190 coming in behind you."

Edwards looked in his mirrors. Acting on advice from Litvyak, he'd had a second mirror placed on top of his cockpit to increase the field of vision aft. It had made his Thunderbolt look a bit like a rabbit but the blind spot behind him was seriously reduced. The dead 190's wingman was boring in fast. "*Jeanie* time for a bait and hook."

Over on Edward's right, *Jeanie* swung left while *Fivebyfive* swung right so that the two P-47s were crossing. Behind them, the 190 picked on *Jeanie*, turning with the big Thunderbolt and obviously believing that Edward's right turn had put him out of the fight. That made *Jeanie* the bait fighter. Both P-47s had put their noses down and were straining to build up speed. Once they did that, the Focke-Wulfs would be left behind. The whole idea was to put pressure on the German pilots to try and get their kills before the Thunderbolts accelerated away from them. That urgency would make them careless.

What the German pilot didn't know was that when an enemy aircraft chose the bait fighter as his target, the two aircraft would turn in towards each other. Only, while one fighter might be the bait, the other was the hook. The two Thunderbolts crossed paths. *Fivebyfive* was the hook and it was just a matter of timing at that point. Edwards gauged his distance carefully and, once their separation was great enough, the two P-47s again reversed their turns, bringing the enemy plane into the *Fivebyfive's* sights. As long as the Thunderbolts kept their speed up, the bait and hook left little chance of escape to even the most maneuverable opponent.

The maneuver had the German fighter 300 yards over to Edward's left. He thumbed the water injection on his engine, felt the cough and then the surge of power as the extra 300 horsepower cut in. At that instant he threw the controls over and felt the *Fivebyfive* skid to the left, her nose coming around in a steady, remorseless swing. The FW-190 was three hundred yards out, exactly the convergence point of his eight .50 calibers. The first few shots went ahead of the aircraft but the rest plowed along the fuselage, ripping it apart in an explosive stream of smoke, flame and shattered fragments. Edwards saw the engine erupt, the propeller spinning off in a wild arc, the undercarriage dropping down and the cockpit bursting open under the torrent of bullets. Then, the Focke-Wulf exploded in a fireball. Edwards was too close to avoid it and had to take his Thunderbolt through the blast. Instinctively he ducked down as he swept through the debris of the destroyed fighter, then he was outside and in the clear.

Once again alongside *Jeanie*, Edwards scanned the battle. The sky was covered with the streaks of brown smoke that told of fighters either going down or heavily damaged and trying to break off the battle. One of the latter was *Slick Chick*, Jackson's Thunderbolt. His wingman had already gone down and his P-47 was trailing smoke from a damaged engine. A 190 was behind him snapping out short bursts as the enemy pilot tried to finish off his victim. Jackson was rolling and snaking in an effort to avoid the gunfire but it was obvious that *Slick Chick* was badly damaged and it would only be a few seconds before the aircraft was destroyed. Edwards swung *Fivebyfive* over and started to make a firing pass on the 190 before it could claim its kill.

He was too late. Despite the ruggedness of the P-47, *Slick Chick* was already badly damaged and her luck ran out before Edwards could get to her. A long burst from the 190s four cannon and two machine guns struck home, setting the engine and wing roots ablaze. The P-47 lurched upwards and Edwards watched as it rolled on its back. Jackson bailed out; dropping clear of the wreck before his parachute opened and he started to float downwards.

The 190 swept past him and then, climbed away, rolled over and made another pass. Edwards could see what was about to happen but was helpless to do much about it. He fired his machine guns in an effort to deflect the German pilot from his pass but the range was over a thousand yards and the effort was futile. All he achieved was to have his gun camera working when the FW-190 strafed Jackson on the end of his parachute. Edwards could see Jackson swinging in his parachute harness, perhaps in a hopeless effort to avoid the gunfire aimed at him. Then, the swings turned to jerks as the bullets struck home. Jackson's parachute collapsed into a white streamer and he plunged downwards.

Edwards was pure, cold-blooded furious. As a child, he had read about air combat over France in the Great War and the code of conduct that had evolved then. When parachutes had become common at the end of the war, aviators did not kill other aviators who had bailed out. One fought the machine, not the man in it. All of that had just been ended by the deliberate murder of Jackson. For the first time, Edwards understood the true character of the Russian Front and why the Russian pilots thought the way they did. Yet, while he did so, he was also planning the destruction of the German pilot in front of him.

The way he was approaching the 190 would put him across its nose at an oblique angle, making it easy for the 190 to turn on to his tail. That suited him fine. *Fivebyfive* swept down, building up energy in its long, gentle dive. Then, as he passed in front of the 190, he pulled the nose up and started to climb away. Climbing wasn't the Thunderbolt's greatest virtue; the big airframe lost energy and speed quickly and its sustained climb rate was sluggish. Both the 109 and the 190 climbed faster than the P-47. Obviously, the 190 pilot behind him couldn't believe his luck and, equally obviously, thought he had a complete novice in front of him. He was climbing after the Thunderbolt and closing the range fast.

Edwards watched his speed waffling downwards and waited for the precise moment he needed. Then he thumbed the water injection switch and felt the engine cough before the extra 300 horsepower cut in. Once again, he threw the controls over to the left, allowing the massive torque of the R-2800 on water injection combine with the Thunderbolt's roll rate and its slow speed to flip the aircraft around in little more than its own length. Edwards heard *Fivebyfive's* wings scream in protest at the maneuver but his nose was coming around fast and he was now head-on to the 190 and his eight guns were hammering out a long, deadly burst. The German was firing too but he hadn't realized what was about to happen and his burst was late. Edwards saw the tracers streaming past his cockpit and wings but the German was second and Edwards was first. In this match, being first was everything.

His .50s tore the radial engine of the 190 apart, then walked back along the fuselage, chewing the enemy aircraft up and sending its cockpit into a mass of flame and fragments. Then, the 190 blew up and for the second time in a few seconds, Edwards had to fly through the fireball of a disintegrating Focke-Wulf.

By the time he was out of the explosion, the battle was over. He looked around the sky; the surviving 190s had broken off and dived into the cloud layer to escape. Three Thunderbolts of the sixteen had gone. The survivors formed up and carried on with their sweep ahead of the bombers. They were, after all, flying Free Chase.

Composite Group, 83rd Infantry Division, Klimovo, Chuvashskaya Bridgehead.

The rain showed no signs of letting up. What had been Company B of the 802nd Tank Destroyer Battalion had now been merged with whatever other troops the local commander had been able to scrape up from the front line fiasco and the whole force had been mobilized to defend Klimovo. In all, there were about 200 men defending the village, a few front-line infantry but most were truck drivers, support troops and other rear area personnel. They had rifles or carbines, a few Browning Automatic Rifles and Searle had his Bazooka. That was about it. Sergeant Perry was not hopeful about the possibility of staging a successful defense. *The front line infantry dissolved in a few minutes under direct attack. Why should this scratched-up group do any better?*

Perry and his men had been deployed to a low hill, Hill 540, to the south of Klimovo proper. Hill 540 was at least 70 feet higher than Klimovo. In fact, it was the highest ground in the vicinity of the village. The problem for anybody attacking the position was that the continuous rain was slowly but surely turning the fields and open ground into the glutinous sea of mud the Russians called rasputitsa. *Oddly enough, our uniforms blend into the rasputitsa very well. On the other hand we're so coated with the damned mud; any color uniform would blend in by now.*

The mud had another effect on the situation. Perry knew very well that the German infantry were severely understrength and their losses the year before had never been fully replaced. The offensive strength of the German Army lay in its mechanized and armored units that hadn't experienced the horrors of the room-to-room fighting in Stalingrad, Moskva and Nizhny Novgorod. Those units now powered the current offensive but they also meant that the German advances were largely road-bound. The road past Klimovo, the only hard-topped one in the area diverted around the village, running north of Hill 540. That defined the German access of advance. It also defined where the battle would start.

The rain had another effect, it was blanketing out sound. There was little warning when a shape materialized in the rain-saturated mist and began to edge out. It was a German Mark IV tank, its 75mm gun questing for a target. It edged forward a few feet and stopped, its crew obviously checking for mines or anti-tank guns blocking the road. *I wonder if the crew have heard about Bazookas yet or what happened to their assault gun earlier this morning.* Perry guessed that the tank crew was obviously reassured by what they saw because their vehicle started to move forward again. Shadowy figures, German infantry in their rainproof capes yet still hunched up against the driving rain, were moving alongside the tank. The lucky ones were on the road but the rest were floundering through the puddles and the growing sea of mud.

Perry waited patiently. Up on the hilltop, Grisham had positioned the bulk of his men so that their fire would cover the road yet they would be on the reverse slope of the hill right up to the time the attackers had turned the corner that skirted the lower edge of the rise. He had the rest of his men covering the flanks of the main blocking force. Perry looked again and saw the tank had stopped once more, its turret swinging again in the same questing manner of a dog hunting for prey. *Go on, Searle, take him down.*

Perry suddenly believed in telepathy for he had only just finished the thought when a streak of red fire flashed out from a pile of rocks and smacked into the side of the tank. Searle's shot was precise and carefully aimed at the same spot he had hit on the assault gun earlier. In fact, it was a bit further forward since the Mark IV had eight roadwheels rather than six but that meant the jet of flame from the rocket warhead penetrated into the ready-use ammunition rather than the engine compartment. This time the jet of flame was preceded by a pyre of brown smoke that was quickly swallowed by a jet of orange flame at least a hundred feet high as the ammunition cooked off. Perry heard the cracking of the machine gun ammunition exploding inside the hull and the duller boom of the 75mm rounds detonating.

Around the tank, the German infantry were going to ground, whether to avoid the rifle fire from the American positions or because of the debris from the exploding Mark IV, Perry wasn't clear. What he did see was that the return fire from the German infantrymen was already engaging his own positions and the German rifle and machine gun fire was deadly accurate. Despite the semi-automatic weapons carried by all the Americans, it was the Germans whose gunfire was quickly dominating the engagement. The German infantry had another advantage; the long wooden handles on their stick grenades meant they could be thrown further than the American hand grenades. Once again, Perry was watching the Americans being driven back.

PFC Jasper Robson was a country boy who had discovered a natural home in the Army. On enlisting, he had found the extra hour in bed every morning most enjoyable while the food was excellent – although he found the meals a little light on such traditional breakfast staples as flapjacks, chops and steaks. He had also found the pleasant, leisurely cross-country walks (which the Army called route marches) a useful form of exercise and he had won much popularity by carrying his comrade's packs when they found the going hard. To his delight, he had found that not only did the Army encourage him to shoot at things but they would actually give him the ammunition to do so. He had been under the vague impression he would have to buy his own. The only thing that had really disappointed him was that the Army range officers had insisted on putting the targets much too close to provide a real challenge.

Now, he had positioned himself carefully in a well-protected dip where two rocks shielded him from incoming fire yet provided him with a good field of fire. He had marked carefully where the Germans were positioning themselves and settled down to earn the extraordinarily generous pay the Army gave him. Briefly, he wondered if any of the Germans below were related to the Hundleys, the Robson's traditional enemies on their mountain. The day before he had left to join the Army, Jasper had shot Roscoe Hundley in the ass at over six hundred yards.

The ranges here were far less than that but the steady rain and swirling mist posed problems all of their own. Robson had been watching the enemy closely and he had noticed that each section of German infantry was supervised and commanded by a single man. Robson did not take to authority kindly and tended to react badly to those who had it. This had caused some problems with his Sergeants that had only been resolved after a long, earnest and damaging conversation behind the ammo dump. He had identified one of those men with authority and he was now settling the butt of his M1 Garand into his shoulder. His prey was pointing upwards, obviously driving the four men in his section up the slope to the American positions. Robson breathed out, steadied the blade of his foresight on the German's eye and gently squeezed the trigger. The man's head snapped back, then he crumpled, lifeless, to the ground.

Robson was already moving, abandoning his previous position and getting to another that he had already selected. A lifetime feudin' with the Hundleys in the Appalachian Mountains had taught him to shoot once and move fast. It was a matter of great sadness to him that the Army instructors hadn't listened when he had tried to drive that lesson home. He'd already come to the conclusion that the Army was a fine institution but he also got the feeling that it needed an urgent shot of reality. From what he had seen this morning, it was getting one.

From his new position, he could see the German infantry were still moving forward although they were more cautious than they had been. Robson picked another German soldier who seemed to like ordering other people around and carefully shot him through the head. In his opinion, that discouraged the Germans greatly.

Watching from below, Perry was of the same opinion. The attack on his unit's positions was faltering as the enemy NCOs were shot down. They'd stopped pressing home and were beginning to drop back. He could sense the surge of excitement amongst the Americans as they saw the Germans actually faltering and retreating. After eight hours of being chased backwards, it was a welcome sight.

"Sergeant, get the men reorganized. That was just a skirmish, recon troops trying to find what they are up against. The kraut main body will be up here soon enough." Lieutenant Grisham looked down at the scene on the slope of the hill. It had been a minor skirmish indeed.

Perry nodded. "They can't get past us until they clear that wreck from the road. That'll need engineers. We've bought some time at least."

"Yeah, thanks to Searle and his Bazooka. What's that kid got against tanks anyway?"

B-17E Memphis Belle *Approaching Kolomna Locomotive Factory*

"Approaching IP now." Colonel Holland relayed the report from the navigator with an unholy degree of relish. This was a maximum effort by three bomb groups and the sky was filled with almost two hundred B-17s packed into tight formation. Far off to the north west, another three bomb groups of B-17s were closing in on the main marshalling yard of Moskva. That meant over four hundred heavy bombers had reached their targets and were starting their bomb runs. The days when a dozen or so bombers approached a target in a ragged formation seemed a long time ago.

Moskva stretched across the horizon in front of the bomber formations. It was a huge city compared with the targets they had struck before and it shone in the sunlight. The rain front was behind them and the visibility, as the weathermen had predicted was near perfect. Below them, the ground seemed to have been laid out as a navigation aid for approaching bombers. The Oka River ran east to west but suddenly turned through 90 degrees, heading due north for almost exactly fifteen miles before making another 90 degree turn to run west for another fifteen miles. Then, the river made a third 90 degree turn to run south. There was another odd feature on that southern leg. About half way down it, the river made a series of hairpin turns that created a finger of land pointing west. The tip of that finger was the IP and turning on it would align the bombers exactly on the long axis of the Kolomna Locomotive Factory. It was the sort of geography that sometimes made LeMay quite certain that God was a bomber pilot.

Kazan Thunderbolts

"Kraut fighters are up. They were waiting for us behind the cloud front but the 356th plowed into them. Shot a lot of them up and forced a lot more back to base to rearm and refuel. Our Little Friends are taking on the rest right now." Holland was watching the dogfights on the outside of the B-17 formations. The Thunderbolts were breaking up the formations of German fighters long before they became a significant threat. The massed machine gun fire of the B-17s was driving off the few that did make it through the fighter escort. Another thing that had changed from the early days. As confidence in the B-17s armament had grown, the escorting fighters had started roaming further and further away from the bombers, sure that they could get back in time to aid any Fortresses that were in trouble.

LeMay grunted as he pulled *Memphis Belle* around on to the bearing that led from the IP right down the center of the Kolomna Locomotive Factory. Up ahead of him, he could see the point where the Moskva River, a large and prominent tributary joined the main river. That tributary, at an angle of 60 degrees to the main river, was as perfect a target marker as anybody could ask for. The Kolomna Locomotive Factory was almost three miles long and three quarters of a mile wide running parallel to the Moskva. It was a near-perfect target.

He looked over to his left and saw *Sally B* making the turn in perfect coordination with his own. Holding formation through rain, flak and course changes had ceased to be demanding and was now just a routine action. He advanced the throttles, accelerating *Memphis Belle* up to just under 300 miles per hour. Speed was the key now, with the bombers fixed firmly on their courses, getting through the attack run as quickly as possible meant everything.

"Jeez, look at that flak." Ahead of them, the sky was turning black. Not with rain clouds, not anymore, but with the evil black-gray balls of smoke from flak bursts. Moskva was a big city and the single most important communications and transport hub for hundreds of miles. It was defended accordingly and intelligence had reported that all the defenses of German-held strategic points were being reinforced with additional anti-aircraft guns. That meant that fewer guns were available to support the troops on the front line. To LeMay that was proof that the way his bombers were constant hammering targets in German-occupied Russia was already having its effects.

Memphis Belle was already starting the bouncing and jerking that marked passage through the flak barrage. This time, it was different; normally the flak bursts close enough to throw the bomber around were rare. Now, they were almost continuous and the motion resembled a ship plowing through a storm rather than the intermittent shaking they had experienced before. The temptation to try and take evasive action was almost overwhelming but LeMay reminded himself that mathematics proved that evasion was as likely to turn the aircraft into a shell burst as away from one. Oddly, that was of remarkably little comfort when he could hear the thrumming noise of fragments striking the fuselage.

Over to his left, the B-17 *Likely Lass* was keeping station in her combat box. One second she was flying normally through the flak bursts that surrounded her, the next the whole wing section between her starboard inner and outboard engines dissolved into an orange ball. *Must have been a direct hit from an 88* thought LeMay. What was left of the starboard wing was spiraling through the air while *Likely Lass* rolled on to her back and started to spin down. There was only one thing the other bombers could do for her now and Holland gave the order.

"Watch out for parachutes."

"Nobody getting out of her." The Flight Engineer had the truth of it and everybody understood that. Once a B-17 started to spin like that, the forces inside the fuselage stopped the crew escaping. There was a vague chance some might be thrown clear when the aircraft finally broke up, assuming it hadn't hit the ground first, but it was a long, long shot.

"*Leadfoot* is in trouble." Holland looked around while LeMay concentrated on holding *Memphis Belle* straight and level. "I can see her, Curt. Inner port engine is on fire, hold that, they've got it out and feathered the prop. She's holding station fine on three engines."

"Bombardier here. One minute to release point."

"Acknowledged, you have the aircraft." LeMay took his hands and feet off the controls and felt the tiny movements as *Memphis Belle's* bombardier started lining up on the target. He could also feel the buffeting as the bomb bay doors opened, exposing the eight 1,000 pound bombs that were the whole reason for making this flight. Without the strain of holding his aircraft in formation, he could look around at the attack group. Several aircraft were streaming smoke from damaged engines but the formation was holding together well.

"*Mollita* is going down." The intercom voice was dispassionate but LeMay could sense the anguish as another B-17 started to drop out of formation. "Tail gunner is out, ball turret gunner out, four more chutes from the bomb bay."

Mollita was already leaving a thick, dark brown trail behind her. Both inner engines were dead, their props feathered. Her pilot was jettisoning her bombs in an attempt to keep the aircraft flying but it was a hopeless task. The fuselage was already starting to burn, the orange fires coloring the smoke trail as the B-17 started its long descent. That was when the wing structure failed and both wings separated from the fuselage. The aircraft seemed to crumple in mid-air and just fell out of the sky.

"Bombs gone." The intercom message just served to confirm the message from the leap upwards as *Memphis Belle* dropped her load. "Aircraft is yours, Colonel."

"All aircraft, prepare to turn on to oh-niner-five."

Memphis Belle started her long turn to starboard. LeMay noted that the turn had thrown the flak guns off for a few seconds; their shells were predicted on the bomb run, not the exit course. It took about ten seconds for the gun predictors down below to come up with their new firing solution and for the shell bursts to surround the B-17s again. *So that was where that ten-second thing came from.* Behind them, the second formation of bombers was turning on to the same course after dropping on the marshalling yards. There was now only a single mighty parade of Flying Fortresses heading eastwards for home.

That was when there was a roar and an impact that sent *Memphis Belle* staggering to one side. LeMay felt an ominous wetness spreading over his face and down the left hand side of his body. *Time for that later.* The inner port engine was burning, the stream of orange flame running back over the wing to leave a comet-like trail behind the B-17. That left no time to worry about anything other than getting the fire out. The designers had anticipated the problem and equipped the B-17s with carbon dioxide engine fire extinguishers. The first step was to starve an engine of gasoline by advancing the throttles all the way to scavenge the engine and fuel lines of gasoline. LeMay then moved the mixture control to idle cut-off and shut down the fuel pump. With the supply of fuel to the damaged engine cut off and the prop feathered, he activated the engine fire extinguishers. It took a few seconds but the stream of flame from the engine flickered, wavered and finally faded away. That gave LeMay a chance to look around the cockpit. The chaos that met his eye was appalling.

It looked as if some of the New York gangs had decided to conclude some family business in the cramped confines of a B-17. The windscreen, instrument panel and side windows were splashed with over-liberal quantities of blood and unidentifiable fragments. LeMay looked down at himself. His leather jacket and flight suit were saturated with sprayed blood and debris and his goggles were unidentifiable masses of remains. In the co-pilot's seat, Colonel Holland was slumped back, obviously dead. A fragment from the shell that had exploded alongside *Memphis Belle* had removed his whole lower jaw and most of his neck.

"Flight Engineer to the flight deck. Radio operator, take over the upper turret."

LeMay looked out to starboard and saw something that shocked even him. A B-17 was slowly falling back through the formation even though all of its engines were running. A hit from a flak gun had taken off most of the nose.

The bombardier and navigator's stations were gone completely and what was left of the cockpit was twisted and misshapen. How the aircraft was still flying was beyond his understanding.

"*Westward Ho*, report status."

The voice that came back was obviously terrified yet equally determined to try and hide it. "We're hit bad. 88 exploded right in front of us. Navigator and Bombardier are gone, they just fell out. Pilot and copilot are dead."

"Who are you? Flight Engineer."

"No, sir. Flight Engineer is wounded. Won't make it. He's all ripped up. Frankie's taken over his position. I'm Sam. We're the waist gunners."

"Waist gunner?" For once LeMay blessed the Bell's Palsy that forced him to keep his voice level. "How many hours have you flying a B-17?"

"None, Sir." The gunner had obviously recovered enough to realize he was speaking with an officer. "I have two hours on a 50 horsepower Piper Cub though."

"That will do." *It'll have to.* "First thing, you must keep up with the rest of the formation. Does Frankie know what he's doing?"

"He thinks so. He used to watch the Flight Engineer when there was nothing else to do. And he used to ride a motorcycle."

Dear God. "Tell him that if you have to abuse your engines by overboosting, or running in auto-lean, at high power in order to keep up, never mind the regs, just do it. You must keep station. Just don't forget to report it when we land. The boys on the field don't mind changing engines, but they can't do it over enemy territory."

"Very good, Sir."

LeMay looked around his cockpit again. The wreckage of Colonel Holland had been removed from the co-pilot's seat and the worst of the blood and pulp scraped off the leather. The Flight Engineer had taken over the position and was looking at the hole torn in the starboard cockpit side. "Sir, that fragment just missed you. Another inch to the rear and it would have taken your head off."

LeMay looked at the hole and growled "it wouldn't have dared."

746th Tank Battalion, Outside Timyashi, Chuvashskaya Bridgehead

Colonel Long thought carefully about the information he had received. He had taken advantage of the slowly-slackening rain to send a patrol out to investigate the enemy positions in Timyashi. Eight men in two jeeps had probed around the area where the Germans were supposed to have set up their defenses and lived to come back with a detailed report that suggested the enemy was holding his defenses with only about a hundred infantrymen, a couple of panzers and one or two anti-tank guns. It sounded like an easy task for even his badly-weakened battalion to drive them out. *If I can do that, we'll have secured this section of the line and that will mean the units to the north will be able to stabilize their part of the front.* He called Major Barndollar over to the tank he had taken over to replace his own.

"All right George, we'll move now. While the krauts still think the rain is holding everything up. I'll take Baker Company and we'll clear the defenses. Get ready to push Able and Charlie companies through the hole we make." *I wish I had my light tanks here to do some scouting. Thank you, Vetrenyy Freddie. Dispersing my battalion all over the place and failing to give us any back-up is really appreciated. Without any real infantry support, I'm going to have to hope that the sight of my tanks supported by truck drivers and field kitchen personnel will scare the Germans into pulling back.*

To Long's surprise, it actually seemed to work. Faced with more than a dozen Sherman tanks moving in on their position, the two Mark IVs in Timyashi started to pull back. The infantry was falling back with them, manhandling what appeared to be a pair of 50mm anti-tank guns. This was a situation that the Shermans were very well-equipped to handle. On Long's orders, the 75mm guns on the Shermans barked, sending patterns of shells into the retreating Germans. The blasts sent some of the men tumbling into the ruins on either side of the lanes through the village. Others abandoned the two guns and ran for cover. The Mark IVs speeded up their withdrawal and ducked through the gulches to the east of the buildings. Long's Shermans accelerated as well, chasing after the Germans in the kind of pursuit of a defeated enemy that all tank officers dreamed of.

Unfortunately, this was the Russian Front and Long was to learn how quickly dreams could turn into nightmares when fighting the German veterans. The village of Timyashi was split into two sections with a large area of deep gullies between them. As the Shermans entered that clear area, German anti-tank guns began firing at them from everywhere. Long barely had time to realize that he had driven into a skillfully designed trap. One shot from an anti-tank gun shattered the forward idler wheel, leaving the track broken. The driver switched into the reverse gear, and the tank drew a short arc, leaving a broken caterpillar ahead, crawled back into a front garden. By sheer luck, the tank finished its escape in a very comfortable position. Long saw that the shell had well and truly mangled the idler and the front roller. There was no way his crew could repair that kind of damage without assistance from the engineering platoon. Sensing the start of an imminent disaster, he ordered the crew to stay with the machine and wait for a maintenance party.

When Long went to see what was happening to the other tanks, he saw it was far worse than he had imagined. One of the tanks was stuck on a gulley slope, its nose high in the air and its crew lifeless around it. Other tanks were already burning from the lethal fire that enveloped them. Behind him, Long saw that the "retreating troops" had rallied, assumed new positions and slammed the door shut behind him. Both of the "abandoned anti-tank guns" had been recovered and repositioned. Now they were shooting carefully and methodically into the almost unprotected rear of the Shermans. Other German infantry units had surrounded the American troops and were methodically cutting them down.

The South was even worse. Baker and Charlie companies, tasked with outflanking the German defenses in Timyashi, had instead run straight into a screen of expertly-placed anti-tank guns and Mark IV tanks. They'd shot the Sherman companies to pieces, leaving the ground strewn with the burning wrecks of the American tanks. The mathematics was very simple. The 746th tank battalion had ceased to exist. The sight filled him with guilt. Now, in retrospect, he could see what had happened. While he had been waiting for the rain to ease off, the Germans had been preparing a small force to act as bait and a screen of anti-tank guns. When the former had retreated, they had led him right into the trap.

Long rejoined his tank crew. There were now ten men in the garden. Major George Barndollar and his crew had managed to bail out of their tank and make their way to cover. A few more survivors were beginning to trickle in but Long knew they couldn't stay very long. Sooner or later, the Germans in the village would finish mopping up the men there and start a sweep to clean out any survivors. The tank crews would have to be gone by then. "Right, we must get out of here."

"Which way, Bill?"

"North. The kraut tanks and panzergrenadiers are passing south of us. The road to Kanash runs there. We'll have to head north, away from them. I've heard some of our boys are regrouping at Klimovo."

Nobody said anything but the small force of surviving tankers started their long walk to the north.

Composite Group, 83rd Infantry Division, Klimovo, Chuvashskaya Bridgehead.

"It's a tank!"

"Don't tell Searle, he'll blow it up."

"He can't. It's a Sherman, it's one of ours!"

173

"He'll still blow it up. He hates tanks. One frightened his mother before he was born."

"Who's Searle?" Lieutenant Jake Fuller was haunted by the sights of the morning. As far as he knew, his tank was the only survivor from the 746th. He guessed there had to be troops from the support echelon somewhere, ones that had been in the rear and had used their vehicles to get clear of the disaster, but he hadn't seen them. He had seen the Shermans in the tank companies getting shot to pieces by the German tanks and anti-tank guns. The suggestion, however light-heartedly made, that he might be in danger from American troops as well was chilling him.

"One of my riflemen. He picked up a Bazooka and turned out to be a real hunter with it." Grisham was also haunted by the events of the morning. Searle's unexpected expertise with the rocket launcher was about the only good thing that had happened. "What's going on out there? We're getting nothing but gibberish from up top."

"You and everybody else. The krauts have broken through all right. The 746th tried a counter-attack down by Lenino. We're the only survivors. From what we saw on our way here, everybody behind you is falling back on Kanash. Holding on here is buying them time to do it."

"So, what's the plan? A delaying action here while reserves move up to Kanash?" Grisham was trying his best to make sense of a situation that seemed to have gone completely to hell.

"There is no plan. And there are no reserves. Vetrenyy Freddie has split all the units up and scattered them across the front. We're being taken apart piecemeal. Everybody is just doing the best they can with where they are and what they've got and hoping something will turn up."

"So, we hang on here as long as we can, then pull back to Kanash." Grisham thought over the situation and could see that was the only way to go. Kolvino was a good blocking point for a holding action but that was all. His map told him just how vital Kanash was. All the roads in the region seemed to converge there. And it was a medium-sized town, not a small village that could easily be overrun.

When something did turn up, it was not what Grisham had wanted. The increasing howl overhead told him that artillery fire was inbound. A scattering of shells landed on Hill 540. There was no concentration to the barrage, no apparent focus to the fire. A few hours earlier, Grisham might have dismissed it as amateurish but he had learned much in those hours and he knew now that the Germans didn't do amateurish. If they had scattered shells all over Hill 540, it was because they had wanted to. *So what are they up to?*

Grisham edged to a position where he could see the road that was still blocked by the wreckage of the Panzer IV. Other than an almost subconscious note that there was not traffic backed up behind the blockage, his attention was focused on Klimovo. The northern and western edges of the small town were disappearing under a rising cloud of smoke as the German guns zeroed in and started their bombardment. Further to the north and west, the ground started to rise again into a quarter-circle of ridges that over looked the town. Grisham knew that was where the guns were. It suddenly struck him that the fact that he could see the whole panorama laid out in front of him showed how much the weather had cleared in the last few minutes. The driving rain had eased off and was now a fine drizzle that seemed to get everything wet without making any real effort.

"Take a look." Fuller had left his tank tucked away on the reverse slope and come up to join Grisham. He handed the infantry officer his binoculars and pointed at the long slope leading down from the ridge to Klimovo. Grisham could see the small groups of German infantry working their way down the slope. Each group would move forward for a few yards, then go to ground and snap out bursts of machinegun fire at the American positions along the edge of the town. That would provide cover for other groups who would make their advances. Then the groups would exchange role. It was a standard leapfrog advance but done with a smoothness and professionalism that neither American officer had seen before. Mixed in with the advancing infantry were assault guns whose crews spotted any major center of resistance and engaged it with direct artillery fire. Grisham could see that resistance along the northern edge of the town was already beginning to crumble.

"They're pinning us down up here while they take the town. Then they'll block the road behind us and take us as well." Grisham could see what was happening; what shocked him was how fast it was taking place. It had been barely an hour since Searle had blown up the Panzer IV and yet the Germans were mounting a planned, integrated assault.

"We got to get out of here." Fuller was watching the German attack reach the outskirts of Klimovo. The assault guns were already edging between the outlying buildings with the infantry covering them from close assault. Any resistance was met by point-blank fire from the 75mm guns on the StuGs. "Get your wounded on the tank, we'll carry them. The rest of you, walk alongside. If we waste any time, we'll never get out of here."

It took barely ten minutes to get loaded up and on the move. By that time, resistance in Klimovo was crumbling fast and the German assault forces were getting close to the town center. Once again, Grisham saw that his troops were being forced back and the knowledge tasted foul in his mouth. Part of the way out led through a small hamlet, Churashevo. There were four American six-by-six trucks there. As the tank pulled up, a group of artillerymen ran out of the buildings towards the Sherman. Fuller descended from the turret and went over to the commander

"Do you need any help?" The detachment commander, a sergeant, was almost in tears and started babbling a confused story. Apparently, the artillery position had been hit by intensive German artillery fire. The troops that were supposed to screen them had run off and left the artillerymen alone without any support. The artillery sergeant pointed to the four trucks and to where a pair of 105mm howitzers were emplaced. That was all that was left of his artillery battery. Four two and a half ton trucks, a ¾ ton truck, a jeep, two guns and 17 survivors. The German artillery fire had been deadly indeed.

"Just get us out of here." The Sergeant was too obviously in a state of shock to do much. Grisham got his men into the trucks while the artillerymen hitched their surviving guns to two of the trucks.

"Hey, Ell-Tee, they've got two rounds of ammunition left." Grisham heard Searle shouting from one of the trucks.

Grisham smiled at that. "Well, we've got one M4 representing a tank battalion so why shouldn't two guns with a single shell each represent an artillery battalion? We'll just have to find some more shells. Now, we need to get the hell out of here before kraut panzers appear in the street.

Control Tower, Airfield 33, Surovka, Moskva Front

"How did it go Ben?" Brigadier-General Clayton Adkins already knew one answer to the question. Fifty four Marauders had taken off for the attack and fifty four had returned.

"Milk run." Major Benjamin Wood couldn't help but compare this mission with the catastrophic attack on the radar station. "We took our bearing from the navigation beacon just like we were told and our ground radars tracked us out. When we were at the right distance along the bearing, they told us to drop and we dropped. Lord knows if we hit anything."

"The heavies are reporting minimal fighter opposition but very heavy flak over Moskva. So your raid did some good." Adkins looked at the line of B-26s again. Their raid had been intended to keep German fighters on the ground while the B-17s passed on their way to Moskva.

"Sir, two B-17s are asking to come in. *Memphis Belle* and *Westward Ho*. They can't land at Tarlovka, the runway is blocked by a wrecked B-17. *Memphis Belle* reports that she's lost an engine and has casualties. Also that *Westward Ho* has had her nose shot off and is being brought in by the waist gunners."

"*Waist gunners?* They can't land her. Tell them to bail out."

"Negative, Sir. They say they have too many badly wounded on board. They say they have to bring her in. The . . . errr . . . pilot on *Westward Ho* is asking for advice on how to do it."

"Ben, take the radio over and talk them in. We better get *Memphis Belle* in first in case this runway gets blocked as well." Adkins paused for a second, "it sounds much better calling the aircraft by name rather than code letters."

Wood was already sitting behind the control tower radio. "Yes, Sir. It does. The odd thing is, some of the crews say they think the aircraft are happier now they have names."

Adkins snorted derisively. "Right. Now, get those B-17s down."

The General returned to the control tower window and watched *Memphis Belle* making her approach. She was coming in on three engines and her radio operator was firing red flares out of the mid-upper hatch. Everybody knew what that meant. *Casualties on board, ambulances urgently needed.*

"There go Wint and Kidd." One of the control tower crew was watching a jeep racing down the runway, meeting up with the crippled Flying Fortress as it touched down. The B-17 made a perfect landing despite the dead engine and came to a virtual halt barely half way down the runway. Then, its three remaining engines picked up and the aircraft turned off the strip on to the taxiway. By the time it came to a final halt, *Memphis Belle* was surrounded by ambulances and fire trucks.

"Would you look at that?" Adkins hardly dared breathe as *Westward Ho* started her approach. He honestly couldn't believe that an aircraft in that condition could still fly. The nose forward of the cockpit had gone completely while the cockpit itself was a twisted tangle of shattered steel and glass. Behind him, Wood was talking the two crewmen flying the aircraft down.

"Is the ball turret gunner out?" Wood's question was critical. If the undercarriage collapsed and the ball turret gunner was still in his position, he would be squashed as thoroughly as a grape in a wine-press.

"Most of him, Sir." A chuckle ran around the tower at the gallows humor coming from the crippled aircraft.

This landing was an entirely different matter from the smooth, professional approach of *Memphis Belle*. *Westward Ho* was skittering from side to side, her wings constantly dipping from side to side as the inexperienced pilot tried to keep her under control. One of the dips put a main wheel hard down onto the runway surface and bounced the aircraft back into the air again. The pilot over-corrected and smacked the other main wheel down, again bouncing the aircraft.

Then, just as the aircraft leveled, the pilot managed to put the wheels down on the runway and the aircraft started rolling to a stop.

For a moment, Adkins thought *Westward Ho* had made it in but the damage from the two heavy impacts combined with the accumulated flak wounds proved too much. The undercarriage collapsed and the aircraft dropped onto her belly, sliding down the runway and slowly turning on her vertical axis as she did so. That turn took her off the runway completely and into the grass on one side. Adkins saw Wint and Kidd in their jeep chasing her through the grass. By the time *Memphis Belle* had come to a halt, they were right alongside the wrecked B-17. They jumped out of their jeep, ran to the wreck and disappeared inside. A few seconds later, they emerged with the first of the casualties. They laid the man down and then went back inside for the next.

By the time the wreck had been evacuated, Adkins could see the butcher's bill. Eight men had got out of *Westward Ho*. Two were obviously dead, their stretchers covered. Three more were being rushed into ambulances. That left just three men unhurt. More ambulances were crowded around *Memphis Belle* ready to take away the dead and wounded. He realized he must have missed something because he could see Sergeant Wint helping a wounded airman out of *Memphis Belle*. He looked around the control tower just in time to see a stocky figure soaked in blood and unspeakable remnants entering.

"Curt, what the hell? You should be in the hospital."

Despite the effects of Bell's Palsy, LeMay's voice had a slight shake to it. "It's all right Clay, none of this is mine. Dutch bought the farm. Flak. Who are those two Sergeants? The ones who came in the birds."

"Wint and Kidd. For some reason, they've made it their duty to make sure as many of the crew get out of the aircraft as possible. If a plane cracks up, they're the first into the wreck and the last out."

"Grandstanding?"

"No. I think it's some sort of vocation with them. Or something like that. It started when we lost all those Marauders in the Lugovskoy mission. Now, they've got their quarters covered with the internal diagrams of B-17s and B-26s and they spend their free time working out the best way into a wrecked aircraft and getting the wounded and dead out. Hell of a boost for morale. The '26 is a hard bird to land at the best of times and bringing in one that's been shot up is a killer. Knowing there's a couple of people who've made it their business to get survivors out makes a big difference. It's going to be a wrench losing those two."

"They being posted out?"

"Think so. Started when I wrote them up a citation each. God knows, they deserve it but there's nothing in the book that covers what they do. Go cold-bloodedly into a burning aircraft to pull the wounded crewmen out? In my book that deserves more than a medal. Anyway, I got a call from Ninth HQ, telling me to send them over there. Look, Curt, get washed up and debriefed and we'll talk more. While you're doing that, I'll get a call through to Bolshaya Tarlovka and tell them we've got two of their birds down here. We can fix up the *Memphis Belle*, enough to get her back to Tarlovka anyway, but *Westwood Ho* is a write-off."

Headquarters, American Expeditionary Force, Seitovo, Chuvashskaya Bridgehead.

"General Fredendall? General Ernest N. Harmon reporting for duty. I have orders to take command of the Second Armored Division and also to act as your deputy Corps Commander."

Fredendall bristled at the introduction. "What Second Armored Division? It's stuck the other side of the Volga. We've got more important things to worry about than a division that's stuck eighty miles away. The krauts have broken through and you can't stop them. Do you understand that, they have broken through and you can't stop them."

Harmon looked at his commander with open disgust. Fredendall was chain-smoking and Harmon could smell whisky on his breath. "May I ask your intentions, Sir."

Fredendall repeated his comment for the third time, his voice rising in near-hysteria. "They have broken through and you can't stop them. I'm issuing orders for a withdrawal from this headquarters to one over the Volga. This installation will be destroyed."

"With respect, Sir, Isn't that premature? The krauts are still some fifty miles to the west of us."

The glare from Fredendall was sufficient to blister timber. "If you think you know so much about the situation here, you take over. I'm getting some sleep."

Fredendall threw a paper with a hastily-written transfer of authority on it to Harmon and then stormed out. Harmon grabbed it and then took a deep breath. *That man is a physical and moral coward. Just what the hell is going on here?* He walked over and looked at the situation map pinned to the wall.

"I wouldn't put any faith in that if I were you." Colonel Ryan Anderson had entered the room as soon as Fredendall had stormed out. "We've got a much better situation map in the communications center. We compiled it from radio intercepts, ours and the enemy's. General Fredendall's orders were indecipherable so our unit commanders are using their own judgment. That boils down to them fighting delaying actions wherever they can until somebody takes charge of the situation. General, you need to speak with General Ward commanding First Armored."

"Get your map brought in here. And arrange for me to speak with General Ward. Colonel if you had to summarize the situation in thirty seconds, how would you do it?"

"I would say that the krauts have broken through the front held by the 83rd and are advancing forward, so far to a depth of at least seven miles. Probably more. They're chewing up our units and what's left of the 83rd is in full retreat. But, their infantry losses over the last two years have made them roadbound and roadblocks are holding them up. The biggest bit of good news we have is the Bazooka. It's caught the krauts completely flat-footed and they haven't worked out how to deal with any infantry outfit down to platoon level being able to kill tanks."

Harmon gave a respectful nod. "Thirty seconds on the nose. What reserves have we got?'

"Combat Command A of the First Armored is positioned here. At Kalinovka. General Fredendall tried to split CCA up and distribute it piecemeal along the front but General Ward refused to obey the order and threatened to go all the way to General Marshall. That's when Vetrenyy Freddie backed down. So, the order still stands but everybody pretends it was never issued."

"What a hell of a way to run a war. Right, Anderson, we've got a complete combat command on the northern flank of the kraut breakthrough. We've got three more combat commands and another infantry division crossing now. I think we can do some good here."

"Getting vehicles over the Volga is way behind schedule, Sir. We've got formations backed up for miles."

"I know, son. We're addressing that right now."

CHAPTER SEVEN: THE PATH BACK

River Ferry Crossing Point, Kazan.

The wail of the air-raid sirens was sudden but never unexpected. All along the great parade of vehicles and equipment backed up on the east bank of the Volga, men ran to their stations and swung the barrels of their anti-aircraft guns skywards. This wasn't the first time German fighter-bombers had raided the columns of troops and it wouldn't be the last. Each time, though, they were finding the opposition greater and their casualties increased. Every American tank, every truck carried a .50 caliber machine gun. The half-tracks used by the infantry always had one and sometimes as many as three. Practice, was indeed making perfect. Or, if not perfect, deadlier.

A small column of five vehicles was passing the long lines of tanks and trucks when the sirens sounded. The central vehicle was an M-20 scout car with two generals in it, one Russian, one American. In front and behind it were two half-tracks, each with a quadruple .50 caliber anti-aircraft mount. At the front and rear of the convoy was an M-8 armored car. The reactions of the troops around the small convoy were mixed. The more pessimistic assumed that the vehicles would draw fire in their direction; the optimistically-inclined believed that the strafing German aircraft would shoot at the Generals, not them.

Up ahead, rolling clouds of orange-red stained black smoke marked the scene of bomb explosions. Wearily, the troops along the road knew what that meant. The German attack aircraft had hit one of the three small Kazan ports that were the loading points for the American troops. They would have sunk at least one – probably more – of the flat-topped ferries that were shuttling between the banks of the Volga. Until those ferries could be replaced, the rate at which American forces could be transferred to the west bank would slow still further. The pessimists thought that was a very good thing since it was already well-known that the Germans were on the attack and going over to the west bank implied that there would be no return trip.

There were six Bf 110s in the formation that appeared through the explosions. Four were flying low, over the road with brilliant flares from their noses showing they were indeed strafing the troops on the road beneath them. The other pair were slightly higher and behind the strafers, obviously protecting them from attack by defending aircraft. The six aircraft seemed to be supported on a pyramid of orange flashes, the tracer fire from the host of vehicle-mounted .50 calibers. Around the 110s were puffs of brownish-black smoke from heavier anti-aircraft guns. There were six American divisions backed up on the east bank of the Volga and they had all positioned their AA guns around the Kazan ferry harbors. The Russians had their own guns there as well, adding to the barrage that turned the dark gray sky black.

Those guns had already exacted a toll. There had originally been eight 110s making the attack but two were already down and a third was trailing thick streams of black smoke from its engines. The pilot was obviously losing control of the machine but he was too low to bail out and the only alternative was to get clear of the road and find somewhere as far away as possible to crash-land. No sensible pilot would want to come down close to the troops he had just bombed and strafed. The damaged 110 curved away, trying to make it over the Volga although this was one of the few areas where the west bank wasn't German-held.

The other three strafers seemed to close in with terrifying speed. The noise of the .50 caliber machine guns seemed to swell and climax as they swept overhead, the road of engines and gunfire being punctuated by the blasts as the 110s dropped their underwing 50 kilogram bombs on the stalled ground units below. Then, they were gone, the silence that followed their departure seemingly profound. It was only broken by the crackle of burning trucks and the shouting of men as they tried to get the wounded clear of the wreckage so they could receive medical attention.

"Where the hell are our airplanes?" The American general shouted the inquiry at an Army Air Force Colonel.

"Sir, the weather is clearing from the west. That means the kraut airbases are clear but our birds are still socked in by bad weather. It'll be three or four hours before all our bases are clear and by then dusk will be coming down. Mostly, the weather is from the east so it works in our favor but this isn't one of those times. The closest airfield we have to the front is 108 here at Kazan but the Thunderbolts based there are on their way back from Moskva."

"They should be supporting our boys in the line." The General sounded very certain of that.

"That's why they are being reorganized. The tactical aircraft, B-26s, A-20s and the P-39s are all part of 9th Air Division. They'll be assigned to close support. Two Bombardment Wings of B-17s and the P-47s are now the 8th Air Division. They're the strategic air. The P-38s and F-5s are being divided between the two." The USAAF liaison officer was painfully aware of the behind-the-scenes fighting that was going on over the way the Army Air Force should be evolving. Splitting the force in Russia into two numbered air divisions had always been intended – eventually – but the infighting had grown so intense, the division had been brought forward.

Listening to the exchange, Colonel-General Ivan Stepanovich Koniev was struck by the sheer volume of resources the Americans were pouring into the war. It seemed as if the American national motto was 'Why choose?' Faced with a choice between tactical or strategic air forces, they supplied both. The army they were passing was another example. When the Americans had started to move forces into the Volga Front, it had been assumed that their divisions were the same size as Russian or German divisions and the Russians had planned transport and logistics facilities on that basis.

This drive had shown him how wrong that assumption had been and the stalled convoys were the result. A U.S. division was three times the size of its Russian equivalent and twice the size of a German division. Even more striking was the fact that the American divisions were completely mechanized. An American infantry division had more tanks than a fascist Panzer division, more artillery than a fascist corps. *Give the artillery to division or corps level of command? Why choose? Give them both all the artillery they need. Once the Americans get their command structure sorted out, shoot a few incompetents and get some experience under their belts, they will be formidable indeed.*

Koniev's reflections were the result of something else he had learned in the last hour or so. The first reports of the American air raid on Moskva were coming back from the Partisans. Making radio transmissions from occupied Russia was perilous and only done when there was gravely important news to relay. The German intercept and triangulation services were too fast and accurate for anything more. The news from Moskva had qualified and Koniev wondered how many Partisans had died to get it through.

According to the first reports, the American bombers had completely destroyed two marshalling yards in Moskva and devastated the largest locomotive production plant in the country. It would be days before the Germans could get trains through the blasted rail network – and Moskva was the only railway center through which the German Army now attacking the Chuvashskaya could be supplied. *As soon as they have burned through their on-hand supplies, the fascists will be out of fuel and ammunition. Remarkable. The Americans have cut off a Hitlerite army corps without moving a single ground unit. For the cost of seven Flying Fortresses and their crews, they have established a strangle-hold on a significant part of the fascist army.*

The M-20 continued to pass the long lines of trucks and tanks stalled on the road. Koniev looked at his companion, noting the thunderous scowl that was clouding his face and the almost electric crackle of anger that surrounded him. *This should be interesting. I haven't seen an American General lose his temper yet. Will he have the men he decides are sabotaging the war effort shot or will he think up something more interesting? Why choose? Perhaps he will think of something more interesting and then have them shot.*

The dock in front of them was capable of handling only a single ferry at a time and it was blocked by one with four tanks already loaded. The crew was moving two of the tanks around in a complex series of patterns, obviously intended to make enough room for a fifth. Their efforts were being complicated by a highly-strung horse that was dancing and rearing in the main ramp area. Three Army men were trying to calm it down and failing dismally. The American general heaved himself out of the M20 and stormed down the ramp leading to the loading docks.

"Who is in charge here?" The simple question was loaded with a stream of obscenities of such virulence and depth that an NCO of thirty years service came over all faint and had to sit down.

"I am, Sir." The speaker was a fresh-faced young officer who was obviously out of his depth and had never heard language like that before.

"Then tell me what the hell is going on here?" The General's voice was slightly less than a full blooded roar but there wasn't much in it. The young officer blanched and stepped back but it didn't help him much. "And what is that Goddamned horse doing on this ferry?"

"General Fredendall's orders, Sir. He demanded that his horse be brought over on the next ferry."

"You mean you've got a twenty mile long column of tanks and men backed up and strafed because of a Goddamned *horse*." This time the General's voice had made it to a full roar. "There are kids dead on the road back there because of you. Are you going to tell their parents their son died because of a God-damned *horse*? I'll show you how to deal with this problem."

The General swung around drawing a single-action Army Colt from his belt. He took careful aim at the sweet spot on the horse's forehead and fired a single shot. The horse went down in a dead heap, a sight that caused a shocked but approving murmur to run through the spectators. "Get that animal butchered and give the meat to any civilians who want it. Now, why is this ferry still here?"

The loading officer had gone completely white and desperately wanted to be sick. "Sir, General Fredendall read that the ferries are rated to hold five tanks so he ordered that no ferry was to leave this side without a full load of five tanks. It takes ten minutes to get the first four on, an hour or more to make enough space for the fifth."

The General glanced at the river. Not only were there lines of stalled vehicles waiting to load but there were ferries lined up waiting for their cargoes. Two had been sunk in the last air raid and three more damaged. "From now on, no ferry will stay at this dock for more than ten minutes. If it isn't loaded by then, send the God-damned thing on its way with whatever it has."

"But General Fredendall's orders . . He said he'd court-martial ,. . ." The officer stopped dead, staring at the muzzle of the revolver that was pointing at his forehead. He had never realized how large .45 of an inch was before and he had a sudden insight into how the horse must have felt.

"You got a choice. Court-martialed by Fredendall or your Goddamned brains blown all over the Volga by me. *Now, get this ferry moving.*"

The officer stepped off the ferry deck and waved it off. The next ferry moved up to take its place and a quartet of Sherman tanks moved up on to it. That ferry was moving in eight minutes and another was already in its place, loading up with half-tracks. The American general walked back to his M-20 listening to the cheers coming from the long line of vehicles, now slowly moving forward as the ferry operation picked up speed.

Colonel-General Koniev looked at his travelling companion with new interest. "Tovarish Georgi, I think you will do well on the Volga Front."

Airfield 108, Privolzhskiy na Volga,

During the sweep over the west bank of the Volga, Edwards's anger had settled into an ice-cold fury. Now, sitting opposite the debriefers, he didn't realize that, for the third time, he was telling the story of how Jackson had been deliberately killed after bailing out of his aircraft while he had brushed off his two and a half indisputable kills in less than a minute. The debriefers, who were a lot more skilled at their task than they appeared to be, had carefully noted the details and compared each version of the story. It wasn't the consistencies they were looking for, it was the slight differences in retelling that tended to confirm the basic truth of what they were hearing. They had the evidence there that they were looking for and so it was time to move back to the subject of kills.

'Lieutenant, we have similar reports from the 4th and 56th Groups. We're analyzing gun camera footage from, all three groups now."

"I'm pretty certain that I got it on mine."

I hope so, anyway, we have to move on. What did you notice about the 190s you intercepted?"

"They were painted differently, normally the 190s have green and dark gray wings with light gray fuselages dappled with dark green, These ones were dark gray overall with medium gray dapple on the fuselage. They also were sluggish compared with the 190s we met before."

"That confirms them being Wilde Sau aircraft. 190s used as night fighters. They've been modified with exhaust dampers and blind-flying radio equipment and extra firepower. 13.2mm machine guns in the nose, four MG-151 20mm cannon. You and Anderson got the first one together? Your stories match in all the important details."

"We did. I'm claiming half on that one."

"And we're allowing it. The second one you and Anderson got with a bait-and-hook? Anything odd about it?"

Edwards shook his head. "The bait and hook works fine. If the krauts get sucked in, they die. Was one thing though, I've noticed before. When the kraut blew up, his wing went first. There was a brilliant white explosion that took the whole left wing off. Then the rest of the plane blew up."

The debriefer nodded. "Again, we're getting confirmation of that from the other groups. There's something about the way the krauts build their fighters that caused that. The Russians have some wrecks they're letting us look at. We'll get to the bottom of it. The third kill was the man who killed Jackson?"

"The one responsible for the murder of Lieutenant Jackson, yes. I wouldn't call him a man." Edwards related the details of the dogfight, using his hands to show how the moves were executed. "I got him good. His 190 blew up with him still in it. My camera gun film should show it."

"I don't think we need that. Lieutenant Anderson was coming in as well and he saw you pull that crazy turn in mid-air. You're not supposed to be able to do that by the way. Anyway, that's confirmation. We're crediting you with two and a half kills. Your total is now five kills. That makes you an ace. First Thunderbolt pilot to become one. We're finished here, go get yourself a drink to celebrate."

Edwards walked away, the rage still eating at him. He stopped off at his quarters, changing out of his sweat-soaked flight suit and changing into his non-flying clothes. Then, pausing only to pick up a small package, he set off for the officer's club. It had stopped raining and the sun was trying to force its watery light through the clouds overhead. Inside the bar, the Yak pilots were sitting around, conscious of the achievements that the B-17s and Thunderbolts had clawed out of the fascist hide while the Russian fighters had been grounded by the weather.

"Tovarish Misha! How went the day for you?"

Edwards returned the wave. "We lost three Jugs to 190s. Got eleven of them in return. We haven't heard from the bombers or the other two Jug groups yet."

"And how many fascists did you kill, tovarish?" Koldunov seemed cheered by the success of the 356th Free Chase mission.

"Two and a half. I finally got the other half-aircraft." Edwards was finding the rough-humored warmth of the Russian pilots was slowly driving the sick fury from his heart.

"Congratulations, bratishka!" Koldunov's voice echoed around the bar. Then his eyes opened wide. "Then you have five kills! For this, you should receive the Order of the Patriotic War."

"Five dead fascists is reward enough." Edwards might have mellowed a bit but the memory of his flight leader being shot on the end of his parachute was still at the front of his mind.

Beside him Lilya Litvyak looked at him hard. Her initial thought was that he was poking fun at the Russian pilots and their loathing for their enemy but that didn't last more than a second. One look at Edwards's eyes was enough.

"What happened, bratishka?" Her voice was filled with sympathy, the first time she had spoken to him with much more than disinterest or casual politeness.

"It was Jackson. The fascists killed him. It was a fair enough fight, he was attacking a 190 and was so fixated on shooting at it he forgot to check his six. Another 190 came in behind and shot him up. Tom bailed out but the bastard shot him on the end of his parachute. Just machine-gunned him." Edwards explained the dogfight again, once again using his hands to illustrate the moves. When he described how he used the torque of his engine to flick *FivebyFive* around, he got a burst of applause, punctuated by glasses being banged on the bar in salute.

"This reminds me. Tovarish Lilya, the advice you gave on the extra mirror was of great value. I believe it might have saved me; had Jackson had such a mirror, he might not have been killed. Allow me to make a small gift to you in thanks for your advice. A gift from one fighter pilot to another."

He took the package out and handed it to her, to the accompaniment of whistles from the other pilots in the club. Litvyak went bright crimson but opened it and took out the white silk scarf within. Her eyes opened wide; the scarf was fully six feet long and more than a foot wide. Moreover it was made of the best silk available to the U.S. Army Air Force. Her own threadbare blue polka-dot scarf was artificial silk and had been left ragged and bedraggled from long hours in her Yak-9. She pulled the old scarf off and wrapped the new one around her neck, luxuriating in the smooth, soft feel of the silk. It was a princely gift for somebody in a country suffering from its third year of war.

"Bratishka, let us raise our glasses to the Americans who died fighting for the Rodina this day."

Her voice echoed around the club. There was a sudden silence as the Russian fighter pilots raised and drained their glasses, then the still was broken by the sound of the glasses being banged on the bar.

"Once, we would have smashed them so they would never be used for a lesser purpose." Koldunov explained. "But now, we cannot afford to sacrifice even a cheap glass."

Gunboat PR-73, Ulyanov'sk Narrows, Volga River.

"The engineers have cleared a passage for us." Kennedy swung the bows of PR-73 towards the gap in the wreckage of the bridge. *One of the advantages of having American troops backed up east of the Volga is that there are lots of units available for emergency assignments. Like the engineers who have cleared a passage through the wreckage or the two battalions of self-propelled artillery that are being moved up to support us. Pity the Marine recon unit got taken away though. Custer was really apologetic about that. He really fancied the idea of a boarding action but he and his boys had other orders.*

"Just how were the krauts expecting to get through this wreck?" Thom found the sight of the wrecked Ulyanov'sk bridge in daylight fascinating. He'd taken the trouble to get his camera from his quarters and was photographing the long, semi-submerged ruin. "The S-boats and probably the MFPs might be able to thread their way through the way we do but no way a converted steamer will."

Kennedy watched the east bank of the Volga rolling past. "Either the steamer is going to stay back here while the smaller craft go on ahead or the whole formation intends to hit this bridgehead. That makes sense, in a way. Nobody ever intended to set this bridgehead up. It just happened with the whole situation growing out of control. The krauts don't like that. They want to think they are dominating everything that is going on. This bridgehead must be irritating the hell out of them."

"So we're going into a battle not knowing what is happening or why." Thom did not sound pleased.

"Oh, we know what's happening. With the Partisans reporting in and now the Air Force running photo-reconnaissance birds over the west bank, we've got good coverage of what the krauts are doing. It's the 'why' that we can't cope with." Kennedy thought that over. *It's the why of things that this supposed scheme to provide a clearing house for intelligence is supposed to solve. Put all the political and military intelligence together and each fills in the holes baffling the other. Only, if that's true, why have just one such agency? If we had several, each looking at the whole issue from their own points of view, wouldn't they fill in the things the others missed? Only that wouldn't give my father and Donovan the control they want. They want to manipulate the decisions that will be made by controlling the intelligence that informs those decisions. The Russians have seen that, recognized it, and realized the dangers. Damn it, they have probably had the same thing happening in their set-up, more than once at a guess. Perhaps that's why Beria met his accident.*

"We have them on radar, Skipper." Maguire interrupted the train of thought with his reported radar contact within seconds of clearing the bridge wreckage. Range three miles, more or less. Big target with four smaller ones in front and six behind. I'd guess that's the steamer with the S-boats up front and the landing craft behind."

"You reckon?" Kennedy's voice was cheerful although he hardly felt that way. "Well, time to screw their plans up. Signal to BK-116 and BK-119. "Tovarishchi! Zagruzite vashe oruzhiye i podnyat' kulaki. Sushchestvuyet rabota, chtoby sdelat' etot den"

"Comrades, load your guns and raise your fists. There is work to do this day." Thom translated the message with an unholy degree of relish. "Skipper's getting to be more Russian than the Russians."

Kennedy overheard the remark. "Well, let's do something about that. Get the largest Stars and Stripes you can find and hoist it. We don't want any confusion. Well, we really want a lot of confusion but none of it over who we should be killing."

"Aye aye, Skipper." Thom had the flag up in a few seconds, streaming it proudly from the radar mast. The roar of the engines running at full power defeated even the underwater exhausts as PR-73 surged forward with BK-116 and BK-119 struggling to keep up. The sheets of rain that had swept across the surface were fading slowly and the visibility was improving proportionately. The first two German craft to edge out of the mist were the small LS boats. They had originally been designed to operate from auxiliary cruisers but that had proved impractical and they'd been sent to the Volga instead where they could operate in more confined waters than the larger S-boats. *They're small all right but they're only armed with a single 20mm cannon. They were supposed to have torpedo tubes but they never got them. They were equipped to lay mines instead. That's what they must be here for, to block the ways through the wreckage of the bridge by laying mines in the gaps.*

BK-116 was the first to open fire on the LS craft. She had two 45mm guns in old tank turrets, a 37mm anti-aircraft gun and two twin 14.5mm machine guns in beam turrets. The 45mm weapons obviously threw a much lighter shell than the 3 inch gun on PR-73, four pounds as opposed to twelve, but it fired fast and BK-116 did have two of them. Also, the crew was behind armor and that made a big difference when one of the LS craft opened fire with its 20mm gun. Kennedy saw the streaks of tracer deflecting off the turret armor before the red flashes were blanketed out by the flash of the 45mm gun. The first two rounds from BK-116's forward gun missed her target but the third smacked home into the bridge. Since the target's only gun was mounted on top of that structure, the single hit had the effect of silencing the German boat completely. BK-116 turned slightly to bring her aft gun to bear and the two guns combined quickly reduced the German ship to a burning wreck.

First blood to us Kennedy thought *and how. But that was the easy bit. Those LS craft have no place being anywhere somebody might shoot back at them. Had no place that is.* The quick amendment was due to the fate of the other LS boat that had been ripped up by BK-119 aided by a generous contribution of 1.1 inch machine gun fire from PR-73 and PR-57. *Three quad 1.1s certainly make a mess of an unarmored target.*

"What the hell is that?" Thom heard the inbound howl and saw the great splashes thrown up by the shells. "Those aren't 88s."

Kennedy made a simple yet inspired guess. "They're five point nines firing under radar control. I guess we just found where the guns from Sengiley went."

Fast Attack Craft S-38, South of Ulyanov'sk, Volga River.

"The auxiliary cruiser is firing."

Oberleutnant zur See Oskar Wuppermann thought that, given the howl of the shells passing overhead, the comment was a little superfluous. The river steamer following them had been converted further south, down the river where the Ami bombers hadn't yet struck, then brought up to be armed at Mordovo. Now, she had four 15 centimeter guns, two 88mm anti-aircraft guns and two quadruple 20mm weapons. Three of the 15 centimeter guns were arranged before the bridge so they could engage an approaching target. Just to add to the mix, the ship had been equipped with radar fire control for her heavy guns. Wuppermann seriously hoped that the combination would be an unpleasant surprise for the American and Russian gunboats.

"LS-9 and LS-12 both reporting severe damage. LS-9 is sinking, crew abandoning ship. LS-12 trying to make it to west bank so she can beach."

So, the Amis drew first blood. Beaching here won't do LS-12 much good, the west bank here is held by the Ivans. I knew those small boats wouldn't be of any use. At least they drew fire away from us. "Prepare to open fire."

There were three enemy gunboats ahead of him, maneuvering to avoid the splashes from the first salvo of shells from the auxiliary cruiser. Off to port, S-

67 was already maneuvering to attack the largest of the three, one that was flying the largest American ensign Wuppermann had ever seen on the Volga. The two smaller boats had both hoisted the hammer and sickle in reply. *Ami and Ivan gunboats fighting together. First time we have seen that. This alliance of theirs is settling down fast. I wish it was settling down the way LS-9 is.*

Gallows humor apart, LS-9 was beyond hope. Her stern was already awash and she was rolling over quickly. Her bows were swinging upwards, leaving her pointing an accusing finger at the sky. LS-12 was crawling across the river, clouds of black smoke belching from her riven hull. Nearer to the east bank, S-67 was already extracting a stern revenge for the destruction of the two small craft. She had swung away from the American gunboat in favor of pinning BK-119 in against the shore and was spraying her with 20mm gunfire. Wuppermann could see the problem though. It was the same one that had plagued the S-Boats ever since the fighting on the Volga had started. The 20mm guns were just not powerful enough to deal with an armored gunboat. In theory, the shells were powerful enough to penetrate the armor but the combination of oblique angles of impact and constant movement made the job much more difficult than it seemed. Most of the shells just bounced off. However, the 45mm and 37mm shots from the gunboat had no such problems when firing on the wooden S-boat. S-67 might have BK-119 pinned but she was still getting the worst of the duel.

That was when Wuppermann saw the thing he dreaded most. PR-73 had curved away from its course up the middle of the river and come to the rescue of its Russian consort. A large fireball erupted from S-67 as a three-inch round plowed into the fragile S-Boat and exploded deep inside its hull. Once again, the armor on a river gunboat proved of greater value than speed or torpedoes. The Ami gunboat had now changed course and was running parallel to S-67, lashing at the torpedo boat with the quadruple 1.1 inch mount aft and the twin machine guns amidships. Another massive explosion rocked the S-boat and it started to slow dramatically. Obviously shell splinters had cut the fuel supply to its diesels. Now, the situation was reversed and, hosed by gunfire from two sides, S-67 was ablaze all along her length and it was her crew that was abandoning ship.

In every disaster lies an opportunity. Wuppermann reflected on the truth of that saying with grim delight. By swerving away to rescue BK-119, PR-73 had left BK-116 exposed. S-38 could use her speed to isolate and overwhelm her before PR-73 could make it back over the river to aid her. Wuppermann looked forward at the 37mm gun sunk into its recessed mounting in the bows. Armed with three such guns now, S-38 was a much more formidable craft than S-67 had been. He felt the hull vibrate with the surging engines as his craft accelerated into its attack run.

Kazan Thunderbolts

It was obvious that BK-116 was unaware of the modifications carried out on the S-boat. The Russian gunboat turned to meet S-38 and started to fire its forward 45mm gun at the approaching German ship. S-38 swerved away slightly, apparently retreating from the 45mm shell bursts around her, but actually unmasking the midships and stern 37mm guns. Once they were able to bear on BK-116, the three guns swamped the Russian gunboat with shells. The armor that had deflected machine gun fire and some of the 20mm hits was penetrated with ease. BK-116 was silenced, her guns knocked out and her waterline opened for much of her length. By the time S-38 had finished her pass, BK-116 was already rolling over and sinking.

Wuppermann had little time to celebrate the success. Three more gunboats had arrived in the midst of the battle. One, the largest, had two of the long three-inch guns and was firing them into the rain-soaked mist that covered the river. He guessed she was using her radar fire control system to engage the still-hidden river steamer that was lobbing her 15cm shells into the battle area. There were two other American gunboats with the big one. One appeared similar to PR-73 but the other was a different type. It had only a short-barrelled heavy gun but that made it easier to handle and the first shells from it were already landing around S-38. S-38 started swerving and weaving through the shell bursts. PR-73 was heading over to join the battle and her forward gun was already lobbing shells at the S-boat. The Volga was 12 kilometers miles wide at this point and that made PR-73's gunfire largely ineffective.

However, it wasn't the three inch guns that did for S-38. The S-boat had used her superior speed and maneuverability to dodge the shells from them but by doing so, she had taken herself close to the three gunboats that had just arrived. Those three had four quadruple 1.1 inch mounts between them and their concentrated fire lashed through the flimsy hull of the S-boat, knocking out internal systems and cutting down the crew at their posts. S-38 lost power instantly and started to drift as the damage mounted. Wuppermann was wounded by splinters from the inside of the newly-armored bridge. The armor had indeed kept the 1.1 inch bullets out but the hits had caused the inside surface of the armor plate to break away. The fragments had bounced around the bridge and done more damage to the men within than penetrating hits would have done. The fragment wounds left him stunned and weak, so much so that the heavy lurch rolling S-38 over into a severe list hardly registered. He simply assumed that it was another hit from the guns on the American ships. By the time he registered that S-38 was returning to an even keel, his command was already in danger. He heard the running steps on the main deck but the mush fogging his mind meant they didn't have the meaning they should. Nor did the shouting on deck register until the hatchway to the wrecked bridge was forced open.

Standing in the hatch was a figure decked in a combination of U.S. Navy khakis and a florid Hawaiian shirt topped by a seriously crushed and disheveled

U.S. Navy officer's cap. One of the surviving bridge crew tried to grab a pistol but the figure was holding a Thompson sub-machine gun and the man was cut down before he had reached the weapon.

"You'd better order your men to stand down, Cap'n." The man had a voice that sounded as if a substantial volume of gravel had been mixed in it. "We hold the decks and the engineering spaces. To be honest, there aren't enough of your men left standing to man a gangplank. We machine-gunned you real good before we boarded."

Wuppermann felt sickened and humiliated but had to face the inevitable. "Oberleutnant zur See Oskar Wuppermann. S-38. I see I have no choice but to surrender my ship to you. . ."

"Lieutenant Quinton McHale. PR-109. I accept your surrender. Gunner's Mate 1st class Borgnine will take command of this tub and get her back to Starry May. And, Ernest, check up on prize regulations while you're doing it."

Gunboat PR-73, Ulyanov'sk Narrows, Volga River.

"We cleaned their clocks but good." Thom sounded exultant. The bad news was that BK-116 had been sunk, BK-119 was aground off the east bank of the Volga while PR-73 had minor damage. On the other hand, three of the S-boats had been sunk and the fourth boarded and captured.

"We haven't done our jobs yet. That was just the escort. Now, we have to get that river steamer of theirs and the landing craft. We're scattered all over the place." Kennedy looked out of his bridge. The visibility had improved significantly since the battle had started and he could now see the river steamer and the landing craft to the south. Jennings in PR-57 had made the best of it and his two three inch guns were making good practice on the steamer. In contrast, the 5.9s on the steamer were not. They were getting their shells close but never quite close enough. *The five-nine is too clumsy for this kind of fighting. I'll bet that steamer is along for river bank bombardment, not engaging gunboats.*

"Signal to Kauffman and McHale, order them to form on us and we'll hit the six MFP landing craft together. Tell Jennings to keep on plastering that steamer. The last thing we need is her trying to protect the landing craft."

The three American gunboats quickly formed into a line abreast, PR-73 in the center, PR-109 on the right and PR-84 over on the left. Behind them, PR-57 was crowding the river steamer against the west bank of the Volga. Kennedy guessed the converted steamer was already in serious danger of running aground. *Once again, the Russians were right. Shallow draft is essential for fighting on the Volga. Converting freighters and ferries into gunboats just doesn't work. Even if they can carry heavier guns than we do, their maneuverability is so restricted they can't use them properly.*

"Skipper, the sun is coming out!" Maguire was pointing at the clouds overhead. The sun wasn't actually breaking through but there was a bright patch in the clouds that marked its position. The rain had slowed down to a fine drizzle that made things damp rather than wet. That meant visibility was drastically improved and, for the first time, Kennedy could see what was happening on the river without having to rely on the radar picture. What surprised him was how late in the afternoon it was. The sun wasn't precisely setting, not yet, but it wouldn't be long before it was.

"All gunboats, open fire on the lead landing craft, port column." The MFPs were in two columns of three and Kennedy was prepared to bet that the commander was in their right-hand column. That made it the port column from his point of view. His own three inch gun fired almost instantly, making him guess that the crew had it loaded ready and the gunner had his finger around the trigger. PR-84 followed a split second later and the two shells made a perfect straddle around the designated MFP. "Keep shooting. Fire at will."

"What we got against poor old Will?" The traditional joke was shouted out from the gun pit. It didn't reduce the rate of fire from the gun crew though and shell splashes quickly surrounded the target. McHale's PR-109 was still too far out to join in the bombardment. The 3 inch 23 caliber gun might be a lot handier than the 50 caliber weapons but it was very short-ranged and lacked punch. *She'd be better off with a second quadruple 1.1 up front.*

"Hit her!" The scream of triumph came over the crashing of PR-73's gun. An orange-red fireball had risen from the targeted MFP and the landing craft was burning.

"PR-84's claiming the hit." Thom sounded disgusted. "Anybody can see that was one of ours."

"Who the hell cares?" Kennedy was annoyed by the grandstanding. "As long as the krauts go down, who the hell cares who scored the hits?"

He swung his binoculars around to look at PR-109. As the gunboats had moved downstream, they had passed the river steamer, now burning from the hits scored by PR-57, and that had unmasked the steamer's stern guns. The two 88s were much more suited to this kind of fighting than the five-nines and they were firing on PR-109 with enthusiasm. Kennedy saw PR-109 lurching as at least two shells plowed into her and the gunboat slowed dramatically, the first clouds of black smoke rising from her engine spaces.

That gave a frustrated five-nine crew the chance they had been waiting for. With PR-109 at almost a dead stop, they threw one of their 100 pound shells directly into the crippled boat. There was a massive explosion that shrouded the gunboat. When it cleared, there was nothing left but floating wreckage.

MFP-253, Ulyanov'sk Narrows, Volga River.

"Ganz und gar beschissen!" Stabsscharfuhrer Johannes Gottschalk couldn't help reflect that the emotion was a common one when Americans were around. They just would not do things the sensible, logical way. The almost-instant destruction of one of their gunboats at the hands of the auxiliary cruiser should have forced them to concentrate on destroying the cruiser while the landing craft slipped past and deposited the assault force on the shore side of the Ulyanov'sk beachhead. Instead, the gunboats had run the heavy guns on the auxiliary cruiser and concentrated on the landing craft.

Only the largest Ami gunboat had stayed behind to pummel the cruiser with its main guns and multiple machine guns. Despite its heavy guns, or, more accurately, because its slow-firing, slow-to-traverse heavy guns couldn't keep up with the low-built, fast-moving gunboat only a hundred yards or so away, the auxiliary cruiser was getting the worst of the exchange. She was listing and fire was spreading in the superstructure and amidships.

The MFPs weren't doing much better. They were armored against rifle-caliber weapons it was true but provided only minimal protection against the twin .50 caliber machine guns and none at all against the heavy quadruple mounts on the stern of the gunboats. Those guns, bigger and more powerful even than the 20mm anti-aircraft guns carried by the MFPs, were punching holes right through the sides of the landing and bouncing round inside before exploding.

Gottschalk could see the inside of MFP-253 was already turning into a butcher's pen with several centimeters of red-tinged river water washing around the transport deck. Their 75mm gun, an obsolete, short-barrelled infantry howitzer, was also silenced. The moment it had fired its first shot, both gunboats had turned their machine gun fire on it with savage ferocity. The gun had vanished under the streams of tracer fire and now it was swung to one side while its barrel drooped lifelessly towards the pitiless gray of the Volga. Lifeless also described its crew; strewn around the mount where they had died in the hopeless battle to serve their gun.

That was something else Gottschalk couldn't understand. Everybody knew the correct way to engage a ship in this kind of battle was to concentrate on its bridge and wipe out the command crew. Once that was done, the target would be out of control and helpless. The Americans hadn't done that. They'd concentrated on the defensive guns mounted by the MFPs, subjecting anything that fired to the same deadly torrent of counterfire. Only now, when the MFPs guns were silenced did the Ami gunboats concentrate on other targets.

Four years before, Gottschalk had been at a briefing where visiting naval officers had explained to members of SS Jagddivision 502 why their mission in

England was so important. They'd spoken of how the Royal Navy destroyers and coastal attack craft would tear apart any invasion force before it got half-way over the channel. Then, the German Navy hadn't even had MFPs. The troops would be crowded into converted river barges with barely a few inches of freeboard. The destroyers, the Naval officers had grimly pointed out, wouldn't even have to fire on those barges. They just had to sail close to them and their wake would swamp the helpless targets.

That was why it was so crucial that the special warfare teams of SS Jagddivision 502 seize suitable airfields in Southern England before an invasion took place. Then, air-landing troops could be flown into those airfields to turn them into airheads from which attacks could be mounted on the coastal ports.

At the time, the SS troopers had laughed off the Navy officers, accusing them of lacking dedication. They had believed they could fight off the British destroyers themselves. Now, on the Volga instead of the Channel, Gottschalk could see how wrong he and his comrades had been. They had tried to mount their machine guns on the sides of the landing craft but the gesture had been futile. The 7.92mm bullets had just bounced off the gunboats but in exchange they had attracted the storm of fire that had silenced all the other weapons. The landing craft were helpless victims, a school of fish beset by two sharks that made repeated passes through them. All of the MFPs were defenseless, all were trying to escape. None had the speed or the maneuverability to do so.

"Herr Stabsscharfuhrer. We must beach our ship now. Otherwise we will sink in mid-channel. If we do that, the survivors of your men will drown. We are south of the bridgehead held by the Ivans. Now, the west bank is friendly territory."

Gottschalk was about to give the naval officer a furious lecture on the need for courage and determination when his rational mind kicked in. MFP-253 was sinking, slowly but surely. His men were heavily loaded with weapons and equipment and they were all excellent swimmers but human bodies had their limit and the width of the Volga made swimming ashore impossible. He also realized that the naval officer was primarily concerned with the safety of the men his ship was carrying and the crew was putting them before their own chances of survival. Gottschalk saw something else; the two Ami gunboats had stopped making firing passes at the MFPs but had started holding station on them and using their heavy gun to sink each craft in turn. MFP-253 had a very narrow window in which to seek some sort of safety.

"Herr Captain, there is, I think, no place in Russia that is friendly to us. But, please, beach this craft and get your men off. We will escort you to the nearest of our bases." Gottschalk felt the engines on MFP-253 surge as the landing craft turned for the west bank. *Once again, the Amis have defeated me.*

Gottschalk raged to himself as the bitterness of a third defeat at their hands sunk deep into his soul.

Gunboat PR-73, Ulyanov'sk Narrows, Volga River.

"Our mortar crewmen are asking permission to open up on the beached landing craft. They feel left out and neglected." Thom sounded as if he could be joking but his face was grim beneath the bandage from a shell splinter that had scoured his forehead. As usual, PR-73 had a lot of trivial damage from machine gun and 20mm cannon fire and several of the men were wounded. The worst damage was along the waterline to port where a 75mm shell had exploded in the water alongside. Fragments had penetrated the armor and caused flooding but the damage control teams were hard at work plugging the leaks. The mortar crewmen were probably helping them but Kennedy could understand their desire to have a crack at the grounded ship. *It is a perfect target for mortar fire and we do have our new heavy mortar to try out.*

"Very good, Larry. That MFP still hasn't struck her colors so we need to finish her. Three inch crew are to leave station and assist damage control The mortar crew are to engage that grounded MFP. We don't want to have to sink her again at any time in the future."

"That we don't, skipper. Mortar crew, open fire on that landing craft."

The heavy whumph of the 107mm mortar followed almost instantly on the order. The shot was well over, landing in the woods behind the beaching site. There was a long pause before the next round followed it. *I bet the watch remaining with the mortar had a round ready to go but they needed the rest of the crew before they could reload and get off another.* When it resumed, the mortar fire was hardly accurate and Kennedy could hear some protesting groans from PR-73's hull members. He watched the shells scattered around the beached landing craft. *The motion from the river and our forward speed isn't helping but there's more than that here. I bet lack of range wasn't the only reason why the Russians rejected this model. I think the short barrel and reduced propellant charge cause excessive dispersion. Doesn't matter to us since we use it for illumination. Supposedly. Well, we missed the MFP but I bet we scared the people who made it on-shore.*

The American flotilla was reforming. PR-109 and both Russian boats had been sunk. PR-57 was heavily damaged with at least two 88mm hits and her superstructure mauled by a quadruple 20mm. PR-84 had taken a 75mm hit in her mortar pit and the whole act area of the ship was a blackened ruin from the ammunition fire. Ahead of them though was the greatest sight the Volga had seen since the war had started. A German S-boat was plowing north with the Stars and Stripes flying proudly over the Nazi flag. Her radios had to be out as well because she was signaling to PR-73 using a lamp.

Kazan Thunderbolts

"Message for the Commodore – that's you Jack. Captain Borgnine is asking for assistance. He says his command, USS *McHale* has engine problems. The diesels are failing and she needs a tow back to Starry May."

Kennedy heard the exultant cheer going up as the name of the captured S-boat spread. "The 57 boat is too badly damaged. Tell Borgnine, the 84 boat will take him in tow. We're the only boat left in fighting trim right now. We need to keep our hands free. Oh, and include our condolences on the loss of Captain McHale."

"Not going be possible, Jack. Got another message, in Morse by flashlight, from the sandbank to starboard. Crew of BK-119 and a couple of survivors from the 109 boat are stranded there. We leave them behind, the krauts will shell them for sure."

"Signal back, we'll pick them up."

"That might be tricky, Skip. We can't get in close enough and they've got too many wounded to swim out to us. And a lot of Russians don't swim."

Kennedy stared at the low-laying sandbank. "Right, we'll do this. I'll swim over there with a lifeline. We can string it between us and that stump in the middle of the flat. The survivors over there can use the line to get to us. The fittest can help the wounded and the ones too weak to make it by themselves."

Thom was about to say something but Kennedy held up his hand. "Don't say it Larry. We all know I'm the strongest swimmer here and all those years fooling about on Long Island Sound had better count for something. Now, give me a lifeline, I'm going over the side."

Kennedy dived into the Volga, feeling the cold of the water chilling his bones. He was indeed an excellent swimmer and his powerful crawl took him through the river current to the stranded men. Despite that, he could feel the strain on his back taking its toll and the feel of sand beneath his toes was a relief. The survivors gathered around him, the two Americans cheering, one of the dozen or so Russians thrusting a flask of vodka at him. Kennedy took a swig, feeling the raw spirit warm him and ease the knotting muscles in his back. "Tovarish, each man must haul himself along the rope back to our gunboat. Those of you who have the strength must help those who do not."

Kennedy looked around the group. Both Americans were badly wounded by burns and fragment. About half the Russians were no better. "Did Captain McHale make it off?"

"No, Sir. He was on the bridge still when that last shell hit us. The whole boat just blew up."

"Too bad. Without your Captain, you two will have to look after each other. Time to move."

Offshore, PR-73 was powering her engines up and down in order to hold still against the river current. The Volga current wasn't that strong but it was uneven and the eddying effects were causing the gunboat to move constantly. The lifeline to the shore thus dipped and then stretched before being drawn first one way and then whipping back to another. Although hauling oneself along the line from the sand bar to the safety of the gunboat was easy to say, the constant flexing of the line made it hard to achieve. For fit men to do so was difficult enough but the few unwounded were burdened with the disabled and semi-conscious. The first group of three, two unwounded men with a third unconscious seaman held between them, were soon in trouble. Kennedy dived back in the river and swam over to their aid. With his help, they were able to make the exhausting journey to PR-73. There, the crew had nets over the side and they helped bring all three men up to the main deck.

By that time, Kennedy had already swum off to the aid of another Russian seaman. Although wounded by bullet fragments in his legs, he had refused help and started to make the trip along the rope on his own. A particularly large movement had whipped the lifeline out of his hands and he had been flicked into the water away from safety. Kennedy swam over to him and cupped his chin with one hand in the traditional lifeguard's position. Then, with powerful kicks from his legs, he had pulled the man back to PR-73 and handed him over to his crewmen hanging on the nets.

The next two men on the line were the two American survivors from PR-109. They were in extreme difficulties and in constant danger of losing their grip on the rope. By the time Kennedy reached them, they were semi-conscious and obviously on the point of slipping away completely. He managed to secure them with his own grip on the line and then started the exhausting process of dragging them through the water towards his gunboat. Two of his men saw what he was trying to do and dived into the water as well. Their strength was the margin that kept the two survivors alive and saw them lifted to the safety of PR-73. By the time the two American sailors and their saviors were on deck, Kennedy had already swum off to bring another wounded Russian sailor to safety.

The rescue had already attracted the attention of the German forces on the west bank. Machine gun and cannon fire plus rounds from field artillery were already splashing into the water around PR-73. The boat's bulk was shielding the men in the water from the shells and bullets but Kennedy knew that it was only a question of time before the Germans brought up heavier guns and got the range more accurately. That added urgency to his efforts and he swam faster and harder from one small group of struggling men to an individual and then back to another group. He heard the dreaded howl of heavy artillery but in his exhaustion, it didn't register that the rounds were going from east to west. Nor did it register with him that the guns were American 105mms.

Then, he realized that the sandbank was empty. All the survivors had been evacuated and not a single one had been lost. There was only one thing left to do. Kennedy untied the lifeline from the tree stump that had done such noble service. He had heard the Russians swear never to leave a single thing behind that might aid the fascists and he was determined to follow their example. That included something as simple as a length of rope. He tied one end around his waist, wrapped the extra length around him and set off on the last swim back to PR-73.

Kennedy knew he was a strong swimmer but he also knew his efforts had exhausted his last reserves of strength. Yet, he seemed to be moving through the water remarkably quickly. It was the pressure on the rope that told him why. PR-73 was moving through the water, leaving the sand bar behind and towing him along behind. Yet, despite the artillery duel now raging overhead and PR-73s three-inch gun firing at the west bank, his crew and the Russian survivors were hauling on the lifeline, bringing him up to the gunboat's side. Their hands reached down, caught his, and hauled him up on board. Once again, it was a swig of vodka from a flask that restored warmth to his body and dulled the agony in his back. Only then did he hear the words that the men hauling him aboard had been singing.

"Ey Ukhnemi, Ey Ukhnemi!
Yeshcho Razik, Yeshcho da raz
Ey Ukhnemi, Ey Ukhnemi!
Yeshcho Razik, Yeshcho da raz
Razovyom my beryozu
Razovyom my kudryavu.
Ey Ukhnemi, Ey Ukhnemi!"

As he was carried below decks, he suddenly felt intensely proud of being considered a true Volga Boatman.

Headquarters, 40th Bombardment Wing, Kolosovka.

"Has anybody any idea what we are doing here?" Gunnery Sergeant Custer looked around his Marine reconnaissance team. "The gunboats wanted our help on the river but we were ordered here instead."

"News to us as well." Sergeant Kidd was sitting in one corner of the waiting room going over the internal schematics of an A-20 with Sergeant Wint. They'd found a way they could get to all the crew members through the side of the aircraft without wasting any time. Recently, they'd started teaching other ground crew personnel the skills of getting into crashed aircraft and rescuing the men inside. "What about you, kid?"

The question was directed at a young sailor sitting erect in another corner, his hat clasped firmly in his hands. "Sorry, Sergeant, I don't know either. I thought I was coming out here to join one of the gunboats."

"Gentlemen, would you please step this way?" The Lieutenant who had emerged from General Eaker's office was speaking with more respect than that normally adopted by officers speaking to a group of enlisted men. To the more experienced and cynical, that spelled trouble. "The General is ready for you now."

The group of men was conducted to a conference room, one considerably more luxurious and better-equipped that the briefing rooms they were used to. General Ira Eaker was sitting on the desk, a female Russian officer sitting beside him on a leather seat.

"Gentlemen, I am General Ira Eaker, currently in command of the Eighth Air Force. This is Major Tatiana Timofeevna Pavlova of the Partisans. You may have heard that we now have obtained confirmation of something we have long suspected. The krauts are murdering our shot-down airmen whenever and wherever they can find them. We also now have proof that their fighter pilots are in the habit of killing our airmen when they bail out of crippled aircraft. We have raised this issue with the Red Cross in Geneva and they have approached the Germans on the subject. The German response was that as far as they are concerned, our bomber crews and anybody who supports them are terrorfliegers, criminals, and deserve execution."

Eaker paused while the palpable anger in the room subsided. "Quite. The Red Cross is unable, or unwilling, to do anything about this flagrant abuse of international law. So, we are thrown on to our own resources. It has been decided, at the highest levels, to form an organization dedicated to rescuing shot-down aircrew. Obviously this means collaborating with the partisans behind German lines. Major Timofeevna will act as our liaison with the partisan groups.

"Gunnery Sergeant Custer, your men are vastly over-qualified for the work you have been performing. You have demonstrated your ability to get in and out of enemy territory without a ripple. Yet, your men are also highly trained in demolitions, scouting and a wide variety of other skills.

"Sergeants Wint and Kidd, you two have shown an uncanny skill in getting into crashed aircraft and rescuing those within. Your dedication to saving the lives of your fellow airmen is both awe-inspiring and humbling to those of us who can only watch you at work.

"Seaman Jeff Thomas here is a new recruit to the Navy but he went into a compartment of his ship, one that was burning and filled with toxic gas, and pulled out three of his fellow seamen who would surely otherwise have died. He impressed his officers, not just by what he did but by the innate skill that allowed him to do so without becoming a casualty himself. In short, all of you have demonstrated that you have the skills and dedication that this new organization will require."

Eaker paused for a second. "This is a new kind of organization, one that consists of members from all our armed services working together to a common aim. The partisans will rescue our pilots and shelter them but it will be you who go into enemy territory – or anywhere else – and bring our airmen back home to safety. If you need equipment, you will get it. If you need resources, you will get them. Your sole and only duty is to rescue our aircrew. If anybody else tries to divert you from that mission, be they ever so high in rank, you are authorized to tell them to take a hike. That authorization comes from the President himself. President Roosevelt added that you should feel free to invoke his name when needed. However, you will have other duties, but only ones related to your primary mission. One of them is to find other men . ."

Major Timofeevna cleared her throat pointedly. To the secret delight of the enlisted men in the room, the General actually blushed. "And women where appropriate. . . in your own image who can expand this operation. Can we, can all the airmen who fight along the Volga Front, count on you?"

And that is a loaded question if ever I have heard one, thought Custer. "What is the name of our new formation, Sir?"

Eaker grinned to himself, knowing that there men were hooked on their mission. "This is a multi-service group with representatives from the Sea, from the Air and from the Land. So, we're going to call you SEALs."

Gunboat Squadron GunRon 5 Headquarters, Staraya Mayna, Volga River.

"They're coming in, Sir." Lieutenant Commander Raymond Blake almost ran into his commander's office. Word of the battle south of the Ulyanov'sk Narrows was spreading far and fast. It was also gaining color with every retelling. It was a classic example of the Bullfrog Tendency at work. Any story would be inflated as long as there was a gullible audience to listen and believe.

"What's left of them are." Farrow was looking out of his window at the port entrance. "Three boats sunk, two shot up so badly they'll be in dock for weeks and one with lesser damage. This was our first real battle on the Volga and we got hurt."

"Not as bad as the Hitlerites." Blake used the Russian expression unconsciously. Ever since the news of the murdered airmen had started to spread, the older terms for the Germans were being dropped. "They lost all four S-boats and three MFPs. One MFP is grounded and the other two plus their steamer are shot to hell. We won by every standard of any importance. And take a look at that. A captured S-boat!"

"I know." Farrow was dry. "What's the betting that a picture of it will be on the front page of the newspapers tomorrow, right up there with the Flying Fortresses bombing Moskva. If you look carefully, right at the bottom of the page in the smallest type the newspaper has, there'll be a note that the U.S. 83rd Division has given ground in the face of fierce German attacks."

"I do not think so Comrades. I can think of much work that a captured S-boat might be used for as long as we are discrete." Napalkov was also looking at the S-boat and his Chekist's mind was already conceiving of devious plans in which she would play a part.

"Tovarish Chekist, you have returned." Farrow sounded pleased which was a good piece of acting on his part. "How goes your investigation?"

Napalkov only just barely stopped himself smiling. He had noted how Americans usually greeted each other with some variant of the phrase 'welcome back' or 'good to see you' a phrase pointedly not used this time. A lesser man might have taken offense at its absence here but a good Chekist never took offense at anything unless it served the interests of the State to do so. "My investigation went well. The arrival of the wrong ammunition at the railway yards here was a blunder. Errors in procedure were compounded by stupidity and poor equipment. That has been corrected. How the ammunition was delivered to this base for shipment south is another matter. Ahh, that is PR-73 coming in is it not? How is my friend John Fitzgerald?"

"It is reported that he injured his back severely while swimming to the rescue of a group of stranded sailors and will require prolonged treatment. Lieutenant Thom will be taking command of PR-73 while Jack recovers."

"I must go and see him." Napalkov hesitated slightly. "Tovarish commander, may I ask a great kindness of you? Our investigations have suggested that there was indeed sabotage in the rail yards here. John Fitzgerald has a working knowledge of railways and how they might be . . . . misused. Perhaps he could be assigned to advise me while convalescing?"

Oh crap. That's what I was hoping wouldn't happen. "I'm afraid that Lieutenant Kennedy will be confined to his hospital ward as soon as he can be taken off his ship. His back has been seriously injured with a pre-existing injury exacerbated by the efforts he made while swimming and the concussion of artillery shells exploding in the water near him. At the moment, I think he will be confined to his bed and under treatment. That means I no longer have authority over him until his doctors release him to me. I'm afraid that he is in the hands of our medical staff right now and you must approach them if you wish his help. Certainly, if they grant permission, he may assist you until he is once more fit for duty."

"I quite understand Tovarish Commander. I will simply ask his doctors if he could read a few files for me and give me any thoughts he might have. His doctors might even appreciate him having something to read, Bored patients make difficult patients and having something to do might make him more . . . . tractable."

Farrow waited until Napalkov had left and then grabbed his telephone. "Get me the base hospital immediately. Chief Surgeon. . . . . Chief Surgeon? Hi, John. There'll be a Chekist called Napalkov over to see you very shortly. He wants Jack to help him with an investigation. Get in his way will you? Yeah, undisturbed bed rest, that'll do. Ohh, Ray's already over there? Great. We want as little to do with CheKa as possible."

Farrow relaxed. He realized that Blake must have understood what was needed, slipped out and made the arrangements while he and Napalkov were still talking. Of such things, good executive officers were made.

Composite Group, 83rd Infantry Division, Yandoba, Chuvashskaya Bridgehead.

Once again, what was left of Lieutenant Grisham's force was defending a ridge. Nobody had told them to do so, but it seemed like an obvious thing to do. The ridge was the commanding ground and the ground it commanded was so obviously vital it would have been negligent not to have disputed it. It wasn't just the crossroads surrounded by a few dilapidated houses that was so essential. A railway line also ran through the same junction. Also, the clear terrain that had led to this area being named the Kolkhoz Pass was necking down with dense forest crowding in. One of the terrain paths that had cut through the forest came in from the north here and added to the bottleneck.

Once, by which he meant earlier in the day, Grisham would have seen the buildings around the junction as a fortress. Now, he knew they were just a trap. The fascists, with their tanks and assault guns could shell any resistance in the buildings into submission before the infantry closed in to dislodge the survivors. In order to act as a fortress, a town had to be large enough to absorb that first blow and still offer a viable defense. Kolvino had been not quite large enough. Kanash would be. The hamlet below came nowhere close.

Instead, Grisham had set up his defense along a ridge behind the hamlet. This time, it was serious high ground, more than a hundred feet higher than the surrounding area. While the crossroads and railway were apparently undefended, he could cover them with fire from the ridge and make them too hazardous to use. His tank was positioned carefully on the reverse slope so that it could edge forward and fire over the crest when necessary. He even had his two howitzers set up. The guns might only have a single round each but he was willing to be that the Germans didn't know that. They'd see a defensive position that was formidable in its own right and was held by troops with artillery support. *Now, if I can make them think that we have more armor up here than we do . . . .*

"Jake, is it possible you could move from place to place behind this ridge and pop up here and there. Make the krauts think there are more of you?"

Fuller audibly sucked his teeth. His Sherman was tucked away on a piece of hard ground, well-concealed by the ridge. "We can do that. In fact, I can offer you something else. We got a lot of high explosive on board. Not much armor piercing and we shot off about half of what we had but we still got our HE. You plan to bluff the krauts with our one-round field guns? Why don't I shoot an HE off at the same time? Old Tinny here has a French 75 as a main gun. It is a field piece, or was, and somebody who has just got hit by three shells isn't going to notice one of the bangs is a lot less than the rest. We can toss others at odd intervals, keep up the bluff that we've got guns here."

Grisham thought that over. "That'll be great, Jake. Are you set up so we can spot for you?"

"We got a telephone mounted on the rear right of the hull. Put a guy on that and a walkie-talkie connection to your spotter and that'll work fine." Fuller looked at Lieutenant Grisham and decided some reassurance was in order. "Look, Irwin, don't sweat this. We're trained for this sort of thing. Back home, they hammered things home to us. Tanks are to support the infantry by direct and indirect engagement of hostile forces. That's why we've got a field gun as our main armament. Taking on enemy tanks is the job of the tank destroyers."

"Twelve miles back in the west, we were the tank destroyers. 90mm guns. Their infantry took us out. Never got to fire a shot."

"Yeah, and we were supposed to be supporting our own infantry only there wasn't any. Not of ours anyway. We took on the kraut tanks instead and got cut to pieces."

Grisham nodded. "It's been a hell of a day. At least it's stopped raining."

"It has that. Odd yellow light isn't it."

"Sun shining under the clouds and reflecting off them." That made Grisham think. "Dusk will be falling soon. That could work for us as well."

"What have you in mind?" Fuller looked at Grisham curiously. He had a feeling that whatever the infantry lieutenant had in mind wasn't going to be precisely risk-free.

"It was something you said. About how you spent all your time training to support the infantry? Well, I've spent all day being pushed backwards by the krauts. Every time we've brushed into each other, we've ended up doing what they want which boiled down to getting the hell out of their way. I'm sick of doing what they want. Why don't we make them do what we want for a change?"

"Go on . . ." *I knew it,* thought Fuller. *My old man sat me down and gave me some advice when I heard we were going overseas. It was 'shut up and never volunteer for anything'. I should have listened to him.*

"Every time the krauts hit us, they did it the same way. They had a light section in front, some infantry and a few small vehicles, mostly those little half-tracks or armored cars. They probed us and found where our defenses were. So, when that recon section turns up, we hit it, hard. We drop our artillery on it, then attack them with your tank in support. By then, it'll be dusk, they won't be able to see much. The sun will be behind them, this weird yellow light will screw everything up. We'll be in near-darkness. With a little luck, they'll make us for a much larger force than they are and they won't know who or what we are. Rather than attack an unknown at night, they'll hang off until morning when they can see what they're doing."

Fuller could hear his father shouting out the warning across most of the continental United States, the Pacific Ocean and a substantial proportion of Russia *Don't do it son. Shut up and never volunteer for anything!* But, the truth was that Fuller also was fed up with being pushed around by Germans. "You might have something there. What'll we do once we've held them for the night?"

"I don't know, Jake, honest to God, I don't know. But, we'll have gained ten hours or so, given the boys a chance to grab some food and sleep and maybe, just maybe, we'll piss off the krauts. Who knows? The brass might get us some help here or maybe the Russians will help us out. Whatever might happen, it won't if we don't do something now."

Grisham paused for breath and saw Fuller nodding. *At least we're going to be doing something.* "We'd better get the boys up and ready."

Motorized Reconnaissance Company, 7th Panzer Division, Yandoba, Chuvashskaya Bridgehead.

"If we've cleared the town, we better move on to check out the ridge." Major Maximilian Hildebrand looked across at where the dark bulk of the ridgeline overlooking Yandoba glowered down at him in the twilight. "I don't like having that thing overlook us like this."

"Our orders were to secure the town. This junction is key to moving forward." Captain Moritz Kneib also looked at the ridge with great caution. His six heavy SdKfz 231 eight-wheeled armored cars would have to lead the way up that ridge and that was a task he did not relish in the growing darkness. *There are rumors spreading that the Americans can knock out even the heaviest of tanks with their rocket launcher. And my armored cars have armor that is as thin as my shirt.*

"And you, Klem?" Lieutenant Klemens Günther commanded the reconnaissance detachment's motorized infantry company. It was a company in name only. Supposed to have 5 officers and 222 enlisted men, he had only two officers, himself and the commander of the heavy platoon. His three infantry platoons were commanded by Sergeants and each had only 24 out of its supposed 42 soldiers. The infantry units had suffered severely in the fighting so far and had lost further men in order to keep the mortar and two machine gun sections up to strength. The mortars and machine guns were the backbone of every infantry unit and that was well understood by every infantry officer.

"This village is too small to defend properly. We need to have that ridge. But, it is nearly night and we cannot fight our way up in darkness if we have to. I think we had better wait until morning. The General's orders were specific, to take and hold this village. He said nothing about going beyond it."

"We would not have to fight our way up. Today has proved the Amis cannot fight." Kneib was still weighing up the advisability of advancing up the ridge. "They retreated faster than the Ivans and made little effort to hold ground. If we attack the ridge, they will abandon it, if they are up there at all of course."

The answer to that implied question came as a shocking surprise. The howl of artillery fire was something the German units were quite familiar with but they hadn't heard inbound fire since they had moved to face the Americans. So much so, it was a split second before they realized the shells were indeed coming at them rather than from them.

The three explosions racked the middle of the hamlet, landing in the midst of the motorized company's support platoon. It had also been badly under-strength to start with and Hildebrand guessed it was a lot more so. Now, that platoon was a chaotic and disorganized mass of men running for cover, crouching down behind the armored vehicles or taking cover underneath them. *Our four mechanics are in there. The battle train and baggage sections don't matter but if we lose those four men, we are in deep trouble. The whole army is short of mechanics and there are long lines of vehicles waiting to be repaired as a result.* The screams and more ominous sounds that followed the explosions of the shells told him that there were wounded in there. Another artillery shell arrived just a few seconds later, still aimed at the middle of the hamlet.

"Tank! There's a tank up there!" Captain Kneib shouted the warning as the echoes of the exploding artillery round died away.

Hildebrand saw that he was right, An Ami Sherman tank had moved up just enough to expose its turret. There was a brilliant flash as its gun fired, sending a brilliant red streak the 1250 yards that separated it from the nearest German armored car. The shot missed, at that range it could hardly do anything else, but its effect was dramatic nonetheless. The driver in the SdKfz-222 was frantically trying to get the little four-wheel armored car started but the engine chose that moment to balk. The sound of the engine turning over but not catching had a despairing note to it. The second shell from the tank that was slowly advancing down the slope from the ridge also missed but was a lot closer and Kneib imagined he could hear the stones and gravel ringing on the armor. The armored car gunner tried to fire back with his 20mm cannon but the range made the effort hopeless. Yet, despite that, the white streaks of his shots sprayed around the tank and one of them actually hit the sloping front of the Sherman only to disintegrate into a shower of sparks.

Hildebrand was so intent on watching the armored car trying to get clear that he had missed the hit scored on the tank. When he did glance away from the struggle of the driver to get his vehicle started, he saw the one thing he didn't want to. The tank had infantry support, the figures of American infantry moving on either side of the Sherman. He could see the brilliant flashes of their rifles, flashes much brighter than those of the Kar98k rifles used by his men, and from them he knew that the advancing enemy had semi-automatic rifles. Behind him, a third shell from the Sherman had hit right beside the armored car, rocking it so badly he thought it might have flipped over. It didn't but its crew decided enough was enough. Their vehicle wouldn't start, its gun was useless and the American tank had it in for them. They bailed out and ran clear. Behind them, the fourth shot from the Sherman sent their 222 into an orange fireball.

"At least a battalion of infantry up there." Günther spoke cautiously although he was an experienced man who had been in the reconnaissance troops since France three years earlier. "That ridge is too important; the Amis won't send their entire force down here. They'll keep most of their men back to hold the high ground. And a platoon of tanks?"

"Probably. An American platoon is five tanks. One up there on the ridge to provide overwatch, the other advancing to support the infantry. Our panzers probably got the rest." Kneib was doing the mathematics as well. "And a battery of artillery, probably short of shells though. They'll be holding what is left for when we attack."

"Just what the hell are they up to?" Günther watched the American infantry go to ground, apparently unwilling to face the 20mm fire from the armored cars. The tank wasn't worried though. It had closed to around six hundred meters and at that range it only took three shots to reduce one of the big, eight-wheeled SdKfz 232s into a burning wreck. Meanwhile, rifle fire from the Americans was beginning to pepper the German unit. It didn't take long for some of the bullets to bite. It was the vicious ripping snarl of the MG 42s that was beginning to dominate the exchange of fire between the infantry though. The streams of white flashes from the machine guns showed how they were pinning the Americans down, making further forward movement impossible. They also gave the Sherman a target for its main gun. Günther saw the tank switch targets from the armored vehicles and carefully put a main gun round into a machine gun nest. The explosion silenced the gun almost instantly.

"They're going to stay back there while that tank reduces our armored cars to wrecks, one by one." Hildebrand watched the Sherman moving into position to shoot up another 232. "They won't come in until they've pushed the armored cars back."

"Either that, or they have more tanks out there and are outflanking us. This attack could just be to pin us in place while they do that." Kneib grinned. "It's what we would do to them."

"And aren't they learning fast." Günther sounded distinctly disturbed.

"I'd noticed. We'll drop back behind the village so it acts as a screen. That way they'll have to close in if they want to fight is and if they are pulling a flanker, we'll be in a position to crack the jaws open."

Emergency Casualty Station, Kanash, Chuvashskaya Bridgehead.

"Incoming!" The howl of the inbound German artillery fire was becoming familiar. Kanash was at the extreme end of the range boasted by the German 170mm guns. The shells were few in number and their dispersion was great. However, they were also unusually powerful and when they did hit home, they did a lot of damage. That combination made them entirely suitable for keeping the troops assembling in Kanash awake and on edge. It was called harassment and interdiction fire.

First Lieutenant Dorothy Hopkins was feeling suitably harassed and interdicted. She, and the three other nurses with her, had set up an emergency aid station in Kanash, initially to treat the wounded from the sporadic shellfire hitting the town. Word that an aid station was available and taking customers was available had spread quickly and casualties were starting to come in from all around. The nurses had done what they could and then more. Hopkins had been overwhelmed and on the edge of despair when a miracle had happened.

Kazan Thunderbolts

Heaven be praised, a couple of real doctors had turned up. Our little shelter turned into a real hospital where wounded could be treated, not just comforted.

"More wounded coming in." One of the other nurses had shouted out the warning. Hopkins hoped the casualties weren't from the artillery fire. There was a special horror in how the shell fragments tore a human body apart. *Come to think of it, though, even rifle bullets can do terrible damage.*

"Where are they from?" The answer she got from the stretcher bearers was just a shrug. "Get them to the tent."

Once inside she approached the nearest of the new arrivals with her best professional smile in place. One calculated to cheer her patient and relax him without giving the impression she was taking his injuries lightly. "Your name, Private?"

"Newman, ma'am. Private Ronald Newman."

"All right Ronnie, what happened?"

"Krauts hit us with mortars. One went off close to me and I got this. Fragment hit my leg. Lieutenant Grisham had me evacuated back here."

"All right, let's get your pants off and have a look." Hopkins found that a nurses professional smile was also a good way of stopping her laughing at her patients reaction to the news that a woman was about to take his pants off. She was so intent on inspecting the wound that she didn't notice the sound of engines outside or the sudden change in atmosphere inside the tent.

"What's wrong with this one, Lieutenant?" The voice was acidic, and had an undoubted air of command. Hopkins looked up and jumped to attention. She'd never actually had any military training, nurses weren't given any and she knew her rank was a courtesy. Officially it was so enlisted men would obey their orders. The enlisted men believed it was so the officers could keep all the nurses for themselves. She took in the man facing her. A General, elderly with a sour, pinched expression on his face as if he had just smelled something very nasty and then found it looked worse than it smelled. His white hair peeped out from beneath a helmet with three stars on it. He was staring down at Hopkins.

"Leg wound from a mortar fragment. The fragment has torn up the tissue and there are major arteries and veins in there. We have to clean the wound and debride it."

The General snorted and peered at the wound with what seemed to be a mixture of curiosity and suspicion. "It doesn't look so bad to me."

"Well, this battle don't look so bad to me." Hopkins was furious at the cavalier dismissal of her judgment.

"You're not a soldier, how would you know?"

Hopkins pointed at the wound. "You're not a doctor, how would you know?"

The General stared at her, his eyes narrowed. Hopkins was suddenly very aware of the two pistols hanging on his hips and how close his hands were to them. Then, two her amazement, the General broke out into a broad grin. "Well, it's good to meet somebody around here with some guts. Now, son, how did you get hit?"

Newman gaped slightly at the sudden change in mood. "Sir, Lieutenants Grisham and Fuller have us on the ridge overlooking the town. All mixed up, just anybody they could find. We've got infantry, truck drivers, a tank and a couple of guns. The artillery is out of ammunition though so the gun crews joined the rest of us. I'm a truck driver. Anyway, the krauts were in the village below us. Lieutenant Grisham thought we ought to do something about that. So we attacked them at dusk. Drove them out of the village and knocked out some of their armored cars. Burned them up real good. They stopped us with mortar fire and machine guns but they still ain't retaken the village so I guess we won that one."

The General nodded. "I guess you did son. You'll get a Purple Heart for that wound. Haven't got the medal for you now but I can give you the ribbon."

He took the ribbon off his own jacket and pressed it into Newman's hand. "Now you get well, son. The Army needs men who know how to attack. Lieutenant, get your nurses together and we'll get you out of here. This place is going to be the scene of one hell of a battle."

"No, Sir. The men need us here." Hopkins thought quickly for a decisive argument that the General would accept. "If we're here, we can get the wounded back on the line a lot faster."

The General nodded. It wasn't an argument he liked or agreed with but it was one he could accept. "Very well, pick out the men who can't fight, and we'll get them out."

"Sir, we want to stay and fight it out right here. If the nurses can take it, we can." Newman's words caused a ripple of approval around the reception tent. That made Hopkins blush brilliant red.

The American General reached down and shook Newman proudly by the shoulder. "That's how an American soldier talks, son."

The General went around the reception tent, quietly speaking to each of the dozen or so wounded men and then left. Outside was the same column of armored cars and half tracks that had crossed the river earlier. It had been a hard drive to get from the ferry point at Kazan to the town of Kanash.

"I have word from our command." Colonel-General Ivan Stepanovich Koniev was smiling broadly. That meant trouble for somebody. "Two infantry divisions and an independent armored brigade have moved into Tugaevo. They will be able to hold the southern shoulder of the fascist salient."

The American General swung into the M-20 command car, took a small box from a recess and replaced the Purple Heart ribbon on his uniform. *All set for the next visit to a field hospital. Now, two Russian infantry divisions and an Independent Tank Brigade are roughly equivalent to an American infantry division. These men are veterans, they know what they are doing.* He thought that over carefully. "Combat Command A of the First Armored is in place at Kalinovka, Combat Command B of the First Armored is moving up and Combat Command A of the Second Armored is right behind them. They'll hold the northern shoulder. Once they're in position, we'll snap the jaws shut."

"Can the 83rd hold? They're beaten."

"No, Tovarish Ivan, they are not beaten. Today they were defeated but they weren't beaten. The shock is wearing off and those boys are getting mad. They know the krauts made fools out of them and they don't like it. They're not beaten men, Ivan, they are getting to be very angry young men. They'll hold this town long enough to make sure the Nazis are in the deepest pile of crap any army has ever seen."

"Unless General Fredendall makes another series of blunders."

"Ahh yes. Vetrenyy Freddie." The American General glared into the darkness lit only by the orange fires of burning buildings and vehicles. The expression on his face, reddened by the light of the fires, chilled even Koniev, a General whose ruthless brutality was legendary in an Army where ruthless, brutal generals were commonplace. He could almost feel it in his heart to be sorry for what was about to befall General Fredendall.

Composite Group, 83rd Infantry Division, Yandoba, Chuvashskaya Bridgehead.

Slowly, the force on the ridgeline was growing. Two more Shermans, survivors of the 746th, had joined *Old Tinny* making a weak but viable platoon. More stragglers had joined the units and been told of how they had kicked the Germans out of the village below them and knocked out their armored cars. Other arrivals had been told how Private Searle had made a specialty of blowing up tanks with his bazooka. Both stories had given badly-needed encouragement to the new arrivals.

Men and tanks hadn't been the only things to arrive. A small group of trucks had pulled up from Kanash and resupplied the two 105mm howitzers with a full load of ammunition. They'd also brought some more 75mm ammunition for the tanks. The same column had brought food, rifle and machine gun ammunition and, to the wonder of all, two more bazookas. Word was spreading of how the bazookas were knocking out the German tanks as soon as they came close enough to the infantry and that was adding to the change of heart that was sweeping through the American units.

Lieutenant Grisham was watching another vehicle approaching. It had drawn his attention as two heavily-masked headlights picking their way up the back side of the ridge and then resolved itself into a jeep with two men on board. When they reached Grisham's position, they stopped their vehicle and dismounted.

"Sir, Lieutenant Grisham, Sir?" Grisham nodded. "Lieutenant Harold Richards and Sergeant Adam Doyle. We've been sent up here to help you out. General Harmon's orders. General Harmon is in charge right now, Vetrenyy Freddie is in a snit and is hiding in his tent. Well, in his heavily-reinforced bunker. Although that won't help him. Word is that a storm is arriving from the East and that he's first on the list of divine thunderbolt recipients."

Grisham snorted with laughter. "Ohh-kay. Welcome to the party. What you bringing? Ma Deuce?"

"Oh no." Sergeant Doyle seemed slightly amused by the suggestion. "We've got something much deadlier than a mere machine gun. The Lieutenant here has a radio. In fact, we have two, one portable, one built into the jeep."

"Ahhhh." Light was beginning to dawn on Grisham.

"That's right, Sir. We're artillery observers. We got a battalion of 155s and two of 105s on the end of these here radios. General Harmon wants this town held and that means holding this ridge. So, you tell us where you want the guns to drop their stuff and we'll make it happen."

Grisham suddenly believed in Santa Claus. "Damn, we haven't seen friendly artillery all day."

Richards seemed solemn suddenly. "General Harmon knows it and he ain't happy about it. Trouble was, nobody knew where any of our units were so our guns were just as likely to hit our own people as anybody else. Your action here at dusk put a hard fix on your position so you were first in line. Now, Lieutenant. . ."

"Call me Irwin and our tank commander is Jake."

"I'm Harry. Show us your ridgeline and I'll set up an observer's position. I don't think the krauts have any idea what our guns can do when they're allowed to."

Headquarters, SS Jägddivision 502, Zhemkovka, West of the Samara Bridgehead.

"Anybody can fail once. Doing so twice is unfortunate. Doing so three times suggests that your competence is seriously in question." SS-Brigadeführer Otto Skorzeny was neither genial nor supportive. He stared at Stabsscharfuhrer Johannes Gottschalk with only very lightly concealed rage. "I had great hopes for you once Johannes, but I must now ask whether you have any future in our unit."

Gottschalk swallowed down his impulse to scream back at his commander. "We were helpless in those landing craft. We tried to fight back with rifles and machine guns but the Ami gunboats were too heavily armored for our fire to have any effect. Once the S-boats escorting us were gone, we were finished. We were able to get back to our own territory and we brought the sailors safely back with us."

Skorzeny admitted to himself that Gottschalk had a point. The original plan to attack the Ami gunboat base at Staraya Mayna had been his but the plan he had proposed had been very different. His concept had been to drop airborne troops at night behind the base and attack it from the landward side. Only, the Luftwaffe hadn't enough transport aircraft to make the drop possible and the growing fleets of American aircraft on the East Bank of the Volga made attempting to use them much too risky. So, the powers that be had changed the operation to a seaborne landing. Then they had switched the target from Staraya Mayna to the bridgehead at Ulyanov'sk. Adding a converted merchant ship armed with 15 cm guns hadn't helped.

None of that had changed the scene of two significant operations that SS Jägddivision 502 had staged coming apart. For a unit that relied on its reputation for infallibility, that was a blow of utmost seriousness. The one thing that Skorzeny did not want was for his pet commando unit to become another line infantry formation, subject to the brutal attrition of the Russian Front.

"As a member of this unit you are expected to face unexpected and unfavorable situations and turn them to your advantage. Three times you have failed to do this. Against the Americans, a painfully inexperienced and inexpert force. They are little more than children on the battlefield yet they have bested you every time you have met."

Gottschalk said nothing. The truth was, there was nothing he could say without sounding as if he was a whining infant making excuses for the inexcusable. Trucks that turned out to be heavily-armed with machine guns; a gunboat that had turned up in just the wrong place and the wrong time for his mission and a thoroughly misconceived operation that had put him and his men in an impossible situation. There was nothing he could see that could have changed any of those yet that was no reason for failure.

Skorzeny pretended to make his mind up although the truth was that he had already done so. Gottschalk had the stink of failure on him now. He was a man who lost. Such a man could not be permitted to remain in SS Jägddivision 502 lest he infect others with his inadequacy.

"Gottschalk, I am transferring you out of this unit. You will be assigned to the SS Infantry Regiment *Germania* forming part of the 5th SS Panzer Division *Wiking*. The official story is that, since this division is formed mostly of volunteers from Norway, Sweden and Finland, veteran German SS troops will provide stiffening and expert guidance. Your particular assignment will be to pass on the skills you have learned here to those volunteers."

Gottschalk knew there was no appeal. Skorzeny's shift from using his first name to his last told him that, no matter what he said or did, he was no longer a member of the SS Jägddivision 502 family. Now, he was an outsider. He saluted and left.

As usual, rumor had spread the word of his expulsion faster than could be explained by the conventional laws of physics. Where once he would have been greeted by his comrades and exchanged some back-chat with them, now he was isolated and alone. He saw some of the men he had regarded as friends avoiding him, changing their path so that they wouldn't have to be obvious in their shunning of him. Worst of all, he saw the supercilious smirk on the faces of the women auxiliaries as they looked at him from their offices and from behind their typewriters. The look made the anger inside him curdle into something very unwholesome.

When he got back to his quarters, it only took him a few minutes to pile his belongings into his pack. He had been with SS Jagddivision 502 ever since its formation over four years earlier. He had been a key in the seizure of the airfields in Britain that had spearheaded the German seizure of the country. In Barbarossa, he had helped seize the vital bridges that had opened the way to the heart of Russia. He almost chuckled at that memory. He and some of his men had simply dressed in Russian uniforms, then walked up to the guards and shot them. It had been that simple.

Now, it was all gone. The successes had been forgotten, the failures were all that were remembered. The bitterness swelled in him again and flooded through his brain. Even the air smelled sour to him.

"Es alles die schuld der verdammten Amerikaner ist." The words raged out of him. "Die verdammte Scheiße amerikanischer fress Bastarde."

He stormed out of his quarters to where a Kubelwagen was waiting to take him to his new posting. He managed to stop himself kicking it. Even though breaking his foot would be the appropriate end to this day.

CHAPTER EIGHT: GAINS WON

Airfield 108, Privolzhskiy na Volga, Moskva Front.

Today was going to be something new. Normally when *FivebyFive* taxied out on to the runway, she had drop tanks under her wings and/or belly. Today, there were five hundred pound bombs under her wings and a single drop tank under her belly. Although the 356th had the highest score of any of the four Thunderbolt groups, it was also the closest to the front line. So, it had been assigned the ground attack mission while the other three Thunderbolt groups would be providing high altitude top cover. They were just one element of the mass of tactical air power that was being thrown into the battle now raging in the Chuvashskaya Bridgehead.

The pre-dawn briefing had been eye-opening. Virtually everything the allies had in the Moskva Front region was being deployed against the German forces attacking in the Chuvashskaya. B-26s would be hitting airfields, staging positions and supply dumps while Russian-flown A-20s were being hurled against the columns of troops and armor moving up. Russian and American P-39s were flying medium and low-altitude cover along with Russian Yaks and Lavochkins. The P-38s were patrolling the east bank to intercept any Luftwaffe aircraft that tried to interfere with air operations. Even the B-17s would be getting into the act, although quite what they would be doing hadn't been made clear.

The 360th had a special assignment. They were to hit one of the most important German airfields, Saransk-North where the Germans were known to have FW-190 ground attack aircraft and Bf 109 interceptors based. The other two squadrons of the 356th were hitting Saransk-South, the main airfield of the sector. They would be following up attacks by the B-26 groups. It was supposed to have Ju-88 bombers and Ju-52 transports as well as a plethora of 109s. The hope was that the B-26s would leave the airfields in chaos, allowing the Thunderbolts to dive-bomb and strafe anything of value left there with particular emphasis on the ground attack aircraft. Once they had finished with their primary target, all the Thunderbolts were to strafe targets of opportunity on the way back. Come the dawn, American and Russian air power would be flooding into the battle area on a scale neither the Germans nor the Russians had ever contemplated.

Ahead of his aircraft, Edwards saw the blue flames from the exhausts suddenly lengthen as the Thunderbolts ran up to full power for take-off. The four-aircraft section ahead of him started to accelerate away. In the dim, pre-dawn lights, their bulk seemed to block out the first points of light from the rising sun as they climbed away. *Another change from the days after we first arrived here. Then we took off, hiding from the fascists and concealing our locations. Now, we don't do that. A second group of P-38s has joined the 55th in its barrier patrols along the Volga. That's something else. It was two weeks between us arriving and flying our first combat missions. The 479th had arrived one day, got a day to settle in and are flying this morning.*

Edwards felt the reassuring clump as his wheels retracted into their housing and *FivebyFive* surged upwards. The initial flight out was to be at eighteen thousand feet, keeping the formations of Thunderbolts well above the light flak from the Germans – and from the Allies come to that. The troops on the ground had a distressing – from Edward's point of view – habit of shooting first and asking questions afterwards. This would be the first time that the 360th squadron had operated low down enough for ground fire to be a problem but the pre-flight briefing had been at pains to point out that some of the P-39s flying over friendly positions had returned from their missions with .50 caliber bullet holes in them.

The long climb to cruising altitude had the effect of making the sun seem to rise much faster than normal. After the foul weather of the previous day, the sight of the sun peeping over the hills of the west bank was glorious. It would also serve to blind the anti-aircraft gunners and the watching ground observers. *Not that they will be in any doubt that we are coming. They can probably hear the engines in Moskva.*

FivebyFive was climbing sluggishly, the bombs under her wings reducing the Thunderbolt's already unimpressive rate of climb. The American pilots would be flying significantly lower today than their usual mission profiles and that had been an issue at the pre-mission briefing. Previously, the Thunderbolts had been in their element, flying at altitudes where their turbocharged engines were at the peak of their performance and their success had reflected that. Now, they had other things to do and they would have to accommodate a different environment. That gave Edwards an uncomfortable thought. *The world is growing up and we're having to grow up with it. Why do I get the feeling that playtime is over?*

Forward positions, Composite Group, 83rd Infantry Division, Yandoba, Chuvashskaya Bridgehead.

The sound of the artillery fire told Searle all he needed to know. *The krauts are coming.* There had been scattered rounds of artillery coming in all night but they had achieved little other than to keep the Americans defending the ridge awake. The barrage that had started with sunrise was different. The number of shells exploding in the American positions had increased enormously and they were being specifically targeted on the likely defenses. Seale was grimly amused to note that the village they driven the German armored cars out of the night before was now being methodically blown apart. In fact, most of the shells that were inbound were either hitting Yandoba or the ground between it and the ridge. And that meant they were being wasted because Lieutenant Grisham had dropped back from that area and now had his defenses laid out on the reverse slope of the ridge. Searle and his bazooka were one of the few left who could see down towards where the German attack was forming up.

The volume or artillery fire seemed to redouble as the Germans started to move forward. Things had changed since the previous day. Then, the infantry had moved forward until they ran into opposition. Once the centers of the defense had been located or pinned down, the tanks and assault guns would move forward and knock them out with direct fire from their guns. Now, the armored vehicles were staying well back and the infantry were scouting for the American positions.

Searle knew that a lot of the reason for the change had been that the earlier attacks had been against locations where the American positions were thoroughly scouted and well-known but he guessed that another reason was that the American bazookas had given the German armor a nasty shock and the changes were a response to that. That thought made him feel ridiculously pleased with himself.

It was obvious that the Germans had brought up reinforcements during the night. The company-sized force in front of Searle was in an arrow-shaped formation with the point aimed almost directly at him while the flanks angled back on either side to protect the seven assault guns following them. They seemed to be moving slowly and cautiously yet the speed with which they were closing on his position was frightening.

Yet, that wasn't the worst of it. Over to his right, a second infantry company was barely five hundred yards away and was already almost up to the crest of the ridge. Searle realized that the Germans had done it again. While the Americans had been hunkered down, waiting for the dawn, they had already started their moves and so gained the advantage. They held the initiative and the American were doomed, once again to be responding to their moves. He was almost unwilling to look to his left but he made himself do so and the sight there made him despair. A third German infantry company was also advancing up the ridge there and it was also well-advanced.

Searle pictured the German assault as an M shape with two infantry assault columns forming the uprights and the V in from of him providing the sweep that joined them. He could see how it would work; the columns would prevent the flanks of the American positions closing in on the arrowhead while the center force would pierce the American line and eliminate the center. Then, the attack would spread sideways to eliminate the remaining force holding the ridge. For the second time in a few seconds, Searle felt ridiculously pleased with himself. In his own eyes at least, he was beginning to think like a soldier.

That thought stayed with him for only a few seconds. The German artillery had paused for that brief interval but now it resumed its bombardment. They were dropping short, sharp bombardments on rock outcrops in front of the advancing infantry. It occurred to Searle that, the previous day, he had used rock outcrops for cover both times he had killed enemy tanks. Today, for some reason, he had found cover in a gully behind some stunted bushes. His sense of satisfaction at having outwitted the Germans, even if by accident, was quickly removed by the sound of machine gun bullets whipping through the bushes and scattering leaves and twigs on his head.

"We'd better get out of here. They must have seen us." During the night, Searle had been assigned an assistant who could reload his bazooka. *Jiminez was utterly inexperienced and as green as they came. Just like I was yesterday.*

"They're shooting up everything that can give us cover. They haven't seen us. Shows we scared the crap out of them yesterday." Searle didn't believe that for a second but it sounded the right thing to say."

Over on the left, the distinctive chattering of a machine gun broke the steady rolling thunder of the artillery fire. Searle realized it wasn't the murderous ripping noise of the German MG-42 but the slower, steady hammering of the American M1919. The machine gun had only fired a few shots before some of the infantrymen on the ridge opened up with their Garands and carbines. The fire cut down the point of the arrowhead marching up the hill, dropping some of them to the ground, sending others rolling down the slope. The rest of the troops on that side of the arrowhead went flat and started to fire on the machine gun position and anywhere that might have given cover to an American rifleman. The troops on the other side of the arrowhead were moving forward to try and get positions from which they could fire upon the defenses. Behind them, the assault guns were turning to add the fire from their 75mm guns.

A red streak shot out from a position on the crestline towards one of those assault guns. Searle shook his head; the rocket was approaching from the front where the armor on the gun was thickest and the range was long. By the time the streak reached the StuG, it was already wavering and moving erratically. It hit the ground just in front of the German vehicle, showering it with gravel and smoke but leaving it undamaged. The assault gun fired back almost immediately. The shell exploded exactly where the rocket had been fired from and Searle guessed that if the bazooka man hadn't got out of there fast, he was now dead. It was a lesson he took to heart.

The resistance over on the left had its effect though. The center sweep line of the German attack was swinging to face the defenders and in doing so, the closest of the seven assault guns was presenting its flank to Searle and his bazooka. The range was longer than he liked but the chance was irresistible. What was more, the fact that the assault gun had its main weapon trained off to the left would give him a few additional seconds to make his escape. He could feel from the weight that his bazooka was loaded so he shouldered the clumsy weapon, took careful aim and fired.

"Carlo, run for it!" It wasn't quite a run but the two men scrambled down the gulley, bounced off the bank where it made a 90 degree turn and continued to get clear. By that time, Searle had heard the explosion of the bazooka round but not the roar of secondary detonations that had accompanied his two previous kills. Once well away from his firing position, he took a chance and stuck up his head to see what was happening. What he saw was chilling.

The rocket must have reached the point where it was beginning to lose stability and start to wander since the hit was much further forward than the sweet-spot by the engine compartment. By the look of it, Searle thought he had hit the gun compartment or possibly even the driver's position. The assault gun was stopped and it was burning but with a slow, almost gentle, fire rather than the spectacular infernos of before. What horrified Searle was that the commander had been trying to abandon the stricken vehicle but had become stuck in the hatch. How, Searle couldn't even begin to imagine. *Perhaps his belt snagged on a projection or something?*

Whatever it was, the man was trapped, half in, half out of his vehicle. In doing so, he had blocked the escape route for the rest of his crew. Searle could hear them screaming inside the assault gun as the fire took hold but he guessed their fate was more merciful than that of the commander. The inside of the assault gun would be filled with smoke and the fire would be burning the oxygen out of the air. They would die soon enough. The commander had plenty of air and there was no smoke to asphyxiate him. Only the lower half of his body would be burning and that would take a long, long time to become fatal.

Searle shrugged to himself and continued to move away from the scene. Behind him, he could hear the screams from the burning assault vehicle diminishing but that was distance and the rest of the sounds of the battle.

Artillery Observation Post, Composite Group, 83rd Infantry Division, Yandoba, Chuvashskaya Bridgehead.

"They're coming up the slope now." Sergeant Adam Doyle was on the portable radio, speaking to Lieutenant Harold Richards in the radio jeep. Richards, in turn, had the allocated artillery waiting on the other end. "Time to show them what they're made of. Fire mission. Freddie Uniform Seven forty-four-twenty six."

"Acknowledged. Guns, Freddie Uniform Seven forty-four-twenty six."

"Received. Big boys on their way." The voice on the radio was cold and unemotional but to those in the know, his words were loaded down with imminent fire and death. 'Big Boys' were 155mm guns, a U.S. infantry division's heavy artillery. The second seemed to creak past as Richards waited for the howl that would announce the inbound shells. The gun batteries were almost twelve miles to the rear and logically he knew that the delay before the bombardment started was not unreasonable. Yet still he started to curse the wait and the minutes that were slipping past. The ironic thing was that when the piercing howl over head arrived, it still made him jump out of his skin. The thunder when the shells arrived on the reverse slope of the ridge made the ground shake under his feet.

"Down forty, shift five mils to the left." Doyle's voice was also calm and uninflected.

Again there was the seemingly unending wait, then the shocking and unexpected howl overhead. This time Richards saw a cloud of smoke rising over the ridge crest. "Adam?"

"On target. Fire for effect. Pour it on Boss, everything we have." Doyle's voice suddenly lost its impersonal tone and there was a fierce relish in his words.

"General fire mission. Freddie Uniform Seven forty-four-sixty six."

"On its way. We're handing over to the small boys after this." The voice on the line was still calm and unemotional.

The howl overhead, when it came, lasted longer and was much, much louder. This time, there wasn't a single cloud coming over the ridge line but a whole series of them< As one started to disperse, two more would erupt to take its place.

"They're breaking, Boss. They can't take it. The whole left flank is breaking up and falling back."

"What's happening on the right?"

Doyle's voice was suddenly much more subdued. "They're breaking through, their column is nearly up to the ridgeline now. One assault gun is burning, another stalled but the other five are about to crest the ridge."

Beside Richards, Grisham got on to his own radio. "Jake, their armor is about to cross the ridge. Time for *Old Tinny* and her friends to get to work."

"Right. All tanks, AP up."

"I'm going to drop smoke all along the ridgeline." Richards explained quickly. "That'll give our infantry cover to pull back and also mean the assault guns will come out of the smoke blind. They can't traverse their guns so our tanks will have the advantage."

There was a brief pause before Fuller's voice came over the radio. "Tell that arty that I love him more than words can possibly say."

There was a burst of laughter around the command post but Richards was already in touch with the 105mms bringing down the smoke screen. He just gave a thumbs-up when the order was in.

Grisham took his binoculars and looked at the men falling back over the ridge. They were falling back, certainly but they were still firing their rifles and holding some semblance of order. *It probably is,* he thought to himself *a long way from being perfect but it's a hell of a sight better than we did yesterday.*

The Americans were half-way down the slope when the howl overhead told Richards that the artillery he had ordered was arriving. This time the effects were very different. The 105mm shells exploded into dense clouds of white smoke that quickly masked off the ridge. His radio bleeped again and he tapped it impatiently. "What's happening up there?"

"Can't see a damned thing, boss. I can hear the engines and tracks but we can't see the tanks. That smoke is blotting out everything."

"That's what it's supposed to do, Adam. Infantry?"

"Moving past us now. We're being outflanked."

"Get out of there, Adam."

"No, boss. You need us up here to spot for you. We'll hold on where we are."

223

Kazan Thunderbolts

Richards grimaced at the other officers around him. "Here we go. The assault guns will be coming through any second now. If they get through, they'll drive right over us."

"They won't do that." Even over the radio, Fuller sounded grim and vicious. "We've got some payback time waiting for them."

"They'll be coming out now." The message came in through the artillery observation network. Richards pointed to the two 105mm guns that had been positioned so they could take the advancing Germans under direct fire. "And we can use these over open sights.

It was as if Richards had given the command himself. As soon as he had finished speaking, small groups of German infantry started to emerge from the smokescreen blanketing the ridgeline. The .50 caliber machine guns mounted on the trucks, half-tracks and tanks opened up, sending a storm of tracer fireflies at the enemy infantry. The range was great, even for the fifty calibers, and the glowing tracers seemed to arc slowly through the air before descending on the targets. Richards could see the enemy going to ground, trying to take cover against the heavy bullets that were striking them down.

He was so intent on watching the almost hypnotic sight that the ear-bending crash of the 105mms firing sent him jumping. Those shells two seemed to arc through the air before exploding in the groups of infantry. What had been men taking cover in an orderly manner was now a wild panic as the shells started their work.

Richards could see the Germans retreating, being pushed back into the smoke by the methodical rake of the machine guns and the punishing blasts of the 105mms. Then, they steadied as the dissipating smoke screen was torn open by the low, raking shapes of the StuG-III assault guns.

Fuller had moved his three tanks around to one flank so that he caught them assault guns at an angle. This allowed him to put his shots through the thinner armor on the vehicle's sides but, more importantly it gave him a few seconds undisturbed practice with his 75mm guns while the StuGs tried to bring their casemate-mounted guns to bear. The shots from the Shermans streaked across the ground in a flat line that made the earlier arcs of howitzer and machine guns seem idle. The first few shots landed short or in front of the StuGs but one of the tanks scored a direct hit on the side of the German vehicle. It stopped dead, its gun barrel dropping down and black smoke rising from the hull. Richards could see the crew bailing out amid the flashing tracers from the American machine guns.

A second StuG took another direct hit, this time on its frontal armor. To Richard's disappointment, the American shot disintegrated with an ear-shattering clang and a spectacular display of sparks. It was enough though. The

German armor had had enough and they were pulling back. The infantry went with them, the American tanks and infantry following at a respectful distance.

"We did it! We held them." Grisham was dancing, jumping up in the air and clapping at the sight.

Richards knew how he felt but innate caution made him less sanguine. "That was easy, Grish. That was too damned easy."

B-26B Marauder Dark Angel, *Approaching Saransk North Luftwaffe Airfield.*

Major Benjamin Wood's firm opinion that the universe was a malignant organism dedicated to his personal destruction, had in his opinion been adequately, if not conclusively, confirmed. Soon after takeoff, his own aircraft, *Delta Rebel*, had a power failure in its port engine. With a feathered propeller, Wood had been only too aware that the aircraft would be unable to keep up with the rest of the group. He decided to return to base and transfer to one of the spare B-26s, *Dark Angel*. It wasn't quite as bad as it seemed; *Dark Angel* had only just been delivered and had been assigned as the Group Commander's aircraft. It had all the latest equipment, additional armor, four .50 machine guns in packages on the sides of the nose to deter frontal attacks and uprated engines. He had radioed the base to make sure the ground crew was waiting, and they had helped the crew of *Delta Rebel* transfer their gear over to the spare plane. Soon *Dark Angel* was airborne and flying at top speed to overtake the rest of the 391st Bomb Group. She had slipped into *Delta Rebel's* place about half way to the target. It had never occurred to Wood not to try and rejoin his formation. The briefing had been quite clear. The 83rd Infantry Division was fighting for its life on the ground and it needed all the help it could get.

By the time Wood had rejoined the formation, the weather conditions were beginning to clear at last. As the B-26s climbed the mist that had almost, but not quite, been thick enough for instrument conditions was fading away. Wood could see his own group, all fifty four aircraft, formed into three tight combat boxes. By the time they had broken out of the mist they found they were crossing the Volga. The sun was up over the horizon and in the growing light, Wood could see other formations of American aircraft in the distance, heading towards targets of their own.

One of the formations had joined his own and was now stationed at 22,000 feet, above and behind his Marauders. He recognized the Thunderbolts and knew they were the second part of the attack formation. A third group, this time of P-38 Lightnings, was prowling in the area, ready to break up German fighter attacks if and when they developed. Technically, they were assigned to stop German formations crossing the Volga to attack the ever-growing number of

Allied airbases on the eastern side. However, nobody had said how far west the German formations should be intercepted.

The 391st continued on towards its target, acutely aware that it was just one part of a massive attack air offensive.   The German fighter controllers apparently were confused by the various bomber trails for the first German fighter planes didn't appear until the B-26s were only a half hour from their target. By then, the B-26s had hit strong headwinds and had been slowed down to a ground speed of around 90 miles an hour. It was that factor that had led to Wood's pessimistic conclusions about the universe.

"*Dark Angel*, kraut nightfighters coming in. Ju-88s. We're intercepting."

Woods could see them The Ju-88s were climbing up ahead of his formation while the P-38s swept past on their way to fend them off. Wood could almost feel sorry for the Ju-88s; they were medium bombers pretending to be fighters and had no place in a daylight battle with a sky filled with real fighters. He was turning his head to watch the Lightnings tear into them when suddenly we could see streamers coming from their wings. He recognized the great trails as they closed in the B-26 formations as some kind of rocket. The Russian fighters sometimes used rockets when they were strafing ground positions but this had been the first time anybody had seen the Germans using them against airborne targets.   They weren't that effective; the B-26s easily avoided them with relatively gentle evasive action

That was when Wood heard the ominous rattling noise of bullets hitting *Dark Angel*. He glanced around quickly and what he saw made him swallow. Around to his right and left were groups of hostile fighter aircraft, fire or five or six in each. By the time he had finished the count, he realized that there were in the neighborhood of 65 enemy fighters besieging his formation. Luckily the attacks were uncoordinated; the escorting Thunderbolts and Lightnings were tearing at the German fighters, harrying them and forcing them away from the bombers. Wood made a private vow to himself. He would never again let a Thunderbolt or Lightning pilot buy his own beer.

One thing had puzzled him; none of German fighters were in a position to attack *Dark Angel*. It took a second for him to understand what had happened – in bobbing to evade the rockets, he had accidentally flown into a stream of bullets from one of the other B-26s. Beneath that was the realization that the German fighters were pressing home their attacks with a ferocity they had never displayed before. "The krauts are coming in closer than I've ever seen before. Check her over Artie."

Lieutenant Arthur McCrary, Wood's copilot started calling the positions in the Marauder, checking the crew. Everybody answered in, except, ironically enough the radio operator.

"Check him," was Wood's terse comment. McCrary went back to the radio operator's position. The man was unharmed; it was simply that his radio jack had broken. McCrary was standing in the radio hatch chatting to the man and trying to fix the communications cord when suddenly the radio operator was knocked off his feet and slammed into his back, knocking him down the passageway that led to the waist gun positions. That put him directly under the upper turret. He tried to heave himself to his feet by grabbing hold of the turret traversing gears but as he did so, the turret started to swing around, trapping his fingers in the turret gears. He screamed as his hand was mashed by the cogs, but he could only see blood curling over what was left of his fingers and washing down the rubber-mats on the floor. One of the waist gunners grabbed him and started trying to stem the flow from the ripped up hand.

"It's OK, Sir, the skin and meat have been torn up but the bones aren't broken." McCrary appreciated the aid and encouragement but he'd felt the crackle as bones broke under the grinding of the gears. And, he had never seen so much blood before. He didn't know where it could have come from. He had never thought a human arm could hold so much yet it was strangely impersonal, just so much red paint over his overalls and on the deck. That was when *Dark Angel* lurched as a burst of gunfire raked her midships section. By the time McCrary had realized what had happened, the waist gunner was crumpled on the floor, his face twisted with pain. The man who had helped him with his crushed hand just ten seconds earlier had been hit by a bullet that had entered through the window in the waist and struck him squarely in the back.

"Sir, get back to the cockpit. I'll take the gun." The radio operator had run back to the waist positions. It was the order of progression; the cockpit had to be manned first, then the gun positions, then anything else. McCrary staggered forward, trying to ignore the slow-burning agony in his hand that was slowly but surely spreading up his arm.

"What happened?" Wood was watching the battle outside his aircraft. In his experience, he had never seen the German fighters attacking with such desperation. Some of the fighter pilots seemed like mad dogs as they recklessly hurtled themselves at the B-26 formation. Wood saw one FW-190 flying at a B-26 in a straight line, ignoring the Thunderbolt behind it that was pouring .50 caliber fire into the German aircraft. There was a brilliant white flash as the left wing of the Focke-Wulf exploded and the plane disintegrated in mid air. It was too late, the B-26 took hits all over its wings and fuselage and disappeared in one giant ball of fire. The sight was sobering. Usually B-26s died hard and fought to give their crews one last chance to bail out. *Betty Boo* had just exploded from the barrage of hits from 20mm shells.

Other B-26s had been forced to swerve to avoid being rammed by German fighters. The intense attacks made it difficult to maintain close formation because of the evasive action being taken by the individual B-26s. Wood guessed that was why this wave of attacks was being forced home; the attempt was to break up the tight formations at all costs. Woods guessed that the German fighter pilots had understood that the chance of saving their homes depended on using every trick possible to stop the bombers.

"At initial point now." The bombardier-navigator shouted the words over the intercom. Wood knew that this was the crisis point. For the next two minutes the B-26s would have to hold absolutely straight and level. Flak was beginning to mushroom around them but that didn't stop the German fighters from trying to get through to the bombers. Nor did it stop the P-38s and P-47s from hunting those fighters and bringing them down. Wood was almost holding his breath for the long straight run to the target. He could see it now, the runways white against the brownish green of the Russian countryside. It was an odd-looking airfield with two parallel runways with taxiways in between. It was orientated so that the axis of the airfield was north-east, almost dead on 45 degrees. The B-26 formations were approaching on a course of two-four-five degrees, a course that would take a curtain of bombs over the center of the field.

Suddenly, in front of them, a FW-190 had swerved in and was lining up for a head-on pass at *Dark Angel*. Wood felt the plane shudder and realized that they were hit hard. A cannon shell fired from an FW-190 smashed into the cockpit, shearing through the armored windscreen. Another thing the Germans had changed. Before, they had loaded their guns with the thin-walled minengeschoss shells. They were made from drawn steel, instead of having the explosives cavity drilled into a solid shot. That technique had allowed thinner shell wall construction and therefore a far greater amount of explosive filler. According to the briefings, the minengeschoss shells had worked well against the poorly-protected Russian aircraft but the heavily-armored American planes had resisted their damage.

Now, the Germans were using armor-piercing ammunition and the rounds went straight through the armored windscreen instead of exploding outside. Wood felt a sharp pain in his face and left eye: a quick glance over at McCrary showed him that the whole left side of his copilot's face was slashed open by fragments from the shot. The head wounds were spurting blood all over the cockpit.

Dark Angel was slowing down as number two engine started to lose power. Oil was spewing over the wing but at least the engine wasn't burning. The FW-190 was still coming in and Wood started to press the firing switch for the new package guns. Before he could do so, a shadow swept over *Dark Angel*. A P-38 raced past them, then dropped in front of the battered B-26. The P-38 had one great advantage over the single-engined fighters; it had all its guns grouped in its nose and that made for a fearsome gun battery. The P-38 was sawing the FW-

190 apart in mid-air and, in addition, taking the hits that would otherwise have finished *Dark Angel* off. The 190 was dead, but the P-38 had been hit hard and was burning. Wood saw the pilot roll his fighter over and bail out.

"Little friend is on the way down." He didn't know if the warning would achieve much but it was all he could do for the fighter pilot who had saved him. *Perhaps, an American or Russian fighter would cover the pilot on the way down, perhaps there would be partisans to help him reach safety. Perhaps he might escape and evade on his own. Perhaps.*

Wood glanced sideways. McCrary was thrashing with his arms and legs, and had slipped from his seat down to the cockpit floor. In doing so he had jammed the control column and rudder pedals. The radio operator came to the rescue and managed to pull him free from the controls and get him out of the cockpit. *He's sure turning up wherever he is needed today.*

"Thirty seconds to drop point." The bombardier-navigator was holding the aircraft steady. The aircraft was shaking steadily from the flak bursts around the formation. Wood knew the rule of thumb; *if you can see it, don't worry about it. If you can hear it, it's close. If you can feel it, it's really close. If you can smell it, it's too damned close.* The smell of cordite from the flak shells was choking him. Then he felt the bomb bay doors opening and the vibration as the stream of bombs left the bay. He could still see the center of the airfield when the first explosions flowered right in the middle, between the two runways. At first he thought they had been badly placed and missed anything vital but the masses of secondary explosions on the ground told him that he had hit at least one parking area. Then, other columns of explosions drowned Saransk North airfield as the B-26 squadrons added their loads to the destruction down below.

By the time they had got clear of the airfield, Wood saw that *Dark Angel* was more than 400 yards behind the group. He put his good engine on maximum power but even with his uprated engines, he still continued to drop back. Up ahead he noticed two other struggling B-26s and wagged my wings for them to close in. They did, and the three stragglers at least had a three-aircraft formation for mutual support. Around them, the P-47s were swarming to cover the cripples. They were three hundred miles from their base at Surovka. Wood couldn't help feeling it was going to be a long day.

Thunderbolt **FiveByFive** *Approaching Saransk North Luftwaffe Airfield.*

The temptation to jettison their bombs and go to the aid of the besieged B-26 formations had been nearly overwhelming. Sitting above and behind the groups of bombers, the pilots of the 360th had watched four of the Marauders going down under the relentless fighter assaults. They had also watched the escorting Thunderbolts and Lightnings going to work, trying to fend off the enemy fighters that kept slashing at the B-26s.

"Prepare to dive." Edwards watched the first flight of P-47s peel over and start the long dive down to Saransk North. The last Thunderbolt started its dive. Edwards counted five Mississippis and then followed them down. He pushed the nose of his Thunderbolt down at an ever-increasing angle until it reached 70 degrees. That was the maximum allowable dive; any more than that and there was a strong chance the Thunderbolt wouldn't pull out in time.

As the nose of his Thunderbolt dropped, Edwards saw the Luftwaffe airfield, or what was left of it, beneath him. The whole area had been pounded by the B-26s; the large hangars had taken multiple direct hits and the clouds of black smoke from the fires that now ravaged them were rolling across the airfield, obscuring much of the target area. Nevertheless, he could see that strings of bombs had plowed up the runways and shattered the taxiways and parking stands between them.

For all the destruction below, many of the anti-aircraft gun positions were still in action. They were already starting to engage the second wave of American aircraft now diving on them. Edwards guessed that the crews of the 20mm guns had been unable to engage the Marauders and were now anxious to take revenge for the pounding the medium bombers had handed out. Their tracers seemed to float upwards before seeming to accelerate and shoot past on either side. He found himself crouching down in the cockpit, attempting to get as much cover from the flak as possible.

At the same time, his eyes were firmly focused on his instruments. It was critical that *FivebyFive* did not start to side-slip or yaw during her dive. Doing either would cause her 500 pound bombs to slide sideways and miss to one side or the other. He kept his turn and slip indicator firmly centered while the flak site under his nose grew steadily. There was another thing that he had to bear in mind. The heavy Thunderbolt picked up speed quickly in a dive and exceeding the red-line on the air speed indicator brought the aircraft perilously close to the dreaded problems of compressibility where the controls would lock solid and the aircraft dive straight into the ground. Edwards was aware that earlier in the P-47s career, several initial production aircraft had lost their tails when diving at high speed and that the problems hadn't been entirely solved. American aircraft designers were beginning to learn that the new generation of 400mph plus fighter aircraft were facing a lot of problems whose existence had barely been suspected.

At 3,000 feet, the tracers were still flashing past his cockpit, not into it. The way they poured up from a point on the ground reminded Edwards of the streams of bubbles in a glass of beer. He pressed the bomb release equipment, feeling his aircraft lurch as nearly half a ton of weight detached from under the wings. As soon as he was sure the bombs were gone, he pulled back on the stick and started to bring the nose up. The controls were mushy yet stiff, as if they were set in rapidly-solidifying concrete. The first sign of the dreaded compressibility setting in. Yet, the nose came up and the big Thunderbolt started to level out. Edwards was vaguely surprised to note that the pull out – and the mandated rate and from the specified altitude – had put him at the perfect altitude for a strafing pass. *Perhaps the guys who wrote the book actually did know what they were talking about.*

At first, all he could see was the torn up center of the airfield, as if the B-26s had left little intact. Yet, as he looked across the wrecked airfield, he began to realize that while the medium bombers had flattened the center of the field, the Germans had parked the aircraft around the perimeter where they had missed the worst of the bombing. *Up to now, anyway*, thought Edwards, *now what do we have here? Twin engine, a long streamlined canopy with a turret on top and a single tailplane. My God, it's a Ju-188. That's a golden kill if ever there was one.*

The grounded aircraft was approaching fast. The opening of the revetment it was parked in faced the runway in order to permit a fast take-off. It was a trade-off, protection against operational convenience but the engineers had never realized that a Thunderbolt would be barreling in above the runway with murderous intent. Edwards squeezed his firing button, felt the kidney-battering vibration of the .50 calibers going off and saw the streaks of tracer going out in front of his aircraft. They seemed to arc slowly downwards before ending in a long track of white puffs that raced across the ground towards the helpless Ju-188. The dust spurts of the impacts suddenly changed to brilliant white flashes as Edwards walked the burst on to his target.

The German bomber was hidden, enveloped in a shroud of grayish-brown smoke that seemed to coil around the stricken aircraft. Just as he thought the aircraft was going to survive the punishment he was handing out, there was a swelling orange-black mushroom of smoke and flame from the revetment that marked the German bomber exploding. Edwards swung his aircraft away from the blast, trying to avoid getting hit by the debris being thrown into the air from the inferno he had created. Then, he was over the trees that surrounded Saransk North.

By the time he had managed to pull his Thunderbolt around, the parking area in the trees was a sea of flames. Edwards guessed the refueling lines had been wrecked by the torrents of .50 caliber gunfire and were pouring aviation gasoline into the burning wrecks of the aircraft. The pyres of black smoke rising into the sky seemed to beckon the Thunderbolts in again, almost audibly whispering *Tovarish Americans, there is more work to do here this day.* This time, Edwards had a very particular target in mind. While pulling out of his dive-bombing run, he had seen that the airfield control tower was still undamaged. He was determined to make sure that it didn't continue that way.

Spotting the control tower again was harder than he had anticipated. It had been camouflaged and it blended into the background well. Not quite well enough though; it was the red of the fires reflecting off its windows that gave it away. Once again, Edwards made his run towards his selected target and watched the sheets of tracers walking across the grass towards the tower. Like most of the fighter pilots, he had stopped loading tracers for his guns a long time ago, *well, it seems like a long time ago*, because all they did was warn the pilot of the aircraft he was shooting at. As a result, the ammunition dump had been full of unwanted .50 tracers and the strafing mission had seemed a good chance to get rid of them all. By happenstance, it appeared that the high tracer loads were doing a good job of suppressing the anti-aircraft fire.

The flight tower seemed to be flimsy. The barrage of .50 machine gun fire was throwing fragments into the air in a spectacular display of destruction. By the time Edwards had to lift his nose to clear the ground, the building was blazing from diesel fuel leaking out of the tanks supplying the generators. Ahead of him a group of figures were running away. Edwards guessed they were the control tower crew who had abandoned their posts in the face of the Thunderbolt bearing down on them. He lined up carefully and squeezed off a burst that shrouded the men in a curtain of dust and sent them tumbling to the ground.

"All aircraft, we're going home on the deck. It's all fascists around here so shoot at anything that moves. In fact, shoot at anything that doesn't move as well." Major Young sounded well satisfied with the attack that had left Saransk North a fair imitation of hell on earth.

Thunderbolt FiveByFive Returning From Saransk North Luftwaffe Airfield.

Everything looked different when looking at the Russian countryside from a few hundred feet up instead of twenty thousand. Ground features that had previously seemed to crawl past far below now approached so fast he could barely make out what they were before they flashed past on either side of his aircraft. One thing had already made a deep impression on Edwards. The Germans were extremely careless about moving round this far behind the front line. Academically, that was something he had already known. The Russian aircraft were tasked with supporting their army and they operated on or near the line of contact. The idea of fighter-bombers roving deep into enemy–held territory was something the Germans hadn't had to deal with and their carelessness showed that clearly. Seeing something though was very different from simply hearing about it.

The situation now proved that point. The line of trucks moving along the dirt road hadn't even reacted to the appearance of the four Thunderbolts. If they had, the rearmost truck would have swerved to a halt and the men in the back would be racing against time to get the quadruple 20mm gun they were towing into action. Instead, Edwards could see that some of the men in the back were waving at him. *I bet they think we are Focke-Wulfs. After all, we're coming from where they used to be based. And, old Robertson back in High School used to say that people see what they expect to see.*

Edwards was almost beside the truck convoy, about three hundred feet up and slowing down slightly to make his turn and dive. He had picked the truck with the anti-aircraft gun as his first target. He had been sorely tempted to make his pass along the line of trucks but his instructors had warned against that. If the trucks were loaded with ammunition and exploded, the blast could easily tear a wing off. The truth was, Edwards doubted that. A P-39 or a P-40 perhaps but not a P-47. All the Thunderbolt pilots were developing an almost religious veneration for the damage their Thunderbolts could take and still get them back to base.

"And now, the perfect example of an 'Oh Crap' moment." Edwards spoke into his radio as he dropped down and squeezed the button to unleash his 50-calibers. The altitude was one he had chosen carefully, low enough to make his pass deadly, high enough so he could dive to bring his guns to bear. The brilliant white tracers seemed to float slowly down towards the truck he had chosen for destruction, describing an almost lazy arc that ended just short of the truck. It, and the gun it was towing, vanished in the gray-brown fountains as the bullets tore into Russian soil. That only lasted a split second before the brown and gray turned black and orange as the hail of armor-piercing incendiary bullets tore the truck and its occupants apart. The smoke billowed upwards in a pyre that reminded him of the day he and some of his school friends had started a bonfire that had gone completely out of control. The Thunderbolt lurched as it passed over the inferno, making Edwards believe he had experienced the much-dreaded munitions explosion but it was just air driven upwards by the heat of the blazing truck.

Behind him, the other three Thunderbolts had taken out the trucks at the head of the column. In between the blocked head of the convoy and the vehicle Edwards had destroyed at the end was a scene of utter and complete chaos. The trucks were swerving to a halt, scattered at odd angles all over the roadway. Some had misjudged their turns and gone into the ditches that lined the track. One had run both wheels off the road and was in process of turning over completely. Yet another had tail-ended the truck in front. Edwards hadn't seen anything like it since his local high school football team had won a completely unexpected state championship victory and all their supporters had tried to drive home while falling-down drunk.

The random thought surprised him, even while he was hauling his P-47 around to the right before making another strafing run. At low altitude and without the torque bonus that came with a left-hand turn, *FivebyFive* was sluggish and took her time to come around. By the time Edwards had his aircraft in the right position, he could see the Germans on board the trucks hurling themselves over the side and abandoning the vehicles. Behind him, Barnes in *Miss Fire* and Walker in *Glory Gal* had seen the same thing and widened their turn so their strafing pass would run parallel to the stalled convoy, hitting the troops running to either side of the doomed trucks. On Edward's wing, Griffin had already opened fire on one of the trucks near the head of the convoy. Edwards selected the two trucks that had collided and opened fire. Once again, he saw the tracers seeming to drift slowly towards their target before being swallowed up by the two interlocked vehicles. This time though, the effects were immediate and both vehicles exploded into fireballs. *Gas tanks must have been leaking and the tracers set them off.*

Edwards quickly debated a third pass but decided against it. The convoy was thoroughly wrecked, most of the vehicles were burning and the sides of the roads were scattered with figures in gray uniforms. *And it's a long way home still,* he thought. *Best to save on ammunition.*

Beside him, the four Thunderbolts of Fox Flight slid in to rejoin the formation. *Tipsy* Lieutenant Russell's bird, led the four aircraft back into position behind and to the left of Edwards's Eagle Flight. George Flight, led by Lieutenant Powell in *Charlotte* was still off on its strafing run. Overhead, providing top cover for the strafing Thunderbolts, was Dog Flight led by Major Young.

"How did ya do, *Tipsy*?"

"OK, I guess." Even over the radio, Russell's voice was flat and depressed.

"*Tipsy*, are you hit." Young's transmission from above was sharp and loaded with concern.

"No." Russell still sounded despondent. "We're all OK."

Edwards glanced down at the map on his knee. The next likely target area on the way home was the railway marshalling yard at Romodanovo. It was marked as an important target and the way home led right over it.

"Plaster, this is *Lailani*. F-5 from Temple." The message was unexpected. "Romodanovo marshalling yard has been hit by B-17s and is a write-off. Lot of light flak down there, stay clear. But, there are four trains trapped on the lines south of the yard. They're not going anywhere for a while. Ready to be plucked."

"Thanks *Lailani.* You heard him, boys. Time to go working on the railroads."

Sickbay, GunRon 5 Headquarters, Staraya Mayna, Volga River.

"Ah, bratishka, I see you have been doing good work in my absence." Napalkov looked over the figure on the hospital bed with a professional eye. *This man has many, many ills. I am surprised his Navy accepted him. But then who are we to speak of such things. What was the old joke about medical inspections for the infantry? First, take his temperature and make sure it is above zero. Second, take his pulse and see if he has a heartbeat. Third, count his fingers to make sure he has at least one to pull a trigger. To pass, score one in three.*

"Ivan Mihailovich, how went your investigation?" Kennedy was in traction but he struggled to sit up. Napalkov put a kindly hand on his shoulder.

"Stay resting, Jack. We need you back on Mother Volga as soon as possible. On the way down, I met with Admiral Nikolay Gerasimovich Kuznetsov. He told me of your exploits and of how you risked your life to save our sailors. As a Russian, I thank you for your bravery and your service to the Rodina. As your friend, please more careful in future. In CheKa we have so few personal friends we cannot afford to lose the ones we have."

Although he didn't show it, Kennedy was surprised by both the comment and by the apparent sincerity behind it. *Is he playing me or is he being sincere? Or both? I suppose a foreigner here with allied forces is the only kind of person with whom a Chekist could have a personal relationship. And, the fact is, I do rather like this man. And that means I will have to keep my guard up still higher.* "I understand you completely tovarish Ivan. I only have a few of me as well and I cannot afford to lose the one I have."

Napalkov burst out laughing. "Very good Jack. May I ask how you were injured?"

"I was a sickly child, Ivan. One childhood disease after another. I had measles at two years old, almost died of scarlet fever when I was nearly three, and had whooping cough and chicken pox shortly afterwards. Later I had diphtheria and constant bouts with flu and bronchitis. When I was 17, I went down with severe spastic colitis and a whole raftload of other stomach and digestive diseases. Back then, the doctors persuaded my father to put me on a steroid treatment for the digestive problems. My father loved experimental treatments." Kennedy sounded extremely bitter and that made Napalkov look at him sharply. "The steroids were a disaster. They gave me a duodenal ulcer and back problems because they drained out calcium from my bones. They also caused gland function problems and really messed me up. Addison's disease they called it. Anyway, my bones, especially in my back were left really weak.

Kazan Thunderbolts

When I was swimming in the Volga, the fascists were firing artillery at us and the concussion from the shell blasts on the water did a real number on me. I've got fractures all down my back. Doctors say I'll probably have to wear a back brace from now on. If so, that's the end of my naval career, afloat anyway."

"That will be a great loss Jack. I am sorry to hear that."

Once again, Kennedy found himself wondering how sincere the apparently genuine regret in Napalkov's voice was. "Bratishka, how did your investigation in Archangel go?"

Napalkov chuckled. "That end of it we solved. A simple blunder of procedure mixed up with errors and oversights. Most of the problem we corrected by giving a secretary a new typewriter and the rest by transferring some of the guilty to the infantry and demoting the rest. There was blame to be assessed there but we could find no ill-intent. So, that side of the investigation is closed. Down here, that is another matter. The wrongly-labeled ammunition arrived here by accident but it was shipped to you for delivery deliberately. That is treason and we must discover those responsible. And punish them in a manner fit for their crimes."

Mentally, Kennedy gulped. *Those last few words had a terrifying ring to them. Just remember, Jack my boy, this man is a Chekist.* "My commanding officer has said that I might assist you to the best of my ability. Not that I have much ability right now."

"I have files on the people who were directly involved in the trans-shipment of the ammunition." Napalkov took out a thick stack of personnel files. "I had them translated to American for you. Perhaps we could go through them together and pick out the more likely suspects?"

"I think it would be better if looked through those files separately and formed our own opinions on who were the likely suspects. Then we could compare lists and see where agreement lies. The more eyes that independently view a situation, the more likely it is that the truth will be seen."

Napalkov nodded. "This makes sense. Much better than funneling all information through a single point, yes? This is why the Rodina has so many intelligence agencies."

Also because nobody trusts any of them because they are all conspiring against each other. Yet, in that balance of power there is great safety for everybody else. Checks and balances we call it. "Bratishka, I think before we look at these files, we had better identify why the guilty may have committed their crimes. Motive may be the key here."

Napalkov thought about that. "Treason is treason. Is there need for greater reason?"

"But why? I will give you an example. Perhaps one of these suspects lost their only son in the fighting. That might emerge as an intense hatred for the invader but it might also have turned him against the Rodina because of suspicion that his son died when he might not have done. Or, perhaps, we have a man who harbors a deep grudge against somebody in the railway yard for reasons that perhaps even he does not remember. Great crimes do not always require great motives." Kennedy hesitated because what he was about to say might sound paranoid. "Perhaps the criminal is somebody who hates us. Americans. We are here in your country and there are always those who would believe we should not be here. Perhaps such a man saw the wrong ammunition and thought that sending it to us would teach us a lesson. Nothing does that more emphatically than running out of ammunition in the middle of a battle."

Napalkov couldn't help but like that idea. Chekist he may be but his stomach still rebelled against a Russian betraying the Rodina to the invaders. *But if this was a misguided protest against another group of foreigners the traitor saw as invaders also, then we can understand how he thought even if we cannot forgive him.* Then, another thought came to his mind.

"Bratishka, you suggest that the traitor might have shipped the wrong ammunition to you in the hope that you would run dry in the middle of a battle? That although we thought this was linked to the attack on Island Ten, that may have just been coincidence."

Kennedy nodded carefully since the effort hurt his back. "That's the size of it. Use foreign ammunition to punish foreigners. It has an ironic twist to it that obsessed people like."

"But, my friend, I remember when we first talked of this, you told me that those organizing dissension looked out for those with exploitable grievances and cultivated them. Suppose our saboteur with a dislike for Americans or a grudge against them spoke of his anger and the real traitors overheard him? They put the idea of supplying the wrong ammunition to your gunboat into his head. He thought he was sabotaging you, not realizing he was actually aiding the Hitlerites."

Kennedy and Napalkov gazed at each other. The ideas Napalkov had explained had a powerful attraction to them both. It explained so much but it also meant something else. Kennedy voiced that thought first. "But that means you have an organized fascist spy ring in that railway yard."

Napalkov nodded thoughtfully. This was turning out to be a hospital visit full of thoughtful nods. Wordlessly he handed the pile of translated personnel files to Kennedy, then took the other stack of Russian originals to a desk on the other side of the room. Silence reigned supreme as the two men worked their way methodically through their respective piles. After a few minutes, Kennedy took one file out and placed it to one side. A minute or two later Napalkov did the same. They were the only ones either man picked out.

Eventually, Napalkov put down the last file and lifted up the one he had picked out. "This one."

Kennedy lifted up the file he had selected and lifted it up. "I agree. This one."

Napalkov opened the file and started to read the contents. "Habarov, Nikolai Pavlovich. Forty four years old. Wife, Nina Klaravina age twenty five. He is a dispatcher at the railway yard and sent the supplies on their way. She is a welder at the Grivka shipyard. She is reported to have had an affair with American sailor stationed there but hasn't been seen for several weeks. This man, we should speak with."

Airfield 108, Privolzhskiy na Volga, Moskva Front.

The left hand tire had been shredded by a 20mm hit on the port wing and that dragged *FivebyFive* over to one side. Edwards hauled on the controls, desperately trying to keep the Thunderbolt on the runway but it was an impossible task. The P-47 swerved off the runway and into the grass to one side. Its tail swung up and its nose dipped, driving the still-spinning propeller deep into the earth. For a moment, Edwards thought the aircraft would flip on its back but it hung nose down for a moment before falling back on to its tailwheel. He breathed a sigh of relief. He was down.

The trains had been a hideous experience. There were four trains trapped in the entrance to the bombed out marshaling yard. Each had three flatcars with anti-aircraft guns, one in front of the engine, one halfway down the consist and one at the end. Each had either a quadruple 20mm gun or a single 37mm and the volume of flak that had gone up was something the Thunderbolt pilots had never seen before. *Eye Candy* had been hit on the run in and had pulled away in a long sweeping curve with the ground fire still lashing at her. She'd reached the top of the curve, rolled on her back and then dived straight into the ground. Edwards had seen *Ive Addit* with flames pouring out of her turbocharger exhaust. He had remembered the lecturer who had said that once that happened, the pilot had 15 seconds to get out before the Thunderbolt exploded. *Ive Addit* had blown apart right on the beat.

Suddenly bright light flooded the cockpit as the canopy was opened from the outside. "All right, Sir. We got you. Are you hurt?"

Edwards shook his head, then felt himself being dragged out of *Fivebyfive*. Once outside, he could see how the left side of the aircraft had been raked by 20mm fire. *Damn, any other aircraft would have fallen apart in mid-air.*

One of the ground crew was under the left wing, looking at where the panels had been torn up by the flak. Suddenly, he started prying at something within the wing structure. After a minute he straightened up, holding something in his hand.

"Well, take a look at this, Sir. Looks like a 20mm shell to me. One of the thin-walled ones. It hit the main wing spar and crumpled up. If it had exploded, it would have taken the whole wing off. You want to keep this, good luck charm."

Edwards took the shell and looked at it carefully. It was indeed a 20mm minengeschoss. "Thank you Sergeant, I'll do as you suggest. How is the old girl?" That's when Edwards frowned slightly. He could have sworn he had heard an aggrieved voice say *Hey, not so much of the old*. He put it down to the stress of the strafing mission.

"She's out of it Sir. Needs a new wing and panel repairs to the aft fuselage and tail. We'll have her done by the end of next week. You'll have to take one of the spares until then."

"Thanks Sergeant." Edwards walked over to where the intelligence debriefers were waiting, took his shot of whisky and then described the mission. He mentioned the help from the reconnaissance F-5 and how it had led them to the most valuable targets. He ended up with the havoc wrought by the flak on the trains and how they'd had to knock the guns out before they could finish off the rest of the trains. When they had got around to strafing the railway cars, the secondary explosions had been spectacular.

"Thank you Lieutenant Edwards. You'll be going out again soon. You'll have to take one of the spare 'Bolts."

"Take *Live Bait* Monty. She's a good bird." Major Young had called over from where he was speaking with the intelligence people. "Get yourself some coffee and donuts. We're going out again in an hour."

Coffee and donuts? Edwards was suddenly aware he could smell fresh coffee and – wonder of wonders – freshly cooked donuts. *That does it, I'm either dead or gone mad. Or both.*

Without the rest of him being aware of it, his legs had followed his nose and he was standing in front of an American school bus. It was painted olive drab certainly but it still looked like a school bus and where the olive drab had been scratched, the orange-yellow of a school bus showed through. One side had been cut open and now formed a counter with a sun-shade above it. In the back of the bus, three women were hard at work brewing fresh coffee, making tea for the Russian pilots and serving donuts to everybody. The word "Clubmobile" was written above the bus windows. Edwards thought that the women looked

239

remarkably thin for people who worked with donuts all day but then realized they were just normal American women. It was just that his months in Russia had accustomed his eyes to the more . . . solidly-built . . . Russian women. Meanwhile, his nose continued to drag the rest of him towards the coffee and donuts.

"Coffee and a donut, hon?" The woman in the converted bus beamed at him.

"I'll have to go to my quarters first. I don't have any money on me. We have to leave anything identifiable here."

"You don't need money, honey. The Air Force wanted us to charge for the goodies but the rich folks stepped in. They're sponsoring the Clubmobiles. Every cup of coffee and every donut we serve, they pay for. So dig in. How would you like your coffee?"

"Milk and sugar? And a donut, please."

"We got cream." The woman watched with amusement as Edwards nodded disbelievingly. "Here you go and come back if you want another donut."

Lilya Litvyak was sitting in one of the cheap folding chairs scattered around the Clubmobile. She had a glass of tea in one hand, a half-eaten donut in the other. Her mouth and cheeks were covered in powdered sugar and there was a small blob of red jelly on her nose. She looked just like a cat that had discovered an unguarded pot of cream. She looked up as Edwards approached. "Lilya, may I join you?"

She nodded, pausing only to take a small bite out of her donut. Edwards knew exactly what she was doing, trying to stretch the delight of the unexpected treat out as long as possible. Edwards sipped his coffee and knew exactly how she felt. The taste of real coffee, freshly brewed with cream and sugar was something he had almost forgotten. He had the weird sensation that the whole of his body was thanking his taste buds. Then he took a bite out of the donut, still warm from the machine and the sensation was redoubled.

"This must be what your millionaires eat." Lilya's sugar-starved body was experiencing a high from the sudden influx of best American powdered confectioner's sugar.

That made Edwards chuckle. "This is the working man's snack, tovarish Lilya. What we call a meal on the run. If we are really short on time, we go into a coffee shop. Spend a nickel - that's five cents – for a cup of coffee and another nickel for a fresh donut. There are some coffee shops, mostly run by Italians I guess, where a man can buy a special coffee for a dime. That's 10 cents. Who's going to spend ten cents on a cup of coffee, I ask you?"

Edwards became aware of Lieutenant Tom Russell standing near them. He was unsteady on his feet and Edwards could smell the alcohol. "Tom, what's up? Come and join us."

Russell slumped into a chair, nearly falling over backwards in the process. Edwards was suddenly aware that this situation was a lot more serious than he had thought. They were due to fly in . . . . less than half an hour . . . and the Lieutenant was obvious too drunk to do so. That was a court-martial situation. "What the hell is the matter with you, Tom?"

"The horses. . . . . Oh Christ, Monty, the horses." He seemed to be about to break down but steadied himself and kept talking. "We were strafing the roads and we saw a kraut column. We started to strafe before we saw that they were all horse-drawn carts. Did you know that our .50s will knock a horse clean off its legs? We could see our guns blowing huge bits off them. Some of those horses that took a full burst were knocked through the air. And that isn't the worst of it. Those carts must have been carrying gasoline on jerrycans because they blew up and burned as soon as our tracers hit them. Those bastard krauts just ran off and left the horses harnessed to the carts. They were trapped there, in the middle of all that burning gasoline. Some were running to try and escape but all they did was spread the gasoline further. I'm sure we could hear them screaming. We were doing passes, trying to shoot them before they burned alive but it was no good. There were too many of them and they all burned. It's the worst thing I've ever seen in my life."

"Russell, you're unfit to fly. Emotional breakdown. Get to sickbay." Major Young sounded and looked worried. He had come from behind Russell as soon as he had realized there was a problem. "Thanks for looking after him, Monty. I'll cover this. Guards Captain Litvyak, welcome to the American tradition of the coffee and donut break. Monty, your guest has an empty hand. I suggest you fill it immediately."

Edwards grinned at the mock reproof but Lilya was regretful. "Thank you, Major, but I've already had my donut."

"Guards Captain, whoever said that you are rationed to one? Our coffee and donuts trucks might be run by the Red Cross but they are sponsored by rich industrialists. I'm told this one is sponsored by a man called Stuyvesant and his family. Never heard of him myself but . . . . So, whenever you have a donut you are helping to transfer wealth from bloated capitalists to honest workers and peasants. Monty, take your guest over to the Clubmobile right now and don't bring her back until she has a fresh, warm, jelly donut. I think they call jelly donuts pyshki in Russian."

"That's Lening . . . . Petrograd, Sir. In my home town, outside Moskva, they were called ponchiki. I missed them terribly."

241

Edwards and Litvyak set off for the converted bus, watched by Young. As soon as they were out of earshot, Young turned to Guards-Major Stepan Petrovich Ganin standing beside him. "You know, those two are the only ones on the base who don't know they are a couple."

Management Office, Admiralteyskaya Grivka Shipyard, Kazan

Electrician's Mate Owen Barton stood at attention in front of the desk that formed the center of the sparse office. A lieutenant from the Office of Naval Intelligence was behind the desk, staring at Barton with interest. "At ease. What happened, Barton?"

'Sir?" Barton was trying to play it cool but wasn't nearly old enough or experienced enough to pull it off.

"Barton, you haven't done anything wrong right now and you may, just may, have accidentally done something unexpectedly valuable. We're not here to investigate you, you are here to help us investigate somebody else. Let's start at the beginning. What do you do here?"

"Repair electronic equipment on damaged gunboats, Sir. Anything that Starry May can't fix comes here. I've been trained to use electrical tools and repair electrical equipment. I know how to charge storage batteries and wind armatures. I can repair telephone circuits. I learned all of that back home, Sir. The Navy taught me to apply first aid in case of electrical shock. That's it, Bring the gunboats in, fix them and send them out. We have PR-59, PR-83 and PR-35 in right now and two Russian boats. They're all badly shot up. You must know all this, Sir."

"I do. Now, do you know Nina Klaravina Habarovna."

Barton's eyes widened as he began to realize, or thought he realized, where this was going. "Nina? Yes. She is a Class One welder, meaning she is qualified to weld armor plate. That's tricky work, Sir. Do it wrong and the armor is ruined. We worked together a few times. Nice lady. Had it rough though."

"What do you mean?"

"Her husband beats her. Couple of times she came into the yard with her face bruised. And she was thin, I think her husband spends all their money on drink then smacks her around when it ran out. I heard the foreman transferred her to the yard down at Starry May so she would have an excuse to get away from him. That must be three, four weeks ago."

"Did you have an intimate relationship with her?"

Barton shook his head. "Sir, she was desperate for affection, any sign that somebody cared about her. I took her to the canteen a few times, put a decent meal in her. I listened when she talked, that's how I know about all her problems. Anything more than that would have been taking advantage. It would have made me just another man exploiting her."

"I see. At any time, did she ask you about your work? About the electronic equipment you worked with?"

"No. Never. We don't talk about our work here. Sometimes she would ask about America, what we ate, what we would do in the evenings, that was all." Barton came to the obvious conclusion, even though he was in error. "You think she is a spy?"

"No." From one corner of the room where he had sat quietly and watched the interview, Napalokov got to his feet and joined the other two at the desk. "We think she was an unfortunate women trapped in a marriage with a drunken and violent man. Something all too common in the Rodina I fear. We think she had the good fortune to meet a sympathetic man who would listen patiently while she poured out her troubles. We think that people with malicious tongues saw that and spread false rumors that had tragic consequences. I think, Electrician's Mate Owen Barton, that you are a good man and that you have nothing to fear from CheKa."

Baron saluted and left. Napalkov thought for a second and turned to the ONI officer. "That young seaman. Are all your young men like that?"

The ONI officer was a bit nonplussed by the question, not one he had expected from an officer in the notorious CheKa. "Not all, no. We have saints and sinners like everybody else. But I honestly think that most of our youngsters faced with a woman in such distress would have supported her with kindness and not taken advantage of her. I hope so anyway. If we have done our work as parents properly, they would do so."

Napalkov smiled slowly. "If that is the case then I think your country has nothing to fear from the future. But, here and now, I think that the husband of Nina Klaravina and those whose malicious tongues spread false rumors about a comrade, they have something to fear from us."

Vorkova Prospekt 47, Kazan

The house was small, built of wood, with a shingled roof. A door on the left, a window beside it. The floor above had two windows. That was it. Major of militsiya Aleksei Nikolaevich Ras'kin nevertheless knew that this was more than many residents of the city had to shelter them. *Ever since the Hitlerites invaded the Rodina they have driven the population eastwards, overcrowding the cities that remain. It will take us decades to repair the damage done over the last two years. More than decades perhaps. But I must not show despair, not with an officer of CheKa with me. This is a crisis for me. If I do well, I will gain the interest and support of powerful people. If I fail here today, I will be in an infantry unit tomorrow.*

Ras'kin strode up to the front door and knocked respectfully. "Tovarish Nikolai Pavlovich, I have urgent news from the front."

Standing unobtrusively, Napalkov made a mental note of approval. *That is cunningly done. 'Urgent news from the front' always means that your son, your brother, your father or perhaps even your sister have given their lives for the Rodina. It is a phrase heard every day in every street. Even the nosiest of neighbors will now shake their head sadly and give the poor bereaved a little privacy for their grief. And that means we can take this man away unnoticed. If there is a saboteur ring here, this would be the first step to rolling it up.*

Ras'kin knocked again. Then, the door opened and he stepped inside. Again, to any casual watchers the user of the house had opened the door, hoping against hope that this was something other than the dreaded news of another Russian dying to save the Rodina. In fact, the Major of militsiya had used his skeleton key to open the door and let himself in. Napalkov waited patiently. There was a brief disturbance from the area behind the house and then there was silence broken by the sounds of any city.

Well almost any city. The sounds were joined by a deep throated roar that seemed to echo from the buildings and doll down the streets. Napalkov looked up and saw the cause. Aircraft were flying overhead, American Thunderbolts. The deep-pitched snarl of their engines was quite different from anything else that flew around this section of the front. Napalkov counted quickly Forty eight aircraft, three formations of 16, each split in four groups of four. The sound of their engines seemed to make the ground shake under his feet as they passed directly overhead. An old woman, her head wrapped in the traditional headscarf stopped quickly to look at the American aircraft.

"My ne odni." Her old voice seemed to gain strength from simply saying the words. "We are not alone."

Napalkov made a respectful gesture to the old lady even though he desperately wanted her out of the way. Together, they watched the Thunderbolts flying overhead and continued to gaze upwards until the sound of their engines was muted by distance. The old lady spoke again. "Amerikanskiye brat'ya. Let us wish them good hunting and a safe return."

"Let us do that, mother. And let us give thanks to the American mothers who have sent their sons here to fight alongside us." To his own surprise, Napalkov found that he was quite sincere.

Once the old lady had gone, a hand emerged from the doorway and waved Napalkov in. Once inside, Napalkov looked around. The place was the kind of dirty, unkempt, sordid mess that only a man on his own who was perpetually drunk could create. And yet, there were signs that a woman had been here once. The obvious question was, where was she now? Napalkov realized that this was not one of those stories that could possibly have a happy ending.

There were two rooms on each floor. Habarov, Ras'kin and two very large privates of militsiya were in the back room of the lower floor. The privates were sitting on Habarov, keeping him firmly pinned to the floor. There was also a senior sergeant of militsiya supervising the arrest. In this case, supervising seemed to involve kicking Habarov every time he tried to move or make a sound. Napalkov approved of the sentiment but felt he had to caution the Senior Sergeant. "Not in the head, tovarish Sergei Sergeevich. We need the information that lies between his ears."

"There was a woman who lived here. She's gone now." Senior Sergeant Sergei Sergeevich Pargamenko was one of those men who deeply and genuinely loved his wife and extended some of that love to women in general. This made him intolerant of those who abused them. He knew in his heart what must have happened to the woman who had lived here and his feelings towards Habarov were black indeed. "I wonder what happened to her."

"She went to Staraya Mayna. She works in the yard there."

"No, she does not." Ras'kin spoke quietly but with great authority. "We checked."

Napalkov nodded again to himself. Ras'kin had destroyed the man's story without giving away more than he had to. A job well done. "What happened here, Major of militsiya?"

"As we came in the front, he tried to leave out of the back window. Only I had my two men waiting for him. They pushed him back inside. All in a day's work for the militsiya."

"Where is she?" Ras'kin asked the question again, managing to convey that he was a man of great patience and that Habarov had better remember the proverb about avoiding the wrath of a patient man. But Habarov ignored the hint and said nothing.

Napalkov watched as Ras'kin strode over to the window and stared out. He could sense the man's frustration and was interested to see how he would handle it. Then, reading the Major of militsyia's body language with the skill of any good secret policeman, he realized that the Major had seen something but hadn't quite worked out what yet.

"Tovarish Chekist?"

"Bratishka?"

"Please tell me what you make of this." Ras'kin was looking out of the window over the vegetable plot in the rear of the house. "It was raining hard all yesterday, and well into dawn. See how there is still water sitting on the surface of the ground where the vegetables grow? Yet, look at the end of the plot. See how the water has drained away. As if the soil is loose and the drainage improved. Yet the plants do not look well. I would not say they are wilted but perhaps they are sad?"

Napalkov nodded in agreement. Encouraged by the approval and by being addressed as a brother by a Chekist, Ras'kin continued. "Would not the plants being dug up and moved, a grave dug there, and then filled with the plants moved back explain this?"

"Come down with one of your men. The Senior Sergeant and the other private of militsya will stay here with the prisoner. We have digging to do."

It took ten minutes to find some spades and another twenty to exhume the grave. Right from the start, they knew that Ras'kin had been right. The soil was loose from being dug over and, as the excavation deepened, the smell became frightful, yet familiar to the men in a country that was suffering its third year of brutal war. Eventually, they exposed the body at the bottom of the pit. It was badly decayed yet was recognizable as a woman, naked and with her hands and feet tightly bound. Her mouth was open in the terrified rictus of a human being who had died screaming. To both Chekist and Major of militsya, it was obvious that Nina Klaravina Habarovna had been alive and fully conscious when her husband had buried her.

"I think she was begging for her life, even while that bastard threw the dirt on top of her." Ras'kin's voice was saturated with loathing. "I dread to think what else he did to her."

"Not all monsters are Hitlerites." Napalkov managed the phrase without a trace of irony in his voice. "We must get a team here to remove this body quietly so we can confirm the cause of death. We also need to get the murderer away from here so he can be interrogated. Thoroughly interrogated. Major of militsya Ras'kin, you have done very well here today and I think it is certain you will receive a commendation for your work. And your men of course. The detection and solution of this terrible murder is your achievement. But, there is much more to this. Nikolai Pavlovich Habarov is the vilest of traitors as well as being the vilest of murderers and his crimes may lead us to others of his kind. So, this will become a matter for CheKa to deal with. And deal with it we will. You can be assured of that."

By the time he had finished speaking, he and Ras'kin had returned indoors. Habarov had been moved to the front room, ready to be collected by the car that would take him to the local CheKa office for interrogation. He remained silent, all the way out to the car. What caused him to break it was something nobody could have organized. From overhead came the sound of aircraft engines. Not the vicious snarl of the Thunderbolts but a steady, all-encompassing drone. Overhead, a wide white band, the contrails left by a massed formation of B-17s spread across the sky. To Napalkov, Ras'kin and the militsiya it was an inspiring sight, one that lifted their hearts and renewed their hope that one day the war would end with the Rodina *and its allies* victorious. They savored those three words *and its allies* with joy indescribable. The effect of seeing the bombers on Habarov was quite different. He was suddenly seized with an inchoate fury that emerged as a tirade of screaming luridly obscene insults directed at the Americans and all who had let them come to Russia. His insane screaming continued all the way to CheKa. *He is getting into practice,* Napalkov reflected.

Sickbay, GunRon 5 Headquarters, Staraya Mayna, Volga River.

"We got the right man?" Kennedy lay back on his bed. He was in visibly worse condition than on Napalkov's previous visit. He had a blinding headache and severe nausea and was suffering from acute fatigue. The nurse responsible for him had been very reluctant to let Napalkov in and had only relented when she had been assured that the Chekist was bringing good news to cheer him. And that the meeting was vital to the war effort.

"We got him and a sad story it is." Napalkov settled down in a chair beside the bed and started to tell the story he had heard. "Habarov is a habitual drunkard and has been for many years. His drunkenness had prevented him from promotion within the railway authority and he remained a poorly-paid official of the lowest grade. What a young woman with prospects like Nina Klaravina had seen in him that had made her marry such an older man is inexplicable. As a skilled welder, she earned more than he did and he came to rely upon her earnings to keep him in his drink-sodden state. When he had spent all her money, he would beat her. Like most men who beat their wives, he had grown skilled at doing so without leaving obvious bruising yet like most drunkards, he made mistakes.

"Nina Klaravina met a young American sailor after a beating that left her with obvious damage. That young sailor saw she was hurt and did what he could to help her. They became friends, that is all. He acted like one good comrade should act towards another in distress. But, there was at least one woman in the shipyard who did not like the sight of a Russian woman with an American man. You know the type of woman I think. One who claims to know everything about everybody and will tell it all to anybody who will listen. Yet all that knowledge never includes anything good about the people they denigrate. This woman jumped to the conclusion that a relationship existed where one did not and went running to tell Nina Klaravina's husband.

"Habarov confessed to what happened next. No, that is not correct, he boasted of it. He attacked his wife when she came home from work, subdued her and spent the next few hours 'punishing' her for her alleged infidelity. In fact, from his own words he cared nothing about her, only for the loss of the money he needed to buy all the vodka he wanted. It was the loss of his beloved drink that drove him into the full madness of anger. When he had finished brutalizing his wife, he buried her alive in the vegetable plot behind his house. Yet even that dreadful act did not assuage his anger. Instead, he transferred his rage and loathing to the American Navy who he saw as responsible for him losing his drinking money.

"The next day at work, he complained bitterly for all to hear about how his wife had run away with an American. It was a foolish story of course; quite apart from anything else, Americans have nowhere to run to here. But, he was already being watched by fascist spies who had marked him down as a likely recruit. They are experts in what they do and they fed his anger and rage at the Americans. Perhaps they guessed his wife was really dead and fed on that as well. We will know when we catch them. But they put the idea into his head that if he delivered the wrongly-dispatched ammunition to the gunboat base, then an American gunboat would run out of ammunition in the middle of a battle and they would thus suffer for what they had done. The illogic of the scheme of course did not register in Habarov's drink-sodden mind. He did not realize that the ammunition could not be for an American gunboat but would be sent on to Russian troops. So he went ahead and did the paperwork needed. To that he has confessed."

Napalkov sighed, deeply saddened by story he had told. "Jack, in America you deride those who pushed through prohibition but when I come across stories like this, ones that are far too common, I understand why its supporters did so."

"Did we get the spies? And what will happen to Habarov?" To Napalkov's admittedly inexpert eyes, Kennedy's condition had deteriorated even while the story had unfolded. Certainly his voice had weakened.

"We have not caught the spies yet. Habarov has not given then information yet. He will. We have deprived him of his drink and soon the absence of alcohol will turn him into a gibbering wreck. And after that . . ." Napalkov suddenly lost all the friendliness and amiability he normally displayed and all that was left was the ruthless Chekist goon. ". . . we have experts ready to indoctrinate him in the intimate relationship that exists between water, electricity and pain."

CHAPTER NINE: PRICES PAID

Headquarters, American Expeditionary Force, Seitovo, Chuvashskaya Bridgehead.

"If you would like to wait in the anteroom, General Fredendall will see you when he . . . . . Oh." The aide had started to speak with completely inappropriate and unwarranted condescension in his voice but an elderly yet very strong hand had pushed him in the chest, sending him flying backwards into an office chair. He sprawled there, watching the parade of stars in front of his eyes. Two of those stars belonged to an apparently smiling and friendly general who wagged his finger at the Lieutenant. "We'll speak about this later, Lieutenant Rawlings."

"Yes, sir, General Eisenhower, sir." The Lieutenant had gone white. Such discussions never ended well for the junior officer.

"A snake rots from the head down." Colonel General Koniev, technically present as a mere observer at this point, spoke quietly. Eisenhower nodded. Any further comment was interrupted by the crash as the leader of the delegation kicked open General Fredendall's door. It flew open, smashed against a pair of filing cabinets and bounced back, only to be kicked again. The sound echoed off the stone walls of the headquarters and rolled down the corridors, freezing everybody within earshot. Ripples from the event spread far and fast with the more astute officers making sure they were both anywhere else and frantically busy.

"Why George, it's good to see you here. I was told you'd be . . . . ." General Fredendall tried to look pleased to see his visitor.

"I've been at the crossing points and up on the front. Not one of our men has ever seen you there. I'll tell you what I did see. A hell of a lot of our guys are not doing their jobs. A lot of them are wandering around behind the lines, dodging MPs, and, when caught, claiming they are either lost or their nerves had 'cracked.' Every man who isn't at the front when he should be, for good reason or not, means one less man doing his job. And that includes you. That means other men have to take up the load they have dropped. Other men have had to take up the load that you dropped." General George S Patton's voice picked up in volume as his anger grew. "You are just a Goddamned coward, you yellow son of a bitch. And because of your spineless crap, the good men who are still trying to hold the line have to carry the extra burden you have laid on them. Yesterday, those brave young men fought and died because you didn't have the balls to lead this army. You're setting the standards for this army and every man who has deserted his post is following your example."

Koniev was watching with fascination. This was, in his opinion, how generals should treat those who failed to live up to their responsibilities. He leaned over to Eisenhower. "Tovarish, why do you not simply shoot him?"

Eisenhower sighed slightly but kept watching Patton with the eyes of a hawk. An unwritten part of Eisenhower's job was to keep Patton under control when the General lost his temper. Nevertheless, Eisenhower could see what Koniev was getting at. "Oh, that we could, tovarish Ivan. Oh, that we could. . ."

The exchange had meant Eisenhower had missed a little of the tirade of insults Patton was pouring on Fredendall, Patton was now standing in front of Fredendall's desk, his hands on the edge supporting his body that was extended over the surface so that he was shouting in Fredendall's face. "You know what our boys on the front call you? Vetrenyy Freddie. Windy Freddie. It makes my blood boil to think that our boys know they are being led by a yellow bastard son-of-a-bitch like you. How the hell can you expect those kids up there to fight when you are skulking inside a mountain back here? I won't have cowardly bastards like you hanging around in our rear. I won't have you showing our boys you haven't got the guts to fight. We'll probably have to start shooting people like you or we'll raise a breed of morons."

"I think he is joking right now, or acting at least. I'm never quite sure when he is joking, acting for effect or genuinely believes what he is saying." Eisenhower was watching the display with a connoisseur's appreciation of a finest-vintage ass-chewing.

Fredendall was speaking but Patton was simply ignoring him. Instead, he spoke to Eisenhower. "It's not important that you know, Ike. It's only important that I know."

Koniev tipped his head slightly in response. "I must warn you all that the Russian Front is a place where violent jokes almost always come true."

In the background, Fredendall was still trying to justify his actions but the truth was, nobody was really listening. "But, an army needs a secure headquarters where decisions can be taken without distractions . . . "

"Distractions!" Patton was now bright red and was obviously reaching boiling point. Eisenhower moved closely to prevent anything untoward happening. Patton lashed out and slapped Fredendall across the face with his gloves. "Shut up with that Goddamned whining. I won't have the brave men here, men who have done their duty and been shot at, seeing a yellow bastard sitting here whining."

He then struck Fredendall again and yelled, to anybody and everybody within earshot. "Kick this yellow bastard out. I won't have this headquarters cluttered up with these sons of bitches who haven't got the guts to fight."

He then turned back to Fredendall, who shaking all over, and his voice was deadly quiet, "You're going to the front lines, Windy Freddie, and you may get shot and killed, but you're going to fight. If you don't, I'll stand you up against a wall and have a firing squad kill you on purpose. In fact," he said, reaching for his pistol, "I ought to shoot you myself, you Goddamned whimpering coward."

Now is the moment, thought Eisenhower. He reached out and put his hand over Patton's. "George, he's not worth it. Do you realize how hard it is to get forty-five long Colt ammunition out here?"

Patton paused and nodded. "Ike. General Truscott, you have twenty four hours to get this Goddamned headquarters slimmed down to a realistic size, mobilize it and get it on the road. We need to be on the front line, not seventy miles behind it."

The cheer that went up across the headquarters was clearly audible. Eisenhower could swear that Patton had winked at him. Patton paused for a second and then continued rapping out orders. "Get the senior medical officer and the head nurse here. I want this place converted into a hospital right now. The boys who took a bullet for their country deserve the best treatment we can give them in the safest possible place. There's nurses up on the front line, treating our boys as best they can in ragged tents under artillery fire. They and their patients deserve better. That's your boys as well, tovarish Ivan. If the wounded are allied, they can be brought here. This Goddamned white elephant ought to be used for something useful."

"Will you be using this office, General?" It was uncertain who had asked the question.

Patton glared at Fredendall's desk and the stunned man still sitting behind it. "No good decision was ever made in a swivel chair. We'll be moving out right now. Ike, cut orders for Vetrenyy Freddie here. He's to go as an observer to the Ulyanov'sk bridgehead. He can learn how to fight by watching real soldiers. Tovarish Ivan, please instruct your men at Ulyanov'sk that General Fredendall will be joining them as an observer and if he tries to command anything they are authorized to Goddamn well shoot him."

"General Patton, sir. We have a critical situation brewing. The enemy is attacking north and south of Kanash and if our flank forces can't hold them, the town will be cut off. Should we organize a relief force?" Colonel Ryan Anderson had quietly entered the room while the destruction of Fredendall had been in progress. "Sir, the best overall picture of the situation is our map in the communications center. We've monitoring radio intercepts, ours and the enemy's all the time and it's as up to date as we can manage."

"Thank God, somebody who knows what he is doing. Anderson? As from now, you're the Situations Officer. I'll need you to expand that situation map. Make it your first responsibility. No relief force. I was up at Kanash last night. They will have to hold out with what they've got. You can bet the krauts are waiting for us to try some sort of relief column. They'll already have some sort of blocking force waiting on ground they've chosen. Never let the enemy pick the battle site. Spread the word, tell everybody to remember, we shouldn't underestimate an enemy, but it is just as fatal to overestimate him. We did the first, now we are doing the second. No matter how tired and hungry we may be, the enemy will be more tired, more hungry. We must keep punching. Just not where he expects us to punch, that's all."

Atnashevo, North West of Kanash, Chuvashskaya Bridgehead.

Master Sergeant Fredrick Merriman did not like the M-10 tank destroyer. It was open-topped, for one thing and he didn't have the comforting sense of being protected by armor. When he had been assigned to a Sherman, he had felt protected but the M-10 was different. Of course, the fact that it had an open-topped turret was mostly responsible for that. Yet, it was that same lack of overhead protection that had saved his life the previous day. His vehicle had been hit by a shot from a Panzer IV that had slashed straight through the thin armor. The explosion had thrown him clear of the vehicle. If it hadn't, he knew that he would probably have died then and there, As it was, his uniform was singed and he had minor burns to his face but he had managed to get clear before the vehicle brewed up. The tank destroyer had continued to burn and eventually the shells inside detonated and blew it apart.

For all that, overnight he had visited his battalion command and volunteered for assignment to another M-10. A scratched-together armored unit was being assembled from the rag-bag of units that were converging on Kanash. And, so it was that Merriman had come back to the M-10. The truth was that while he didn't like the M-10, he did like its three inch gun. It was much more powerful than the 75mm equipping the Shermans. The previous day, Merriman had used it to good effect, tearing up the fascist Panzer IIIs and IVs. He had actually found it an interesting battle until his commander had made a dumb mistake and let them be flanked by that Panzer IV.

Kazan Thunderbolts

Now it was the next battle with the surviving tank destroyers supporting the troops defending Atnashevo. The village was blocking a German advance against the main road that linked Kanash with the towns further east and, eventually, to Kazan, Seven M-10s and four Shermans had been deployed to support a company of infantry that had been tasked with holding the position. Merrimen's M-10 was one of three that had been placed in a fan formation over on the right flank of the position.

The key to the defense was a river, more like a small stream, that cut across the battlefield in front of the American position. All three M-10s were fairly close to the river bank, and positioned close together so that the firing sectors of the tank destroyers overlapped. Overnight, all the M-10s had been dug in by the engineers. The pits had been big enough to hold the tank destroyer so that most of its hull was below ground level with just the turret exposed The barrel of the three-inch gun was only a few inches above ground level and the whole position had been camouflaged with some bushes. The engineers had sloped the rear of the pit so that the M-10 could back out when it needed to. They'd even dug a small pit under the vehicle for the crew to rest in. The M-10 was too small for the crew to rest in when it was in a defensive position. So the crew had taken it in turns to keep watch while the rest of the crew had slept in the pit under their vehicle.

The impending attack wouldn't be the first that day. At around 4 o'clock in the morning, a quick German artillery bombardment had set some of the town houses on fire. The brief bombardment had been followed by an infantry attack in company strength supported by three assault guns. Two things had quickly become apparent; one was that the attack was being pressed home with great ferocity, the other that the troops involved lacked the sublime skill with which the German infantry had routed an American division the day before. Anyway, the Germans open fire and commenced an attack from the village graveyard. It was also obvious that word of the American bazookas hadn't spread to the German unit yet. The three assault guns drove right up to the outskirts of the town and were promptly knocked out by bazookas. The rest of the fight had been bitter but it had ended with the Germans being driven back. That was when the Americans had found they were up against an SS division.

The Americans had found something else. Moving forward to retake the areas overrun by the SS, the American troops had found, written on the white wall of one ruined hovel with a charcoal: "Rocketmen, don't let us take you prisoner, we'll cut you to pieces while you're still alive." And nearby they had found the bodies of a bazooka operator and his loader, a star carved into their foreheads, their arms broken, theirs eyes gouged out and their genitals cut off and stuffed into their mouths. Word of that had spread around the perimeter very fast.

253

"They're coming again." Merriman heard the warning on the radio and a single look confirmed the message. There were a lot more Germans than before and they had real tanks with them, not assault guns. He took a harder look at the tanks and identified them as Panzer IVs. *Well, those we can handle.* He cranked the turret around and felt the M-10 vibrating under his feet as the driver gunned the engine. *A lesson from yesterday, when we need to move, we need to move very fast and right away.* Meanwhile, he was spinning the turret and brining the long-barrelled three inch gun to bear. He centered the telescopic sight on the center enemy tank and looked at it again. Something seemed a bit off about it but he mentally shrugged the worrying thought off.

"Target identified. Firing." The three inch gun snapped out its round and the red streak behind made it easy for Merriman to follow it all the way to the target. It was a beautiful shot, dead centered on the frontal armor of the tank. Only, instead of the brilliant flash of a penetration, there was a shower of sparks as the shot disintegrated on the armor plate. "Load AP, NOW."

Beside him, the loader was frantically pushing another armor-piercing round into the breech of their gun. Merriman laid the gun with exquisite care and fired again. Yet, the result was the same. Through the dust kicked up by his gun, he could see the shot hitting the front of the German tank and bouncing off.

"What the hell? Our shots are just bouncing off the damn thing. I might as well be shooting spitballs at it!"

"Those aren't Mark IVs. They're too damned big for that."

The German tank fired, its shot screaming so low over the top of the M-10 that Merriman could swear that he felt it sucking his helmet off his head. The M-10 commander was screaming "back up, back up" when another shell hit their revetment. Merriman felt his teeth clacking together from the explosion and a spray of shrapnel raked the open turret of the M-10. The loader went down, spraying blood from his face and neck. The M-10 commander helped Merriman slap a field dressing on the wounded man. Merriman guessed that was about the most useful thing he could do right then since the shrapnel had wrecked his gunsight. Out in front of his position, the Germans are already advancing with their tanks shooting at the American positions. A black pyre of smoke already marked where one of the Shermans had been destroyed. All too quickly, it was joined by a second and a third.

"Just what the hell are those damned things?" Merriman watched in frustration as two more armor piercing shots bounced off the German tank. "Let's get the hell out of here"

That was when the M-10's luck finally ran out and a shell slashed straight though the earth embankment in front of the tank destroyer, sliced through the frontal armor and sent the engine spiraling backwards out of the hull. Flames erupted through the ventilation grills on top of the engine and started to spread through the hull. Merriman knew form previous experience that he had only a few seconds to get clear. He shut his eyes, heaved himself over the rim of the turret and was just far enough to one side to avoid the flames that engulfed the tank destroyer as it exploded. The blast threw him at least five yards and rolled him through the bushes. That probably saved his life because the German tank was using the machine gun in its bow to rake the area around the tank's victim. Somehow, he managed to turn to avoid getting hurt by the fall.

Somehow, he couldn't quite work out how, he was holding his Colt M1911 and he had an insane urge to fire it at the German tank. One look told him that the whole area occupied by the tank destroyers was covered by a net of tracer rounds, and enemy shells were exploding everywhere. Common sense, for once, prevailed over insanity and Merriman crawled away, heading for the riverbank where there would be some cover.

A couple of minutes later he looked back at the scene he had just barely escaped from. There was nothing left of his M-10. The vehicle had completely fallen apart, only the gearbox was recognizable; it had been thrown clear and was burning in a pool of blue flame. What shook him was the German tank just a few feet from the wreckage. It was huge, making the tank destroyers look puny. Then Merriman saw that a German tank crewman was half-fallen out of one of the hatches. For some reason. the German tank came up and another M-10, hidden between two buildings, had scored a direct hit right in the side at point blank range, at most from 10 yards away. The second M-10 was already burning; obviously it had been hit while it was killing the giant German tank. Two survivors from the crew were heading backwards, both wounded. One had obviously been hit in the arm, while the other had blood streaming down his face from a wound in the cheek.

By the time Merriman got the survivors of the three M-10s to the medical station the German advance had reached the outskirts of Atnashevo but it was quickly losing momentum. Six of the seven M-10s and al the Shermans had been destroyed but they'd got two of the German tanks. One was the vehicle killed by the M-10. The other had been shot in the rear by a bazooka crew. Nobody was playing games there, not after what had happened earlier. The SS men in the tank had been killed as they bailed out of the burning vehicle.

"Master Sergeant, take some of these men, go out to the left. We need to know what's down there. Try and take a prisoner." Merriman looked around, hoping that there was another Master Sergeant who was the subject of the orders. There wasn't, Merriman guessed that he was it. The men he was supposed to take with him were a group of four soldiers, all with wounds of some kind or another. Compared with some of the men being shoveled back into the inferno around the northern edge of Atnashevo, they were in good health.

There was a pile of weapons in one corner of the aid station, taken from the casualties who had been brought in. Merriman picked up a Thompson submachine gun and as much ammunition as he could find. The men he had been assigned helped themselves as well. By the time they had sorted themselves out, they had reached the point of exchanging barbed insults over their choices of weapon. Then, they shrugged at each other and set off down a gulley towards a grape orchard further along the river bank. According to the Russians, these usually had bunkers converted out of wine cellars and made a good defensive position. As they closed in on the position, Merriman saw something on the ground near what looked like one of the cellars and figured that maybe it was a fascist.

"Is he dead?"

One of the four looked carefully at the object. "Nah, Sarge, it's just a big heap of straw. There's a doorway behind it though."

The building's door was half-open; Merriman started to open it with his Thompson barrel, As he did so it gave out a piercing squeak.

"Well, if anyone had been inside, they would sure have started shooting."

Merriman nodded in agreement. "Cover me, just in case."

Then he opened the door and went in. He was sorely tempted to go in firing but the training officers had warned that the massive muzzle flash of the Thompson would light him up as a target if he tried. A quick sweep with a flashlight showed there were no grapes in the hut. There was, however, the body of a dead German. Merriman searched him, finding some matches on him, a handkerchief, a torn newspaper and something resembling a letter. He also had an automatic cigarette maker, that Merriman pocketed. "Well boys, the krauts have got to here. That much we know. That means they've already flanked us and cut the road out of Kanash. Take all his stuff; even if we didn't get a live prisoner, at least we have proof of some contact with the bastards."

125th Independent Tank Brigade, Balabash-Baishevo, Southern Flank, Chuvashskaya Bridgehead

Colonel Mihail Fedorovich Lapturov hauled himself out from the dugout underneath his tank. Normally it was where the crew lived while they were not on the move. At the moment though, he and his crew were getting their T-34/76 ready for battle. Every tank crew serviced their tank themselves. They refueled it, loaded it up with ammo and performed any necessary maintenance. Nobody was exempt from the hard, brutal work. Even the zampolits, the political officers, worked together with the rest of the crews. In fact, more so now than ever.

The whole attitude of the political officers had changed since last winter. Once they had been guardians of political orthodoxy, ears always open for sounds that might be construed as treason or defeatism. Once, they had contradicted orders or issued their own and undermined the authority of the regular army officers. Then had come the day when unified command had been restored. Some of the Zampolits had disappeared, never to be seen again. The rest had become morale officers, tasked with building up spirits, of looking after the men rather than watching them.

Now they were forbidden to interfere with the command structure of the units they served. Leading by example was the current motto and so, the brightest of them were first to volunteer for the hardest work and dirtiest labor. Lapturov couldn't help but think that studious attention to their new duties might be seen by them as avoiding the fate that befallen others of their number.

Whatever the motive, the zampolit was indeed refueling a tank alongside the men. Lapturov had heard that American tank battalions had special trucks modified to refuel the tanks. The Soviet Army had no such luxuries. A normal flatbed truck would bring fuel barrels near to a tank, roll them down the tail ramp and move on. The tank crews had each been issued two ten-liter pails. Two men would fill the pails, a third one would take them to the fender and a fourth would pour the fuel into the fuel tank. When Lapturov had become a company commander, he had decided that it was unbecoming to his new rank to carry the pails so he had taken over the job of filling them from the barrels. Then when he had ascended to the command the tank brigade, he had given himself the job of pouring the diesel fuel into the fuel tank. *Lifting fifty ten-liter pails was certainly a way for a man to build up his strength!*

After they had topped up the oil, then the same pails would be used to lift the ammunition into the turret. Before that though, the shells had to be degreased. Normally it was a task for the radio operator- machine gunner. After degreasing, one man would pick up a shell, another one standing on the fender would take it from him and hand it to a third one standing inside the turret and a fourth one - the gun loader, would stack it inside. Now, three years into the war, it was a smoothly operating drill.

Lapturov called his men in. The tanks were ready to go and there was time for the men to eat before they went in to action. Normally, they would eat in the evening when they would have breakfast, lunch and dinner all at once. But, the rations had included American bacon and the cooks had found some small fresh potatoes dug up that very morning. So, they fried the potatoes with the bacon. It was the men's favorite frontline dish and they all knew that many of them would not be alive by evening to enjoy it. So, Lapturov had arranged for them to eat now. They had vodka as well, two pints for each tank crew.

Lapturov was keeping a close eye on his wristwatch. He'd timed everything so that his men could eat properly, fortify their spirits with some of the vodka they had been issued and get their tanks ready for battle. He'd even allowed time for the crews to have a few brief minutes of quiet, officially so they could steady themselves although unofficially it was admitted that most would use it to pray. In fact, Lapturov had heard that some units were even starting to have open prayers before going into battle. He was going to watch and see what happened before he committed himself there. Anyway, it was time for him to make the expected speech before the brigade bounced off.

"Bratishka! How much longer does the Rodina have to suffer from the Hitlerites? Let us attack them! Let's give it a try. Let our tanks speak for us and exact revenge for all our comrades who have died. Do we have mortars? We do! Do we have antitank guns? We do! Do we have submachine gunners? Do we have machine gunners? We do! What else do we need? Open the ammunition boxes, take everything that will help kill a fascist. Cock your hammers! Raise your fists for we have work to do this day! We will strike the bastards with a blow any who survive will never forget! Tank riders. Get to ready to board your tanks!"

Ahead of the 25th Independent Tank Brigade was the target of today's operation. The Brigade had moved up the night before, shifting from its previous position near Tugaevo specifically to take advantage of an opportunity that had opened up the evening before. A German tank battalion had got into a fight with an American tank battalion. They'd chewed the American up and spat them out, of course, but they'd got mauled in the process. Nobody in the Russian units was laughing at the Americans for the defeats they had suffered the day before. All too many of them remembered the dreadful days that had started in May 1941 and never seemed to end. The Americans hadn't performed any worse than Soviet units had back then and had done better than many.

The sight before Lapturov was an example of that. The remains of a German tank battalion, some 30 tanks, mostly Mark IVs were standing near the woods. The word was they had been moved to this location to refit after the slugging match the day before. Thirty tanks out of seventy one. Lapturov rolled that number around in his mind. *Just how many tanks did the Americans kill yesterday? All the fascist units were understrength but how many tanks had they started with?*

From the top of the ridge that concealed his forces, Lapturov was looking at the Hitlerites with bated breath. They were still working around their hauling ammunition, refueling with gasoline. Just what Lapturov and his men had been doing a few minutes before. The fascists had every comfort that could be imagined: thermoses, chairs, tables, all spread around the vehicles. Russian soldiers may sleep on the ground or under their tanks, but the fascists had all the comfort of home, as if they were out hiking. *The Hitlerites are strange people,* Lapturov thought. *They don't make small mistakes. When they do make a mistake, it's a huge one. I bet fascist husbands tell their wives that their new dress makes them look fat.*

Lapturov glanced at his wristwatch again. It was about time. A quick glance around showed that the T-34 and their crews were ready, the tankriders crouched behind the turret. A strong westerly wind was blowing, a leftover from the storm that had passed through the day before. Soon, the wind would swing around and blow from the east. It would be a cold wind, one that would send the temperatures downward. Lapturov deeply hoped that was prophetic. The same wind had swept all the sound and smells of a Soviet unit away from the fascist position. And the hundreds, no thousands, of aircraft the Americans have thrown in over the battlefield have swept the fascist reconnaissance aircraft from the sky. Surely the Russian Army supported by American aircraft can withstand an attack by any enemy! And isn't that exactly what we have here today?

As if in answer, the howl overhead was deafening. *The artillerists are right on time.* The artillery plan had taken most of the early pre-dawn hours to prepare and had been a long expedition into a hall of mirrors. As soon as scouts had reported the Hitlerite tank battalion moving into place, the planning had started to drive it in. Once the T-34s were rolling forward, it would take them five minutes to cover the ground between their selected marshalling area and the German defenses. So, the artillery would have to keep the fascists under fire for that time. After the first three minutes, the tanks would be in range and they could start firing on the fascists. So, it had been decided that the artillerists would continue firing for four minutes before shifting targets.

But what then? Where would the fascists go? What would they do? Under heavy artillery fire, they would have to move. They had really only two choices, through the dense woods to the north or west, along the southern edge of those woods. There were only two roads, fairly close together, with forest either side impenetrable to tanks. If the fascists retreated along those, then artillery fire would destroy them. If they retreated to the east, they would be moving in open ground and could retreat to a position where they had a ridgeline to fight from. But there wasn't a suitable ridge! The nearest good defensible terrain for a tank heavy force was a series of ravines where the tanks could go hull down and move from firing position. That was it! That was where the artillerists should concentrate their fire next!

Kazan Thunderbolts

"But wait!" The artillerist colonel had said. "Suppose the fascists guess that we would not believe they would retreat through the woods and would go east? So they might decide to go north and escape us!"

And so it had gone on. If we do this, then they do that but they may guess we would think that and do the other. And that would mean we would have to do something else. And so, an artillery plan had slowly emerged by which the guns would track the fascists from projected position to projected position.

Lapturov had no illusions about the plan that had finally been agreed. If it worked, it would inflict great harm on the invaders. The Soviet Army's artillery was an immensely powerful weapon but it was sluggish and unresponsive. Once it was committed to a firing plan, that was it. Change didn't happen and if the battle went in unexpected directions, then all that artillery power would be ineffective.

At least the battle was starting well. He could see the fascists freeze as they heard the howl overhead, a welcome outbound howl for the Russians but a dreaded inbound howl for the Hitlerites. They rushed to their tanks as the ground erupted around them. The fuel trucks flared up, the ammunition trucks exploded. To Lapturov's delighted eyes it seemed as if utter chaos had broken out in the fascist unit. "Forward bratishka, lest the artillerists do all our work today and claim the honor of our victory!"

He actually felt a bit embarrassed by the bombastic message but it would sound good in the after-action report and such dramatic touches did fire the hearts of the men. Anyway, sending messages like that seemed like fun. Three kilometers in front of him, the fascists were still in utter chaos as the unexpected artillery barrage tore at them. Some of them even seemed to be abandoning their tanks and trying to get away from the artillery fire on foot. The T-34s were surging forward, rushing over the ridgeline and accelerating to maximum speed as they descended the long, smooth slope. It was a race, a desperate race to get the tanks close to the fascists before they came to their senses and started to fight back. And before the heavy guns ceased fire and started to engage the next pre-planned target.

Lapturov's brigade was still halfway down the long slope when the fascists came back to their senses and began firing back at the oncoming tanks. The artillery barrage had done its work; the tank crews were scattered and gone to ground, mostly away from their vehicles. Nevertheless, the fascist unit was already getting itself organized and was beginning to open fire. Over the roar of the T-34s diesel, Lapturov could hear the dull whumph of mortars being fired and the vicious flat crack of antitank guns. He could even hear the rasping of machineguns joining the battle. *Ublyudki! What could those do against my tanks? No artillery. A few mortars against a tank brigade are complete garbage!*

Now, there was far too much work to do for Lapturov to think about anything. A T-34/76 tank commander had to do everything himself; fired the gun, commanded his own tank and delivered orders to the rest of the brigade on the radio. Very often the commander was so busy that it was only when a solid shot knocked out his tank that he realized that it had been hit.

Once, long ago a journalist from Pravda. . . . or was it Izvestia?. . . had asked me if leading my tanks against the Hitlerites was scary. I had given him the standard heroic answer, full of the spirit of the New Soviet Man defying a brutal invader. Yet, there was truth in what I said. It wasn't scary for me inside the tank. Of course when receiving an assignment there was inner stress. I always knew that we would be on the attack and the odds were that I would die. That thought itched my head and I couldn't get away from it. Yet, once I got inside my tank the anxiety was still there, but there was so much to do when the battle started, I found I forgot about that. There was no time for fear inside the tank when you were so busy fighting to stay alive. So I never had fear inside the tank at all. It had been frightening when my tank was knocked out and we had to evacuated the burning wreck. Now it is happening again. We are advancing on the fascists. For once they have blundered and hung one of their units out in the cold.

It was easy to get carried away with the battle. The fascist unit was within range, yet the heavy artillery fire that was pinning it down still had not finished pounding them. This was another subject of debate, when should the artillery fire cease? Too early and the Hitlerites would recover, man their guns and inflict a blood price from the attackers. Too late and the artillery fire would inflict casualties of its own on the advancing tanks. Lapturov was one who favored keeping the artillery firing until the last possible moment. Yet, despite that, there had to come a time when the guns would cease fire and swing to their next target.

When the guns ceased fire, the smoke and chaos that had enveloped the fascist position cleared quickly. Lapturov could see at least one of the Mark IVs had its crew on board and was starting to move. *It is time to stop advancing and fire the gun.* He was very proud of his crew; they were veterans and had been well-trained. The drill for firing the gun was very well established and was carried out with slick precision.

"On target! Firing!" The platoons of T-34s were trained to follow their commander's lead and engage a single target. The Soviet Army knew that its gunners were nowhere near as skilled as the Hitlerites so they went back to the ancient Russian truth that quantity had a quality all of its own. Three other T-34s followed Lapturov's lead and engaged the slowly moving enemy tank. The shots went all around it, spraying it with dirt and clods of earth.

Kazan Thunderbolts

"Shortstop!" The shell from his tank had exploded directly under the bow of the Mark IV, sending it rocking on its suspension and its return shot high into the air. Lapturov fired off one more shot that streaked past the enemy tank's turret and then another. He was spinning the turret around, first swinging the 76mm gun from right to left, then back again as the targets became visible. As each type of enemy approached, he was shouting out the rounds he needed out: "Armor-piercing round! Fragmentation round!" The engine was roaring at maximum power for in a knife-fight with fascist tanks, anybody who slowed down for any reason would die. T-34s were dying, intellectually Lapturov knew that, but the shell bursts were something he never heard any more.

In any case, the crash of his gun had completely disrupted his hearing. He guessed that in future years his hearing would go completely to the great amusement of his children and grand children but the despair of his wife who would note that his deafness grew worse when there were chores to be done. The shape of the turret seemed to focus all the sounds of the tank into Lapturov's ears and sent him into a world of his own, a world that consisted only of his gun and the turret that contained it. He had long since stopped hearing what was going on outside. It was only when the shattering noise of a high-velocity round hitting the armor and the screech of it being deflected away pierced all the other noise that he realized somebody was firing at you also.

All the time, gunpowder fumes were accumulating inside the turret. In wintertime, fans kept up with extracting those fumes, but in hot summertime weather they didn't. Suddenly, Lapturov's cry out to the gun loader: "Fragmentation round!" went unanswered.

The loader was supposed to respond: "Aye, fragmentation round, sir!" but more usually just yelled "UP!" but this time there was neither. Just silence.

Lapturov pushed him and repeated the order "Fragmentation round!"

There was still no answer. Lapturov looked across the turret and saw the loader unconscious, sprawled out across the main gun ammunition rack – stifled by those fumes. Whenever an intense battle was going on it was a rare loader who could resist the fumes. He was moving around more than other crew members but he was also the furthest from an escape hatch. Either the commander or the driver had to get out before he could and so his general stress level was very intense. That made him breathe in more of the cordite fumes. The radio operator/machine gunner, commander and the driver/mechanic never passed out that way.

He reached down, slapped the loader awake and sat him back on his seat. Then he opened the top hatch to try and get some air into the tank, painfully aware that every second he spent away from his gun was a second that a fascist could be sending a shot his way.

That fact was driven home suddenly and completely unexpectedly when there was a teeth-battering slam and the whole tank rocked. For one second more, Lapturov thought his tank had been hit by one of the dreaded fascist 88s. The rest of his crew had thought so as well and they were already half-way out of their hatches. By opening the hatch to get air for his loader Lapturov had a head start.

What he saw and his head came out of the turret was quite different. A Mark IV was directly in front of him and his T-34 had rammed it, plowing directly into the side where the turret joined the hull. The Hitlerite's gun had obviously been trained on the T-34 but the long-barrelled weapon was wedged against the T-34s turret, its muzzle safely behind the turret. The fascist commander had been thrown against the rim of his cupola and was looking goggle-eyed at the T-34 that had so suddenly come out of the smoke and dust. Then, he realized what was happening and tried to grab the machine gun in front of him.

Lapturov couldn't help but think of the old Russian principle that a guest should have the best of everything. *I suppose that applies to uninvited guests as well.* While thinking the flippant thought, he had drawn his TT-33 pistol and emptied the magazine into the fascists head and shoulders. *My TT-33 is a fine pistol so tradition has been observed.* That thought sprang into his head as he slid back into the turret,

"Back up Bratishka! Load armor piercing!"

"Up."

"Shoot!" And the Mark IV exploded into flames.

The distance between the two groups of tanks was no more than one hundred meters. There was no more maneuver, no more tactics. The tanks hunted each other in the smoke and dirt, each with a round ready to go and he who shot first lived. It was not war, but tank slaughter. The tanks crawled and they fired and they died.

Everything was on fire. An inexpressible stench was in the air of the battlefield. Everything was so covered with smoke, dust and fire that it seemed that twilight had fallen. Radio communications had broken down. Someone had been transmitting a voice radio signal and suddenly got killed. The radio had been left in transmit mode and cause the radio channel to be blocked. Switching to the reserve radio channel would be required, but whoever knew when?

That was when Lapturov's tank was knocked out. A shell flew from somewhere and hit the tank's side, knocked off an idle wheel and a primary roller wheel. The tank stopped, veering slightly. His crew bailed out even though the vehicle wasn't burning yet, and went crawling towards a shell crater.

Kazan Thunderbolts

Any repairs were out of the question. If a tank was immobilized it had to be abandoned. *If you were not killed at once the next enemy tank would come up and finish you off.* His crew got into a shell crater and sat there, ready to shoot back. No Mark IV turned up to kill the stranded tank and all around was the rattle of submachine gun fire as the tank riders swept along the forest, shooting down the fascists as they tried to retreat. Eventually, the shooting subsided and Lapturov was able to reorganize for the next stage in the battle. It had been a good day so far. Out of sixty-five tanks in the brigade forty were still operational and an unusual number of tank crewmen had survived the destruction of their vehicles. The battle had lasted ten minutes.

Lapturov knew the battle was only half over. The back of the armored unit had been broken but the tanks had covered the retreat of the rest of the force to the gullies where they were already setting up a defensive position. Rooting them out would be hard work for his battered tank brigade. He commandeered another T-34 and started to get ready for the charge.

"Tovarish Colonel. There is a message from Corps. We are to hold here. Air support is on its way. We are to attack as soon as the bombing is completed."

"Well done, bratishka. Acknowledge the message and order the tanks to wait." Overhead, Lapturov could already hear the drone of approaching aircraft. A few second later, he recognized it, and then heard the cheering as the Sturmoviks swept overhead. They made a pass, spotted the designated target area and started to circle it, keeping well out of range of the light flak. Every so often, one of the Sturmoviks would break from the circle, dash in and fire its rockets or drop its bombs. Others would make their runs with their wing-mounted 23mm cannon. Slowly, they whittled down the anti-aircraft fire until it was sporadic and ineffective. By that time, four of the fifteen aircraft had been hit and sent limping home.

"Wait there is still more to come." Lapturov could see that; from high over the battlefield he could see the black dots in their 70 degree dives. They grew quickly, becoming recognizable shapes despite the fact he had never seen them before. They were American Thunderbolts. The blast of their bombs could be felt even through the armor of the T-34s. *Five hundred kilos at least and they drop with precision even the Stukas would envy.* "All right, Go bratishka, Now is our time!"

The Thunderbolts kept making firing passes at the fascist defenses right up to the time Laptorov's tanks crunched through the forward positions. As a result, the long vicious fight he had expected was over in minutes and at minimal cost. There was no doubt why; Hitlerites were stunned by the bombing and strafing and their resistance was perfunctory at best.

As his men raised the Red Flag over the enemy's final redoubt, two Thunderbolts returned and did a low pass over his unit. They rolled as they passed over and waggled their wings in salute. Lapturov hoped for only two things. One was that the pilots could see his men cheering them and the other was that they could see the fear on the fascist's faces when the big American fighters had started their run. As he looked at his men, he could see exactly what they were thinking. *With the Russian Army and the American Air Force fighting together, there will be no power in the world that can beat us.* That was when the glorious thought filled his mind. *Isn't that exactly what we have? We are going to win this war.*

There was still work to be done. Not all the Hitlerites had been killed. Some had lived to surrender and were sitting on the ground, their hands on their heads. *It is a strange thing that the fascists seem so diminished by defeat. We think of them as giant monsters, ruthless superhuman destroyers yet now they have surrendered to us, they look just like young, frightened boys. And they are young. Some are still arrogant but most look as if they are broken inside. Soon, the rear area security people will take them. The rules are strict, killing them in the fighting is fair enough and we should do what we should do. Killing them after the battle is over is forbidden. This is not kindness on our part but our leaders know that one day this war will be over and the prisoners can be put to work repairing what they have destroyed.* Lapturov looked at the prisoners being formed into a column and marched off and a strange thought crossed his mind. *Why do I think these are the lucky ones?*

CheKa District Headquarters, Metallist Prospekt 16, Pestretsy

The demented screaming rang through the headquarters building, echoing off the concrete walls and piercing the ears of everybody inside. For all that, it made the men and women working in the building feel a little better. The previous evening, morale amongst the CheKa workforce had taken a grave blow when the hideous details of Nina Klaravina Habarovna's brutal death had leaked out. Death was a familiar thing to the operatives of CheKa, if not precisely a comrade, certainly a co-worker. But, Nina Klaravina had been a skilled worker whose services had been of great value at this time of national crisis. She had served the Rodina well, had been awarded the Soviet Medal for Labor Valor and the titles of Stakhanovite and Dvukhsotniki. That somebody who had served the state with such dedication should meet her death at the hands of a wrecker and a fascist saboteur challenged their idea of justice.

The evening before, while Nikolai Pavlovich Habarov had sat in a bare cell, undergoing a forced cold-turkey cure for alcoholism, some wives of the Cheka agents had been confused and more than a little suspicious when their husbands had brought them small presents or been unusually attentive and considerate.

Kazan Thunderbolts

The CheKa agents had cheered up a little when Habarov had been dragged from his cell and down to the interrogation rooms in the basement. The first screams from below had told them that in death Nina Klaravina was receiving the justice that she had been denied in life. That cheered them a bit more. One of the interrogation team, coming up to wash his hands, had noticed the change and promised "the electrocution will continue until morale improves."

He had kept his promise but now his work was done. The agents had seen him hurrying to Napalkov's office with a file in his hands and they knew that the prisoner had broken. The file contained all of the names he had revealed and those of the people those names had associated with. There was fine judgment involved in this; recognizing the point where the prisoner had told the truth and no more. Any interrogation beyond that point would simply result in him lying to try and stop the interrogation team doing their work. The interrogator knocked on Napalkov's door and handed the file over.

"We've got a major breakthrough here. The primary contact handling the traitor Habanov is Rassadkin, Vasilii Stepanovich. A Volga German deported here after the fascist invasion. There have always been doubts about his loyalty. Not so much because he is a Volga German although that would be cause enough. Because he is a member of a small group of such people who are secretive and do not welcome outsiders into their number. We have lists of all the members of that group. Your predecessor in this office, tovarish, was concerned by them and kept the whole group under surveillance. We found they have links to other groups, in Saratov and Samara. I have lists of the names we identified in these groups here.

Napalkov looked at the lists. There were about three dozen names in total on them, a few being obviously their wives. Napalkov looked at another file on his desk; that of Nina Klaravina Habarovna. The picture stared back at him. She had been a plain woman, lacking even the prettiness of youth. A complete lack of other suitors might be why she had taken the fateful decision to marry the traitor and saboteur Habarov. But, lack of beauty was no reason why she should have died the way she had. "Bratishka, you have done well. We will arrest all these people. But, in honor of the sacrifice Tovarish Nina Klaravina has made, treat the wives gently when you interrogate them. I suspect, a cup of tea and telling them of the fate of Habarov's wife with the implication their husbands might have been about to do the same to them could be all you need."

The interrogator nodded slowly. "That will be a good strategy. A freely made confession is always better than one obtained under pressure. We could even turn ourselves into their protectors, having rescued them from that awful fate."

That gave Napalkov a great degree of satisfaction. Whatever outsiders thought of the organization, CheKa's self-image was one of protectors and defenders, The Chekists saw themselves as agents who had to do a hard and often distasteful job in order to protect Soviet citizens from the work of fascists, saboteurs and wreckers. Napalkov had good personal reasons for believing that more than most, reasons that had cost him one of his eyes. None of the higher-ranking Chekists were naïve simpletons; they knew well the nature of their profession. Yet, the self image of being protectors was strong within them and helped them accept the worst aspects of their work.

"And once a dog leaves home, it never returns to its old master. We could turn them all into double agents and that would lead us to more spies and saboteurs. That would be a good memorial to tovarish Nina Klaravina."

Napalkov strode out into the corridor. "Comrades, raise your fists, for there is work to be done. We have identified a ring of fascist spies and saboteurs. We must arrest them all and bring them in for questioning. Speed is of the highest priority, bratishka, for as we make our first arrests, word will spread and the wreckers will try and flee. We must make a clean sweep, none must escape. The memory of Tovarish Nina Klaravina demands that we strike without mercy. Now, go to work and show our people and our allies how good, vigilant, Chekists treat those who aid our enemies!"

From his office window, Napalkov watched the snatch squads leaving the headquarters compound. Some still used the black pre-war sedans inherited from the NKVD while others were driving brand-new American jeeps obtained under lend-lease. Personally, Napalkov thought the earth-brown with red stars that comprised the Russian paint job looked a lot better than the American olive drab with white stars. The stream of vehicles leaving the compound drove home to him just how big an operation this was turning out to be. *And all from one gunboat that found one drum of the wrong ammunition. If they had not spotted it and reported the problem, we would not have investigated and this whole business would never have been discovered. Truly from the smallest seeds do the mightiest forests grow.*

"Ivan Mihailovich, a moment please?" His secretary was standing at the door, her notebook in her hand. Napalkov nodded. Like most good administrators, he realized that his secretary was a vital partner in keeping things running smoothly. "I have called our brother office in Samara and they are hard at work making arrests down there. They have contacted the underground office in Saratov and they will do what they can."

Napalkov knew that Saratov might be occupied by the fascists but there would be a CheKa office still there, even if perhaps there was only one agent left. That one agent would be watching for collaborators and saboteurs and doing what he – or she – could to bring them to justice. "Thank you, Mariya Makarovna. Your hard work is of great value to the state and to every agent who works from here. Sometimes we might forget to thank you for your efforts but we never forget their value."

She smiled gently. Napalkov hadn't been the only person to say something like that this day. The death of Nina Klaravina Habarovna had affected everybody. That brought up another issue from her to-do list. "The Doctor is waiting to see you."

"Send him in please."

Doctor Egor Vasil'evich Taltanov actually liked doing autopsies on murder victims. They were a way that he could exercise his medical skills, one that his normal workload could not provide. Soviet law stated that everybody who died should have a death certificate issued. Nowhere did the law say that the death certificate had to be accurate. Doctor Taltanov had a pre-filled selection for people who died in CheKa custody. "Heart failure" for those who were electrocuted, "shortage of breath" for those who were drowned and "cerebral hemorrhage" for the ones shot in the back of the head. The file he had in his hands, the autopsy report on Nina Klaravina was something of much greater importance to him. It was an honest investigation and report on the cause of death.

"I have completed the autopsy, tovarish. As we suspected, the victim was indeed buried alive. I found dirt in her mouth, throat and in her nasal cavities. The body was badly decayed and most of the other evidence has been lost as a result. Enough remains to tell us that what her husband did to her before her death was . . . . horrible. Tovarish, I beg you, let us keep that a secret. Let her keep some dignity in her death."

"All the evidence and details have been recorded?"

"They have." Taltanov lifted the file.

"Then let that file be sealed. It will only be used if the evidence is needed. Leave it with me."

Taltanov left, his spirits a little lighter. Napalkov carefully put the file in his safe. It would be very effective in turning the women in the fascist spy ring into double agents.

Headquarters, 40th Bombardment Wing, Kolosovka.

"Another railway yard has gone. Nothing left of it. From what I can see, the battlefield is fairly well isolated." Major Richard Gonzalez was a familiar figure at the 40th Bombardment Wing headquarters. The 40th and 41st Wings each had a 4-plane detachment of F-5B Lightnings attached to them for bomb damage assessment runs. Other F-5Bs were still assigned to the mundane but vital task of photo-mapping the front on which the U.S. Army was fighting. All were starting to steer the P-47 fighter-bombers to lucrative targets whenever they had a chance. Gonzalez honestly believed that the unarmed F-5Bs were contributing as much to the war effort as any of their more glamorous partners.

"Not yet." General LeMay hadn't let promotion, long overdue by everybody who knew him, affect his terse manner. "All the easy ones have gone. Getting to the rest will be tough."

Gonzalez nodded; the main railway marshalling yards were much further west than the ones that had been hit to date. Even the Moskva yards had been easier targets than the complex LeMay had in mind. "You mean Tula. That's six hundred miles in."

"Tula. Can *Lailani* make it there?"

There was a minute's silence while Gonzalez computed distance, fuel consumption and time in his head. He might be cheerful and irreverent but he was a professional to his fingertips. The big problem would be fighters. There were five major fighter fields near Tula and if his F-5 came under sustained fighter attack, he would have to run at full power for extended periods. That might mean he would run out of fuel before getting back. "Yes, sir. But it will be tight, very tight. I'll need the biggest drop tanks we have. And won't my run tell the fascists where we'll be going next?"

"They'll know anyway. Only a few of the big yards left. The range is a bigger problem. The Thunderbolts can't take us all the way in. We'll have to do the last hundred miles on our own."

"P-38s?"

LeMay shook his head. "Too few of them. They're a lot of trouble. There's pressure to convert the two P-38 groups to P-47s and convert the '38s to F-5s. There's a feeling the loss rate on F-5s is going to start climbing."

"How so, Sir."

"Intell says the krauts are moving some specialized high-altitude 109s in. We can pick them out, they're painted duck egg blue all over. Yesterday, the 41st reported they were being shadowed by 109s high up. So they're here. Also, Gonzalez, news for you. The krauts know about you and they've put a price on your head."

Gonzalez broke out into a great beaming smile and pumped his fist in the air. LeMay looked at him. "You are pleased about that?"

"Of course, Sir. Where I come from, it's the biggest compliment around to have your enemy put a price on your head. Can I tell my mother, Sir? Please, Sir. She'll be so proud."

269

Kazan Thunderbolts

LeMay nodded. "Richard, however did we beat you people?"

"You didn't, Sir. We stopped fighting. There's a difference."

Airfield 108, Privolzhskiy na Volga, Moskva Front

"They're coming in!" The cry from the control tower could be heard all over the airfield. Sixteen of the twenty four Thunderbolts on the base had gone out for a late evening strike. Now, they had been sighted returning, the American ground crews dropped what they were doing and ran out to see the planes land. The Russian crews working on the Yak-9s also stopped their work and scanned the sky for the first black dots to appear."

"Tam oni! There they are!"

The first group of P-47s was already swinging in to their approach. All across the field, the ground personnel could be heard counting them as they touched down. "Four! Five! Seven! Eight!"

Lilya Litvyak was standing by her Yak, in theory at least supervising some minor repairs and watching another white rose being painted under her cockpit. It was her twenty third confirmed kill, a Heinkel 111 that had been part of an attempted raid on the Kazan ferries. It had been a blood-bath; American P-38s and P-39s, Russian P-39s and Yak-9s had converged on the fascist formation and ripped it apart. In theory, the Yaks and P-38s should have driven off the escorting fighters while the P-39s used their heavy cannon to drop the bombers. It hadn't worked out that way; the heavily outnumbered German fighters had been driven off, then everybody had converged on the bombers. Several Heinkels had crash-landed east of the Volga. The wrecks were being guarded by Russian troops but soon, there would be a scavenging hunt for "trophies". The swastika cut from the tail surfaces was a favorite.

In reality though she was watching for Edward's Thunderbolt to land and everybody knew it. When he had touched down and given his account to the debriefer, she would "accidentally" meet him and they would have coffee, tea and donuts together. It was a tradition she found hard to admit to, not for any political or disciplinary reason but because she knew she was tempting fate. Every friend she had ever made had been killed.

"Fourteen! Fifteen!" Lilya could see *Live Bait* on her final approach, wheels down safely, tires undamaged, no smoke trailing from a damaged airframe. She and the other Russian pilots knew that if a Thunderbolt got its pilot this far home, the chances were the pilot would make it. She could only think of two cases where Thunderbolts had crashed and killed their pilots when landing. In both cases, the big radial engine had failed at just the wrong second.

Live Bait was down safely, rolling to the end of the recently resurfaced runway. Airfield 108 looked nothing like the airfield she had known only a few

270

months before. All signs of concealment were gone, new buildings were everywhere and the constantly rotating antennas of the defensive radar systems dominated the skyline. As one of the most forward airfields, the base was now ringed with anti-aircraft guns, American 90mm and 40mm weapons with Russian female crews. The challenge was obvious. "Come and get us. Try it. If you dare."

Over at the debriefing tables, Edwards had finished his report, declined the free shot of whisky and was looking around for Lilya so that he could "accidentally" meet her. He happened to be walking past her Yak when she stood up from examining a patch where a 7.9mm bullet had drilled into the rear fuselage. "Bratishka, how did you do?"

"We shot up more supply trains and dive-bombed an artillery position. We're working with your Sturmoviks now. We make a great team – dead fascists everywhere. Hey, you got a new kill?" Edwards was slightly jealous. The fact he was doing almost all ground attack missions these days meant he was stuck at nine kills. Lilya's score was slowly but surely mounting.

"Heinkel 111. There was a full staffel of them but we broke the raid up completely. I did a nose on pass . . . . . " Her hands moved in the traditional fighter pilot's gesture as she showed Edwards how the battle had gone. "I think I killed the pilot and copilot because the bomber reared up and just fell out of the sky."

Edwards couldn't help but remember the conversations he'd had with girls back in the States. He was reasonably sure that none of them had involved comparing notes on how to shoot down German bombers. "I think we ought to have a donut to celebrate. You going out again?"

She shook her head. "We are finished for the day. You?"

"Same here. Hi Liz, two hungry fighter pilots here."

Elizabeth Richardson, the Red Cross woman running the Clubmobile looked at her two latest customers and tried to stop herself smirking. She knew that she smelled of doughnut grease and that her hands were red and raw from scrubbing the coffee urn and the tea samovar clean. Her work required much more than the mundane chores of serving doughnuts and coffee. Only one applicant in six was selected for work in the Clubmobiles. Yet, she considered her role to be nothing compared with the couple in front of her. The crew of the donut truck were running a pool on how long it would be before these two ended up in the sack together. They left the alternative unsaid. That one or both would be killed before that time came. So, she put on her brightest smile. "Lilya, you got another kill today. Hey, do you like lemons?"

Lilya nodded. "I love lemons but I haven't had any since the war started."

Kazan Thunderbolts

Liz reached into the freshly-baked trays while one of the other women in the truck got Lilya's tea. She bit into the donut she had been given and her eyes opened wide with delight. The donut was filled with lemon-flavored custard. Behind her, Edwards had picked up his jelly donut and the two made their way towards a table with two seats that had somehow remained unoccupied. After they sat down, Edwards saw that his guest had a large drop of lemon filling on her nose. He reached out, took it off with a fingertip and held it out. Lilya leaned forward and licked it off. Around them, those who had picked dates a long time in the future of the pool looked resigned to losing their bet.

"Lilya, did you hear that there is a Glen Miller concert over at Bolshaya Tarlovka in ten days time. The USO is staging it for us. Would you like to go?"

"What is a Glen Miller?" Lilya had never heard of the group.

"He's a very famous band leader. Plays a lot of really swell music. Open to us all. We each get to take one guest." Edwards didn't mention that command had made it clear that although the invitations were "one American serviceman plus one guest", that guest had better be a Russian. Lilya though, who was a lot more politically shrewd than he was, guessed that was the case. Nevertheless, she also guessed that even if that provision hadn't been made, he would still have invited her.

"I would love to go. But, Bolshaya Tarlovka is 180 kilometers away. How would we get there?"

"Command thought of that. There's a transport flight laid on. We drew lots for who got a seat. Well, who got to sit on the floor, it's a cargo plane. And I got lucky."

Lilya looked excited, her smile flashing and relaxed. For the first time since Edwards had known her, the hint of madness had gone from her eyes. "So, this is an American date?"

Edwards looked at her and grinned. "You know, I guess it is."

Sickbay, GunRon 5 Headquarters, Staraya Mayna, Volga River.

"You can't go in there."

One of the great questions of experimental physics is the conundrum of the result of an irresistible force meeting an immovable object. In the corridors of the U.S. Navy hospital, Staraya Mayna, this question was subjected to a scientific experiment when a CheKa officer who wanted to do something met an American naval nurse determined to protect her patient. The irresistible force lost hands down and slunk away with its tail firmly between its legs. Chekist Napalkov decided that regrouping and trying a different approach was on order.

"Tovarish nurse, could you tell me what is happening with my friend John Fitzgerald?"

"We are not supposed to disclose medical information to anybody except the patient's family and/or their commanding officer." Lieutenant Kushala Norroso was not going to give an inch of ground. Then she detected genuine concern on Napalkov's face and decided to give a little bit after all. "He lost consciousness this afternoon and slipped into a coma. If you promise me, on your honor as a communist, that you will not try to enter his room while I am away, I will get one of the doctors dealing with the case to talk to you."

Napalkov nodded in agreement. Norroso looked at him with an eyebrow raised. He sighed slightly. "I promise, on my honor as a member in good standing of the Communist Party of the Soviet Union, not to enter John Fitzgerald's room until you return."

Norroso gave a slight smile of satisfaction and set off in the direction of the doctor's offices. Napalkov, on careful reflection, decided that he had better remain exactly where he was. The nurse was only gone for a couple of minutes when she returned with a doctor. She saw where Napalkov was standing and gave a very self-satisfied smirk.

"Chekist Napalkov, you have come to see Lieutenant Kennedy?"

"He is a friend, and I hear he is very ill. Doctor ?"

"Walter Swenson. I believe Lieutenant Kushala explained the situation to you?"

"She did. But, we have been working together and we became friends. Even if he is unconscious, I would like to visit him. Does not working together make us brothers? That is what we call each other on the front line. Bratishka. Brother."

"Very well. Firstly Lieutenant Kennedy is not unconscious, he is in a deep coma. He has one of the diseases we call meningitis. That means he has an acute inflammation of the protective membranes covering the brain and spinal cord. We do not know the cause of this infection yet. The inflammation may be caused by infection with viruses, bacteria, or other microorganisms, and less commonly by certain drugs. Meningitis can be life-threatening because of the inflammation's proximity to the brain and spinal cord.

"Until very recently, we had no proper treatment for meningitis and the chances of the patient recovering were very low. Therefore, the condition is classified as an extreme medical emergency. However, we are working on the presumption that this is bacterial meningitis, probably the result of his swim in the Volga. He may have swallowed contaminated water or have been infected by way of cuts in his skin.

"He's a lucky man on two counts. One is that he was brought here due to his other injuries and we recognized the symptoms as soon as they started to present. The other is we have a new drug here, called penicillin that is supposed to work wonders in cases like this. It is something very new and we know little about it other than it is an excellent remedy for infections.

"The bad news is that Lieutenant Kennedy is in very poor health to start with and has abnormally low resistance to infection. Frankly, he should never have been allowed to enlist. How these factors will play out, we will have to wait and see."

"May I wait with him?"

Doctor Swenson thought for a second. "Very well, you may. But the great danger is further infections. Therefore, you must promise me that you will wear a surgical mask and not touch the patient or his equipment."

"I will do all of that, Doctor." Napalkov donned his surgical mask and went into the room. He took a chair near the bed, then drew his Tokarev pistol and put it down on the nightstand beside him. That was when he saw the doctor and nurse staring at it and thought he had better explain. "This man has fought courageously for the Rodina. If death comes for him, there will be a fight."

Napalkov sat stolidly and unmovingly in his chair as the minutes and hours ticked by, apparently as unresponsive as Kennedy himself. But, the Chekist's eyes missed nothing as the work of the hospital continued around him. He watched as a casualty was rushed in from one of the gunboats with wounds sustained in an engagement with some of the fascist troops on the west bank. Some of the gunboat crew had come with him and now they stood around waiting while the surgeons did their work.

The minutes continued ticking by and a surgeon came out, his scrubs still bloodstained. Napalkov watched him shake his head sadly as he spoke with the sailors. The wounded man hadn't made it. *Does that mean Death has taken his quota from here? That my friend will now live?*

That thought made him take a quick, guilty look at Kennedy. It seemed to Napalkov that his color was slightly healthier and his breathing was a little less labored. Norroso came in after a while, took his temperature and readings from some instruments and looked much happier. *That has to be good.* He was about to say something when she put her finger on her lips and waved him outside. Once in the corridor, she carefully shut the door.

"There is a theory that people in a coma can actually hear everything that goes on around them. We know that hearing is the last sense to be lost when a patient is dying so it may well be true. Anyway, we nurses don't take a chance. We never speak about a patient's condition where they might hear us."

"We could speak in Russian?" Napalkov was intrigued by this nurse.

"Or we could speak in my language but I very much doubt if you can." She smiled at him, a smile that had a strange undertone of menace in it. Rather like a ferocious wolf being friendly.

Napalkov looked at her carefully. She didn't look like the other Americans. "Your language? You don't look quite like an American. You look a little like us, especially Russians from the south and east."

"I am not an American. I am from The Nations. A Ndendahe Apache and my language is Chiricahua. Anyway, Lieutenant Kennedy is responding to treatment. His temperature is down, the stiffness in his neck is fading and the muscles in his legs are relaxing. These are all very good signs. Tovarish Chekist, if the theory about patients in a coma being able to hear is right, your friend must have heard you say you would stay all night to guard him. That friendship might have given his spirit the extra strength he needed."

That made Napalkov feel good. "Lieutenant Norroso . . ."

"The name is Kushala, Lieutenant Kushala. Apache do not have two names but the Navy insisted on two so I gave them my father's name as well."

"I am sorry, Lieutenant Kushala. May I ask why the Apache are here? All I know of your people is what I have seen in films and I do not think that is accurate."

Kushala laughed. "No it isn't. But, when Washington declared war, all the elders of the tribes, the Navajo, Western Apache, Chiricahua, Mescalero, Jicarilla, Lipan, and the Kiowa all met in debate around a great campfire. They discussed the Nazis and what they had done. They read the book of the Nazis, Mein Kampf and argued about what it said. They watched newsreels of their great parades and listened to the speeches made by their leaders.

"They spoke of these things with great seriousness and thought carefully for a long time. Then, they decided that, all things taken together, it would probably be best if we killed them all."

Napalkov erupted into laughter. "I see we are alike then."

"Perhaps." Kushala looked over his shoulder at her patient, then went into the hospital room.

When she came out, she was nodding contentedly. "His temperature has started to fall. I think the crisis is passing."

"As long as it does not fall too far." Napalkov decided to risk a small joke. "Falling to room temperature would not be a good sign. Now, I will resume my guard."

Kazan Thunderbolts

Motorized Reconnaissance Company, 7th Panzer Division, Yandoba, Chuvashskaya Bridgehead.

"What do you mean we haven't any fuel?" Major Maximilian Hildebrand was just reaching the point where he would take the greatest pleasure from ripping the supply sergeant's head off, sucking the bones dry and discarding the desiccated hulk on the black soil of Russia. Soil he was beginning to cordially hate.

"I'm sorry, Sir, but there isn't any fuel coming up. Or any ammunition. Or food. The Amis are strafing and bombing everything they can see and some things they can't. Nothing is getting through."

"We've never had this problem before and the Ivans have more aircraft than the Amis do."

"Do they, Sir? I really would question that. Think of how many we've seen just today. But it's not how many aircraft they have, it's how they are using them. They're going deep into our territory and shooting up everything in sight. As your supply sergeant, Sir, I know all my opposite numbers in every unit on this section of the front. We have a network for comradely support and assistance."

If by that you mean scavenging, black marketeering, stealing and making sure ends meet with a worthwhile overlap, then I do know what you mean. "Go on Sergeant."

"Well, Sir, in the last eight hours, over half those men are dead. Most of them burned alive when the Amis strafed our fuel convoys. They fire incendiaries from their machine guns and the fuel trucks just explode. And that's not the worst of it. Those big bombers of theirs, the viermotoren? They have hammered every railway yard this side of Moskva. There isn't one that's handling a tenth of the cargo it used to before the Amis got to work. The nearest intact yard is at Tula, 800 kilometers to the rear. The way I hear it, supplies being sent forward are stacking up there and the whole city has become a giant fuel and supply dump. The supply lines are trucking our fuel and ammunition forward from there. You know how it works, Sir. They're using five liters of fuel to get one to us and that's before the Amis set it all on fire. The Luftwaffe has given up; they're moving back to bases further west. The Amis keep bombing and strafing their front-line airfields and the fliers are running out of fuel as well. If they find the fuel to fly, they must fight against heavy odds, if they do not, they get destroyed on the ground."

"Sergeant, be very careful what you say. If the wrong people overhear you, it will not end well for you. Such talk could be considered defeatist." Hildebrand shook his head slightly. *What is the Heer coming to when a man cannot give his officers information they need to know.* "Moritz, we must try another push up that hill. Can your armored cars support us again?"

Captain Moritz Kneib shook his head. There had been fighting up and down the ridge all day. The German attacks hadn't been pressed home with any great determination since they were aimed at keeping the force on the ridge pinned in place while the rest of the 7th Panzer and the Wiking SS Division surrounded the town of Kanash. The latest word was that Wiking had broken through at Atnashevo and cut the road leading east. The bad news was that every time they had made one of their pushes up the ridge, they'd lost a handful more men and another vehicle or two. Now, Kneib's unit was down to two of their armored cars and the infantry company had lost a third of their remaining strength. The forces that had been attached to them earlier in the day had already been withdrawn and reassigned. *And that isn't the worst of it. Every time we tried a push, the Amis sitting on that ridge got a little bit better at what they are doing. They're learning and we're teaching them the lessons.*

"Max, our armored cars are down to a quarter of their fuel capacity. Some of them, less than that. That's barely enough to defend ourselves if we get attacked and we can only do that once. If we use our fuel to go up that slope again, then we we'll run out up there. And then there's ammunition. We're pretty much out. Laying down suppressive fire against those rocketmen uses up the basic load fast. That's their real effect, not the vehicles they kill but the way they slow us down and make us expend ammunition. Anyway, it's late evening. The sun is setting behind us, the Amis are in darkness and we're silhouetted against the setting sun. Going up there again won't get us anything we haven't already achieved and will leave us helpless to defend ourselves if we get counter-attacked. And that would mean the Amis could break out."

"Moritz is right, Max." Lieutenant Klemens Günther was enthusiastic on that point. "I haven't enough men left to stage an advance. We've got our machine guns and our mortars still but that's it. We've lost the riflemen. There's nothing we can . . . ."

His words were interrupted by a howl overhead, one with which the Germans were becoming increasingly and wearily familiar. American artillery. Their guns were in the habit of firing a few rounds at the German positions every so often. The intervals were unpredictable but the accuracy of the fire was disturbing. The guns were slowly making it impossible for the German troops to move and the casualties they caused were steadily mounting. That alone caused everybody at the impromptu council of war to dive for cover. The half-dozen explosions that followed impacted on the ruins of the village, shattering what was left of the buildings. The screams told their own message, that the butcher's bill had taken another step upwards.

"I think that was American for 'good night.'" Hildebrand was frustrated by the nature of the battle. He was acutely aware that his unit was occupying the same ground as it had the night before. For all their efforts, they hadn't moved forward by as much as a centimeter. For some reason, that worried him.

A-20G Havoc "For Marina Raskova", 588th Night Bomber Regiment, Over the Chuvashskaya Bridgehead.

Captain Nadezhda "Nadia" Vasil'yevna Popova had decided she liked the American A-20. The 588th was an all-women unit that had been equipped with the ancient Polikarpov Po-2 biplanes. The old aircraft had their virtues; they could operate from anywhere and were ridiculously easy to maintain. Their offensive capability, though, was derisory. They could do barely 150 kilometers per hour, were armed with a single rifle caliber machine gun on a pintle mount and carried 300 kilograms of bombs.

One day, a few months after the Americans had joined the war, the 588th had received a visit from a delegation of VIPs, some of whom were American politicians. One Senator looked in horror at the flimsy biplanes and had muttered something like "we can do better than that."

A week or so after the visit, the Regiment had received a complete set of brand-new A-20Gs via the ALSIB (Alaska-Siberia) air ferry route. They had been delivered by American female ferry pilots who had given the Russian women a quick course in how to fly the new aircraft. Maintenance and ground crews had arrived by one of the big American four-engined transports and started to instruct the 588th ground crews on the feeding and watering of A-20s.

The 588th never stopped flying missions but fewer and fewer were flown by Po-2s and more by the new A-20s. The new aircraft hadn't been entirely popular; the Po-2 could be flown through the treetops and was a much harder target than casual observers had suspected. But, the A-20 could do 550 kilometers per hour, carried a thousand kilograms of bombs and was armed with four 20mm cannon and four .50 machineguns firing forward and two .50s firing aft. The new aircraft had won even the most stalwart supporters of the biplanes over.

"We're about twenty kilometers out." Lieutenant Evgeniya Maksimovna Rudneva really liked the A-20. In the Po-2, her navigator's seat had been a metal circle in an open cockpit without even a screen to protect her from the slipstream. In the A-20, her navigator's station was enclosed and had a comfortable leather-trimmed seat. Even better, she had two .50 caliber machine guns to defend the tail of the aircraft. In fact, Zhenya, as she was universally known in the Regiment, had come to the conclusion that Americans were very fond of navigators. "Come around to one-five-five. The lake should be right in front of us."

Their initial point was an oddly-shaped lake, one that looked like a man running away with his hands in the air. If the A-20 made its run exactly between the raised arms, the next thing they should see would be two smaller rectangular lakes right in front of them. They would lead the light bomber directly to the positions occupied by the German unit that was their target for tonight.

"There it is!" Nadia Vasil'yevna saw the lake glimmering in the faint moonlight. Her navigator had brought her in perfectly between the two arms and at right angles to the nearest edge of the square lakes. She reached down and throttled the two R-2600 engines back so that they were barely whispering. The dominant noise now was the whistle of the wind over the airframe. If this went right, the fascists wouldn't even hear her coming in.

In fact, she had probably left the throttle-back a bit late. The two R-2600s made a lot more noise than the old Po-2 had done and it had alerted the Hitlerite gunners. Their tracers arched upwards, flashing past the dark brown A-20. The flashes were disturbing but tracers always worked both ways. Nadia Vasil'yevna now knew where at least one flak gun was placed and it was conveniently close to being directly in front of her.

She made the course correction, gunned the engines to maximum power and squeezed the firing buttons that set the four 20mm cannon in the nose and the four machine guns on the side of the fuselage to work. Her guns were loaded with the usual one-in-five of tracer and she walked the impact points on to the anti-aircraft gun. It was silenced very quickly, to her delight the secondary explosions from the gun site came before the four cannons jammed. *The Americans make fine aircraft but they cannot build a 20mm cannon to save their lives.* She pulled the nose up and opened the bomb bay. The 50-kilo bombs inside dropped clear, spreading across the target area in a ripple of orange-red flowers.

By the time they subsided, her A-20 was well on its way home.

Motorized Reconnaissance Company, 7th Panzer Division, Yandoba, Chuvashskaya Bridgehead.

"Damn those Night Witches!" Hildebrand was furious. The light bomber had come out of nowhere, wiped out his 37mm gun and spread its bombs all over his command. One of the two remaining SdKfz 231 heavy armored cars had taken what was close enough to a direct hit and was burning furiously underneath a pyre of smoke. The rest of the bombs had bracketed the area where what was left of his infantry had bivouacked. *They were mauled badly enough already. They didn't need that as well.*

"Sir, we have ten dead and a dozen wounded. I'm sorry, Sir, but Lieutenant Günther is dead as well. The bombs caught him as he ran for an anti-aircraft gun."

Hildebrand looked at the ridge that glowered down on them in the darkness. *I bet the Amis enjoyed watching that.*

CHAPTER TEN: DER TAG, AN DEM DIE EXPERTEN STARBEN

Headquarters, American Expeditionary Force, Seitovo, Chuvashskaya Bridgehead.

"Congratulations on the star, Curt." George S Patton reached out with his riding crop and gave LeMay's new stars a sharp blow each to 'tack' them in place. "Now, I need to borrow your Goddamned bombers."

LeMay was staring at the big situation map that now dominated one wall of the room. It had been carefully prepared by Colonel Ryan Anderson and showed the latest positions of the American and German units. As soon as Vetrenyy Freddie's ad-libbed codes and cryptic remarks had been abandoned, the information had come flooding in. What the map now showed was completely different from the scene 48 hours earlier.

"The krauts are swinging South East." LeMay's quiet voice contrasted sharply with Patton's bombastic delivery but there was no difference in the level of professionalism between them. They'd both seen what the map was telling them and realized what it had meant. "What the hell are they supposed to be doing?"

"I've seen this before, in the Louisiana and Tennessee Maneuvers. Ground up north is open and it's closer to our main airfields. The kraut supply columns are getting the worst of the air attacks up there and their units are short of fuel and ammunition. Down south, the roads are running through heavily wooded areas and they're further from our bases. So, their units are better supplied. So, the whole advance wheels south east. It's the same thing that the Goddamned krauts got wrong in 1914. You'd think the dumb bastards would learn." Bereft of an audience to impress with his bluster, Patton was comparatively thoughtful as he assessed the situation. "They wanted to go for Kazan but the battering they're getting from Quesada's Ninth Air Division is deflecting them south. An opportunity is opening up here Curt; we've got a chance to kick their damned ass but good. Only I need your big boys to do it."

"Where?"

The terse reply didn't faze Patton at all. He tapped the map with his crop. "Here, up in the north where the salient joins the original front line. The bastard krauts have left that area thin but we've moved up three combat commands, almost all the armor we have this side of the river. There's one defense position, here at Sinyal-Yaushi. The krauts have set it up as fortress and use mobile forces based there to patrol the flank. It's what they do when they have too much front to cover for the forces they have available. I want your bombers to pound on that base until the Goddamned Huns are bleeding out of their assholes."

"That's Quesada's job."

"Know that. But we have another problem. What's left of the 83rd is cut off at Kanash and the damned krauts are strangling them. Quesada's B-26s are supporting our boys trapped there. I need your big boys, Curt."

"We're supposed to be going to Tula next. The whole city is one enormous supply dump. We got aerial pictures back this morning. Fuel and ammunition are piled up in the streets, waiting to be shipped out. We could burn the whole city and everything in it to the ground. Leave every kraut unit in the Chuvashskaya unable to move or shoot."

"Won't help our boys right now, Curt. It's the next couple of Goddamned days that are critical. We got an open flank. You blast a hole in it for us, we can go right through. That's when blowing up the kraut's fuel and ammunition will be critical. How many boys you sending to Tula?"

"The whole of the 40th and 41st Bombardment Wings. Five hundred B-17s. We'll have to do the last hundred miles on our own. " LeMay thought about that for a second. *If we leave this tactical mission until after Tula, we might not have enough bombers left to plaster Sinyal-Yaushi. Yet, we'll have heavy fighter cover all the way to Sinyal.* "George, I'll have to clear it with 8th Air Division but there shouldn't be a problem. If I can borrow your communications here, I'll get it rolling. We'll need to change the daily orders and Quesada will need to return the Thunderbolts but, assuming that happens, we'll fly your raid late tomorrow afternoon. That fit your plans?"

Patton nodded, very briefly. "It will. We got the orders cut last night. All we need to do is fill in the time. I'll take you to the Comms Room. If it's still there of course. We'll be moving out of this Goddamned tomb just about the time your boys will be turning Sinyal-Yaushi into one."

Patton and LeMay left the office. As they did so, a Captain was walking fast in the opposite direction. Patton's crop lashed out and smacked the wall in front of him. "Captain, where is your Goddamned tie?"

"Sir?" The captain was bewildered by the sudden downpour of nausea that was engulfing him.

"How do you expect your men to obey orders when you don't have any regard for them yourself. There is only one type of discipline, perfect discipline and it applies to everybody. There is only one way to do something and that is the right way and everything should be done that way." Patton looked around. "Ike? Issue a general order. All officers are to wear ties, gaiters and helmets. Being caught without them means a 25 dollar fine. Each. You're lucky son, you just scraped in under the wire. Now, get yourself into your uniform."

A very relieved captain scuttled off to get his tie and helmet. Patton watched him go, then turned to his companion. "If men do not obey orders in small things, they are incapable of being led in battle. They will not obey orders when it really counts. If they do not get into the habit of doing small things right, they'll fail at the big things."

"And once they do things right, we have to keep them doing it right. All the time, not just some of it. It's the same in the Fortresses. If the kids do things right without having to think about it, a lot more of them come home." LeMay and Patton exchanged looks, the youngest General in the U.S. Army and one of the most senior understanding each other perfectly.

CheKa District Headquarters, Metallist Prospekt 16, Pestretsy

"Donuts?" Napalkov lifted a quizzical eyebrow.

"Donuts. Or rather pyshki. One of those converted busses the Americans call Clubmobiles pulled in. The women in the back told your deputy that they had just been unloaded from the train and needed to test all the equipment. So, to avoid waste of course, could they offer tea and donuts to the men and woman here?" The head of the interrogation team watched Napalkov grinning. They both knew that the Americans were trying to be as tactful as they could and not boast about how much they had and how little did the Russians. "Anyway, so they pulled in and started making us our tea and pyshki. Do you know how much sugar the Americans put in their donuts?"

Napalkov shook his head. His vigil at the hospital had cost him his first taste of American donuts but he believed it had been an investment worth making.

"Well, it's a lot. And the people here haven't seen sugar for three years. We did what you ordered, tovarish Ivan Mihailovich, and treated the six women on the arrest list with kindness. The first woman was crying and nearly wetting herself with fear when she was brought in to the interrogation room. But, our interrogator sat her down, gave her tea and offered her an American donut. That calmed her down and they talked of inconsequential things, her job, her history, how her children were doing in their school, that sort of thing. During that time she ate two more donuts and the overdose of sugar after so many years without nearly caused her to float out of the window."

Napalkov and the interrogator burst out laughing at that. Quite a few prisoners of CheKa and the NKVD before it had been killed by 'jumping" out of a high window while "trying to escape" but floating out on a sugar overdose was new. Napalkov liked it. "And she told us everything?"

"Not quite yet. The sugar overdose made her careless and so they talked of more sensitive things and she gave much away. But our interrogator watched her carefully and when he saw the first signs of her sugar crash, he said to her, 'Anna Ivanovna Sokovets, I can see that you are innocent of wrongdoing and so you have nothing to fear from CheKa. But, you still have much to fear and the danger comes to you from your very innocence. You know, perhaps, Nina Klaravina Habarovna? She too was innocent but the head of the fascist spy ring gave orders that wives and children not committed to their cause should be killed in a way that would teach all waverers a lesson. Read what her husband did to her on his orders.' And then he handed her the file and let her read it. He didn't tell her the rest of the story of course."

"And that was when she told us everything." Napalkov dipped his head in respect.

"Everything, tovarish. She would not have told us to save herself but the effects of her sugar crash and what she thought was the terrible danger to her children brought her around. She gave us every name she knew and the brats have gone to arrest them now. That procedure also worked with all the other women we have picked up. Tovarish Ivan Mihailovich, we have broken what must be the biggest Hitlerite spy and sabotage ring uncovered since the war began. And all due to an American sailor who checks cargo manifests carefully and American women who make sugary donuts!"

Napalkov and the interrogator burst out laughing again, both pleased beyond measure at how well the day's work had gone. *And yet it is only morning* Napalkov thought, noting that some CheKa agents had been hanging around close enough to overhear the report and were laughing as well. *Ahh, well. Once a Chekist, always a Chekist.*

"And the women, bratishka? They are being well care for?"

"Of course. They have been given comfortable rooms to stay in and Tovarish Mariya Makarovna has found them new clothes, high-quality civilian wear, not prison garments. They have also been told that their children will be placed under our protection in the child center used by our own families." *Where, of course, everything they say will be carefully recorded.* The interrogator smiled impishly. "The process of turning the women into our agents is well in hand. They know, without being told of course, that loyal service to CheKa will erase the stain on their records."

Napalkov managed to keep a straight face at that. *A stain on a record would never be removed. CheKa never forgot and forgiveness could always be rescinded.*

On the way to his office, hoping that Mariya Makarovna had kept a donut for him, he met a familiar figure. A good Chekist never forgot a face. "Tovarish Senior Sergeant of militsya, Sergei Sergeevich Pargamenko. Welcome to our local headquarters. You have work to do here?"

"Tovarish Chekist, I have brought some men to help look after all of the prisoners."

"Why, thank you, Bratishka. I remember you well from the arrest of the spy and saboteur Habarov. You rendered the Rodina good service that day. You know, we have all the information we need from him now. If you would like to go to his cell, you may kick him as much as you wish."

"Thank you, Tovarish Chekist." Pargamenko beamed at Napalkov's back. *What fine fellows these Chekists are! How I have misjudged them in the past!* He took a few practice swings with his foot, and then set off to find the saboteur Habarov's cell.

Emergency Casualty Station, Kanash, Chuvashskaya Bridgehead.

"You should have got out of here while you had the chance." Captain Martin Anderson was being deadly serious. "The krauts have slammed the back door on us. Unless our boys can break through from the east, we're in trouble."

"We'll be all right." First Lieutenant Dorothy Hopkins was nowhere near as confident as she sounded. *These are krauts and in the last war, they shot Edith Cavell. They could do the same to us.* "We're protected by the Red Cross."

"I hope so. I do so hope so." Anderson looked at the next casualty that had been brought in. "Damn, this one's taken some shell splinters in the gut. He'll take hours to fix. If he can be fixed."

There was a grim decision to be made and Anderson had to make it. There were wounded men backed up outside and the time spent that might save this one would cause the death of at least half a dozen. "Take him to the waiting area and make him comfortable. Next."

The next patient in had been shot at least twice and his leg was hanging by a thread of skin and muscle. Neither doctor nor nurse needed to say that the leg would have to come off. Somebody had used a belt as a tourniquet and that had to come off fast before what was left of the leg went gangrenous. The nurse acting as the anesthesiologist had already gone to work and the patient was slipping under. It would only take a single quick cut to remove what was left of his leg. The doctor had just started when there was the dreaded whistling howl overhead.

"Inbound!" The warning cries filled the air. Even so, the crash as the shells exploded all over Kanash drowned out the yells. Hopkins noted grimly that the explosions were smaller than the big shells that had harassed them during the night but there were a lot of them. And they didn't stop arriving. There was something else. The thunder of the guns firing was a lot closer than it had been only a few minutes earlier.

"What's happening out there? Does anybody know?"

"Krauts are attacking all along the eastern perimeter." One of the wounded men spoke up. "The SS are out there and they've got the biggest tanks I've ever seen. They blew up the M4s and Teedees like old tin cans. We're tryin' but we can't hold them."

Overhead, the artillery fire suddenly had competition from a formation of four aircraft that flew overhead. Hopkins recognized them. Airacobras, painted earth brown with red stars on their wings and fuselage. She could hear the dull, rhythmic thumping of their 37mm cannon. That told her how close the SS had to be.

His work done, at least while the next patient was being readied for surgery, Anderson was looking up at the Airacobras. "Russian P-39s. The Russians don't often use them for ground attack; they think of them as top cover fighters. If we didn't think things were bad before, we know they are now. I'd suggest we get ready to move but there's nowhere to go."

Headquarters. 83rd Infantry Division, Kanash, Chuvashskaya Bridgehead.

"It's like a piston sliding into a cylinder." There was another comparison that Lieutenant Colonel William Long could have made but he had decided not to. It would have been . . . indelicate. "Two Heer divisions are north and south of us and the SS are advancing along the corridor between them. Those troops the boys on the Yandoba Ridge are holding back are just the backstop, there to prevent us breaking out."

"The SS are trouble. It's not just those big tanks they have. The Russians say they are called Tigers by the way. They've been seen before, down south around Stalingrad, but never this far north. There's more to the SS than that. They're fanatical Nazis. All they want is death and glory and the Heer are happy to let them have some of the latter if they also get a lot of the former. The

Russians say we can expect a lot of very bad things if we're up against an SS unit. And we are."

"The intelligence we missed out on because of Vetrenyy Freddie." Major General Tillman was frustrated. "The Air Force took their advice, the Navy took their advice, why the hell did Fredendall ignore them? Thank God, Gorgeous George put that right."

"I hear he slapped Vetrenyy Freddie right in the face." The story of Patton's meeting with Fredendall had spread across the American front with the speed of light. It had put some cheer into an army that was close to being demoralized by defeat. Long had walked for almost 36 hours after his tank battalion had been chopped up and that story had been the first thing he had heard. It had made the walk seem worthwhile.

"We need something that can stop those damned Tigers." Tillman could see what was going to happen over the next few hours. The Tigers would push through his defenses until they'd got their infantry up to the built up areas of Kanash. Then, they'd use their 88s to cover the SS infantry as they fought through the streets.

"We've lost the Shermans and the TeeDees. We've assembled the survivors from the TeeDee battalion into assault teams to close in and destroy enemy tanks on foot using magnetic mines, explosives and so on. They were supposed to be trained to do that but like so much else, it got overlooked. I'll tell you this, Sir, the last few days have been one hell of a wake-up call.

"I know, Bill, I know. It's just that I've got a bad feeling we're not going to be the ones to benefit from the lessons. Not unless we can find a way of stopping those tanks. And the infantry they are supporting." Tillman was interrupted by a rolling thunderous sound from the east. He paused to listen to it. "That's Quesada's B-26s at work. At least we know one thing. We've got the air support side of this thing working. If we're going to stand any sort of chance, it'll be the bombers that give it to us."

Thunderbolt Live Bait *Over Shikhazany, Chuvashskaya Bridgehead.*

The bottom tier of the formation consisted of the Il-2 Sturmoviks. They were skimming along over the tree tops to prevent fascist fighters from coming at them from below and behind. The same low altitude also prevented the fascist anti-aircraft guns from engaging for longer than a brief interval. Above them was the medium-altitude cover, the Yak-9s of the 866th Fighter Aviation Regiment flying at 2,000 meters. Their job was to prevent Hitlerite pilots from interfering with the Sturmoviks as they went about their work. Then above the Yak-9s was the high cover. P-39 Airacobras flying at 4,000 meters. Their job was to guard the tails of the Yaks from fascists coming in from above, using the superior altitude performance of their Me-109s and FW-190s to strip the escort away. This was the normal formation of a Soviet close support mission, the tiered ranks of aircraft all tasked with one overriding mission, to allow the Il-2s to support the infantry on the ground.

Today was not normal.

Today, there was another layer to the formation, the sixteen Thunderbolts of the 360th Fighter Squadron, 356th Fighter Group were covering the whole attack group from 7,000 meters. Back on escort duty at last, Lieutenant Edwards was scanning the sky around him for enemy fighters. He had spent an hour the previous evening with a drill and screwdriver mounting a second rear view mirror over the cockpit. Now, *Live Bait* had Rabbit's Ears, just like *FivebyFive*. It was the extra arc of rear vision caused by those dual mirrors that allowed him to see the brilliant flash as sunlight reflected off the windscreens of enemy aircraft above and behind them.

"All Plaster aircraft, bandits at six o'clock high." His warning was directed at the top cover flight but it went out to the whole formation.

"Acknowledged. All Plaster aircraft engage." Young's voice on the radio was steady, as if the incoming fighters were routine.

Of course, by now they are. Edwards thought. He took another look over his shoulder at the enemy aircraft closing in. His eyesight had always been perfect and he could swear that they were 109s. Then, it was his turn to drop his tanks and pull his Thunderbolt around to the left. That would start the head-on run that would open the furball. At that moment he happened to turn his head to the left and saw a dozen or more Me-109's coming up behind out of the clouds on his right at high speed. *Oh crap, they've foxed us. They were stalking us, waiting for that turn that would let them come in from behind.*

"All Plaster aircraft, we've been had. They're coming in from behind us as well." The thought flashed through Edward's mind. *They've been hunting us, waiting until we were low on fuel and ready to spring the trap on us.*

His mind was suddenly icy cool and he could see the tactical picture as clearly as if he was ten thousand feet over the scene. *This can't be all there is. We've got fascists on two sides of us, there has to be a third group coming in.* His mind had all the positions of the aircraft firmly fixed, arrows from each giving their cause and speed. Every piece of information was telling him that there was another formation of 109s coming in, ready to scythe through the trapped Thunderbolts. *If I was them, I'd be coming in from over there, using the cloud banks as cover. To avoid being hit I've got to veer steeply to the left and get into those clouds as well. If we can do that, we will gain the advantage and get that third formation as soon as they burst out of the cloud cover.. It's a good job we have the speed. We can turn this around quickly enough if we use our heads.*

Edwards didn't climb; the Thunderbolt wasn't in its element doing that. Instead, he held *Live Bait* level as he headed for the part of the clouds that he was sure held the third German formation. Off to his left, the two P-47s led by *Francesca* were drifting wide on the outside of their turn. That was allowing them to pick up speed while *Live Bait* and *Gypsy Rose* bled speed off in their much tighter arc. It was time to do something about that. Edwards hit the water injection button on his Thunderbolt and felt the engine cough before his aircraft picked up speed.

He was barely a hundred yards from the cloud formation when the expected group of Me-109s burst out for their ambush. They were almost close enough for Edwards to make out the fascist pilot's faces. He guessed that they thought the Thunderbolts were closer than they were, misreading the P-47's size as being that of normal sized aircraft unusually close. The 109 pilot in front of Edwards never got a chance to correct his mistake. A blast of fire peppered bullet strikes all over the Messerschmitt, rupturing its fuel tanks and sending it into a spinning ball of flame.

To his left, Edwards saw *Gypsy Rose* rip her target into fragments. *Francesca* and *Honeychile* had reversed their turn and were running across the German formation, raking the gray-green fighters as they went. Edwards had just time to see the bright yellow paint on the noses and rudders of the 109s before all four Thunderbolts plunged through the cloud.

There was no doubt in Edwards' mind that two of the eight 109s were dead and more were badly damaged. He was equally certain that the survivors wouldn't come into the clouds after him. The fascist pilots had received too many bitter lessons about the devastating effects of even a short burst from a Thunderbolt's eight fifty calibers to risk a fleeting encounter in the clouds. The picture in his mind of where everybody was and what they would be doing was still clear and he ran through the tactical options. *Climbing, not on. The Jugs aren't good at that and the 109s outclimb us. Nothing to be gained by going up. We can outdive almost anything else flying but if we do that, our sluggish rate of climb will leave us out of the battle. And, the rest of the boys are outnumbered two or three to one.* That was when Edwards realized something that shocked him. *If I abandon our bratishka, I'll never be able to look Lilya in the face again. That only leaves holding this altitude and taking those 109s on again. No great problem there.*

In the seconds it had taken him to make that decision, his flight had formed up and he led them into a U-turn in the clouds. Once heading for the clear air again, the four Thunderbolts flew a little further on then dived below the clouds. As soon as they emerged, Edwards saw that the Germans had anticipated his decision and used the climb rate of their 109s to get above him. Highlighted against the blue sky were, flying in line astern, two pairs of Me-109s.

Kazan Thunderbolts

The leader of one of the pairs spotted the P-47s and side-slipped into a long dive aimed at the American fighters. They started firing much further out than was usual; Edwards guessed that the fascist pilots realized they weren't fighting Russians anymore and holding fire to point-blank range just allowed the Thunderbolts to get their blows in first. There was something else; the gunfire looked different. Instead of the rapid streams of tracers, the two nose machine guns were firing more slowly but the blobs streaking towards him seemed larger. The big change though was the central engine-mounted gun. Instead of the rapid barrage from the 20mm cannon mounted there, the tracers were much slower, more widely separated and arced downwards.

For a brief moment, Edwards thought he was facing an Airacobra in German markings but he dismissed the idea. *The P-39 is a vicious little dogfighter below 12,000 feet but, up here at 20,000, I'd rather fly a turkey* after it had been stuffed and roasted. That's a 109 with different guns.

Over by the cloud formation, the lead pair of 109s were firing on *Francesca* and *Honeychile*. The Thunderbolts were rolling and jinking to avoid the inbound fire but *Francesca* mistimed an evasion and caught one of the big blobs on the aft fuselage. The explosion was impressive and blew a cloud of fragments away from the P-47. It lurched in mid-air but kept flying, its .50s lashing out with a hail of gunfire at the 109 responsible. The fascist fighter blew up in mid-air, its flaming wreckage tumbling out of the sky. *Francesca* turned and staggered away, the areas of her fuselage stripped of skin by the shell hit clearly visible.

Edwards wanted to watch her, to make sure she was safe but there was no time to do so. The remaining 109s were already coming in behind the streams of tracers from their nose guns. He managed to head off the leader of the second pair with a burst of fire that raked the 109's fuselage, then turned with him. The crippled 109 was sluggish and that allowed Edwards to get him in his sights and loosed several more bursts at him. There was the usual brilliant white explosion that blew the left wing completely off, then the 109 rolled over onto one wing and went down.

Edwards realized the fascist plan. *Those bastards want to run us out of fuel, to force us to climb high then shoot us down or at least force us to crash for lack of fuel.* In front of him, the surviving Thunderbolts of the 360th squadron were in desperate straits. At least four appeared to have been short down and the survivors were besieged by a flock of the yellow-nosed 109s. With the rest of the squadron outnumbered three or four to one, Edwards really didn't see he had any choice. With the battered *Francesca* struggling to keep up, he led his flight of four aircraft into the maelstrom.

The dogfight going on was something he had never experienced before, not even when he had been flying Free Chase in front of the B-17 formations. There were at least a hundred aircraft involved, the yellow-nosed Me-109s on one side, the remaining Thunderbolts from the 360th on the other. Some of the 109s had already broken away from the high-altitude fight with the P-47s and were closing in on the P-39s and Yak-9s providing medium and low altitude cover. None of the fascist fighters had broken through to the Il-2s yet but the situation was desperate. *That's somebody else's problem. We've got enough people trying to kill us here.*

That thought was driven home by the dull thrummm noise of bullets hitting *Live Bait.* A 109 was behind him and was flailing his Thunderbolt with his nose mounted machine guns. Edwards spun his aircraft left in an effort to get clear but the 109 pilot anticipated his move and shifted his point of aim accordingly. More bullets struck the rear half of the Thunderbolt, the impacts on the armor protecting the back of the pilot's seat clearly felt through the thickness of the plating and the padding of the seat.

It was time to do something different. Edwards flipped his controls over and did a right hand barrel roll, pulling himself out of the stream of fire and away from the fascist fighter. The 109 pilot had obviously been expecting him to break left again and went the wrong way. Edwards used the high rate of roll of the Thunderbolt to reverse his turn, putting him perpendicular to the 109 so that the German fighter was crossing his nose. The fascist pilot had obviously realized his mistake and was trying to get away but it was too late. Edwards made a perfect deflection shot, his first few bullets passing ahead of the Messerschmitt but the rest walking along the fuselage with all the destructive effects of a buzz-saw. He could hear the dull whoomph as the enemy fighter's fuel tanks exploding.

Up above him, he saw something that chilled his soul. More fighters were coming in, their blunt noses telling him they were Focke-Wulf 190s. For a second, he didn't know what to do; the Thunderbolts were already seriously outnumbered and running low on fuel and ammunition. The new waves of fighters were the end of it. Then he took another look; the newly-arrived aircraft were diving very fast and black dots showed they were dropping their auxiliary fuel tanks. Then he saw the blue-and-white striped nose paint and realized the truth. They were Thunderbolts, the whole 56th Fighter Group of them.

Zemke's Wolfpack had arrived.

They tore through the surviving 109s with the savagery for which the 56th was already becoming famous. Each flight of four was picking a target and saturating it with gunfire. Faced with the deadly barrage from 32 fifty-caliber machine guns, each of the 109s broke off, trying to flee from the dogfight that had so suddenly turned into a massacre. In doing so, the 109 pilots had made a terrible mistake; no other fighter could out-dive a Thunderbolt and the Wolfpack was not known for allowing enemy mistakes to go unpunished.

Kazan Thunderbolts

"All Plaster aircraft, execute 555. The Wolfpack will take it from here."
Edwards heaved a sigh of relief. 555 meant return to base. It was not before
time; his fuel gauges were showing he was very low on fuel and it would only
be a few minutes before he was running on fumes unless he did something about
it. He leaned out his engine as quickly as possible and cut back on power. That
would bring him enough time to get home. Then, he looked around at the rest of
the formation. Of the 16 Thunderbolts that had started the mission, only nine
were left and all of them showed damage. He looked around quickly and saw
his wingman, *Gypsy Rose* formatting on his aircraft. *Honeychile* was also
formatting on the other side of his aircraft but there was no sign of *Francesca*.
The damaged Jug hadn't survived.

One eye firmly fixed on his fuel gauge, Edwards started out on the flight
back to Privolzhskiy na Volga. About five minutes later, breaking out from
another patch of cloud, he saw a Yak-9 flying a parallel course but streaming
black smoke from its engine. Even from far above, it was painfully obvious that
the Yak had been mortally injured and stood no chance of making it back to the
Volga. What was equally obvious was the group of three 109s closing in on the
cripple. Edwards shook his head. Fuel shortage or no shortage, his flight
couldn't let this situation stand. He rocked his wings and then nosed over into a
long, high speed dive.

On the way down, he felt the controls stiffening with the onset of
compressibility. He ignored the sensation, concentrating on the peril of the lone,
crippled, Yak-9 below and studiously avoiding any speculation as to who the
pilot might be. Instead, he fought the glue-like controls of his Thunderbolt and
focused on the three 109s that were also closing in on the Yak. Their pilots had
made a classic mistake, one that every pre-flight briefing warned about. And yet
one that even the most veteran of pilots still made. They were so concentrated
on the easy kill in front of them, they forgot to look behind at what might be
sweeping down from above.

For one of the yellow-nosed 109s, the simple mistake was completely fatal.
Three Thunderbolts concentrated their fire onto the center aircraft of the three,
sending it spiraling into the ground in a fireball of smoke, fragments and debris.
The other two, skilled enough to realize that their position was hopeless and all
they could do was to get away, broke off the pursuit and ran. It would have
been a foolish mistake high up but this was close to ground level and the speed
advantage of the Thunderbolt over the Me-109 had gone. Acutely conscious of
how much precious fuel he was burning, Edwards pulled up next to the Yak.
Relief flooded through him; it was No. 75, Aleksandr Ivanovich Koldunov's
aircraft.

Koldunov waved at him a bit weakly. Obviously he was fully aware that
the rescue by the Thunderbolts was a very brief respite. His Yak was going in,

the engine was pouring black smoke and bits were falling off underneath. That's when inspiration struck Edwards. There was a long straight road ahead, not well finished for no roads in Russia were. Not by American standards at least. But, there was also a long strip of smooth, open ground beside it and there didn't seem to be any Hitlerites around. Edwards waved back at Koldunov and pointed down, his fingers in the traditional "walking" sign from training school that warned a pilot he had left his undercarriage down.

Koldunov had understood the message and his Yak-9 headed downwards. Edwards thumbed his radio "Cover me, I'm going to pick Alex up."

"Christ, Boss. We're going to need some help here."

Edwards had brought his Thunderbolt around so that he was lined up with the road below and was dropping into the landing procedure. Alongside the road, Koldunov's Yak hit the ground, bounced high, then squashed down on its belly. It smashed through a stone wall before its wing caught on something that spun the whole aircraft around. The aircraft nosed up, hung for a moment with its tail in the air, then crashed down. Koldunov heaved himself out of the cockpit and, staggering slightly, started to run for the road.

By this time, *Live Bait* had her undercarriage down and was coming in for a textbook landing. Overhead, *Gypsy Rose* and *Honeychile* were circling overhead, ready to strafe anybody who tried to interfere with the rescue. Edwards glanced up and saw they were being joined by a flight of four American P-39s. That was good news; down at this altitude the P-39s offered a level of dogfighting capability the Thunderbolts couldn't match while the 37mm gun in the Airacobra's nose offered at least some capability against any armored vehicles that might appear. They flashed over *Live Bait*, rocking their wings in salute as they passed. Then they opened up with their machine guns at an unseen target near the woods. Obviously, there were fascists around and the sooner this operation was completed the better.

Live Bait stopped and Edwards threw his cockpit canopy back. Koldunov had reached the aircraft and was scrambling to try and get aboard. The sheer size of the Thunderbolt was a problem here and Koldunov wasn't familiar with how to get on board. Edwards released his harness, reached down and grabbed him by the scruff of his neck. A quick heave brought the Russian up on to the wing root and from there he was able to pile into the cockpit. Now, the size of the Thunderbolt worked for them. Neither Edwards nor Koldunov were big men and Republic had sized the P-47's cockpit around the largest pilots America had to offer. In fact, most pilots complained the cockpit was too large. Not this time, there was enough space for them both but only just. Edwards threw his parachute out to make sure there was enough room, then gunned his engine and started to move forward.

That was when there was another roar and a trio of Yak-9s flew past, joining the aircraft covering *Live Bait* while she made her escape. Edwards saw the large white rose painted on the nose of one of the Yaks and felt the incredible surge of pride that only comes when a man knows his girl is watching him doing something truly heroic.

Koldunov guessed exactly how Edwards was feeling. He pointed up at Lilya's Yak-9. "You have certainly won her heart now, my friend. There is nothing a Russian woman admires more than manliness and audacity."

"We have to get out of here alive first. If we get shot at, run around inside the cockpit." Edwards was already pushing the throttles forward in an effort to get *Live Bait* off the ground before the Germans reacted to the pick-up.

Squeezed into the cockpit, Koldunov laughed at the memory of their first conversation weeks earlier. Then he pointed at a dial that appeared to be resting on zero. "Is this the fuel gauge here?"

"It is. We might have enough to get back home. Just." Edwards was actually gambling on something that nobody knew existed. It was rumored that Republic had designed the Thunderbolt with a tiny bit more fuel capacity than they or anybody else admitted. It wasn't much, ten gallons or so, but it gave the pilots a last desperate chance to get home. They called it 'gas for momma' but its existence was soundly and emphatically denied.

Live Bait lifted off and set course for Privolzhskiy na Volga. He was using every trick he knew to stretch his fuel out and, even so, he was slightly surprised to see the Volga in front of him. The other pilots, two Thunderbolts, four Airacobras and three Yak-9s were bunched around him, boxing him in. They understood that there was no way he could fight with two people crammed into the cockpit and they were sending a message loud and clear. Anybody who wanted to get to him would have to get past them first.

By the time they saw the Volga ahead of them, the needle on the fuel gauge had made its last despairing little flick and was resting on the 'empty' stop. At least now, Edwards had a 'Plan B' in case the engine started to cough and backfire. The Thunderbolt had only one pilot-killing vice; if the engine cut out on final approach, the plane would just fall out of the sky.

Now he was over the Volga, if the engine started to cough from fuel starvation, he would land on the nearest piece of flat ground he could see, before he lost power completely. But, hope was slowly growing; he might be flying on gas for momma but he could see the thin black pencil stoke that marked the runway at Airfield 108. It grew, gaining width and length and he was lined up perfectly for the landing. There was going to be no messing about, he was coming straight in, his companions very considerately staying out of the way.

It was a split second after his wheels touched the runway that the R-2800 that had brought him home coughed and stalled. By then, he was down and rolling along the length of the concrete. *Live Bait* had to be towed off the runway on to the taxiway, but they were home, surrounded by cheering ground crews and the rest of the base personnel.

Koldunov climbed out of the cockpit first and stood by the wing root while Edwards climbed down. Then he very solemnly saluted and shook Edwards' hand before seizing him in a bear-hug that lifted him off his feet. The cheering around the Thunderbolt redoubled in volume and Edwards felt his spine quaking with the pounding of back-slaps he was receiving.

The four Airacobras had also landed and would have to borrow fuel to get back to their own base at Borisoglebskoye. Before that though, their pilots made a point of joining the celebration around *Live Bait* and pump Edwards' hand. The trio of Yak-9s were already down and taxiing to their own dispersal point.

All but one, that was. Lilya's Yak halted just by the party and she ran through the crowd to grab Edwards around the waist and smack a kiss on to his mouth. That really sent the cheering to stratospheric proportions and mixed the acclamation with laughter. Her head resting on his shoulder, she turned to the audience.

"Moy muzhchina." She pointed at Edwards just so nobody would misunderstand. "My man!"

JG-52 Operations Room, Savasleyka Airfield, Vyksa, Ryazan.

It had been a catastrophe. That afternoon JG-52 had sent seventy two Me-109G-6s to intercept an enemy raid. Only thirty had returned and four of those had crashed while attempting to land. The losses of pilots were just as bad. The Amis were fighting like Russians now; they used the cockpit as an aiming point and continued firing on their target until it blew up or burned.

On the great chalk board that recorded pilot availability, large areas were now blank. Gerhard Barkhorn and Günther Rall, the two leading experten of JG-52, were both dead. Johannes Wiese, Gruppe Kommandant of I/JG-52, was dead, Helmut Kühle, Gruppe Kommandant of II/JG-52, was missing, presumed dead.

The door slammed behind the base commander. Without looking away from the decimated board, the general asked the one question that still plagued his mind. "Did he survive?"

"No, Herr General." The aide's voice was shaking as the enormity of what had happened sank in. "His Gustav ground-looped as he landed. He was trapped inside when the aircraft burned. The ground crew pulled him out but . . . Perhaps he was lucky not to have lived."

The general nodded and took the damp cloth that was used to erase out-of-date data. With a single swipe he removed Erich Hartmann's name. Then, he took the chalk and wrote in the daily comment's section, "Der tag, an dem die experten starben."

CHAPTER ELEVEN: TESTING TIME

Headquarters. 83rd Infantry Division, Kanash, Chuvashskaya Bridgehead.

"Colonel, we've just had confirmation. Major General Tillman is dead. He took a bazooka and went hunting tanks. He got a Tiger, sir, fired at it from the roof of a three-story building and hit the tank in the engine compartment. It burned and blew up but then he got trapped up there and the krauts killed him."

Colonel Long looked at the map pinned up on the wall but it didn't tell him anything he didn't already know. His ears had already told him that the game was nearly up. Where once he had heard only the dull ramble or artillery fire and the thunder of bombing, that barrage had been joined by the flat crack of high-velocity tank guns and then the ripping noise of German machine guns. Now, he could hear the softer popping noise of submachine guns and carbines.

The resistance in Kanash was collapsing quickly, embarrassingly so. The American troops were holding a rectangle about a mile long by half a mile wide with the long side to the north aligned with the railway. It was an odd battle; as the Americans lost ground to the SS troops advancing from the east, they were gaining it to the west. So, the American pocket was slowly crawling westwards in an effort to link up with the troops that were still holding the Yandoba Heights. The problem was that German resistance was slowly strengthening along the western face of the pocket as well.

"Why did he do it, Sir? Hunting tanks with a bazooka isn't a job for a General." Major William Barndollar was bewildered by the situation that had developed in Kanash. Years of service in the peace-time Army hadn't prepared him for this. Nor had it prepared General Tillman for the situation he had faced.

"Why did he do it?" Colonel Long suddenly looked inexpressibly sad. "Because he knew we were not going to be getting out of this mess and he didn't want the first battle fought by an American division on Russian soil to end with the commanding General of that division being captured. Being killed is one thing, captured quite another. So he made sure he went down killing a Tiger."

"Damn." Barndollar was shocked by the cold-heartedness of Tillman's decision.

"We've got worse problems now. I've just had the latest reports from the troops along the Sportivnaya Ulitsa. The krauts are moving into the Kanash Town Park. They haven't started to push out of there into what's left of the area we hold but it's only a question of time."

Barndollar looked at the map pinned to the wall and saw the problem instantly. "If the krauts advance from the town park towards the railway, they've got a wide, straight road to do it down. It leads them right into the bottleneck between the lake and the railway. They'll split our defense zone in two."

Long really wished Barndollar hadn't said that. It was true, but he hated being reminded of the fact. There was a large lake in the middle of Kanash and the gap between its northern point and the railway was barely a hundred yards wide. *The Tigers could drive up the road from the Park, firing their 88s to either side, and seize that gap any time they wanted. Without the Shermans and the TeeDees, there is virtually nothing to stop them. Only the bazookas and the Germans are getting the measure of those. They advance slowly now, thoroughly machine-gunning any areas that might hide a bazooka team. The rocket launchers had slowed down the krauts but they haven't stopped them.*

"Oh great." Barndollar had received another message slip and read the contents.

"What's the matter Bill?"

"Message from Lieutenant Grisham up on the Yandoba Heights. He's reporting that the krauts reinforced the troops in front of him last night, relieving the recon battalion that was there with panzergrenadiers and tanks. They've slammed the door behind him and he's isolated on the Heights."

"Oh crap. So even if we break out of here, we've still got nowhere to go." Long looked at the map again, trying to force himself into believing it was showing something it wasn't.

"In a few hours at the outside, we're going to be cut up into three separate pockets, none of which are mutually supporting, all running out of fuel and ammunition and none of which have the strength to break out on their own. Tillman was right, this is over. We can hold here for the rest of the day, no more than that. Will, start burning all the division's confidential books, smash the code machines and destroy anything the krauts might find useful."

Airfield 108, Privolzhskiy na Volga, Moscow Front

"Got a few minutes, Monty?" It was a polite request from Major Young, or so it was phrased, but it was still an order.

"Yes, Sir." *Uh-oh.*

"We might as well walk over to the maintenance hangar. I guess you want to see how the repairs on *FivebyFive* are going? And I need to talk to you about yesterday. You got credited with three kills. Brings you up to a round dozen."

"That was a rough fight, Major. Those boys were better than anything we've run into before. They tore us up real bad."

"They should be good. They've been identified as JG-52, Goering's Fire Brigade. They're an elite unit that gets pushed to whatever section of the front that's in danger. Full of aces, experten the fascists call them, or was. A lot of them bought the farm yesterday. We lost a dozen Thunderbolts between ourselves and Zemke's Wolfpack, the Russians had seven Yaks brought down and we also lost five Airacobras. Twenty four aircraft, but we got forty of theirs. JG-52 also flies the latest model 109, the G-6. It's got a 30mm engine cannon and two 13.2 mm machine guns in the nose. Your report remarked on the slow-firing low-velocity nose gun?"

"I flew between the shots one time. The 20mm gun was more dangerous. That new gun did for *Francesca* though."

"Got good news there, Bill got out and the Partisans have him in hiding. We got word from them last night. Heard something else as well from Wing. You've been put up for a Silver Star for that pickup you did yesterday. You'll get it too, an American pilot doing a pickup on a downed Russian is too good for morale. Now, don't take this the wrong way, Monty, you deserve that medal and not just for a politically convenient pickup. But, did you think you were picking up your girlfriend when you pulled that off?"

"No, Sir. I did not. I saw a damaged Yak going down with three 109s on his tail. We went down to cover him. I'll be honest, I was afraid it might have been Lilya but that didn't have any bearing on the decision. Nobody even thought about who or what. One of our bratishka needed help and we had his back. Then I saw the number on his tail and knew it was Koldunov. He was going in anyway, too badly shot up to get very far. Everything was in the right place so I did it. The truth is, I wasn't thinking who it was by then. I was too damned scared."

Young snorted with laughter at the mental picture. "All right. Look, Monty, your relationship with that girl is causing concern at Wing. We all know relationships between Russian women and American men are going to happen. How we handle it is still up for discussion. There was even talk of a non-fraternization policy but nobody wants to issue orders that won't get obeyed. If you two make this work and it doesn't interfere with your duties, it'll make things easier for everybody. Now, let's look at your other girlfriend."

Inside the hangar, Edwards could see *FivebyFive* up on trestles. The nose cowling and left wing were new and unpainted and there were other subtle changes as well. The most obvious was the propeller. It was bigger than the standard and paddle-bladed. Then he realized something. It wasn't that parts of the aircraft were unpainted, it was that the maintenance and repair crews were taking the paint off. The give-away was that the nose art had been replaced over the bare metal of the new cowling. "What are they doing, Major?"

"There's another new fascist unit around. It's designated 1/JG-3. They're specialists in high altitude flight. They have specially-equipped Me-109G-3s with boosted engines, a pressurized cockpit and a different VHF radio. Some of the reports are that they've been doing ops at over 28,000 feet."

Edwards whistled. "We get up there easily enough and the Jugs are in their element. Never seen the Huns up that high though."

"They don't usually; the Russians never fly above 12,000 – 15,000 feet and all their aircraft are running out of steam by then. Even our P-39s aren't much good above 16,000. So, all the fighting has been down there. We broke the mould with our Jugs but up at 24,000 with the Fortresses is as high as we go. Now, what those high altitude 109s do is fly high above our formations and coordinate attacks on us. Our Jugs don't climb so well and by the time we get up there, the 109s have kicked in the boost and gone. When we go back down to the bombers, they come back. The powers that be have decided to do something about it. You cracking up *FivebyFive* gave us a chance. Russ McNeely here is an engineer from Republic. He'll tell you all about it."

The middle-aged man looked out of place in a Lieutenant's uniform. It was a thin disguise but it had worked. "We've pretty much fixed your bird, Lieutenant, but we've made some modifications to save weight. We've taken four machine guns and their ammunition from the wings and almost all the armor plate. All in all, we've saved nearly two tons. We put on a new, experimental paddle-bladed prop from Curtiss that they claim makes a big difference. Also, we've put in a new engine. Originally, *FivebyFive* had an R-2800-21 that gave you 2,000 horsepower up to 25,000 feet. Now, current production P-47s have an R-2800-59 with a new turbocharger that'll give you the same power up to 27,000 feet. We've given *FivebyFive* an R-2800-77C that will give you 2,800 horsepower up to 29,000 feet. With water injection of course. We've also taken off the drop tank pylons and removed the paint. If our calculations are right, this baby should climb like a homesick angel."

"What's the catch?" Edwards knew that there had to be one somewhere.

"The obvious ones. Firepower is halved and the only protection the aircraft has is its self-sealing fuel tanks. Beyond that, it will be even more of a gas hog than the Jug usually is. You've only got a single drop tank so you'll have to turn back early. The Superbolts are a very specialized aircraft for a specialized job. We'll keep them back for that job alone."

"Superbolts?"

"That's what we're calling them." Young looked sympathetically at Edwards. "You won't be getting *FivebyFive* back unless we need the Superbolt flight, Monty, and even then the other pilots will be rotating that duty. You'll be flying *Live Bait* most of the time now."

Combat Command B, Second Armored Division, North of Sinyal-Yaushi, Chuvashskaya Bridgehead.

"The bombers have reached their IP. They're starting their bomb run now." The liaison officer from the 40th Bombardment Wing (Heavy) was sitting in a radio jeep, listening to the lead pilot in the approaching formation.

"Pass the order. All units get ready to attack. We'll go in as soon as the Fortresses release their loads." General Harmon knew that moving that soon would mean that his tanks would be following right behind the bombing and it wouldn't take much for some of the bombs to hit his own troops. It was the same principle as following a creeping barrage; the closer one followed the barrage, the more casualties one suffered from one's own side but the fewer one took from the enemy. *And if the last few days have proved anything, it's that German Army is much better at killing its enemies than we are at killing ours. That will have to change.*

Harmon was looking at the German position through his binoculars, wondering if the fascists had any idea what was about to happen to them. He was in no doubt that they knew the Flying Fortresses were coming but he guessed that they thought they were on their way to a target further west. After all, nobody had ever used massed formations of heavy bombers for a tactical bombing strike before. There were three villages in the area forming an equilateral triangle. Sinyai-Yaushi was to the north and formed the point of the position closest to the impending American onslaught. Oykas-Yaushi was to the east and Bolshiye-Yaushi to the south. The Germans had taken them on the first day of their offensive and converted all three into a single major fortified base, linked by perimeter ramparts and wire. There were undoubtedly minefields there as well but that was something the assault engineers would have to deal with.

"All units, advance at full speed on Sinyai-Yaushi! Give them HELL!!" Harmon yelled the order into the microphone and felt his half-track lurch as it started to roll forward. He was doing something that generals hadn't done for decades at least and most certainly were not expected to do today. Not only was he leading the charge of three combat commands of the United States Army, he had unfurled the flag of his own division, the Second Armored "Hell on Wheels" Division from his half-track and stood up to watch it streaming in the wind as every armored vehicle in Combat Commands A and B of the First Armored Division and Combat Command B of the Second Armored streamed forward.

It was an incredibly stupid thing to do and Harmon knew it. Generals had better things to do than lead what amounted to a cavalry charge straight at a heavily defended enemy position, let alone in a vehicle so clearly marked as one of critical tactical importance. And yet his actions, although stupid bordering on the insane by normal standards, were actually logical in the extreme. Harmon was determined to root out the malaise brought on by Vetrenyy Freddie. *However stupid my actions are here, allowing the breakdown in confidence of the troops in their commanders to continue would be far, far worse.*

The objective was closing quickly. Harmon could imagine the reaction within the defense perimeter as the American armor had streamed over the ridgeline to the north and was pouring towards the defenders. They would be running from their quarters to man the defenses and get their guns into operation. As if to confirm that guess, the first brilliant streaks came from the fascist defenses as the anti-tank gun crews got to work,

In response, the Sherman tanks and the M-3 half-tracks had opened fire with their own guns, 75mms from the Shermans, .50 caliber machine guns from everybody, and the air between the American armor and the German defenses seemed filled with the massed fireflies of high velocity ammunition seeking targets.   Sure enough, an unseemly proportion of the incoming seemed to Harmon to be aimed at his half-track. All three of the .50s mounted on the vehicle were firing back, most fire going wild but enough was hitting the defenses of Sinyai-Yaushi to pin the fascists down. Surrounded and engulfed by the roar of gunfire and engines, intoxicated by the feel of the charge, Harmon forgot what was happening overhead.

Thus, it was a complete surprise when all hell exploded on earth.

Three combat boxes of B-17s from the 305th Bombardment Group, a total of 57 Flying Fortresses had released their loads simultaneously on Sinyai-Yaushi. Each had been carrying 20 five hundred pound bombs. To the crews, this had been a milk-run. It had been a short-range mission with all of the flight path taking place over friendly territory. There had been no fighters to worry about, they were too high to be worried by the light flak that guarded the target. Their bomb runs were undisturbed and their concentration was deadly. The equivalent of over 5,700 155mm artillery rounds were already descending on their target and they would all arrive within two minutes from first impact to last. Nothing like it had ever been seen on the Russian Front before.

In front of Harmon, the whole of Sinyai-Yaushi appeared to lift in the air on top of a black, rolling cloud of explosions before the apparent mass of the village disintegrated into a storm of fragments that rolled out from the impact area. The blast wave from the ripple of explosions built up with each extra bomb that was added to the inferno until nothing could stand in its way. When it struck the advancing American vehicles, it rocked them on their suspensions and made their armor ring as if the tanks and half-tracks were vast, misshapen bells. The vehicles kept on ringing as fragments from once had been a fortified village rained down on them.

Harmon knew that the bombers had made their run from east to west and he could see the results of that decision. To the west of Sinyai-Yaushi, a thinning train of explosions marked the impact points of bombs that had been dropped late or had hung up in the bomb bays of the Flying Fortresses. As he had feared, some of those explosions were in the front ranks of the advancing Americans and he knew that at least some Americans had died from the bombs released by their own aircraft.

No matter what he felt about that as a man, General Harmon knew that it had been a price that was justified by the results. The defensive position of Sinyai-Yaushi had been completely silenced. Over to the east and south, he could see the great pyres of smoke that marked where the 19th Bombardment Group had repeated the performance on Oykas-Yaushi and the 35th Bombardment Group had erased Bolshiye-Yaushi from the map. The tanks and half-tracks picked up speed again after the shock from the bombing had passed and surged through what was left of the outer defenses. There was no resistance, no resistance at all.

Once inside what had once been a combined collective farm and village, Harmon could see why. The whole area was nothing but a maze of interlocking bomb craters that had erased any sign of the community that had once been here. From the air, Sinyai-Yaushi had resembled in inverted M, its three roads pointing north and joined at the south end by a single crossroad. All of that was gone. Only shattered fragments of buildings formed fingers that pointed at the sky. All around the American vehicles was destruction.

On the outskirts, a few Germans who had been sheltered from the ferocious bombing or had simply been lucky were staggering around as if drunk. They were incapable of any kind of organized resistance. A few tried to resist, a few shots were fired by them, but those who did so were mown down by the waiting .50 calibers. The rest, left apathetic and bewildered by the unprecedented destruction, were collected together and started off on the long march to the rear and to the waiting Russian POW camps.

"We must move on, General." A Russian colonel, the liaison officer assigned by Koniev, was urgent. "Already the Hitlerites will be assembling forces to block our advance south. Of all the things they do, that is perhaps the most important to remember. An officer, a sergeant and a few men, they will gather others, sweep up support troops and they will block the way for a few hours. In that time, another officer, another sergeant, a few more men will do the same and the way will be blocked again by a stronger force. Every minute we lose is critical. We must get as far as we can before the fascist defenses solidify."

"I know, tovarish." Harmon couldn't help grinning at the situation. "That's why we're not going south. We're going west. Our first objective is Kalinino. Once we have the crossroads and railhead there, we'll have a stranglehold on the whole northern flank of the fascist salient. I wonder how long it will be before the Hitlerites realize they solidified their defenses in the wrong place?"

Sickbay, GunRon 5 Headquarters, Staraya Mayna, Volga River.

"If that bastard comes here and sets foot in my hospital, I will kick his ass so bad his head dents the ceiling. I will not have that arrogant piece of crap telling me what to do with my patients. I don't care who he is or what he thinks he is. If he or anybody acting on his behalf tries to enter here, shoot them."

Entering the hospital by the main doors, Chekist Napalkov could hear the infuriated administrator shouting with pure undiluted rage at whoever it was who had provoked the outburst. He looked over at the admissions officer who was trying to hide behind his desk. "That isn't me is it?"

"No, no, Tovarish Chekist. This is a Navy matter." The Lieutenant looked nervously at the double doors leading to the main part of the hospital. "I've never seen our administrator so angry. I'd stay out of the way if I were you."

It was too late. Captain Harvey Sutton slammed through the doors with eerily cheerful Lieutenant Kushala following behind. He was about to start shouting again when he saw Napalkov and tried to calm down. Even so his voice was still shuddering when he greeted the Cheka officer. "Tovarish Ivan Mihailovich, welcome back. I must apologize for the situation here but we have been trying to deal with a serious and intractable problem."

"Can CheKa be of any help?"

"Do you have the authority to execute senior American politicians?" Sutton sounded hopeful.

Napalkov thought about that. "Not yet."

The comment was taken as a joke and the resulting laughter defused much of the tension in the air. For a moment, Napalkov didn't quite realize that the

Americans around him had assumed he was joking. When the realization sank in, he laughed as well. "But I can offer you some CheKa or militsya guards if you wish? In case Russian civilians become involved somehow?"

"Your offer is much appreciated, bratishka, but we have Marines coming to make sure the . . . . person . . . . in question does not make a nuisance of himself. After all, the welfare of our patients comes above everything else."

"Doctor, may I ask what has happened here?" Somehow Napalkov knew that he was on the verge of finding the information he had been fishing for over the last few weeks.

Sutton stared at him for a few seconds and came to a decision. *Perhaps having CheKa involved would have advantages. And sticking it to Joseph P Kennedy might be one of them.* "Come with me, bratishka. We should talk in private."

Comfortably seated in Sutton's office with glasses of tea in hand, Sutton and Napalkov looked at each other, summing the other up. Both came to the conclusion that there was more to the other than met the eye. Sutton opened the conversation. "You are aware, of course, that Lieutenant Kennedy's father is a very important man in American politics?"

"Joseph Patrick Kennedy? I am, although I believe that his importance has diminished somewhat following his numerous questionable statements."

"It has, although everybody wishes somebody would tell him that. His influence now resides in his ability to organize the Irish and Catholic votes on behalf of the Democratic Party. In truth that does give him a lot of influence in high places. He's one of those people who thinks that his position means he can have anything he wants, he can't accept there are things he can't have and can't understand that there are things he shouldn't have."

"We have suffered similar problems." Napalkov spoke the words with great gravity but the chuckle underlying them was obvious.

"I don't doubt it. Well, this time he surpassed himself. Early yesterday evening we got a telegram from Joseph P Kennedy ordering – ordering us mark you – to return his son, John F Kennedy to the United States for treatment. An identical telegram was received by Commander Henry Farrow, Lieutenant Kennedy's commanding officer. We each replied, in broadly similar terms, that he had no authority to make such demands nor would doing so be tolerated. I believe Commander Farrow's response was somewhat more incendiary than mine.'

Sutton paused and sipped his tea. "Probably as a result of his instructions being spurned, Kennedy went to the offices of Admiral Ernest J King and ordered him to recall Lieutenant Kennedy to the United States."

Kazan Thunderbolts

"Dear God." Sutton lifted an eyebrow at Napalkov's remark. Napalkov saw the gesture and hastily added. "As we used to say. I hear Admiral King is not an even tempered man."

"On this occasion, he was very even-tempered. He started the discussion with Joseph P in a raging incandescent fury, continued it in a raging incandescent fury and ended it in a raging incandescent fury. More to the point, he ended it with four Marines dragging Kennedy from his office and throwing him down the steps. Then, Kennedy sent another telegram to his son, ordering him to leave the hospital and return to the United States. Lieutenant Kennedy responded by reminding him that it is a very serious criminal offense to attempt to persuade a U.S. officer on active service to desert his post. We're now anticipating he will either come personally or send representatives to drag his son back to the states. I'm afraid that the stress from this incident has caused Jack's health to deteriorate sharply. When he does recover, he will be promoted, decorated and assigned to a command position here at Starry May."

Napalkov was having a hard time stopping himself laughing. *Why did I never realize that American politics is so much more amusing than ours? But, this has played right into my hands.* "May I see Tovarish John Fitzgerald?"

"Of course. But I must ask you to be considerate and if he grows tired, to let him rest and recover."

Once Napalkov reached Kennedy's room, he could see that the strain of the night's events had affected his friend greatly. Kennedy was lying back in his bed, his head resting on a pile of pillows. He opened his eyes when Napalkov entered and smiled a welcome. "Welcome, tovarish Ivan Mihailovich. I suppose you have heard of our problem here?"

"I have indeed. I mean no offense to your family bratishka, but your father's conduct appears inexcusable."

"No offense taken, bratishka. Inexcusable is one of the milder words applied to my father's conduct towards others. He is a bullying thug, a man devoid of any sense of decency or honor. All my life he has been hounding me to do the things that he wants, that suit his aims and fill his pockets. He cares for nobody but himself, has respect for nothing but his own ambitions. If he cannot gain something for himself, he will try and put a puppet into place who will do his bidding – and woe betide that puppet if he does not. In my father's eyes, everybody around him exists for the sole purpose of serving his interests. He is a monster, Van'ka, a true monster and I am well rid of him. I will be only too happy if he never speaks to me again. Please forgive me if my bluntness is impolite but . . . ."

"I understand, Jack. My father also was a monster in human form." Napalkov paused a carefully gauged instant. *Now is the crisis, this is the point I have been working for. Can I get Jack to reveal something truly dreadful against his father so that we can crush the policy proposals he supports.* "Have I ever told you of my family background?"

Kennedy shook his head. Napalkov continued after appearing to collect his thoughts. "I come from the province of Perm and my people are the Bashkirs. In years past, before the revolution freed the people from the tyranny of the priests, we followed the teachings of Islam."

"I didn't know you were a Muslim, Van'ka."

"I am not, I am a good communist and I have no time for outmoded religious superstitions. Nor have my brothers and sisters. We were all members of the Young Pioneers. This is a youth organization like your Boy and Girl Scouts only Young Pioneers get to use real tools to build things, they get to fire real weapons, drive real tanks and some even learn to fly real aircraft. One thing about Young Pioneers is that all the girls and boys are together so they learn to work together without problems. And, being youngsters doing exciting things and being taught in ways that were both entertaining and productive we all grew to be friends. Religion was a forgotten thing; instead we learned things of practical value from the books provided by the state. Perhaps we were arrogant because we regarded the old people who still practiced religion as being stupid and outdated. If we had been more perceptive, perhaps a great tragedy might have been averted.

"You see we never noticed how our father was becoming more angry over life in our village. His father had been the Imam before the revolution had ended the authority of the religious teachers. I think he felt deeply the loss of prestige and felt belittled by the new secular society that was growing around him. I think he hated the fact that his children cared nothing for the religion that was the center of his life and all this ate away at him. He started to listen to subversives and saboteurs, those who demanded a return to the strictest forms of his religion and that came to dominate his waking moments. He started to harass my sisters because they were Young Pioneers and associated with the boys from many backgrounds on equal terms. He even started to tell them they should wear veils, something the Bashkiri women had never done. They didn't listen to him of course and that made matters worse.

"One day we had been out hunting. We had rifles that looked like the three-line Mosin Nagant but were really .22s. We used them to hunt squirrels and other rodents. When we came back, most of us went to return our rifles to the armory but my eldest sister Anechka and two of her friends went ahead to help prepare dinner for their families. Then, we heard the other two girls screaming. We ran over to them and they told us that my father and two of his brothers had seized my sister and dragged her into the house. We ran in and what we saw scarred us all.

Kazan Thunderbolts

"Anechka had been pinned on a table by my uncles. My mother was holding her hair and had dragged her head back to expose her throat. My father had a great knife and was trying to cut off her head. We of the Young Pioneers immediately went to Anechka's aid. Two of the girls dragged her away from my mother and father, a third used her red scarf to bind the wound around her throat. Us boys, we fought my father and uncles. Unarmed boys against full grown adults with knives.

"Here in Russia, if there is a fight, men will wind their belts around their fists with the prong of the buckle held forward. That was how my father had armed himself when he hit me in the face and the spike blinded me in one eye. My friend Seryoga was slashed across his face and left scarred. Irinushka was shielding my sister with her body and was stabbed in the back. It was looking bad for us but the militsya came to our aid and arrested my parents and my uncles.

"We were all rushed to the hospital. Anechka survived but was left unable to speak. My eye was ruined and would never see again; Irinushka had a knife penetrating her lung and was ill for many months. The CheKa, it was called the OGPU then, considered my parents and my uncles to be enemies of the state. At their trial they claimed they were defending their families honor and that Anechka deserved to die because she was immoral. The judges wouldn't allow that to stand, found them guilty of attempted murder and they were executed in the town square. Yes my friend, I know what it is like to have a monster as a father."

Kennedy leaned back a bit further in his bed, allowing his head to sink comfortably into the pillows. *That was a truly inspiring story. Courageous youngsters defending their sister against a murderous assault by a monstrous, brutal father. I wonder if there is a single word of truth in it. But, this is my chance to make sure that justice catches up with my father for all the foul things he did.*

"Bratishka, let me tell you something about my father. I have a sister, Rose Marie, but we all call her Rosemary. She was a wonderful girl but she had learning problems. She twice failed to advance from kindergarten on schedule. She could read but really didn't like doing so but she enjoyed dancing and outdoor sports. She really did well when she was presented at the British court. Her real problem was that the part of her brain that tells us when we're doing something dangerous didn't really work and she just didn't know when she was doing something unwise. That got worse as she grew up; she became increasingly assertive and rebellious. She had her stormy moods and her behavior became more reckless. For example, she began to sneak out at night from her convent school in Washington. As I said, she didn't understand that

Kazan Thunderbolts

her actions were unwise or might have bad consequences. My elder brother Joe and our younger sisters looked after her though and kept her from harm.

"Then one day, she told my father that she was having no part of one of his schemes and wouldn't do what he wanted. There was a terrible row. I was away at the time but I heard what happened next. My father said that my sister was insane and needed 'treatment'. Remember I told you he liked experimental "treatments"? well, that "treatment" was to have her lobotomized. That's right, Van'ka, he had her brain cut up.

"When I had left for basic training, I had a sister who was attractive, lively and enterprising but who was also slow and reckless. That was a bad combination but all she really needed care from people who loved her. When I got back, she was a helpless vegetable with a mental age of two who would have to spend the rest of her life locked away in a home. My father had completely destroyed her and I will never forgive him for it."

"That is a truly awful story, bratishka." *And it gives us everything we need. With it, we can put an end to efforts aimed at establishing a single intelligence service for our alliance.* "Let us speak of more cheerful things. We have won a great victory against the fascist spy ring. It had spread to many towns along the Volga but we are rolling it up. There have been many arrests and, as the saboteurs are interrogated, they implicate many more. Of course, many of those they implicate are innocent and those we release but this is the greatest victory we have ever scored against spies, saboteurs and fascists.

"Now, may I ask a favor? Quartermaster 3rd Class Ed Mauer who first realized your gunboat had been sent the wrong ammunition? My superiors would like to place an article about him on the front page of Pravda. With a large picture of him in U.S. Navy uniform of course. The article would tell of how his dedication to duty and meticulous care spotted the wrong ammunition and how his prompt report of the error to his commanders led to the problem being solved. It will give him the credit for having saved our garrison and the defeat of a fascist attack. Will this be satisfactory to you?"

"I haven't the authority to approve something like that, Van'ka. You'll have to go to Henry Farrow and he'll probably have to kick the decision upstairs. I can't see any objection though. Just a matter of formalities."

"I thought I would check at each level, Avoid people thinking I had gone over their heads on this." Napalkov paused. "I will be honest with you bratishka. . . . . "

That will be a first thought Kennedy.

"Seeing how you Americans work, how you approach problems, has been a great education to me. There is so much we have to learn. The Rodina has shut

309

itself off from the world for too long. We should open our doors and learn everything the outside world has to teach us if we are to defeat the fascists and throw the Hitlerite invaders out of our country."

"And we also have much to learn from you." *Including the fact that even friends should not be trusted.*

CheKa District Headquarters, Metallist Prospekt 16, Pestretsy

"The English officer is here." Chekist Mariya Makarovna announced the arrival of Napalkov's visitor. Napalkov had arrived back from the American base at Staraya Mayna and she had just finished typing up his report. There was no doubt in her mind; her superior had just scored a great coup and that would mean she would shine in his reflected glory.

"Ahh, Commander Fleming. Welcome to CheKa. We share an interest I believe. In ensuring the plans of William Donovan do not reach fruition."

"The problem is not Donovan, tovarish Chekist. The problem is that he has political support from powerful people. Those people, in turn, are in debt to Joseph P Kennedy for the political support he organizes for them from the Irish and Catholic communities." Ian Fleming paused. "There are two things in this world I can't stand. One is fried eggs gone cold and the other is cheapskate American politicians who think they are God almighty."

"Well, I think we can help you with the latter one." Napalkov slid the report containing the information he had received from Kennedy earlier across the table. Fleming picked it up and read it. As he did so, his eyebrows rose until they nearly merged with his hairline.

"Dear God, this is incredible. There have been faint rumors along these lines for a couple of years now but this is solid confirmation. If this gets out, it'll completely destroy our friend Joseph P. The way the man treats his family will destroy him with the Irish and the Catholics will loath everything that lobotomy stands for. They won't just kick him out as an organizer, they'll do the opposite of what he says out of sheer disgust. As soon as his patrons realize he doesn't organize those votes any more, they'll drop him like hot bricks. The entire family will be out in the political wilderness for generations. And with it, Kennedy's support for Donovan's plan for a single centralized intelligence service will be crippled. He won't have political backing any more. Being associated with Kennedy will make him political poison."

Fleming leaned back in his seat, smiling happily at the load which had been lifted from him. Unaware of how mightily CheKa had labored on his behalf, he thought that the arrival of the report was merely a fortunate coincidence.

Napalkov also smiled happily. "I must also say, Tovarish Ian Lancaster, that the government smiles greatly on your alternative plan where a committee, comprised of representatives from all our intelligence services, will be formed to coordinate activities but where all the information will be available and those who dissent from the majority verdict will have the opportunity to file a report of their dissent. May I ask a return favor of you? I think it would be best if Joseph Patrick Kennedy was advised of this report by a member of a Commonwealth of Nations intelligence service, with perhaps a hint it came from fascist sources in Britain. The very people he associated with when he was Ambassador there? Given his background, it would have more credibility I think, coming from British officialdom. Assuming of course that he is foolish enough to cause us to release it."

Commander Ian Fleming smiled even more happily. "My dear fellow. I would be only too pleased to oblige."

Composite Group, 83rd Infantry Division, Yandoba, Chuvashskaya Bridgehead.

"It's over, isn't it, Sir." Private Eugene Searle could read the signs as well as anybody else. "We've nowhere to go and nothing left to do."

Lieutenant Grisham looked across the shrinking perimeter on the side of the Yandoba Heights. The Germans were edging forward, slowly and carefully. Earlier in the day, they'd been reinforced by troops from Kanash including at least five of the monstrous Tiger tanks. That was ominous in several ways; it showed that the Germans were gaining the upper hand in the battle for Kanash and that resistance in the town was collapsing. It also meant that the Germans were also gaining the upper hand along the ridge. They'd occupied the crest, finally, and the newly-arrived reinforcements had seized the foot. That had left the Americans sandwiched on the slopes. The Tigers had methodically picked off the three Shermans and the two 105mm guns. *Old Tinny* had been the last to go; she'd died bouncing 75mm shots off the front of a Tiger and then held off brewing up just long enough to allow her crew to escape. *The only option left is to try and break out. And that's not going to be possible.*

"Take a word of advice, Searle. Dump your bazooka, there's no more ammunition for it anyway, get as far away from it as you can and pick up a rifle. A Garand for preference. There's enough of them on the ground. Make like an infantryman."

Searle's mouth turned down with dismay. In the four days this scratched-up bag of misfits had been holding the ridge, he'd killed two more tanks, bringing his total to three tanks and two assault guns. That made him an ace. The unwieldy bazooka had turned him into a man of consequence on the ridge and losing the long tube made him feel as if he was throwing himself away with it.

Grisham picked up the expression and understood it. "There's something you need to know. The krauts hate these bazookas and the men who operate them. We hear that if they catch you, they have a game called loading the rocket. They cut off your dick and force it down your throat until you choke on it."

Searle gulped. "I'll get rid of the launcher right away."

Any further conversation was ended by a call from the forward positions. "Ell-Tee, there's one of those German jeeps coming over. It's flying a white flag."

"Right. Let the kraut through."

The Kubelwagen stopped a few yards from him and an officer in a mottled camouflaged uniform got out. Grisham took the man's appearance in; fair hair, blue eyes, rugged face. "Good afternoon Herr SS-Sturmbannführer. I assume you have come to surrender? We are a bit short of men to guard all the PoWs but if you would order your men to stack their arms over there, we will do our best. And could you give the keys to your Tigers to our own tank crews please? Since you blew up all our Shermans, we'll have to make do with them until we can get some replacement M4s."

The German officer blinked and looked confused. He started to say something, changed his mind, took in a deep breath, started to same something different and changed his mind again. After three attempts, he finally managed to get started.

"Lieutenant, the position of your regiment is hopeless. You are surrounded, we have a direct line of fire into every part of your position. We have tanks and artillery, now you have none. All resistance in Kanash has ended. Last night, we split your defense perimeter there into two. The first pocket surrendered early this morning, the other a few minutes ago. I have here a formal written request for the surrender of this regiment in order to avoid further unnecessary loss of life. We will grant all the honors of war. Please take it to your commanding officer. I will wait here for a reply."

"This is not a regiment, Herr SS-Sturmbannführer, this is a composite force that gathered here. We do not have a formal command structure. But, I will discuss this with my fellow officers and bring you a response when we have made a decision. In the meantime, could we offer you a cup of coffee?"

"Thank you, but no."

Grisham went over to where Lieutenants Fuller and Richards were watching. They made a show of debating the issue with the appropriate displays of histrionics and striking of poses but the truth was they had very little choice and fewer options. The American force was out of food and water and had very little ammunition left. With German forces moving up and backed by the seemingly-invincible Tigers, surrender was inevitable.

"Herr SS-Sturmbannführer, based on your note containing the offer of proper terms and full honors, we have concluded that it is in the best interests of our men to surrender before more lives are needlessly lost."

The German nodded in acknowledgment. "Please order your men to stack their weapons and equipment here. We will need you to march to an assembly point where you rejoin the rest of your division. From there, you will be taken by truck to a railway and then by train to a PoW camp in Germany."

Headquarters, 40th Bombardment Wing (Heavy), Kolosovka.

"Gentlemen, final briefing for today's mission. This is a maximum strength effort. All three of our groups will put up the maximum number of aircraft available, three combat boxes of 18 aircraft and the low box of 21 aircraft. We will not, on this one occasion be, keeping back a cadre. In addition, the 11th Bombardment Group is being declared operational for this mission and will be adding its aircraft. In total, we will be throwing three hundred B-17s at our target. Behind us, the 41st Bombardment Wing will be doing the same, reinforced by the 401st Bombardment Group."

A whistle of disbelief went around the room. *Six hundred B-17s were going on their way to hit their targets.* A mere three months before, a single bomb group hitting a railway marshalling yard had been considered an achievement. The more thoughtful members of the assembled crews reflected on the sheer scale of the effort needed to organize a bombing mission like this. Trains carrying fuel for the Flying Fortresses and their escorts, bringing the bombs for the B-17s and drop tanks for their escorts. Tons of ammunition for the machine guns and everything else the bombers would need. Other trains, containing troops, food, everything else needed by the burgeoning U.S. Army in Russia, would have been shunted to one side to make this mission possible.

Up on the stage, the curtains were pulled back, exposing the mission that had been planned. It was instantly obvious that this raid was going much further west than any previous strike. The other obvious difference was that the planned flight path didn't go to a single target. Instead it split into two.

Colonel Phillip Hall waited for the noise to die down. "Our target is the first of two strikes forming a double-tap raid. We will be hitting the railway marshalling yard at Tula, well to the west of Moskva. Tula isn't just the most important distribution point in this sector of the front but it is also the key railway terminus for the main rail lines heading west. Trains come in from western Europe carrying ammunition, fuel, everything that the German army uses to fight along the Volga. Those trains go back loaded with food and loot. The Hitlerites have made a policy decision to strip Russia bare of everything edible as part of a policy to eliminate the entire population here. By taking out Tula, we won't just make the job of our boys easier, we will be saving huge numbers of allied lives, military and civilian.

"The good news is, we've been interdicting fascist supply routes so thoroughly that most of the supplies that came to Tula are still there, piled up in the streets." Hall flipped on the projector and showed pictures of drums of fuel and crates of ammunition blocking the streets of Tula. "It is our considered opinion that this is the most inflammable target on earth. That's why we'll be dropping a lot of incendiaries as well as thousand pounders.

"The other target will be hit by the 41st Bomb Wing (Heavy). It is the Vyksa Steelworks at, funnily enough, Vyksa. This is one of the largest steelworks in the world, built between 1933 and 1937 as part of the Second Five-Year Plan. To give you some idea of how important this plant is, it contributes some ten percent of Germany's total steel production. Not only that, but it produces some 45 percent of the highest grades of steel available to Germany. Without supplies from Vyksa, the fascists will be unable to support their present levels of munitions production. Vyksa must go."

Hall coughed and drank some water from the glass on his podium. "All right, that's what we want to do. Here's how we'll do it. The outbound flight will take you to the divergence point here. You'll be escorted by the P-47s of the 356th and 56th Fighter Groups with the P-38s of the 55th running ahead on Free Chase. At the divergence point, the P-47s will be running low on fuel and they will be turning back. The 40th Bomb Wing will make its run on Tula and the 41st on Vyksa without escort. That will mean you will have to fight your own way through for about a hundred miles to your targets. Once the bomb runs are complete, you will have to fight your way back to the convergence point where the P-47s of the 4th and 357th Fighter Groups will be waiting to escort you home.

"Defenses. The Tula railway yard is defended by 175 88mm guns; mostly ones that have been stuck there because they can't be taken forward." Hall looked at the bomber crews listening intently. "They are not short of ammunition either. Flak will be intense and prolonged. The defenses also have 140 20mm and 37mm guns but we don't have to worry about those. We also believe there are six 105mm flak guns on railcars in the center of the marshalling yard. They will be your aiming point. The Vyksa steelworks is even more heavily defended. They have at least 240 88s there and a dozen or more 105s. Look on this a different way. Every gun defending these targets and the rest of the target set we have within range is one less gun facing our armies. I know that isn't much comfort right now, but it is really important to our long-term prospects. We out-produce the fascists in war material by a level so high we can hardly credit it and yet we haven't even begun to really mobilize. So, the more we force the Hitlerites to spread themselves out, the sooner we can punch through."

"What about fighters, Sir?"

"Ahh, now there we have got lucky. Yesterday, the 356th got into a bare-knuckle prize-fight with JG-52. They're the highest scoring fighter outfit in the world, the ones the krauts send to critical areas. They turned up here, draw your own conclusions. After Zemke's Wolfpack joined in, we downed at least forty of their aircraft including five of their top aces. We lost twelve Thunderbolts. JG-52 are out the battle. There'll be four fighter groups around but the odds are a lot better than they were this time yesterday. So, we know we can expect to Me-109s and FW-190s, possibly some heavy fighters after the Thunderbolts have to turn back. And, remember we will have the P-38s on Free Chase."

"You coming along, Sir?" It sounded an impertinent, bordering on insubordinate, question but Hall had carefully planted it.

"Of course." Hall sounded indignant. "I'll be flying in the lead ship, low box, lead group on the Vyksa mission. And, before anybody else asks, General LeMay will be flying the lead ship, high box of the 305th on the way to Tula."

Combat Command B, Second Armored Division, Sayavalkasy, Chuvashskaya Bridgehead.

Harmon looked at the map on his lap and suddenly realized the situation was historic. The lead elements of the American formation were west of the Chuvashskaya Bridgehead. Not much, that was true. Just a mile or so but that mile was of critical importance. It meant that the daily situation report could honestly and truthfully read that American forces had broken out of the Chuvashskaya and were pursuing defeated German units westward. Actually, south west since the plan was still to link up with the Russians and cut off the whole fascist force that had launched their offensive earlier. It was just that the link-up point was further west was normally the case for an encirclement of this kind. That was important, Patton's chief of staff had explained why clearly. Eisenhower had told Harmon that when this battle was over, the front line had to be to the west of its position the day before the fascist offensive had begun. That would mean that the U.S. Army could, despite the defeats experienced in the first few days, could fairly claim to have won its first major battle in Russia.

The mood of euphoria evaporated with a single radio message. "General Harmon, Sir. Message from Reaper. We've just had word that what's left of the 83rd infantry has surrendered at Kanash."

Harmon felt the blow as if it had been a punch to the stomach. *That message is not really true though. A lot of the 83rd escaped eastwards and the division is reforming at Urman. They were able to do that because of the boys who held Kanash and the Yandoba Heights for long enough to cover their escape.* "Any word of prisoners?"

There was a pause while his aide read the message. "We think about three hundred. We know about a thousand men were holding out in Kanash and Yandoba but the casualties in the street fighting were brutal. We're expecting to hear from the krauts sometime soon."

"Do not place any faith in that, bratishka." The Russian liaison officer had a grave note in his voice.

"Under the Geneva Convention, the German Army is supposed to send us a list of the name, rank and serial numbers of any prisoners taken by way of the Red Cross in Switzerland." Harmon felt naïve and innocent even while he spoke the words. He had been in Russia long enough to know that the Hitlerites were not playing this war by any civilized set of rules. The only question in his mind was whether the Germans intended to make any distinction between Russians and Americans. He had an ugly feeling he already knew the answer to that.

"The fascists have repudiated that agreement long ago, tovarish. We have never received any such lists."

Harmon was almost relieved when the conversation was halted by the vicious clang of an armor-piercing shot bouncing off a tank's glacis plate penetrating the roar of the engines. Ahead of him, an M-3 light tank had been stopped by a direct hit on its armor plate. He couldn't tell if the shot had penetrated or not but he could see that the crew had bailed out. The tank wasn't burning and that was important; a tank that did not burn could be salvaged and put back into operation within a few hours. A tank that burned was a write-off, fit only for scrap.

There was another factor as well, of course. A tank that didn't burn gave its crew a better chance of escaping. The last few days had revealed something that, to the American commanders, was very important. The Shermans gave their crews a much better chance of escaping than Russian or German tanks. Having the entire crew escaping a knocked-out vehicle was commonplace.

Quite apart from anything else, that meant the much more of the experience gained by the crews was surviving to be passed on to newcomers. Some of that experience was already showing. A few days earlier, the tank and half-track crews would have tried to see where the fire was coming from. Such subtleties had gone. Now, everybody was firing at everything that might conceivable hold an anti-tank gun. The noise was incredible, the roar of the massed .50 machine guns mixed in with the crash of 75mm guns and the flat, vicious cracks of the 37mm guns on the light tanks. The area between the advancing American armor and the scattered cover in front of them was a continuous flicker of red streaks and flashing lines as the suppressive fire did its work.

Incredibly, despite the hail of fire that was being directed at the Russian countryside in general, the German anti-tank gun fired again. The brilliant red streak hit a Sherman square on the frontal armor but the shot bounced off with an ear-piercing scream. The shot had been ineffective for the Germans for the Sherman continued to move forward as if nothing had happened. It had, however, given the American crews a positive indicator of the enemy position, a ruined farmhouse surrounded by rolling grassland. It was now the focus of the American gunfire as the tanks pummeled the wrecked building with fire from their 75 millimeter guns. The half tracks were refusing to be left out of the battle and were pouring machine gun fire into the building as well. Harmon could swear he saw an officer in one of the half tracks draw his pistol and fire at the farmhouse.

Not a bad idea come to that. Harmon thought as he drew his own pistol and emptied the magazine in the general direction of the building. He knew it was coincidence and it was unlikely that the slow, heavy shots from his Colt had even reached the building but he still felt ridiculously pleased when a secondary explosion wrecked what was left of the building. *The anti-tank gun and its ammunition going up.*

The explosion seemed to have knocked the wind out of the defenders. A white flag, hoisted on the end of a stick started to wave from above the shattered remnants of the building. One of the M-3 half-tracks pulled up a few yards short of the wreckage and two figures got out of the back to take the surrender. The Russian Liaison Officer saw them and jumped up, shouting "Nyet, bratishka!"

He was too late. An MG-42 machine gun opened up from a loophole in a pile of rubble and cut down both Americans. In doing so, the long tongue of flame from the muzzle out clearly revealed its position and revenge was instantaneous. A Sherman fired a 75mm round into the loophole from a few dozen feet away and the site of the machine gun vanished in a cloud of smoke and splinters. The Russian looked at the scene sorrowfully. "Bratishka, never act on a surrender from the fascists until they are standing in the open and you can count two hands for everybody. Remember that it is the hands that will kill you. They can hold pistols or hand grenades. If you cannot see those hands clearly, assume the worst. You will rarely be wrong."

While the small sideshow around an anti-tank gun and an infantry outpost had taken place, another Sherman had taken a hit in the side and slewed off the road. Once again, the response was immediate with all the tanks and half tracks taking the possible ambush locations under fire. Within a few minutes, the position had been overwhelmed and its defenders killed. Harmon, though, realized the real problem. Each of these engagements was slowing his advance down and giving the fascists more time to set up their defenses. *The armored warfare doctrine book might speak about 'shock action unit emphasizing*

Kazan Thunderbolts

mobility and firepower' but how does one do that on a battlefield where every tree might hide an anti-tank gun? That book is useless, written by theorists who had never had to command a real armored unit in a real war.

That was when Harmon realized he had taken the first step to true wisdom. He understood now how little he knew.

Secondary School 18 "Alexander Ignatyevich Molodchy", Kazan

The children had a game. When they heard aircraft approaching, they would try and guess what kind of aircraft it was, just from the sound of its engines. At first, there had been much dispute accompanied by pushing and shoving over the claimed recognitions but as the war had ground on, the children had become so familiar with the aircraft that recognition was prompt and unanimous. The game had been revived when the Hitlerites had come within range of the city only then it had a new, ominous tone. Were the aircraft friendly fighters defending the city or fascists coming to burn and destroy?

The winter and spring of 1943 had caused the children to become experts again and often they recognized the approaching aircraft before the anti-aircraft defenses did. The Soviet Army, desperately short of resources and oddly willing to listen to children when other adults might not, had taken advantage of the expertise and acted on the identifications. And so, Secondary School 18 had won the honorific "Alexander Ignatyevich Molodchy" after the heroic bomber pilot. The school had also been awarded another prize, one the children appreciated far more. The black swastika cut from the tail of a crashed He-111, reputed to have been shot down by the famous "White Rose" herself.

Spring had passed, the hated Hitlerites had failed even to come close to the city of Kazan and the game had suddenly had yet another revival on interest for more aircraft had arrived to be identified. American aircraft and in numbers the Russians could scarcely credit. The names were strange and different. The two-engined *Maroder* and *Molniya*, the single-engined *Kobrushka* and the mighty *Grom*. Yet of them all, the one the children found easiest to recognize was the huge *Krepostny*, the four-engined giant that battered the fascists without mercy. The schoolteachers had pointed out that the Soviet Union had built bigger aircraft than the Flying Fortress but they'd only built a handful of them. The Americans had built hundreds and they had sent them all here to help defend the Rodina.

"Amerikanets!" The children's call was made early because this was the easy one. Only the great *Krepostny* made the ground tremble like that and they were only flown by the Americans. And so, the cry of *Krepostny* followed without any delay. Then, there was an eerie silence as the children watched for the first sight of the aircraft. Would they keep their reputation for infallibility?

Would the artillerists still have faith in them? Then, fingers pointed upwards as the first aircraft came into sight.

They were indeed the Flying Fortresses and the reputation of Secondary School 18 was safe. The first groups of bombers passed over Kazan, much lower than usual, their engines laboring because every aircraft was carrying a full load of fuel, bombs and ammunition for their machine guns. Thus, their rate of climb was well down. The lower altitude meant they were escorted by P-39s and Yak-9s at this point, the Thunderbolts would be joining them later, as far west as possible. Every mile the Thunderbolts went westwards before joining the big bombers was a mile they could get closer to their targets before the fighters had to turn back.

On the ground, the children were counting the bombers as they passed overhead. They'd seen enough American bombing raids going out to know that they flew in groups of 18 with the odd 21-plane group. They knew that they flew in multiples of three groups, that 57 aircraft was a small raid, 114 was a medium one and 171 was a major attack. Sometimes there would be a huge formation, 340 aircraft, and that would cause much rejoicing because a raid that big meant many, many fascists would die.

Yet, to the children's amazement, this time the great parade of bombers never seemed to stop. For every group that passed overhead, two more would appear on the horizon. The number passed three hundred and still kept climbing upwards. By now, the first groups to appear were long past yet the Fortresses continued to overfly the city. By the time the last one had vanished into the sky to the west, over six hundred heavy bombers had passed.

With the continuous throb of the engines gone, the silence over Kazan seemed almost oppressive. The children looked at each other, awed by the sight of the long stream of bombers, knowing that they had seen something that they would, one day, tell their own children about. After the vast parade of heavy bombers, the sight of the B-26s heading west also seemed an inconsequential thing. Then the school bells rang and the day returned to normal.

B-17E Flying Fortress "Memphis Belle", Over Khyrkasy, August 17th, 1943

"Need more power." General LeMay checked his instruments, confirming that the stream of B-17s had leveled off at 24,000 feet. The altitude, like everything else on this raid, had been carefully chosen. It was high enough to sharply reduce the performance of the most feared German fighter, the Focke-Wulf 190, and that of the Messerschmitt 109 by a lesser amount but the turbocharged Thunderbolts would be at the peak of their performance envelope. It had still been a long, hard climb to get up here. LeMay knew that the B-17s had been pushed right up against their maximum authorized take-off weight and he suspected quite a few of the bombers were well above it. The crews, knowing they would be flying through enemy airspace for almost 90 minutes without fighter escort, had stuffed their aircraft with all the ammunition they could fit on board. Some had cannibalized wrecked B-17s for extra machine guns. Replacing the single guns in the waist with twins had been a popular move. Others had their noses modified to mount extra guns to guard against head-on attacks. The extra weight was slowing the aircraft down.

"The new Fs have got improved engines." Colonel Albert Cox was also concentrating on the instruments. A bitter lesson had been that the copilot had to be ready to take command of the aircraft instantly if the pilot was killed. Delay could, would, be fatal. "Dash 97s with 1380 horsepower. They need it with the extra weight."

LeMay knew what Cox meant. The B-17F incorporated the early lessons from operations over Russia. The waist gun positions were staggered and equipped with twin mounts. The nose had been re-profiled so that aircraft could carry a twin .50 in the upper section of the transparency - provided they didn't have to carry a Norden bombsight as well. A total of 15 .50 caliber machine guns. Just as importantly, the engines had been protected by extra armor plate and a heavy bulkhead installed in front of the pilots. "At least they cured the tail-heavy problem."

"Little friends arriving. Hey, two of them are silver."

The Thunderbolts were forming up around the long stream of bombers. The red and blue checkered cowlings of the 356th group seemed to LeMay and the other 305th crews to be old and trusted friends. The blue and white stripes of Zemke's Wolfpack were less familiar but the Wolfpack had a ferocious reputation. Then there were a pair of silver P-47s. Both were from the 356th and they had the blue/red nose but the rest of the paint had gone. The silver finish made the aircraft oddly difficult to see; it picked up the color of the sky around it and the eye just slid past the aircraft. LeMay made a note of that for future consideration.

"Course change coming up." The navigator was working hard to keep the formation on its planned course. They'd been heading a bit north of west since take-off and were now passing north of Cheboksary. Now, the plan had them swinging to south of west so that they would pass due south of Nizhny Novgorod. They'd continue on that course until they swung west for the divergence point. "Get ready to swing to two-four-seven."

"Ready."

"Execute." LeMay moved the controls and *Memphis Belle* swung elegantly on to her new heading. Behind her, the entire bomber stream changed course.

The coordination wasn't perfect and the turn made by the two new groups was ragged but they had made a valiant effort.

"No fighters yet." Cox was twisting in his seat trying to see everywhere at once.

"Sit still. Gunners will tell us when the fighters arrive. Won't be soon. Most kraut forward airfields have been taken out. Tactical has pushed the Luftwaffe back. Opened the door for us."

"Top gunner. We've got a pair of bandits following high up."

Cox looked over at LeMay. "And so it begins."

Superbolt FiveByFive Over Lyskovo, Moskva Front.

"Superbolt flight, take the spotters out." The voice over the radio was calm and clipped yet the relish in the order was obvious. The two-plane spotter flights had been annoying the Thunderbolt escorts ever since the Germans had started using the tactics. At first, they'd used standard Me-109s but after the escort fighters had nailed a few of them, I/JG-3 had been sent in. The P-47s lack-luster climb rate had made it impossible to shoot them down but it was obvious Major Young hoped that was about to change.

Edwards reached down and got ready to blow his drop-tank and ram the boost up to the highest possible setting. At this point, he really needed three hands because he had to cut in the water injection. He craned his head upwards, watching the lazy figure-of-eight being flown by the 109s high above. Eventually, one of their turns put the pair of Superbolts behind them. That was the key. Edwards pushed the engine boost up to the maximum allowed by the modified controls, knowing he was starting to tear his engine apart. Then, he kicked in the water injection system, feeling the cough and thump of the boost mix and the screams of protest from his R-2800 engine. One press on the release and his drop tank fell away, separating cleanly from the modified P-47 that was already soaring skywards faster than Edwards had ever climbed before.

By an oversight, the climb and dive indicator had remained unchanged. Now, it showed the needle resting firmly against the 6,000 feet per minute climb rate, Edwards didn't believe that; his experience was that at the top end of performance, aircraft instruments grossly overstated speed and rate of climb/dive. Nevertheless, the speed with which he was closing the range on the 109 told him he was climbing at over 5,000 feet per minute. The seat of his pants also told him the massive boost was damaging his engine every bit as badly as he had feared. The R-2800 was running noticeably rougher now than it had been at the start of the balls-to-the-wall climb.

Ahead of him, the 109s had made another turn and they had finally spotted the two Superbolts closing in below and behind them. They looked strangely different from the 109s Edwards was used to seeing, painted light duck egg blue overall instead of the usual green/grey mottled mix. He already had the lead aircraft in his sights and he squeezed the trigger just as his target started its left-hand turn. Edwards made the slight adjustment needed to compensate for the turn, then pressed the firing button. The bright flashes of hits on the tail section immediately registered and began to walk along the fuselage. He kept expecting the 109 to disintegrate. Then, he realized that he had become used to the instant destruction meted out by the eight-gun battery on the Thunderbolt. The Superbolt's four guns had nothing like the same shattering effect. The line of impact points reached the 109s cockpit and he held the burst there. That was when the 109 blew up in the usual white flash and went spiraling down in multiple pieces.

The other light blue 109 had made the usual mistake of trying to dive away from *Lewd Lucy*, the other Superbolt. This time, though, the 109 seemed to be getting away with the blunder. The lightweight Superbolts picked up speed a lot more slowly in the dive and they were having trouble catching up with the 109. Edwards felt the controls becoming heavier as the dreaded compressibility built up. The 109 was still out of range when the control forces reached levels that prevented the surfaces moving at all. This was the critical point; the Thunderbolts were unable to pull up.

"Full tabs. Now." Edwards gave the order, following the advice Republic had handed out for just this situation. Both pilots spun the elevator tab controls to maximum deflection and saw the nose of their aircraft lift slightly. That eased the vice compressibility had on their controls and they were, slowly and painfully, able to pull out. At first, Edwards was disappointed that the 109 had got away but then he saw it, still in its steep dive. He guessed what was happening, the pilot fighting controls that compressibility had locked in place while he was pinned in his seat. Edwards watched the 109 go all the way down until its dive ended in an orange explosion on the ground far away.

"Superbolt flight. Execute 555. You're both trailing black smoke." Young's voice sounded concerned. The two Superbolts turned around and headed for home, leaving the bomber stream behind them.

B-17E Flying Fortress "Memphis Belle", Over Sarov, August 17th, 1943

"Divergence point approaching. On my mark, come around to two-two-eight." The navigator sounded as if he was holding his breath in anticipation of the hailstorm of fighter attacks that everybody on board the six hundred B-17s were sure that would engulf them all the way to their target.

"Ready."

"And execute." LeMay brought the controls over and swung *Memphis Belle* on to the new course that would take her all the way to Tula. The 41st Wing was turning to three hundred degrees for the run to the steelworks at Vyksa. Out of the corner of his eye, he saw a 41st Wing B-17 accidentally follow the 40th Wing aircraft, realize the mistake and then scuttle back into place.

"This is Plaster and Wolfpack. We're turning back now. Time is 11:41 local. Good luck Big Boys."

"Thank you Little Friends. See you soon. We hope." LeMay looked at where Cox was sitting. "Well, Al, we're on our way. For years we have said we could gun our way through to a target. Now, it's time for us to find out if we knew what we were talking about."

"I just hope we don't find out we were wrong in a blizzard of bullets and shells."

LeMay looked at Cox sharply then saw the grin on his copilot's face. "I don't know what you are complaining about. We've got fighter escort all the way to our target. It's just they've got crosses on them."

"Estimated time at target, 12:30 local." The navigator's voice was studiously level. "IP in forty five minutes."

"Bandits approaching, two o'clock low." The ball turret gunner really didn't want to be the first to break the news but the battle was starting. "Two squadrons, I count twelve Me-109's and eleven FW-190's climbing like they're on some kind of elevator."

"I got them, They're turning into us. Second is following."

"Bombardier. More bandits, many of them eleven o'clock very low. They're climbing fast guys. All I can see is their noses."

"*Black Widow*. Many more enemy aircraft deploying on the other side of the formation. They're boxing us in."

LeMay looked out to one side and saw an Me-110 holding the same level as the bomber formation but sitting out of range. He guessed the twin-engined fighter had been brought in to replace the two high-altitude fighters shot down by the Superbolts. He also guessed that the 110 was going to stay with the 40th Bombardment Wing all the way to the target, apparently radioing their position and advising fresh fascist fighter groups waiting farther ahead of weak spots developing in the formations. He had an uneasy feeling that the Hitlerites had been tipped off or at least had guessed the 40th's destination and had set a trap for the Flying Fortresses. He knew that the aircraft had already penetrated the normal defensive fighter belt. Obviously, there were many more fighters than intelligence had estimated.

"There's more than we thought." Cox had obviously been thinking along the same lines as LeMay.

"They have moved a lot of squadrons back and they must have been saving up some outfits for the inner defense that didn't know about. It's a fluid, flexible defense in depth. We're not the only ones who are learning."

"Fighters coming in. Two Me-109s, 12 o'clock high." Mid-upper gunner called out the warning.

"Bandits, two Me-109s with yellow noses. 2 o'clock high, Coming in fast." It was one of the waist gunners. Both waist gunners had twin .50s using guns salvaged from *Westward Ho* and he was itching to try them out.

"Bandits, two Me-109s, 1 o'clock high. Yellow nosed bastards want a piece of us do they?"

LeMay could see the situation developing as the twelve-ship squadron of yellow-nosed 109s started swinging around in a wide U turn. It left the Messerschmitts came in from twelve to two o'clock in pairs. LeMay knew the main event was on and resisted an impulse to close his eyes. It was at times like this that he blessed the Bell's Palsy that froze his face into a ferocious scowl.

Two 109s were coming straight at *Memphis Belle*. They were obviously more experienced pilots than those the 40th had met on previous missions. They were coming in on frontal attacks with a noticeably slower rate of closure, apparently having throttled back to obtain greater accuracy. The blobs of tracer from the nose machineguns were larger than before and the engine cannon tracers were large and slow. LeMay marked that up to intelligence; they'd already passed through the warning about the new heavy guns on the 109s. He settled down and stared ahead, the very epitome of grim determination to steer his Flying Fortress through the attack.

Next to him, Cox jumped nearly six inches out of his seat when *Memphis Belle's* top-turret gunner started hammering at the 109s dead ahead with both his .50s. The twin muzzles blazing out their streams of gunfire barely a foot above the flight deck gave a realistic imitation of cannon shells exploding in the cockpit. It was something every B-17 crew quickly became accustomed to. The mid-upper gunner, bombardier and navigator were all firing at the lead 109, wrapping the aircraft in a sparkling red cocoon of tracer fire. It rolled, its engine spurting black and white smoke as it dropped away from the attack. In exchange, LeMay felt and heard the rattle of machine gun bullets striking *Memphis Belle* followed by a loud explosion. The aircraft lurched in his hands but he quickly corrected the movement.

"Radio cabin. That was one of the 30mm shells. They got a lot more moxie than the 20mms."

Over to the right, a 305th Bombardment Group B-17 was hit by a rapid succession of cannon shells. The bomber turned gradually out of the formation to the right, maintaining altitude. In a split second it completely vanished in a brilliant explosion as the fuel tanks erupted into four balls of fire, the fuel tanks that were consumed as they fell earthward. All that was left of the B-17 was a shining silver rectangle of metal that sailed past *Memphis Belle's* right wing. LeMay recognized it as main-exit door. Seconds later, a black lump came hurtling through the formation, barely missing several propellers. LeMay saw it was a survivor from the downed bomber, clasping his knees to his head as if he was a diver making a triple somersault to win an esoteric competition. LeMay could see the man so clearly that he saw a piece of paper blow out of his leather jacket. What he didn't see was the man's parachute open. *Perhaps he is making a delayed jump.*

All around him, the air battle was picking up in intensity. More and more fascist fighters had joined the battle; the alert calls from the B-17 crews picking up in intensity as the fighters pressed home their attacks. It was obvious to LeMay that the German defenses had realized the objective of the attack and the pilots were inspired with a fanatical determination to stop the American bombers before they reached their targets. Many pressed attacks home to 250 yards or less, or bolted right through the formation wide out, firing long twenty-second bursts. These fighters often presenting point-blank targets as they tried to make their breakaways and the number of long black streaks across the skies showed that the Flying Fortress crews were exacting a toll. It was also obvious that the level of skill demonstrated by the German fighter pilots was declining. Some committed the fatal error of pulling up instead of going down and out and their fighters were gutted by the .50s as they exposed their vulnerable bellies.

The attack patterns were becoming recognizable. The most dangerous attacks, pressed home with almost fanatical determination, were the head-on passes aimed at the lead elements of the combat boxes. It was obvious to LeMay that the defending fighters were desperate to break up the B-17 formations and disrupt the coordinated gunfire that was beating off the attacks. Other fighters, seemingly the less experienced ones, were coming in from astern, dueling with the tail and ball turret gunners. He saw several of the 190s trying deflection shooting, carrying out on side attacks from 500 yards on the high boxes, then raking the low boxes as they made their breakaway. Some of the pilots even kept their noses cocked in a side slip, trying to keep the B-17 formation in their sights longer.

Sitting motionless except for the movements needed to keep *Memphis Belle* on station, LeMay stared out of the cockpit windows, his instincts working overtime to gauge the sense of the battle. The air around *Memphis Belle* was filling with debris from the battle, so much so that the airplane was endangered by emergency hatches, exit doors, prematurely opened parachutes, bodies, and assorted fragments of B-17s and fascist fighters. The wreckage seemed to streak past the bombers in their slip stream. All around him, LeMay saw B-17s in every stage of distress, from engines on fire to controls shot away.

Yet, it was becoming apparent that the fighter attacks were failing to halt the close-knit juggernauts of the Fortresses, and that the fascist fighters were paying a grim price for their determination. LeMay saw two fighters explode not far beneath *Memphis Belle*, disappearing in sheets of orange and white flame. They joined the streaks of smoke across the sky and on Russian soil far below, a long line of black funeral pyres of smoke from fallen fighters and B-17s, marking the trail of the 40th Bomb Wing as it fought its way through the German defenses.

"Will you look at that?" Cox's voice was awed by the sight around him. The sight of the desperate air battle was highlighted by white dots of more than sixty friendly and enemy parachutes floating down. He believed that nothing like this had ever been seen before; a sky where disintegrating aircraft were commonplace and nothing was worth a second look.

"Fortress on our right going down." LeMay's response was deadpan neutral. He watched a B-17 turning slowly out to the right, its cockpit a mass of flames. The copilot crawled out his window, held on with one hand, reached back for his parachute, buckled it on, let go and was whisked back into the horizontal stabilizer of the tail. LeMay know that, despite the desperation of his escape, the copilot had been killed by the impact. His parachute didn't open.

"190 coming in, six o'clock low." LeMay took *Memphis Belle* up slightly, clearing the arc of fire from *Sally B* beside. The 190 was caught in the crossfire from two ball turrets and the *Sally B's* tail guns, turned over on its back and spun out in a dive that ended with a brilliant white flash that blew its left wing off. It had been a neat piece of shooting by Sally B whose streams of gunfire had missed *Memphis Belle* by only a few feet. Yet, despite the attack, LeMay felt suddenly that the bombers were winning the battle. The skill and élan of the first waves of fascist fighters had gone and the follow-up attacks were much more pedestrian. While there was still no letup in the volume of attacks, the precision and flair had gone. The fighters queued up like a bread line and took turns firing at the bombers. That meant each second of time had a cannon shell in it but the gunners were having an easier time gauging the attack runs of the fighters and pouring fire into them.

Yet for all that, the strain of being a target at the end of an aerial shooting gallery was becoming intolerable. *Memphis Belle* shook steadily with the fire of its .50's, and the air inside was clouded with smoke to the point where breathing was becoming difficult even through the oxygen masks. LeMay swept his eyes across the engine instruments for the thousandth time and saw the readings. All normal. As far as he knew, there were no injured crew members. Yet.

B-17E Flying Fortress "Memphis Belle", Over Gorodnoye, August 17th, 1943

"IP in fifteen minutes." Cox sounded shaken by the stream of almost 200 individual fighter attacks that had besieged the bomber formation for almost half an hour. In the last few minutes, though, the pressure eased off. Although hostile fighters were still in the vicinity, they'd stopped pressing home their attacks. External fuel tanks were visible under the bellies or wings of some of the attacking aircraft. *At least that explains how they've been able to sustain their attacks on us so far from their bases.*

"Acorn calling in." They've reached IP and report it clear of fighters. The radio operator paused briefly and when he resumed his voice was incredulous. "Acorn is reporting they've sighted a formation of Dornier 217 bombers heading for us."

"They're throwing everything in." LeMay was his usual taciturn self. Beneath it, he was contented with the situation. The 40th wing had lost aircraft, that was true, but they were taking the fight deep into enemy territory and forcing the German defenders to react to them. The bombers had the strategic initiative and were dictating the terms of the air battle. They were also forcing the Luftwaffe to throw in its last reserves in the battle to stop the bombers. This was what the theorists had predicted before the war when the concept of strategic bombing had started to evolve. Previously, once an army had invaded another country, all the death and destruction of war had taken place on the invaded country's territory. Now, the homeland of the invader was being opened to the same horrors. Once the B-29 came, the bombers could reach Germany itself.

"Heavy fighters coming in up ahead. 12 o'clock high." The mid-upper turret gunner was first to call them in.

"Acorn reports that Tudor is strafing the Luftwaffe base at Dyagilevo. Caught Dornier 217s and Heinkel 111s taking off. Also report Heinkel 177s on the base. They're shooting the crap out of them."

"Krauts are throwing their heavy bombers in?" Cox had settled down again and was watching the twin-engined fighters above and ahead of them beginning their curve. "Dyagilevo is a heavy bomber base. What do you think they're up to, Sir?"

Cox's voice had a certain degree of contempt in it. To American eyes, anybody who could consider the Do-217 or He-111 to be heavy bombers was touched in the head. The He-177 was closer to the mark but American analysts had assessed it as a failure. There had been intelligence reports that it had major problems with its engines and a tendency to fall out of the sky without provocation. Nevertheless, as the largest German bomber around, it was a high-priority target. Cox had little doubt that the P-38s of the 343rd Fighter Squadron were spending their time destroying the 177s.

"It's Curt on the flight deck." LeMay growled. "Either evacuating the base or throwing them in the battle. We'll find out. Now watch those Ju-88s."

Ahead of the B-17 boxes, a dozen or more twin-engined fighters were starting head on attack runs. They were concentrating on the low box of the 305th's formation. The low box was the most exposed of all the formations and it normally had 21 bombers rather than the usual 18. Only, two of its B-17s had already been shot down and others were damaged. On the other hand, all of the B-17Fs received by the 305th were concentrated in the low group.

As it happened, it didn't matter. The Ju-88s approached the B-17s in a steady formation and fired air-to air rockets at the low group from well outside .50 caliber machine gun range. To LeMay's quiet and unspoken pride, none of the B-17s in the low group tried to return fire. It turned out that the Ju-88s had opened fire from outside machine gun range but also from outside the range of their own rockets. The grey streaks of smoke faltered well short of the B-17 group and plunged to earth harmlessly. The front ranks of Ju-88s peeled away and a flight behind moved up to fire its rockets with equally little effect.

"It's a caracole!" Cox was astonished by the reappearance of a tactic that hadn't been credible since the 16th century.

"What" LeMay snapped the word out. He didn't like people using arcane words when trying to explain things. Clarity and conciseness were virtues, pretentiousness was not.

"Caracole, Curt. Old cavalry tactic. The cavalry would gallop up to the enemy line and then fire pistols at them. Single-shot flintlocks. Then they'd turn away and gallop to the rear while the next rank rode up and fired. The idea was that the steady volley of pistol fire would break up the defense and let the lancers charge through. Or something like that. That's why the single-seaters are holding back; they're waiting for the rocket-shooters to break up our formation."

"Going to be a long wait, Al. Look how that low box is holding together."

"Message from Acorn. Three Tudor aircraft were lost strafing Dyagilevo but they took out almost two dozen aircraft on the ground including all six 177s. Acorn reports all their aircraft are running low on fuel and they need to return to the barn."

328

"I guess we're really on our own now." Cox was watching a formation of German twin-engined aircraft approaching from ahead. They were only a few hundred feet higher than the B-17s but they were heading directly in, pressing their attack home and holding a steady heading. That contrasted sharply with the ineffectual rocket salvoes from the Ju-88s. LeMay had a feeling that the Ju-88 heavy day fighters had felt the lash of the B-17s defensive gunfire before; the Dorniers had not. Whatever the reason, they held their course until they were directly over the lead combat box of the 40th Bombardment Wing. That was when it became obvious that the Germans were attempting a new wrinkle in their efforts to break up the B-17 formations.

The Do-217s were making an attempt at air-to-air bombing. Their bomb bays open and a cascade of small bombs tumbled out. They had obviously been equipped with time-fuses since they exploded in small gray puffs at the right altitude but well off to one side of the formation. In exchange, the upper turret gunners on the B-17s had a field day firing on the large slow targets only a few hundred feet over their heads. Two of the dozen or more 217s exploded, probably as the armor-piercing bullets ripped at the contents of their open bomb bays. Others started streaming smoke from their wing-roots and engines before losing altitude or spinning out of control.

Oddly, one Do-217, spinning downwards with both engines on fire and its crew bailing out achieved what the air-to-air bombing had failed to do. It passed through the low box of the new, partially-trained 11th Bombardment Group, causing the box to splinter as the B-17s swerved to avoid it.

A group of single-seat fighters were quick to exploit the chaos as the disrupted combat box tried to reassemble itself. For a few minutes, the B-17s in the low box were on their own and the inbound fighters tried to cut out the most vulnerable of them. Cox looked at the new wave of fighters intently. They were quite different from the 109s and 190s that had carried out the earlier attacks. "What the hell are those things?"

LeMay looked at them and the shape of the wings clicked in his mind. "They're Spitfires. British-built Spitfires. Krauts use them as trainers or give them to their allies."

Given the clue, Cox saw the strangely-shaped yellow crosses on the wings. "They're Romanian."

Despite the disruption caused by the crashing Do-217, the Romanian fighters were unable to tear up the combat box the way 190s would have done. Going by the gun flashes and streams of tracer, the Spitfires still had their original armament of eight .30 caliber machine guns and they were of only marginal value against the heavily-armored B-17s. It was only when the reassembled combat box was nearing the initial point that a crippled B-17, all four engines either dead or burning, dropped out of the box. Three of the Romanian Spitfires circled it closely but held their fire while the crew bailed out. LeMay heard the litany from his own crew.

"Tail gunner out."

"Three out of the bomb bay."

"Two out of the aft door."

"Three more out of the bomb bay.

That left only the pilot and LeMay guessed he was fighting the controls, holding the bomber steady while the crew escaped. Two of the Ju-88 heavy fighters that had put up such an ignominious display earlier were closing in on the crippled and doomed B-17. To his amazement, two of the Romanian Spitfires broke away from the bomber and flew straight at the Ju-88s, forcing them to break off their attack. Meanwhile, *Memphis Belle's* crew broke out into cheers as the last parachutes emerged from the bomber. A split second later, the aircraft went out of control and started its last long dive down.

"Damn, Curt, did you see that? Those Romanians weren't attacking that bomber, they were protecting it while the crew bailed out."

"Approaching IP. Prepare to turn to three-five-five." The navigator was clipped and unemotional. From this point on, flak would be the enemy, not enemy fighters. "Execute."

LeMay brought *Memphis Belle* around on to the final course for the bomb run. Behind him, the weary, battered column, now with 15 bombers gone but still holding the close formation that had brought the remainder to the target, made the same turn. LeMay knew that the bombardiers in the lead bombers of each combat box were searching for their target below so they could synchronize their sights on the great marshalling yards lying below the B-17s as they swept over the outskirts of Tula.

"Bombardier. I have sighted our target. Taking control of the aircraft."

"All yours." LeMay was quietly exultant. They had done it. The bombers had fought their way through to their target. It had been costly and raids like this could not often be repeated, but it could be done. Strategic air warfare had become a reality. For the enemy, it meant that nowhere within 600 miles of an American airbase was safe.

There were no individual sounds of explosions from the flak barrage. Instead, there was a continuous roar as the sky turned black around the bombers. One B-17 suddenly lurched in the air before its left wing and tail were enveloped in a sudden gout of flame. The aircraft rolled to the left as its wing structure failed under the intense heat of the fire and it spun downwards. There were no parachutes. Another lost its wing from the right hand wing root outwards, rolled over and broke up in mid-air.

The lurches as flak bursts shook the aircraft were no longer identifiable but were part of a constant vibration and the thrumming of fragments hitting the fuselage was a constant hum. Suddenly, *Memphis Belle* gave a slight lift and LeMay thought the bomber had taken a serious hit. Then, he saw the red light on the instrument panel that told him their bombs were away.

"Pilot, you have the aircraft."

"Acknowledged." LeMay turned *Memphis Belle* away from the target, towards the flight for home. Behind him, he could see a beautiful sight – huge rectangular columns of smoke rising from the huge marshalling yards. Only the novices in the 11th Group hadn't got the concentration demanded; their bombs were scattered over the town. That had been anticipated and their bombers had been loaded with large numbers of incendiaries and 250 pound bombs. Even from the great height of the B-17s, LeMay could see that Tula was already ablaze with fires and secondary explosions spreading through the streets

Reassembly Point, Over Sorokino, August 17th, 1943

"My God, do we look that bad?" Cox was looking at the formations of the 41st Bombardment Wing and they fell in behind the 40th. Multiple bombers were trailing smoke or had engines shot out. Others had bits missing. Tailplanes shot off, rudders destroyed, holes and gashes in the fuselage from fighter gunfire and flak.

The B-17 *All American* had a huge gash in its fuselage that looked as if it should have completely severed the tail. Somehow, it hadn't and the aircraft was still flying. Colonel Hall had reported that *All American* had been in a mid-air collision with a 109, probably with a wounded pilot, that had struck the B-17, tearing off the left horizontal stabilizer and left elevator. The vertical fin and the rudder had been damaged, the fuselage had been cut almost completely through connected only at two small parts of the frame and the radios, electrical and oxygen systems were damaged. There was also a hole in the top that was over 16 feet long and 4 feet wide at its widest and the split in the fuselage went all the way to the top gunner's turret.

The crew had used the webbing from their parachutes and some bits of the 109 to hold the tail in place. There was no reason why the aircraft should be flying but it was and it had even managed to complete its bomb run despite the damage.

The 40th Bomb Wing had lost 24 B-17s. Fifteen had gone down on the way to the target, six had been lost to flak over Tula and three more had been shot down on the way back. The 41st Bomb Wing had lost 32 B-17s. The double-tap raid had cost the 8th Air Division 56 aircraft and 560 crew members. There were at least a dozen more dead and many more wounded in the surviving bombers. In addition, a half-dozen P-38s and two P-47s had been lost.

"Big Friends, this is Horseback. We're joining you now. Please don't shoot at us." The red-and-white checkered noses of the 4th Fighter Group's P-47s were just about the most welcome thing Cox had ever seen.

"Big Friends, this is Roundtree. We're moving in above and behind you."

LeMay twisted in his seat and saw the green-nosed Thunderbolts of the 357th Group moving in to provide extra cover. "Welcome back, Little Friends. Good to see you."

Headquarters, 40th Bombardment Wing (Heavy), Kolosovka.

"So far the P-38s are claiming 13 aircraft shot down and another thirty shot up on the ground. The P-47s are claiming nineteen kills."

"And how many are the gunners on your B-17s claiming?" Major Gonzalez had arrived with the processed after-strike pictures. They showed massive damage at both targets although huge clouds of smoke were obscuring large parts of the Tula target area.

"Two hundred and eight-eight. Probably means we got thirty to forty." LeMay was growing increasingly cynical over the claims of the B-17 gunners. "I can't see much on the Tula pictures."

"Too much smoke. The fires down there are covering most of the city. I can tell you they are oil fires; the heavy black smoke shows us that. So, the fuel stored there has gone up and that implies the other stores there are burning as well. The yards though are complete wrecks and the fires there will finish them off. We'll send another F-5 to have a look tomorrow. Can't use *Lailani*, she is in the repair shed."

"Flak?"

"109s. That high-altitude bunch you mentioned. I had to go to thirty thousand to dodge them and they got a few licks in before we broke clear. Anyway, *Missouri Outlaw* got good shots of the Vyksa Steelworks."

"Couple of interesting things. Bombing patterns are tight but they only cover about a third of the plant. You'll have to go back and get the rest later. Also, look here to the east of the plant. See those white trails? They're on the ground. I think the krauts tried to mask the plant with smokescreens. I'm not sure whether that is intended to stop you hitting the plants or me from taking pictures of them."

"Both." LeMay put the pictures of the Vyksa Steelworks to one side and went back to the ones of Tula. "How many casualties on the ground?"

Gonzalez thought about that. "The smoke makes it hard to say but I suspect a lot. Those fuel drums piled up in the street will spread the fires and people who've taken shelter will get roasted. I think it was pretty bad down there for everybody. We could be looking at hundreds of dead, possibly thousands. Plus the six hundred we lost of course, I sure hope this raid was worth it."

"What you don't know is that Tula wasn't just a supply center and marshalling yard, it was the headquarters for most of the rail repair units in Russia. All those skilled railway engineer personnel were billeted in the areas we targeted. With luck, most of them are dead."

"We deliberately targeted civilians on the ground? That's a change in policy isn't it?"

"It is. An inevitable one. Back in Washington, a friend of mine studies these issues. He believes that taking out warmaking industry means taking out almost everything. I'm beginning to think he's right."

Gonzalez sighed. "It's a hell of a war, isn't it?"

"They all are Richard, they all are. This one is just worse than most. It'll get worse before it gets better."

LeMay paused for a second. "That brings us to another subject. I've had a request from the top. The Philippines is set to become independent in 1945 and we're building up their armed forces so they can look after themselves. Over the last few months, you've built yourself a hell of a reputation; Hap Arnold himself has his eye on you. You've turned photo-reconnaissance from an almost-forgotten niche into a weapon of strategic importance.

"Now, General Arnold wants you to go to the Philippines and take over their reconnaissance force. Watching what is happening in that area of the Pacific, especially what the Japanese are up to, is critically important so we're giving them new F-5Gs. You'll be seconded from our air force with the permanent rank of Colonel. It is a career opportunity of a lifetime."

"That'll mean leaving Russia, Sir. We haven't even started to do the job here let alone begin finishing it. It doesn't sit right with me, Sir, going home while the bomber crews are still at work."

"Richard, this war goes a long way beyond Russia and there's more to it than smashing everything we can find with a black cross on it. This posting you're being offered is important, more so than you realize now. You accept this offer now, you get all the incentives and benefits on offer. Turn it down, in a week or so, you'll get an official transfer. No incentives, no benefits. My advice is, take the offer now."

Gonzalez sighed. "I'll go pack my bags. I'm sure going miss working with you, General."

"Oh, I think we'll work together again. I'm quite sure of it." LeMay sometimes wished he could smile. He stretched out his hand instead and the two men solemnly bid each other farewell. "Good luck until we do."

CHAPTER TWELVE: REPERCUSSIONS

Headquarters, Army Group Center, Spassk-Ryazansky, Russia

"How did this happen?" Generalfeldmarschall Ernst Busch was furious, with his staff, with his command and most of all with the Americans. "We defeated the Amis in the Chuvash."

There was an uncomfortable shuffling of boots and a rustling noise as everybody present glanced at somebody, anybody, else. Eventually, General der Infanterie Gotthard Heinrici who was famed across the Heer for his complete lack of tact took the lead. "I don't think the Amis accept that is the case. Given the lamentable performance of their army, I don't think they have the experience or expertise to understand the situation they were in."

"Then how are we in this scheissloch!" Busch almost screamed the question. "What has happened?"

"Bombers, Herr General. American bombers. Their heavy bombers have destroyed all the railheads feeding the troops on the front. Their medium bombers destroyed airbases and other transport centers. Their jabos strafed and bombed all our supply lines. We cannot move in daylight without getting shot up. The only supplies that get to the front line move at night and even they are at risk from the Night Witches. Our losses in trucks and railway rolling stock have been astronomic. And yet, every day, more American fighter and bomber groups arrive. Our intelligence says the only thing slowing them down is a lack of capacity in available airbases. They are, of course, building more. We assume so anyway; they keep shooting down our reconnaissance aircraft. It would be helpful if we could shoot down theirs once in a while." Heinrici looked reproachfully at the Luftwaffe field commander who was flushed red at the remorseless exposure of the Luftwaffe's failures.

"We have done what we can." General Carl-Alfred Schumacher protested at the thinly-veiled accusations. "We have lost almost half our operational strength since the Americans arrived and replacements do not even begin to make good our losses. The replacement aircraft we receive are obsolete. Reichsminister Speer has greatly increased aircraft production but he has achieved this by standardizing on types and resisting demands for improvements. We still receive Me-109G-2 fighters armed with two rifle caliber machine guns and a single 20mm cannon. The machine guns are useless against a B-17 and it takes between 20 and 30 hits from the 20mm gun to bring down one of those bombers. We have begged for the G-6 version with a 30mm cannon since we can bring down a Flying Fortress with only five to ten 30mm hits but we are told the gun is in short supply and the G-6s are available only to special units. In the great raid yesterday, we lost almost eighty fighters and thirty bombers and claimed sixty Ami bombers. With modern fighters we should have done much better."

"Ahh yes, the great raid. How bad is the damage?" Busch had regained his equilibrium. Just.

Hans Schmidt had just completed a preliminary study of the damage from the previous day's bombing raids. Before revealing the results, he had made sure he had a clear path to the door leading out of the conference room and a good chance of getting away completely. "Gentlemen, my technicians have finished inspecting the damage to the Vyksa steelworks. Its capacity has been reduced by approximately sixty percent. The electrosteel smelting capacity has been destroyed completely and with it much of the high-performance alloy production. Once repairs start, we should have the normal steel capacity restored to seventy five percent within two months and back to pre-attack levels within three. Electrosteel capacity should be restored in phases over six months. Once, we can start repair work."

Schumacher picked up on that. "What do you mean, once you start repair work?"

"We can consider ourselves very fortunate the American raid on Vyksa dropped mostly high explosive bombs. They did much damage but what they did can be repaired. At Tula, they dropped large quantities of incendiaries and this, combined with the huge amount of fuel and ammunition backed up there, set most of the city ablaze. It is still burning and we cannot get in there to assess the damage. However, the heat of the fires is such that we can be certain that the rails have been ruined by the fires; they will have to be replaced and the old rails used for scrap. Tula is the key marshalling yard for the rail system west of Moscow. We must repair that before we can bring in the equipment we need to repair Vyksa. Unfortunately, the nearest place that can produce the rails we need is – Vyksa. We cannot repair the plant until we rebuild the yard and we can't fix the yard until we reconstruct the plant. Yesterday's raid was very well planned by people who knew exactly what they were doing."

"How did we not know it was coming? We have been alerted to impending Ami raids before." Heinrici was on form, asking questions nobody wanted to admit existed.

Schumacher drummed his fingers on the conference table. "Before, we have known there was a raid coming even if we did not know where it was going. This allowed us to ready our Jagdgeschwader and ensure the maximum number of fighters were serviceable. Let me explain. The Amis have two heavy bomber Geschwader, each with around two hundred heavy bombers. They fly those alternately so that each group flies one deep penetration mission per week and one shallow penetration per week. In other words, those heavy bombers hit us every other day. Usually, they keep a third of their strength back. Yesterday, they flew both Geschwader at once and threw every bomber they had in. We were not prepared for a raid that size."

"Why not?" Busch's question had all the quality of an armor-piercing shot from an eighty-eight.

"Because our warnings came from a spy ring we had organized inside the Soviet railway system. They would keep us advised of the quantities of aviation fuel and munitions that were arriving. American aviation fuel is higher-octane than Russian so we knew what was going where. That ring of agents has now been destroyed by Soviet counter-intelligence and the information it provided has gone." Abwehr agent Lorenz Gabler looked grim. "Herr General, the reason why this invaluable resource has been lost is something we must discuss in private."

That caused a prolonged silence. Eventually, Busch pointed at the map on the wall. "So, what do we do there?"

The silence grew, if anything, even more profound. Once again, it was Heinrici who led the charge where nobody else dared to tread. He strode over to the situation map and tapped the long salient jutting into the Chuvashskaya Bridgehead where the American 83rd Division had collapsed. That salient had started as a finger pointing at Kazan but it had been deflected south and now the finger was crooked. The fingertip was the perimeter around Kanash. "We must pull out of this salient. It is indefensible. The Amis and the Ivans are already counter-attacking at its shoulders. If we are not very careful we are the ones who will be cut off in a pocket."

"We already are." Schumacher caused a stir with that. "I am beginning to understand how the Amis think. We see this battlefield as something on the ground but they do not. They see a battlefield as three-dimensional. Where we see movement on a map, they see movement through a volume. They see going over our defenses just as viable a tactic as going through them."

That was when Schumacher suddenly stopped. He had a strange feeling that he had just said something critically important but he couldn't think what it was. The sensation left him chilled to the bone. "They have cut off that salient from the air. Completing the process with ground troops will be just a formality for them. Those troops must withdraw now; every hour they delay the evacuation will make it harder to complete."

Heinrici looked at the map again, seeing how the American and Russian forces were slowly advancing, blasting their way through the German defenses with air power and artillery. *How does the old expression go? This is a war of flesh and blood against steel and iron. Mobility, a mobile defense, is the answer to that kind of assault. Don't be where the blow is landing.* "I agree. We must pull back to our original lines. Otherwise we will lose everything in that salient."

Busch nodded in agreement. "Then, we are agreed? We will present this whole operation to the Fuhrer as a successful raid into enemy territory. A raid that is now completed and we return to our normal positions. Issue the orders. Lorenz, please wait here."

Once the conference room was empty, Busch turned to Gabler. "What happened?"

"Skorzeny happened. That's what. That commando division of his has access to all too much secret information, He found out about a load of ammunition that had been misrouted to Kazan and ordered that some of it be diverted to the Ivans defending Island Ten. He'd been tasked with seizing the place and hoped it would cause the Ivans to run out of ammunition in the middle of the battle."

"Did he have authority to do that?'

"No. He did it anyway. An Ami sailor on the gunboat delivering the ammunition spotted it was the wrong type and reported the error. The Ivans investigated and exposed our ring. A few agents, mostly women, escaped and one of them reported what had happened. We didn't quite believe it at first, the danger of double agents permeates situations like this, but there was a Pravda article this morning about the sailor in question. Usual thing, stirring tale told as an example of how carefulness and attention to detail saves lives."

"Nothing about our spy ring?"

"Nothing. Just a homily about doing one's duty and the need to show that Russians can be as meticulous as Americans. There are a lot of articles like that at the moment, extolling American virtues and how hard their men work to help defend the Rodina. That's what makes us believe it."

"Skorzeny." Busch thought for a minute or so. "I think this gives us the opportunity we've been looking for."

Headquarters, SS Jägddivision 502, Zhemkovka, West of the Samara Bridgehead.

"Sverdlovsk" Otto Skorzeny was staring at a map of eastern Russia and, in particular at two thick red lines that went from the eastern ports around Vladivostok to Kazan and Yaroslav'l. "Sverdlovsk is the key."

"Key to what, Otto?" SS-Standartenführer Stephan Bähr was used to cryptic comments from his commander. Usually, they were the first sign that some new scheme was forming in his mind.

"American supply lines. According to the Abwehr, more than sixty percent of American logistics runs from Vladivostok along the Trans-Siberian Railway. Twenty five percent is coming in by convoy across the North Atlantic into Murmansk and Archangel. The balance comes in by way of Iran. Now, we can't do much about Iran right now although the potential for stirring up trouble remains. The navy is attacking the convoys but the truth is the Canadians and British are good at beating off their submarine and air attacks. They're losing a percentage of the supplies that come that way but it's not a big percentage. In any case, the big prize is the railway. I've been looking at it and I've seen a weakness we can exploit."

"It turns out we have a really good source in Japan. Several, in fact. The Japanese know a lot about this railway for obvious reasons and our source got hold of most of it. The original line runs to the south along the Chinese border. It was single-track but the Ivans double-tracked it after their 1905 war with Japan. In 1929, they also started a second railway further north but up until mid-1941, their funding for it was sporadic. After Barbarossa, the Americans poured money and railway engineers in. Pretty obviously they anticipated the need for a secure supply line. Anyway, they built a lot of track and built it fast. That whole northern line is complete and it's double tracked as well. The Americans also built cross-connections between the two lines so they can switch around and major marshalling yards here at Khabarovsk, at Komsomolsk and all along the net. Impressive bit of construction.

"The northern line goes north of Lake Baikal; the southern line goes south of the lake. They join here, at Krasnoyarsk. Another huge set of marshalling yards. The line goes through Tomsk, Omsk and Sverdlovsk. At Sverdlovsk it splits into two routes again. One goes south by way of Kazan, the other goes north by way of Yaroslav'l. Eventually, they crossed the Volga at those points before heading to Moscow and joining there. They don't do that anymore of course, the bridges have been blown up.

"The critical bit is this stretch between Krasnoyarsk and Sverdlovsk. It's the bottleneck in the whole system. A single stretch of double-track railway with few sidings and marshalling yards. All the supplies the Americans unload at Vladivostok have to go along that railway track. That's why their build-up has been so slow, they can't get the stuff they need forward fast enough. I'll bet there are supplies and troops backed up at Krasnoyarsk that make the dumps at Tula seem poverty-stricken."

Bähr looked at the map. From this perspective, the Trans-Siberian rail network looked like an hour glass with the bulbs at east and west but a single thin neck joining them. He could see what Skorzeny was driving at. It was indeed a critical weakness. "Otto, the Amis must have seen this as well. Their Army may be pathetic but they have more experience at building long-haul railways than anybody else. I can promise you they will be fixing this bottleneck. They're probably quad-tracking it all the way."

"Don't underestimate the Amis, Stephan. They may have a vast amount to learn but they have very little to unlearn. They will get the hang of fighting this war soon enough. And, yes, they will be enlarging and quad-tracking all the way from Krasnoyarsk to Sverdlovsk. But, it's not ready now and this opens a window for us. It's 2,400 kilometers, Stephan, even the Americans cannot rebuild that length of railway overnight. But, that's not the interesting bit. This is. It's 950 kilometers from the ground we hold west of the Volga to Sverdlovsk. We can handle that distance."

"What do you mean we can handle it?" Bähr had a terrible feeling he knew where this discussion was going.

"We can deliver the division there. We can use Kondors and Ju-290s to carry paratroopers who can seize an airhead and other transports can fly reinforcements in."

"Otto, how do we get back?"

"We don't. That's the beauty of it. Once we've assembled the division and taken Sverdlovsk, we destroy everything of value there. The city is a mass of marshalling yards, railheads, factories and assembly plants. Just losing the city and its facilities will be a crippling blow to the enemy. But, that's just the start. Then, we retreat to the countryside and organize a guerilla war against the railway. Spread the whole division out into small groups and recruit local tribesmen. Train them as guerillas and give the Soviets a taste of their own medicine. The Amis won't just have to rebuild 2,400 kilometers of railway, they'll have to guard every centimeter of it as well."

This is madness! Bähr was only just barely managing to keep the horror off his face as Skorzeny fleshed out the details of his plan. *Am I expected to take this plan seriously? Is this some kind of test, to see if I will have the fortitude to point out the obvious impossibilities in this fantasy scheme? Or has the General really gone mad?*

"How many airfields are there around Sverdlovsk, Otto?"

"Four. Two south east of the city, two in the north. We can seize them easily. Here." Skorzeny handed over the pictures he had found.

Bähr looked at them carefully. *Three landing strips and one major, well-equipped airfield. The problem being, these pictures were taken in 1928. This confirms my worst fears. We are heading into this operation without any accurate, up-to-date intelligence.* "The Luftwaffe has sixty Ju-290s, the only transports we have with the range needed to get to Sverdlovsk. Over the range in question, they can carry forty eight paratroopers each. That means we are trying to seize a major industrial city with a force of three thousand men. Less than that, we'll lose at least ten percent just from drop casualties. Allowing for men who scatter on the drop and the fighting while landing, say two thousand men. We have already learned that fighting in a Russian city is a meat grinder. Two thousand men will just disappear."

"We took our airheads in Britain with less than two thousand men. We're not trying to take the whole city, Stephan, just airheads. Then we can fly in the troops who will seize the city."

And that is what really lies behind this scheme. Bähr thought. *The invasion of Britain was the one great, indisputable success of SS Jägddivision 502. We did the impossible; we seized the airheads in Southern England and held them long enough for the Luftwaffe to fly in air landing divisions to consolidate our hold. Then, with airheads already in England, we were able to attack and seize small ports and land more troops there. Yes, we pulled off the impossible; we staged a successful invasion of England. Yet, it took two years of planning and preparations and elite troops pre-positioned in key areas. Even then, the fighting was vicious and victory was in doubt right until the end. Everything else this division has attempted has either failed or been of dubious value. Otto is determined to find the one operation that will show that our success in England was not a fluke. And determination is becoming desperation.*

"Seizing the English bases was using prepositioned troops already on the ground and in place. Dropping paratroopers is a very different thing. We will need far more than a weak battalion of light infantry for each of those bases yet we lack the lift for anything more than that."

"We could use Me-323 to reinforce the lift. And the 321 gliders."

"The Gigants don't have the range to even get there, let alone get back. Also, it'll take the transports at least four hours to get there and they'll be attacked by fighters all the way. Gliders? The only effective tug we have for the Me-321s is a trio of Me-110s. They have very limited range and the operation is very dangerous. Otto, they just won't get there. It's not like England where the transport aircraft were twenty minutes flying time from our airheads and could land once they got there."

Skorzeny sighed and reluctantly accepted the inevitable. "Sverdlovsk is out then. We can't do it. But we can still try and stir up a revolt of the local population and attack the railway that way."

Bähr bit his lip. *Once, we might have done but it's too late now. In 1941 when people didn't know us and enough thought we could bring freedom from the communists for them to side with us, we could have done this. In 1942, perhaps. But this is 1943 and every Russian and every other person living here knows we mean their extermination. And then there are the Americans. They offer people a third choice, between us and the communists. A friendly choice, dispensing gifts and gold in quantities we cannot equal. In the last year we have recruited a handful of Ukrainians to help fight the partisans back there. That's all. No, Otto, this scheme will not work either.*

"We will still need long-range transports and they are in very short supply. The only one suitable is the Ju-290 and the navy get two out of every three built for long-range maritime reconnaissance. The Luftwaffe is demanding more aircraft to meet Army demands for airlifted supplies. Still, I will examine the situation and see what resources we can find. I am afraid we will have to tailor the scope of this operation to the availability of resources."

"Very well, Stephan, do that. And get a plan to me as soon as possible."

Parking Apron, Bolshaya Tarlovka Airfield, Russia.

"Welcome to Tarlovka, ladies and gentlemen." The Sergeant had boarded the C-54 as soon as it had come to a halt on the parking ramp and a set of steps rolled up to the passenger door. The aircraft had been commandeered from Western Airlines almost a year earlier and its civilian interior had been mostly stripped out in favor of payload. Its present cargo was 80 examples of the self-loading variety and were mostly sitting on the floor. It hadn't been a comfortable flight but free tickets to a Glen Miller concert were worth a little discomfort. The fact that the ticket included a twenty four hour pass, something rare for Americans and unheard-of for the Russians, was an added incentive.

"What sort of aircraft is this?" Lilya had been looking around the transport in disbelief. The fact that Americans had provided a four-engined transport aircraft just to take personnel to a concert and dance was something she could never have imagined.

"It's a C-54. A Douglas airliner that was just being introduced when the war started. The Air Force promptly took all the completed ones over and commandeered the production line. Airlines weren't very happy about that. They threatened to take legal action against the government but it didn't happen. Hold on, we're getting off."

Around them, people were getting to their feet as the aircraft started to unload. Lilya carefully gathered her overnight bag. It contained her only civilian dress and a few carefully hoarded items of make-up. Most of the Russian women on the aircraft had similar bags with equally treasured contents. In most cases, those bags represented their only remaining contact with civilian life in a pre-war world. A life that they had already guessed would have little or no place for them should they survive to return to it.

"Your aircraft back will be leaving at 1000 tomorrow. It will take off promptly at that time and anybody who isn't on it will be AWOL." The sergeant was reading from a card he had been given. "We have a recently-completed barracks block here, assigned to a B-26 group that will be arriving next week. You have been allocated rooms there. Please check your room assignments on the list pinned up in the building entrance. Any questions?"

"Sergeant, are we using the same aircraft back?" Edwards was curious about the arrangements that had been made.

"No, Sir. This bird is being fuelled up and having casualty litters installed. She'll be on her way back Stateside in three hours." The Sergeant looked at Edwards and his guest and realized they were both pilots. "She'll be stopping at Zheleznogorsk and Anadyr, then overflying the Bering Strait to Anchorage. There, she'll transfer her load to another aircraft for the flight down to Seattle, get a day's maintenance and then turn around to bring cargo back. She'll be back here in five days with 15 tons of supplies. One round trip a week. Your aircraft tomorrow will be arriving with a load of sparking plugs for R-1820s, then take you back to Airfield 108. After you disembark, it will be loading up some priority passengers from Kazan and starting the long haul home."

"Thank you, sergeant. May I ask, what were you doing before the war?"

'Airline scheduler, sir. Couldn't you guess? Now, if you'll excuse me . . .'"

Edwards and Litvyak joined the scrum of people around the pinned up lists in the new barracks building. The party from Airfield 108 were on the second floor. Edwards found his name first. "I'm in 212 with Andrews, Burwell and Cooper. The ABC Gang."

Lilya looked at him curiously. "The ABC Gang?"

"From their initials. Those three were trained on the West Coast. They hang together, always fly together and if there's something unregulation happening, they're at the back of it. Who are you with?"

"227. With tovarishchi Nadezhda Vasil'yevna, Evgeniya Maksimovna and Tatiana Timofeevna. The first two are a crew from the 588th Night Attack Regiment; I do not know the third." Lilya was hard put to stop herself laughing at the disappointed look on Edwards' face. Russians, particularly in the armed forces, had low expectations of privacy and if a couple wanted to have sex, they would do so and those around them would pretend not to notice. She doubted very much that Americans would be comfortable with that. *Well, that's his problem. If he wants it, he'll have to find a way of getting it.* "Look, it says that the concert and dance starts at 1900 in Hangar Four."

"That's good. I'll pick you up at 1845?"

"That will be perfect." Lilya smiled at him and made a kiss-kiss motion with her lips. *If that doesn't stir his creative juices, nothing will.*

Hangar Four, Bolshaya Tarlovka Airfield, Russia.

Hangar Four was new, unused and huge. It had been designed to hold four B-17Fs at a time so they could be maintained under cover during the approaching Russian winter. Three more hangars like it had already been completed and were in use, two more were still under construction. Hangar Four though was clean; there was no oil dripping on the floor to cause unwary dancers to slip, no dirt or debris to spoil the evening. A single B-17 had been towed in and placed at one end of the hangar and the band had set up underneath it. All that the party needed was for the guests to arrive.

"You look beautiful, Lilya." Edwards was speaking the truth. Litvyak had spent the time between their arrival and Edwards knocking on the door of her room getting herself ready. It had taken far longer than she had once needed for it had been literally years since she had attended a party like this.

"You mean I do not always look beautiful?" Lilya pretended to look affronted. *And so the game starts*, she thought.

Edwards was equal to that gambit. "Every day, Lilya, you are the beautiful huntress who find the fascist beasts and kills them. Tonight, you are the beautiful princess, admired and envied by all."

"Nice catch-and-serve, Monty." Lieutenant Nick Rogers was a P-39 pilot from Borisoglebskoye, also the home base for the 588th. He was escorting Nadia Vasil'yevna while another P-39 pilot from the same base had Zhenya Maksimovna on his arm. If one ignored the USAAF "pinks and greens" uniforms, they looked like any other young couple out for the evening. The others were different. The man was Charles Schultz, obviously a USAAF officer but he had the distinctive bearing and character of a mustang, an enlisted man who had received an officer's commission. His guest was Tatiana Timofeevna. Obviously the two were friends yet where the other three couples were holding each other, the woman clasping the man's arm or his arm round her waist, Schultz and his guest walked beside each other, close but never quite touching.

It was the perfect time in the evening, there was still enough light for clear visibility yet the approaching dusk had softened and tinged the air with calm. It wasn't even civilian twilight yet but the promise of night was already evident. Lilya lifted a finger. "Any time now."

That was when a faint drone could be heard from the east. The runway lights flicked on, adding grounded stars to the approaching night. Far off in the east, Edwards saw the flashing of navigation lights. They never seemed to move and for a moment he thought he had made the classic night-flyers error of mistaking Venus for another aircraft. Then, the flashing lights did seem to move, accelerating until they resolved into a C-54 on its final approach, The transport touched down, its engines roaring as the pilot reversed pitch, then it turned away on to the transport aircraft parking apron. The runway lights vanished and the world went back to its pre-twilight calm. Around the transport, unloading crews were already surrounding the aircraft.

"Every hour, on the hour." Lilya sounded subdued. The precision of the American transport operation was even more impressive than its scale. After flying for two days with three intermediate stops, the transports were arriving almost with clockwork regularity.

"Twenty four hours a day, tovarish Lilya." Rogers spoke quietly so he wouldn't sound boastful. "Three hundred or more tons of priority cargo every day. Douglas is working triple shifts to build as many C-54s as they can."

Despite the distance separating the base from enemy-held territory, the black-out was still in place and the slowly gathering dusk was beginning to turn the buildings into shadows. The main doors of Hangar Four were closed but two side doors were open with military police checking the documents of those lined up to enter. There were also three White M3 scout cars parked nearby; two with .50 machine guns, one with a 37mm anti-tank gun. Edwards looked at two of the military policemen by the scout cars. "We expecting trouble?"

"No, Sir. We're too far behind the lines for any real possibility of attack. But, General LeMay insisted we set up a guard perimeter just in case and treat it as a base security training exercise. We got live ammunition though."

Edwards noted two other things; one was the hum of a portable generator in the background, making him guess that the power supply to the hangar hadn't proved adequate for the demands of the concert. The other was the unmistakable smell of roasting beef was drifting across the parking apron. Edwards smiled to himself; he had been expecting that as soon as he had seen 'refreshments' between the formal concert and the dance that would follow it.

He had anticipated one problem that would emerge and had already taken some countermeasures.

Inside, the Glenn Miller Orchestra was already in place and tuning up for the concert. By the time everybody had taken their seats, they were ready to go. To a roar of applause, Glen Miller appeared from a side door, looking rather diffident and shy. Yet, with every step he took towards the podium in front of his band, he gained presence and authority so that by the time he picked up his baton, there was no doubt as to who was in charge. He rapped his baton sharply on the podium and silence fell on the improvised concert hall. He turned to the audience, bowed slightly and then addressed them. "Comrades, welcome to this concert and thank you for coming tonight. I would also like to thank the officers of the United Service Organization's Camp Shows program who worked long hours to make tonight's concert possible."

He then turned back to his band, rapped the baton again and ordered, "Gentlemen, prepare to play, 'St Louis Marching Blues.'"

As the last notes of the opening instrumental died away, the music segued to 'Moonlight Serenade' and then to 'In the Mood', 'Tuxedo Junction', 'Pennsylvania 6-5000' and 'Chattanooga Choo Choo' before ending with 'A String of Pearls', 'At Last' and finally 'Kalamazoo', When Edwards glanced at his watch, he was shocked to see than forty minutes had passed while he had been wrapped up with the music and Lilya's head resting on his shoulder. In the silence that briefly existed between the last chords of music and the thunderous applause from the audience he could hear another C-54 landing. 2000 hours.

"The band is going to have a quick break now. I'll let you into a musical secret; playing wind instruments really dries the throats of the musicians and the only thing that can keep their mouths and throats moist enough to continue playing is beer." Glen Miller paused for a beat. "Well, that's what they tell me. Anyway, we have three ladies who'll be singing with us in the second part so I'd like you to welcome Miss Anne Shelton and Miss Dinah Shore. I would also like you to give a great hand to comrade Klavdia Shulzhenko currently appearing at her season in Petrograd but who has made a special trip in an A-20 to sing for us here tonight."

Miller paused while the applause died down. "Now, while we get sorted out, Miss Dinah Shore and her quartet will give a short recital."

Edwards wasn't familiar with the tune from Dinah Shore's backing quartet and he hadn't heard the song before. But, as the singer's voice soared over the audience he found a lump forming in his throat.

"There'll be bluebirds over the banks of the Volga,
Tomorrow, just you wait and see.
There'll be love and laughter and peace ever after.

Tomorrow, when the world is free
The shepherd will tend his sheep.
The valleys will bloom with grain.
And Sasha will go to sleep
In his own little room again.
There'll be bluebirds over the banks of the Volga,
Tomorrow, just you wait and see."

Edwards slipped a look sideways towards Lilya and saw that tears were running down her face. *After more than two years of war, peace must seem an impossible dream. We've been here three months and it does to us. Before I left for Russia, pop and I had a long talk over his special bottle of whiskey. He'd been a doughboy in the first war and he passed advice on from a veteran to a new arrival, not as a father to a son. One thing he told me was that the only way to stay sane was to look on oneself as the walking dead. He said that living and dying isn't the real issue, staying sane is. Those who cling to life become consumed with fear of death and their wits get clouded. If you accept that you died the moment you arrived on the front line, then you can accept everything that happens while your wits stay sharp. He said to take each day as a gift that probably won't be repeated and make the most of it. Yet, we need to be reminded why we are here sometimes and that's what has just happened.*

"Now, comrades, a big hand for Miss Dinah Shore and her string quartet. Our wind section being suitably refreshed, we can carry on with the second half of our recital. To start with, we'd like to play for you the current number one single on the Billboard Record Chart for the last three weeks. Gentlemen, we will start with Cossack Patrol sung by Klavdia Shulzhenko ."

The first chords from the orchestra were instantly recognizable and brought a gasp from the Russians present. The traditional Russian 'Cossack Patrol' had been reset to swing music and scored for an American-style big band. After the opening instrumental, Klavdia Shulzhenko's clear voice swelled out to fill the hangar. Behind her voice, Edwards could hear a humming noise that kept perfect time with the music. A glance at Lilya told him it was the Russians in the audience proving a base note that rounded out the performance. As the tune ended, the orchestra switched to an arrangement Edwards didn't recognize.

"Tachenka." Lilya whispered, "Machine-gun Cart."

The Russians make fantastic military music Edwards thought. Then he noticed that as the music for Tachenka died away, the lights were dimming. The last few notes sounded a signal for a group of spotlights mounted in the roof to flick on. Each spotlight was trained on one of the defensive gun positions on the Flying Fortress. Edwards noted that the guns had been mounted for the show; usually they were stored in the armory. The bit of theater was met by a barrage of whistles, cheers and foot-stamping. By the time it had subsided, the orchestra had segued into its next song.

> *"One of our planes was missing, two hours overdue*
> *One of our planes was missing with all its gallant crew*
> *The radio sets were humming they waited for a word*
> *Then a voice broke through the humming and this is what they heard:*
> *We're comin' in on a wing and a prayer, comin' in on a wing and a prayer*
> *Thought there's one motor gone we can still carry on*
> *comin' in on a wing and a prayer."*

That astonished Edwards. From the moment American troops had started to arrive in Russia, they'd been told that Russia was an atheist society and they were to keep quiet about religion. Yet, even in the short time he had been in the country and the limited perspective he had of it, he could sense that the old religious practices were still there. Even so, the blatant references in the song were completely unexpected.

Lilya noticed his confusion. Sometimes, although she had been too well-brought up to admit it, his political naivety annoyed her. "Misha, you can be very sure every song at this concert has been approved by everybody at every level."

While the first half of the concert had been entirely instrumental, the second part had the orchestra accompanied by one or more of the singers. America and Russian melodies were mixed together and, once again, Edwards lost track of time. He felt an almost physical sense of loss when finally the program ran to its end.

"Comrades. We will need about thirty minutes to clear the floor for dancing. There are refreshments being served outside, courtesy of the Texas Cattlemen's Association and the Coca Cola Company. It's just a few minutes before 2100; the dance will begin at 2130 and end at 2300. We have to clear the hangar then; it will be needed for operational purposes tomorrow.

Meaning a B-17 raid is going out. Even after losing sixty bombers in a single mission, the Flying Fortresses are going back in. I just hope to God, we're there to take them all the way in. It makes us sick to leave them unescorted.

The Texas Cattlemen's Association had done the concert proud and the base cooks had stretched their skills to the utmost. The standing rib roasts had obviously been top-quality to start with and they had been roasted with skill and tender attention. One of the cooks was starting to carve, the paper-thin slices falling on to a strategically-positioned serving plate. Another was slicing loaves of bread while a third was peeling portions off a huge wheel of cheese. It looked like the USO had done the concert party proud. Unfortunately, as the expression on Lilya's face showed, there was a problem. A freshly-cooked roast beef sandwich was bound to be drippy and meat juices falling on a dress would leave stains that would never come out.

"Will this help, Lilya?" Edwards reached into his jacket and pulled out a large sheet of Nibroc paper he had scrounged from one of the maintenance benches. It was 26 inches wide and 30 long. It was easily large enough to allow Lilya to eat a sloppy sandwich without ruining her only dress. Nibroc paper was also processed to resist oil so was unlikely to break while used. The Corbin Paper Company almost certainly had never envisaged this use for their product but it was about to save the day. Some of the quicker-witted of the men around the sandwich bar were already on their way to the engine repair shops to get rolls of the paper. The Mess Sergeant was also sending some of his minions to do the same.

"How would you like your beef, Sir?" The cook assembling the Edwards' sandwich was piling an inordinate amount of meat on to the bread. In the background, the mess minions had arrived with a large roll of Nibroc paper. One immediately set to work cutting off 30 inch lengths while the others went back to the maintenance shops for another roll. "You've saved our necks, Lieutenant. All the planning that went into tonight's concert and nobody thought of that problem. More sandwiches for you and your lady?"

Edwards glanced over his shoulder and saw Lilya nodding emphatically. "Thank you, Sergeant. Another very rare and one well-done please."

"Here you go, Sir. When you get to the Coke cooler, tell the corporal there I sent you and he'll slip you two an extra bottle or so."

Lilya looked at the black contents of the Coca-Cola bottle with a degree of suspicion. "Drink up Lilya, that's America's national drink."

She tried the contents and looked thoughtful. "So sorry, but it lacks something. I know!"

She reached into her bag, pulled out a flask of vodka and poured a good shot into her Coca-Cola bottle and then added some to Edwards' drink. He tried it and had to admit the vodka had made the Coke – interesting. "Lilya, do you Russians go *anywhere* without a large supply of vodka?"

She thought about that for a moment and came to a carefully-considered opinion. "No."

Behind them, another C-54 touched down and taxied away.

By the time two more C-54s had arrived, the dance was ending. What had started as a formal dance with classical steps had slowly settled down to a nightclub shuffle in which the couples moved slowly, more or less in time with the music, with the woman's arms locked around her partner's neck. Schultz and Tatiana Timofeevna were the only exceptions; they were still in the classic dancing pose with a small but distinct gap between them. Lilya caught Edwards looking at them and whispered in his ear. "I have seen this before. She has been raped, many, many times. So much so that she cannot bear to be touched. She is fortunate that she has found a man with whom she feels safe and secure, doubly fortunate in that he is a good man who understands her needs and does not put pressure on her. And so, he has become the rock on which she tries to rebuild her life."

It was the last dance. Glen Miller once more returned to his podium with the now familiar rap of his baton. "I am sorry, Comrades, but we must now bring this evening to a close. Thank you once again for coming. Now, gentlemen, we will play The Internationale, followed by the Star-Spangled Banner."

Walking back to the accommodation block, they stopped to look at the stars scattered across the dark blue sky, Lilya pointed upwards at one group of stars. "That's Vodoley."

"We call it Aquarius." That was the start and they were soon pointing the constellations to each other, exchanging their names in American and Russian. "What do you call that one?"

"Bol'shoy Pos." The game was interrupted by another C-54 arriving. The one aircraft every hour rate was being held with a degree of precision that Lilya found both heartening and deeply disturbing. It was good to know that the Rodina had such a powerful ally but quantity of military equipment that was pouring into her homeland and the wealth it implied showed how far behind the times her country had drifted. *What happens if peace comes and they refuse to leave? Will we not have replaced an invader with an overlord? And if Americans are so clever, why has he not found somewhere we can go so he can spread me?*

In fact, it was that very issue that was preoccupying Edwards at that very moment. His first idea had been to 'borrow' a B-17 but all the available aircraft had ground crews working on them. That had left the possibility of disappearing into the open ground between the runways and the parking apron but he'd already seen several other couples heading that way. He was also sure that Lilya didn't want to get grass stains on her clothes. "Lilya, perhaps we should go into the barracks? So you can change out of your dress?"

"You mean so you can get me out of my dress?" Lilya looked at him sideways. "It will be hard to find somewhere to ourselves there."

In fact, the solution to the problem was much easier than Edwards had anticipated. Passing Room 212 he saw a note stuck to the door with a large M scrawled on the front. He opened it and burst out laughing, before reading the message to Lilya. "Monty, we're bunking elsewhere tonight. So, you'll have the room to yourself. Or perhaps not. The ABC Gang."

He opened the door and Lilya slipped through after him, closing it behind her. She took a quick breath and let it out while her fingers started to unfasten the buttons down the front of her dress. "Promise me one thing Misha. Promise me you won't get killed for at least three months."

He slid his arms around her waist, under the dress now hanging loosely from her shoulders. "Before I came to Russia, my father gave me some advice. He said that he had learned in the trenches to take each day as a gift that probably won't be repeated and to make the most of it. Whatever tomorrow brings, Lilya, we have tonight and that is a gift beyond price."

Headquarters, SS Regiment "Germania", Kanash, Chuvashskaya Bridgehead.

SS-Standartenführer Kurt Meyer had received his orders from divisional command. They stated that he was to withdraw his regiment from Kanash starting that night and retreat to the original pre-offensive positions 'with maximum possible speed'. As would be the case with any competent officer, his first action had been to call his senior NCO to discuss how the orders could be best achieved. And so, SS-Sturmscharführer Johannes Gottschalk had been summoned to Meyer's office to join the staff meeting.

"If were able to retreat directly back to Oraushi, it would be 40 kilometers. Only, we can't do that. There are no roads on that route and if we try to go cross-country, we would be slowed to a crawl. We've lost a lot of trucks already and many of the ones that are left have little cross-country ability. We have to follow the roads. That means we have to pull back 50 kilometers. I propose we use the trucks to tow our guns and mortars and to carry as many of the men as possible. The rest can ride on the tanks and assault guns. Gottschalk, how soon can we move?"

"If we start loading up now, Herr Standartenführer, we should be able to move by 2200. That will give us seven hours to dawn. Assuming we do not run into any trouble, we should be able to make a good start in getting back to our original lines. But, Herr Standartenführer, I must draw your attention to a problem. We have well over four hundred American Army prisoners of war. We have no transport to move them and we cannot march them back to our lines. And there is something else as well. . . "

"Speak up, Gottschalk, that's why you are here."

Kazan Thunderbolts

"Sir, the men have been heard discussing how it is better to be taken prisoner by the Americans than the Russians. That to be taken prisoner by the Americans means sitting out the rest of the war in comfort."

"I see. We must discourage that attitude from spreading. I think, perhaps, getting rid of those prisoners would be a good start in doing so. One that would solve many other problems as well. See to it, Sturmscharführer."

Large field west of Karmamei, Chuvashskaya Bridgehead.

"Attention American Prisoners of War. We will soon start moving you to the railway yard at Lesnik. From there you will be taken by train to PoW camps in eastern Germany. The first group of five trucks will be arriving shortly. Each group will take 100 prisoners. Gather any belongings you might have now so we can load quickly." Gottschalk climbed down from the back of the Kubelwagen and put down the loudhailer he had been using. He had to admit to himself that after the humiliations he had suffered at the hands of the Americans, this assignment was giving him great personnel pleasure.

Generations of feuding in the Appalachian Mountains had given PFC Jasper Robson a keen sense of danger and it was screaming warnings at him. He looked around the field that had been the temporary American PoW camp outside Kanash for the last couple of days. His eyes took in the six foot high stone walls and the fact there was only one gate out. It had obviously been used as a stock pen at one time. Almost by instinct, he picked out somewhere a bit safer than the rest of the field, somewhere a man might take cover when everything went to hell. He settled on a small pit close to one of the stone walls, one that seemed to have a concrete pipe or something running from it. As inconspicuously as possible, he started to drift over to it.

"I don't like the look of this, George." Lt Col William E Long was beginning to believe that surrendering had been the worst mistake he had ever made.

"They say they're going to take the first hundred out in a few minutes but they haven't started to separate them out yet." Major George Barndollar was used to dealing with administrative matters as the battalion exec and what he was seeing wasn't how it was done.

The same thought had occurred to Hill, Curtis and Martin. The word that they were being moved out had left them profoundly unimpressed. There was something about the way the SS man had spoken that made them distrust everything he said. So, they drifted over to where the four nurses had made themselves a small lean-to. "Ma'am, we don't like this. If things go to hell, we'll try and boost you over the wall so you can get clear. If we manage it, run for the woods and keep running. No matter what happens, don't stop."

"What about you three?" First Lieutenant Dorothy Hopkins was forced to ask the question. In her heart, she knew there was no way this was going to end well.

"We'll do what we can ma'am. Let's hope it doesn't come to that."

"There's the first group of trucks." Sergeant Jeremy Perry pointed at the small column of trucks that was pulling up outside the field. He recognized them as British-built AECs, a sound cross-country truck that featured many small but ingenious forms of sabotage from its manufacturers. The trucks stopped in a line along the road, then backed up so their rear drop-gate was close to the stone wall. Then, the canvas tilt was rolled up to reveal the water-cooled M'08 machine gun and crew in the back of each.

Private Eugene Searle was one of the first to realize the ghastly truth. He was close to the line of trucks and in the middle of the field, far from any possible hint of cover. It was his position in the middle of the field that bought him a few instants of extra time. The SS machine gunners had started their fusillade of fire from the sides of the crowded mass of American prisoners and worked towards the center. For a split second, when the slow, relentless hammering of the water-cooled machine guns started, he thought that he was hearing road work in progress. It was only when he saw the men at the edges of the group start to go down that he realized what was happening. Sheer disbelief took the few heartbeats that were left. By the time Searle started his desperate attempt to get away, it was too late. A dozen or more bullets cut him down and left him lying on his back in the mud. Almost instinctively he rolled over and reached out for his bazooka so he could take down one of the trucks but there was no strength left in his arms.

Sergeant Jeremy Perry was much faster on the uptake. He dropped flat as the first pass of the machine guns reached him and the bullets passed over his head. As soon as they had swept over him, he was on his feet and running towards the trucks by the wall. There really was no point in running any other way and his only thought was to try and get at least one lick in before the machine gunners killed him. He did it; he had picked up a rock and he hurled it at the crew in the back of the nearest truck. He thought he heard the clang as the rock hit the steel helmet of one gunner before the sweeping arcs of gunfire cut his legs out from under him. As he bled to death on the ground, all he could think was that this wasn't how soldiers were supposed to die.

Lieutenant Irwin Grisham saw his Sergeant go down as the streams of tracer fire from the machine guns criss-crossed the field. There was little he could at that point; he had the feeling that the gunners had been told to kill the officers first. He started to run one way, changed his mind and started in different direction and then changed his mind again. He was hit before he had made any

Kazan Thunderbolts

significant move in any direction. He was still trying to think of the order that would get his men out of this as he died.

Hill, Curtis and Martin fulfilled their promise. Their first action when the gunfire started was to grab hold of First Lieutenant Dorothy Hopkins and try and thrust her over the six foot stone wall. They had boosted her up to the top and started to push another nurse up to join her when their attempt to escape was spotted. Two of the machine guns broke their long, methodical sweeps and concentrated on the lean-to and the knot of figures around it. The three men were standing erect and virtually motionless when the concentrated fire hit them. The nurse they were lifting didn't live any longer than those trying to help her; she was in the worst possible position and the bullets tore into her chest. Hopkins was three quarters over the wall when her legs and hips were struck by a dozen bullets or more. She slid back down to join the bodies of the men who had tried to save her and watched helplessly from the ground as the slaughter continued.

Lt. Col. William E Long knew he was dead; the machine gunners would kill him first. He'd been in the army long enough to know that the Hollywood picture of men dying from gunfire was hopelessly wrong. They didn't go flying around or make dramatic gestures. They simply lost all the strength in their bodies and crumpled to the ground. He felt as if his legs had ceased to exist, as if there was nothing between his knees and the ground. He felt the impact as he hit the ground face-first and that was all.

Beside him, Major George Barndollar went down at almost exactly the same time. His first instinct had been to try and get as much distance between himself and the machine guns as possible but he simply never had the time. He had only half-completed his turn when a group of bullets hit him in the head. He was dead before he hit the ground.

Corporal Larson's last thought was that he hoped the German gunners hadn't done their paperwork properly. As company clerk, he thought he would feel properly avenged if they'd screwed up the ammunition requisition and got court-martialed. He'd heard the German Army was very strict on doing its paperwork properly. Suddenly, as he fell face-first to the ground, he was completely and totally sure that they had indeed screwed up their paperwork.

Private Colin Green was unaware of Larson's last thoughts. He was, however, absolutely sure in his own mind that the fascists would pay for what they had done today. That the U.S. armed forces would mark this day down and never stop hunting the people responsible. That was when he remembered the time he had an in-growing toenail treated at a Navy Hospital in Starry May. One of the nurses had come from the Apache Nation and he remembered her wolfish smile. The smile seemed to grow in menace and gain a radiant glow in his memory before it faded away to blackness.

354

PFC Solomon Yablonski had never had any illusions about surviving captivity. He knew it wasn't a question of whether he would be killed but when and how. The Army had offered him a false set of identity tags that identified him as one Samuel Yates, an Episcopalian but he had refused them and the ones he wore bore his own name and the Star of David. His reply to the machine guns echoed across the field.

> *Exalted and hallowed be God's great name*
> *in the world which God created, according to plan.*
> *May God's majesty be revealed in the days of our lifetime*
> *and the life of all Israel -- speedily, imminently, to which we say Amen.*
> *Blessed be God's great name to all eternity.*

Solomon Yablonski died praising his God and asking for His blessings upon the comrades who were dying alongside him.

PFC Jasper Robson nearly made it to the hideout he had picked. Nearly, but he was just a few feet short when a burst of machine gun bullets raked across his back. He went down, tried to crawl a few feet further but all his strength had gone. As he died, he could almost bring himself to feel sorry for the Germans who had just started a generations-long blood-feud with the entire population of Appalachia.

Lieutenant Jake Fuller really missed his tank. Even though the Shermans had proved grossly inadequate against the massive, heavily-armored Tigers, one Sherman and five men could turn this whole situation around. He could see the crowd of American PoWs thinning rapidly as the water-cooled machine guns did their work. He started to run for the closest of the stone walls, not with any hope of surviving but simply to irritate the German gunners by making their job more difficult. As he ran, he felt the strange thuds in his side and ahead he thought he could see *Old Tinny* waiting for him.

Private Ronald Newman never stood a chance. Badly wounded and almost immobile, he went down with dozens of bullets plowing into him. For all that, he was fortunate. The SS troops had already burned down the American field hospital in Kanash with its patients still inside it.

Lieutenant Harold Richards had already experiences the attitude of the SS troops. When they had found he had smashed the radios in his forward artillery observer's jeep and burned all the code books, they had been extremely angry. He had the bruises and other injuries from the beatings they had handed out to prove it. One thing the SS had never asked him was how much artillery the American Army had brought with it. Richards thought that it would be a nice surprise for them.

Kazan Thunderbolts

Sergeant Adam Doyle saw his officer being cut down by the relentless sweeping of the heavy machine guns. He was one of the last men to be hit. His one thought was that he would show these damned Hitlerites how a true Irish-American died. His shout of "May the Lamb of God stir his hoof through the roof of heaven and kick you in the arse down to hell" echoed across the field before the machine guns cut him down as well.

SS-Sturmscharführer Johannes Gottschalk jumped down from the Kubelwagen and looked across at the bodies strewn all over the field. "You men, check every body; make sure they are all dead. There's nothing I hate more than survivors."

Headquarters, Army Group Center, Spassk-Ryazansky, Russia

"SS-Brigadeführer Skorzeny, we are here to discuss the future operations of SS-Jagddivision 502." There had been furious competition amongst the headquarters staff of Army Group Center to chair this meeting with Skorzeny. General Heinrici had won by complete lack of charm, inordinate guile and knowing where all the bodies were buried.

"You have read my proposal for an assault upon the Trans-Siberian railway?" Skorzeny thought than Stephan Bähr had come up with a plan that was insufficiently daring given the resources that would have to be committed and the gains that could be made. Nevertheless, it was probably the one that stood the best chance of being accepted.

"We have." Heinrici sounded magisterial. "We assumed you were drunk when it was assembled. In that, it shows much resemblance to the other plans generated by SS-Jagddivision 502. Operations that are so badly planned they are ineffectual or require major commitments of resources that are badly needed elsewhere. In most cases, your demands for those resources has prevented other elements of the Heer from carrying out operations of much greater significance. In examining the operations of SS-Jagddivision 502 over the last year, we are forced to the consideration that your formation's presence in Russia is a net negative for our strategic position."

"What about England?" Skorzeny was only just keeping control of his temper. "Without our assistance, we would still be stuck on the French coast and Britain might well have rejoined the war against us!"

"Even if that were true, Fall Seesäugetier was last year. What have you achieved *this* year? Let us see. An attack on a truck convoy that failed. A simple task any unit of the Heer could have achieved. An attack on a defended island. A difficult mission to be sure but your failure was total. The attack on the Ami gunboat base at Staraya Mayna. Not just a failure but a major victory for the Amis and Ivans. I will tell you what you have achieved this year, SS-Brigadeführer Skorzeny, one failure after another. The cost to us has already

356

been too great to continue. Now you want us to commit our entire long-range airlift to a guerilla war against a stretch of railway. To add this to the list of strategic assets that have been lost due to your inflated opinions of your own importance. Had your command had a long record of success, we might consider it. SS-Jagddivision 502 has no such record."

"What about England?" Skorzeny's voice sounded as if he was chewing concrete.

"Even a blind pig can find a truffle now and then. Your division achieved nothing before Fall Seesäugetier and has achieved nothing after it. We are suffering from the consequences of your actions now. Without any authority and without any consideration of the consequences, you endangered the operations of a spy ring on the east bank of the Volga that was feeding us vital information. You didn't just endanger it, you get it destroyed, depriving us of vital operational information. The great American air raid just a few days ago succeeded because we had no idea an operation of that magnitude was planned."

Heinrici looked down at his papers and tried to hide the ghoulish delight in his voice. "It has been decided that the entire concept that lies behind SS-Jagddivision 502 is fallacious. We also note that both Heer and SS formations are desperately short of manpower. We cannot afford to have an entire division of our best soldiers sitting behind the lines doing nothing most of the time and failing when they do try to achieve something. SS-Jagddivision 502 is disbanded as of now. The orders and reassignments are already going out to your sub-commanders.

"SS-Brigadeführer Skorzeny, you are being transferred to Army Group Vistula where work will be found for you. I assume that this will be linked to the continuing attack on Petrograd. Look on this return to mainstream military operations as a chance to redeem your sorely-tarnished reputation. You may leave."

Skorzeny stormed out of the meeting. Heinrici grinned to himself and picked up the telephone. "Hans, I will have a wienerschnitzel for my luncheon, with a bottle of the good white wine. Now send in SS-Standartenführer Stephan Bähr."

Once again, Heinrici made great play of reading a file when Bähr entered his office. "Sit down, Stephan. Now, if you have not already heard, SS-Jagddivision 502 is disbanded and its officers and men will be dispersed amongst regular formations. Why do you think this division was a failure?"

"Because it was too large and its objectives were excessively grandiose. There are occasions when an operation of the scale envisaged for SS-Jagddivision 502 would indeed have major strategic impact but they are very rare. Probably, Fall Seesäugetier was the only one we will see in this war. 502

Kazan Thunderbolts

was oversized; commando units need to be small and the men carefully chosen. In 502 there was a constant drive to justify our size and requirements and that meant we took on operations that were ill-planned and unsuited to the nature of the force."

"That agrees with our assessment." Heinrici sat back in his chair, apparently considering military options but actually anticipating his wienerschnitzel. "Stephan, there is a role for a commando unit that can undertake special operations but not a whole division. Army Group Center has elected to replace SS-Jagddivision 502 with a company-sized force, no more than 100 officers and enlisted men. It will operate under strict control, reporting directly to Army Group Center Command. This is a smaller unit than your rank entitles you but it may well be the last chance a commando unit has to prove its worth in our armed forces. It needs a good man, one with a sense of realism, to command it. Would you take on this post?"

Bähr didn't even hesitate. "Yes, Sir."

"Good man. Why don't you stay to lunch? I believe Wienerschnitzel is on the menu, with one of our better bottles of wine."

"Thank you, Sir. That would be most enjoyable." Bähr, smiled to himself; wienerschnitzel was his all-time favorite dish.

Officers Quarters, 360th Fighter Squadron, Airfield 108, Privolzhskiy na Volga.

My Dearest Mom and Pop, August 22, 1943

Mom, it's been a long, long time since I last wrote to you. I'm really sorry about that and I will try and do better in future. I'm not allowed to tell you where we are based other than that we're on the Volga Front. That tells you nothing since the Volga is more than two thousand miles long so I suppose that's why we're allowed to say so. Censorship is very strict; everything we write is read by censors and if we step out of line, the letter gets sent back to us with a tail-chewing. Pop will tell you it was the same in the Great War I guess.

First thing you want to know is that I'm healthy, unhurt and doing real well. I got promoted to First Lieutenant a few days ago and they're going to give me a Silver Star. Please be careful if a reporter from the local boiler sheet talks to you about the award. Just say I am in a Fighter Sq. 'Somewhere in Russia'. Mom, to give you an honest answer to the question you asked, yes, what we are doing here is dangerous. The Hitlerites are skilled and very experienced. The good news is that we've been superbly trained, we are well-led and our aircraft are much better than theirs. Best of all, our Russian bratishka have all the experience they've gained in three years of war and they pass on everything they know.

The living conditions here were pretty rough when we started. We had tarpaper shacks and that was all. Since then, the Army engineers are everywhere building away like beavers. Not long ago, we moved into new barracks and boy, are they a swell place. They're built of stone, real stone just like some sort of castle. Why stone? Well, there's a lot of it here so it's cheaper building material than brick and the local workmen know how to do stone.

I'm sharing a room with three other officers, George, Will and Terry. They're great guys, absolutely the best. All three come from the West Coast. The Russians we work with every day are great people. Nobody here had much to start with and they've have lost almost everything because of the war. Yet, they see one of us; they will give us whatever they have because we are their guests and their allies. They will go hungry to give us a crust of bread. They also have this sense of humor that is hard to describe. A Russian joke doing the rounds here is about a worker who is captured by the fascists. He immediately volunteers to work for them saying he would rather work for a hundred fascists than one American. Every time he is asked, he keeps saying he would rather work for a hundred fascists than one American. Eventually, somebody asks him what his job is and he answers, "I dig graves."

The Army looks after us pretty well and we get all of the basic stuff we need. You asked about what I wanted so you could send some parcels. Well, shaving stuff would be nice, the army soap is bad and I keep cutting myself. Fresh-knitted new socks are always golden; it can get cold up high. We get plenty of food but it's the same every day so candy, dried sausages or jerky will always be appreciated. We don't really go off-base so recreation items like decks of playing cards, small books or copies of the Bible will help us a lot. The last probably surprises you; we had to leave everything like that behind because we thought the Russians wouldn't like us having them. The truth is, they don't care very much. And family pictures, please. If the kids do drawings, I'd love to see them as well. Some of the guys have kids and we pin the pictures they draw up in the O-Club. A new picture from the kids back home is cause for a party. When our Russian comrades come to our O-Club, they go straight to the picture wall to see the latest arrivals.

OK, Mom. Here it comes. After I fly a mission, I take out the pictures you sent me of our family, spread them out on my bed and just sit there looking at them. Well, we'll have to take a new set now because there's one more person to be added to the family picture. You see, I got a girl over here. She's Russian of course. Her name is Lilya and she comes from a town outside Moskva. This is serious so you obviously want to know about her. Well, Lilya is 23 years old 'a daughter of workers and peasants' which is the Russian way of saying 'an average family'. She looks very Russian, a squarish face with short, tightly curled blonde hair and grey eyes. She can look very serious most of the time but her whole face lights up when she smiles. Like most Russians here on our base, she speaks fluent English. Most importantly, she is a fighter pilot just like me. She first soloed when she was 14. Now, she flies a Yak and has 24 kills. I'll send you some pictures as soon as they are passed by the censor.

Pop, I never really thanked you properly for all the advice you gave me before I left. It was all good and has helped me a lot. You were so right; people who haven't been here can't imagine what it is like. Just please make sure Mom knows that I really am fine and things do look good over here. We rule the sky our side of the Volga, and the fascists have stopped trying to say otherwise. When we first came here, they were very aggressive and tried to attack us whenever they could. Not anymore. Now, they run and hide in the clouds when they see Thunderbolts coming. We're taking the battle to the enemy. I mean we are hunting them and making them pay for everything they have done here. We were novices when we came here but now we are fully trained and just want to be sure we are doing our part.

I hope all is ok at home. Tell everyone hello for me. I remain.

Your loving son,

Monty

"You didn't tell your mother that George, Will and Terry move out whenever they can so we could have the room to ourselves for a while." Lilya had been touched by the other officers' gesture. She saw it as an act of supreme generosity, one that must have required immense effort to get the stamp of official approval.

The fact that they just went ahead and did it without getting approval had never occurred to her. Or that when Major Young had spotted the unofficial change, he'd just smiled and shrugged. Later a quiet word had come down *'be where you are supposed to be when you are supposed to be there and doing what you are supposed to be doing. For the rest, use common sense.'*

She was lying on the bed, reading Edward's letter home and quietly smiling to herself at all the things he was leaving unsaid. "There is another version of the story about the grave digger you know."

"What's that Lilya?"

"A woman of the town is selling her body for a kopek each to the Hitlerites. Eventually, one of her customers gives her the kopek and asks why she charges so little. She tells him that she would rather service one hundred fascists a night for a kopek each than a single American for ten thousand dollars. Again, he asks her why? And she replies 'because I have syphilis.'"

Edwards burst out laughing. "That's good, but I can't tell it to Mom. Pop perhaps. Not Mom."

Lilya had read the bit about herself and was laughing, kicking her bare feet backwards and forwards in delight. She knew that everybody who was aware of her stays in Edwards' room assumed that they were making love all the time. In fact, they usually spent time relaxing, talking, getting to know and understand each other. She would read American magazines from the O-Club or read him Russian folk stories from a book she had brought over. Slowly, she was beginning to teach him to speak Russian. Making love would come, they were both young adults after all, but it would come later when the stress of flying missions, of hunting other humans and being hunted in turn, had faded away.

"Would you like to eat in the O-Club mess tonight?" Despite the close relations that had developed between the Russian and American groups, Russian officers could eat in the American O-club only as guests of an American officer who would be liable for their tab.

"I have a better idea." Lilya was smiling brightly. "Why do I not take you to our mess tonight? Tonight is our Monday meal, a tradition to get the week off on good start. Perhaps you will find Russian food to your taste?"

Edwards was about to say no when realization struck him. By Russian standards he was a rich man and lived a rich man's life. Lilya probably felt guilty about him taking her to the O-Club all the time and didn't want to give the impression she was using him. Suddenly he understood that it was very important to her that she should return his hospitality when she could. "I'd like that very much, Lilya. A little later of course."

"Of course," she agreed.

Kazan Thunderbolts

Officers Canteen, 866th Fighter Regiment, Airfield 108, Privolzhskiy na Volga.

Lilya led the way to a table that had three seats unoccupied. Edwards carefully seated her and then took the chair beside her. Koldunov saw them arriving and hurried over to make up the foursome. The table, now being fully occupied, meant that they were eligible to start eating. Over by the kitchen, one of the cooks took note of the fact and issued the necessary instructions.

"Do we have to collect our own?" Edwards asked quietly.

"No, Misha, a cook's assistant will bring our trays over to us." Lilya was trying to hide how hungry she was. The Monday meal was when the cooks always tried their hardest.

"Once, a very powerful general was inspecting an airbase but he got very, very drunk. When he reached the canteen he slipped on the floor, fell and injured himself quite badly." Koldunov seemed to have remarkably little sympathy for the stricken officer. "From his hospital bed, he issued orders that all pilots should be brought their food at the table."

Edwards joined the laughter and then looked at the tray that had been placed in front of him. It seemed remarkably well-filled and for a moment he thought it had been prepared for him but a quick glance around showed him the Russian officers were getting the same.

Lilya pointed to the various plates. "First we have a salad with a hard-boiled egg and a slice of Kashkaval cheese. Then, we have Schav; a sorrel and kidney soup followed by a sausage with kasha and pickles. Then, to end with, bread, butter and cherry preserves. The cherry harvest must be starting."

Edwards picked up the bowl containing his salad and looked at the contents. He didn't know what the green vegetable leaves within it were but the grated carrot was easily recognizable. The cheese was a milky white color and there was a whole freshly-boiled egg on the top. What surprised and delighted him was that the salad was fresh; the vegetables still crisp from the fields. Compared with the powdered eggs he had become used to, the idea of a whole fresh egg was a luxury.

"Lilya, this is great. It's been months since I had a fresh salad. How do you do it? Everything we have is tinned or preserved."

Her eyes sparkled with pleasure and relief. "Our army supply lines are . . . ." She paused, fumbling for a word.

"Non-existent?" Koldunov offered the English helpfully.

"Not quite, but everything goes to the troops on the front line. Because we are in the rear, we must look after ourselves. So, every day, the cooks and their assistants go to the local Kolkhozs, the collective farms, and buy fresh produce from them. Others go to the woods and fields to see what they can find. We have an excellent cook and he has picked skilled assistants so they look after us well. We are rationed of course, the cooks have a budget per man and we can only take so much from each Kolkhoz. We can only have two eggs per person per week. For the rest, we must hunt and scavenge to add to that."

"The winter of 41/42 was terrible." Koldunov's voice was tragic. "The fascist advance had dug deep into our country and we had lost almost all the harvest. Nobody had enough to eat; even the generals looked thin and starved. Many, hundreds of thousand, died from starvation. If it hadn't been for the food you sent us, and the Australians and the New Zealanders, the dead would have been in millions. Things are better now but we will never forget those who stood by us in our darkest hours."

"There is so much to be grateful for. That is why it pleases us so much that you are here with us this evening." The fourth man at the table looked up. "My apologies, I am Captain Valentin Yakovlevich Rukosuev, the Zampolit for the 866th."

"Political officer." Lilya spoke the words quietly.

"Good evening, tovarish Valentine Yakovlevich." Edwards spoke carefully to make sure he had the pronunciation right. "It is a pleasure to be here. Fresh food is a gift to be treasured. May I ask one thing? I noticed that a table is only served when all the seats are occupied. Why is this?"

"Ahh, for us, the evening meal is the most important of the day. It is one where the whole family gathers together and the food is only served when the last member has arrived. So, our little ceremony of filling tables here brings that back to us."

"Thank you," Edwards sipped his soup. Like most Americans he tried to avoid meat too closely associated with the urinary tract but he assumed that every effort was made to eat every part of every carcass. He was surprised to find that the taste of the sorrel and sliced kidney blended well. "It is much the same with our families. The children come home from school, father returns from work and we all eat our evening meal together. American hours are very regular so a wife knows when to have the family dinner ready. Her husband will call out 'Honey, I'm home' and by the time he has changed out of his work clothes, dinner will be served."

"What does your father do, tovarish Misha?"

Kazan Thunderbolts

"He is an estimator for a steel company; when the company is negotiating a contract to supply steel, his job is to calculate how much steel is needed so the bid can be made. If his estimate is too high, then the company will put in too high a bid and they will lose to another. If it is too low, then the company will lose money on the contract."

"It is the same in ours! We do not have profit and loss of course, but the amount of steel supplied by the factory is measured against the resources it consumes. If it is not an efficient user of the resources it is allocated, then the reason for the problem is investigated." Rukosuev concealed his delight at how the conversation was going. On being assigned to his post, he had been told he would be in close contact with an American group and given his instructions. *We must show that Russians and Americans are not so different. We may not look like Americans, dress like Americans or believe in the same things as Americans but we are still decent, ordinary folk, just like them. We're defending our families and Motherland from the Nazis, and like them, we do not want to die but are not afraid to do so if called upon. What I never knew when I took my post here is that the task is easy because all of that is true.* With a sudden flash of insight, Rukosuev realized that, around this small table and many like it along the east bank of the Volga, something much greater than a simple alliance was being created.

Combat Command B, Second Armored Division, Approaches to Kalinino, West of the Chuvashskaya Bridgehead.

The lead elements of CCB were just two miles short of the outskirts of Kalinino. It was more significant than that; they had seized the ridges that overlooked the town and were moving self-propelled artillery up into position to start the bombardment that would precede the expected assault. The guns would fire all night and in the morning, the infantry would move in. Harmon knew he would be working far into the night, trying to come up with the various options available to the fascists and what he would do about them. One by one and/or collectively. It didn't help matters that he had been getting increasingly irate messages from AEF Headquarters wanting to know why he wasn't advancing more quickly. A week ago, he wouldn't have had an answer. Today he did but he wasn't sure the people he would have to explain it to would like it.

There was a roar of engines and a sudden storm of activity outside his tent. The flap swung open, causing a sudden gust of wind that threatened to scatter his papers and maps on the ground. He stabilized his desk just in time to see General Patton storming in.

"Ernie, just what the hell do you think you are doing? You're supposed to be ten miles west of this Goddamned town by now."

"George, the goddamned plan is a pile of steaming crap." Harmon was beginning to get into the technique of handling General George S Patton. When he pushed, push back, harder. The fatal thing was to give in, or worse, compromise. "Anyway, operational plans are for the guidance of wise men and the blind obedience of damned fools. We're not damned fools here and I'm not going to get my boys killed just to comply with a few pencil marks on a piece of dirty paper."

Patton couldn't argue with that. Harmon was quoting him and both Generals knew it. "Fine, Ernie. Now tell me what is happening and why."

"The what is simple and you put your finger on it. We can't do the fast advances and sweeping movements the pre-war books said we should. They're not possible; they never were. Certainly not when we're fighting Hitlerites and probably not against anybody. All that crap the Brit general, Fuller I think his name was, is just that. Crap. People took his books as if he was some sort of God but they forget nearly everything he wrote was theoretical. Just like everything we wrote before we got here was theoretical crap. Let me show you something. The deadliest weapon in the fascist arsenal, as far as our tankers are concerned anyway." Harmon reached into a desk draw and pulled out a stake, painted white. "Here it is; cost us more boys than anything else until one of our privates found it and realized its significance."

Patton looked at the piece of wood curiously. "A marker for a minefield?"

"Close. The fascists love stay-behind forces. Nothing grand, one of their older anti-tank guns and a couple of machine guns to cover it, all manned by whatever men they can scrape up. The gun is usually a 37mm or perhaps a 50. They keep the 75s and the 88s for their main line of resistance. Those old guns are just barely adequate to handle a Sherman and they know damned well they get one crack before we flatten the area the shot came from. So, they pre-measure all the ranges and they drive markers into the roadside at the optimum point, close enough to kill the tank, far enough out so we have a job to see where the shot came from.

"Now we've understood the significance of the stakes, our boys watch for them and if they see one, they know a stay-behind group is deadly close. That warning has reduced our tank losses and it also means we can move a bit faster between stakes. That isn't very far, there are a lot of those stay-behind groups and as fast as we take them out, the Hitlerites scrape together a few more men, give them whatever junk they can find and send them out. God help us when they get bazookas. They must have captured some by now and they'll copy them.

"What this means is that we can't go plunging around. If we try, we get nickel and dimed to death by those stay-behind groups. What we have to do is keep a steady pressure constantly moving forward, destroying the stay-behind forces as we go. That way, the fascist front stretches like a rubber band and will eventually run out of strength and break. Like a rubber band, when it breaks, it'll go completely and when it does, that's when we get to move fast. That's not now."

Patton gazed at Harmon, pleased at what he had heard. A considered and carefully-evaluated analysis of the situation. *Now, the next part.* "What do we need to do, Ernie?"

"Tank formations need more infantry. I could make a case for replacing the light tank company with an armored infantry company. Having more infantry on point with the tanks will speed us up, not slow us down. When we spot one of those damned white stakes, the infantry dismount and scout ahead on foot with the tanks as overwatch. George, could you spread the word? Infantry must dismount and attack on foot, with the tanks and half-tracks up front to suppress the fascists with 75s and machine guns. Also, we need to isolate the battlefield. We're doing that on an operational level already but we need to do it everywhere. If an American unit is fighting, we need to make sure that nobody else gets in or out of the battlefield. It's odd, the Russians do tactical isolation but not operational or strategic, we do operational and strategic but not tactical. We both had half the answer but not the whole thing."

"The Sturmoviks and Thunderbolts are teaming up more often now. They work well together. I'll talk to Eaker and Novikov, see if we can step that program up. Novikov is a damned good guy for a Soviet and he's a personal friend of President Zhukov. He gets things done. For your ears only, more Thunderbolts are coming. Two more groups by the end of next month and four groups of B-26s. We'll have three full P-47 wings by the end of October. Anything else I can get done?"

"Sure George. Can you put on one of your shows? We've still got Fredendall Disease here. Most of the boys think that nobody up top knows or cares what is happening out here. Just showing them you're here will be worth an extra battalion of artillery. And a public commendation for Private Southard? He's the man who tumbled the white stakes."

"Good. Have him washing the headlamps on my armored car in five minutes. Ernie, write up everything you've told me and anything else you think of and send it to me. I'll get my people to hack it into a tactical handbook and we'll get it to every goddamned man on the front line. I'll not have a single dumb bastard die on my watch because nobody told him what he needed to know."

Five minutes later, the voice of a Sergeant echoed across the camp. "Southard? Go wash the headlights on General Patton's car. And do a good job, if he drives into a ditch and breaks his neck, we might get Vetrenyy Freddie back."

Patton waited for the proper moment and strode out to his vehicle, his bearing carefully set and his 'war face' firmly in place. Standing on top, he looked at the men gathering around him. A second's thought told him that 'extemporized speech number three' would suit this audience best.

"At ease. Get something straight. No bastard ever won a war by dying for his country. You will win this one by making the other poor dumb bastards die for their country. That means pushing hard then harder again. I believe that an ounce of sweat now will save a gallon of blood later. That's because the harder we push, the more fascists we kill. The more fascists we kill, the fewer of our men will be killed. Pushing harder means fewer casualties. I want you all to remember that. Even if you are hit, you can still fight. That's not just crap. I want men like the lieutenant in a skirmish a few miles back who, facing a kraut with a machine gun, swept aside the gun with his hand, jerked his helmet off with the other and busted the hell out of the fascist with the helmet. Then he picked up the gun and he killed another Nazi. All this time, that man had a bullet through his lung. That's a man for you! That's an American soldier!

"When I tell you that, don't think that the real heroes are all storybook combat fighters. Every single man in the army plays a vital role. So don't ever let up. Don't ever think that your job is unimportant. What if every truck driver decided that he didn't like the whine of the shells and turned yellow and jumped headlong into a ditch? That cowardly bastard could say to himself, 'Hell, they won't miss me, just one man in thousands.' What if every man said that? Where in the hell would we be then? No, thank God, Americans don't say that. Every man does his job. Every man is important. The ordnance men are needed to supply the guns, the quartermaster is needed to bring up the food and clothes for us because where we are going there isn't a hell of a lot to steal. Every last damn man in the mess hall, even the one who boils the water to keep us from getting the GI runs, has a job to do. Take Private Southard there. He saw the white stakes and realized their importance. He reported his insight to his commander and now that is being spread across the whole Goddamned army. Take a look around you, all of you. Some of you are here tonight because Private Southard did his duty and then a bit more. General Harmon, why is Southard still a private? Promote him at once. Corporal at least.

"All right, you sons of bitches. You know how I feel. I'll be proud to lead you wonderful guys in battle anytime, anywhere. That's all."

Patton jumped down and went around the front of his armored car. "What are you doing Southard?"

"Washing your headlights, Sir."

"Thank you." Patton dropped his voice so that they couldn't be overheard. "I'll see to it that your parents get a letter telling them how well you are serving your country and how proud I am to serve with you."

"Sir, if I could ask a favor, could you put the code DESIGN on the back flap?"

Patton's eyes narrowed slightly. "I know SWALK, EGYPT and BURMA, but not DESIGN. What the hell does that mean?"

"Don't Sweat, Its Good News. To our families, most military letters aren't, Sir."

That made Patton think. "More good advice, son. Carry on this way, and you'll be a General by the end of this Goddamned war."

CHAPTER THIRTEEN: A TERRIBLE DESIRE FOR REVENGE

Office of Joseph P Kennedy, Washington D.C.

"There is an officer to see you, Sir." The office receptionist had a strong feeling this would have been a good day to call in sick.

"Has he an appointment? Who is he anyway?"

"It's a Commander Ian Fleming of the British Royal Navy. He hasn't got an appointment."

"Then throw him out."

"Sir, he stresses that this is very urgent. He says it is a matter of Lieutenant Craig."

The receptionist could hear the sudden pause and catch of breath. "Oh, very well. Send him in."

"Thank you for seeing me, Sir. I apologize for barging in on you but this really is an item of the greatest urgency. I have just returned from Great Britain and there is some information I was given there that you need to see right away."

"England? Who did you see there? Halifax?"

"No, Sir. I am sorry, but I am sworn not to disclose their names to you. I can say they are people with whom you are familiar from your stay as the Ambassador in London. They asked me to hand you this file." Fleming handed the file over. It was in a standard Directorate of Naval Intelligence cover. Both cover and contents were the real thing and had been carefully put together at the Free Royal Navy headquarters in Ottawa while Fleming had been flying in from Kazan. The meat of the file was the material John F Kennedy had revealed to Chekist Napalkov in the hospital at Staraya Mayna but it had been augmented and disguised to conceal its source. Some deliberate mistakes had even been included in order to mask the fact that a family member had disclosed the situation.

Fleming handed over the file and watched Joseph Kennedy reading it. *He's been very patriotic about it.* Fleming thought, *He's going red, white and blue in that order and is now proceeding to purple.*

When Kennedy finally spoke, his voice sounded like the crack of doom. "How dare you use a family tragedy in this manner. I should have you killed for this."

"Sir, I am just the delivery boy here. The truth of the matter is that the people who asked me to bring this to you do not feel that you have held up your end of the whatever bargain they think they have with you – assuming any such bargain exists at all. After all, Sir, these people have made one political and military mistake after another for the last three years. I think that their activity here is another blunder of immense proportion and consequences and I would try and assist you in controlling the damage that will result from it. Frankly, Sir, I am disgusted by having to bring this file to you and regard the people responsible as despicable in the extreme. Even touching that document makes me want to wash my hands in carbolic soap."

"Then why did you do it?" Kennedy's voice was quivering with rage but there was a new undertone of curiosity.

"Sir, I am not an officer in the Royal Navy, I am an officer in the *Free* Royal Navy. I am also a member of the Resistance. My brother, Peter Fleming, is a *leading* member of the resistance. As such we are aligned with the Commonwealth. Britain's membership of the Commonwealth was suspended in June 1940 and what was the British Commonwealth is now the Commonwealth of Nations. I can honestly say that when representatives from every member of the Commonwealth saw this repulsive document, they were as appalled as we were. The Indian attaché in Ottawa went as far as to say 'it was not quite cricket'. They wish to assist you in any way they can. The more time they have, the more they can do."

"If you're resistance and Free British, why did they pick you to bring this filth to my desk?'

Fleming mentally held his breath. This was the crux, the crisis point. If he could get past this, it wouldn't quite be game over but it would be a huge step in that direction. "Sir, I am in the resistance. My survival depends on that fact remaining unknown. To the people in London, I am a loyal Royal Navy officer. Should they learn otherwise I am dead."

"That's your funeral." Kennedy didn't seem to realize the humor in his comment. "What do the people in London want, anyway?"

"People like me don't get funerals, Sir. Our bodies get thrown in a shallow, muddy hole in the ground. As to what the people in London want, it's quite simple. They want you to use your power and influence to orchestrate an American withdrawal from the war. If you do not, they will release all of this to your enemies in the press."

"That's out of the question; impossible." Kennedy exploded again. As he did so, Fleming watched the color in his face change again, this time from red to green as the full implications of the trap he was in sank in. If the contents of this file were released to the press, he knew he would be destroyed, finished forever as a man of power and influence. If he did as he thought the Halifax Government was demanding, he would also be destroyed. There was simply no way he could bring about any American withdrawal, not now and the time for thinking about it had gone. It was a repeat of the same mistake the Halifax clique had made in 1940; what would have been acceptable and even popular in January 1940 was anathema in June. Fleming thought that if there was any truth at all in the story he was spinning, it would have been a brilliant political ploy to ruin Kennedy. "You said the Commonwealth wanted to help me. Why? What's their price?"

"No price, Sir. This is just a matter of common decency. And practicality of course; if this sort of thing becomes accepted diplomatic conduct, then international diplomacy will go down the tubes. Also, Sir, consider our help a demonstration of good faith."

Kennedy was relaxing slightly. He knew he was being sold something but wasn't quite certain what. He did know he was being offered a way out of the trap he was in. "What do you plan?"

"There is one thing we need put in place for us to be able to squash this idea. The Directorate of Naval Intelligence in London is not enamored of this blackmail ploy either. To be honest, Sir, we're not quite certain why this plan is being run through them. Normally it is something the Secret Intelligence Service, outsiders call it MI.6, would run. We can't explain it. Be that as it may, DNI can squash this, What will happen is that the contents of the file will somehow be replaced by a rehash of stories about your ill-advised speech in 1940, It'll get to the press, they'll take one look, stamp it as old news and spike it. Problem gone."

"So, what's the piece you need." Kennedy was calming down again.

"We have to offer DNI London something in exchange. They'll be risking a lot of men's lives and it needs to be worth their while. Frankly, Sir, you mean nothing to them; we have to offer them something that does have meaning. The

Kazan Thunderbolts

only thing that will be of use to them is intelligence; they need it to plan anti-German strikes as a part of the Resistance war. That's the problem. Brigadier General Donovan's plan for a centralized Russian-American intelligence service will cut the Commonwealth out of the intelligence loop. Coincidentally, I think its coincidental although I could be wrong on that, it will also deprive the Commonwealth intelligence services of the ammunition they need to aid you by crushing this blackmail scheme.

"There is an alternative scheme called Goldeneye. This proposes an intelligence committee made up from representatives of all the allied intelligence services, and all the services report to that committee. This will give the Commonwealth the access it needs to crush the report being used to blackmail you. As I said, Sir, this is not a demand or a bargain; the Commonwealth will help you regardless. But this is the surest and quickest way of getting you out of this jam. And everybody wins."

"Except Brigadier General Donovan."

"Has he demonstrated any good faith to you, Sir?"

"No he has not. Just made promises. Very well, Commander Fleming, I will use my influence to work on behalf of the Goldeneye plan. You should see the first results of my moves in a month or so. Will that be adequate to gain the assistance you need?"

Fleming nodded. Kennedy pressed the button on his intercom. "Please advise the reception staff that Commander Fleming is to be granted access to me at any time, with or without an appointment.

Fleming managed to contain his smirk as he left Kennedy's office. *When the war's over, I'll have to start writing spy novels,* he thought. *If I can sell that pile of steaming horse manure, I can sell anything.*

There was an official limousine waiting for him. Fleming climbed in and gave the man waiting in the back seat a triumphant 'thumbs-up'.

746th Tank Battalion, 83rd Infantry Division, Kalikovo, Chuvashskaya Bridgehead.

Master Sergeant Fredrick Merriman was back where he belonged, in a Sherman tank. The 746th had been reconstituted with new tanks and mostly new crews. There was a hard core of survivors from the old 746th and they'd been spread out amongst the new tanks.

"Stockade, stockade, stockade!"

The warning blasted out across the tank battalion and its supporting infantry. Somebody, somewhere had spotted one of the threatening white stakes

372

by the roadside and shouted out the code-word. Merriman's driver had immediately thrown the tank into reverse and was backing up. So were all the tanks behind them. The infantry were debussing from their half-tracks and taking cover, ready to assault the blocking force. For all its speed, the response was only just fast enough. Merriman swore that the red streak of an armor-piercing shot had passed through the slot bounded by the tank's gun barrel, the top of its hull and the front of its turret.

"Load smoke, engage treeline 11 o'clock, 300 yards." Merriman had guessed the position by the angle of the red streak and the range on the assumption that the enemy was a PAK-50. The M4 was already swinging as the driver turned the turret to face the expected direction of fire. That way, the thickest armor on the tank would be facing any inbound rounds. The tank was still turning when the 75mm gun cracked. The red streak of the outbound shell carved a line that ended in the billowing white cloud of a smoke round. The treeline in question seemed to erupt all along its length as a mixture of smoke and high explosive rounds blanketed the area. Immediately, the tanks and half-tracks started to edge forward.

Once, the inexperienced American tankers would have rolled in as fast as they could with the infantry in their half-tracks behind them . Those days had gone and the experience that had replaced the old habits had been bitterly bought. The tanks were moving forward at walking pace, constantly on the lookout for an ambush. Between them, the half-tracks kept pace, firing their machine guns in a continuous barrage intended to force the enemy to keep their heads down. The infantry were moving on foot, using the armored vehicles for cover. A lot of fire was coming out of the suspected fascist position but the choking clouds of smoke made it little more than random. The machine gun fire was ricocheting off the armor of the tanks and half tracks while the occasional red streaks from the anti-tank guns were too high and mostly between the vehicles. Only one tank was hit and it shrugged off the 50mm round.

It took only a few minutes for the armor to reach its overwatch position, about 50 yards out from the fascist outpost. At that point they stopped and concentrated on pummeling the sources of inbound fire. The infantry behind them picked up the pace, passed between their supporting vehicles and advanced into the treeline. There was a brief, savage exchange of rifle and machine gun fire punctuated by grenade blasts before the triumphant message came over the radio. "Position taken. Enemy force eliminated."

Merriman's report was succinct. An enemy stay-behind position had been encountered, attacked and taken. Fascist forces eliminated, two anti-tank guns, three machine guns, 15 men dead. Friendly casualties, 12 dead seventeen wounded, one tank hit but not damaged. *The fascists are still outfighting us but the margin by which they do is shrinking all the time. Thank God none of those*

Tiger monsters was here; they seem to have vanished as mysteriously as they appeared.

"Loophole 5, this is Tenderfoot. We are ordered to advance on the next small town. It's called Karmamei. We're to take the town and hold it."

Merriman looked at his map. Karmamei was just over two and a half miles away. "Got it Ell-Tee. Recommend if we swing northwest, the track takes us west then southwest, straight into the town."

There was a pause that made Merriman sure he could hear maps rustling in the background. "Loophole 5, Duderanch confirms. Do it – and take point. Matchlock 3 will follow you as infantry support. Watch out for stockade."

"Affirmative, Tenderfoot. We're moving out now."

The two tanks in the light section of the platoon pulled out, followed by three half-tracks. A short-cross-country drive took them back to the track. As the map had promised, the pathway, it could scarcely be called a track, much less a road, led northwest before swinging due west and then southwest. Every man in every vehicle was scanning for the tell-tale white markers – or anything else that looked odd or out-of-place. Somebody, somewhere had realized that it wouldn't be long before the Hitlerites guessed that the Americans now understood the significance of white stakes and use something else. Merriman realized something else, the path he was following skirted a long finger of forest that ran due north. It defined the southern edge of the Kolkhoz Pass, the gap in the forest through which the 83rd Infantry had retreated. The road they had used was barely a mile to the north and the Yandoba Ridge where the composite group had made its stand was almost three miles to the east.

When Karmamei swam into view, Merriman ordered his detachment to halt. The town seemed peaceful enough but it never hurt to make sure. "Sarge, we're here, look."

The driver was holding out a map. His finger was pointing to a small rise on the path, just before a large, stone-walled field. "We're where we are supposed to be. One thing, this field here. Why's there black smoke rising above it?"

Merriman looked hard. There was a faint black smoke above the walled field. He hadn't seen anything quite like it before; it wasn't burning oil, gas or shot-up vehicles. It was far too faint for that. Suddenly it occurred to him that his binoculars had been issued to him for this kind of situation. When he lifted them to his eyes and looked carefully, he realized what he was seeing.

"Joe, that ain't smoke, those are crows. Hundreds and hundreds of crows."

There was a reason why any gathering of crows had, for centuries, been regarded as the worst kind of bad luck. Crows swarmed wherever there had been a disaster and there was meat to be scavenged. Merriman's loader was from Texas and he summed it up perfectly. "Sarge, back home, we see buzzards circling, there's something dead out there. See a flock like that, there's sure a lot of dead there."

The small column started off again and made its way down the path towards the entrance to the field. It took only a few minutes with any kind of opposition conspicuous by its absence. By the time the tank pulled up again, the stench was making Merriman gag. He looked from the turret, through the gate and across the field. What he saw completed the process and he vomited over the side of his tank.

"Sarge?"

"It's our boys, the fascist bastards have massacred them. There's hundreds of them, all over the field. The bastards killed them all and left their bodies to rot." That's when Merriman's mind started working again; he grabbed the .50 machine gun mounted on the turret and fired a burst over the field. With fear overcoming greed, the crows swarmed into the sky. Some were so fattened with meat they were unable to make it into flight and they tried to waddle away. "Matchlock Three, dismount and secure that field. Don't touch anything, we need to gather every shred of evidence we can."

Merriman turned as a figure ran up beside the column of vehicles. "Sergeant, I'm Robert Capa, combat photographer. Can you tell me what is . . . . . . Holy Mother of God."

"Capa, take every picture you can. Scenes and of each body. Duplicates of each and as many rolls as you need. I'll get more film for you. Oh Christ, there's going to be hell to pay for this. Tenderfoot, this is Loophole 5. Sir, you need to get here fast. The fascists have murdered hundreds of our PoWs. . . . That's right, hundreds. . . . . No I am not exaggerating, the bodies are all over the place. . . . . Left to rot, the birds were eating them. . . . . I have Robert Capa taking pictures now. . . . . . Hold one. Capa, what kind of film d you need?"

"Kodak, if you have some of the new Kodacolor . ."

"Did you get that, Sir? Kodak and any Kodacolor we have. We need the top brass down here, right away. And a film crew. And ambulances, trucks, everything we can find. . . . . No, I don't think there are any survivors but we're checking now. We need MPs as well. When word of this gets out, the order of the day will be 'Kill'em all.'"

Kazan Thunderbolts

Merriman put the radio down and stared across the field. One thought was dominating his mind. The night he had made his night patrol, the fascists had already captured the center of the American position. He had been faced with a choice, go east and link up with the American forces there, or to go into Kanash and help with the defense of the town. He had gone east. He knew, with heavy certainty, if he had gone west, his body would have been lying in this field.

River Gunboat PR-73, the Ulyanov'sk Narrows, Volga River.

There were more gunboats in the Volga south of the railway bridge than Jack Kennedy had ever seen in one place before. At least two 125-foot Huckins boats, six Elco 92-footers and a dozen Russian craft. One of the Russian boats was an old, pre-WW1 steam gunboat, the *Krasnoye Zhelezny* with 5.1 inch guns. The veteran was providing the heavy punch, lobbing shells behind the ridge that provided the town proper with cover from artillery fire originating from the east bank. The American gunboats were doing fine work with their three inch guns. They'd been positioned to the south so that their flat-trajectory guns could reach behind the ridge. Finally, much closer to the river bank, the Russian gunboats were supplying pinpoint fire from their 45mm cannons and heavy machine guns.

"Landing craft are on their way, Jack." Lieutenant Thom, now formally confirmed as commander of PR-73, was watching the Higgins boats making their way across the Volga from the river port at Krasnyy Yar. The destruction of the Hitlerite spy ring in the rail yards had meant that the arrival of the Higgins boats by rail had gone unnoticed by the fascists. For once, the allies had the operational initiative. They had scraped up a landing force from various detached U.S. and Russian Marine units. Combining them on a tactical level had proved problematic until a U.S. Marine had remarked that the Russian Marines were just naval infantry, not real Marines. By the time the inevitable brawl had ended, some five hours later, the Russian and American marines had consolidated themselves on a basis of mutual respect. Now, that new spirit of cohesion was about to be tested.

"Any counterfire?" Kennedy knew that the Higgins boats would take more than half an hour to cross the Volga and the execution properly-handled coast defense guns could wreak in that time would destroy the whole operation. That was why the gunboats were pummeling the shore so hard. One thing running for them was that the 600 foot high ridge that lay along the west bank of the Volga. The combination of the very narrow river bank plain and then the steep rise made it difficult for the defenders to position artillery close to the river and the ridge provided valuable dead ground for an attacking force.

"Not yet." Thom was watching intently for any signs of resistance. It was largely pointless; Thom knew that the fascists were too wily to give positions away when they didn't need to. Most of the fire that was being directed into the landing area was intended to pin down the defenders. If they were goaded into returning it, so much the better.

"Aircraft inbound, bearing oh-nine-oh, estimated strength 50, altitude angel 12." Ensign Ed Mauer was still trying to get used to the fact that the Navy had gone and made him an officer. It hadn't made any difference to PR-73 or the work he did on her. The truth was that the copies of Russian newspapers that described how he had spotted the sabotaged ammunition shipment, exposed a fascist spy ring and thus saved hundreds of Russian and American lives meant far more to him. He had sent copies of all the papers that carried the story back home along with English language copies supplied by the CheKa agent who had conducted the investigation. He had got a simple letter back that had read. "Son, your mother and I, and every man and woman in this here town are proud of you." It was the first time that his father had ever said that.

"They're B-26s. Right on time." Boatswain's Mate Joe Palazzolo was the first to spot the inbound medium bombers. They were right on time, part of the sequence of actions that were intended to keep the Hitlerites occupied until the landing craft could make it over. Compared to the lethargic crawl of the Higgins boats, the Marauders seemed to cover the ground at a rapid pace, eating the distance to the drop point. The bombers were heading straight and level, obviously already running in from their OP back on friendly territory. That struck Palazzolo as a strange contrast. The operation presently in hand was the most complex and dangerous the riverine forces had ever attempted. Yet, for the aircraft passing overhead, this was a milk-run, little more than a training exercise.

A scattering of black puffs erupted around the bombers, as if to remind Palazzolo that this wasn't really a training exercise. The fire was dispersed and inaccurate, but one of the Marauders suddenly developed a stream of white smoke from one of its wings. The bomber was obviously hit but it was holding its place in formation and maintaining its bomb run. The formation of aircraft continued on course until it was well over the west bank. Then, it suddenly turned sharply and headed east again, for home and safety. Palazzolo saw smoke starting to rise over the ridge and began to count seconds. 15 Mississippis later, the rumble of explosions echoed across the water. *3 miles*, he thought, *that's the kraut airfield gone. One of them, anyway.*

By now, the stricken B-26 was obviously in dire straits. The trail of white smoke had become thicker, wider and was now shot with brown and black. The Marauder had dropped out of formation in a long, sweeping curve and was taking the shortest possible route for the east bank. It was helped by the wind blowing from the west that was taking it back to friendly territory. From Palazzolo's perspective, it had made it to safety and, if confirming that assessment, the white dots of parachutes appeared behind the descending

377

bomber. The inevitable count started with a qualified sigh of relief as the sixth chute opened. Qualified because the Marauder carried a crew of six or seven men. Palazzolo kept watching until, after a nail-biting pause, the seventh chute appeared. Obviously the pilot had remained at the controls to ensure the aircraft remained stable while his crew bailed out. Then, he'd taken the chance of setting the Marauder on autopilot so he could jump himself. The risk had paid off, for his crew at least. Not so for the aircraft; its turn and descent rate both increased, the aircraft dropping in a spiral until it vanished behind the east bank ridge. A second or two later, the billowing explosion of a crashed aircraft rose over the crest of the bank.

By that time, the Higgins boats had finally crossed the Volga and were making their run at the river bank beside Karamzina. This was where the shallow draft gunboats came into their own. They accompanied the landing craft in, maintaining steady fire from their guns on the buildings that lined the shore. That made Kennedy distinctly unhappy; the buildings in question were from the 19th century or older and had a character that modern Soviet architecture lacked. He guessed that this had once been the "resort" area of Ulyanov'sk, the place where the richer or better-connected had their holiday homes. He assumed they had now been taken over by officials of the Communist Party and that relieved him of some of the guilt that had come from the knowledge that there would soon be nothing left of the waterfront.

The Russian gunboats ahead of PR-73 had now swung sideways to the shore. They had been modified for this operation with a 16-barrel Katyushka launcher replacing their aft 45mm gun. Now, those rockets justified the trouble and expense that had gone into installing them. They streaked across the water in short, flat arcs that terminated in a rolling barrage of explosions. The riverfront buildings that Kennedy had admired so much a few seconds earlier dissolved in the blasts, seeming to tumble to the ground in slow motion. At the same time, the Higgins boats grounded on the shingle beach, driving in until their bows were lifted high out of the water. The Marines scrambled out, over the bows and sides, waded through the surf with their rifles at high port and started to infiltrate into the town of Karamzina. Kennedy knew that the next generation of Higgins boats had their bows redesigned to include a dropping ramp that would ease disembarkation.

"Radio message from the landing force sirs." Mauer still had his enlisted habits in place. "There's no resistance in Karamzina although the town is heavily booby-trapped. The Marines are beginning to scale the ridge behind the buildings."

"Artillery boys did their work." Thom was sweeping the landing zone with his binoculars. He could see the small groups of Marines working their way upwards. "Made the town untenable so the fascists abandoned it. I guess the leathernecks won't get any serious resistance until they reach the crest."

"Sirs, you better read this." Thom looked around at Mauer. The man was white and shaking. "This came in, top security cipher. We got a resend and checked the decoding three times. It's accurate."

Thom took the message flimsy and read it. By the time he had reached the end, he was also white with shock. His hands were trembling as he pressed the send button on the speaker system. "Attention all hands, attention all hands. We have just received a message from AEF Headquarters in Kanash. The bodies of 486 American PoWs including four Army female nurses have been found in a field outside Karmamei. Eye witnesses to the massacre state they were murdered by the SS. That's all the information I have right now. I'll pass more through as we receive it."

Ridgecrest over Karamzina, Ulyanov'sk.

Marine Lieutenant Yevgeny Petrovich Brusilov had brought his entire platoon through the ruins of Karamzina without losing a man. Long, bitter experience of fighting fascists had taught all his men that anything – literally anything from a piece of debris to a man's body or more – could be booby-trapped. So, they touched nothing, checked every door, every window, every culvert for mines and fragmentation charges. Any that they found were marked and left for bomb disposal workers in the penal battalions to deal with. That could take weeks before the town was safe for the return of its inhabitants.

The long climb up the 100 meter high ridge that marked the end of the riverbank had also been relatively cost-free. A few men had fallen to snipers and stay-behind parties and a few more to mortar round lobbed over the ridge crest but the Marines, Americans and Russian, were nearing the top and preparing a defense line in place. The fascists would be expecting them to swarm over the crest and start the advance down the reverse slope towards the grass-runway airfield that lay at its base. Four kilometers beyond that was a second airfield, a pre-war field with concrete runways. It had been bombed, and hopefully neutralized, by the American medium bombers earlier but it was obviously a prime target. Brusilov glanced at his watch; the unexpectedly low level of resistance had actually put him ahead of schedule. There was time to dig in and get ready for a counter-attack. The fascists would launch one, he knew he could rely on that. If they got the chance.

As the hands on his watch touched the hour, there was a long flicker of lightning along the east bank of the Volga. This was it, the start of the main attack. For all the resources poured into it, the landing by the Marines at Karamzina was a diversion, intended to draw the Hitlerites south, away from the main attack into the heart of the city of Ulyanov'sk. Brusilov couldn't help reflect that he knew more about this operation than any since his war had started. The American briefing had been complete and careful, so much so that the Russian officers, imbued with the need for security, had been distinctly uncomfortable. *Still, it is nice to know what the plan is and how we fit into it. Makes deciding on things easier.*

The rumble of the guns firing rolled down the Volga, echoing off the banks. It coincided with the awe-inspiring sight of the massed guns landing their shells on the long slope leading up from the existing bridgehead to the crest of the ridge. That slope was heavily dominated by fascist fire and had been impassible ever since the riverbank had been seized weeks before. Now, the slope itself was invisible under the hail of shells that were pounding every square inch of it. The allies had assembled every gun they could find; the artillery of the First Kazakhstan Front, the artillery battalions of the American divisions still backed up on the east bank, even the first battalions of the American corps artillery.

Trainloads of ammunition for the guns had arrived and were now being delivered with unholy enthusiasm. The Russian artillerists were starting a rolling barrage that would cover the infantry while they advanced up the slope. The American gunners had started with the general barrage but were now switching to point fires on targets of key interest. Soon, they would shift again to picking off targets appearing unexpectedly. Overhead a small light aircraft was circling over Ulyanov'sk. Brusilov wondered if the fascists had yet associated those light aircraft with the uncanny accuracy of American artillery.

"The Ponchiki artillerists know their trade well." Sergeant Petr Ivanovich Lashkov was watching the massive artillery bombardment with something very close to awe. The Russian troops were developing the habit of referring to the American soldiers as Ponchiki, the nearest Russian translation to "dough boys" but also a reference to their consumption of doughnuts and their generosity in handing them out to any Russians who happened to be around when the trucks arrived. "Do you feel that, tovarish lieutenant?"

A strange hot wind, air displaced by the ferocious artillery bombardment had started to blow down the west bank of the Volga. The artillery had been firing for almost 15 minutes and the time for the next stage of the assault was due. Infantry, mostly Russian but with a regiment of Americans attached, were to assault up the bank. Following closely behind the rolling barrage. As they neared the ridge crest separating them from the town of Ulyanov'sk, the guns would shift to the town itself.

That left the problem of the reverse slope, the one that was the center of the fascist defense of Ulyanov'sk. It was the same problem that Brusilov and his men faced at Karamzina; the forward slope was almost untenable for the fascists but once the allies crossed the crest, their own artillery would be useless and they would be exposed to the full fury of the Hitlerite guns. Only, at Ulyanov'sk, the Americans had a solution for that. Two hundred B-17s were going to dump over a thousand tons of bombs on that reverse slope. The briefers had called it "the Big Dump", something the Americans present had found hysterically funny. Brusilov reflected that the American sense of humor was hard to understand sometimes.

He could see the ridge under attack from his position. At Ulyanov'sk, the riverbank ridge was twice as high as high as it was at Karamzina and was a formidable defensive position. Despite that, the red flares being sent up as the advancing infantry seized the key positions on the ridge. The advance stopped just short of the crest; like Brusilov, the American and Russian commanders knew that the reverse slope defenses would be far more formidable than those they had faced so far.

"Bratishka! There they are!" Lashkov was pointing upwards, at the mass of white contrails that pointed straight at Ulyanov'sk. It was easy to see the thick, straight white lines of the Flying Fortresses and the sweeping curves of the fighters that protected them. Brusilov watched them approaching, seeing them holding a straight and level course despite the black spots of flak bursts beginning to surround them. From his time on Island Ten, he had seen the B-17s developing their skills and discipline. Every time he had seen them, their formations had been tighter, their courses more threatening and determined. Only now, he was sure he could see one of the groups of six bombers drifting behind and to one side of its correct position. Even so, he was shocked to see the explosions on the reverse slope of the ridge being joined by a pattern that landed deep inside the ground just seized by the Russian and American infantry.

REPORT ON THE ACCIDENTAL BOMBING OF ALLIED TROOPS BY THE 401ST BOMB GROUP.

Conclusions

This report has considered the events that led to the release of 96 500 pound bombs well short of the designated aiming point by a single section of the low box, 401st Bombardment Group.. A total of 36 officers and men of the 84th Infantry Division were killed in this accident and seventy wounded. It was very fortunate that the errant bombs dropped far behind the leading edge of the allied advance in relatively unoccupied ground otherwise casualties would have been much higher.

At this point, it must be stressed that the air raid in question was exceptionally successful and the bombing carried out by the 41st Bombardment Wing blasted a hole right through the German defenses in front of Ulyanov'sk. No significant resistance faced allied troops until they had reached the center of Ulyanov'sk. There was bitter fighting in the rest of the city but German resistance ceased after three days. The disruption caused by the bombing extended well south of Ulyanov'sk and allowed the Marines landed at Karamzina, initially intended as a diversion, to advance inland, seizing two airfields and cutting the roads leading west. It is considered likely that it was the Marines swinging west of Ulyanov'sk that finally caused the German command to abandon the city. Overall it is believed that the number of casualties resulting from the poorly-aimed bombs is far exceeded by the number of allied lives saved as a result of the bombing attack.

This leads to our first primary conclusion. The use of the B-17 heavy bomber for tactical support is a devastating weapon that should not lightly be abandoned. Although B-17s are being withdrawn from strategic roles as a result of increased deliveries of B-29 aircraft, it is our recommendation that B-17s should be retained in theater as long as enough aircraft remain available.

Secondly, it is apparent that the 401st was a novice bomb group at the time of this attack, this being only the second mission it had flown. The tactical bombing missions are regarded by the 8th Air Force as being 'milk runs' and used for training purposes. As a result, many of the crews are inexperienced replacements being seasoned before undertaking more demanding raids. Due to the precision required by close-support operations it is our second primary recommendation that this practice should cease.

The sequence of events that led to the mistargeting have been found as follows. *Madeline*, the lead bomber of the third flight, low box, was hit by flak early in its bomb run. Although the aircraft was not seriously damaged, its radio room was knocked out and the radio operator wounded. As the B-17s started their bomb run, they unexpectedly ran into unforecast headwinds and were slowed accordingly. This caused the drop time to be delayed, a fact that was communicated to the rest of the formation. Due to the damage to *Madeline*, the message was not received by that aircraft and the bombardier assumed the original schedule held. Due to inexperience of its flight deck crew, *Madeline* had also drifted out of position. The aircraft in the low box was supposed to release their bombload when the lead bombardier dropped. Two of the three flights did so. However, the bombardier of *Madeline* saw the originally-scheduled release time come up and dropped on that. As a result, his release was some 90 seconds premature. The rest of his flight followed on his release.

This gives rise to our third primary recommendation. A period of retraining should be given to the entire 401st, ensuring that they understand the need to bomb on the lead bombardier's release, not on their own estimates.

Our final recommendation is based on the loss of the most senior U.S. officer killed in this unfortunate event. Major General Lloyd Fredendall was following the advance in an M-3 command car that received a direct hit from a 500 pound bomb. It is our recommendation that should any parts of General Fredendall be found, they should be returned to the United States for interment in the Arlington National Cemetery.

Combat Command B, Second Armored Division, Kalinino, West of the Chuvashskaya Bridgehead.

"Sir, you'd better come and look at this."

General Harmon was glad of the excuse to stop reading the dispatch advising him of the massacre at Karmamei. At the same time, the way the call was being phrased made left him profoundly uneasy. "Where?"

"In the rail yard, Sir. And the truck park next to it." Captain Greer was outraged by what he had found and wanted to get the word out as soon as possible.

"This had better be important so, or you'll be shoveling horse puckey for months."

Greer led the General to the vehicle park that sat in the square formed by the railway line and six roads that converged on Kalinino. The roads were what made the town important; the railway yard itself was too small to be of great significance but the roads allowed the supplies brought in to be quickly distributed. Kalinino had been cut off before the fascists could evacuate most of the vehicles and the park was still filled with an esoteric mixture of trucks. German Opel and Henschels, British AECs, Bedfords and Scammells, French Citroëns, Panhards, Peugeots and Renaults. There was even a U.S. Army 6x6 in the mix.

"Be careful what you touch, Sir. We're still clearing booby traps. We've checked over these dozen vehicles here in case there were wounded in them."

The 'dozen vehicles' were Opels and AECs filled with van-style enclosed truck beds. Large white squares with a prominent Red Cross had been painted, crudely and hurriedly, on each. Harmon looked at them suspiciously. The way their suspension was compressed seemed to indicate they were heavily loaded. A private guarding the nearest vehicle opened the back doors.

"Sir, those wounded soldiers seem to look remarkably like drums of fuel and crates of ammunition to me. We've searched them all carefully and the only thing we can't find in these so-called ambulances are wounded or medical supplies. And, Sir, if the unit markings on these trucks are genuine, these belong to the Heer, not the SS."

"Damn. Captain, have you heard about Karmamei?"

"There are rumors going around, General. Nothing confirmed yet."

"Considered then confirmed. There's been a bloody massacre down there. The Red Cross has a team recording the details. We'd better get them up here right away. If anything, this is worse. Make sure these vehicles are sealed and under constant guard."

Harmon turned away and called out to an aide. "Get me AEF HQ right away. General Patton himself if he's there."

Airfield 108, Privolzhskiy na Volga, Moscow Front.

"Yebesh', yego vozdushnyy nalet!" Lilya's venom-filled shout nearly drowned out the wail of the air-raid sirens. She and Edwards had just reached his room, cheered by news that the other three pilots who shared the quarters with Edwards had let it be known that they were elsewhere for the evening and wouldn't be back for at least three hours. For all the kindness and good intentions of those three officers, she and Edwards hadn't had a chance to get out of their flying clothes before the sirens had gone off. "We must get the fighters off the ground."

Lilya had been through air raids on the bases she flew from many times before and had absorbed the hard-learned lessons. She had grabbed her flying helmet and was putting it on as she went through the door of the room. Edwards had done the same and was close behind her. The Tannoy system was already giving the alert; radar had spotted the German formation while it was still over the west bank and P-39s based in the Chuvashskaya were intercepting. The Thunderbolts and Yaks on Airfield 108 were to get airborne without delay. The Americans had listened to Russian advice on that point; it was better to get airborne and fight than stay on the ground. The Hitlerites didn't use that philosophy; they relied on dispersing the aircraft on the ground and ringing the base with flak.

By the time Lilya had reached her Yak, the lead Thunderbolts were already taxying out towards the runway. Others were enveloped in clouds of black smoke as their starters turned over the R-2800 engines. Her own Yak-9 was surrounded by a ground crew getting the fighter ready to go. She scrambled up the wing, into the cockpit and fastened her harness, feeling the familiar pressure on her waist and shoulders as she tightened the straps. She also felt the Yak come to life as her crew went through the starting procedure.

"Blocks away!" The taxiway was crowded with Thunderbolts and Yaks, all attempting to get airborne before the Hitlerite air raid arrived. The allied aircraft were nose-to-tail even while they attempted to make their take-off runs. Lilya guessed that it would only take one aircraft to crack up while taking off for there to be an avalanche of collisions that would produce a spectacular pile of wreckage. She sagged slightly with relief when her Yak lifted off, leaving the stampeding herd of aircraft below here. She rotated right as her undercarriage retracted, allowing her to clear the Thunderbolts. The American P-47s had a much longer take-off run than her nimble Yak-9. Already, she was in Free Hunter mode, her eyes scanning for enemy aircraft. A flash of light off a cockpit canopy far to the west gave her the information she needed. The Hitlerites had broken through the barrier patrols along the Volga and were coming for Airfield 108.

Thunderbolt Live Bait *Over Airfield 108, Kazan.*

"Enemy aircraft coming in from the west. Bearing 300 degrees." Edwards hadn't even lifted off the runway when the fighter controller's voice came over his radio. There was no indication of range so he had no idea when the enemy aircraft would appear in front of him. It was, in his opinion, the time to get off the runway as quickly as possible. He was just above take-off speed so he pulled the stick back enough to give a minimal rate of climb. Then, when his wheels were just clear, he slapped his landing gear up.

As if that had been a signal, an FW-190 burst out from above the trees directly in front of him, crossing from right to left. Edwards made a minor cause adjustment and let fly with his battery of .50s. Normally, his bursts started by passing ahead of his target and then plowed back along the fuselage. This time, he had so little warning that his first shots passed behind the 190 but the torque from his R-2800 pulled him around so fast the stream of bullets tore into the tail and walked along the rear fuselage. The enemy fighter rolled inverted and broke up in a flaming explosion that touched the ground. Edwards looked down and realized that the kill had been so fast his undercarriage doors were still closing. More critically, his wingtip seemed to be only inches above the ground. That suggested to him that it was time to level out and get some altitude before making another turn.

Yak-9D White Rose *Over Airfield 108, Kazan*

A few hundred feet above the growing dogfight, Lilya quickly assessed the enemy formation. It was badly broken by the barrier patrols that guarded the Volga and she guessed that the P-38s and P-39s had bled the inbound formations badly. The 190s were coming in small groups, two or three aircraft each with equally small groups of Me-109s trying to cover them. The Yaks were already streaking in to face the fascist 109s head-on. Lilya picked her target carefully, one well out on the right so that she could make her escape away to the side if the attack did not go well. The 109 was already firing at her Yak but she held her own burst until the range was point-blank. Then she let fly with her 20mm cannon and single 12.7mm machine gun. The tracers seemed a thin and paltry blow compared with the thick streams from the Thunderbolts below her but they started to do the work. She saw the brilliant flashes of bullet strikes on the engine cowling and cockpit canopy and a stream of black smoke start to pour out of the engine.

The 109 tried to turn away but the mistake was fatal for him. Lilya used the turning ability of her Yak to fasten herself on his tail, only ten or twenty meters away from her prey. Her guns snapped out short bursts, knocking pieces off the German fighter's tail. The 109s engine was still streaming black smoke but she paid little attention to that. She knew if the fascist pilot pushed the throttles forward too hard, the over-rich mixture would cause that streamer. Anyway, she was more intent on putting her shells and bullets into the cockpit.

The 109 had already started to burn but Lilya stayed with it, still methodically shooting the enemy aircraft apart. Suddenly, it flipped over on to its back and the pilot bailed out. She watched dispassionately as he plunged earthwards, his parachute failing to open before his body slammed into the ground. *One more good fascist*, she thought grimly before turning her Yak to face another group of Me-109s.

Thunderbolt **Live Bait** *Over Airfield 108, Kazan.*

Not quite certain whether he should be elated by his early kill or terrified that he had come within inches of flying into the ground, Edwards climbed to a safe altitude before heading east to intercept the formation of bombers being tracked by the ground control radar. The barrier patrol had reported at least a dozen Ju-188s had attempted to cross the Volga but five had already been shot down and two more sent limping home. Downing the rest would be up to the first P-47s to get airborne while the remaining P-47s and Yaks dealt with the fighters.

Up ahead, Edwards could see six black dots, the surviving fascist Ju-188s. He could count six, obviously one of the claimed kills had been over-optimistic. There were four P-47s heading to intercept them. Both groups of aircraft had settled into formation, the Thunderbolts in their standard finger-four, the 188s in a group that seemed familiar to the American pilots. As they closed, the reason became clear. The 188s were in a rough copy of the combat flight used by the Flying Fortresses. Whether they were trying to mislead the defenses into thinking they were B-17s, simply copying a proven formation or something else wasn't clear.

"OK boys, they're copying our tactics, we'll copy theirs. We'll hit them head-on, in formation from 12 o'clock high. Blast the center and left aircraft in each V then we'll turn around and get the other two."

"Gotcha, Boss." Edwards heard the acknowledgment and took his flight of Thunderbolts upwards. By the time he was in position, the Ju-188s were closing fast. They were a lot lighter on their feet than the B-17s but in comparison with the sheets of fire from the Flying Fortresses, the barrage the fascist aircraft put up was decidedly unimpressive. The Thunderbolt flight had split into two pairs, one for each flight of Ju-188s. Edwards saw his intended target approaching fast, its long greenhouse cockpit with a machine gun turret perched on top growing rapidly in his gunsight.

At 300 yards, he squeezed the trigger and watched the stream of bullets tear the sleek greenhouse cockpit apart. The 188 staggered in the air, disintegrating under the flail of the eight .50s. Streaming a mixture of orange fire and black smoke, the crippled bomber fell out of the sky far too low for its crew to stand any chance of bailing out. The wreckage plowed into a field and exploded, sending a fountain of dirt and debris upwards. Edwards climbed away and looked around for the surviving Ju-188s. He could see three more pyres of smoke and flame that marked an aircraft downed but no flying aircraft. Then, he realized that in the attack he had somehow got switched around and he was looking east rather than west. Once he looked the right way, he could see two surviving twin-engined aircraft fleeing for the Volga and, although they didn't yet know it, the waiting Airacobras.

"Back to the airfield. Leave the fascists to the barrier patrol." Plaster, the fighter controller on the ground, gave the order with a harsh level of command in his voice.

"On our way, Plaster."

Yak-9D White Rose *Over Airfield 108, Kazan*

The Focke-Wulf 190s were the ground attack version, more heavily armored than the fighters Lilya normally engaged. They had 13.2mm machine guns in the nose and 20mm cannon in the wing roots but the outer wing cannon had been deleted in favor of bombs or drop-tanks. The 190s had been trying to strafe the base but there was no sign of them having dropped any bombs. They'd probably carried drop tanks instead given the distance to their bases. Lilya cursed to herself as another burst from her guns caused flashes from strikes all over the rear fuselage but the 190 seemed to shrug them off. It was another example of a long-standing complaint of hers; the Yaks were too lightly armed for the work they had to do.

She took a deep breath and steadied herself before squeezing off another burst at the fascist in front of her. This time she had shifted her aim and walked the stream of strikes along the 190s left wing. The change was successful; her gunfire blew the entire left wing blew off in a brilliant white explosion and the 190 rolled onto its back before diving into the ground.

Lilya relaxed for a split second before feeling a heavy slam on the patch of armor plate that protected her head. Simultaneously, a line of holes appeared in the wing of her Yak. She looked behind, through the bubble cockpit that gave her improved rear vision and cursed, violently and profanely. She'd fallen for the oldest fighter pilot's trick in the world. While she had been fixated on killing the 190 in front of her, four Me-109s had closed in on her and boxed her in against the ground. She was painfully aware that if it hadn't been for the patch of armor introduced on the Yak-9, she would have been killed instantly when they opened fire.

Even so, her position was desperate. No matter how she turned, one of the 109s behind her was able to get in a good deflection shot; if she tried to climb away, the 109s could keep up with her and would tear her apart. She couldn't dive; she was barely 200 feet up. She had only one chance and that depended on her Yak staying together long enough to use it. Ahead of her was one of the anti-aircraft batteries that protected the airfield. She skidded her Yak right to try and avoid the fire from the fascist fighters behind her then immediately reversed the skid and went left. It bought her a little time and left her close enough to see the anti-aircraft guns in front of her. The battery captain was already pointing at her. *Tovarish Captain, please don't shoot at me. I have enough problems. The fascists are behind me. Do your duty this day.*

Her Yak was in desperate trouble and she knew it. There was smoke coming from the engine in front of her, she could smell the unmistakable tang of burning wood and varnish. Worse, the controls were getting sloppy and the aircraft was slowing as it lost power. She skidded again feeling the growing lack of response from her controls. Then, red streaks from the anti-aircraft guns started passing her. For a hideous moment she thought they were indeed firing on her but a glance to the rear reassured her. The bursts from the guns were right amongst the 109s pursuing her and caused them to break off the attack and scatter. Even better two Thunderbolts and three Yaks were coming to her aid and it was now the 109s that would have to fight for their lives.

Lilya looked around; *White Rose* was finished. She was leaving a great black smear of smoke behind her and the controls were getting worse by the second. She brought the dying fighter around, lining up with the runway beside her. The undercarriage lever was useless; it just flopped in her hand when she tried to pump the undercarriage down. *So, it's going to be a belly landing then. This just gets better and better.*

Slowly, the brown expanse of the runway came into view under her nose. By now, her windscreen was black with burned engine oil and the smell of the fires in her aircraft was choking her. The loss of engine power had already dropped below the critical point and her crash landing was imminent. She reached up and tried to pull the cockpit canopy back in readiness for the fastest exit she had ever made from a Yak. It wouldn't move.

"Chertovy fashisty! We'd finished for the day! I was supposed to be on my back by now!"

Her scream of outrage and the way fate had conspired against her coincided with the slam as her fighter hit the end of the runway and started to slide on its belly down the length of the strip. The force of the impact threw her against the forward frame of the cockpit canopy, dizzying her. She could feel the blood running down her face as she slumped back in the seat. By now, the Yak had slowed enough to dig one wingtip into the ground and that stared to spin the aircraft.

There was nothing she could do. With the cockpit canopy jammed, there was no way out. The wreck of her fighter was sliding out of control with the fire from the engine spreading fast. The wooden structure of the Yak had its advantages but once it started to burn, the fires quickly engulfed everything. The fascists knew that of course which was why they carried incendiary ammunition.

Eventually, the Yak stopped, just off the runway. It seemed to rear slightly as if it was going to somersault but it crashed back on the ground. Lilya could hear the dull whoomph noise as the fuel tanks in the wing roots exploded. They were nearly empty and the outboard tanks had been drained but there was still enough fuel left to cause a sheet of flame to erupt on both sides of her cockpit. She was trapped by the fires. Instinctively, she pulled the heavy collar of her flight jacket up to protect her face but she knew it was hopeless. She'd heard the screams of pilots being burned alive in their aircraft and had always decided that she wouldn't allow that to happen to her. As the temperature in the cockpit climbed and the smoke choked her, she started to feel for her Nagant revolver.

Before she could find it, the wreckage of her Yak lurched sideways. *There go the outer wing tanks. Sorry, Misha, this is the end.*

Then, her cockpit seemed to explode around her.

Thunderbolt Live Bait *Over Airfield 108, Kazan.*

"My God, look at that!" The scene around Airfield 108 was indescribable and unforgettable. The black pyres of smoke from shot-down aircraft ringed the base and were scattered across it. The comment from *Miss Fire* was nothing more than a reasoned response to an awesome situation.

389

Kazan Thunderbolts

"All Plaster aircraft, come in to land. Watch out, there are wrecks all over the field; mostly fascists. So far, we've counted 26 hostiles down for a P-47 lost and a crashed-landed Yak-9 to the left of the main runway, surrounded by emergency vehicles. *Live Bait*, be advised the wreck is *White Rose*. We have no reports from the crash scene yet."

"*Live Bait*, land now. We'll follow you in." Major Young's voice on the radio was sympathetic but there was an undertone of caution to it, He had known that this situation, or something like it, would happen one day and how these two, or the survivor thereof, handled it would determine the answers to a lot of policy decisions.

Edwards glanced around the sky and noted two of the Thunderbolts were trailing smoke and obviously shot up. "With respect, Sir, *Miss Fire* and *Lewd Lucy* are both in trouble; whatever has happened down there has already happened. Those two need to get down now."

The reply had the caution replaced by quiet respect. One of Young's questions had been answered the way he hoped it would. "Very well; *Miss Fire* and *Lewd Lucy* land now; clear the runway immediately for *Live Bait*.

Edwards was running on instinct when he put *Live Bait* down in a perfect three-point landing. All he could see when he passed the wreck of *White Rose* was a group of emergency vehicles, some olive drab, others earth brown, around a pyre of smoke and flame. The fire was one of the fiercest he had ever seen at a crash site; a legacy, he guessed, from wooden construction and aviation fuel. His mind was continuously generating images of what he might find when he got to the scene. *Lilya's blackened, twisted corpse, charred to a husk? Or worse, her charred body still alive and screaming?* The latter image nearly made him vomit into his cockpit.

He completed the shut-down procedure and was about to run over to the crash site when a jeep pulled up beside him. Koldunov was at the wheel although the jeep was American. "Get in. I'll get you over there."

Koldonov was as good as his word; indeed the ride over to the crash showed he had a degree of driving skill that Edwards had never suspected. His borrowed jeep swept across the runway, exploiting a gap between the Thunderbolts coming in, and broadsided to a stop. Edwards leapt out to run to the burning Yak first of all. The fires were dying down and all he could see left were the engine block and the cockpit seat. It was empty, the charred husk he had feared wasn't there.

"Lieutenant, over by the ambulance. We got her out." Two sergeants were standing by a smoke-blackened and badly damaged jeep. They'd been writing notes down on a pad and comparing impressions and actions. Edwards took in the uniforms, noting the odd unit patch on their arms. It was a seal balancing a ball on its nose. Then he took off on a run for the ambulance.

Once he got there, he slowed down. A group of figures were clustered around a figure on a stretcher, working furiously. He was about to join them when a hand grabbed his arm.

"Stay away for a few minutes, Lieutenant. The doctors have work to do this day." Guards-Major Stepan Petrovich Ganin sounded reassuring.

"How is she, Sir."

"A great debt is owed to those two sergeants back there. They drove a jeep into the fire and rammed the wreck, pushing it clear of the burning fuel. Then one of them stood on the hood and smashed the cockpit open with a sledgehammer. They pulled her out before she started to burn. Then they backed the jeep out through the fire. I believe Guards-Captain Litvyak has only moderate injuries but I fear the jeep is mortally wounded. The doctors are waving, you had better go to them."

"Lieutenant Edwards? Guards-Captain Litvyak has been asking for you."

"How is she, Doc?"

"She has severe smoke inhalation; we have her on oxygen for that. We've been washing her eyes out; they were filled with smoke particles and there is some danger her corneas will have been scratched. We'll have to do vision tests to find out. Minor burns to her hands, they'll heal fine. Big worry is her head. She took a severe blow when her head hit the cockpit frame and her forehead is lacerated. She'll have more scars there to add to her collection. I guess she's crashed Yaks before. She has a severe concussion and will be off duty for a week or more because of that alone. You can go to her now but don't expect her to make too much sense. As I said, she has a bad concussion. We'll take her to the base hospital and keep her there until we're sure she won't get any worse. We'll also X-ray her head and make sure she hasn't got a skull fracture."

"Thank you, Doc. For everything."

"Don't thank me, thank those two sergeants. What they did was just about the bravest thing I've ever seen. Now, have a quick word with your girl before we put her in the ambulance."

"Oh Misha. Ya oblazhalsya." Then, Lilya remembered who she was speaking to. "Misha, I made a mistake. I didn't want to burn, I was going to shoot myself."

"I know. Why do you think the Army gives us these?" He tapped the .45 Colt in its shoulder holster. "It isn't so we can shoot it out with the entire Hitlerite Army."

Edwards reached down and took her hand. Her gloves had protected her fingers but there was a band of burns around her wrists where the skin had been exposed. "At least you're out safely. The Doc says you have concussion but you'll be fine. They're going to keep you in hospital overnight."

Edwards watched her carried in the ambulance and driven off to the base hospital. Theoretically it was an American facility but Russian medical care was primitive although they had a surprising number of personnel trained in basic first aid. So, the Russian area was used as first-aid center for minor injuries while the American hospital was used for more serious incidents. Once her ambulance was over the runway he went back to where the two sergeants were sitting. "Sergeants, I don't know what to say. We owe you more than there are words to express. Thank you seems hopelessly inadequate."

"Our job, sir. I'm Sergeant Kidd, this is Sergeant Wint. We're SEALS, our part of the operation is to go around and teach people the best ways to get crews out of crashed aircraft. The first thing we learned today is whoever designed that Yak-9 really hates pilots. It's near-impossible to get out of that thing without getting burned up."

"This time, we were lucky." Wint looked up from his notes. "That thick flight gear with the big collar we made fun of? Turns out it's more fire-resistant than our coveralls and Guards-Captain Litvyak had the presence of mind to pull the collar up to protect her face. That's one piece of advice we'll be passing on. Another is, don't crash land a Yak. Bail out. With fuel tanks in front and on either side of the pilot, it's a ready-made roasting oven."

Suddenly light burst on Edwards. "I know you two; you wrote that pamphlet we got on how to put a Thunderbolt down. That saved more than a few guys here."

"Glad to hear it." Kidd sounded a little embarrassed. "You wanted to know how to thank us, well, telling us that will do nicely. Anyway, this is a pretty good job for Government work. The SEALS have top priority, anything we want, we get. Wint and I have top travel priority. A few days ago, we had to go up to Zheleznogorsk; people running the Air Bridge are worried a loaded C-54 will crash and they want to know what to do when it happens. We're still studying that. Anyway, we bounced two people off a C-54, one a Major General, the other a Brit naval commander. The General took it good, just wished us luck. The Brit was as mad as hell. I don't think he'll ever forgive us."

Edwards Household, 548 Spruce Street, Hellertown, Pennsylvania.

"Honey, I'm home." William Edwards carefully hung up his outdoor coat. With clothes rationing just introduced, he had a feeling it would be a long time before he could get another. His hat followed his coat.

"There's a package from Russia, Bill." Alice Edwards had carefully put the package to one side so she and her husband could open it together. She had a feeling it would contain pictures of her son's new girlfriend, a person of whom she had the darkest of maternal suspicions. She had already checked the back flap and her heart had stopped pounding when she saw the code DESIGN written there.

Edwards opened it and tipped out the contents. There was a long letter in there, one which they would both read carefully before storing it with the others. There were also some pictures sandwiched between two thin wooden boards. A frustrated carpenter, Edwards noted the intricately beautiful grain pattern and instinctively knew that this was genuine Siberian pine.

"Oh, isn't she pretty!" Alice Edwards was holding up a picture. It was of Lilya climbing out of the cockpit of her Yak looking straight at the camera. "She seems such a nice girl."

Privately Edwards doubted that. Not by middle class American standards anyway. A woman at war couldn't be nice and survive. There was another picture of her, a close-up that had obviously been taken by a skilled photographer. That made her beautiful rather than just pretty but the photographer had also caught a look of ruthless determination in her eyes. *I would not want this woman hunting for me.* "They're good pictures. There's one here of Monty in his Thunderbolt. Why don't I varnish these pieces of timber and then use them as a frame for the photographs. We can put them on the mantelpiece, one each side of the clock."

"What a wonderful idea! Do you think we'll meet her, Bill?"

"Of course. He'll bring her home as soon as he gets enough leave." Edwards was lying and he knew it. The memories of the trenches in WW1 closed in on him. *We'll never see our son again and we'll never see his girl. The Russian Front will swallow them just like the trenches swallowed the kids my age who went to war in 1917. Same enemy, different generation. In the name of God, let's finish it properly this time.* "Why don't we listen to the game on the radio while we eat dinner, then I'll go to my bench and make the frames."

His wife smiled and went to get the evening meal. She still wasn't quite used to rationing but she was quietly proud of having put together a tasty, filling meal. Behind her, she heard the squeal and crackle of the radio being tuned in.

"We interrupt this program to bring you a special news bulletin. The German Army has murdered four hundred and eighty six American soldiers taken prisoner near the town of Kanash on the Russian Front. The dead include four female Army nurses. President Roosevelt has announced there will be a national day of mourning for our murdered men and women. American troops advancing on Kolinino as part of our counter attack in the Chuvash found the bodies left to rot in a field. We take you now to Washington for the latest news."

A different announcer cut in. "No more details of the Kolkhoz Gap massacre are available at this time although an official statement is expected in a few minutes. The White House released the news in a brief statement to reporters read by Stephen Early, the President's press secretary. Wait please . . . . We have just been informed that elements of the U.S. Army Expeditionary Force advancing in the Chuvash have captured large numbers of German Army trucks disguised with red crosses but loaded with fuel and ammunition. We return you now to your scheduled broadcast but will bring you more news as it becomes available."

"Oh my." Alice Edwards had nearly dropped their dinner when the news broadcast had started. "What does it mean, Bill."

"It means we had better finish this war a bit more finally than we did the last one."

Astoria Cinema, 235th Street, Cicero, Indiana.

"Can we sit nearer the screen please? My eyes are a bit tired." Annie Nelson was using the standard excuse used by girls who didn't want to go into the back row. *Next date, perhaps.*

Raymond Searle mentally raised his eyebrows and submitted to the inevitable. By the time he and Annie had settled down, the lights in the cinema had dimmed but the program didn't start. Instead the cinema manager stepped out on to the stage. "Ladies and Gentlemen, we have just received a newsreel film direct from Russia with a government request it be shown immediately. The staff hasn't seen it ourselves yet, but in view of the radio announcement a few minutes ago, we can guess what it contains."

The projector clicked and whirred, the images forming on the screen. It was a field, surrounded by a high stone wall. There were Army vehicles, trucks, tanks. Russian, American, all around the entrance. There were also Russian civilians, watching what was happening impassively. The commentator was speaking with grave solemnity.

"Ladies and Gentlemen, this is a news story I thought I would never have to cover. This is a field in the Kolkhoz Pass, on the Russian Front. Here, the bodies of four hundred and eighty six American men and women, taken prisoner after defending the town of Kanash, lie where they fell, murdered by German SS troops." The commentator hesitated. "No, I am sorry, I cannot call them troops. Soldiers have a sense of decency, a sense of honor. They respect their opponents even while they fight them. The men responsible for this massacre have no decency, they have no honor. They do not deserve the title of soldier –

I ask if they can even be considered men. Here, men, real men, from American ambulance units have assembled to recover the bodies. They have been joined by our Russian allies, soldiers, partisans and civilians to help in the grim work. There are volunteers from the Red Cross here as well, trying to aid the soldiers with this terrible scene."

The commentator moved back towards the entrance to the field, the camera crew following him. As they moved up to the entrance, the camera span swept across the field, showing the piles of bodies littered across the grass. A gasp went up from the audience as the full horror of what had happened in the field sank home. The dead were being inspected by medical personnel, photographed, checked for identity documents, then placed on a stretcher and covered with a blanket. As the first of the dead was brought out through the gate, his arm fell clear of the blanket and the fingers trailed in the dirt. A Russian woman ran from the watching civilians and took the hand in hers. The cinema audience was expecting her to push the hand under the blanket again but, instead, she held it all the way to the waiting truck. When the stretcher was loaded, she went back to the gate. Already a line of women was forming and each of the bodies was escorted by a Russian woman who held his hand until he was loaded.

"Ladies, gentlemen, I have no words for what we are seeing here. I have heard of things like this but actually to see our young men murdered in their hundreds. . . . I don't know what to say. Now we know what the Russian people have suffered for the last two and a half years. We knew, but we didn't know. Only now to see this. Somehow, to see this, now we know. Somehow we thought this wouldn't happen to us; that we were different. Well, we're not. This is what Nazis do and they'll do it to us as well. I'm sorry, I can't go on."

Probably to cover the commentator's loss of composure, the cameraman zoomed in on one of the bodies that was about to be loaded on to a stretcher. The man was on his face, his head covered by his arms so that the birds hadn't got to him. When the stretcher-bearers rolled him over to load him, the features of his face were clearly visible.

"Oh my God, it's my kid brother. That's Gene!"

"Ray's right. I was on the high school football team with him. That's Gene all right, no doubt about it."

The newsreel had been watched in dead silence but that suddenly ended as the audience saw one of their own amongst the murdered men. A ripple of rage started to spread, a bear-like, low-pitched growl that mixed in with the sobbing from the women. The volume might have started low but it was increasing steadily. When the cameraman filmed the dead nurses, what had been a low growl was very close to being a roar. By the time the newsreel had ended, the theater manager was seriously worried that he had a riot on his hands.

"Ladies and gentlemen, please. We were going to show the romantic comedy 'Heaven Can Wait' with Don Ameche and Gene Tierney but after what we have just seen, we can't. We just can't." The manager broke down and took a moment to compose himself. "We'll refund your tickets at the booth."

"Buy war bonds with the money! Give them to the American Legion." It was the same voice that had confirmed the identification of Eugene Searle and his words brought a roar of agreement.

"Yes, of course." The manager turned to his secretary who had run on to the stage with a piece of paper in her hand. He read it quickly. "This is from the owners. They say that they will match the money raised for war bonds tonight, here and at the other theaters they own. The theater that raises the most will get the total doubled again. We'll collect the money in the foyer."

By the time Ray Searle and Annie Nelson got to the foyer, it was crowded with men emptying their wallets into the collection buckets, Annie took the get-me-home money her mother made her carry in case a date went really bad and added that to the totals. Most of the women were doing the same. Then, the chaos was frozen by the sound of the volunteer fire company siren sounding. The company commander ran in. "All fire company members, get ready. Somebody has just tossed a trio of gasoline bombs into Schreiner's Grocery."

The company members looked at each other. Helmut Schreiner had been an immigrant in the 1920s and a prominent member of the German-American Bund. Even after the war had started, he'd gone around saying that the Bolsheviks were the real enemy and that Americans should ally with the Reich against them. Nobody was surprised that his business had been torched. The Company Commander sensed the reluctance of his men to turn out. "Come on boys. The fire might spread."

That was the deciding factor and the Volunteer Fire Company turned out. Across the road from the burning store, the Army recruiting office was opening up to handle the crowd of young men trying to volunteer. The Navy recruiting station had beaten them by a couple of minutes and Ray Searle was already inside, signing up for flight training. He left the station with his enlistment papers in his hands and started to take Annie home. They'd have to walk, they'd already given all the money they had on them to the war bond drive.

Across the road, Helmut Schreiner, his wife and children were sitting on the side of the road, dimly lit by the red glow of the fires that had destroyed their business. They had lived above their store and the gasoline bombs had taken away everything they owned. Three or four of the men in the street had found themselves baseball bats and tire irons and were descending on the family. Patrolman Nathaniel Malone saw them and stepped in their way.

"Back off. You can't do this."

"You saw what these krauts did, Nate. Time for some payback."

"I didn't say you *shouldn't* smash their heads in. I said you *can't*. Now, get out of here."

For a second, it seemed as if his order would be defied and Malone decided if they were, he wasn't going to get himself beaten down as well. Fortunately, the men backed off, dropping their weapons and retreating into the shadows. Malone looked around, it had been a small victory but the situation still had the potential to turn into a murderous riot. He stared hard at the Schreiners, acutely conscious of the weight of his pistol on one hip and his nightstick on the other. "You can't stay here. I'm going to take you to the police station and put you into protective custody.

"What are you arresting us for? We're the innocent party here." Schreiber was blustering furiously.

Malone just stared at him. "No, you're not."

Carinhall, Schorfheide, Brandenburg.

Early morning was Reichsmarschall Hermann Goering's favorite time of the day. It was quiet so he could mull over the issues that troubled him in peace. He was alone so that he could think without worrying about how the inevitable audience would use his musings to their own advantage. Most importantly, having been at rest for so many hours, the pain from his wound was at its lowest ebb and he didn't need his morphine to dull the grinding agony. He knew all too well what the day would hold. As his activities increased throughout the day, the pain would increase and then he would resort to his morphine. His mind would become clouded as the pain grew worse and he resorted to greater and greater doses of the drug. Soon, he would become incapable of doing anything and his staff would take over, using his authority towards their own ends.

One of his maids entered his room, as quietly as she could so that the Reichsmarschall would not be disturbed. It would amaze those who only knew Goering's public persona to learn that he was popular and well-regarded by his domestic staff. They knew of his public character of course, the founder of the Gestapo, the organizer of the concentration camps, the creator of the slave labor system not to mention the assiduous collector of other country's art treasures. They never saw that side of him. All they saw was the affable, considerate and generous employer who went out of his way to look after 'his' people. One of the maids still spoke of the time her parents had been trying to buy a house and a particularly obnoxious official had obstructed them at every turn. Goering had resolved the issue by cosigning the loan documents himself. When the official had seen the signature he had wet his pants.

"Your breakfast and the newspapers, Herr Reichsmarschall." She put the tray beside him, gave her most pleasant smile and quickly left the room.

Goering was in no real hurry to start the day. He ate his scrambled eggs and drank his tea first, then looked at the first of his newspapers. One of the greater secrets of the Reich was that the Reichsmarschall had a serious fondness for reading the Wall Street Journal and getting him the current copy was a major exercise. Ten seconds after he had picked up that copy, any members of his staff seeing his face would have had no doubt he was capable of, and had committed, every single one of the dreadful crimes of which he had been accused. And many more besides. The single word "MURDERED" in bold type had seen to that. The picture below it had just finished the job of destroying any sense of tranquility he might have had.

The full story was inside the paper; so much so that most of the company and economic news had been deleted. That wasn't unusual; the corporate data had been growing steadily thinner as more and more had become related to war work and was thus classified. Goering read the details of the mounting German atrocities with something akin to horror. Air men deliberately shot as they bailed out of crippled aircraft; hunted down, captured and executed on the ground or taken to interrogation centers, tortured for information and then killed. First individual soldiers being brutally murdered after they had surrendered then the mass murder of whole surrendered units. Using Red Cross markings to smuggle munitions, fuel and other war supplies. It wasn't the fact of the atrocities that perturbed him; after all such conduct had been the normal state of affairs in Russia since the first day of Barbarossa. Nor was it the number of killings; his own personal score of political enemies killed was far in excess of the number of American dead described in the newspaper. It was the sheer stupidity of the massacres that overwhelmed him. *Damn them. If I can see this is the ultimate stupidity, why can't they?*

Once, long ago, before his health had started its downward spiral, Goering had been a keen huntsman. One morning, just after dawn, he had been hunting in the Schorfheide forest when the post-dawn mist had come down unusually thick and fast. Within seconds, the weather had changed from the usual pre-dawn twilight, dark yet clear, to a clinging blanket of white that masked out everything. It had been so dense that it was quite possible to walk into a tree without seeing it. Within minutes he had been hopelessly lost and in grave danger of stumbling over a ridge or falling down a steep slope. He had stumbled through the woods, racking up a slowly increasing total of minor injuries and fighting down the onset of panic. Then, without warning, the sun had broken through the fog and swept it away. The forest around him was suddenly crystal clear, so much so that he could see the individual water droplets on the leaves and the tiny rainbows they caused in the morning sub. That moment of crystal clarity, made all the more amazing by the clinging blanket of fog that had preceded it, slowly faded as well and the day reverted to normal.

Now, it was happening again and Goering felt the clouds roll back from his mind and he could see everything around him with pitiless clarity. He knew what was happening; one of his doctors had told him that one day this would happen. He would have a moment of absolute clarity in which he would see everything around him the way it was, he would see himself as he was and for what he was. The same would apply to the people around him, he would see them for what they were and how they regarded him. His vision had become unclouded by the drugs that befuddled him and allowed him to gain a deep understanding of the truths that had been out of reach for so long. Long ago, one of the doctors tending him, Erhard Wetzel, had warned him that one day such a moment would come. He had said it would be his brain making one last desperate plea for help before the damage to it became irreversible.

Goering suddenly became aware of another presence in the room. It was a young man, in the old-fashioned uniform worn by pilots in the First World War. His face was twisted with scorn and contempt. Goering realized that he was seeing himself as he had been once, as a young and successful fighter pilot on the Western Front. Through the eyes of that younger self, he also saw himself as he was now. A morbidly obese, buffoonish, arrogant, incompetent braggart who was held in contempt and derision by his professional colleagues. In short, the sort of man his younger self would have taken great pleasure in beating into a pulp. It was that insight that made him decide to take action.

"Find Dr. Erhard Wetzel and bring him to Carinhall." His order down the telephone was clear and decisive, something the operator had not heard for a long time.

"He's already here, Herr Reichsmarschall. He attends the domestic staff, guests and the local townspeople."

"Then send him up to see me. Immediately."

A few minutes later, Dr Wetzel knocked respectfully on the door and waited to be summoned in. "Doctor, once you told me I would have a moment of clarity and this would be my last chance. That moment is upon me and I wish to take account of the warning. I need your help."

"I will be honest Herr Reichsmarschall. Your condition today is far worse than it was when I gave you that warning. We may be too late; even if we are not, then we have no time to waste. You need surgery to correct the basic cause of your problems, the bullet wound you suffered in 1923. We need to find out what that quack Breitbarth has been giving you."

"Dihydrocodeine."

"And? The symptoms you have described suggest you have been taking a cocktail of drugs. We need to find out what is in that cocktail."

"We shall find out the easy way. Doctor Breitbarth will tell us himself."

Ten minutes later, a sample of Goering's medication was on its way to a laboratory for analysis, Goering was on his way to his morning staff meeting and Doctor Breitbarth was on his way to the Russian Front.

Once in the conference room, Goering looked at the participants. "We have only two items for the agenda this morning. One is that I will be away for some time due to ill-health. In my absence, Generalfeldmarschall Milch will act for me. General der Jagdflieger Galland and Generaloberst Jeschonnek will report to Generalfeldmarschall Milch on matters relating to fighter and bomber matters respectively. Generalleutnant Herrick, your report on an air defense system for the Reich was interesting. Produce a plan for its implementation and submit it to Generalfeldmarschall Milch.

"And now we come to the more important matter. What is your excuse for this?" Goering threw the copy of the Wall Street Journal on to the conference table. "Dolfo, what would you do if given the order to strafe pilots that bailed out? Or to murder them on the ground afterwards?"

Galland stood up and his voice rang with indignation. "I would never obey that order. I would do everything in my power to ensure that everybody else refused to obey it."

Goering gave him a slight but very noticeable dip of the head. "And I'd do the same. The conduct described here is both disgusting and stupid. What excuse do the rest of you have?"

He listened to the denials and claims of ignorance, some of which he believed, and the excuses and justifications from the SS and Army representatives. Listening to the self-righteous posturing, he found the lack of understanding for the nature of their new enemy quite astounding. Eventually, he slammed his hand down on the table with a crash that silenced the room. "Dolfo, you will stamp this behavior out. Shoot a few Geschwader commanders if you have to. And make it clear nobody who indulges in this behavior will be granted the title of 'experten'.

Goering turned around and started to storm out of the conference facility but at the door, he stopped and his voice hissed across the table. "You damned fools! I can think of nothing that would enrage the Americans more that the wanton slaughter of unarmed prisoners and the murder of helpless aircrew after they had bailed out of their machines. They will *never* forgive us for this. All you have done is to waken a sleeping giant and fill him with a terrible desire for revenge."

EPILOGUE

Office of Joseph P Kennedy, Washington D.C.

"Joan, I need some coffee right away. It's been a long night." For Joseph Kennedy it had been. The introduction of rationing on gasoline, tires, clothing and many other war-essential items had brought with it a host of problems for the people he regarded as his constituency. He had worked until the small hours of the morning, calling in favors, striking deals or finding solutions for the people who lacked the contacts and gravitas to solve them for themselves. In Kennedy's eyes, it was his duty to them just as it was theirs to vote for him or the causes he supported.

When his secretary came in, her eyes were rimmed bright red and she kept dabbing at her nose. Kennedy looked at her with concern. She was, after all, one of his people. "What's the matter, Joan?"

"Sir, didn't you hear the news bulletin last night?" She went on to describe the radio broadcast and cinema newsreel that had enraged an entire nation. "I've got a copy of the Post. It's all on the front page."

To Kennedy's eyes, there was no doubt about that. The single word "MURDERED" dominated the front page over a picture of a field strewn with dead bodies. And that was all the front page was. It didn't need to be anything more.

As Kennedy read the articles on the inside pages, the cold rage inside him built up to bursting point. Not just about the massacre although that would gnaw at him. It was the way he could have been so easily destroyed by the ham-handed maneuver from the Halifax machine in London. *Those bastards. Those ineffectual simpering bastards. If I'd done what they wanted, I would have been linked to the anti-war, pro-German cliques just as news of this atrocity came out. My family wouldn't just have been destroyed politically, there's a good chance some of us, probably me, would have been lynched. And there will be lynchings over this. If it hadn't been for the warnings from the Commonwealth and that Brit naval commander, what was his name, Fleming, we could have been ruined. All right, we can welsh on gambling debts and financial loans can always be defaulted but political debts must always be repaid.*

"Charles." Kennedy called out for his chief of staff. "First, go through all the dead in the Kolkhoz Pass massacre, there must be some Irish-American kids in there. Damn it, add in any who were Catholic. Draft a letter to their parents, usual thing, grieve for their loss, courageously fought for their country, will do all we can to see their loss is not in vain. Add in a note that this letter is an invitation to visit us here any time if they are in Washington so we can talk about any assistance they may need. If any of them take us up on it, schedule them for twenty minutes and a staffer takes them to lunch. Bring those letters to me, I'll sign them personally.

"Secondly, draft me a speech about this horror. Deeply shocked, angered beyond measure by the murderous attack on prisoners of war. Deeply appreciate sympathetic gestures by Russian people. Massacre shows us how much we have to learn from each other. Now, United States, Russia and Commonwealth are fighting side-by-side, we must share all the knowledge we have and we must all have a voice in how to prosecute the war.

"Thirdly, tell our cellar manager that he is to find absolutely the best bottle of whisky we have, with or without an E, pre-prohibition of course, and send it to Commander Ian Fleming, Free Royal Navy, Ottawa.

"Oh, and fourthly, send a telegram to Jack in Russia. Message reads, 'you are right, I was wrong.' Got all that? Good, Get on with it."

With his office once again empty, Kennedy reviewed his actions. *So, we're making nice with the voters and the speech will tell the Commonwealth I'm on their side in the intelligence question. I'll smooth Donovan over later. And I've patched things up with Jack. Now, how do I screw over those jerks in London?*

Main Street, Hawkins, Tennessee

When the Robsons came to town, men would step aside. When the Hundleys were around, the womenfolk would hide (quite why was a good question since the rules of Feudin' outlawed harming women unless they'd elected to take an active part in the dispute). The point was both families believed that the point of a gun was the only law they could respect. And when it came to shooting straight and fast, both families were mighty good.

So it was that when Micah Robson and two of his sons walked down Main Street towards the Town Hall and met Ike Hundley and two of his sons, also heading for the Town Hall, the sheriff put up a sign reading "Gone Fishing" and left by the back door. Everybody else on the street took cover.

The six men stood facing each other in silence. These were hard-eyed, hard-faced men who used words sparingly and weighed each one carefully for its value. They stood facing each other, neither willing to make way until Ike Hundley broke the silence. "Heard about your boy, Micah. Weren't right what them Narzees done."

Micah Robson nodded in acknowledgement. "Cowards wouldn't fight him fair. Took his gun first then shot him."

"Remember Jaspar shot me in the ass when I was takin' a dump. Musta been six hundred yards that shot."

"Shut up boy. Elders are talkin'." Ike looked at his son Roscoe sideways, his comment without anger or venom. Roscoe had made a strong point. A marksman who could shoot a squatting man in the ass at 600 yards could have blown his head off just as easily. "Micah, my boys goin' to enlist. Be right with you if they get a couple of Narzees each in Jasper's name?"

"Why, I'd take that right kindly, Ike. Beth too."

"How's she takin' it?"

"Government telegram arrived, she took to her bed cryin'. Still weepin'. When she heard they killed the nurses. . . ."

The six man nodded slowly. When a feud was running, a man getting killed was an everyday possibility and the Robson-Hundley feud had been running for generations. Only, here, in the Appalachian Mountains of Tennessee, nurses were regarded with a veneration that verged on worship. It was the town nurse who turned out in the middle of a storm when one of the womenfolk was in labor and held the line until a doctor arrived. It was the nurses who stayed with the sick during an epidemic, at risk of their own lives. It was nurses who watched over ailing infants when their mothers were desperate for a little sleep. Nobody ever laid a hand on a nurse. Or if they did, every man's hand would be turned against them until the day they died. Which wouldn't take long.

Ike Hundley knew what that code meant. "Micah, seems to me we got bigger problems with them Narzees than our own difference."

Micah Robson grasped the approach immediately. "Right, Ike. Them Narzees need killin'. Need it real bad."

The two men stretched out their hands in a movement so perfectly coordinated that nobody would ever be able to claim that the other family had reached out first. They solemnly shook hands and at that moment, on the Main Street of Hawkins, the Robson-Hundley feud ended after almost 150 years.

The recruiting Sergeant wasn't surprised to see the Robson and Hundley boys come in together. All over the Appalachians, old feuds were being set aside or buried so that the young men could unite against the greater enemy. "Hello, boys. You want to enlist? What service had you in mind?"

Kazan Thunderbolts

"Where we get to kill most Narzees." Roscoe Hundley spoke for them all; he had earned that right from the .30-30 scar on his left buttock.

"That'll be the infantry, son." The recruiting sergeant knew the way to a young Appalachian man's heart. He took a gleaming M1903A4 Springfield sniper rifle with a telescopic sight and handed it to the nearest of the four recruits. "Being as you're a backwoods man, we'll give you one of these. Normal recruits just get a Garand but you boys deserve something special. Take these here papers to the clerk and he'll get you sworn in. Army will come and collect you in a couple of week's time.

The four boys left, and the Sergeant gazed at their fathers. "You two were doughboys in the First One, right? Well, you got two weeks, more or less. Teach them everything you can about real soldierin'. They'll need it."

Prisoner of War Camp, Maimyzh, Kazakh Front

"Raus, raus, raus!" The American guards were pounding gongs with their nightsticks, creating an unholy cacophony of noise. "Parade outside in five minutes."

Oberleutnant zur See Oskar Wuppermann heaved himself out of bed and pulled on his uniform jacket. It wasn't precisely cold, not yet, but there was a chill in the air that showed the dreaded Russian winter was approaching. It was like seeing a thundercloud on the horizon, knowing that the arrival of the storm might be a time coming but arrive it surely would.

Still, he thought, *things could get worse.* The food in the American-run PoW camp was as good as he would have been receiving in German naval service. The camp buildings were solid and the guards themselves were reasonable men. Or had been; that had changed quite suddenly. Now, they were hostile and Wuppermann felt that quite a few of them were looking for an excuse to start shooting.

He fell in with the other officer survivors of S-38 and heard the guards doing the count. Each section reported in as soon as the roll call was completed and the numbers of prisoners tallied. When the process was finally over, the Camp Commander stepped out on front of the parade.

"As the result of an agreement signed yesterday between the Russian and American governments, the custody of German prisoners of war held by American forces will be transferred to the forces of the Union of Soviet Socialist Republics. A group of trucks will be arriving shortly to transfer you to a Russian-run prisoner of war camp further east."

A column of American Studebaker trucks was already entering the camp. They drove past the parade, turned away from it, stopped and then backed up towards the waiting men. Wuppermann was surprised to note the sudden wave of fear sweeping the ranks of German Army prisoners. The trucks stopped again and the back of the canvas canopy rolled up.

The trucks were empty and the relief from the German Army prisoners was palpable. Two NCOs jumped down from the back of each, submachine guns hanging from their shoulders. Once again, Wuppermann got the feeling they were looking for an excuse to start shooting. The Camp Commander resumed his address. "Start to board the truck in front of you. Walk directly to your truck in single file. A step to the left, a step to the right will be considered an attempt to escape. Give your name and rank to the NCO by the tailgate."

Wuppermann fell in behind the small group of prisoners that had been on the left. As the first one of that group reached the tailgate, the leader gave his name. "Stelian Vasilescu, Captain, Romanian Air Force."

"Wait a minute, you are Romanian?" Vasilescu nodded. "What did you fly?"

"A Spitfire Mark VI. I was shot down by a P-39."

"Are all the men in this section Romanian Air Force? And are they the only Romanian prisoners here?"

"Yes, Sir."

"Then fall out. Romanian prisoners are being kept in American custody. We'll be shipping you back to Canada."

Wuppermann reached the NCO. "Oskar Wuppermann, Oberleutnant zur See, German Navy."

For a moment he too thought he would be told to stand to one side but the American NCO simply made a tick by his name before jerking his thumb at the back of the truck. It was then that he realized his life was about to get a whole lot worse. Then, the canvas back to the truck was rolled down and he felt the jerk as the truck started on its way.

Behind him, Captain Vasilescu went over to the Camp Commandant and saluted. "Sir, I believe I am now the senior ranking PoW here."

"Captain Vasilescu, our airmen have reported that on a recent bombing mission Romanian Spitfires protected crippled B-17s while their crews bailed out. We have also been informed by the Red Cross that aircrew taken prisoner by Romanian forces have been moved to Bucharest. The same message confirmed they are being treated properly. We have also received the mandated lists of such prisoners. You did right by us, we'll do right by you."

The camp commandant jerked his thumb at the departing truck convoy. "They didn't."

Kazan Thunderbolts

Gunboat Squadron GunRon 7 Headquarters, Ulyanov'sk, Volga River.

"Congratulations, Jack. You've got your own base and your own squadron. Well, you've got a wrecked base and the boats are under construction."

Kennedy looked at the wreckage of the harbor at Ulyanov'sk. The Russians had done a thorough job of blowing the facilities, then the fighting when the Germans had taken Ulyanov'sk had wrecked most of what was left. Then, when they had been forced out of the city again, they had finished the demolition of the little harbor. Kennedy had been particularly struck by the way the German demolition engineers had made two cranes twist around each other as they had brought them down. Finally, everything that was left had been booby-trapped. "I'm going to split the boats between the small anchorage north of the bridge and this one. We'll convert the cargo area here to a maintenance area. You hear we're getting the Elco 100-foot boats?"

"I did. Sorry I had to turn you down for PR-73, Jack, but she's Thom's boat now. He deserves a shot to make her his own and if he came here, she'd always really be yours. Also, we can't name this base after McHale, the Navy is naming a 2250 ton destroyer after him." Commander Henry Farrow gazed at the intricate pile of wreckage that had once been the cargo handling area of the small port. "God knows, you've got your hands full here. When this base is open for business, we'll control the whole length of the Volga, both banks, between Kazan and Ulyanov'sk. First job will be to link up with the Chuvashskaya Bridgehead, then expand south to join up with the Samaraskaya. We know how to expand that now; a series of small amphibious bites each one moving just far enough to flank the fascists without moving out of support range. That's for next year though."

They were interrupted by the sound of sirens out on the river. On the ruins of the Ulyanov'sk Bridge, a new trestle section was being swung into place. It marked the start of the reconstruction of the bridge and the establishment of a new supply line over the Volga. More significantly, it was a full, permanent repair. As such, it was a visible sign that the high tide of the German advance had passed and the Allies were now moving forward.

"How long do you think it will take us to get to Berlin, Henry?" Kennedy sounded as if he would have preferred not to know the answer.

"Don't ask me. My guess is ten years and five million dead. But, we'll get there."

CheKa District Headquarters, Metallist Prospekt 16, Pestretsy

"I wish I could tell you of how much tovarish Nina Klaravina achieved for the Rodina." Chekist Napalkov spoke with all the sincerity he was capable of, which wasn't actually very much but he was good at faking it. "Although she

406

lost her life in doing so, her exposure of the Hitlerite spy ring was a key part of us recovering Ulyanov'sk and establishing a new bridgehead on the west bank of the Volga. In achieving that, she was also responsible for saving the lives of hundreds of our soldiers and as many Americans. One day, when the war is won and the Rodina is free of foreign invaders, her story will be told and future generations will be inspired by what she achieved against all the odds facing her."

"She was never a beautiful girl and her looks faded very early." Her father's grief for a dead daughter was compounded by guilt. "She was desperate to be married and when Nikolai Pavlovich asked for her hand, she was only too pleased to accept. My wife and I we should have suspected something but we also were pleased to see her finally settled. If we had only been more suspicious, she might not have died. What happened to Nikolai Pavlovich?'

"He was found guilty of the worst kinds of murder, treason, sabotage, aiding an enemy of the state, spying and defrauding the State Liquor Authority. He had been cremated and his ashes scattered." Napalkov looked saddened by the tragic outcome of the case. Actually, he was feeling a little guilty about the administrative oversight that had resulted in Nikolai Pavlovich's execution being overlooked prior to him being placed in a cheap coffin and pushed into the crematorium. Tovarish Mariya Makarovna comment on the error had been "he kept saying he wasn't dead, but everybody knows what liars those fascist spies are." *Still, the error did have a poetic justice to it.*

"Anyway, the state will pay for the cremation of Nina Klaravina and a special marker has been commissioned that will record the fact that she rendered great service to the people of the Rodina. We have selected a fine place for her to rest; a small cemetery overlooking the Volga and the city of Ulyanov'sk. She will be at peace there I am sure and she will be close to your home so you may tend to her as she sleeps."

After the office door had closed, Napalkov sat down and opened the next file on his desk. The sheer speed with which Ulyanov'sk had fallen, mostly because of the way the American B-17s had blasted a hole in the defenses, had resulted in the capture of many fascist records. Some would, Napalkov was sure, reveal the identities of more traitors and saboteurs. That thought made him sigh. *Truthfully, the work of a Chekist is never done.*

Officers Canteen, 866th Fighter Regiment, Airfield 108, Privolzhskiy na Volga.

"Oh Bratishka, what have you been doing to our tovarish Lilya?" Koldunov looked mournfully at Edwards. Lilya had been released from hospital with a more or less clean bill of health, physically at least. The hospital staff members were convinced that she was just about at the end of her mental strength and was suffering from severe combat exhaustion after flying on the front line for more than 18 months without a break. There had been a quiet conference amongst her friends about how best to help her. The conclusion had been that they should create as normal an atmosphere around her as they could, including all the banter and teasing that went on. Sympathy and compassion would be counter-productive. So Koldunov had grabbed her arm and was currently holding it up to reveal the thin red ring of burns where the heat from her flaming Yak had crept between her gloves and the sleeve of her flight suit. "Have you been tying her up again?"

"Surely a good Russian woman would have to be securely bound before she would submit to the embraces of a foreigner?" Valentin Yakovlevich was joining in the fun. He also had recognized how close to a breakdown Lilya was and wanted to ensure something was done to help her. To do so, he had rushed approval of an American request through the bureaucracy. In the meantime, the rough comradeship of her friends would have to work as well as it could.

"You have it all wrong!" Edwards was trying to sound defensive. "It is to protect us poor foreign men from the savage bites, purple bruises and deep scratches that are inevitable when one's lover is a Russian woman!"

He stole a glance at Lilya while the group erupted into laughter. She had gone bright crimson with embarrassment at the merciless teasing but was joining in the merriment. Then, as the laughter went on, hers changed from the normal sound of a young woman at the center of a friendly party to an ugly sound that was closer to crows cawing over a field full of dead mixed with whooping yelps as she tried to draw breath. Her eyes began to show panic as she couldn't stop the cycle. Edwards "mistook" the sound for her choking on a drink and patted her firmly on the back. It was enough to break the repetitions of the noise and bring her back to normal. Nevertheless, Lilya was scared by the vivid demonstration of how close she was to coming apart.

"Sorry to break up the party bratishka, but Major Young wants to see you, Monty and you, Lilya in his office right now."

"Uh-oh. This does not sound good. Come on Lilya, let's see what is going on here."

Guards-Major Ganin was also waiting in Major Young's office, leading to even more apprehension. Young was reading a file that he put down as soon as the two pilots entered. "All right, let's start with you, Edwards. The brass has set the length of a combat tour at 200 operational flying hours. You're getting close to that now."

Lilya's jaw dropped open. The idea of leaving the front while still alive was completely foreign to her and she had never even considered the possibility that he might simply go home. "You're leaving Misha?"

"No, tovarish Lilya. Edwards had already volunteered for an extension tour that would keep him on the Volga for another 200 mission hours. And that request has been granted. However, signing on for an extension also entitles him to two weeks leave back in the States. Frankly, after flying both ways, he'll be lucky if he gets four to six days there. There is a solution to that though.

"Monty, your Silver Star citation was published yesterday. It got buried by this massacre business, but John Ford, the film director saw it and he wants to make it the theme of his next movie. He urgently wants to get a march on his competitors by making the first Russian Front war film. He's asked the Army for a couple of technical advisors. They thought about it and suggested that you might want to volunteer. It would be a two week stint in Hollywood but your travel time there and back would come out of the Army's pocket so your two weeks at home will be a real two weeks."

Ganin took over smoothly. "The fact is, Lilya, nobody in Hollywood knows anything about Russians or what it is like to fight out here. Nor, to be frank, do they have any idea of what it's like to be a woman fighter pilot. Now, Mr. Ford wants this film to be realistic, to show Americans what is happening on the Volga. So, our Army command wants you to tell them. In other words, they want you as the other technical advisor. Remember how few of our pilots actually speak fluent English. So, it's two weeks in Hollywood for you as well; that is an order.

"Now, in recognition of your valiant service over the last 18 months, the people have decided to award you two weeks leave to be spent in America after your Hollywood duties are over. You'll have to do some radio interviews and speak at some war bond drives of course but your speeches will be written for you and you'll find the audiences very sympathetic."

Edwards looked at Lilya. "Bratishka, two weeks living in the finest hotels, doing everything first class and having a film studio pick up all our checks? It's a filthy, horrible job but somebody has to do it. Then you can come home and meet my parents."

"Right, it's all arranged then." Young spoke briskly. Things had come together well and this way everybody got what they wanted – and what Lilya needed very badly. He wanted to get the arrangements fixed before anything went wrong.

"One moment," Edwards wanted a couple of things cleared up. "Is the casting for this film done?"

Young looked at his file. "Lilya will be played by Anne Baxter, you by Dana Andrews. Apparently Bogart wants in so they are writing a part for him. George Sanders is the villain, a hideously evil Hitlerite. He shoots a puppy in the first two minutes. The scriptwriters are having a problem; every time they think they've made him evil enough, the Hitlerites keep raising the bar."

"We're in, aren't we, Lilya?" She smiled and nodded. "OK then. What is this film called, by the way?"

Once again Major Young looked at his file. "Kazan Thunderbolts."

THE END

APPENDIX: AIRCRAFT AND SHIPS

P-47 Thunderbolt

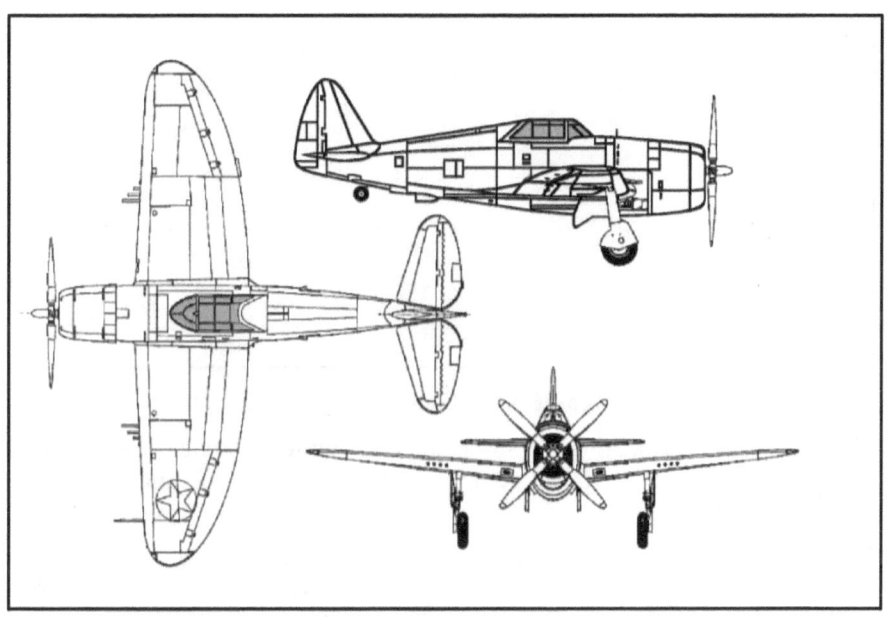

Engine: One Pratt & Whitney R-2800-21 twin-row radial engine delivering 2,000 hp (2,300 with water injection).

Performance: Maximum speed 433 mph at 30,000 feet, and 353 mph at 5000 feet. Service ceiling 42,000 feet. Initial climb rate 2780 feet per minute. Range at maximum cruise power 640 miles at 335 mph at 10,000 feet. Range with a 166.5 Imp. gal. drop tank was 1250 miles at 10,000 feet at 231 mph..

Dimensions: Wingspan 40 feet 9 inches, length 36 feet 1 inches, height 14 feet 3 inches, wing area 300 square feet. Weights: 9900 pounds empty, 13,500 pounds normal load, 14,925 pounds maximum

Armament: Eight 0.50-inch machine guns with 500 rpg and two 1000-lb or three 500-lb bombs

Notes: Historically, the P-47 was an extremely important part of the American fighter fleet. In Kazan Thunderbolts, it maintains this position although the low-altitude fighting characteristic of the Russian Front limits the value of its supremacy at high altitude. As a result, the P-47 is used primarily as a bomber escort and a fighter-bomber.

Kazan Thunderbolts

Yak-9D

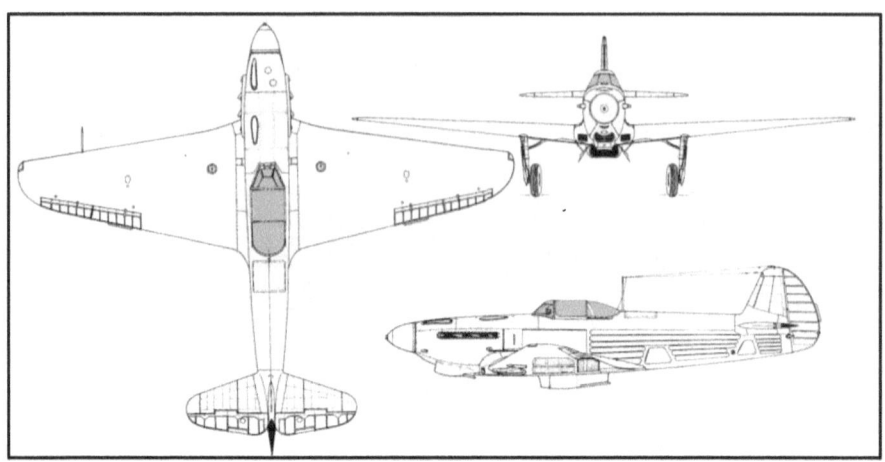

Engine: One Klimov M-105 PF V-12 liquid-cooled piston engine, 1,180 hp

Performance: Maximum speed 367 mph at 12,000 feet. Service ceiling 30,000 feet. Initial climb rate 2690 feet per minute. Normal range 562 miles. maximum range 838 miles

Dimensions: Wingspan 31 foot 11 inches, length 28 feet, height 9 feet 10 inches, and wing area 185.1 square feet. Weights: Weights 5170 pounds empty, 6,380 pounds normal loaded, 6,858 pounds maximum

Armament: one 20 mm ShVAK cannon, 120 rounds, one 12.7 mm UBS machine gun, 200 rounds

Notes: The Yakovlev Yak-9 was a single-engine fighter aircraft that replaced the Yak-1 and Yak-7 from the end of 1942. The Yak-9 had a lighter airframe, lowered rear fuselage decking and all-around vision canopy. Its worst limitations were its weak firepower and susceptibility to fire. The Yak-9D was a long-range version of Yak-9, with a maximum range of 1,360 km (845 mi). Combat usefulness at full range was limited by lack of radio navigation equipment, and a number of aircraft were used as short-range fighters with fuel carried only in inner wing tanks. This situation remains unchanged in Kazan Thunderbolts although the provision of large numbers of American and Canadian-built fighters under Lend-Lease reduce the significance of the Yak and Lavochkin aircraft.

B-17E Flying Fortress

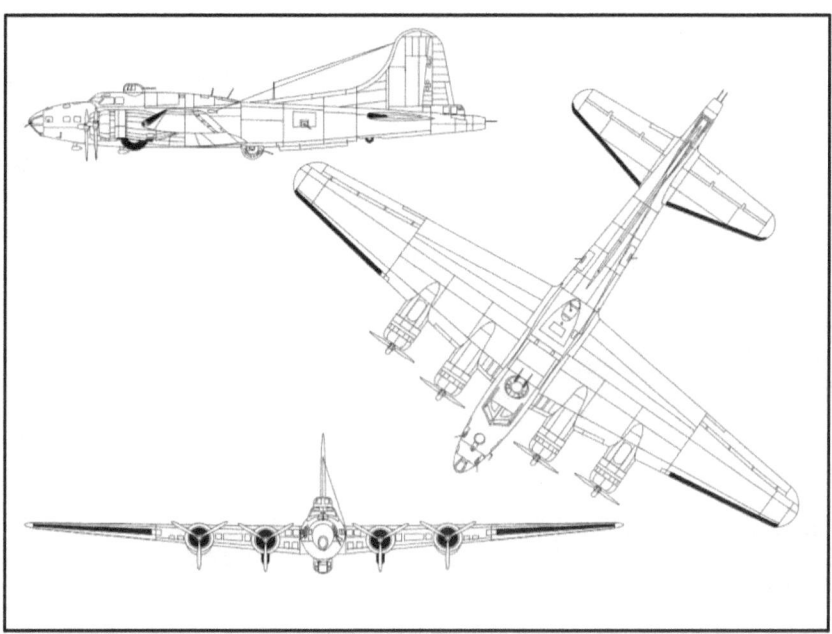

Engines: Four Wright R-1820-65 Cyclone radials rated at 1200 hp for takeoff and 1000 hp at 25,000 feet

Performance: Maximum speed 318 mph at 25,000 feet. Cruise speed 223 mph Service ceiling 36,600 feet. Normal range 1,300 miles with 6,000 pounds of bombs, 2,000 miles with 4,000 pounds of bombs, maximum range 3,300 miles

Dimensions: Wingspan 103 feet 9 inches, length 73 feet 10 inches, height 19 feet 2 inches, wing area 1,420 square feet. Weights: 32,350 pounds empty, 40,260 pounds normal loaded, 53,000 pounds maximum

Armament: Twelve .50 caliber machine guns in nose, cheek, dorsal, radio cabin, waist, tail and ventral ball turret positions. Maximum bomb load 8,000 pounds.

Notes: Historically, the B-17 was the mainstay of the bombing campaign against Germany until the end of the war in 1945. In Kazan Thunderbolts, the B-17 is already nearing the end of its production career with many bombardment groups starting to convert to the B-29. Despite this, the B-17 groups were responsible for developing most U.S. strategic bomber doctrine and originated the strategy of using massed formations of heavy bombers to punch holes in German defenses.

413

B-26B Marauder

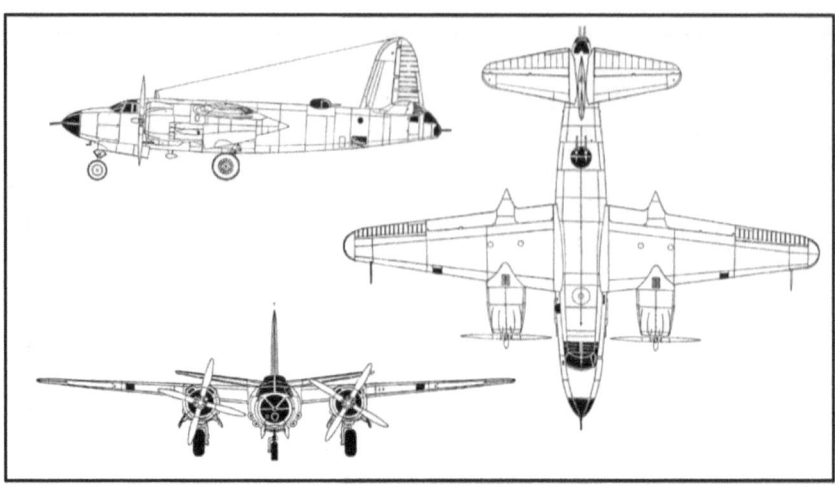

Engines: Two Pratt & Whitney R-2800-43 eighteen-cylinder air-cooled radial engines with two-speed superchargers, each rated at 1920 hp for takeoff and 1490 hp at 14,300 feet.

Performance: Maximum speed 270 mph at sea level, 282 mph at 15,000 feet. Cruise speed 214 mph Service ceiling 21,700 feet. Normal range 1150 miles at 214 mph with 3000 lbs of bombs, maximum range 2,850 miles

Dimensions: Wingspan 71 feet, length 58 feet 3 inches, height 21 feet 6 inches, wing area was 658 square feet. Weights: 24,000 pounds empty, 34,200 pounds normal loaded, 37,000 pounds maximum

Armament: Eleven .50 caliber machine guns in nose, cheek, dorsal, waist and tail positions. Maximum bomb load 5,200 pounds.

Notes: Historically, the B-26 got off to a poor start due to a high accident rate but eventually became a widely-used and successful medium bomber in the air war against Germany. In Kazan Thunderbolts, it is the primary U.S. medium bomber used on the Russian Front. In addition to its operational importance, the B-26 is an important part of the deception campaign that hides the B-17 and B-29 are being produced in lower numbers than public statements suggest and that much of U.S. bomber production capacity is being diverted to the top secret B-36 program. Public statements allege that the B-26 Marauder has proved so successful that it is being produced in preference to the larger aircraft.

FW-190A

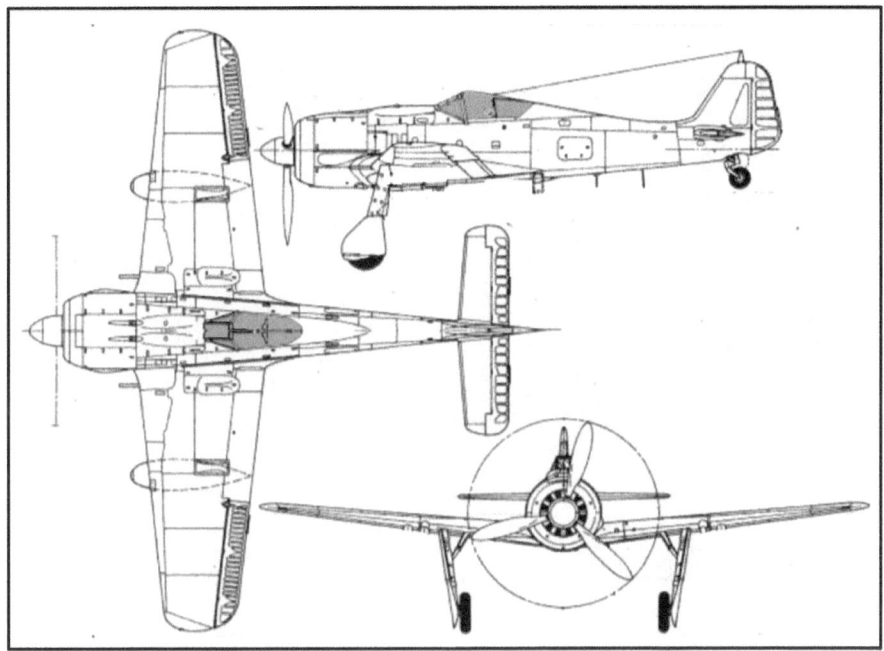

Engine: One BMW 801 D-2 radial engine, 1,650 hp

Performance: Maximum speed 408 mph at 19,500 feet. Service ceiling 37,430 feet. Initial climb rate 2950 feet per minute. Normal range 500 miles.

Dimensions: Wingspan 34 foot 5 inches, length 29 feet 5 inches, height 12 feet 10 inches, wing area 196.9 square feet. Weights: 7060 pounds empty, 9,753 pounds normal loaded, 10,800 pounds maximum

Armament: Two 7.92mm machine guns in nose, two 20 mm MG151 in wing roots, two 20mm MG/FFM cannon in outer wings (later, 13.2mm machine guns were fitted in the nose and MG151s were mounted in the outer wings)

Notes: Historically, the Fw 190 was the backbone of Luftwaffe Fighter Force along with the Me 109. The Fw 190A series' performance decreased at high altitudes, which reduced its usefulness as a B-17 interceptor but its heavy armament gave the fighter enough firepower to bring down a B-17 given the chance. In Kazan Thunderbolts, the P-47 pilots find the FW-190 their most dangerous opponent although the P-47 has a marked edge over 20,000 feet.

Me-109G

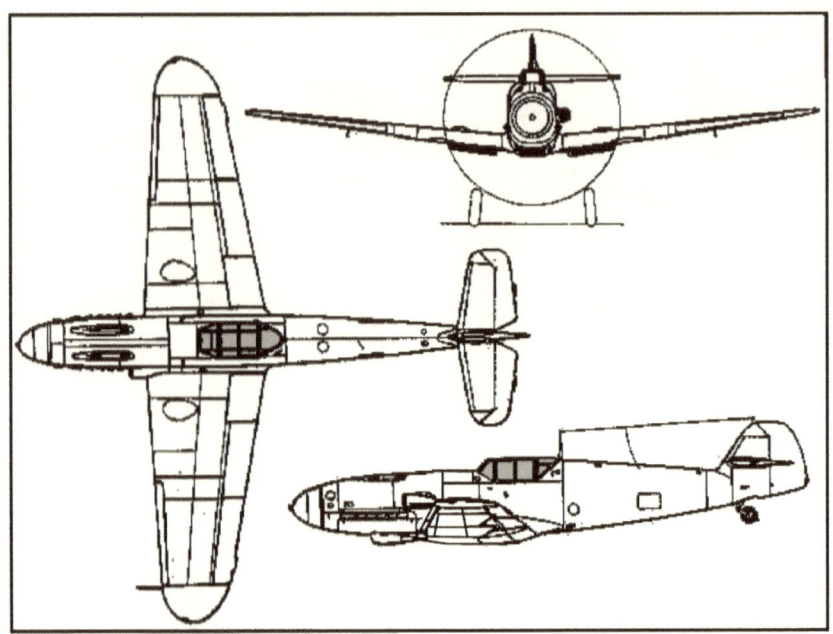

Engine: One Daimler-Benz DB 605A-1 liquid-cooled inverted V12, 1,455 hp,

Performance: Maximum speed 398 mph at 20,669 ft, service ceiling 39,370 feet. Initial climb rate 3345 feet per minute. Normal range 528 miles, maximum range 621 miles.

Dimensions: Wingspan 32 foot 6 inches, length 29 feet 7 inches, height 8 feet 2 inches, wing area 173.3 square feet. Weights: 5,893 pounds empty, 6,940 pounds normal loaded, 7,495 pounds maximum

Armament: Two 7.92mm machine guns in nose, one 20 mm MG151 firing through propeller (later, 13.2mm machine guns were fitted in the nose and a 30mm Mk.108 in the propeller boss).

Notes: Historically, the 109A to D series were called the Bf-109 while the E to K versions were the Me-109. Luftwaffe records show that during Operation Barbarossa, German pilots claimed 7,355 kills on the Bf 109, for exactly 350 losses in aerial combat, a ratio of just over 21:1, and the highest achieved by the Germans on the Eastern Front. The Luftwaffe considered that five kills on the Russian Front were equivalent to one kill on the Western Front. In Kazan Thunderbolts, the heavily-armed, heavily armored P-47s with their well-trained pilots have a major advantage over the Me-109Gs.

U.S. NAVY GUNBOAT PR-73

Elco 92 foot River Gunboat, Lt (jg) John F Kennedy Commanding

Length 92 feet, beam 28 feet, speed 26 knots. Powered by two Allison V-1710 engines

Armament one three inch L50 Mk 22, one quadruple 1.1 inch L75 Mk 1, two twin .50 M-2. One 60mm army mortar amidships for illumination.

Armor, 25mm on bridge, engine rooms and 3 inch magazine.

Notes: The 1940 plans for the U.S. Navy expansion included large numbers of PT boats intended for service in the Philippines and elsewhere. When the U.S. started to arrive in Russia, these PT Boats, primarily Higgins designs, were sent in for service on the Volga and the northern rivers. They were quickly found to be of limited use since their torpedoes were unusable, their speed was of little value and their gunpower inadequate. By June 1943 the orders for PT boats were cancelled and replaced by river gunboat orders. The Higgins gunboats were conversions of the PT Boat design without torpedoes but with extra guns. The Elco boats were purpose-designed for riverine warfare and were much more effective. The problem was armament and the boats were equipped with whatever happened to be available. Likewise, the crews are more or less slung together from wealthy amateur yachtsmen who didn't fit anywhere in the real navy and troublemakers, hard cases and the terminally ill-disciplined who nobody else wanted. What they didn't realize was that was a marriage made in heaven. The U.S. Navy gunboat crews quickly made life on the Volga hell for the German Navy and Army.

Later, once the importance of the gunboats was established, the Navy started scouring its recruits for people with experience of life on the river. Also, as experience with riverine warfare grew, the 92 foot Elco was replaced by the 100 foot Elco design. This had a turret from an M-10 tank destroyer forward, initially mounting a 76mm gun but later a 105mm howitzer, The 100 foot Elco also mounted a twin 40mm gun aft, two single 20mm guns amidships and a 107mm mortar for illumination.

S-38

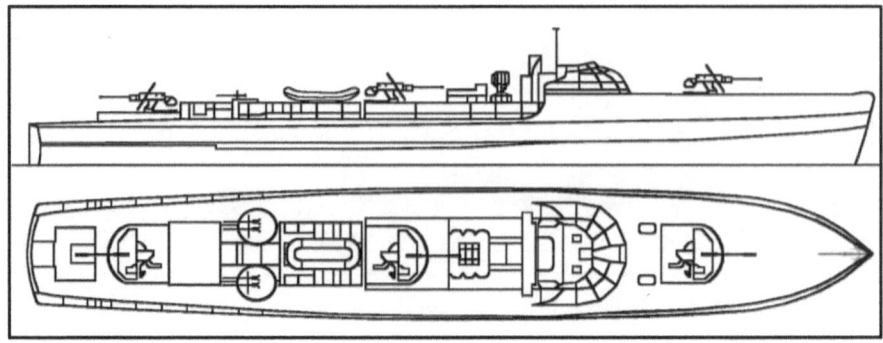

Schnellboot S-38, Oberleutnant zur See Oskar Wuppermann, Commanding

Length 114.5 feet, beam 16.5 feet, speed 44 knots. Powered by three 20-cylinder 2000 hp Daimler-Benz MB501 diesels driving three shafts

Armament three 37mm singles, two twin MG42.

Armor, 12mm on bridge, otherwise none.

Notes: The German advance across the Soviet Union had been harassed all the way by river gunboats that used every available stretch of water to attack the advancing enemy. The gunboats continued to operate against the Germans even when they had been isolated deep in the enemy rear. Despite this experience, the Germans found the level of gunboat activity on the Volga a severe shock for which they were completely unprepared. The Volga was far wider than they realized and the gunboats were present in great numbers. Worse, from the German point of view, large numbers of American-built gunboats had already arrived.

The German Navy attempted to counter their presence by sending a squadron of S-boats and a dozen experimental light S-boats. All these craft proved to be failures in the conditions of riverine warfare. Their lightly-built hulls were ripped up by American .50 and 1.1 inch heavy machine guns while their high speed and torpedo armament proved of no appreciable value. By the time the Volga iced over for the winter of 1943/44, the German Navy had been defeated and its riverine force annihilated. S-38 had been modified with additional 37mm guns in place of its 20mm weapons but this modification was of little value.

www.ingramcontent.com/pod-product-compliance
Lightning Source LLC
Chambersburg PA
CBHW031142050726
47495CB00018B/387